STAR WESTERN

A TREASURY OF 22 OF THE BEST IN PULP FICTION BY THE MASTERS OF THE WESTERN STORY

JON TUSKA

EDITOR

GRAMERCY BOOKS

New York • Avenel

This 1995 edition is published by Gramercy Books,
distributed by Random House Value Publishing, Inc.,
40 Engelhard Avenue,
Avenel, New Jersey 07001.

Random House
New York • Toronto • London • Sydney • Auckland

Printed and bound in the United States

Library of Congress Cataloging-in-Publication Data
Star western / edited by Jon Tuska.
p.   cm.
ISBN 0-517-14688-6
1. Western stories.   2. West (U.S.)—Social life and customs—Fiction.
3. American fiction—20th century.   I. Tuska, Jon.
PS648.W4S73   1995
813′.087408—dc20   95–14139
                                    CIP

10 9 8 7 6 5 4 3 2 1

CONTENTS

———⋆———

INTRODUCTION

---☆---

In 1930, with the Great Depression well under way, pulp magazines bearing the names *Battle Aces, Detective Action Stories, Gang World,* and *Western Rangers* were launched. It was an inauspicious time to begin anything, but the magazines thrived. In time, *Star Western*—a longer, more expensive (15¢ instead of a dime!) magazine of western fiction came on the scene. The first issue was October, 1933, and from the beginning, the magazine became known for its colorful and outstanding western cover art and the excellent quality of its stories.

The Golden Age of pulp magazines was the period between the two world wars. For fifteen cents, *Star Western* gave its buyers a substantial amount of reading material by writers who knew how to please their audience. The January, 1939 issue carried the front cover line: "The magazine of Longer Stories—Five Novelettes by Five Famous Authors!" By June of the same year, the buyer was getting "Seven Complete Novels in Every Issue." With the advent of World War II and its concommitant paper shortage, the number was reduced to six complete novels, ranging from 15,000 to 20,000 words each. In keeping with the patriotism of the stories themselves, the editors at the time explained to their readers that this reduction was the magazine's way of helping the war effort.

Then, in September, 1944, the cover promised "Five Complete Novels" with the sixth slot again given to a short story, and this alternating between five and six novels remained for two years. The price of the magazine went up to 25¢, but the pages increased so the novels got longer.

In time, with the introduction of the paperback novel, *Star Western* tried to compete with the increased violence and more explicit sexuality that appeared on the paperback covers and which were proving to be extremely stiff competition. Despite market changes, despite cover changes, the literary quality of the novels and stories never diminished, but finally, with the September, 1954 issue, *Star Western* ceased publication.

The twenty-two stories that follow, one for each year that *Star Western* was published, have been selected in all but two cases from actual issues of the magazine. The two exceptions are the stories by Alan LeMay and Ernest Haycox. LeMay never appeared in *Star Western*, but he did have stories published in *Dime Western* under a byline fashioned as an anagram to his real name: Alan M. Emley. Ernest Haycox has been included because it was his stories in *Collier's* that greatly influenced authors such as Luke Short, Cliff Farrell, Peter Dawson, Wayne D. Overholser, Frank Bonham, among others, who did write for *Star Western*.

Among the stories themselves, I have chosen several which deal with similar themes, but whose resolutions are as different as their authors. I believe that the development of the Western story is the single most important literary movement in the history of the United States and that it comprises the only unique body of literature which this country has contributed to the wealth of world culture. The Western story is unique to this country because of where it is set: in the American West. There was no place in all history quite like it before and there is no place quite like it now. The American frontier experience will always live beyond its time.

The heart of the Western is that it is a story of renewal, and that is what has made it so different from any other form of literary endeavor. It is refreshing, revitalizing, even spiritually encouraging to contemplate those generations where individual, cultural, and ethnic differences were abundant, where not one culture but many co-existed even if warfare between them was unceasing. We have benefited from that time. There is no one idea and no one cause that can possibly ever win endorsement from everybody. We still live now with that reality of the frontier as part of our social existence.

Above all, the greatest lesson the pioneers learned from the Indians is with us still: that it is each person's *inalienable* right to find his or her own path in life, to follow his own vision, to achieve his own destiny—even should one fail in the process. There is no principle so singularly revolutionary as this one, and it grew from the very soil of this land and the peoples who came to live on it. It is this principle which has always been the very cornerstone of the Western story.

The West of the Western story is a region where generations of people from every continent on earth and for ages immeasurable have sought a second chance for a better life. The people forged by the clash of cultures in the American West produced a kind of human being very different from any the world had ever before known. How else could it be for a nation emerging over centuries from so many nations? And so stories set in the American West have never lost a sense of hope.

What alone brings you back to a piece of music, a painting, a poem, or a story is the mood it creates in you when you experience it. The mood you experience in reading a Western story is that a better life is possible if we have the grit to endure the ordeal of attaining it; that it requires courage to hope, the very greatest courage any human being can have. And it is hope that distinguishes the Western story from every other kind of fiction. Only when courage and hope are gone will the Western story cease to be relevant to all of us.

Jon Tuska

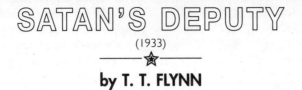

SATAN'S DEPUTY

(1933)

—————— ☆ ——————

by T. T. FLYNN

T. T. Flynn *was born in Indianapolis, Indiana. He was the author of over a hundred Western short novels for such leading pulp magazines as* Western Story Magazine, Dime Western, *and* Zane Grey's Western Magazine. *His short novel, "Hell's Half Acre," appeared in the issue that launched* Star Western *in 1933. He moved to New Mexico and spent much of his time living in a trailer while on the road exploring the vast terrain of the American West. His descriptions of the land are always detailed, but he used them not only for local color but also to reflect the heightening of emotional distress among the characters within a story. Following World War II, Flynn turned his attention to the book-length Western novel and in this form also produced work that has proven imperishable. Five of these novels first appeared as original paperbacks, most notably* The Man From Laramie *(Dell First Edition, 1954), subsequently made into a memorable motion picture directed by Anthony Mann and starring James Stewart. Flynn was highly innovative and inventive and in such novels as* Night Of The Comanche Moon *(Five Star Westerns, 1995) or* Rawhide *(Circle Ⓥ Westerns, 1996) he concentrates on deeper psychological issues as the source for conflict. Flynn is at his best in stories which combine mystery with suspense and action in an artful balance. The world in which his characters live is often a comedy of errors where the first step in any direction frequently can, and does, lead to ever deepening complications. "Satan's Deputy" appeared in* Star Western *(12/33), the third issue.*

☆ | ☆

*P*allor lay gray-white on Sundown Daly's face as he stepped into the warden's office . . . prison pallor. They had prisons in the cow country in those days.

The lack of sunlight and fresh air which had caused that pallor had not touched the man beneath. Sundown Daly's shoulders were as broad and massive as the day he had entered the barred prison gates two years before. He was thinner, leaner, harder. Corded muscles stood out under his rough prison shirt, and his hands were callused with toil. One thing about him was new; one thing prison had stamped deep: cold bitterness . . . etched in the lines of his face, burning deeply in his steady gaze.

The warden's office was high-ceilinged, filled with heavy black hardwood furniture. The windows were high and narrow. Not much light came through them. It was a shadowy office, heavy with rigid rules, lost liberty, little different from the gray stone cell-blocks where men smoldered in sullen resentment.

Two other men were in the office. Before the rolltop desk sat Warden Bursey — short, pompous, pudgy, an irascible political cipher who had been placed over helpless men, for better or worse.

The second man, slouched low in a chair beside the window, was long and broad-shouldered, with iron-gray hair. His face, behind a black mustache, was lean, hard, and deeply tanned by sun and wind. A pair of worn riding boots reached up inside his trousers. A cartridge belt and holster were slung under his coat. A dusty Stetson was tossed on a chair nearby.

All that Sundown Daly saw with one quick glance. Then his eyes went past the warden, past the seated man, out the window to the sunlight and open range.

The warden wheeled in his chair and stood up. "So, it's you, Daly. You're going out in five minutes. Twelve o'clock, noon." He glanced at the wooden clock ticking on the wall above his desk and repeated: "in five minutes."

Daly pulled his eyes away from the scene beyond the window. His glance smoldered as it rested on the warden.

"You don't have to tell me," he said without emotion. "I've had the day an' hour marked for two years."

The warden's plump cheeks reddened. "No back talk!" he snapped. "You're still a prisoner!"

Daly looked down at the warden and a thin smile of contempt came over his face. "I can wait five minutes," he said softly.

The warden's plump fingers flicked the edge of his desk angrily. "You prisoners all assert your liberty as soon as possible! But I won't have it in here! Understand?"

"I hear you," Daly yawned.

The warden scowled helplessly, reddened. "There are a few details!" he snapped. "The state allows you mileage to the town from which you were sentenced. And we are holding some money for you."

"Three hundred an' seventy-five dollars . . . and six bits," Daly nodded.

The warden opened a drawer and laid a brown manila envelope on the desk. "It's in here, with stage fare to Las Piedras, where you were committed."

Daly took the envelope, scanned the contents briefly, thrust it in a pocket of his ill-fitting prison suit. "Anything more?" he asked slowly.

"Yes. It is my duty as warden to give you a few words of advice."

Daly shrugged. "Spare your advice, Warden. I've listened to you bleat and whinny before. Your little lecture makes most of the boys laugh. It'd only spoil the taste of the ham an' eggs I'm gonna buy."

The tall stranger lounging by the window pushed back his coat and brought out tobacco and papers. He had been watching the interchange. A sheriff's badge, pinned inside his coat, showed briefly, but the prisoner did not see it.

The warden was almost apoplectic. "Damn your impudence! I wish it were possible to put you on bread and water for that! I merely wanted to warn you that you have paid your debt to society! From now on the rest is up to you! We don't want to see you in here again!"

Daly's gaze wandered out the window again, then came back to the warden, steady and cold. "I reckon you'd like to have me back in your private hell hole, Warden. It'd do that mean little soul of yours good to see me bulldogged an' hog-tied again. But you won't! This society you bleat about is only crooked law. I wasn't wanted on Las Piedras range, so they hustled me off. Dealt me jokers an' aces an' called the play. Now *I'm* dealin, Warden." Daly leaned forward. His voice rang bitter, terrible on the quiet of the room. *"They made me an outlaw . . . and I'm staying one! Savvy?"*

"You're talking like a fool, Daly!"

Daly doubled his great hands into great fists, flexed his arms so that the mighty muscles writhed and crawled under his shirt. And he laughed at the warden again. It was not a nice thing to hear, that laugh.

"Don't cross my gunsight, Warden. An' to give that crawling little mind of yours something to think about, I'm riding to the Red McKays in the mountains east of Las Piedras. Throw that in the teeth of this society you're representin' without much credit."

"The Red McKays!" exclaimed the warden angrily. "Then I'll have the pleasure of hanging you before long, Daly. Wallace, you heard this man!"

The big gray-haired figure in the chair nodded slowly, inhaling deeply from his cigarette and seeping smoke slowly through his mustache. His eyes roved over the prisoner appraisingly.

"Daly," he said calmly, "if you join the Red McKays, you'll get shot or hung sooner or later. I'm the new sheriff up that way. And I'm going to clean out that nest of buzzards before I leave office."

Daly's gaze narrowed as he studied Wallace. There was no fear or surprise in his manner, rather cool estimation, as if weighing a man he would one day meet.

"Much obliged for the warning," he said laconically. "Come with your guns out when you start after me."

"I'll be lookin' for you when I get back, Daly."

"I'll be there."

The wooden clock on the wall slowly chimed twelve strokes. Daly's great chest swelled as he breathed deeply. His shoulders went back.

"That lets me out, Warden. An' I'll see you in hell on judgment day. Bad luck to you till then."

Daly swung on his heel and strode out of the dingy office. The warden choked out an oath as the door closed.

☆ **II** ☆

FOOD FOR THE GALLOWS

*I*t was late afternoon when the big black splashed across the sandy shallows and muddy trickle that was the Rio Osito — Little Bear River. The low sun was still hot. Spurts of dust drifted up behind the black's hoofs as he climbed the rise beyond the river.

The country around was rolling, broken, gaunt bare breaks and flat topped mesas, pebbly red soil, barren and dry. Scant bunch grass, rabbit weed and greasewood struggled to live in that dry soil; and now and then stunted *cholla* cactus and scanty prickly pear showed defiant spines.

It was a dry world, a harsh, lonely, desolate world — to the casual eye. No houses, no cattle, no life, save one lone hawk sailing low on motionless pinions, fiercely scanning the ground for unwary rodents. But to the impassive rider on the big black it was not lonely, desolate, or harsh. This was everything he had waited for, lived for.

Two days of sun had already struck hard at the prison pallor. Sundown Daly's great shoulders were squarer, his movements freer, his glance quick and alert.

The black shied suddenly. A dry warning rattle broke out on the ground. With a single effortless sweep Daly plucked the revolver from his right leg and fired. And, as the black cantered on, dark coils thrashed and flowed helplessly on the reddish ground.

Daly laughed aloud with satisfaction as he holstered the .45 and reached to the spotted-hair vest for makings. "If that had been a man, he'd've stayed there," he said aloud.

A new person rolled that smoke deftly and flipped the match away. A changed person from the ill-dressed prisoner who had thrown defiance in the warden's teeth. A black sombrero, already well-powdered with dust, sat jauntily on Sundown Daly's head. A scarlet handkerchief hung about his neck. Fancy-stitched half boots and gay silver spurs were on his feet. A rifle was thrust into a leather saddle-boot. Two guns swung at his hips. Behind him a saddle roll was lashed, with coat and slicker on top. All new — bought in those first few hours of freedom.

He was a lean, hard, eager man, this Sundown Daly, who journeyed toward those distant mountains with a cold fixed purpose. Hughie Jennings had given him the key to the Red McKays. Hughie Jennings, who had ridden with the McKays, and was now doing life inside the high brick walls of the prison.

A rash man would have ridden straight to Las Piedras. Two years had taught Daly caution. They would be expecting him at Las Piedras. If they had framed him once, they could again. Las Piedras could wait.

The sun dropped low to the western skyline. The heat began to fade. There was a road somewhere ahead, leading to a rude collection of adobe huts called Paradise. Daly knew its two saloons and one general store which served the ranch country hereabouts. A drink at one of the bars, a few needed purchases, and he'd push on and sleep out.

So he rode steadily and the sun sank from sight. Heavy purple twilight came rolling out of the east. The swift chill of night dropped down. But there was light enough to show the cloud of dust moving along the road ahead. Daly marked it, ignored it. His mind was on other things when he rode around a tumbled mass of eroded rock and the winding road confronted him a few yards below.

A quick pull on the reins stopped the horse. The stage which had raised the dust stood there in the road. The four horses were still blowing hard from their run, champing bits, throwing their heads. And something was wrong. Very wrong!

Four, no, five men were lined up beside the stage. A lone rider on a short-coupled roan confronted them. Daly hardly needed the glimpse of a red bandanna mask and drawn revolver to get the truth. His first instinctive move brought a gun into his hand. Then he remembered this was none of his business.

The passengers lined up beside the stage stared at him. The masked rider shot a quick, oblique look. Just an instant he was off guard. In the dim light a man's hand snapped down to his vest. A tiny Derringer barked as the masked rider looked back.

The shot struck square. The bandit swayed in the saddle.

"Got him!" Daly muttered. "Good shot!"

A second spat of the Derringer was drowned in the louder roar of a belt gun. The rash passenger fell back against the rear wheel, crumpled to the ground. The others were already scattering out of range. The masked rider fired twice after them — high, evidently, as no one dropped. Then he reined his horse behind the stage, spurred off beyond the road. Daly saw that he gripped the saddle horn with one steadying hand as he went.

Daly rode down to the stage, holstering his gun. The rash owner of the Derringer lay crumpled and still in the dust.

"Hey! Come back!" Daly called to the passengers.

His answer was a gun shot over a large rock ahead of the stage. The bullet whined viciously past his head. Daly ducked, shouted: "You damn' fool! Stop that! I ain't. . . ."

A second shot cut his words off. Splinters flew as lead raked the edge of the open stage door. Another gun behind another rock barked out. The bullet tore through the high crown of Daly's sombrero. Too close for comfort. He reined about and spurred for safety, using the stage for cover.

The light was poor, the men excited. They threw shots after him — and all missed. He made the first curve safely, and without warning found himself riding directly into a bunch of horsemen racing up the road toward the stage.

They were all about him an instant later. Six of them — cowmen by their looks — and none too friendly. A chunky man in overalls reined in close, resting a big Colt across his saddle horn.

"What's all the shootin' about, stranger?" he demanded truculently. "How come yo're hightailin' down the road thisaway?"

Daly grinned at them. "Running to keep my hair," he said coolly. He removed his sombrero, poked a finger through the bullet hole in the crown. "Stage was held up," he explained. "I came along an' got mistook for the rannigan who did it! They opened up on me, an' I left."

"Mistook, eh? Ride back with us, stranger, an' we'll see. We thought somebody had took a crack at that stage when we heard the shootin'." It was the chunky man with the gun speaking. And his manner brooked little argument. Daly had none to give. "Let's go," he nodded.

The stage passengers were gathering by the prone figure in the dust when they rode up. A tall, lanky man with a shotgun in one hand stared at them, and then called out, "Why'n hell didn't you boys get here sooner? I knowed you was behind us an' was hopin'. Might have saved Weber's life."

The chunky one beside Daly exclaimed: "That Dan Weber on the ground?"

"Uh-huh. Drilled through the neck."

"Who done it? This feller?"

The man with the shotgun looked hard in the gathering darkness and then shook his head.

"Nope. His pardner done it. This un stayed hid up there by the rocks an' held a gun on us."

"You're loco, stranger!" Daly snapped. "I didn't know it was a holdup till I rode around them rocks. I never laid eyes on that curly wolf before."

"Lyin' won't help you any!" was the curt answer he got. "We all seen you over there holdin' a gun on us. An' didn't you hightail down the road?"

"You'd've left twice as fast if you'd been on my end of all that shootin'," Daly retorted.

The man with the shotgun spat on the ground.

"You've had time to think of a good story, mister. But it won't go. Chuck, you an' the boys better bring him into Paradise. There's a deputy there can take him for murder . . . if the boys don't lynch 'im first. Dan Weber was well thought of around here."

"Sure, we'll do that," the chunky one growled, and said to Daly, "Gimme your guns, an' ride peaceable or we'll save the law trouble!"

In the black dusk Sundown Daly's mouth twisted in bitter humor. Two years in prison — two days out, and back for murder. He wouldn't have a chance. His record, his statement to Warden Bursey, would give the lie to any defense.

"Gimme your guns!" the chunky one demanded again roughly. He leaned over to empty the nearest holster.

Daly caught his wrist, yanked hard.

The chunky one yelled: "Get him, boys!" as he toppled from the saddle and grabbed leather.

Raking spurs sent Daly's horse lunging into the next animal, driving it reeling. They caromed into a third horse, burst through the circle of riders, and bolted past the rear of the stage.

It was sudden, unexpected. The men were jammed in too close for wild gunfire. Once more the stage screened Daly for a few seconds while he left the road and spurred up the bank beyond. Gathering dusk closed in behind him as a fusillade of shots erupted on the road. He fired back twice as the drumming hoofs of the big horse carried him over the low hogback and out of sight.

They followed. Stray shots at first, searching the night, then the steady pounding of hoofs. But darkness came fast and there was no moon.

Daly plunged down a steep arroyo bank and pounded along the twisting sandy channel. When he reined up and listened, the night lay silent and heavy about him. The pursuit had blundered off in some other direction.

He rode another half mile in the arroyo and then turned out and headed west, away from the road, away from Paradise and the route he had been following.

An all-night ride lay ahead if the horse could stand it. A posse would probably be on the trail before long. Daly smiled wryly as he settled himself in the saddle and faced the night.

"Two days out of that stone corral and they're ready to stretch the Daly neck," he said aloud. "The warden must've had a vision when he warned me."

The black nickered as he trotted easily through the darkness, sure footed, willing. But a little later, when skirting a patch of brush, he shied, snorted.

Nearby another horse snorted, stamped uneasily. Daly's gun leaped into his hand. Dimly he could see the shadowy bulk of the other horse.

"Speak up!" he warned the darkness sharply.

Two long seconds passed without an answer — and then a gasp came from the ground beside the shadowy horse.

"I got you covered!" a voice choked. "Keep ridin' or I'll drill you!" A strangling cough was followed by harsh, labored breathing.

Daly could just see the darker splotch of a form on the ground. Slowly he holstered his gun.

"You've got lead in your chest," he guessed shrewdly.

The strangling cough broke out again. The man on the ground cleared his throat with difficulty. "I ain't answerin' questions, or askin' none. Head off from here an' travel fast."

"Your the rannigan who held up the stage," Daly guessed coolly. "I seen that feller plugged you with his Derringer. You couldn't make it beyond here so you fell off to sit it out."

A bitter oath was an answer. "I've still got a gun!" the labored voice threatened from the ground. "Ride on before I make it two I've plugged!"

"Sure, sure," Daly agreed hastily. "Calm down. That won't help you none. They're ridin' this way. They'll cut your trail or mine sooner or later."

"What's your trail got to do with it?"

"I'm the *hombre* who busted in on your little play," Daly said brusquely. "They opened up on me after you left, and ran me down the road into a bunch of waddies smoking along to see what the excitement was. It seems I was helping you, and they figgered a bird in the pot was worth two out in the brush, so they elected me to hang for you. I never did like to hang, so I lit out. And now, stranger, you'd better drop that gun, if you've still got strength to raise it. You made me an outlaw back there. Some *hombre* said there's honor among thieves, so we might as well talk it over!" And Daly swung to the ground.

"You know too damn much to be makin' it up," the stranger admitted with an effort. "But if you're fixin' to double deal me, I'll plug you yet!"

"You wrong me, stranger," Daly said ironically. "Where'd he hit you?"

"In the chest."

The stranger was lying there on the ground, the reins hooked around an arm. He moved slightly as Daly squatted beside him. The faint click of a trigger cocking nicked the night sharply.

"Hold on," Daly warned calmly. "I'm gonna scratch a match so we can get better acquainted."

He flicked the match head with a thumbnail, cupped the flame cautiously in his hands. In the faint yellow glow a young face, tortured, white, sprang out at him. Crimson stained the mouth corners. The sunken eyes were bright with fever, suffering.

Even while the match flared, another choking cough racked the figure, so badly this time that the cocked revolver dropped on the ground and was forgotten. Flecks of bloody foam appeared. When the spasm was over the youth — he was little more than that — lay limp, exhausted on the ground.

Daly flicked the charred end of the match and swore. "Hell . . . you're only a kid! And you're hit bad. I'll see what I can do about it."

"Save your trouble," was the muttered response. "A doctor couldn't help. It's in the chest, near the heart. Hole's closed up and bleedin' bad inside. I'm cashin' in an' I know it!"

And Daly knew it for the truth. He rolled a cigarette in the darkness as he squatted silently.

"What's the name?" he queried with odd gentleness for the man the world knew as Sundown Daly. "I'm Daly, just out of two years in the pen, and headin' for a necktie party if the posse catches up with me."

With a panting effort the young man stirred and lifted his head. "Sundown Daly?" he husked.

"Uh-huh. Don't say we've met."

"No, but I've heard about you," the boy muttered. "I remember when they tried you at Las Piedras. You shot a deputy."

"That's what they said," Daly agreed. "Found my gun by the water hole where it happened. An' next day I showed up with a bullet in my shoulder. I was lucky to get off with two years."

"I heard talk that maybe Yance Claggett knew more about that than you did."

"You hear talk," Daly agreed, but in the darkness his face went hard.

"I figgered that talk was right."

"Mebbe so," Daly grunted. "Let's forget about me and the Claggetts. What's your name? How come a bright young feller like you lined up a stage full of passengers and made guntalk? Just tired of working for forty a month?"

Another spasm of coughing — and the voice came, weaker this time.

"Wanted money. Wanted to go home with my pockets full. My old man needs it bad."

Daly was noncommittal.

"I've heard Sundown Daly was a square shooter."

"I knew him when he was." Daly said briefly.

"Listen to me." A hand groped weakly to Daly's knee. "I ain't gonna leave here. What the posse'll find won't do 'em any good. This ain't any of your business . . . but a dyin' man rates a favor. Take that bag back of my saddle an' hand it to my sister. Tell her . . . anything . . . but leave the stage out. I ain't known around here. I reckon they won't take much trouble to find out who I am. Will you do that?"

And Sundown Daly, whose hand was against every man's, who rode now toward the Red McKays, man-killers, rustlers, terrors of the high range east of the Las Piedras, found himself answering gruffly, lying earnestly: "I'll take it to her if you can't make it, but you'll pull out of this, son."

Another spasm of coughing shook the boy. "Nope!" he gasped. "No need to lie to me. My number's up. I'm slippin' fast. I can feel it."

Daly did not argue. The boy was right. And no man ever faced death more calmly. "What makes you so sure I'll do it?" Daly asked evenly.

"Sundown Daly would."

"Thanks," said Daly briefly. He inhaled, dribbled smoke through his nostrils. "Where does your sister live?" he asked abruptly. "What's her name?"

☆ III ☆

NIGHT RIDERS

*T*he darkness hid the boy's sigh of relief. His voice was choked as he said: "You're white, Sundown Daly. Go to the Wagon Wheel Ranch an' ask for Jordan Lee."

Daylight would have shown startled surprise on Daly's face. The blackness hid it now. His voice came casual. "Wagon Wheel brand, eh? Seems to me I've heard of it. Feller by the name of Enoch Lee owned it."

"My father."

"Jordan Lee," Daly mused. "That's a purdy name, and a queer one. Never heard a girl called that before."

"The old man went to the Bible to name us. I'm Mark Lee. Ride up an' ask for Jordan. Give her my saddle bags. Tell her I always thought she was a pretty swell sister . . . even if I never said much about it." Mark Lee's voice ran off into a laboring whisper, lapsed into the silence.

The horses moved restlessly, shook their heads now and then. Far off into the west the weird yapping of coyotes drifted through the night intermittently. It was dark here, lonely, and the cool breeze seemed chillier with the tragedy that was drawing in quickly and certainly.

Sundown finished his cigarette, rolled another, lit it. The match light showed young Mark Lee resting with his eyes closed, barely breathing. Sundown shook his head regretfully. The harsh lines in his face were softer. He was about to flip the second cigarette away when the distant, almost inaudible, pound of horses' hoofs drifted through the silence.

"They're coming!" Sundown said aloud.

No answer.

"You hear me, kid?"

Young Mark Lee lay still, quiet. Sundown leaned forward, found a wrist that had no pulse in it. He got to his feet, drawing a deep breath. It was over. Mark Lee had gone, leaving the burden of his transgressions behind him for another man to face.

It was characteristic of Sundown Daly that he wasted no time. He searched the body for papers, found none. Swiftly he moved the saddle bags to his own horse. The riders were nearer now, probably searching blindly in the darkness, but nonetheless grimly.

Sundown took the reins of Mark Lee's horse and swung up into his own saddle. Silently he rode away, leading the extra horse. It was well he did. The hard day's ride had weakened the black. It was not long before he began to tire. Sundown shifted to the other horse and rode on.

The gray false dawn found horses and man sodden with weariness. They were in the foothills now, treading through piñon and cedar that shut them in and barred out the world beyond. In the gray semidarkness of dawn they came to a narrow stream tumbling out of the higher hills.

Sundown let the horses drink sparingly and then rode for some two miles up the winding, rocky watercourse. There he cut off to the left to higher ground. Some fifteen minutes later he paused in an open space at the crest of a hill. Beyond, other slopes rolled up and up into the scarlet and gold glory of sunrise. Below, the green, piñon-covered slopes over which he had come met the dry mesa that stretched as far as the eye could reach.

The panorama was stupendous, with hazy purple mountains rimming the far horizon. But Sundown's bloodshot eyes looked for other things than beauty. He saw no dust that marked riders, no moving dots that looked suspicious. With a grunt of relief he clambered out of the saddle, tied the two horses to a piñon tree, and dropped on the ground beside them. They would have to wait for food and water, staying close and secure where he could be in the saddle in a moment's notice.

Within two minutes he was sound asleep.

Sundown was up at high noon, grimy, unshaven, but refreshed. The horses drooped where he had tied them. Sunlight and shadows checker-boarded vividly back through the trees. Below, over the mesa country, the heat haze thickened into the far distance. And once more there was no sign of pursuit.

Sundown stretched, yawned, tilted his black sombrero over his eyes to break the sun glare, and inspected the horses carefully. They were gaunted, worn, obviously needing rest, forage, water. But there was still hard riding left in their wiry muscles. Sundown mounted, took the reins of Mark Lee's horse, and rode off, whistling softly through his teeth.

All that afternoon he rode through the foothills, climbing the descending steep slopes. And always he made his trail among the piñons and tall cedars. But when the sun dropped to the western horizon, and the shadows were long, and the night not far off, he angled down into the grass and easier going.

The country had changed about him. The grass was greener, taller. Small bunches of white faces were grazing here and there. In the far distance, another three hours' riding, was Las Piedras. Not far ahead was Cowpen Creek and, if one followed the sprawling, sandy bed of Cowpen Creek, one came to the Wagon Wheel Ranch, to Jordan Lee who had been a fine sister. Sundown rode to Cowpen Creek.

The water was low, a mere trickle in the wide, sandy bed. The sand muffled his progress as he rode into the dusk. A little more and he'd be at the Wagon Wheel, his errand discharged, his way free into the hills.

Sundown's face went harder, his shoulders drew back as he thought of that. In the hills was freedom and men who laughed at the law which sought them. And as he thought of that he heard the low bawl of cattle nearby, and close on that the sharp explosion of a gun.

Sundown neck-reined the black over to the bank and up into the shelter of a juniper clump. Gunshots meant trouble.

Other shots, swift, staccato, venomous burst through the dusk as he rode to shelter. There was no whine of lead. The shots were coming from across the stream, beyond the rise of the opposite bank. Rifle in hand, Sundown waited, searching that wooded rim with narrowed eyes.

And then, of a sudden, a horseman burst into view against the skyline. He was riding hard, leaning low in the saddle, slashing with the romal ends, spurring furiously. A sombrero fell from his head as he thundered down the slope toward the sandy creek bed. He ignored it. Sundown saw a belt gun glint in his hand, saw him throw one hasty glance over his shoulder, and then set himself as the horse plunged over a two-foot bank into the creek bed.

There were no more shots, but one knew instinctively that death was not far behind the fleeing man. And as suddenly as the first man appeared, two more riders burst into view at the top of the slope. They reined sharply, their horses sliding to a halt. They carried rifles. They whipped them to their shoulders. Their drumming reports smote almost as one shot.

The horse shied, whirled off at a tangent. And the rider toppled from the saddle, struck the damp sand full length. He rolled limply, gun flying from his hand, stopped on his face, shuddered, lay still. The horse bolted up the slope, reins flying loose, stirrups flapping.

Sundown's led horse shied, snorted. "Hold still!" Sundown said savagely, and yanked the rebellious animal in close.

But it was too late. He had been seen. Two rifles covered the spot. A voice shouted: "Ride out in the open and let's see you!"

"Not while you're droppin' men out of the saddle like that!" Sundown called back. "If you're aimin' to pop me, try it from there!" It was a tense moment. The two men spoke to each other in low tones. They seemed undecided. "If it's guntalk you want, open up. If it ain't, ride back, or come down to the water and meet me!" Sundown called to them.

"Hold it!" one of them shouted. "We're comin' down!"

Slowly, watchfully, they walked their horses down to the bed of Cowpen Creek. And Sundown rode equally as slowly and watchfully to meet them. Three rifles covered targets. Three fingers crooked tense for the first sign of treachery as they met by the limp form on the sand.

Sundown asked coolly: "What's all the excitement about?"

The man on the right was small, slender, stoop-shouldered, with a wizened shrewd face, and a tangle of uncut hair showing beneath the brim of a worn, battered Stetson. He wore one gun and a belt knife. A manila lass rope was tied at his saddle horn. His cowhide chaps were as worn as his Stetson, and he sat silently, watchfully as his companion answered: "We're dealin' questions here, stranger. What's your handle an' your business? You ain't a Wagon Wheel man."

The speaker could have made two of his companion. He was a big man, lean and rangy. A young man, with a carefully trimmed red mustache. Something of a dandy too, in gay chaps decorated with silver conchos. His saddle was fine leather, his bridle studded with silver conchos also. A silk handkerchief was tied about his neck. A big sombrero was cocked at a rakish angle. Two guns, slung low on his hips, had mother-of-pearl and silver inlaid in the handles.

His voice was harsh, commanding. He showed no regret or excitement at having killed a man. His eyes did not even drop to the body on the ground.

Sundown watched them both narrowly. He had a vague feeling that he should know them, but could not place the men. Sparring for time, he asked: "Is this Wagon Wheel range?"

And got a gruff reply: "I reckon you know where you are, stranger. Speak up while you got time! We're in a hurry!"

The little man watched Sundown intently. The round hole in the muzzle of his rifle was like an unwinking eye, threatening, vicious. The wizened face was a mask, a killer's mask.

Sundown weighed the odds swiftly. He might get one in a showdown. The other would probably finish him off. They were not men who bluffed. They had killed once and could easily do so again.

Sundown shrugged and dismissed the odds. His face was hard as he rasped: "They call me Sundown Daly. There's a posse lookin' for me. I'm just out of two years in the pen. This *hombre* you plugged is your business. We'll let the deal stay that way. If you don't like it, call your bet."

The two exchanged a quick glance. The tension visibly relaxed. The little man lowered his rifle, said softly: "I reckon it's him, Rex. Didn't Hughie Jennings write he shaped up about like this?"

And Sundown placed them then. He smiled thinly and lowered his rifle also.

"You're Rex McKay," he said to the big dandy, "old Jupiter McKay's youngest. That mustache fooled me. Hughie Jennings said you were clean-faced."

The little man chortled dryly. "He's grown up."

That got him a scowl. "Shut up, Salty! Your humor gives me a pain in the neck."

"You'll be Salty O'Shea," Sundown said to the little man. "Hughie Jennings says you'd rather shoot a man than eat a sirloin."

Salty O'Shea grinned, in no wise offended.

Rex McKay was still suspicious. Rifle ready, he growled: "Where'd you meet Hughie Jennings?"

"In the pen. He's doing life, but figgers he'll be out before long."

"Where you headin'?"

"To your outfit. Any arguments?"

"Put up your gun," said Rex McKay. He slipped his own rifle in the saddle boot. Sundown followed suit. Salty O'Shea did the same. But Sundown noted that Rex McKay hooked a thumb in his belt within easy reach of the pearl-mounted gun handle as he eyed him narrowly. "You're headin' away from the McKay range," he pointed out curtly. "How come?"

"Business at the Wagon Wheel ranch house, then I'm ridin' back in the hills."

"What's your business at the Wagon Wheel, Daly?"

"Private," Sundown said calmly. "Tend to your own business an' don't pry in mine. It ain't done in polite society."

Rex McKay raised a hand and brushed his mustache. "You a friend of Enoch Lee's?" he challenged abruptly.

"Never saw him."

"Then ride with us and be damned to your business with an old psalm singer. We're turnin' back in a little while."

"I'll ride after when I'm through at the Wagon Wheel," Sundown stated coolly.

Rex McKay let out an explosive oath. His face twisted in ugly lines. "McKay men take orders!" he said angrily. "I tell you not to go to that Wagon Wheel ranch house. Mebbe you're Sundown Daly an' mebbe not. I ain't takin' chances."

Salty O'Shea said softly: "He's Daly all right. An' he's fixin' to join the McKays. He got a raw deal in Las Piedras two years ago. He never kilt that deputy. Hughie Jennings ain't sendin' a man to us unless he's all right. It's gettin' dark. We'll be through in a little while. What's to stop us from ridin' on to the ranch house with him? We can wait until his business is done an' take him back with us."

Rex McKay rubbed the palm of his right hand slowly over the top of the saddle horn, and considered. Suddenly snapping his fingers, he decided: "We'll do that. Come on, ride with us, Daly."

☆ IV ☆

THE NOOSE

*S*undown rode along. The men were not unfriendly. Rather, they ignored him. There were three of them now besides Salty O'Shea. Five men, scattered out in the gathering darkness, drifting a seasonable bunch of yearlings before them.

Now and then one of the men detached himself and drove several of the yearlings off from the main body, rushing them out of sight, returning empty-handed each time. They repeated this move again and again, without looking to Rex McKay for orders.

Puzzled, Sundown rode and held his counsel. They were on Wagon Wheel land. They were drifting Wagon Wheel yearlings as he had noted by the brand. They were heading deeper into Wagon Wheel range, and instead of rounding up the yearlings, they were scattering them out.

Had they been rustling Wagon Wheel beef, Sundown would have understood it. Had they been heading toward the hills and keeping the small herd compact, it would have made sense. This did not. He did not ask.

In half an hour the last of the yearlings were scattered. The riders gathered about Rex McKay. It was almost dark now. The big fellow's face was barely visible as he said casually to them: "Here's a man to take Hughie Jennings's place, boys. He's riding to the Wagon Wheel for a little business. We'll side him for comp'ny an' take 'im back with us. Daly's his name. Sundown Daly. He's been in the pen with Hughie Jennings."

That was all. No comments were made. But as they rode through the night, Sundown sensed the riders were close about him, ready, he guessed, to see that he made no attempt to break away. He was not accepted as one of them, despite Rex McKay's words.

Sundown ignored it. He could understand their caution. But he wondered about the dead man back on Cowpen Creek. Why had he been killed? Who was he? What were these McKays up to?

They topped a rise of ground. Dimly lighted windows were visible a quarter of a mile away. A dog barked, fell silent.

Rex McKay said in a emotionless voice: "There's the Wagon Wheel headquarters. I don't reckon you'll be long, Daly?"

"Can't tell. Be back when I'm through," Sundown said shortly.

"Better leave your guns with us," Rex McKay said in the same detached manner. "Bad things to be carryin' on a friendly call. They might misunderstand you."

Sundown said dryly: "I doubt it. I'll take 'em. I'm partial to 'em."

The men were crowded close about him in the darkness. He heard a stir behind. Without warning the hard muzzle of a rifle touched his back. Salty O'Shea said mildly: "Red wants 'em, friend. You wouldn't disappoint him, would you?"

"When you put it that way," said Sundown gently over his shoulder, "I wouldn't. But some day soon, Salty, old friend, we'll powwow over your rambunctiousness. You're too free with a gun to suit my taste."

"Shore," said Salty, affably. "Always ready to talk over little things like that. Meanwhile, jest hold still an' easy while the boys get your hardware."

Rex McKay chuckled softly, as guns were slipped from holsters. "You'll learn to take orders if you trail with the McKays," he commented. "We'll be waitin' here for you, Daly."

Sundown rode toward the Wagon Wheel lights.

A chorus of barks and snarls greeted him as he came to the low adobe building which was obviously the ranch house. An open door let a shaft of light out on a portal. A man stood framed there, peering into the night. "Who is it?" he called, gruffly.

"Stranger," said Sundown. "I'm lookin' for Jordan Lee."

"Light an' come in."

Sundown dismounted, untied the saddle bags, walked to the portal with them. As he approached, the man disappeared. His voice could be heard calling the girl.

She stood framed in the doorway a moment later, peering out at him questioningly. Sundown felt himself growing speechless, awkward as he looked at her.

Jordan, her father had called her, after a river across the seas. And she was like a river, this girl who stood in the doorway with the light behind her. A river, smooth and clear with soft curves and unexpected depth beneath the beauty of the surface. A river, flowing gently and easily, with the capacity to become a raging torrent.

That was Jordan Lee as Sundown saw her first. Height barely to his shoulders. Brown hair waved soft and close to her head. Her eyes, dark and questioning, in a young face that was oddly mature.

"You wish to see me?" she asked.

Sundown grinned at her. For the moment bitterness left him and he forgot the past. Forgot the Red McKays, the outlaw brand he wore. "If you're Jordan Lee, I brought these saddle bags to you," he said. Sundown held them out.

She took them in slender, strong hands that were no strangers to work. Eyebrows lifting in a puzzled frown, she said: "For me? Why?"

Awkwardness descended on Sundown again at the pain he was about to bring her. "They're your brother's, Mark Lee's. He asked me to bring them to you."

Her face lightened with eagerness. "Mark! Where is he?"

Sundown stumbled over it. He had never done a harder thing. "He's . . . you see . . . I hate to bring you the news . . . he's dead," Sundown said heavily.

The joy and eagerness fled from her face. Disbelief, grief, misery came then. Her hands trembled. She swayed. He thought she was about to fall, and put out a hand. But she drew a deep breath and was the master of herself once more.

"Come in," she said. And Sundown, who should have been on his way at once, followed her into the house.

He found himself in a large room with polished tree trunks across the ceiling. Deerhides, bearskins, and Navajo rugs were on he floor. A great stone fireplace was built into the back wall. There were books about, lithograph prints on the walls.

Jordan Lee laid the saddle bags on the table and looked at him. Her eyes were glistening, her face pale.

"Tell me," she commanded.

Sundown lied bravely. "A horse, ma'am. Hadn't been broke right. He fell over backwards on Mark. It was over in a minute. He asked me to bring the saddle bags to you, and to tell you he always thought you was a fine sister, even if he hadn't said much about it."

It was hard going. She questioned him. Sundown lied with a straight face as he told of the happening down south, near the border. She listened, hanging on his words. When he finished, she said brokenly: "Poor Mark. I can't believe he's dead."

A harsh voice behind Sundown exclaimed: "Mark's dead! What talk is this?"

The door had opened soundlessly in time for her words to be overheard. Sundown had seen Enoch Lee before. There was no change now. The same stern, ascetic face, with cold eyes under bushy black brows. The same stubbly chin beard and mustache, graying slightly now. A stern man, upright, righteous according to his convictions. An honest man, without fear. Harsh to the breaking point with those who transgressed the code by which he lived. Enoch Lee demanded again, loudly, of them both: "What is it about Mark? Who is this man, Jordan?"

Jordan Lee pointed to the saddle bags. "Mark's, Dad. He sent them by this man before he died. It was down near the border. A horse fell on him."

"That's right," Sundown nodded to Enoch Lee's fierce look inquiry. "I was there. He was a good boy, hard-working, steady. We all liked him. And now I'll be going, if you don't mind. I rode out of my way, and I'll have to be getting back."

A cool, amused voice at the door where Enoch Lee had been said: "It's a good story, Daly, but it won't work. Put your hands up! You're traveling into Las Piedras with me. Sheriff Wallace wants you for murder!"

Sundown swung around, hands instinctively lifting from his side to show that he was unarmed. He recognized the voice before he saw the man, and found he was right. It was Yance Claggett, standing there in the doorway with a big frontier model Colt in his hand. Yance Claggett, big and debonair as ever, handsome too. For a day's ride in any direction there were no finer-looking men than the Claggett brothers, Yance and Gil. Yance was the older, and he was not more than thirty-five. Sinuous where Sundown was powerful, smooth-tongued where Sundown was blunt. A man of ready laughter, of shrewd deals that somehow bred no animosity, Yance Claggett was well on his way to wealth. He bought cattle, traded ranch land, owned the biggest saloon in Las Piedras, had scattered interests that were not public knowledge. And there had been bad blood between him and Sundown for years.

Yance Claggett's smooth-shaven, handsome face was smiling slightly behind the level gun. But his eyes were flaming watchfully.

The bitter lines settled in Sundown's face once more. His eyes became coldly blank, his voice expressionless. "I'm not armed," he pointed out.

"Put 'em up!" said Yance Claggett. "You're a tricky one, Daly. You've probably got a Derringer stuck around you some place, like that fellow over by Paradise yesterday."

"What is this, Yance?" Enoch Lee questioned brusquely. "This man seems to have brought news of Mark's death. Do you know him?"

"Every inch of his worthless hide," Yance Claggett stated smoothly. "His name is Sundown Daly. Remember his trial two years ago for shooting Tom Means, the deputy? He just got out of prison several days ago. He hasn't been near the border in years. He an' another man held up the stage over by Paradise yesterday afternoon. They killed one of the passengers and made their escape. Sheriff Wallace got Daly's description this afternoon and recognized it. I was in his office at the time. Wallace was at the prison when Daly left, and tells me Daly said then he was turning outlaw. I don't know what brings him here, but I'll take him in to Wallace."

Jordan Lee had looked startled at sight of Claggett's gun. She stood rigid, questioning, while he spoke. Now she said in an unsteady voice: "But he brought Mark's saddle bags."

She opened them swiftly, emptied the contents on the table as she finished speaking. Two small canvas bags of coin chinked heavily. There was a packet of old letters, a razor, two pairs of socks. Not much. A few pitiful personal possessions. The canvas sacks held only silver dollars when she opened them.

"That's my razor that Mark took when he left!" Enoch Lee said in a dead, brittle voice. His stern face might have been carved from rock. His voice broke, unsteady for an instant. "My razor . . . my boy! And . . . and this man, Daly, and another held up the stage yesterday?"

Yance Claggett nodded. "One of them was shot with a Derringer and wounded badly. Daly here knows," he said, "what happened to the man who was with him."

Enoch Lee turned on Sundown with all the fury of a prophet of old.

"You led my boy into a thing like that!" he blazed. "He was young, willful, wild! A man like you could sway him!"

"Hold on!" Sundown protested. "You're on the wrong trail, mister."

"Damn your black heart!" Enoch Lee thundered. "I'll take you in to the sheriff myself! I'll be standing there when they put a noose around your neck and spring the trap! Verily, vengeance shall be mine!"

Sundown looked at Jordan Lee. What Yance Claggett thought did not matter. Enoch Lee's righteous answer was in keeping with the man's character. But somehow he wanted this clear-eyed girl to understand. She was standing stiff, straight, white-faced. Her eyes were hard with scorn.

"So it was all lies!" she said. "A horse didn't fall on Mark. He was shot while holding up the stage and killing a man. You went from prison to *that!* And then came here with lies on your lips. Couldn't you even be honest about . . . death?"

Yance Claggett stood there soberly. But dancing lights of satisfaction gleamed in his eyes as he looked at Sundown, and then spoke to her.

"I'm sorry, dear. I should have kept quiet. But when I heard his little story, I couldn't keep still. Leave us with him and we'll handle him."

"No, Yance. I . . . I'm all right."

Yance Claggett had made a conquest, not the first Sundown knew about. Somehow this one irritated him. She was too good for Claggett, and always would be. A man could look at her and know it.

Enoch Lee said harshly: "I'll get some of the boys out of the bunkhouse."

Claggett lifted a protesting hand. "No need of that. You won't even have to ride in. I'm a deputy. I can handle him. I'll put a rope around his neck."

Sundown, catching the grim note of satisfaction in Yance Claggett's voice, knew that he had small chance of getting into town alive. Claggett had put him out of the way two years ago. Claggett was afraid of him. This golden opportunity was made to order. Even should he reach Las Piedras, he would probably be sentenced to hang in short order. The facts were too damning.

None of that showed on Sundown Daly's face. He was cold, deliberate, as he looked at Yance Claggett and Enoch Lee and let his gaze wander around the room. Rex McKay had his guns. He damned the big, red-faced outlaw to himself.

Enoch Lee said grudgingly: "If you can get him in alone, Yance, go ahead. It's late to be ridin' into town an' back. I'll come in tomorrow."

Then Sundown saw the looped end of a cartridge belt showing over the arm of a horsehair upholstered rocking chair at the end of the room. He could not see the holster from where he stood. But cartridges were in the belt loops. It was reasonable that the gun would be in the holster. It was a full twenty feet away, past the table where Mark Lee's saddle bags lay in the light of a big, nickel-finished oil lamp.

Sundown shrugged helplessly, said to Yance Claggett: "Looks like you're running this show. I'll have my day in court. Before I leave here's something Miss Lee had better see."

He stepped to the table and picked up the packet of letters and in the same motion he swept the lamp off the table and dropped to the floor. Claggett's gun shattered the quiet of the room.

☆ **V** ☆

DEATH'S HEAD MINE

*T*he bullet grazed Sundown's shoulder as he went down behind the table. The glass lamp shade and chimney crashed into bits on the floor. The lamp flickered, went out, plunging the room into pitch-blackness. Claggett's gun roared three more times as Sundown hurled himself away from the table across the floor. Lead raked into the table, smacked into the floor behind him.

Sundown's outstretched fingers struck the rough horsehair upholstery of the chair — found the gun belt — found the holster on the chair seat. He jerked the weapon out, sprang up with ringing ears as Claggett's shots ceased.

Powder smoke was rank in the room, mixed with the reek of spilled oil and the charred wick. Claggett's excited voice said loudly: "If I didn't get 'im, then I will soon as I see him! Jordan, are you all right?"

She answered from before the big stone fireplace: "All right, Yance. Did . . . did you kill him?"

"I hope so," Claggett replied. "He's a bad one."

Empty shells struck the floor near Sundown. He heard Claggett thumbing fresh ones in. Assuming his man was unarmed and probably wounded, Claggett was reckless. Sundown moved forward noiselessly toward the table. Matches flared brightly in Enoch Lee's hand.

Yance Claggett's handsome face stood out sharply. A spasm of surprise crossed it; and quick, panicky fear as Claggett looked into the muzzle of the gun, and past it at the mirthless grin on Sundown's face.

"Drop it!" Sundown rapped out.

"Yance, watch out!" Jordan Lee cried.

Enoch Lee stood rooted to the floor, three bunched matches blazing in his fingers. And Yance Claggett's gun jerked up, shot.

Sundown felt the bullet strike his side violently, tearing through cloth and flesh. He shot an instant later. Yance Claggett staggered as the gun spun from his fingers and thudded to the floor. He cried out in pain. Enoch flicked the matches out, dodged from the spot where he was standing.

Blackness closed in about them once more. But Sundown was already around the end of the table. Two long strides and he found Claggett, who was still cursing as he bent, searching for his gun. Sundown caught a handful of heavy black hair, jerked him up, jammed his gun in Claggett's middle.

"Easy on it," he snapped. "Let's have some light before I get nervous an' plug this good-lookin' snake!"

"Strike a light quick, Enoch!" Yance Claggett gasped. "He'll do it!"

Matches flared once more. Yance Claggett's face was a pain-twisted mask, a grimace of fear.

In a quick little rush Jordan Lee reached his side. She caught Claggett's arm, blazed at Sundown: "There's been enough of this! Get back! You . . . you shall not shoot him!" The placid river had indeed become a torrent. Her anger was beautiful, reckless, unheeding.

"Jordan, get back!" Enoch Lee cried hoarsely.

Yance Claggett said nothing at first. Blood was dripping from his fingers. His face showed fear, and now bewilderment. He had tried to kill, and he expected the same.

The matches burned low in Enoch Lee's fingers. Sundown stepped back, bent and snatched Claggett's gun from the floor. He laughed as the blackness fell about them again.

"Take him!" he said to Jordan Lee. "Hide him behind your skirts! Let him lie to you. A woman can't see the dust for the smoke she raises when she falls in love. Enoch Lee, you Bible-shoutin' old hypocrite, your boy made a wrong step, but he died like a man. If Yance Claggett takes his place, don't look for the same. He's a different breed."

"I'll have you hunted down like a dog!" Enoch Lee said harshly in the darkness.

Sundown laughed. "Miss Jordan, are them your sentiments?"

"I hope," said Jordan Lee passionately, "you get all you deserve!"

"That would be poison to your pretty boy," Sundown chuckled. "I'm wishin' you good luck with him. You'll need it."

He stepped out on the portal, closing the door behind him. How many men had been within earshot he had no way of knowing. As he left the portal, men came running around the end of the house. Sundown ran for the black, caught reins and saddle horn, and swung up.

A loud voice demanded: "What's all the shootin' about?"

"Trouble inside. Enoch Lee wants you."

"Hey, where are you going?" the voice demanded as the black wheeled and leaped to the rake of spurs. "Who are you?"

Enoch Lee's voice shouted from the front door: "Stop him!"

Guns barked loudly. Bullets whined close. Sundown emptied one revolver back at them, and rode hard, leaning low.

The five men were waiting where he had left them. Rex McKay hailed him as he galloped up. "What's happened? We heard shots?"

Sundown reined up by the speaker.

"Gimme my guns!" he demanded in cold fury.

They were returned.

"What happened?" Rex McKay demanded again.

"My business! An' the next man who asks for my guns'll get trouble instead! Your damn foolishness almost put a rope around my neck! Ride on if I'm goin' with you!"

They obeyed him. His cold fury and manner held them silent as they rode off into the night. Even Rex McKay held his tongue.

They rode fast and far, back into the hills, the mountains, along trails strange and unknown to Sundown. They threaded the pines of the upper slopes, traversed narrow, deep-walled canyons. Came finally to a high, windswept shelf on the upper slopes.

The dark loom of buildings bulked in the waning starlight. Lighted windows gave life to the deserted night. And the tangle of pines, aspen, and undergrowth formed a leafy wall on three sides of the open space. They came to it out of a narrow defile, and Sundown knew where he was. Long ago gangs of men had mined silver and gold from this high mountain shelf. It was the Death's Head Mine, so-called because a grinning white skull had been found on the original vein outcropping.

The gold had played out. Silver had dropped in price. The mine and all the surface buildings had been abandoned for many years. And here the Red McKays were nesting, like eagles in a mountain aerie.

They stopped before a two-story building that had been a saloon and boarding house for the miners. It was a big, gaunt, frame pile. They tramped across porch floors that creaked underfoot, entered a long front room that had been bar and lobby. The bar glass was cracked, gaping blank in spots. The floor was dark with the grime of years. Cobwebs and age lay thick on every side. But the tables and chairs were still in place, and the ornate brass chandelier lamp was burning over the bar.

Five men were playing poker at a big round table. They greeted the newcomers with boisterous salutations, eyed Sundown narrowly. Every man was armed. They were a hard-boiled lot.

He had only a moment to look them over. A high pitched voice called: "Who's that with you, Rex?"

At the end of the room, stairs led up to the second floor. The speaker was on a lower landing, legs braced apart, hands hooked in a gun belt, head bent forward in inquiry. Spindle-shanked, pot-bellied, pink-cheeked, with a glistening bald skull fringed by coarse red hair, he looked not more than forty. The Red McKays terrorized a vast expanse of range country. And Jupiter McKay, their leader, would have made a stranger laugh at first sight. But Sundown did not laugh. He knew too much about the man.

What mattered the bandy legs and pot belly, the feminine voice and pink cheeks? Sundown's eyes marked the lean, powerful hands hooked on the gun belt, the tight-lipped mouth, the cold eyes staring fixedly under coarse red eyebrows.

Hughie Jennings had told him what other men had paid dearly to learn. Jupiter McKay was tireless in the saddle, swift, powerful in action. A dead shot. For all his thin voice he was harsh, cruel when necessary, iron-willed, cunning.

Rex McKay said meekly as he walked with Sundown to the steps: "He's Sundown Daly that Hughie Jennings wrote about. He says a posse's after him, an' he was headin' here."

"So," said Jupiter McKay mildly, "Daly, eh?" His eyes drilled Sundown. His tight lips pursed thoughtfully, smiled suddenly. "Glad to see you, Daly. We can always use a good man. Rex'll give you a room upstairs. We're livin' in style just now. There's grub in the kitchen. Black Sam'll feed you."

It was a simple as that. Rex McKay led him up to a little cubby-hole room. It held a rickety old chair and a cot; blankets were rustled for him. A grinning black giant in the kitchen downstairs warmed him a plate of grub.

Other men drifted in and out of the big room during the next hour. Fifteen or twenty of them, Sundown judged. Horses were corralled at the back of the building. No women were about. The Red McKays were a compact, mobile group that moved far and fast when occasion warranted.

Sundown turned in early. He lay for a time, thinking of that rider who had died on Cowpen Creek. He had known the Red McKays dealt in death and terror. He had been willing to accept it. But shooting a fleeing man in the back was different. Sundown's last thoughts were of Jordan Lee, and her blazing anger.

☆ **VI** ☆
BLOTTED BRANDS

*T*he new day was clear, sunny, peaceful. The front of the clearing dropped a thousand sheer feet into an abyss. One looked off a hundred and fifty miles over the rolling range country to hazy purple mountains on the horizon. There was a certain activity going on today. Men came and went on mysterious errands. In the evening they played cards, drank moderately, talked, even sang. And yet one felt the ever-present tension in the air. They lived with death and violence, and it marked them and their actions.

Few questions were asked Sundown. No hostility was shown after Jupiter McKay accepted him. The next afternoon Sundown saddled the black and rode out unchallenged. High-frowning walls bounded the narrow defile through which he had entered the clearing, forming an impregnable gate to this lair of the McKays. It would be a bold posse that would try to fight through. And it was the only way in from the lower country.

Two guards on duty at the entrance waved at him. One of them called: "The old man's down there somewheres. If you see him, tell him Mike Reeder rode in a little while ago."

"I'll look for him," Sundown promised.

He rode slowly down an ancient road, badly eroded. Birds flashed through the trees. A doe bounded across the road ahead. Sundown grinned, breathed deeply. This was freedom.

He watched for Jupiter McKay. Three miles down the road he saw a big white stallion tied in a grassy clearing. A second horse stood beside it. Sundown rode there, looked about.

Jupiter McKay was not in sight. A narrow path led back into the brush. Somewhere near a small waterfall poured musically. Sundown followed the path. He walked perhaps fifty yards — and stopped abruptly, drawing back into the shelter of a bush.

Sunlight dappled the grassy bank at the base of the waterfall. Two men were sitting there, smoking, talking. Jupiter McKay — and Yance Claggett!

Neither had seen him. Their words were audible. Jupiter McKay's high-pitched voice was saying tartly: "You got no kick comin', Claggett. Rex figgered you might be in the house, an' sent 'im up without his guns. If you couldn't handle him, it's your own fault."

Yance Claggett spat, swore. "He was too tricky for me. Now you've got him, an' it's up to you. I don't want him around. He's dangerous. Get rid of him, or have him turned over to the sheriff."

Jupiter McKay laughed, tossed his sombrero to the ground, ran his fingers through that belligerent red fringe about his bald head. "Plenty of time for that. He's not lookin' for trouble. What about the Wagon Wheel? I'm tired of waiting. I've done my part an' now it's up to you."

Claggett shrugged. "They started their roundup yesterday. I've already advanced the old man five thousand on his beef. Soon as they're in the shipping pens, I'll set off the fireworks. Got it all arranged. Won't be any trouble. That'll give us the Wagon Wheel and a clear way through to Surprise Canyon. I'll be able to handle all the beef you can throw in on Wagon Wheel range. We'll both be sitting pretty."

"What about Lee's girl?" Jupiter McKay asked slyly.

Claggett grinned. "She'll go with the deal. I know where I stand. Now about this Daly. Are you sure you can handle him? He'll make trouble if he gets half a chance."

Jupiter McKay raised a sinewy fist, brought his fingers together in a crushing grip. "Like that," he said. "Forget about him."

Sundown moved into the open. "Stand up, you bald-headed old curly wolf, while I cut your toe nails!" he said aloud.

They came upright, grabbing for their guns. One look at Sundown's crouching figure behind his level belt guns was enough. Their hands shot in the air. Claggett cursed softly. Jupiter McKay blinked, forced a smile, said heartily: "Hello, Daly. Havin' a little fun? Put up them guns an' set down."

Sundown walked slowly to them, holstering one gun. "I made a mistake," he said through his teeth. "I thought I was comin' into good clean company when I headed for the McKays. I knew you was buzzards, but I didn't figger you'd eat your own meat. Unbuckle your belts an' chuck 'em on the ground."

Jupiter McKay's face reddened, his cold eyes under the coarse red brows gleamed. "Daly, I've had about enough of this. Git on your hoss an' ride if you don't like the McKays!"

"I'm ridin'," Sundown agreed, "but I'll pluck your tail feathers first. Jump, you pot-bellied old buzzard!"

Yance Claggett's right hand was bandaged heavily. With the left he unbuckled his gun belt and tossed it on the ground. Jupiter McKay hesitated, then slowly did the same. His eyes never left Sundown's face. His thin, bloodless lips barely moved. "You're a dead man now, Daly! No man ever did this to me an' lived to tell about it! I'll have you ridden down an' dragged behind a hoss!"

"I know," said Sundown. "You're a bad actor. But right now I'm poison! Walk out to your horses, gents. An' don't look so green about the gills. I don't shoot men in the back."

They went unwillingly. A lariat was tied to Jupiter McKay's saddle.

"Climb on an' hang your belly across the saddle," Sundown ordered Jupiter McKay. "Claggett here'll tie you on so you won't fall off."

Jupiter McKay began to swear in rising fury. It did him no good. In the end he was forced to climb awkwardly over his saddle, head and shoulders hanging down on one side, legs on the other.

Claggett, white-faced, took the lariat reluctantly and tied him. Sundown looked on with grim humor, inspected the job critically, then nodded with satisfaction.

"You look like a haunch of bad meat," he said to Jupiter McKay's purpling face. "Some of your men will ride by an' find you before long. Claggett, fork your horse and smoke down the trail ahead of me."

"What are you going to do?" Yance Claggett asked through stiff lips.

"I don't know," Sundown confessed, "but it'll probably be plenty before I'm through. I can't stomach your breed and McKay here's almost as bad. Get going, Claggett!"

It was two hours later before Sundown and Claggett stopped before a small log cabin in the foothills. Their horses were blowing. They had ridden hard down the rough mountain trails. Claggett shifted stiffly in the saddle and asked: "Now what?"

"Light," said Sundown briefly. Gun in hand, he waited until Claggett stood by his horse's head, then swung out of the saddle himself. "Inside," he ordered.

The door was unlocked. A faint look of hope on Claggett's face died away as they entered and found the interior deserted. A rough bunk in one corner, frying pan and coffee pot, and a shelf of canned goods over a small sheet-iron stove comprised the major furnishings.

"Saw this the other day," said Sundown. "Figgered it was a line rider's cabin. Everyone'll be at the roundup now and we can make ourselves at home. Climb on that bunk, Claggett."

Yance Claggett's sullen face darkened with anger. "This had gone far enough!" he exclaimed furiously. "What are you up to?"

Sundown grinned at him. "You'd be surprised. Get on that bunk. Should be some spare rope around here."

In a box that served for a table and catch-all, he found a lariat that had been broken, spliced, broken again, and discarded. Also several worn pigging strings. With the pigging strings he tied Claggett's ankles, his wrists and elbows behind him. And if the knots were loose he apparently did not notice.

"Now wiggle an' squall till you get a frog in your throat," he commented.

Claggett suddenly looked haggard, no longer debonair. "Let me go!" he begged. "I'll bargain with you."

"You're wigglin' quick," said Sundown.

Claggett suddenly seemed to realize that talk was wasted. Apprehension increased on his face. "This won't help you any," he said. "There's over four hundred dollars in my pocket. Take it an' leave the country. I'll keep my mouth shut."

"I'll bet you will," said Sundown. "An' then gobble up the Wagon Wheel. You won't get it, Claggett. You've been crooked long enough. I figgered on turnin' outlaw . . . but it only turned my stomach. I've elected myself a deputy an' I'm goin' to raise hell on the Las Piedras range till you hunt for a hole an' crawl in it. You an' the McKays."

"You'll be hanged so quick you won't know what happened if you stay around here, Daly."

"First off," said Sundown, "I'm going into Las Piedras an' get your brother Gil. He'll talk quicker than you. I'm going to take him to the Wagon Wheel an' pull the truth out of him before Enoch Lee. When the old man hears your brother talk, he'll hit the warpath. You'll be finished then. Figger that out while you're takin' the rest cure here."

Sundown went outside, unsaddled Claggett's horse, and ran it off. Taking the broken lariat, he rode off.

Wagon Wheel cattle were soon in evidence. He looked each bunch over and rode on. In the head of a small draw half a dozen cows, calves and two yearlings, were grazing. Sundown spurred toward one of the yearlings.

He had crudely spliced the rope as he rode, making it fast to the saddle horn. The black rushed the frightened yearling through a tangle of brush, down into a dry arroyo bed, and closed in swiftly. An underhand cast to a hind leg, and the yearling went down in a tangled heap as the black stopped short.

Sundown lit running, caught the other hind leg and flipped the yearling over, revealing the brand. He studied it intently, passing his hand over it. And straightened, frowning to himself.

He rolled a cigarette, flicked a match with a thumbnail, and inhaled. Without warning a crisp, even voice ordered: "I'm covering you, Daly! Don't move!"

It was Jordan Lee speaking. She had emerged from a tangle of piñon and brush on the right arroyo bank above him. She stood there, slim, straight, eyeing him along the motionless barrel of a .30-30 carbine.

The sun wrinkles at the corners of Sundown's eyes deepened as he lifted his hands, smiling thinly. "It's like wishing for an angel and having one drop out of the sky," he said. "I was thinking of you."

He was close enough to see the color leap into her cheeks. He saw her lip curl with scorn. "What are you doing with that calf?" she demanded.

Sundown looked at it, at her. "Trying out my arm," he said. "Got him neat the first throw. Step down an' be sociable, Miss Jordan. Your arm'll get tired holding that gun."

She wore soft leather boots, a divided riding skirt, and a short buckskin jacket. Her head was bare. Flying tendrils of hair framed her face, and she was taut, angry, threatening.

"I'm coming down!" she flared. "And I'm going to take your guns away and herd you in to the sheriff! I'll shoot you if your hands drop below your ears before I say to!"

"They won't," Sundown assured her gallantly. "They're hooked right up there in the air, ma'am. You don't need a gun to keep 'em there."

She came down the bank cautiously, stepped to him, holding the rifle steady. Sundown turned his back obligingly. She plucked the guns from his holsters. He chuckled over his shoulder at her. "You do it like an old hand," he said approvingly. "Now can I haul my fists down?"

"Step away from me before you do. And, remember, I'll shoot you with less provocation than you killed Dan Steele two days ago."

Sundown moved three paces away, lowered his arms slowly, and faced her with a quick frown. "Dan Steele? I don't know him."

"One of our hands," she said. "He was riding circle day before yesterday. His horse came in without him in the night. We found Dan at Cowpen Creek this morning, shot in the back."

"I see," said Sundown softly.

"I see too!" she blazed. "Dan was a hard worker. Steady. He was to be married next month. You shot him in the back and came to me with lies about my brother! Oh, don't bother to deny it!" she said scornfully as Sundown started to speak. "They backtracked on your trail. Your horse had one crooked hind shoe. They found its mark beside Dan Steele's body. When I think of Dan's girl crying her heart out, I could drop you where you stand!"

Cheeks flaming, voice shaking with anger, she was beautiful as she stood there. She was not afraid of him. She despised him.

Sundown drew a deep breath, smiled crookedly. "Put up your gun, Jordan Lee," he told her. "I've been to prison, and I'm accused of murder. Another one don't matter much, I guess. I happened to see your man shot, but I didn't have a hand in it. I couldn't have saved him. If your men looked close, they found other tracks beside him. Why should I shoot a man I never saw before . . . and then come on to tell you about your brother?"

"You shot him because you were afraid of him!" she retorted swiftly. "You knew men were looking for you."

"Shot him in the back while he ran away from me?" Sundown said dryly. "And then came on to your house where your hands could grab me? You reason like a woman: I'm no good so I naturally have to be guilty. Put up that gun and tell me why the Wagon Wheel is rustling cattle."

Her mouth opened soundlessly. Then fresh anger swept her. "What do you mean?" she demanded.

Sundown grinned at her. "This yearling is wearing a Wagon Wheel brand. Look close and you'll see someone has blotted a Double Anchor into the Wagon Wheel. It's peeled and healed, but you can still tell the fresh parts from the old."

Sundown knelt, drew two quarter circles in the sand with his finger, and connected them with a straight line. "Double Anchor," he explained. With a circular motion he turned the two quarter circles into one full circle. Two more lines through it made a six spoked wagon wheel. "That's how it was done," he said, straightening. "The Double Anchor range is north of you. Ben Salazar used to own it. Who holds it now?"

She stared at the brand he had drawn in the sand, then turned to the yearling and studied the brand on its hip. Her watchfulness had not abated, but she seemed suddenly worried, uncertain.

"Wallace, the sheriff, owns the Double Anchor now," she said slowly. "He bought it from Salazar about two years ago. We haven't bought any cattle from him. I . . . I don't understand it. Who did this?"

"Wallace will ask that," Sundown told her. "There's a lot of these blotted brands among your beef. It's clumsy work, and too fresh to pass. When it shows up at the roundup, there'll be trouble. They'll say your old man is a rustler."

"No one will believe it!" she flamed.

Sundown shrugged. "They'll believe what they see."

And by the swift misery flooding her face, he saw she believed him. All the anger had gone from her now. She looked suddenly frightened.

"It would kill him!" she burst out. "Everything we have is here on the ranch. Dad has fought and worked for it. The last few years he's been almost at the end of his rope. Everyone knows it. They'll . . . they'll think he rustled cattle to keep his head above water."

Sundown prodded: "What makes you so sure he didn't do it?"

Her chin lifted proudly. Her eyes scorned him. "He's my father. I know him!"

"Too bad you don't know me as well," said Sundown calmly. He bent, loosened the rope, watched the yearling bolt off along the arroyo. He coiled the rope, dropped it over his saddle horn, turned to her. "The McKay gang did this," he told her. "Day before yesterday I watched them run these yearlings in on your land. They shot your man. I guess he cut their trail and they wanted to shut his mouth. That's what brought me back today. I couldn't figger why the McKays would be bringing cattle onto your range."

"You're a strange man," she said. "I don't understand you or the things you do. But I believe you. You couldn't have had a hand in this. Get out and don't come back."

She dropped his guns in the sand, turned away.

"Wait a minute!" Sundown said sharply. He picked up his guns, asked as she paused: "What are you going to do?"

"Find Father at once and have him go to the sheriff at once."

"Yance Claggett is thick with the sheriff, isn't he?"

"What has that got to do with it?" her eyes smoldered.

"Nothing," Sundown denied hastily. "But if Wallace knows about this, he'll laugh at your father."

"Why should the sheriff know about this?"

"Your father owes money. If word gets around he's a rustler, they'll come down hard on him. He'll lose the ranch. Maybe Wallace wants more land. He may be mixed up in this."

"Dad would fight!" she said furiously.

"Wouldn't do him any good. Wallace is backed by the law. If the McKay gang is hooked up with the sheriff, your old man is bucking a stacked deck. My story won't help. They'd swear I was lying. Where's your father?"

"At the house."

"You better go to your father," said Sundown. "Tell him about the blotted brands. Have him call his men in from the roundup. Tell him I warned you. The McKays are riding today. They're playing for the Wagon Wheel. No telling what will happen."

"What are you going to do?"

Sundown grinned at her. "If anyone asks you, tell 'em I'll be at the Wagon Wheel sometime this evening."

☆ VII ☆
SATAN'S DEPUTY

*Y*ou came down off the mesa through a welter of great rocks, frost-riven, weather-worn, and Las Piedras was there, flung along the rocky bank of Monterey Creek. The stores and saloons, the bank, and eating place of Fat Lee, the wizened Chinaman, were all there in a cluster not more than two hundred yards long. At the end of the street, under towering cottonwoods, was the shabby little courthouse. For Las Piedras was the county seat.

It was twilight when Sundown rode off the mesa, and the shadows were even longer in Las Piedras. Lights were burning behind windows. Horses were racked before stores and saloons. But there were few people in the open.

He rode slowly along the streets, unrecognized. For a moment he paused before a small frame building whose front window bore the legend: Claggett Land and Cattle Company. The office inside was dark. Sundown rode on along the street to the courthouse. His face grew hard as he looked at the two-story brick building, with jail and sheriff's office on the ground floor. There, two years ago, he had sat through a trial and heard sentence passed on him. Many things had happened since.

Sundown turned to the right, passed the cottonwoods on the courthouse lawn, up the slope of the hillside. Beyond, straggled out for a quarter of a mile, were small adobe houses and gardens with, now and then, a small picket corral. A two-story frame house beyond the courthouse grounds was his destination. A light was burning inside. A dog barked as he rode to the side of the house and dismounted.

In the back a door slammed, feet crunched. A short, swarthy Mexican came out of the gathering dusk and peered at him.

"Gil Claggett inside?" Sundown asked.

"No, *señor. Señor* Claggett ees at hees saloon, I theenk."

"I want to see him . . . here," said Sundown. "Here's a half a dollar. Tell him, and then buy yourself a drink."

"*Gracias, señor.* You weel come eenside to wait? I am thee house man."

Sundown smiled grimly in the dim light. "Sure. Just the same."

The Mexican escorted him to the front door, showed him into a small parlor where an oil lamp burned beneath a great shade. The Mexican was swart, dark, with Indian blood showing in his coarse features. His eyes were alert, shrewd, his bow ingratiating.

"You please to estay here, an' I weel get thee *Señor* Claggett," he promised, hat in hand.

"Sure. And don't stop to buy your drink before you get him," Sundown grunted as the Mexican hurried out.

He rolled a cigarette, paced back and forth for several minutes, smoking, and then swung on his heel and went outside. Minute by minute it was getting darker. The aromatic smell of cedar smoke from kitchen fires hung low, pungent. Sundown slipped his guns from the holsters and inspected them.

The front porch of the Claggett house was almost hidden by a screen of morning glory vines. Sundown went into the blackest corner of the porch and took up his position. He was waiting there, silent, invisible, when a man reached the porch steps on his toes and came up almost inaudibly. It was Gil Claggett, almost as big as his brother Yance. Instead of opening the door and entering, Gil tiptoed to the parlor windows and peered in. He seemed puzzled at seeing no one inside, pressed his face closer to the glass to see better.

Sundown spoke softly. "You're wastin' time, Gil. I figgered you'd do something like that." He closed the space between them as he spoke. His left hand snapped out, knocked Gil Claggett's hand from the gun butt to which it had streaked. His right shoved a gun in Claggett's middle. "Take it easy," he advised. "I don't want to kill you before you get a chance to talk an' save your dirty hide!"

The swift intake of Gil Claggett's breath was audible. Rigid, he peered.

"It's me, Sundown Daly. I reckon you and Yance knew I'd show up one of these days."

Gil Claggett's voice came hoarse. "What do you want, Daly?"

"You," said Sundown. "Where's Yance?"

"Don't know. He rode out today on some business."

"I know," said Sundown gently. "I left him hog-tied in a little cabin up in the foothills. He's tamed and full of talk, Gil, and he ain't here to help you tonight. I'll tell you what he already knows. You Claggetts are through."

The darkness hid Gil Claggett's face. His sneer was audible. "The sheriff's looking for you, Daly. If you've dry-gulched Yance, it'll be something else to answer for."

Sundown took Gil Claggett's gun and thrust it behind his belt. He holstered his own gun. "Let's go, Gil."

Gil Claggett swung on him with the speed of a striking snake. A fist caught Sundown on the cheek. His left hand grabbed Sundown's gun wrist, blocking the draw. And as Sundown staggered, Gil snatched for the gun behind Sundown's belt.

He was as big as Sundown. Quicker, if anything. A shot would bring men running. Sundown thought of that as he reeled from the blow. Then, throwing himself forward against Gil Claggett, he got at his left gun and drew it. The barrel swung up against Gil Claggett's head with a dull impact.

Claggett suddenly went limp and staggered over against the house. He would have fallen if Sundown had not held him up. It was some moments before he was himself.

"Ought to have shot you then," Sundown said through his teeth. "Next time you'll get it."

Gil Claggett went with him without further protest. Sundown led the black behind them as they walked down the street. Fifty yards off they met Claggett's Mexican. He peered at them, hesitated as if waiting for an order. Gil Claggett ignored him. The Mexican went on toward the house.

A light was burning in the sheriff's office next to the jail. Sundown left the horse at the hitch rack in front and took Gil Claggett to the door. Wallace was at a desk at the side of the room, smoking a cigarette, writing busily. A prodding gun muzzle sent Gil Claggett in ahead of Sundown.

Wallace looked up, came quickly to his feet, reaching for the gun belt lying on top of his desk.

"Steady, Sheriff," Sundown warned.

Wallace dropped his hand, faced them. The cigarette was steady as it raised to his lips.

"Might have expected something like this, Daly. What's the matter with your head, Claggett? It's bleeding."

In the light Gil Claggett looked much younger than his brother. But as big, and good-looking. He burst out violently: "He trapped me on my porch and bent a gun barrel over my head! And brought me here! What are you going to do about it?"

Wallace smiled thinly under his black mustache. "Not much right now, with a gun in my face. I'm no fool. Daly, what's on your mind? I've been looking for you."

"I heard," Sundown agreed. "You and Claggett sit in them chairs against the opposite wall where you won't be tempted to start anything."

He reached back without taking his eyes off the two men, pulled the curtain on the door, and slipped the heavy bolt, then moved over a step and did the same to the window shade.

The sheriff and Claggett dropped down in the chairs. Wallace was gnawing the end of his black mustache now and frowning. He said curtly as Sundown walked to the door at the rear of the room and bolted it: "This has gone about far enough, Daly. I don't like to be held up in my own jail."

"Too bad we don't get everything we like," Sundown said. "I didn't like to be blamed for holding up that Paradise stage. Might have done it if I needed the money, but I just happened by in time to get the blame. If anybody'd taken time to look back on my trail, they've seen where I was riding alone all day. Those jaspers didn't give me time to say it."

"Lie down with the hogs and you get up with mud," Wallace said bluntly. "You aimed to run with the McKays, and that gets you all the dirt in the territory. The sheriff over Paradise way read your sign next morning and sent out word you might not be the man they wanted after all. I'm ready to forget it. But I want you for killing a Wagon Wheel man on Cowpen Creek. That crooked hind shoe on your horse is a dead giveaway."

"And he had the nerve to threaten *me!*" Gil Claggett snorted.

"Shut up," Sundown said. "The McKays shot that Wagon Wheel man, Sheriff. I just happened to be there. They plugged him in the back after he busted into a little play they were making. Rex McKay and a cold-eyed little gun shark by the name of Salty O'Shea dropped him with their rifles."

Wallace raised his cigarette deliberately, inhaled, and let smoke dribble up through his black mustache. "That so? You just happened to be around when trouble busts, don't you?"

Gil Claggett sneered. "It's always a good idea to blame everything on the Mc-Kays."

Sundown fixed him with a cold eye. "Mebbeso, at that, since you an' your brother are runnin' with the McKays. An' the sheriff, too."

"*What's that?*" Wallace slammed his cigarette to the floor and came out of his chair. "Damn you, Daly, what do you mean by that?"

"You heard me, Wallace. I said you were running with the McKays, too. Calm down."

A startled look flashed over Gil Claggett's face — apprehension, uneasiness. But as Wallace sank back in the chair angrily, Gil Claggett shrugged. "He's crazy as a locoed steer, Wallace."

"I believe it!" Wallace agreed violently.

"Mebbe you can explain them Double Anchor yearlings the McKays threw over on Wagon Wheel land the other day," Sundown said mildly. "Somebody's taken a running iron an' blotted 'em over into Wagon Wheels."

"You're lying!" Wallace said savagely. "None of my cattle has been rebranded this year! And none of them has been thrown over on Enoch Lee's range!"

Sundown said dreamily: "I saw the McKays drive 'em on Enoch Lee's land. I saw the blotted brands. Dan Steele busted into it an' got shot in the back. I heard Yance Claggett go over the deal with Jupiter McKay this morning. You're mixed up in it too."

"The hell I am!" Wallace shouted, pounding the arm of his chair. "If any man said so, he lied!"

"And so," Sundown said in the same dreamy tone, "seeing Enoch Lee was gettin' knifed in the back by his friend Yance, and my number was up as soon as Jupiter McKay got around to obligin' Claggett, I appointed myself unofficial deputy of the county. You're hereby relieved from office, Wallace, and as acting-deputy I'll ride herd on the job. First, we'll throw Gil in a cell where he can't leak out. An' then we'll round up a posse and go lookin' for trouble."

"I told you he was crazy!" Gil Claggett snarled.

"Gil, where's Yance?" Wallace asked suddenly.

"Saw him this afternoon," Gil lied glibly. "He dropped in at the house for a minute, an' then rode out again."

Sundown sighed. "When you lie like that, Gil, it make me envious. I tried to be a skunk too, but I can't stand the stink. Git back in your cell and, if I hear one yip out of you, I'm comin' in an' pistol-whip a new face on you. Wallace, put him in."

Wallace looked at the pistol, and stood up obediently. "Sorry, Gil," he said. "Looks like there's nothing else to do."

"You're not going to lock me up!" Gil Claggett said furiously.

"Git!" said Sundown. "Peaceable too. I been waiting two years to get at you. I'm fightin' temptation now."

Muttering under his breath, Gil Claggett walked back into the small cell block. He was the only prisoner. Wallace locked him in and returned to the office silently. Sundown ejected the shells from the sheriff's gun, emptied the belt loops and held the useless gear out.

"Wear it, so you'll look regular," he directed. "Now make me regular deputy with a deputy's badge."

Wallace took a nickel badge from a desk drawer. "I'd better swear you in," he suggested.

"Shoot."

It took but a moment. Sundown grinned wryly. "I've come a long way since they let me out of the pen. Now pay attention, Wallace. I want a posse. You give the orders." Sundown holstered his gun. "I'll be at your elbow. Don't get careless. I want all the men you can raise in a half an hour. We're riding to Enoch Lee's first."

"And then?" Wallace asked with an expressionless face.

"We'll see," said Sundown. "I'm gamblin' on what a couple of crooks will do. Bein' crooked, they ought to think just one way."

"I'll have to know what the posse's riding into," Wallace said stubbornly. "There'll be married men in it. Friends of mine. I'll lead them into no trap, Daly."

They faced one another, equally big and broad-shouldered. Wallace, gray-haired and rock-like in his responsibility and resolve. Sundown, lean, hard, muscular, younger but equally as hard-faced. The clash of wills struck tension in the small office.

"You said you were going to clean the McKays out before you left office," Sundown said abruptly. "You're doing it tonight, Wallace. They've been hiding out at the old Death's Head Mine. Yance Claggett is workin' with them. I left him tied up back in the foothills. I'm out to bust him and the McKays tonight."

"I'll not lead a posse up to Death's Head Mine tonight," Wallace said flatly. "I know the place. You have to go through a trap to get to the mine. Half a dozen men could hold it."

"Not even to prove you ain't feeding at the same trough with the McKays?"

Wallace's face grew bleak, angry. "What are you driving at, Daly?"

"Skunks," said Sundown laconically. "Couldn't stand them in the pen and I can't now. That takes in the Claggetts, the McKays, and this Wagon Wheel deal."

Wallace nodded, reached for his Stetson. "Let's get the posse together," he said briefly.

☆ VIII ☆

DEATH AT THE WAGON WHEEL

*T*hey rode out of Las Piedras an hour later, the clash of hoofs on the rocky ground striking against the night as they topped the mesa and rode southeast toward the Wagon Wheel range and the mountains beyond.

Wallace rode at the head, Sundown beside him. Eleven armed men followed — all the good riders that Wallace had been able to gather without turning to the ranchers. Wallace's gun was still empty; he carried a rifle, but had no cartridges for it.

Sundown had been standing beside him, grimly silent, in those moments in front of the jail when Wallace told the men they were riding out after the McKays who had killed Dan Steele on Cowpen Creek.

"Enoch Lee will have his men ready," Wallace had told them bluntly. "I'm leaving Harvey Greer behind to round up more men. The McKays are hiding out at the Death's Head Mine up north of Surprise Canyon on Boulder Mountain. They've killed one man. They rustled a lot of my beef, and they're evidently set to raise hell on Las Piedras range for some time. If we meet 'em, there'll be guntalk. Any man who hasn't the guts for it better drop out now."

That was what Sundown had told Wallace to say. Wallace himself had towered before the men sternly. No one had dropped out.

There were men among the eleven who recognized Sundown. Several who had been his friends greeted him cordially. All had noticed the deputy's badge on his shirt. They were curious. They discussed it in asides among themselves. But no man questioned his right to be at Wallace's elbow, apparently by Wallace's wish.

Wallace spoke out of the corner of his mouth as they rode. "This is a queer play, Daly. I haven't forgotten you set out to join the McKays. If this is a double cross and we're trapped, I'll hunt you down myself!"

"*Gracias*," Sundown said. "Thanks, Wallace. I'll have the whole Las Piedras range yappin' at my heels if this keeps on. I'll give you fair warning . . . look for trouble anytime. Pull up your posse somewhere along here and I'll tell you what to do."

Wallace stopped his men after the next quarter of a mile. A low-voiced request took him off a hundred yards with Sundown.

"We'll cut the Wagon Wheel house road just ahead," said Sundown. "Tell your men to drop back a mile or so, and follow us easy. You and I'll sashay on alone."

"It doesn't make sense," Wallace objected irritably. "What are you up to?"

"I'm gamblin' that a smart crook always overreaches himself. That's why they get hung or land in the pen so often."

"Meaning me?"

"Meaning everybody connected with this Wagon Wheel deal, Wallace. Tell 'em."

Wallace reined back to his men, gave his orders curtly. Then the sheriff and Sundown rode on ahead alone.

Sundown passed his sombrero over to Wallace as they went. "There's a double handful of cartridges in it, Wallace."

Wallace passed the hat back empty a few moments later. "Nothing to stop me from taking you in now, Daly."

"Nope," Sundown agreed. "Why don't you?"

"I want to see what you're up to."

"You will," Sundown promised.

His words were prophecy. They rode a mile further, topped the rise on the narrow dirt track they were following, and the Wagon Wheel lights were in the near distance. A horse nickered at the side of the road. The stir of riders off in the dark paralleled their course.

A voice called: "That you, Daly?"

Sundown drew his gun in the darkness and called back: "It's me. Who is it?" and a second voice, close by, laughed shrilly: "It's me, Daly! Jupiter McKay! We been waitin' for you!"

Wallace uttered a round oath furiously. "I was looking for something like this, Daly! By God, I'll kill you first!"

"Damn you, ride for the ranch house!" said Sundown. "An' argue later!" His gun blast laced the night with orange fire, in the direction of Jupiter McKay's voice. He drove the spurs deep. The black leaped forward.

The night was thick about them, hiding the men offside the road. Jupiter McKay shouted: "Gil Claggett, drop back an' we'll get him!"

Close on the heels of that the drum of quick pursuit was drowned in the clash and roar of gunfire. Bending low in the saddle, Sundown heard the vicious whine of lead lacing the darkness about him.

They had been lined up alongside the road, the whole McKay gang it seemed. They rode a gauntlet, a gauntlet of death, and only the quickness of their getaway and the darkness saved him. Sundown emptied his belt gun and reloaded as he rode. Wallace swept up beside him, firing as he came. No words were spoken. But the suspicion and distrust that had lain between them was no more.

The gunfire behind them slacked off. Later Sundown was to know that the McKays had been confused by Gil Claggett's failure to join them. They had received strict orders that no harm come to him.

The pursuit swept down the long slope after them and the lights of the Wagon Wheel ranch house quickly drew near. The McKays were dropping further and further behind, though, seeming in no hurry to close up against the flaming guns they followed. And that too was quickly explained.

Spurring, slashing hard, they swept up to the ranch house, standing silently, quietly. The front door was closed. The windows were shut. No horses or men were in evidence. Only the barking dogs that warily kept their distance as they clamored.

"Something's wrong!" Sundown yelled to Wallace as they rode up.

"What?" Wallace queried.

Sundown reined sharply before the portal, struck the ground running, and made for the front door.

"Who's that?" a sharp, familiar voice demanded out of the darkness.

"Daly!" Sundown panted mechanically. "Where is everybody?"

"Where they won't do any good, you damn meddler!" the voice snarled.

Sundown dodged, grabbing for his gun, as he recognized the speaker. It was Rex McKay!

Surprise — absolute, complete. Orange flame and the roar of a shot drove aside the portal shadows the next instant. Sundown spun half around as a hammer blow struck his shoulder. The shock dazed him. He knew he was badly hit, and for fatal seconds his body refused to function as he staggered and almost went down. His whole left side had been numbed by the impact of the heavy lead slug.

Two paces away a split instant later Wallace's gun thundered, a brace of shots sounding at once. The dull thud of Rex McKay's dropping revolver was audible. His strangled gasp was barely understandable.

"Claggett . . . don't you know me? It's Rex McKay! You . . . you shot the wrong man!"

"I don't reckon so," Wallace said harshly.

He was not answered. Rex McKay groaned once, and then fell heavily.

"I got him!" Wallace said with satisfaction. "Daly, I apologize. Back there I had figured you'd led me right into a trap. I was set to plug you when you cut loose at the McKays. What's going on around here? Where's Enoch Lee and his men? Did McKay get you?" Wallace stepped close.

Sundown said through clenched teeth: "In the shoulder. Guess I'm all right. I can move my arm a little now. Something's wrong here, Wallace! Enoch Lee and his men should have been waiting! They'd've been out here now if they were here. Enoch Lee and Yance Claggett thought I was coming here this evening with Gil Claggett. Claggett told the McKays, like I figgered he would. I wonder what . . . what's inside the house?"

The door opened abruptly as Sundown finished in a swift rush of words. A small, slender, stoop-shouldered figure stepped out, peering. The tangle of uncut hair under his worn Stetson was silhouetted against the light that struck through the doorway; and his gliding progress, gun in hand, his wizened mask of a face stamped him for what he was — a killer.

"Get him all right, Rex?" he asked with no concern in his voice.

"Too bad, Salty!" Sundown said softly. "Drop your gun an' reach high!"

The McKays were coming up with a rush as Sundown spoke. The action at the portal had flashed by in a few brief moments. And Salty O'Shea moved with the speed of a striking rattler, snapping his gun toward the direction of Sundown's voice before his body turned.

Sundown, a scant two paces away, was in action at the first move. His gun swung up, dropped down and smashed Salty O'Shea's gun wrist with a terrific blow as it came around. Cursing with pain, the little man grabbed at a broken wrist as the gun fell from his helpless fingers. He tried to dodge. Sundown tripped him.

"Get him, Wallace!" Sundown bit out. "Take him in the house! They'll corner us here on the portal in a minute!"

Wallace pounced on the scrambling, cursing figure of Salty O'Shea and jerked the little man roughly upright. Gripping O'Shea behind the neck, he booted him through the doorway. Sundown caught up the fallen gun and followed hastily as the drumming rush of the McKays pounded up to the house. A stout wooden bar stood in the corner beside the door. Sundown dropped it into heavy brackets as men dismounted and hurried to the portal. He paused a moment, listening.

Jupiter McKay's high shrill voice said excitedly: "They ain't here! That musta been them went in the house! What's the matter? Rex didn't get him? There was shootin'!"

"Mebbe Rex dropped him an' took Claggett inside," another voice suggested. "Strike a match, somebody!"

And a moment later there were exclamations, oaths. Jupiter McKay's shrill voice rose into a fury of grief. "*It's Rex!* He's dead! Daly killed him!"

"That Daly," one of the men said violently, "must wear a horseshoe around his neck and a rabbit's foot in his pocket. He's hell for luck, an' a shootin' fool!"

Jupiter McKay raved: "He's in there! Get him out! I'll tear his heart out with my own hands! I'll drag him from here to the mine on my own rope! Break in the door!"

Sundown flattened himself against the wall and called: "You old buzzard, it ain't healthy in here! That worthless whelp of yours didn't get all the hell that's loose tonight!"

"Get 'em!" Jupiter McKay yelled.

Guns barked on the other side of the door. Lead ripped and poured through the planks. Sundown shot back twice through the door. For a moment the shooting ceased. He seized the instant of peace to slide along the wall to the door of the living room. As he stepped through, they opened up on the door from an angle.

Yance Claggett had been evidently standing in the living room with his arm about Jordan Lee's shoulder when Wallace entered with his prisoner. Yance Claggett was staring at Wallace as if seeing a ghost.

"I thought it was Gil coming in," he said in a queer voice as Sundown stepped into the room.

Wallace took a tighter grip on his squirming, cursing prisoner, and lightly cuffed him with the barrel of his revolver. The sheriff's voice was expressionless as he spoke to Yance Claggett. "You thought it was Gil, Yance. Why?"

"Why . . . why, Daly said he was going to bring Gil back," Yance stammered.

"And that's why these McKay gunmen were waiting at the front door?" Wallace questioned.

Jordan Lee slipped out of Claggett's arm. Her face was pale, her eyes big. But in that moment, before she spoke, Sundown got again a feeling of a river rising behind barriers, ready to burst.

"McKay gunmen?" she said to Wallace in a tight voice. "You must be mistaken. They were waiting to see my father about some cattle. Yance knew them. We've been talking to them in here."

"I never saw them before, Jordan!" Claggett denied harshly. "You were mistaken!"

Salty O'Shea, gibbering with pain and helpless anger, snarled: "Damn you Claggett! You don't walk out on me like this! If you had any guts, you'd've' been out there with a gun, backin' me up! You said Daly was coming back with your brother. An' he brought the sheriff! I think you double-crossed us. Daly, I wish I'd've' shot you back there on Cowpen Creek the other day!"

Yance Claggett looked like a drowning man, snatching at straws. "Wallace," he said hoarsely, "the man's lying! He doesn't know what he's saying! I'm a deputy! I'm with you on this! Let me have him an' I'll lock him up while you hold those gunmen off outside. Where's Gil? Why didn't you bring him? He's a deputy too."

"Gil had his eyeteeth pulled," Sundown drawled. "He's locked in a cell back in Las Piedras."

"That right, Wallace?" Yance Claggett asked gruffly.

Wallace nodded. "That's right, Yance. And it looks to me like you're going to join him. Miss Lee, where's your father?"

The firing outside had ceased. Curtains had been drawn over the living room windows, shutting off the gaze of anyone outside. And while Sundown stepped swiftly over to them and listened, Jordan Lee answered Wallace.

"Dad took his men and rode to Las Piedras to find you, Sheriff. They took the shortcut. They must have missed you." She swung on Yance Claggett. "*You* told Dad to go. You said you'd stay with me and see that everything was all right. And all the time you were working with the McKays!"

Yance Claggett winced at the blazing scorn in her voice. Then he whirled around, crouching, as a heavy crash sounded at the back of the house. They heard wood splintering, giving. . . .

☆ IX ☆
FIRE!

*S*undown jumped for the open hall door, stopping just before he reached it. He heard Wallace cry out sharply: "Come back, Yance! Don't try it!"

There was a door near the great stone fireplace in the back wall of the room. Yance Claggett had leaped for it, was wrenching it open as Sundown looked over his shoulder. Wallace raised his gun, hesitated.

And in that moment Yance Claggett whirled out of the room. But only for a moment. Loud beyond the door a gun exploded twice. Claggett cried out, staggering back against the door, then reeled back into the room.

Jordan Lee cried out too, involuntarily, as she saw his face. A bullet had struck him below the eyes. For one awful instant the bulging eyes, in that face that had once been so handsome, looked at them glassily. They were the eyes of a dead man who still moved. Yance Claggett's mouth opened, emitted a hoarse, unnatural croak, wondering, dazed.

"They shot me!" Yance Claggett got out. His bandaged right hand lifted jerkily toward his face — and never reached it. Yance Claggett fell there in the doorway, and no one could have helped him if there had been time.

From the next room a yell came. "That was Claggett, Jim! You plugged him!"

"Hell!" said Jim. "I thought it was Daly! Why didn't he yell?"

Wallace was at the doorway by then, pumping shots through it across Yance Claggett's body. He was answered only once and the bullet knocked splinters from the door edge by his shoulder. A door at the back of the next room slammed heavily.

Wallace hauled Yance Claggett's still form aside and closed the door, saying disgustedly: "They wouldn't shoot it out."

Salty O'Shea had been left standing helpless in the middle of the floor. He ducked as a gun spoke out in front and glass crashed, and a bullet smacked against the opposite wall. Beady-eyed, watchful, tense, he turned from Wallace to Sundown, scanning the room with the light of desperation in his eyes. Other shots came from the front, the bullets crashing through the window panes and smacking into the brick wall.

Ignoring them, Wallace walked to Salty O'Shea. His tanned, hard face showed no emotion as he said: "You're in the way here now. Can't bother with you." Wallace reached out a big hand, caught the smaller man to him and calmly swung the butt of his revolver behind Salty's ear. Salty went limp. Wallace let him drop, said simply: "He's dangerous."

Sundown grinned. "Mister, I take your dust for ever thinking you were hooked up with the McKays. Fact is, I never did really think you were, but I couldn't take any chances. You wouldn't have believed me anyway, or brought a posse out here if I hadn't dealt the cards."

"Glad to see you're gettin' some sense," Wallace grunted. "Guess you're right at that. I'd have slapped you in a cell if I'd gotten to my gun first."

They could hear steps tramping at the back of the house, voices speaking loud and unafraid. Jupiter McKay's shrill, bawling tones rose above all other sounds. "Get in the hall there! Block all the ways they can get out!"

Jordan Lee had been backed into the corner by Sundown. She had cried out involuntarily as Yance Claggett had reeled back into the room, then had stood silently. Now she reached to the corner behind her and caught up a light rifle leaning there, and came toward the door where Sundown was standing. He swept her back with an arm.

"Get down where you'll be safe!" he rapped out. "This ain't your game!"

She knocked his arm away. Her dark eyes were blazing. Her brown hair hardly came to Sundown's shoulder. But she became more than a slip of a girl as she answered him. More than the slender little beauty he had first seen. Once more her young face was oddly mature, tense, stubborn, angry. "They're in my house!" she declared. "They've come to kill! Do you think I'll stand helplessly by like . . . like a silly child while they do this?"

Standing there with his blood-soaked shoulder and the pain stabbing with every move, Sundown grinned at her. It was like a fragment out of a dream. Men tramping and shouting at the back of the house, shots crashing through the window panes and raking the room. Death all about the house, closing in on them — and yet for a few moments they seemed apart from all of this, alone.

"You win," he said, and Sundown didn't realize then how gentle his voice was for the first time. Jordan Lee did. "I guess maybe we'll need you after all, before this is over," he said, and whirled to the door as feet rushed along the hall. A man, two men, guns held ready, appeared.

Gun steadied across his forearm, Sundown shot deliberately in a tearing crescendo. The first man plunged to the floor. The second dodged back out of sight, then caught an ankle of the fallen man and dragged him back too.

Powder smoke was drifting in hazy, acrid waves through the room. The air never seemed to lose the crashing reverberations of gunfire. Sundown moved back a step and awkwardly reloaded his gun, wincing as he had to move his left arm.

"Got him in the hollow!" Sundown said. "He'll be reformed from now on."

There was no cessation of the raking fire through the windows. But it was blind shooting, for the curtains still held up. A bullet smashed the lamp shade and chimney, and glass cascaded to the floor. Wallace crossed to the lamp and blew it out.

"Time that was done anyway," he said.

The half light in the hall, reflected from an open door in one of the rear rooms, was eerie, ghost-like. Jordan Lee's rifle barked suddenly at one of the front windows. She had crept there, lifted a corner of the curtain, and shot without warning.

"I think I hit him," she said calmly over her shoulder as she pumped a fresh shell into the breech. "I fired at the flash of his gun."

Jupiter McKay's shrill shout was clearly audible. "There's only two of them in there! Burn 'em out! Here's a can of coal oil!"

One of the men protested hoarsely: "Salty O'Shea's in there!"

"Damn Salty O'Shea! He had no business gettin' himself caught that way! If he'd been half the man I thought he was, my boy wouldn't be dead now!"

And it was plain by Jupiter McKay's voice that the man was half mad with grief and fury.

Wallace showed emotion for the first time, and worry. "If they burn us out, we're done for," he said. "They've got the house surrounded. We haven't got a chance to fight out that way. I wonder where my men are?"

"We were a couple of miles ahead of them, travelin' fast," Sundown said. "We've only been here a few minutes."

"It seems like a longer time with all this hell bustin' loose," Wallace grunted in the darkness. His voice grew more worried than ever. "McKay has a lot of men out there. More than the eleven we brought. I don't know whether they can do much if they do come up. They're outnumbered. I hate to think of them walkin' into a thing like this an' gettin' shot to pieces." Even then, with death closing in inexorably, Wallace the peace officer was thinking of his men.

"Somebody has to get shot," Sundown said coolly, "an' you can't bust up the McKays by standin' off wondering what will happen. I figgered Enoch Lee an' his men would be here, waiting for us. But as long as old Jupiter McKay's hand is called, we might as well see how many cards he can lay on the line. We got to do one thing, though, Wallace. Get this girl out. They're a bad lot, but they won't hurt a woman. They've got no quarrel with her. Let's yell for a truce while she walks out."

"You will not!" Jordan said defiantly in the darkness. "I'm here, and here I'll stay! I wouldn't trust them, and I won't leave you two."

"I'd put her out," Sundown suggested through the darkness to Wallace, as he watched the faintly lighted doorway.

"Try it!" she flared.

She had hardly finished speaking when the hallway beyond Sundown glowed suddenly with the fierce red light of sweeping flames.

"Here we go!" said Sundown dryly. "Our own private little bonfire!"

The words were hardly out when there came a muffled swish of flame. A cloud of fire and sparks sailed through the air and struck outside the door, flaring up wildly to the height of a man's shoulder. It was a bundle of blankets saturated with kerosene, burning more fiercely each instant. The red glare struck into the room. Heat followed. And the choking smell of burning wood rolled over them.

Sundown kicked the door shut with his foot. "No use to drag it in and try to put it out," he commented calmly. "And if I stick my nose out the door, I'll get it shot off."

"They've pitched one outside this door too," Wallace said. "These pine doors will burn through in no time."

Sundown sighed. "It's as hard on them as us. The smoke goes both ways."

"We'll be burnt out like rats in a trap if we don't do something!" Wallace fumed.

"We'll get shot up with McKay lead if we bust out an' try to do something," Sundown retorted cheerfully. "We're damned if we do, and damned if we don't." He began to whistle softly through his teeth.

Wallace had judged the doors correctly. The dry, pitch-filled pine caught instantly. The panels cracked. Smoke began to seep through. The red glare glinted ominously through the cracks.

Jordan Lee moved close to Sundown, put her hand on his arm. "It's going to be pretty bad," she said. "I'm not afraid, but . . . but I want to be near someone." Her voice was a bit unsteady, frightened.

Hearing it, Sundown felt red rage stirring for the first time. It swept away his cold bitterness. It made the thing personal and, in his throat, unspoken, he damned Jupiter McKay savagely. But he holstered his gun and took her hand, her small, strong hand that had not been afraid of work. It lay cold in his, and clung tightly, as if she found strength in the contact. "Some way, somehow," said Sundown with a confidence he did not feel, "we'll get out of this. The McKay luck has held too long. It's due to bust tonight."

"I wish I thought so," she said uncertainly. Her fingers clung tighter in his.

Her heady presence was like wine — and there might be no tomorrow. Sundown swept her close, roughly, and kissed her with fierceness born of gunfire, of flame, and of death.

She gasped, and for a moment lay limp in his arms, against his chest. Her cheeks were satin smooth, her mouth soft, yielding. And then she was out of his arms, laughing in a choked rush.

"Sorry," Sundown muttered.

Her groping hand caught his again. It was no longer cold. "I'm not," said Jordan Lee. "I'm glad! I'll always be glad!"

"I'm a jailbird!" said Sundown hoarsely. "A no-account, worthless, lowdown rannigan!"

"You are *you*," she said.

She was like the river come to the sea, broad and deep as it met the tide and pushed to the deeper depths where there was peace.

Flying lead smashed through the window panes with vicious smacks. The crackling roar of flame eating through the doors rose higher. Glowing red spots drove back the blackness with a crimson glow. The heat was greater, the smoke thickening about them.

Wallace swore aloud. "I'll make a break for it before I roast in here!"

Sundown said to Jordan Lee: "The only way out is through these two doors?"

"Yes," she replied. "There used to be a door on the other side of the fireplace, into a bedroom, but Dad made a store room out of it, and put a bookcase in the doorway and a closet on the other side."

Sundown touched her arm. "Come over to the bookcase. Duck low when you cross the room."

He went first. "Wallace," he said, "come here. I've got a surprise for you." Wallace joined him by the bookcase set into the wall, and filled solid with volumes. "Throw the books on the floor, Wallace!"

And when that was done, Sundown ordered: "Take out the shelves." It was done.

Boards were nailed across the back. "Kick them out at the bottom!" Sundown directed.

Wallace drove a boot through the bottom board; nails gave. In short seconds he had kicked two boards loose at one end. His powerful hands wrenched them free. There was room now to crawl through.

Sundown knelt at the opening, listened, heard nothing on the other side. He wriggled through, stood upright in a tangle of hanging clothes. He opened the door cautiously, peered into a black, silent, deserted room. "All right," he husked over his shoulder, and groped forward.

Boxes and trunks were stacked about. Shelves lined the walls. He found a single window, curtained. Wallace and Jordan Lee joined him there.

"Get her out!" Sundown urged Wallace. "They won't be watching this end of the house."

"You're coming too?" she asked.

"Sure, I'll follow."

Wallace pushed the window up softly, climbed out, caught her in his arms as she followed. Sundown heard the soft patter of their steps for an instant — and then they were gone in the night.

A man came running from the front of the house. Sundown's gun slid over the window sill. But the fellow passed unseeing to the rear.

The high pitched voice of Jupiter McKay sounded back inside the house. Sundown turned and crossed the room. He found a door in the corner. It was unlocked, the key on the inside. He opened the door cautiously.

A blast of heat and the smoke struck him in the face. The red glare of fire enveloped him.

The room was empty. Fire blazed furiously about the door at the front of the room. At the back a door stood ajar and it was through there the voice of Jupiter McKay was coming. It sounded as if McKay were just outside the door.

Sundown gulped a deep breath, hunched his shoulders, and plunged into the heat and smoke. Face set grim, gun steady in hand. He reached the door, kicked it open with his foot. Jupiter McKay was standing a scant arm's length away, his back to the door.

On sudden impulse Sundown jammed his gun in the holster, reached out. Jupiter McKay felt his presence, or felt the sudden wave of heat. He started to turn. Sundown's big hand clamped on the back of the outlaw leader's neck at the same instant. With a mighty yank he brought McKay through the door and spun him back into the room.

McKay struck a chair, half fell, and came up with the quickness of a cat, whirling around to the door on his bandy legs. He saw Sundown and venom and fury boiled across his face. In that moment his spindle-shanked, slightly grotesque figure, with its pink cheeks and coarse red eyebrows, looked like something monstrous. A thin, high-pitched cry of fury burst from him.

They faced each other through the roiling smoke. And between them tension hung at the snapping point.

Sundown held his good hand breast high. His face was a grim mask. "Here I am, you double-crossin' old wolf!" he said. "You wanted me, an' now you got me. Go for your gun, McKay! You got a chance!"

☆ **X** ☆
THE LAST OF THE RED MCKAYS

*J*upiter McKay's tight-lipped mouth went to a slit. He hesitated, his cold eyes wavering. And then one lean, powerful hand flashed to the gun at his hip.

He was fast, a dead shot, and starting on even terms. But that taut, raised hand of Sundown's dropped like a passing shadow. His gun leaped from the holster like a thing alive. He shot while the muzzle of Jupiter McKay's gun was still lifting.

The monstrous, bandy-legged figure reeled forward through the smoke. The gun exploded into the floor. And an instant later Jupiter McKay pitched forward, face down, gun flying from his fingers.

Coughing, choking from the smoke, Sundown stepped to him, caught a leg and dragged the prone figure into the store room. He was not an instant to soon. Men boiled through the doorway from the hall as he straightened up. A yell announced that he was seen. A gun jerked in his direction.

Sundown fired a snap shot from his hip, leaped aside as a second shot answered. He felt the bullet tear the hair vest and then the wall hid him. They would have to come through the door to get him. Sundown waited grimly, wiping the back of his hand across his watering eyes. The smoke was fast filling the store room, too.

In that moment the thunder of drumming hoofs drifted through the open window. Men whooped loudly. The sharp crackle of gunfire burst out all around the house.

"Trouble boys! Everyone outside! Get the horses! McKay's dead! It's every man for himself!"

Sundown reloaded his gun and followed them. Not a McKay man was in sight as he entered the back hall. Outside the shots and yells continued. Men cried out with pain, with unintelligible orders, and requests. Horses galloped off furiously.

No need to wonder what had happened. Wallace's posse had swept down in belated but startling surprise. Without a leader the McKays scattered like chaff before a wind. Through the back door, as Sundown reached it, burst the stubby, bearded figure of Enoch Lee, brandishing a revolver. Recognizing Sundown, he shouted hoarsely: "Where's my daughter?"

"Outside. Safe," Sundown told him. "I thought you were Wallace's posse."

Enoch Lee raised a shaking hand and pushed his hat onto the back of his head. No longer was he the stern, ascetic, righteously hard man. Fear had broken through his shell of reserve.

"We followed the posse from Las Piedras," he said unsteadily. "Caught up with them on the road, talked a few minutes and then took our time following Wallace. Are you sure Jordan is all right?"

"Wallace got her out of here a few minutes ago. As soon as the McKays are on the run, get some men in here to put these fires out."

The McKays were already on the run; some were shot down as they ran from the house, others scattered into the night afoot, and a few on horseback. The shooting stopped almost as quickly as it started. Enoch Lee shouted orders, sent men into the house to attack the flames.

Wallace came out of the night with Jordan Lee. Later, when the fire had been beaten down with blankets, and killed with buckets of water, and the wounded and dead were being collected by the posse and the Wagon Wheel men, Enoch Lee faced Wallace, Jordan, and Sundown. From them he heard what had happened during his absence. He was a sobered man, Enoch Lee. "I didn't believe the McKays would come to the Wagon Wheel tonight," he confessed. "I wanted to see you about those blotted brands, Wallace."

Wallace shrugged. "It was no doing of mine. I've questioned a couple of the McKay men we've got tied up. The McKays rustled them off my land. They wanted your land. You wouldn't sell. The Claggetts, who have been working with them for years buying rustled cattle, lent you money so they could foreclose. The Wagon Wheel is a natural entrance to Surprise Canyon and then through the mountains. It was a smooth deal to get you out of the way without violence. But thanks to Daly, here, it misfired. He saved you tonight, Enoch Lee, although I'm not clear yet how he knew what he was doing."

Sundown grinned sheepishly. "The McKays were after me. I tied Claggett up in the hills and ran his horse off, but fixed it so he could get loose, figgerin' he'd walk in to the ranch here, or run across the McKays and tell 'em I was going to bring his brother out to the ranch tonight and tip their hand. If they went to town tryin' to catch us, they might miss us. All they had to do was wait around the ranch and jump us when we showed up. I figgered you'd be here with your men, armed and ready, Mister Lee. Wallace and I left the posse back a ways and came on alone, like I was bringin' Gil Claggett. I figgered they'd jump us and we'd have the McKays caught between the posse and the men here at the ranch." Sundown shrugged. "I didn't figger on you being away."

Enoch Lee fingered his beard. "It seems I was a rash and headstrong man," he admitted. "I distrusted you, Daly. I thought harshly of you. But I'll make amends. There's a place here for you at the ranch, if you'll take it."

"No," said Wallace. "I made him a deputy. I like his style. I'll keep him. We'll keep the McKays on the run until they're all cleared out."

Jordan Lee spoke then, with the calmness of certainty. "First you'll be a deputy, and then a cowman. Time for both."

Sundown grinned. "The ayes have it. But there's one thing that can't wait. I'll settle that while my shoulder's being bandaged."

"What's he talkin' about," Enoch Lee demanded with some asperity, when he and the sheriff were alone a moment later. "And why's she holdin' him up with her arm around his waist? He can walk all right."

Wallace grinned. "He's a man from boots to hair," he said. "I reckon he'll settle everything all right. Reckon, too, he's a little weak right now, while he leads up to it."

YELLOW DOG

(1934)

———— ☆ ————

by MAX BRAND

Max Brand was born Frederick Faust in Seattle, Washington. He wrote over 500 average-length books (300 of them Westerns) under nineteen different pseudonyms, but Max Brand ™—"the Jewish cowboy," as he once dubbed it—has become the most familiar and is now his trademark. In 1917 Faust met Robert H. Davis, an editor at The Frank A. Munsey Company, and began contributing stories and serials to All-Story Weekly and The Argosy. In 1920 Faust expanded the market for his fiction to include Street & Smith's Western Story Magazine and his popularity helped increase its circulation from a half million copies an issue to over two million. It was not unusual for him to have two serial installments and a short novel in a single issue under three different names. Popular Publications agreed to buy 200,000 words by Max Brand in 1934 and a good part of this fiction consisted of the seven short novels featured that year in Star Western. "Yellow Dog," which Rogers Terrill retitled "Gunman's Bluff," was the first of them. It was hoped Max Brand's popularity would do for Star Western what it had done for Western Story Magazine a decade before. It worked so well that in the bad times of the late 1940s Popular Publications started a new pulp called Max Brand's Western Magazine. It lasted as long as Star Western did.

Some of Faust's Western stories recently published for the first time in book form include Sixteen In Nome (Five Star Westerns, 1995), Luck (Circle Ⓥ Westerns, 1996), and three collections of short novels and stories published by the University of Nebraska Press. These days a work by him is either newly published or reprinted every week of every year in one or another format somewhere in the world.

☆ | ☆

*O*f what good is a ham-strung horse, or a blind dog, or a hawk with clipped wings? And when the right hand of a gunfighter has lost its cunning — the right hand, that almost thinking brain — freedom and hope are gone from the victim.

That was what Dr. Walter Lindus was thinking as he examined the big fellow who had come in half an hour before and asked, a little uneasily, for treatment. He sank his fingertips into the strands of muscle that sprang from the base of the man's neck and ran in broad elastic bands over the shoulder. At the point, just above the shoulder blades, where the muscles curved from back to front like the grip of a many-fingered hand, the doctor encountered the gristle scar-tissue and felt the flesh shrink from his grasp.

He looked hastily up into the brown face of his patient and saw that the smile persisted on the lips of this young man, but that the eyes had grown suddenly stern.

The patient had stripped to the waist for the examination, and the pain had been sufficient to make his belly muscles pull in and the chest expand a little.

"How did you get this?" asked the doctor.

"Hunting accident," said the patient.

"Rifle bullet?"

"Yes."

"The other fellow was careless, eh?"

"Yes."

"Those things happen. I would have said, though, that the other fellow had been careless with a forty-five caliber Colt. Eh?"

The youth said nothing. His calm blue eyes moved without meaning across the face of Doctor Lindus, then journeyed through the window and over the roofs of the houses of the town, through the shimmer of the heat-waves that made the mountains tremble in the distance.

Doctor Lindus ran exploring fingertips through the lower muscles of the arm. Even above the elbow they were firm; below it they twisted into a beautiful tangle of whipcord. Lindus stepped back. In addition to the scar in the right shoulder he saw a long white streak over the left ribs.

"Another hunting accident?" he asked, pointing.

"Had a fall from a pitching bronc and hit a rack," said the patient.

The doctor walked around his man. Across the left shoulder blade was a white zigzag, inches long. It was a very old wound.

"And this . . . another fall from a horse?" he asked, touching the place.

"I suppose so."

"Out of sight, out of mind, eh?" asked the doctor.

"That's it."

The doctor permitted himself to smile. He faced the man again.

"Mister Jones," he said, "does this right arm feel a bit numb?"

"Yes."

"Tingling, now and then, as though the muscles were asleep, eh?"

"Yes."

"Anything else you can say about it?"

"No. It's just the damned left-handed feeling that's come into it. I've got two left hands. And that's no good."

"Particularly for you, Mister Jones. I mean . . . for a fellow who runs into so many accidents?"

Mr. Jones said nothing.

From the beginning of the interview he had said little. He seemed to be one who looked first and spoke afterward. Now his blue eyes turned almost gray with light as they thrust into the mind of Doctor Lindus.

"There's a big nerve up here," said the doctor. "It branches out here. That nerve has been injured."

"How long will that right hand be crippled?" asked Jones.

"I don't know," said Lindus slowly. He saw that he had struck a heavy blow, but the lips of Mr. Jones continued to smile. The shock appeared in his eyes, only.

"You don't know how long it will take to fix me up?"

"Sorry, my friend. I really can't tell."

"Perhaps you mean, Doctor, that I'll *never* get that arm back in shape?"

The doctor drew in a long and very soft breath. Out here on the range he was accustomed to handling big, powerful men, but he had never seen a specimen like this youth, strong as a bull but looking swift as a deer, also. The head was magnificent, too, and it was carried with the lofty pride of an unbeaten champion. That was why the doctor had to pause a moment before he said: "No, I don't mean that. The arm may get all right in time. It ought to improve, anyway. Give it a lot of massaging, though. Up here . . . dig into these muscles . . . dig right in and work on them every day. It'll hurt . . . but it ought to do you good. Patience and time . . . they work wonders."

"Instead of getting better, it may get worse?" asked Jones.

"Why, no. I hope not. Of course it won't get worse . . . I hope."

"You think it's a bust," insisted Jones. "Go on and let me have it between the eyes."

The doctor was sweating profusely. "Injured nerves are serious things. They have to be cared for, worked over. And . . . even then one cannot always tell."

He put his hand on the big, bare arm of the youth and looked at the stone-white of his face.

"By God, old fellow, I'm sorry!" said the doctor.

"That's all right," said the young man who had said his name was Jones.

"If I were you," continued the doctor, hastily, because he was moved to the heart by the cheerful calm of his patient, "if I were you, I would start at once turning my left hand into a right hand. I'd start in spending hours every day in attempting to make the brain hitch up a straighter wire to the left hand. I'd keep on working with the right, too. I'd never give up hope. But I'd even start trying to write left-handed. It can be learned."

Jones was pulling on his undershirt. He straightened it, dragged over it the thick blue-flannel outer shirt which served also as a coat, except in the most bitter winter weather. Now that he was dressed and had retied the bandanna about his throat, he looked a trifle less formidable. The narrowness of his hips belied the real weight and power of those shoulders, once the shirt obscured their bulging muscles. One might have almost described this man as tall and *slender*.

He picked up his belt, last of all, and buckled it on. It hung loosely, canting high on the left thigh and low over the right, with the time-polished holster of the Colt hanging low down, convenient to the touch of his hand. As his fingers brushed across the worn leather, now, he turned that hand palm up and stood there silently, looking down as though he were seeing it for the first time.

"It's just a wooden leg, you might say," suggested Mr. Jones, in his soft and pleasant voice.

Then he added, as cheerfully as ever: "What do I owe you, Doctor Lindus?"

"Three dollars," said the doctor.

"Ah . . . more than that, I guess. Five dollars would be closer, wouldn't it?" asked Jones. He pulled out a wallet which he had begun to unfasten, but the fingers of his right hand kept fumbling and stumbling and slipping on the strap. He made another very brief pause and looked at that hand again. The smile never failed to curve his lips, slightly, but in the eyes there was a sort of frightened agony. Then, left-handed, he opened the wallet and gave the doctor a bill.

The doctor frowned. "I wanted to add a bit more advice," he said huskily.

"Go right ahead, partner," invited Jones.

"The weather around here . . . it may not be right for that arm of yours," said the doctor. "Summer *or* winter . . . it would hardly do for you. I'd go some place where the altitude is less . . . and the extremes of temperature not so great."

Young Jones was looking fixedly at him, searching his mind, until finally the doctor broke out: "I'd go somewhere else . . . where there aren't so many Martins around!"

One of those pregnant silences continued for a moment. "You know me, Doctor Lindus?" asked the man who had said his name was Jones.

"I know you, Cheyenne," said the doctor.

"You knew me all along?" he asked.

"No. But an idea about you kept building in me, and all at once I knew. If you stay around here, the Martins will certainly get you. They'll never forgive you for the killing of Danny Martin, and the shooting of Chuck."

"They asked for it. What was I to do?"

The doctor brushed away philosophical considerations. "That's all right," he said. "But there are other things. If the Martins got another mob and pulled you down, public opinion would probably call it 'self defense.' "

"Because I'm Cheyenne . . . because some folks call me a gunman? Is that it?"

"You've put a long life into mighty few years," remarked Lindus.

"It's really been a quiet life," answered Cheyenne, "except for some people's foolish talk."

"It seems to me that I can remember a good many times when your life wasn't so quiet. There was that affair of the Tollivers."

"I was just a kid and I got excited when the three of them began to put the pressure on me."

"There was Rip Morgan."

"Rip was a bad *hombre*. And I was young enough to feel that I ought to get myself a little reputation."

"What did I hear about Larue?"

"He was only a Canuck," said Cheyenne.

"And there were two men over in Tombstone. And some others here and there!"

"One of those in Tombstone was a crooked gambler. But I'm not arguing. I just wanted to tell you that it's been a pretty quiet life. I've lived by punching cows, not by shooting men."

"Nevertheless," said the doctor, "if you'll take my advice, you'll disappear out of this part of the country before some of your enemies find out that you've only got a left hand!"

At this, Cheyenne glanced out the window, and the doctor saw the softening of his eyes as they rested on the majestic heights of the nearby mountains.

"You love your range, Cheyenne. Is that it?"

"Well, I've had Old Smoky and some of those other mountains in my eye all my life, Doc."

"You'll have to take 'em out. You'll have to go somewhere and get used to a new landscape for a while . . . till you're cured."

"Cured?" said Cheyenne. And he smiled suddenly at the doctor in a way that brought a lump into the throat of Lindus. "You're right," went on Cheyenne. "I've got to get out. And I'm going to. Thanks, Doc."

He went to the door, put on his hat with his right hand, pulled it down with the left. "So long, Doc," he said.

"Good luck to you, Cheyenne," said the doctor, anxiously.

☆ **II** ☆

GUN CHALLENGE

*O*utside, in the street, Sideways was still waiting for him with her head high. The gray mare pricked her ears in welcome now, and came toward him as far as the tethering rope would let her. The lines of her beauty and her strength filled his mind as a fine tool fits the hand of an artisan, but above all he loved to see the wild brightness melt out of her eyes when she looked at him after an absence.

Well, before he was safely off this range, he might need all the windy speed of her galloping hoofs, all the strength of her heart. He should, he knew, get out of town at once. Yet he could not start until the shoe that had loosened on her right forefoot was tightened.

He untied the rope and she followed him across the street, making sure that he was indeed her master by sniffing at his hand, at his shoulder, at the nape of his neck. He would have smiled at this persistent affection, but the dread of people for the first time was clotting his blood and benumbing his brain with fear.

Every window seemed an eye that stared at him and perceived instantly that he was not what he had been. His height and his weight were what they had been before, but he was a shell that contained no substance, a machine whose power could not be used. His right hand was gone.

He passed through the open double-doors of the blacksmith shop into the pungent, sulphurous clouds of blue smoke that rolled away from the fire, beside which the blacksmith was swaying the handle of the bellows up and down with the sooty weight of his arm. The smithy, who was big and fat, wiped the sweat off his forehead and left a smudge behind. He was so hot and so fat that grease seemed to distill with his sweat.

"Shoeing all around?" he asked.

"Just tighten up the right fore shoe," said Cheyenne.

He started to make a cigarette, but suddenly changed his mind and crunched the wheat-straw paper inside his left hand, letting the makings dribble to the ground. For no man must be allowed to see the brainless clumsiness of his touch.

He stood at the head of the mare, saying to the smith "Be easy with her. Move your hands slowly or she'll kick your head off."

The blacksmith, with the forefoot of the mare between his knees, was pulling off the loose shoe, wrenching it from side to side. The gray flattened her ears and breathed noisily out of red-rimmed nostrils, until a word from Cheyenne quieted her.

The smoke was rising to the soot-encrusted rafters, and the slanting sun began to illumine the interior of the shop. Which was why the newcomer who stepped just then in from the street looked to be more shadow than human.

But Cheyenne sensed the danger even before he recognized the man, a fellow with wide, heavy jaws and narrow, squinted eyes beneath a sloping forehead. It was Turk Melody. He had been a great friend of Buck Wilson who, only three months before, had made his play to win a great name by matching draws with Cheyenne. He had not wanted to kill that wild young fool. He had put a bullet through Buck's hip. But the bullet had glanced upward, and Buck had died — despite the doctors that Cheyenne had brought to him.

Turk Melody had not been present at the time. He had arrived only in time to look at the dead man and to swear, with his right hand raised, that he would avenge Buck the first time he met Cheyenne. It was a public statement. That was the trouble with it, for men who make public statements on the range often have to die for them.

Turk, as he saw Cheyenne, snatched at his gun. And Cheyenne did nothing. Lightning messages were ripping from his brain to his right hand, and back again. His right hand twitched, but that was all.

Even if he pulled the gun before he was dead, he knew that he would not be able to hit a target with it. Frosty cold invaded him. The back of his neck ached with rigidity. His stomach was hollow. Something like homesickness troubled his heart. It was then he realized that he was afraid!

He could thank God for one thing only — that the smile, however frozen, remained on his face. He was going to die. Turk Melody was going to kill him, driven on to action by the promise he had made to the world.

The blacksmith felt the electric chill of that moment. He straightened suddenly and growled: "Now, what the hell's up?"

At that Turk Melody cried: "Fill your hand, Cheyenne! Damn you . . . fill your hand!"

His voice was a scream. It quivered up and down the scale. And Cheyenne could see that his whole body was shaken.

Fighting his own fear, Cheyenne walked forward slowly: "You poor scared fool," he said. "Your hand's shaking. I don't want to murder you, Melody. You! . . . get out of here before I start something."

The eyes of Turk Melody widened. His face drained of color, became white and drawn. Then his glance slowly wavered to the side and found the blacksmith. It was pitiful, as though he wanted advice, and the blacksmith gave it.

"If this here is Cheyenne," said the smith, "don't you go and make yourself a dead hero. Go on away and wait till you've growed a bit."

The right hand of Turk Melody left his gun. The gun sank slowly, as though reluctantly, into the holster. And then Turk turned his back and walked out of the shop, leading his horse. He had turned his back on praise. He was walking into scorn and infamy.

"No more sense than a mule, that Melody," said the blacksmith.

Cheyenne said nothing. He could not speak. His tongue was frozen to the roof of his mouth, and he dared not turn around at once, for fear that the blacksmith might see the departing shadow of terror on his face.

☆ **III** ☆

TWO KINDS OF FEAR

*T*here was no joy in Cheyenne as he rode out of town, for he knew that a man cannot keep on bluffing forever. Not on his home range, for there were too many fellows like Buck, always ready to gamble with life and death for the sake of making a quick reputation. His eyes were dim as he headed Sideways vaguely toward Old Smoky.

Something began to swell in his heart and, though he kept on smiling, his teeth were set hard. He had heard Blackfeet squaws screaming a dirge for a dead man, a chief, and that lament kept forming in him and rising into his thoughts. For he was dead with life still in him. He had been a master of men. He had always been able to herd them as sheepdogs herd sheep. But now any fifteen-year-old stripling could knock him out of the saddle or beat him hand to hand in fair fight. Moreover, the sheep had felt his teeth too often; they would be ready to rush him and drag him down when they learned that he was helpless. But looking back he could honestly say that he had never sought out trouble. When trouble came his way, he had accepted it. That was all.

He determined to make a compromise between a straight retreat from his home range and a direct return to it. Into it he dared not go, because the Martins would certainly get him. They were a fighting clan, and they would never forgive him for that day when Danny Martin and Chuck attacked him, full of red-eye and murder. He had killed Danny. But Chuck lived, after putting the bullet through Cheyenne's shoulder. With the pain of the wound grinding like teeth at his flesh, he had waited for Chuck to go on with the gunwork. But Chuck had lain still and played 'possum — the dog! And Cheyenne could not pump lead into a man too yellow to fight.

Well, the Martins would certainly be at his throat if he returned to the range, but he felt that he had to ride once more under the mighty shadow of Old Smoky mountain. He could take a course that angled off the base of the peak and soon find himself headed far into the north. Perhaps in another day he would see the last of his mountain turning blue on the southern horizon. After that, he would pass out into a foreign world.

Clouds began to roll out of the northwest. They closed over the head of Old Smoky. They rolled down across the wide slopes, like the dust of a thousand stampedes roaring into the north.

Cheyenne was in the pass before the shadow swept over him. Looking back, he could see it slide over hill and valley, while the voice of the storm began to reach him, then an occasional rattle of raindrops that made him unstrap his slicker and put it on. Small whirlpools of dust formed over the trail, blew toward him, expanded, and dissolved. The whole sky was darkened, by this time, and the dust which had been sun-whitened was now gray, speckled with black. The acrid smell of it under the rain joined with the wet of the grass. A troop of crows flew low over a hill, flapping their wings in clumsy haste, and dived into a heavy copse.

Then the heart of the storm came over Old Smoky and blotted it out to the feet.

Behind that running wall of shadow, glistening with the streaked and sheeted rain, Cheyenne could still draw accurately the picture of the mountains. But it was time to get to shelter. The long southward slant of the rain showed the force of the wind that had hitherto reached him only in occasional gusts. He remembered a nearby cave that as a boy he had often explored and made for it now.

The brush at its entrance had grown taller in the years since he had last seen the cave. His mustang held back, snorting and suspicious, at that mouth of darkness. But a heavy cannon-shot of thunder, followed by a drumroll of distant echoes, drove her forward into Pendleton's Cave. Then the rain fell against the cliff face, like wall against wall, an unending roar of ruin.

Jets of light sprang from heaven to earth. The brush at the cave mouth flashed from blurred shadow into flat silhouette and back again. Hail came, blast on billowing blast of it, making the cave icy cold in a breath or two. So Cheyenne got the little hand-axe out of his saddle pack and chopped down some brush. When he used his right hand, the blade kept turning. Once the force of the stroke knocked the tool out of his nerveless grasp. And his heart sickened as he began the work with his left hand only. There was no sense, no power of direction in that hand. Yet it was surer than the right. It seemed to Cheyenne that half his brain had resided in the exquisite precision, the delicate touch of that hand. Now half of his brain was gone.

Awkwardly, he managed to get a fire going in the cave. He was standing before it, his hands stretched toward the warmth when, outside, a horse whinnied through a thunder roll. Hoofbeats came crackling over the rocks. Cheyenne, now at the mouth of the cave, saw the misty figure of a rider heading toward him. Lightning poured down on the night, cracking the sky with a jagged rent, and the rider swayed to the left, suddenly shrinking.

Cheyenne wondered at that. Riders of the hill trails are not usually ones to fear lightning. But the speed of the horse rushed this stranger into his vision, and he saw at once that it was a girl. She swung out of the saddle and ducked forward as through not rain but bullets were showering around her. Her horse came right in behind her. It went over and touched noses with Cheyenne's mustang, while the girl threw back her dripping slicker and crouched down instantly beside the fire.

She was in a blue funk. She seemed to think that the fire would give her protection from the lightning; the hands she held over the warmth she lifted as extra shields against those sky-ripping thunderbolts!

Cheyenne looked down on her with infinite disapproval. Women had never entered a page of his life except for a sentence or two. If he went to a dance, it was because there was an excitement in the air, and whiskey, and music, and many men with the look of adventure in their eyes. He held his dancing partners lightly, both with the hand and with the heart.

He felt he knew a lot about girls and he had always thought them both weak and foolish. When Cheyenne looked down upon this girl who had sought refuge from the storm, he saw that she had all the weakness of her sex. Her eyes were not bad, because they were the blue of a mountain lake — though they were foolishly large. Her lips had not yet been stiffened and straightened by the labors, the dangers, and pains of life. Her mouth was softly curving, like the mouth of a child. Her first words revealed all her weakness in one breath.

"Isn't it terrible?" she said, and sobbed in fright.

And Cheyenne, with mounting contempt in his heart, suddenly found his thoughts journeying inward through his own soul. The lightning out of the sky filled her with fear. Yet he, like the coward he had become, was ready to run away from the lightning that came from the eyes of angry men. This thought staggered and sickened him. The stature of his soul was no greater than that of the trembling girl beside him and, if he gave her comfort now, it was a cheap gift from a weak nature.

☆ **IV** ☆

A PROMISE TO DIE!

*T*he sky opened now, like the mouth of a dam, and let fall a blinding cascade of lightning. Thunder shook Old Smoky to the roots. The vibration was great enough to detach a few rocks from the ragged roof of the cave and drop them heavily.

The girl had sprung up as the explosion began. With its continuance she shrank against Cheyenne. He put his arm around her, loosely. She was all full of twitching and shuddering like the hide of a sensitive horse. And, after all, there are even quite a few men, otherwise courageous, who are afraid of thunder and lightning.

"Hey, it's going to be all right," said Cheyenne.

"I . . . I'm afraid!" she whispered, and it took her seconds to get the last word out, she stammered so badly on the "f."

"You want company, eh?" said Cheyenne. "Come here Sideways."

His gray mare came over at once, sniffed at the fire, pricked her ears at the next river of lightning, then gave her attention to the girl. She put one hand up and gripped the mare's mane.

"What's your name?" asked Cheyenne.

She said her name was Dolly.

"Dolly is short for Dorothy, isn't it?" asked Cheyenne. "Well, Dorothy, get hold of yourself."

"I shall . . . I'm going to!" she declared. But she only got a stronger grip on Cheyenne. "I'm going to be all right," she said. "You won't leave me, will you?"

"No," said Cheyenne.

"Oh, what must you think of me? What *can* you think of me?" she moaned. Cheyenne, thinking of his own weakness, colored but said nothing. "Say something," she demanded. "Talk to me! I'll get hold of myself, if I have something besides thunder to listen to."

He sighed. A child might have talked like this. And except for years, of course, she was nothing but a child. He said: "When you came and leaned on me at first, I was sort of reminded of something."

"*Do* tell me," pleaded the girl.

"Yeah, I'm going to," said Cheyenne

A new outbreak of madness in the sky knocked Dorothy into a shuddering pulp again. He patted her shoulder, which seemed to have no bone in it. Strange to say, it was a compound of softness and roundness. Stranger still, from the patting of the girl's shoulder, a ridiculous feeling of comfort and happiness began to run up the arm of Cheyenne to his heart.

"Up Montana way," said Cheyenne, "I was riding one time with some *hombres* who were aiming to run down a big wild mustang herd which didn't have a stallion at the head of it. There was a gray mare, instead. She had black points all around, and she was smart as a hell-cat. Many a remuda she busted up and took away the faster half of it."

There was such a frightening downpour of thunder here, that the cave was revealed in one continuing, quivering glare of white brilliance, and the uproar stifled the outcry of the girl. So Cheyenne, with a sigh, sat down on a rock. It would be much easier to endure the leaning in that posture. She sat beside him, using his shoulder and one of her hands to shut out the sight of danger.

"Go on, please . . . don't stop talking," she said.

He went on: "We got on the heels of the herd and followed it for quite a spell, and one day with a good relay of horses, we gave the mustang herd a hard run. Then I discovered that the gray mare was no longer leading. Instead, she'd come back to the rear of the herd and, as the rest of the band shot by, there she was left, standing, looking at us, pricking her ears. It was the queerest thing I ever saw. Horses have fast feet so that they can run away, but it looked as though that she-devil intended to charge us to drive us away from her herd.

"I just had time to notice that she was big with foal when Art Gleason, off on my right, jerked up his rifle and sank a bullet in her. Well, she didn't budge. She didn't even put her ears back. She just stood there and looked.

"Gleason and the rest, they went charging along, but there was something about the way the old girl pricked her ears and faced the world that stopped me. I pulled up and saw the blood running out of her where Gleason's bullet had gone home. I wanted to go up and help her, and try to stop the bleeding, and then I saw that she was hurt where help would do her no good. As a matter of fact, she should have been dying right then and there. You understand?"

"No," said the girl, faintly.

"The maternal instinct . . . it was stronger than death. She was dead, all right. Gleason's bullet had killed her. But she wouldn't die. She kept her ears pricked forward, looking at happy days, it seemed to me. And when the foal was born, that mare laid down and died. While I stood by and wondered over her and damned the buzzards that were beginning to sail into the sky, that foal came over and leaned on me. It was a queer thing . . . soft . . . it was all soft. It poked its nose into my hand and sucked my thumb. It had its legs all spread out to keep on balance. And there I was, a thousand miles from no place."

The lightning shot from the sky in such a mighty stream that all the other displays had been nothing. The thunder plunged like iron horses in an iron valley. But through the tremendous tumult the girl, as though unaware of fear now, threw back her head and cried to Cheyenne: "But what did you do?"

Not by the glow of the fire but by lightning he saw her face suffused and her eyes shining wide open. "I started to go for the nearest ranch," he said. "But the doggone filly started after me, with its legs sprawling every which way. It was the doggondest thing."

"And then?" said the girl.

He found that he had been dreaming the scene all over again, silently. He smiled back into the face of the girl and she smiled, in expectant excitement, in return. "Well, we both got to the ranch," he said, at last. "It was a pretty tight squeeze, and that filly needed a good lot of helping along the way. She pretty near had to be carried the last stretch. But we both got there, and with a few days of care, she began to come around on cow's milk, with some sugar added." He kept on smiling at her, and she smiled back.

"*I* know something!" she said.

"Do you?" said Cheyenne, with something in his voice which had never been there before — an uneasy joy working in his throat.

"Yes, I know something. That filly of the poor gray mare . . . she's the very one you have here! *This* is that same filly grown up!"

"Not so grown up, either," said Cheyenne. "She still doesn't know enough to keep her nose out of my pockets. She'll try anything from Bull Durham to paper money."

"Ah, the darling!" cried the girl, and she sprang up and put her arms around the neck of the gray mare.

Something had been filling the heart of Cheyenne for a long time, perhaps, and now he discovered that it was full to the brim and running over with a foolish excess of happiness. He stood up, also. Thunder pealed more gently, running to a distance in the south. Plainly, the storm was no more than a heavy squall. And now, far beyond the mouth of the cave, he saw a shaft of golden sunlight streaming down on the earth.

They went out with the horses into the open. The northern sky was tumbled white and blue; to the south the storm fled, with its load of thunder.

The girl could hardly leave the gray mare. "What's her name?" asked Dorothy.

"Sideways. Sideways is the way she bucks. She's got some pretty mean twisters up her sleeve, too."

They mounted and rode out onto the trail. The rain still dripped on the cliffs, and the sun made them shine like dark diamonds.

"You haven't told me your name," she said.

"John Jones," he said.

"Is it? Well, I never would have guessed that. I would have guessed something . . . well, something else."

"Which way?"

"I'm taking the southern pass."

"I ride north," he said gloomily.

"You're not leaving this part of the range? You're not just riding through, are you?" she entreated, and she held out a slim brown hand toward him to prevent the wrong answer.

"Well. . . ," he began.

"I wish you were going to be somewhere around till Saturday," she told him. "There's going to be a dance that day. How I wish you were going to be there!"

"I shall be," said Cheyenne. He listened to his voice say that, and was amazed. It could not be coming from his own throat! If he were to go on living, he must be far away by Saturday.

"You *will* come? How happy I am! The dance is at Martindale."

He heard the word, but would not believe it. The picture of the old town ran again through his mind. He knew every inch of the place, and Martindale knew him. It had been named by the first of the Martin clan to settle in the mountains. It would be far better for him to attend a dance in a nest of rattlesnakes than to go to Martindale.

"And you? Your name?" he asked, slowly.

"I'm Dolly Martin. I'm Ned Martin's daughter," she said.

He pulled off his hat and took her hand in his. The warmth of her touch seemed to re-sensitize that half-dead right hand of his. Saturday night," he said.

"I'll be looking for you every minute. Thank you a lot. I'm sorry I was so silly."

He could not believe what he was saying: "Lots of men are afraid of lightning, too. A fellow can't help being that way."

"It was a beautiful story!" said Dorothy Martin. "I loved it. I love Sideways, too, the darling. Good-bye!"

That was Monday. It gave Cheyenne five days to get his right hand in working shape.

☆ V ☆

PREPARATION

He found a deserted shack up on the south shoulder of Old Smoky and lived there. The forage for Sideways was good. There was a bright little cascade, making its own thunder and lightning, not far away. As for game, he could go to chosen spots and wait, his revolver, in his left hand, steadied across a rock until meat walked into view. This was not sportsmanship, but perhaps he was never again to be a sportsman.

He began his days with the first faint light of the morning and ended them very late, by fire light. He practiced writing, left-handed and right-handed — and found that left-handed was easier. He tried his axe left-handed and right-handed. Left-handed was easier. Whatever he did with his right hand seemed to blur his brain with the effort. It was like walking over a straight road that is deep with mud.

Once — it was on the third day — as he patiently worked the pencil with his left hand over the paper, he looked down at the formless, scrawling line that he had made and suddenly leaped up with an oath. He beat his fists against the wall of the shack and cursed the Martins, the girl, the doctor — and finally himself.

Afterward he went out into the sun and sat down. The sun was hot. The wind carried life into his nostrils. Off at the side, he saw from the corner of his eye the silver flash of the cascade which kept on talking, high or low, by day and by night. It was better, he decided, to live up here, secluded, than to go down among men and be slaughtered. He could see now that, although there was a special peril in Martindale, there were other perils in all places for him. His hand had been too heavy, and it had fallen on too many people.

He could remember, now, the men he had fought against in other days — men with white, strained faces, distraught and desperate as they faced odds against which they knew they could not triumph. He had thought, in those other times, that these fellows were simply cowards. Now he knew better. He could feel the strain coming into his own face, as he merely thought of undertaking battle against normal fighting men.

On Wednesday he made up his mind that he would not go down to Martindale, no matter what he had promised the girl. On Thursday he was assured that it would be madness for him to enter that town. On Friday he stood out with his revolver in his right hand and tried three shots at a big rock. Twice the bullets hit the air. One slug hit the ground ten feet away from the base of the boulder.

Sick-faced, he stared down at hand and gun. He tried left-handed. All three shots hit the rock, but he had to fire slowly. In the time he needed for firing one shot with any accuracy, he could have poured in eight or ten in the old days, flicking home the shots with an instinct that was like touch.

Saturday morning a deer actually walked across the clearing. He had a chance for three shots — left-handed. The third wounded the deer in the shoulder. It fled, three-legged, for a mile. He had to follow and put it out of its pain. Then he had to cut up the carcass — left-handed — and bear the burden of the meat back to the little shack. Four shots to kill a deer!

But the best part of this was that he had plenty to do in fire-and-sun drying the venison. He would keep himself occupied while this day wore away, and the time of the dance with it. Then the sun went down.

He tried to busy himself about the shack, but the beauty of the sunset drew him to the door where he stood at watch. That turbulent rising of mountains west and north, that far flowing of the hills to the south made his mind flow that way to the picture of unseen Martindale.

He had been in that very dance hall, more than once. He knew every house and shop in the town. He had been a welcome visitor there. But now Danny Martin was dead, and Chuck Martin walked with a limp. Every time Chuck Martin limped, the Martins were sure to set their teeth and renew their bitter, silent resolve to take his life.

He began to think of Danny Martin, handsome and savage and treacherous, making an easy living through his crooked skill with the cards. Try as he might, he could not be sorry that he had planted a few ounces of lead in Danny's lithe young body.

They would be lighting their lamps in Martindale, now. They'd be polishing the floor of the barn which served as a dance hall. And the girls of the town would be decorating the old place, stringing long sweeping lines of twisted, bright-colored paper streamers along the rafters and walls.

Cheyenne took a step outside the door of the shack. The night was coming. It was rising out of the earth, and the day was departing from the burning sky. There was a coldness and sickness in him. And he knew that that was the stranger: fear. But there was a joy in him, too; and that, he knew, was the picture of Dolly Martin. He found himself saddling Sideways.

Then he was scrubbing his hands, working on the nails to get the impacted grease out from under them. He was taking a bath in cold water, using roughness of hard rubbing in the place of hot water and soap. Yet all the time he told himself that he would never be such a fool as to go down to the dance in Martindale. And all the time he knew that he would go.

☆ **VI** ☆

CHEYENNE RIDES TO TOWN

*C*heyenne, riding steadily through the night, tried at first to keep his mind from Martindale and the dire test he knew awaited him there. He thought of the old days when he had been as strong as other men; of the night in Tombstone when he had won five hundred dollars — and killed a man. But he found scant comfort in such memories and the new, cold fear in his heart at last drove all other thought from him. After all, was he not like a condemned prisoner passing to the gallows?

He expected to find himself tense, trembling when he entered the street of the town, but as a matter of fact the moment he passed the first house he was at ease. Not without pain, but it was as though he had squared off at another man and received the first blow which shocks the panic out of the mind.

Then he heard the music which throbbed out of the barn. He heard the burring sound of the bass viol and the thin shrill song of the violin, and above all the long and brazen snarling of the slide trombone. The beat of the drums was almost lost. It was a pulse in the air, and that was all.

Under the trees in front of the Slade barn the long hitching racks had been built. And horses were everywhere. He heard them snorting and stamping — those were the colts. And he saw, also the old veterans of the saddle, down-headed, pointing one rear hoof.

He picked a gap in a rack near the lighted entrance, dismounted. Other men were about him, getting ready to enter the barn. He saw a gleam as of metal, and his heart leaped. But it was only the sheen of a bottle tilting slowly at the lips of a man.

He walked in toward the door, passing many figures in the darkness. He came into the little framed off ante-room where coats and slickers and guns were left. He hung up his hat and his gun belt. The room was an armory.

The orchestra had paused. Now it began again. And the idlers were drawn suddenly back into the barn to the dance. He went up to the window and saw Jud Wilkins selling tickets. Jud was a long-jawed humorist with twinkling eyes. But his eyes did not twinkle when he saw Cheyenne.

"My Lord. . . ," he murmured, then he pushed a ticket across the sill and took the money.

"Sort of a warm night for the dance, eh?" said Cheyenne.

"Yeah . . . kind of . . . but . . . my Lord!" muttered Jud Wilkins.

Cheyenne went inside. The roof of the barn was so high and black that the illumination under the lower rafters looked like rising rust. It was a tag dance, and he saw men running into the crowd and touching other men, sometimes slapping them resounding thwacks on the back or the shoulders. No one seemed to notice him. Then he found Dorothy Martin.

She was dancing with big Lew Parkin, who danced slowly. There was a slight bend to his head and shoulders, as though in proper reverence to his partner. She seemed to be enjoying her dance with Lew Parkin. She kept looking up at him and smiling a little. But now and again her glance went to the door of the barn.

Now her look fell straight on Cheyenne, and the smile she sent him set his heart to a thumping. He walked through the crowd, stepping lightly.

Some voice, a man's voice, said behind him: "Excuse me . . . a gent just went by that looked almost like. . . ."

Well, that would be the beginning of the whisper and the deadly preparation for the fight. But it seemed to Cheyenne that this would be the easiest night of a long lifetime for death. He felt that when bullets struck him he could still be laughing. In fact, the faint smile which was characteristic of him was on his lips and in his eyes as he came to the girl and tapped Lew Parkin on the shoulder.

Lew stepped back and almost threw up his hands. "You?" he gasped.

He looked like a hero in a cheap play, confronting the villain.

The girl stepped into Cheyenne's arms, and they moved off. His feet found the swinging rhythm of the waltz. He usually danced on the outer edge of the floor, but he kept to the inside, now, on the verge of that slight vacuum which always forms toward the center of a big dance floor.

"I was hoping that you'd come earlier," she said. "But this is better than nothing at all. Did you have a long distance to come? I've saved supper for you. You'll have supper with me, John? Won't you? I haven't told anyone about you. Not a soul. Not even Mother. I want you to be a surprise, I didn't even talk about being driven into a cave. No one knows a thing. How surprised they will all be! People are looking at you, John. They're looking almost as though they know you. But you haven't said . . . you're going in to supper with me?"

"I can't stay," said Cheyenne. "I can only stay for this one dance."

"Only for this one? Only *one* dance, John!"

The light threw the sheen of her hair down over her forehead, over her eyes. And if one had been unable to understand a word that she spoke, it would have been a delight, nevertheless, to watch the parting and the closing of her lips.

The fluff of her sleeve fell back up her arm almost to the shoulder. Other women had sharp elbows, and the flesh of a girl's arm pinches away toward the shoulder, or else it hangs flabby. But hers was rounded, brown. She seemed to be brown all over.

"How did you get so brown?" he asked her.

"We have a swimming pool behind the house."

She laughed a little and looked up at him. "We're clear around the floor, and no one has tagged you yet."

"No one is going to tag me," said Cheyenne.

"But look, John . . . half the people are off the dance floor!"

More than half had stopped dancing. In a tag dance, every girl ought to be busy; but now they were drifting off the floor, looking back over their shoulders. The music of the slide trombone screeched and died in the middle of a note.

"What's wrong?" asked the girl. "What's happening, John?"

☆ VII ☆

ONE AGAINST THE MARTINS

Everyone in the big room seemed to be asking the same question at the same moment; and the rest of the crowd rapidly stopped dancing and drifted away to the sides of the barn. The orchestra died away piece by piece, following the example of the slide trombone. The drums, the cornet, the bass viol went silent one by one, and the only music which remained was the thrilling voice of the violin.

The violinist was old Tom McKenzie, seventy years old with a rag of white beard on his chin and eyes which still danced faster than young feet ever performed to his music. The good old man had been sitting down, sawing away at the strings with his head canted a little to one side. But when he saw the crowd breaking up and pouring away from the single pair that remained, he jumped to his feet and began to play such a waltz as he never had played before to woo those two dancers to continue.

The drummer snarled at his shoulder: "Don't you be a fool, Pop. There's gonna be guns bangin' away, pretty soon. Out yonder, that's Cheyenne who's dancing with Dolly Martin."

"Is that Cheyenne? Well, God bless him! If he's gonna die, he'll die to all the music that I can give him!" answered Pop McKenzie, and he made his fiddle whistle more sweetly and loudly than before.

"What is it?" the girl was repeating to Cheyenne. "Everyone has stopped . . . even the music . . . except Pop McKenzie. Do you know what's wrong?"

"I know what's wrong," he said.

"Please tell me."

"I'm what's wrong."

"You? John Jones?"

"I'm not John Jones."

He held her a bit closer. "What do you care about the name? Well, you'll start hating me in another five minutes, Dorothy. But up to then, while the fiddle plays, why shouldn't we dance?"

"I'll never start hating you," she answered him.

Her father was a Martin, he knew, who had moved into the community only a year or two before, and perhaps the reputation of Cheyenne might not be such an outrage to his mind and to his daughter as to the rest. But they knew — all men knew — about the recent killing of Danny Martin.

"I'm a man that all the Martins are bound to curse," he told her.

"All the Martins? Then I'm not really a Martin. How they are staring!"

"Dolly!" shouted a loud voice.

Cheyenne saw a tall, gaunt, stern-featured man standing at the side of the hall, holding up a hand. He was of middle age. There was a brightness in his eyes that made Cheyenne recognize him as the father of Dorothy Martin.

"Dolly, stop dancing! You hear me?"

She stiffened inside the arms of Cheyenne.

"I've got to stop," she said.

"One more round. It'll be the last one," said Cheyenne.

She came back to him, though she said: "It's my father!"

"I know it," said Cheyenne.

"Ah, but they're staring at us."

"It's a good way to use their eyes."

He hardly needed to touch her with his hands, she was so close, so balanced in a perfect rhythm. And all about them he heard a rising sound such as the muttering of trees far off across a forest. But this was composed of the voices of men and women. It gathered in strength. Tall Ned Martin was striding across the floor.

"Dolly, d'you mind what you're doing . . . dancing with Cheyenne?" he shouted.

One might have thought that she had known the name all the while. There was no touch or stir of shock in her. He looked into her eyes, and they were the unalterable blue of mountain lakes.

"Did you hear him?" he asked.

"I heard," said the girl.

"And there's no difference?"

"There'll never be any difference," she said.

Long ago, years and years before, he had thought she was no more than a child. He began to understand, now, that he'd been wrong.

They moved straight past the outstretched arm and the stunned face of Ned Martin. Some of the men were starting out from their places along the wall as Cheyenne stopped in front of the entrance. The anteroom was crowded. Men out there had guns in their hands. They had grimly waiting faces. Between the barn and Sideways there was a distance of thirty steps which could be thirty deaths for him.

"Look," said Cheyenne, "you're the bigger half of things from now on. It may not be long, but you're the bigger half of things. Good-bye!"

"You came because I asked you," she was saying. "You knew. . . ."

He turned on his heel. If she had understood why he had come, it would make the going easier.

They were all there about him. He saw Chuck Martin back in the crowd with his head lowered a little. And as he saw the face of Chuck, the right arm of Cheyenne seemed as heavy and lifeless as lead. He remembered how Chuck had fired the bullet on that other day, dropping to his knees behind a table, where the return fire of Cheyenne had made him sprawl on the floor.

He saw the Glosters, father and son. They were Martins, to all intents and purposes. Everyone in Martindale lived in the town because they were bound together by strong ties of blood. Fifty men were ready for Cheyenne.

He walked right into their ranks, thronging the door into the anteroom. They receded on either side of him. He said: "All right, boys. Look me over. And bid up my price. There's only one head of me, but I want the price of a herd."

They spilled away on either side, like water from the prow of a ship. And then he was standing buckling on his gun belt.

Someone said: "You grab him, Charlie. Dive at his knees!"

Charlie Martin kept scowling, his huge shoulders stirring, but he could not quite force himself to take the final step.

Out of the dance room Dorothy Martin cried: "Let me go to him, Father. He came here because I asked him. I didn't know . . . and he wouldn't explain. If anything happens to him. . . ."

"Something is gonna happen to him!" cried Charlie Martin.

Cheyenne pulled his hat over his eyes and walked up to the speaker. With his left hand, he struck Charlie across the face. The blow left a white patch between the cheekbone and the chin. "Why don't you move a hand?" asked Cheyenne, then added: "Give me room . . . stand back, will you?"

They stood back. The sound of the blow which Charlie had endured without protest still seemed to be echoing through their brains. They had chosen big Charlie for a leader, and Charlie Martin was remembering too well that the gun of Cheyenne was a fatal thing. Perhaps he had courage enough to fight and to die but he could not be a leader. He fell back, and the others receded around him.

That was how Cheyenne came to the outer edge of the crowd. Between that edge of that sea of danger and Sideways there was one open space. He would die as he crossed it, Cheyenne knew. The bullets would strike him from behind.

"Dolly!" called the frantic voice of Ned Martin. "Where you going? Come back here . . . !"

Then she was outside, running toward Cheyenne. She was a flash of white coming to him. She put an arm around him. She walked, leaning against him, looking back at the mass of her armed kinsmen.

"They won't dare to shoot, now . . . but faster, faster, Cheyenne!"

"You ain't gonna let him get loose?" yelled Chuck Martin. "Oh, you damned rats, you ain't gonna let him get loose, are you? Gimme a chance to get through! Lemme get at him!"

There was a stirring and a movement in the crowd. Men began to exclaim. Everyone had a voice and a thought. None was the same. And always Ned Martin, pushing forward among the rest, was shouting to his daughter to return.

But she stood with Cheyenne at the side of his mare. "Only because I asked you, would you have come into this!" she said. "Ah, John, you could have died! Be quick! Take Sideways. Oh, Sideways, carry him safe and fast!"

There was need for speed. The Martins, having been held by the hypnotic power of this man's reputation, had remained with all their strength dammed up in front of the dance hall. Now that he was at a distance, perhaps he was smaller in their eyes. They came out with a rush, and their voices rose in one increasing, gathering volume. But Cheyenne, aslant in the saddle, was already making Sideways fly down the street through the night.

A good bluff could be made to stick. Cheyenne carried that lesson away with him, as Sideways cut swiftly along the dark trail. Perhaps, with consummate skill and nerve, he might be able to go the rest of his life without being brought closer to a showdown than he had been at that moment in Martindale.

He lived! There was not a scratch on him to show what he had done. And the thought of Dorothy Martin rollicked through his mind like the music of game old Pop McKenzie. Once more he realized that he should take the northern trail. But he was more than ever loathe to leave. If he could continue to bluff his way out of situations as tight as that one tonight. . . . So he went straight back to the shack on the side of Old Smoky.

☆ VIII ☆
FRIENDLY WARNING

*H*e awakened the next morning with the sense of something missing. Before he tasted food, he sat down at his table and wrote a letter. He could not sweep it off in a few easy gestures, as letters had formerly been for him. The right hand could not manage the pen. Therefore, with the left, he printed out the words as neatly as he could.

> *Dear Dorothy:*
> *You pulled me through the worst of it. You were great.*
> *I'm not riding north. This range is good enough for me as long as you want me on it. If you can see me, say when or where. Address me at General Delivery, Crooked Foot.*
> *Yours,*
> *Cheyenne*

Instead of cooking a breakfast, he took some jerky and chewed it on his way down the mountain to Crooked Foot, on the western side of the peak. There he mailed the letter to Miss Dorothy Martin, at Martindale. The whole sound of the name was different to him, now. A light had been shed from within upon all the Martins, young and old. They were distinguished people in the eyes of Cheyenne.

In the days that followed, Cheyenne fell into a frenzy of labor again. It had been important enough before to restore his right hand and put cunning in his left; but now there was a double necessity, for he carried the voice of Dolly Martin in his ear, and the picture of Dolly Martin in the forefront of his brain. He would not willingly have been without that extra weight, but because of it he wanted to redouble his strength.

Once an hour he massaged his right arm, chiefly about the scar tissue in the shoulder. He used hot water, as much as he could stand, then kneaded the flesh with grease. Sometimes sharp tingles shot through the entire arm as his fingers touched a nerve. After each massage the arm was sure to feel lighter, more alive.

And every day there was the constant practice. He used his gun with either hand. He tried chopping wood, hewing to a line also, with either hand. And he was constantly writing, big and small. The result was that the left began to improve rapidly. When he used axe or gun in it, he no longer had such a strange feeling of being off balance, of being only half present. But in the right hand he could see little improvement or none at all.

He endured that disappointment without the leaden falling of his heart which he had felt at first. This was a task that might take a year, two years. It was one to be persisted in. And he had a goal before him.

After three days he went down to the post office in Crooked Foot, but there was no letter waiting for him at General Delivery. He came slowly back up the hill, walking most of the way. He liked to have the pretty head of Sideways at his shoulder, nodding as she worked up the slope. Whenever he looked at the gray mare now, he would think of Dolly Martin, and that made him turn perhaps fifty times a day and whistle to her, so that she would jerk up her head from grazing and look back at him with those bright, steady, fearless eyes.

Old Sam was waiting at the shack when he got there. Sam was the trapper of Old Smoky. He was associated with the mountain almost as closely as the mists that blew around its head. When Cheyenne came in, the old fellow was leaning his height above the stove, cooking. He had bacon in the pan along with plenty of squirrel meat. Squirrels are good eating if you know how to cook them properly.

Sam, without turning his head, greeted Cheyenne by name.

"Eyes in the back of your head, Sam?" asked Cheyenne.

Sam turned slowly. His face was covered with beard that began just below the eyes. It was like gray wool, never barber-trimmed, but hacked off to a convenient length from time to time with a sharp knife. The result was a series of gray knobs and hollows.

"Cheyenne," he said, "there's a deer out yonder, somewhere. I got a look at it through the door a while back. Go and fetch it in."

Cheyenne went outside. It was the heat of the day, and a gray mist was rising from the ground that had recently been soaked with rain. Only the mountains close by could be seen; the more distant hills were lost. He hunted casually up the mountain for the deer, then turned a bit to the east and circled back toward the hut to report failure.

He was drawing near the shack when saw a man skulking ahead of him from rock to rock and from bush to bush, with a rifle pushed before him. Cheyenne, frowning, shifted the revolver to his left hand.

"After something, partner?" he asked.

The other jumped. As he turned, Cheyenne had sight of a handsome young face as brown as his own. But the sudden start of the stranger made him step wrong. A stone rolled from under his feet. His rifle exploded in mid-air and its owner rolled twenty feet down the slope before he was able to halt his fall.

Then he stood up, dizzily. "Kind of didn't expect you behind me," he said.

"Were you expecting me in front?" demanded Cheyenne.

"I was deer-stalking," said the other. He came up the slope in small steps, the way a mountaineer should do.

"Good thing you weren't carrying dynamite," said Cheyenne. "Time for you to eat?"

"I could eat raw meat," said the stranger.

"You can have cooked squirrel instead," said Cheyenne. "Come along."

He took the stranger into his shack. "I'm John Jones," he said. "This is Old Sam, who owns Old Smoky."

"Jim Willis is my name," said the stranger, and instantly made himself useful in bringing wood to feed a failing fire in the stove.

"You seen a deer out there, did you?" asked Old Sam.

"Coming over the eastern shoulder. I thought it must be heading this way. Of course, if I'd known about the cabin being here, I would have cut down the slope and across the ravines. That's where he is, by now. A big devil," he commented, ruefully.

"You from these parts?" asked Old Sam, as he began to dish out food.

"I'm from all around," said Willis.

They sat down to eat in front of the cabin. Cheyenne found himself operating on the meat without thought. The last thing that he wanted was to permit people to see his more than childish clumsiness with a fork; but without thought he had already skewered a squirrel with an iron fork held daggerwise, while he slowly carved the meat with the knife in his left. Once having started, it was foolish to try to hide the facts; Willis had already marked them with a blue-eyed stare that sent ice-worms up the spine of Cheyenne. But Old Sam was too busy talking about the reduction in the bounty on wolves to take heed of other things, apparently.

Willis went on to find his venison immediately after lunch. He thanked the two hosts, and was gone quickly.

But Old Sam remained to smoke a pipe. "Some folks would have stayed to clean up the dirt they made," he suggested.

"There's only a tin plate and a cup and a fork," said Cheyenne.

"Little things make a big difference, sometimes," observed the trapper. "Right hands, is one of them. Who took your arm off at the shoulder, Cheyenne?"

The blunt question made Cheyenne start. "It's a little out of kilter, is all. I . . . sprained the shoulder a while back."

"Sprained it?" said the other. "Humph!"

Then he went on, as he finished his pipe and rose to go: "You'd think that a gent that comes from all around would be finding his venison down on the hills, without having to stalk all the way up the side of Old Smoky."

"Something wrong about that Willis?" asked Cheyenne, sharply.

"I dunno," said Sam. "I was just thinking."

"Thinking what?"

"That they've lowered the bounty on wolves, but there's still a mighty high bounty on a lot of human scalps."

"What'd you mean by that, Sam?"

"Well, there's some gents that are free targets. Some have a bounty on their heads that'll be paid by the law, and some have a bounty that's only the glory that the killer gets."

Cheyenne stared. "Meaning me?" he asked.

"Son," said Old Sam, "I been looking down through the brush up there day after day and seen you waltzing around down here. I seen you shooting. I seen you chopping wood. And that right arm of yours ain't worth a damn. Me seeing it don't matter, but another gent has seen it, now. If I was you, I'd head right *pronto* for some healthier climate."

☆ IX ☆

BITTER MEDICINE

*C*heyenne determined to take Old Sam's good advice and move on, while he still could. Also, he definitely shifted the holster which carried his Colt from the right thigh to the left. Since one stranger knew that his right hand was a numb, half-dead thing, would not the whole range know it soon? It was time for him to travel. He would, he decided, go south, passing the town of Crooked Foot so that he might inquire once more for a letter at General Delivery.

Crooked Foot was well away from the realm of the Martins, but even in this town there was danger. It was not from the Martins only that he could expect trouble. That was why he spent one solid hour on the shoulder of the mountain working with the gun in his left hand. What he should have learned before became apparent now. Any attempt at speed was fatal. The swift throw of the gun ruined the aim but, if he pulled out the Colt with a calm and unhurried precision, he could rock the hammer with a touch of his thumb and crash a bullet into a target almost as accurately as he had been able, in the old days, to turn loose the deadly stream of lead from the right.

It was consolation, but a small one. For in that interval which was filled with deadly slowness, any man familiar with the quick draw was certain to begin pumping lead into him. And how did men quarrel? A chair pushed screaming back from a card table, followed swiftly by the thunder of guns.

Speed was the thing that meant life or death, and for speed he needed brains in his fingers. But the brains of his right hand were gone; and the left, it seemed, would never be more than a half-wit!

It was hard to keep smiling on the way down to Crooked Foot that day, but he managed it. Half the strength of character is the force of habit, perhaps. It was a day half dark, because of the steaming clouds that poured away from the white head of Old Smoky. Crooked Foot itself lay in the shadow and Cheyenne, with a rather childish touch of superstition, felt that this was a friendly omen.

But at the post office there was nothing. He had turned gloomily away from the door of the little building when a bright voice hailed him — a cheerful voice with just a slight element of strain in it, which might be surprise only. It was Willis, striding across the street toward him, waving a hand.

"Hello, Jones," he said. "Glad to see you again! Step in and have a shot of red-eye with me, will you?"

Cheyenne accepted with a wave of his hand. He was still lost in wonder because his letter to the girl had brought no response. It was the sort of a note that demanded an answer. It was the sort of a note she would have been sure to answer, he kept telling himself.

They went into Tom Riley's saloon. Half a dozen cowpunchers were in there, off the range. It was a bad season with less work to be had than there were workers. In the old days Cheyenne would not have worried about that. No matter how pinched a rancher's wallet might be, he was always glad to find room for a man like Cheyenne. But all of that was ended now.

He might be a damned dishwasher, somewhere. No, because he'd break too many dishes. In some far away camp, he'd become the clumsy greenhorn — the "Lefty" of the outfit.

He was at the bar, leaning not his left but his right elbow on the varnished top of it. He took the whiskey.

"Here's how," they said together in deep, rather apologetic voices, putting down that brown-stained fire at the same moment.

As he put the glass back on the bar, Cheyenne saw that the eyes of Willis were dropping to his left thigh, where the Colt now rode. There was a meaning in that glance. There was a stinging meaning in it.

"Have one on me," suggested Cheyenne.

Willis did not answer. A cold light made his blue eyes paler. His nostrils flared.

Then an unseen man entered through the swinging door.

"Slip Martin!" he called. "What you doin' in this part of the range? Why. . . ?"

"Hello, yourself," said the man who had called himself Willis. But his eyes never left the face of Cheyenne. And he raised his voice to say in the snarling tone which means one thing only: "You're Cheyenne!"

It was the invitation to the fight. Old Sam had been right. There was no good in this "Willis." He had not been stalking deer on the shoulder of the mountain. No, it had been other game that he had been after. A scalp with a price of high glory on it.

But how had he known that his quarry was on Old Smoky? How *could* he have known that Cheyenne was near Crooked Foot, unless the girl had published her information?

"Cheyenne!" someone said in a corner of the saloon. "It *is* Cheyenne."

"If it's Cheyenne," said Tom Riley, behind the bar, "and if you're really a Martin, don't you go and make a damn' fool of yourself. Don't you go and get your insides spilled all over my floor."

"Keep away!" shouted Slip Martin.

He leaned forward a little. His right hand hovered, wavered like a stooping bird, over his gun. It was not a clumsy, half-witted left. It was a right hand that was poised there.

"Keep back and gimme room!" Slip Martin was crying. "I got him where I want him. I'm gonna open him up, and I'm gonna show you that Cheyenne's a dirty, sneaking, yellow dog!"

Cheyenne said nothing. Slip Martin had him. There was no doubt about that. He was gone. He was already as good as dead. And somehow that would have been all right, too — if only the girl had written back to him, if only that hollow uncertainty and disappointment had not been in his soul.

With every second of his silence, of his movelessness, he could see a savage hysteria of joy working more and more deeply into the face of Slip. The man looked like a beast now.

"If you're a man, and not a dirty, low, sneakin' murderer, go for your gun! Fill your hand, or I'll. . . ."

Slip paused there, trembling on the verge of the draw. And Cheyenne did not move.

"My God," said a sick voice, "Cheyenne's gonna take water!"

It was only a murmur, but it fitted perfectly into the sickness of Cheyenne's soul.

"Yeah. . . ," gasped Slip Martin. "I was right." Murder was in his eyes, and then something more cruel appeared there. "I was right. You're only a yellow dog!"

He took a quick half step forward and flicked the back of his left hand across the face of Cheyenne. It was the ultimate insult. Cheyenne thought of Charlie Martin in the crowd at the dance. Charlie had stood white and appalled, working physically to burst away from the controlling hand of awe that gripped him. But he, Cheyenne, was still smiling. The smile would be the most horrible of all. Punch-drunk men in the ring smile like that as they stagger before the conqueror.

"He is!" said someone. "He's yellow. Cheyenne's taking water!"

Cheyenne straightened. He turned to the swing-door. He turned toward all those faces — his back was to the gun of Slip Martin who had called himself "Willis."

The world would never know how Slip had learned that this famous gunfighter was now helpless. Slip Martin would become famous. It was better than shooting a man — to make him back down by the sheer force of cold, hard nerve.

Between Cheyenne and the door there stretched the distance of five paces, but they were five eternities to him. On either side were the horrified faces, but the grin of a ghastly pleasure was beginning to dawn on some of them.

This was a thing to remember. This was a thing to be talked about. Eye-witnesses of the fall of Cheyenne would be valued all over the range. And hungry-eyed men would listen, their lips curling with disdain. And other men of guns and might throughout the mountains would listen with horror, wondering if their own nerve might one day run out of them like water through a sieve.

He got to the swing-door, pushed slowly through it into the open day. He would never again be a happy man. He would fear the eye of every man, because every man might know. He halted, standing stiff and straight.

It was better to go back into the saloon and have the thing over with. It was better to rush back. Then he heard the outbreak of the voices inside, a noise that rose, and one man began to laugh, pealing laughter.

"Slip!" shouted one. "That was the finest, coldest piece of nerve that I ever seen. You're the greatest fellow that ever rode this range."

The king was dead. Another king was reigning. . . .

Cheyenne knew that now, if ever, he ought to ride south. He knew — but the face of Old Smoky, above him, was like that of an old friend. He turned toward it for comfort, and kept traveling up the trail that direction.

A cottontail jumped up from behind a rock. He pulled the revolver with his left hand and counted: "One!" Then he fired. The cottontail turned over in mid-leap, struck a rock heavily, and lay still, a blur of red and fluffy gray. Cheyenne pulled Sideways over to the spot and picked up the meat.

If he practiced with a rifle, he might become a hunter, because his eye seemed even better than ever. It had to be, now that the hand was gone. But whatever he hunted, it could never be a man.

☆ **X** ☆

COWARD'S BRAND

Every day Cheyenne tried to leave Old Smoky. Every day the thought of the outer world was poison in his brain. But on the evening of the third day, he went down the trail at last to make a third and final try at the post office in Crooked Foot. He came in from behind the building, waited until there was no one in sight, then walked in to ask. The postmaster was a cripple, with a pale and sneering face. His deformity was in his eyes as well as in his body.

"You're John Jones, are you?" he asked. He leaned forward a little to scan the man. "You *look* big enough!" he sneered. Then he threw a letter across the counter. It skidded down and hit the floor.

Cheyenne said nothing. He picked up the letter and ripped it open. The address was in carefully formed, delicate writing. The brief note was written with the same school-care, like a specimen for a copy-book.

Dear Mr. Jones, or Cheyenne:
  I thought you were a man. The Martins have no use for cowards.

Yours very truly,
D. M.

Cheyenne came out into the early darkness with the paper in his hand. On the edge of the village he read the thing again by match light. The matches kept shaking, and the paper kept shaking. He lighted a dozen matches, reading and re-reading the brief note.

"*I thought you were a man. The Martins have no use for cowards.*"

That, he thought, was because she was a Thoroughbred. Common people have common reactions. They are open to pity and foolishness. So was she, until the crisis came. But in the pinch she would show the steel.

She was the sort to fill a man with a gentle happiness. But in time of need would she not be as stern and strong as any man? She would be like a child among her children, one day, until the emergencies came. And then they would see her ready for battle. He could see the picture of her altering, her head raising, her eyes changing.

"*The Martins have no use for cowards!*"

He had no use for a coward either. He pulled out the Colt and put the cold hard muzzle of it between his teeth. It was not fear that kept him from shooting, because everything was finished. His world was reduced to the horse that he rode on. But there was suddenly a good practical reason against this destruction of himself. Yonder there was that consummate traitor — Slip Martin — big and brown and blue-eyed and handsome. He was famous in his world, now. Would it not be better to die trying to repay Slip for the thing that had happened, for the perfection of Slip's treachery? The more he thought of this, the more convinced he became that it was the thing to do.

Slip would kill him, of course. But if he could brace himself against he shock of the bullets — if he could stand straight against a wall so that the impact of the lead would not knock him this way and that — then he might, as he died, drive one bullet fired by the left hand through the heart of Slip. It was better to die trying. He turned the head of he mare toward Martindale, far away.

As he rode, he tried to keep his mind off the letter from Dolly. It was well enough to call it the fine scorn of the Thoroughbred, but there was another name for it, also. "Coward" is strong language. After the cave and the dance at Martindale, "coward" was too strong. He put the letter inside his shirt. The crinkling of it there against his skin would help him, in the last moment, to stand straight against the wall, and shoot back.

So he drifted Sideways slowly through the night. It seemed to him that there would remain only one regret when he stood against the wall and fought his last fight. That regret would be for Sideways. Some other man would have her.

When Cheyenne came into the town, he let the mare swing into a canter, because it was not his purpose to be spotted in some ray of lamplight and so have the alarm spread before he was ready for it. The scene of his death he had selected with care on the way from Old Smoky. It was to be in Jim Rafferty's saloon. He had had his beer in Rafferty's many a time, back in the days when he was only a youngster, a growing name. Rafferty had been a friend, then. He was big, burly. He had been an ex-prizefighter, and at the end of his barroom there was a narrow blank wall. Against that wall, Cheyenne would stand and take whatever was coming to him.

When he pulled up in front of Rafferty's, no other horses were standing at the racks. He got down, threw the reins — why make sure that Sideways waited for him in that spot, or in any spot? — and he lingered for an instant beside the good mare. There were enough splintered rays of lamplight to show him the outline of her head and the gleam of her eyes, like black glass. She and the girl were the only things that had ever stepped into his heart. She and the girl and Old Smoky. The girl had stepped out again of her own volition, though the bright ghost of her remained.

But horses and mountains — they are the things that a man can count on. Whatever love you give them, they give back, as a mirror by the nature which God bestowed on it must return all the light that falls on its face. If his life were not at an end, if he had a new start to make with two good hands, he would do things differently. But that — well, that was all gone — everything was finished.

So he rubbed the soft muzzle of the mare in farewell. He spoke a few foolish words over her, then walked into Rafferty's.

Rafferty was not there. No one was in the barroom. It was empty. Empty as a coffin, say, with only the bright image of the bottles in the mirror behind the bar. He walked heavily to the bar. Rafferty came in from the back room, wiping a brightness of grease from around his mouth. He was still chewing, but his jaws stopped working as he looked at Cheyenne.

"You, eh?" he said.

"How are you, Jim?" asked Cheyenne, with that smile of his.

"Well, I'll be damned!" said Rafferty.

He came hastily around the bar and faced Cheyenne. His big jowls trembled with excitement.

"You know what town you're in?" asked Rafferty.

"Good old Martindale, eh?"

"Well, I'll be damned!" said Rafferty again.

"I hope not," said Cheyenne. "Let's have a beer."

"A beer?" muttered Rafferty. He drew one, ruled off the fine bubbles of the excess head. "You have your beer, but I'll take a whiskey. I need it."

He threw off his drink, filled his glass again, and emptied it the second time. Then he resumed his study of Cheyenne.

"This here bunk they been telling me," said Rafferty. "About" — he waved his hand — "about Crooked Foot . . . about Slip Martin . . . what's there in that?"

"Slip Martin?"

"You know what's being said?"

"That I took water from Slip?"

"By God, that's what they're saying, son. Knock me dead if that ain't what they're saying."

"Jim, you've been here long enough to remember Danny Martin."

"I knew the two-faced twicer," agreed Rafferty.

"You remember that he and Chuck Martin jumped me, one night?"

"I remember the night, all right. I remember where Danny dropped dead . . . yonder . . . right in that corner."

"You're going to see another Martin die tonight, I think," said Cheyenne. "Mind inviting him in?"

"Who?"

"Slip Martin. Is he in town?"

"Yeah! Where would he be except swelling around this town, drinking the free drinks. You want him here? You mean it?"

"Not if he's drunk," said Cheyenne. "If he's sober, tell him that I'm waiting in here for him. Tell the other Martins, too."

Rafferty tore off his bar apron. "I been sick at the stomach ever since I heard about Crooked Foot," he said. "Cheyenne, what you say makes me feel like a man again. I'll get Slip. I'll get everybody. Leave it to me! And I'll frame your getaway, afterward! There ain't gonna be no murder on top of this here fair fight!"

☆ XI ☆
DOCTOR LINDUS

*E*arlier that same night, Dorothy Martin has slipped out of her father's house by the side door. She went around through the corral and got hold of her bay mare. All the others scattered at her coming, stampeding into a far corner, where they swirled like currents of conflicting water for a time, then poured out again in a wild stream to either side.

The kitchen door opened. The loud, angry voice of her father bawled into the night: "What in hell's wrong with those horses? Steady, boys!"

But her father was not likely to come out to investigate because he had with him, tonight, the very head and topmost authority of the Martin clan — old Jefferson Martin, who ruled his community like a king. His authority was much reinforced, just now, because of the glory that had come to Slip Martin, his son.

Dorothy led her mare by the mane, carrying her pack slung over her shoulder. When she came to the shed, she did not venture to light a lantern. What she wanted, she could find. Her saddle always hung on the third peg from the door. She found it and swung it over the back of the bay. Usually she got one of the men to cinch up the girths tight. She did it herself tonight, patiently waiting for the bay to let out some of the air with which she swelled her chest against the pressure of the cinches. When she had the girths drawn up, she got the bridle on easily, the good mare opening her mouth and reaching for the bit as though she liked it.

There would be a frightful commotion when they found her note. There would be a still greater excitement when she returned. Perhaps her reputation would be gone after that single excursion into the wilderness. A breath can sully a mirror and a word can destroy a girl. She had thought of all that before she started from the house. She had added up facts and feelings, and she faced the cold of the future steadily and without fear.

Now that the mare was ready, she started toward the door, pulling the horse after her in the direction of that dim speckling of starlight. But the mare, pulling sidewise on the bridle, bumped against the open door. The flimsy wood sounded like a stricken drumhead, and the whole mass of horses in the corral began snorting and racing again.

As she lifted her foot to the left stirrup, she could hear the stamping feet of men and their raised voices inside the house. The kitchen door flung open again and her father strode out, swearing, a rifle in his hands.

"There's some damn coyote around here," he said, "and I'm going to settle it. Don't go and disturb yourself, Jefferson." Then he shouted: "You there! You on that horse . . . hold still or I'll drill you clean, by God!"

She checked up the mare with a gasp.

"Get down off that horse and stick your hands up and come walking to me, dead slow!" shouted Ned Martin.

"Father!" said the girl. "It's only I. . . ."

"Hey, now what in thunder?" he demanded. "What are you doing out there at this time of night. . . ?"

"I'm only going for a jog down the road," she said. "I'll be right back."

"Stop that horse!" he shouted after her.

She reined in again. Such a weakness came over her that she began to tremble. Now the tall silhouette of her father bore down on her.

"You're going to jog down the road, this time of night, after dark? Dolly, what in thunder is in your head? What's the matter with you? What's *been* the matter with you, these last days? Get off that horse!"

She slipped to the ground.

"Nothing's the matter," she said. "Only, I wanted to get out alone for a few minutes."

"What's tied on behind that saddle?"

His hands fumbled there. Afterward he faced her in the darkness, and she heard him breathe once or twice before his voice came.

"Dolly, you've tied a pack on behind the saddle. You were going some place."

She did not need a light to see the pain in his work-starved face. The years of his tenderness and his love poured sorrowfully over her.

"I was going away for two days," she said.

There was another pause.

"Going away? For two days, Dolly?" he asked her. "Where?"

"I don't want to tell you."

"Would you mind coming back into the house?" said Ned Martin.

She wondered why his broken voice did not bring the tears into her eyes; but there was a deeper sorrow in her heart, a coldness of misery which had lain there for days. She walked back silently beside that tall, long-striding form. She was thinking of her childhood and her big father coming in from the cold and the wet of a winter night, with the steam of his breath blowing over his shoulders. She was remembering, strangely enough above all, her first struggle with algebra, and how his huge hand had cramped itself small to hold the pencil as he labored beside her, not helping but at least suffering with her, as he made his figures fine and small, like copy-book writing almost.

They went through the kitchen. The Chinaman grinned and bobbed his head at her. Chinamen never understand anything except how to be kind, she reflected. And that's the lesson which the world needs most.

They went into the dining room, one end of which was usually the family living room, also. There, by the cold stove, sat "Uncle" Jefferson, the father of Slip. Because of his fatherhood, the girl could not look at him squarely.

"Jefferson," said Ned Martin, "looks as though my girl was about to take a trip away from home. I thought that maybe you could reason with her."

How strange that her father should ask Jefferson Martin to "reason" with her! He, the father of Slip!

"What kind of a trip away? Where you goin', honey?" asked Jefferson Martin. He was a mountain. Time had worn away some of the sloping flesh, but the rocky frame remained, immense and awe-inspiring.

People said that he could be a savage when he was angry. But she looked into his craggy face without the slightest feeling of apprehension. Such blows had fallen on her, silently, that no words of Jefferson Martin could add to her burden.

"I can't say where I'm going," said the girl. "It would only make unhappiness."

"Ned," said Jefferson, "looks like you gotta bear down a mite on that gal."

Ned Martin reached out his bony hand toward Dorothy, then smiled, and shook his head. "How would I bear down on Dolly?" he asked.

"By the ripping thunder!" shouted Jefferson, his wrath flowing suddenly as he smote the edge of the table, "I'd give her a command and I'd see that she yipped out an answer! Dolly, where you planning to go?"

She said nothing. She merely watched his face curiously, fearlessly. Other people knew nothing about pain. How could they know?

"By God, Ned," said Jefferson Martin, "if it was a brat of mine, I'd up and lambaste her, is what I'd do. She ain't too old for it. If she was, I'd make her younger, a damn sight! Stand there and look you in the eye and say nothing, will she?"

The hoofs of horses and the light rattling of wheels drew up in front of the house. In the silence, during which Ned Martin sorrowfully examined his refractory child, there came a knocking at the kitchen door. The Chinaman opened it. He never could learn to ask questions. Every inquirer, even the most ragged tramp, was instantly brought by Wong into the heart of the family. So Ned Martin strode hastily to block away this interruption. But he was too late. Already the stranger stood in the dining room doorway.

Ordinarily, all that one sees at the first glance is eyes and mouth and nose; but what the girl saw in this stranger was a forehead so high and so wide, that it gave his face a bald look. The eyes glimmered rather vaguely behind thick glasses, and the lower part of his face was refined almost to femininity. His hands were pale and thin. He could be no hand on a ranch. But he had stamped on him an air of authority which would have made him pass as current coin — and gold at that — in any society.

"I've been looking for Mister Jefferson Martin," he said, "and I was informed that I could find him here. I am Doctor Walter Lindus, from Martindale."

"Hello, Doctor Lindus," said Jefferson Martin, getting to his feet. "I've heard tell of you. I've heard fine things told of you. It's a happy day for Martindale to have a doc like you in our town."

They shook hands. The introductions went round and, when the doctor shook hands with the girl, she felt his glance linger on her a little, as though in surprise. They were inviting this distinguished guest to sit down; they were assuring him that dinner would be on the table in a few moments. He cut straight through this hospitality.

"I can't stay," he said, "because I have to turn back immediately. I'll have to wear out my team, as it is, and drive practically all night. I simply have five minutes' talk on hand for you, Mister Martin."

"We'll step into Ned's front room," suggested Jefferson Martin.

"I can say it here just as well," said the doctor. "I'd rather speak with more witnesses, in fact. I've come over here because I've heard of the damnable outrage your son committed, Mister Martin!"

This sudden stroke, a blow in the face, caused the big rancher not to recoil or straighten, but to lean a little forward with a darkening brow.

The doctor was not deterred by this attitude of Jefferson Martin. He went straight on, with that wonderful air of a man who is in control. He said: "Murder is a horrible crime, Mister Martin. But there are worse things, it appears. Your son has been guilty of one of them. He has taken advantage, publicly, of a helpless man. I refer to his cowardly behavior in a saloon in the town of Crooked Foot."

"Coward? Him a coward? My Slip a coward?" shouted Jefferson Martin, getting his voice up by degrees to a roar. "You mean my Slip . . . a coward? Him that faced down that man-murderin' Cheyenne? What kind of fool talk are you makin'?"

The doctor lowered his head a little. The highlight danced slowly on the big, bald knobs of his forehead. All that the girl could feel about him was brain, brain, brain. He was a man who knew; and whose knowledge could not be wrong. And suddenly a wild hope had come up in her heart and was pouring out toward him, clinging to him and his next words.

He was actually shaking his finger at Jefferson Martin. "You mean to say," he was exclaiming, "that you didn't know that poor Cheyenne is a helpless man? You mean to declare to me that you and all your tribe didn't know?" The doctor looked his disbelief. "I've been hunting for you," he said, "because I was told that you're in control of your clan. You mean to tell me, Jefferson Martin, that all of you are not perfectly aware that the right arm of Cheyenne is no better than half paralyzed?"

A dreadful stroke came in the throat and in the heart of Dolly Martin and beat her right down to her knees.

"What would you mean by that?" demanded Jefferson Martin. But the assurance was gone from him, now. "Paralyzed?"

"But, of course, you know all about it!" exclaimed the doctor. And he lifted his head, suddenly, and stared around him with a fine contempt for them all. "The eyewitness who told me about the thing distinctly described the holster that Cheyenne wore as being on his left hip. You must have been told the same thing. And your scoundrel of a son, sir . . . do you hear me? . . . I say that your coward of a son took a shameful advantage over a defenseless man whose spirit may have been broken forever, for all I know. And I am here to warn you Martins, individually and as a clan, that if a single finger is ever lifted against him in the future, I shall make it my business to publish the shameless facts all over this range!"

There was no question that the doctor held them all, easily, in the palm of his hand; and the girl began to get back on her feet.

"Cheyenne!" she said to the doctor. "Do you mean that he'll never be well again? Do you mean that his right hand will never be good again?"

"He has one chance in three . . . or in ten," said Walter Lindus.

"I knew he had a need of me!" cried Dolly Martin. "That was why I was starting to go to him tonight. There was a voice in my heart that told me to go. . . ."

Her father, at this, turned as pale as a blanched stone. But before another word could be spoken, the kitchen door was dashed open and the voice of Sanders, one of the hired cowpunchers, roared out in the next room: "Wong, gimme a hunk of cheese and a lump of bread. No supper for me. Ted Nolan's gone by with the word that Cheyenne is in Rafferty's place! Cheyenne is there . . . waiting for Slip Martin to come. My God, think what a fight it'll be! Cheyenne ain't a yellow dog after all, it looks like. He's right there in Rafferty's, now. Gimme that bread and cheese. I'm gonna get goin'. It'll be the greatest fight that ever was! It's a *duel,* Wong!"

Doctor Lindus was struck aghast. "Cheyenne waiting? Cheyenne challenging Slip Martin? Cheyenne standing up to a normal man? He's mad!"

"No, no," cried the girl. "Not mad . . . but he'd rather die like a normal man than live to be shamed. And here we stand . . . while he's being murdered!"

She went swerving past her father and raced through the kitchen and outside. The door creaked slowly back behind her and struck with a heavy bang.

☆ XII ☆

THE GREAT HEART

Martindale converged on Rafferty's saloon. Not all of Martindale, for the women and the children remained at home, of course, and they formed the whispering chorus against which the tragedy was to be enacted. The men headed for Rafferty's saloon, quickly, in steady streams.

Rafferty had found Slip Martin in a lunch room, eating pork chops and sauerkraut and French fried potatoes. Slip was washing down a mouthful with a good swallow of coffee and hot milk when the barman came in. He kept the cup at his mouth for a moment while his eyes dwelt on the face of Rafferty.

In that moment his mind jumped like a running rabbit through many ideas. The whole affair up there in the cabin on the side of Old Smoky had been a lead-on and the affair in the saloon at Crooked Foot had been a fake. These affairs were to draw him on for a killing — because nobody would blame Cheyenne if he killed Slip Martin, now. No, everyone would praise him.

And yet that business of managing the fork in the right hand, that surely had not been faked. The wobble of the fork, held like a dagger — that was not playacting! Perhaps like a beaten champion, the injured Cheyenne could not resist one more call to the ring. Well, this time Slip would kill him. This time Slip would put him down and out forever.

Rafferty left the lunch room, and a murmur began to spread up and down the street. The murmur would grow into shouting, later on, when Cheyenne was dead.

And Slip Martin went on with his meal, slowly. People would talk about that, later. They would tell how Slip Martin received the news about Cheyenne, and calmly finished his meal, then went out and killed Cheyenne like nothing at all. It isn't what a man does so much as the way he does it. The style is the thing.

His meal done, Slip made a cigarette. He felt fine. He went out across the dark of the street and around the back way, then looked into the side window of Rafferty's place. He saw the whole room filled with people. They were plastered up against the bar and they were pooled against the side wall, but no one stood near the end wall, opposite the swing-door, for Cheyenne sat there at a small table, sipping a glass of beer. Cheyenne was turned a little to the left, in his chair. And Slip Martin saw now that the holster was on his left hip.

Therefore Cheyenne was a dead man! Slip Martin, grinning, went on studying details. He saw the beer glass raised in the right hand of Cheyenne. The glass wobbled. Cheyenne dipped his head a bit to meet the drink.

Slip could not help laughing. If he had been privileged to set the stage, he would have put no other people on it. Everyone in front of whom he wanted to appear great was there. Everyone, that is, except Dolly Martin. But a man can't have the world with a fence around it.

Slip turned away and rounded the front corner of the building. Against the darkness he could still see the image of Cheyenne's handsome face, perfectly calm, with a faint smile carved about the mouth. The man was brave. If only those people inside could *know* how brave he was!

Slip pushed open the swing-door and stepped inside. It was so easy that he could not help smiling. There was no hurry. He could beat any left-handed draw by half a second; and he could not miss a target that was only ten steps away. He would reduce that distance to make sure.

But, as he took one stride forward, Cheyenne said: "Stand fast!"

Cheyenne was rising, and Slip halted. At the authority in that voice, something stopped in his heart. For Cheyenne spoke like one who cannot fail, who must be right. Slip was still smiling. When he had both hands at his service, who in all the world would be fool enough to go up against this great champion?

He could not believe his ears — he could not believe that the deep, calm voice of Cheyenne was saying: "Friends, this fellow called me a yellow dog once. I've been trying to keep that down, but it won't stay. Slip, I'm going to do my best to kill you. Fill your hand!"

What made this man so calm, so sure that he offered the first move to an enemy? Had he managed to conjure into his left hand all the skill that had once resided in the right?

He stood tall and easy, close against the end wall of the room. His quiet smile had, surely, both disdain and surety in it. And the courage in Slip Martin rushed out of him, suddenly. He wanted to run. He knew that if he did not act quickly, he would flee. His own garb of hero was being torn to pieces, and his fear could be seen by everyone through the rents.

He screeched out in a queer, womanish voice: "Then take it, damn you!"

His gun was out as he yelled. But he triggered too rapidly. The first bullet ripped a long furrow down the flooring. The second was wide to the right. He was shaking. He could never hit his mark. And then he saw that the gun of that smiling, tall, handsome man was only now, gradually, leaving the holster. Left-handed? Cheyenne might as well have been trying to use the gun with his foot! That was why the third bullet from Slip's rapidly firing gun tore through the left thigh of Cheyenne.

Low, and too far to the left — even so, the man should have gone down. But he did not fall. His wide shoulders were pressed back against the wall, and his gun was tipping smoothly forward out of its holster.

Higher this time, thought Slip Martin, and more to the right. One more slug, properly placed, would fix Cheyenne for all time. The fourth bullet, more truly aimed, crashed straight into the body of Cheyenne.

Why didn't he fall? Why didn't he crumple, or pitch forward, or slump weakly to the side? No, the wall upheld him — and the fourth bullet had only drilled through his right shoulder. And with the wall supporting him, as a screech of horror came from the throats of all who saw this smiling giant, slow of movement, endure without reply the fusillade from the weapon of Slip — now, as that yell began, and as the fourth bullet drove home, Cheyenne fired.

The bullet jerked the gun out of Slip's right hand and flung it back into his face. The impact knocked across his eyes a cloud of darkness mixed with sparks of shooting fire.

He was on his knees when his vision cleared. Blood streamed down his face from a rent in his forehead. And through the whirling mist he saw not the body of Cheyenne, still erect, but only the stony, smiling face, and the poised revolver.

"Don't shoot!" screamed Slip Martin. He wallowed on his knees in an agony. All of life that was about to leave him, imprinted its sweetness on his lips. The taste of it made him shriek again: "Don't kill me, Cheyenne. I'll tell 'em I was a yellow dog. I'll tell 'em how I knew your right hand was no good. Don't murder me, Cheyenne. I give up. . . ."

He began to crawl toward the swing-door, and the gun of Cheyenne did not explode. Slip leaped to his feet and fled. The impact against the swing-door let him escape, staggering, into the open might. And he ran for his life, with the blood from his forehead blinding him.

Inside the saloon, Cheyenne was saying: "You fellows have chalked Danny Martin up against me. I give you Slip, for an exchange. Does that make us square?"

He had no answer to this. For the Martins, with sick faces, were pouring out of the saloon into the open. So he got hold of the chair from which he had just risen, and lowered himself into it. The warmth of his blood was flowing all over his body and streaming down on the floor. Numb agony wakened momentarily into living pain.

He picked up his beer glass and drank off what remained in it, tipping his head back slowly. That was what Dolly Martin saw as she sprang through the doorway. She saw big Rafferty, like a portrait in stone, leaning paralyzed over his bar; she saw the crimsoned clothes of the wounded man, and the beer glass tilting at his lips.

Jefferson Martin and Ned strode in beside her. But she was the first to reach Cheyenne.

He said: "Dolly, things are all right. I'm only winged in a couple of spots. Don't look like murder . . . there's nothing very wrong. Only, the old left was pretty slow."

They laid him out on the bar. The blood ran down onto Rafferty's floor and into his wash sink, as they cut away clothes and got at the wounds to stop the bleeding. And as they got off his shirt, the letter came with it, half soaked in crimson.

"The Martins have no use for cowards." Then Cheyenne was adding, faintly: "Leave that with me. It's the reason I had to come."

"I wrote it, Dolly," admitted her father, with a wretched face. "When I saw the writing of a stranger on an envelope, I looked inside. And I couldn't have you writing to Cheyenne . . . not after what you did that night of the dance. I was too scared."

She waved him away. Because what he had done was in the past and all that really counted was the present and a certain golden glory which, she knew, was to make the future.

"I didn't write it, John," she cried above Cheyenne. "I didn't do it. It wasn't mine! It isn't my handwriting!"

His eyes had been closing and glazing with pain and with weakness. Now he opened them and looked suddenly up at her with understanding. "I should have known," he said. "You'd write a bigger hand! You'd write a lot bigger hand!"

The buckboard of Dr. Walter Lindus, by the grace of chance, came through Martindale some time later, and it was Lindus who searched and bandaged the wounds of Cheyenne. It was he who said to the girl at Cheyenne's side: "I don't know. That wound in the right shoulder may counteract the effects of the old wound. Or it may make the effects worse, but after this, he's safe enough on this range. No man will ever take another chance against him, my dear girl."

"Dolly," said Cheyenne, "could you keep on caring for a one-handed man?"

She drew her breath in sharply, instead of letting it go out in words. He looked up into the blue of mountain lakes. He could keep on looking into them for miles and miles. He began to smile. The girl smiled back like an image reflected. They said nothing.

As this silence endured for a time, the doctor saw that it was full of a meaning greater than music or speech, so he withdrew softly from the room and went into Rafferty's kitchen. There he stood as one stunned, unheeding poor Mrs. Rafferty who was busily offering a chair, and a drink beside it. The doctor was seen to look down at his own pale, thin hands. Then he said a thing that the Rafferty's never quite understood.

"The great heart," said the doctor. "Never the hand, but always the great heart!"

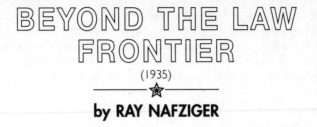

BEYOND THE LAW
FRONTIER

(1935)

★

by RAY NAFZIGER

Ray Nafziger was the nom de plume *used by Robert Dale Denver everywhere except in* Ranch Romances. *Fanny Ellsworth, long-time editor of this magazine, was quite vocal about how fine a writer she thought Nafziger was and perhaps, as a sort of tribute, she insisted he always use his own name as a byline. Denver was born on a Kansas farm during, in his words, "one of those summers of the period of the great hot winds." His father was a farmer and feeder in southern Nebraska as well as a rancher in the sand-hill country of the Platte River. Denver's education was varied; he attended George Washington University and Columbia University as well as colleges in the West. Following his service in the U.S. Army during World War I, he worked for the Department of Agriculture in Washington, D.C., and later was a forest ranger in New Mexico. A partnership in a dude ranch in the Jemez Mountains near Santa Fe lasted only three months, but it was during this period that he began writing Western stories, first published in* Ace-High Magazine *which, like* Ranch Romances, *was a Clayton publication.*

According to his own count in 1939, in the previous fourteen years he had published over five million words. Most of his work during the 1930s and early 1940s appeared in Dime Western *and* Star Western *and his stories were usually showcased on the covers. He earned a sufficiently good living from writing that he eventually owned, although he did not directly operate, a cotton and alfalfa farm on the Rio Grande in New Mexico. He commented wryly that "my own bale-an-acre cotton average puts me to shame in a neighborhood of the two-bale-an-acre cotton growers. But I have a two-daughter family that makes up for cotton production deficiencies." Those who have enjoyed Ray Nafziger's Western stories have always regretted that he only produced two hardcover Western novels — Hell Roarin' Texas Trail (Macaulay, 1932) and Gun Smoke at Dawn (Harrap, 1949), both under the Robert Denver byline — and I cannot recall a short novel or short story of his ever having been previously collected. "Beyond The Law Frontier" was first published in* Star Western. *(4/35).*

☆ **I** ☆

On a bare flank of the Gallows Mountains a black area of burned brush had left a queer freak. Always there had been two clefts falling straight from a black rim and making a huge standard, with the rimrock as crossbar. Now below the rim a fire, set by lightning, had burned grass and brush to reveal another cleft, midway between the other two and falling straight from the rim.

The two deep clefts, the rimrock as a cross-piece, and the third cleft looked on the mountain like nothing else than a huge gallows and a dangling rope. This was gruesome enough, but below the rope the same fire had blocked out something more sinister — the giant figure of a hanged man.

Scaffold, rope, and hanging figure could be seen plain from the town of Tarrash in the valley. For years the range had been called Gallows Mountains; no one in Tarrash had known why. But everyone knew now. At some time, maybe when the first American trappers had passed in search of beaver, that brush area had been burned over to show the hanging man. Gallows Mountains, the range had been named, and the name had stuck.

The people of Tarrash nodded grimly at the grisly sight. A fit symbol, they thought, for the hard people who inhabited those towering peaks and high-rimmed canyons. A gallows breed, all of them.

Long ago, many an outlaw had found security in the Gallows range. All of them had drifted out, but according to the people of Tarrash, the ranchers in the Gallows canyon now were just as hard a lot as the outlaws had been. The ranchers rode always with hard-hitting rifles on their saddles and belt-guns at their waists. Quarrels among them, so Tarrash gossip ran, were frequent, and the reason why the resulting deaths did not come to light was because the ranchers of Gallows range hated the law more than they hated each other.

There were two family groups ranching the Gallows rising country: the Clauntons and the Guards. Only one ranch had changed hands in recent years, bringing in a big, square-jawed red-head, named Rann Tate, to take over a small outfit lying between the Claunton and Guard clans.

With him had come his mother and the twelve-year-old orphaned son of his sister. A fit resident for the Gallows range, Tarrash agreed, this red-headed Rann Tate. It was said that he had served a prison term under a different name and, in his gray eyes when he first came into the country, there seemed to lay something somber, sinister. Perhaps it was the shadow of prison walls.

Tarrash always eyed Rann Tate speculatively when he drove to town with his mother, a sweet-faced little old woman whom Rann Tate, for all his hardness and prison sentence, lifted in and out of his buckboard with all the tenderness that a mother might give a baby. But behind his gray eyes and under his curly red hair lurked a devil, so Tarrash agreed. If that devil were ever unhobbled, he'd make his own hell in the deep canyons of the Gallows range.

The ranch for which Rann Tate had traded was known as the Gallows ranch, running a small brand that was a miniature of the scaffold on the mountainside, without, of course, the image of the hanged man. The brand had been adopted perhaps by some cheerful outlaw who had cheated a gallows and swinging rope and, when ownership of the ranch and brand fell to Rann, he had laughed and continued to use the mark for his cattle.

As for the ranchers in the Gallows range he found them no better, no worse than people in other sections. The Clauntons to his west were none too sociable and, he figured, would steal a few of his cows if they had a chance. The Guards to his east he liked whole-heartedly. An honest group of people, friendly, rollicking, with a strong strain of Danish blood, they had heartily welcomed their new neighbors.

Several of the wives and daughters of the Guard families had volunteered to help Tate's mother get settled in the big adobe house. And later, during the summer, they continued to drop in, bringing fruit from their orchards and vegetables from their gardens. They liked Rann Tate's spry, gentle-voiced mother.

She had never known of Rann's prison sentence; he had spared her that by using a false name in the trial. Had she been brought into the courtroom at his trial, her presence would have freed Rann. As it was, she knew only from his face that he had been through some trouble, during that time when she thought he had been down in the Argentine.

He had returned to her then, bitter, sullen, but she saw that fade as he rode these grimly-named mountains. And the shadow of those prison walls disappeared altogether when he looked at a girl, Judith Guard — dark of hair, blue of eye, pretty — the kind that would stick to a man to the backlog of hell.

Rann changed back altogether to his light-hearted old self after knowing Judith Guard. And seeing his happiness with the girl, Rann's mother sighed contentedly. There was no jealousy in her, the little old lady. She had lived her life; there remained for her only the concern for Rann, and for her daughter's orphan son, twelve-year-old Jimmy, who was always nine months of the year attending school in a town fifty miles distant. Someday Rann and young Jimmy, for whom Rann had all the affection of a father for a son, would be partners.

That was the future that Rann Tate's mother saw for Rann Tate and her grandson, until war flamed suddenly in the Gallows Mountains. A bullying rider, Dud Claunton, claimed a calf that plainly belonged to a cow wearing one of the Guard brands. Les Guard, unarmed, braver than he was wise, protested, maybe cursed Dud Claunton. The argument ended in gun-play when Les Guard, badly wounded, had fled from Dud Claunton and his relative, Lin Saugus, while they raced after him, trying to shoot him from the saddle.

Rann Tate had heard the shots of that chase, and had watched it from a low benchland. He reached for his rifle and sent two shots over the pursuers' heads to haze the pair back. Then he rode out and lifted Les Guard down out of his blood-soaked saddle and carried him into the Tate ranch house. Before a doctor could arrive, Les Guard gasped out his story and died.

That killing was a flame in a powder keg, although the Guards kept their heads and decided to stay within the law. The hot-bloods of their clan wanted to settle personally with Dud Claunton and Lin Saugus, but Jep Guard, Judith's father, and his brother, both oldish men, rode down to notify the authorities.

The sheriff at Tarrash looked at the warrant that had been given him and shivered, knowing that the Clauntons would never give up Dud and Lin. He had not served a warrant in the Gallows Mountains during his term of office and had prayed often that he wouldn't have to. Now that he had to go, sheer folly made him deputize Jep Guard and his brother to help make the arrest.

Jep Guard protested, pointing out that the Clauntons — if they would surrender the pair at all — would not surrender them to the kinsman of the slain rider. The sheriff argued that he could get no other deputies to go against the Clauntons, that the Guards were interested parties and should share in the risk. Being brave men and determined that punishment should be meted out to the murderers of Les Guard, they agreed finally to go.

The expedition ended in tragedy. The Clauntons promptly opened fire on the sheriff and the two Guard brothers. At the first shot the sheriff fled at top speed, while the two Guards, outnumbered, fought. Jep Guard returned home alive, bringing his brother tied to his saddle, dead. After that it was war.

Faint echoes of the battle came to Tarrash in the form of riders clattering into town at night to buy cartridges or sometimes to summon a doctor for a bullet-punctured man. Into this whirlpool of violence Rann Tate was drawn. It was impossible for him to stay neutral. The Guards never asked him for help and, when he offered it, pro-tested that it was not his fight. It was their private quarrel and the fact that Rann and Judy Guard were engaged to be married made no difference. But after a group of Clauntons shot at Rann one day, it was settled: his fortunes thereafter were those of the Guard clan.

Weeks of guerrilla warfare followed. Ambushes, long-range gun battles leading to a pitched fight one day at an old sawmill, with a dozen or more men on each side. That day the Guards found that their ally, Rann Tate, was a fighter, a one-man army, master of the tricks of an Apache in brush fighting.

Almost single-handed he sent the Clauntons in flight, turning into a panicky stampede what the Clauntons had planned as a bloody ambush. After that battle the bloody score which had been running in the Clauntons' favor was more than evened.

The echoes of that gun-fight reached Rann Tate's mother, and left her trembling for Rann's safety. Her grandson, Jimmy, was fifty miles away at school and safe, but from now on Rann would be in deadly danger. The Clauntons would consider him their bitterest enemy.

Ten gunmen at fancy wages were imported by the Clauntons. The Guards hired no extra riders nor men; they asked no one to risk their lives in their behalf. They played a waiting game, riding patrols in pairs along the boundaries of their cattle range to make sure that no invading parties of Clauntons had passed through. The Guards were not killers, even after all their losses. They wanted to be left alone, and they hoped that the trouble would soon end.

None of the Guard forces wished for peace more than Rann Tate, taking part in the patrols with his lone rider, Tom Cornwall. Such a war, he knew, might go on to extermination and he had other plans than feeding the buzzards. His chief desire right then was to marry Judy Guard. And as week after week went by without further trouble, he began to hope that it was ended. On the day that he had been helping Jep Guard's boys chase cattle out of the Duck Creek brakes, he returned home in high spirits.

No smoke was rising from the chimney of his ranch house. A little uneasy, frown-ing, puzzled, he hurried up from the corrals and ran into the house. In the kitchen he found his mother. Two packed valises were beside her, and she was dressed in her best black, her little flat, black bonnet on her head, her plaid shawl over her thin shoulders.

She sprang up as Rann came in, and suddenly he halted at sight of her face. It had aged ten years since morning. "Rann," she said tremulously, "we've got to leave here right away. This . . . this fighting . . . our staying on here will only end with your being killed!"

He took her in his arms and looked down at her, trying to puzzle out the strange, tense look on her face. Usually she was as light in spirit as a young girl. "Leave?" he repeated. "What for? The war's all but over. Why, Ma, there hasn't been a shot fired for a long time!" He smiled assurance at her, an assurance that, for some strange reason, he did not feel.

She winced at this. "Rann," she went on, "this war *isn't* ended. It never will be. It will go on and on. People like the Clauntons don't quit killing, once they've started. They'll fight to the last man, and those who are left . . . if there are any . . . will be tried for murder and hanged. That scaffold on this mountain and that hanging figure were put there as a brand for these people. The breed here is a gallows breed, Rann. You don't belong with them, and they'll kill you if you stay. And then . . . I'll have no one."

"There'll be Jimmy," he reminded her. "They won't get him, over at school. What's happened? You were never like this before. You were singing as you got breakfast this morning."

The voice that she had been keeping steady broke now. Tears began rolling down her lined cheeks. "Rann, I never asked much of you, did I?"

"You never asked anything," he returned gently. "You always gave to me. Ever since I was born, you've been giving."

"I'd like to take something back, then. Just a little, Rann. I want you to leave with me tonight, now, to make a fresh start somewhere else. You know that Jake Ellerman owes us money. He'll give you part of his range to square the debt; he's offered to several times. They don't fight up there where the Ellermans live. Please, Rann. I'm all packed to go. Let's leave the rest and go away and never come back again. I . . . I can't stand it here any longer."

"I couldn't do that," he said slowly. "You wouldn't have me run away. But you've had too much of this. I'll take you over to stay with little Jimmy for a while and you can see how he's doing in school."

She paused a long time at that. She seemed to tremble all over at mention of the boy's name. "No, I'm not going to stay with Jimmy," she said firmly. "It's you, Rann, I'm worried about. You'll go with me, won't you? It's the only thing I'll ever ask you, Rann. We'll go up to the Ellerman ranch and you'll make a fresh start there and later you can send for Judy."

"She wouldn't come to marry a coward," he said miserably. "Ma, don't you see that you're asking the one thing I can't do. I've joined up in this war. I can't back out now, leaving Judy's father and the rest to handle it by themselves. I'm to meet Bronc Guard tomorrow morning at Bear Springs to ride patrol."

"You can send word by Cornwall that you won't be there. Please, Rann, tonight you and I . . . we'll leave. We'll go to the Ellermans', and on the way we'll talk it over."

"All right," he agreed. "I'll start you out tonight and you'll stay with the Ellermans until this is over. Cornwall is just ridin' in. I'll give him a note to take to Jep Guard; he'll notify Bronc that I won't meet him tomorrow at the Springs."

He stepped to the door and yelled to his none-too-ambitious rider, Tom Cornwall, to bring in the pair of bay broncs that Rann drove to the buckboard. Cornwall, a relative of the Guards, had been in a sweat for fear since the feud had begun. He helped hook up the team and took the note which Rann had written.

"You going away, Rann?" he asked. "Too hot for you in this country, eh?"

"I'll only be gone for a day," said Rann impatiently. "Never mind about me running away; you see that note gets to Jep."

Cornwall nodded, but he was plainly not convinced that Rann did not intend flight. As Tate whirled away in the buckboard with his mother beside him, he saw

Cornwall running to saddle a fast horse. The man evidently did not like the idea of being left alone on the ranch. The bay team took a trot, and kept it down the steep, stony trail to the valley and out under a star-strewn sky.

Tate had planned to stop after dark at a valley ranch, but his mother wanted to put all possible distance between them and the home where she had only known terror. She insisted that they go on. Rann humored her, knowing she was under some strain, either from shock or fright.

Maybe, Rann thought, she had seen an armed band of Claunton riders pass the ranch, and yet that was not enough to shake a woman who, when she'd been younger, had helped fight Apaches. His arm held her in the bouncing rig, while she pillowed her head against his shoulder. After midnight he insisted on stopping at a ranch. She went to bed, but before daybreak she was up again, urging him to go on. Her ordinarily pale face was flushed. She sat silently during the ride across the valley and through the foothills toward the Ellerman ranch house in the higher mountain slopes.

As Rann lifted her down, she collapsed suddenly in his arms. Put to bed, she developed almost immediately a high fever, and in two hours she was babbling in a delirium as she lay, small, child-like, in an enormous bed. The doctor who came could do little except give her heart stimulants.

The slow hours drew on to night and dragged on to a gray dawn and Rann Tate still sat by the bedside. Even delirious, his mother seemed to know whether he was in the room. When he stepped out, she called his name, as if fearing that he might slip away and return to the Gallows country.

Her fever was haunted by nightmares of the threats of the Clauntons to her son. A few lucid intervals came when she smiled wanly at Rann, and she seemed to want strongly to live. Then she sought to strengthen her feeble hold on life, not for what it meant to her, but so that she could keep Rann out of danger. Living, she believed that she would have a chance to save him from the Claunton guns.

Days and nights melted together until Rann lost track of them. Only a few snatches of sleep broke his vigil, when he dozed uneasily in the chair by the bed. He knew there was no hope and one night, when his mother began talking in a clear but painfully weak voice, he knew instinctively that the end was near.

For the first time she began talking about little Jimmy. And as the meaning of the broken sentences came to Rann, he sat up and leaned forward to listen intently, trying to piece together what had happened on the day when his mother had wanted to leave the Gallows country. She had been in the yard that afternoon when she had seen her twelve-year-old grandson come riding home on his pony. There must have been a vacation at school and Jimmy was using it to return for a visit.

When he had been not far from the house, six of the Clauntons had ridden out of the brush behind the boy. And then as a sight almost unbelievable, Rann's mother had witnessed the six raise their guns, had heard the crash of the weapons. She had seen Jimmy fall, blasted from the saddle. Had seen his small, twisted form on the ground — a pitiful still, bloody heap.

Rann Tate sat like a statue, rigid, gripped by horror. Twelve-year-old Jimmy, who was more like a son to him than a nephew, killed by the damned Clauntons, six of them. Butchered!

Rann Tate's mother had picked up the riddled boy, had brought him home and, unaided, had dug a grave for him. When it was finished, she had wrapped the boy in blankets, buried him, and covered the grave with pine needles. The pony she had turned into a pasture where Rann would not see him; the saddle she had hidden under the hay in the stable. Rann, she had intended, should have no knowledge that Jimmy had come home, knowing that when he found out, he would try, single-handedly, to slaughter the six that had killed Jimmy. And attempting that, he too would meet a bloody death. Only the treacherous delirium had wrung from the woman her secret.

Six men, and she had seen them all, had identified each one. The names tumbled from her lips. Dud Claunton and his cousins, Towner and Gray Claunton. Lin Saugus and Sam Tovrey, sons-in-law of Gris Claunton. And lastly, George Fitton, a Claunton rider. These were the six who had killed a twelve-year-old boy as he had ridden across the open park below the Tate ranch house. All were equally guilty. They had all laughed as the boy fell from the saddle.

Rann gripped the arms of the chair hard, seeing in his mind's eye the bullet-riddled little body, his mother concealing it all and attempting to get Rann out of that country of cold-blooded killers. It was near morning. The Ellermans had run out of kerosene for their lamps and a candle was burning in the sick room. Rann's mother in a last faint flash of strength sat erect, called Rann's name. His arms closed about her. Then a little breeze stirred through the house making the candle flicker wildly. The woman's courageous spirit slipped away, as if on the same light current of air.

Two days later, leading one of the bays and riding the other, changing his saddle at intervals to make greater speed, Rann Tate was racing back towards the Gallows Mountains. To his ranch, his friends, and revenge. . . .

☆ **II** ☆

ONE-MAN WAR!

*I*t was a still afternoon in late fall when Rann Tate rode back to the Gallows range and, passing the fork in the trail that led to his ranch, he headed toward Jep Guard's Bar 7 outfit on High Creek. There Jep Guard lived, in a big log house which the Guard women kept bright and clean and home-like.

It was not in Rann Tate to whimper, but he wanted to be with friends, with people who had received him as one of themselves. Judith would be there too — Judy Guard who had promised to marry him, with her quick sympathy and understanding which he had never needed more in his life.

Dropping down the canyon through the scattering growth of pines, he came upon the well-kept outfit at the foot of a red cliff. The sight of its pole corrals, the big log stable, and the house itself of peeled white aspen logs, gave him a comfortable feeling of warmth. For him thereafter this was home and its people, his only family.

Horses were tied at the corral, with gun-stocks sticking up from saddle scabbards. As he rode through a little clump of aspens, he could see men coming from the house, and there was a glint of color among them, the familiar scarlet scarf worn by Judy Guard. Tate raised his hand as he saw them, but there was no answering friendly gesture from the men or the girl.

Puzzled, he rode on, weighed by a fear of some unknown disaster to add to those of the deaths of his mother and Jimmy. They were going directly to their horses. Jep

Guard, his bearded face deep-lined, his eyes like Judy's, clear blue flames, was leading the little group. They were ignoring him, as if he and his horse did not exist.

There was a silence, heavy with hostility, as they swung into saddle leather. A happy people, the Guards, save in times like this when they were all ice, Judy included. He started to speak, but old Jep's hand gave a short gesture, indicating the trail that led to Rann's ranch.

"You ain't wanted here, Tate," the rancher said curtly. "We never want to see you again."

Without a word more the men rode off and disappeared in the brushy canyon bottom. For a dark moment he stared after them, then he turned.

In the doorway of the house Judy Guard's mother looked out at him calmly, and then went back indoors. Bewildered, hurt, he was left facing the girl, who was regarding him as an utter stranger, a stranger to whom she did not even want to speak.

"What's happened, Judy?" he inquired helplessly.

She answered in a voice, low, vibrant with deep feeling. "You ought to know. We depended on you. You ran away without telling us that you had gone. You were to meet Bronc near Bear Springs to ride patrol. Instead the Clauntons met him and bushwhacked him. No one but you and Bronc knew where you were to meet. The Clauntons knew, some way."

Rann thought back to the day when he had left Tom Cornwall, the distant relative of the Guards, with orders to deliver the note telling Jep that he had been called away. He knew instantly that it had not been delivered.

"What happened to Tom Cornwall?" he asked.

"He was last seen in Tarrash," she answered. "He said you had quit and he had quit too."

"Cornwall ran away!" he burst out. "He didn't ride to tell you? And Bronc was killed? Why, I gave him. . . ."

He stopped. What was the use of explaining about Tom Cornwall? He had lost not only his immediate family but the Guard family also. He had lost everything that made up his future. If he explained to her, there was no reason why she should believe him. He could tell about Jimmy and about his mother, and the note sent by Cornwall on whom he had every right to depend, since Cornwall's own kin was concerned. But it would be his word against Cornwall's. Both were cowards in the eyes of the Guards. Anger flared in him suddenly. He did not care to explain; if they had lost faith in him that easily, then they could go to hell!

"You don't act as if you'd want to listen to my side of that," he said. And then noticed the girl's rifle. "You're not riding, too?"

"They need me," she said in a small, hard voice. "There must be patrols. The Clauntons have hired more gunmen. They've got twice as many men."

He had changed utterly in her eyes. He had run away and in some way had revealed to the Clauntons that Bronc Guard would be at Bear Springs. Maybe they even thought he had deliberately betrayed Bronc to his death.

"You don't believe that . . . I . . . ?" he stammered.

"What else is there to believe?" she said, but she hesitated a moment, checking her horse as if waiting an explanation. And he was too sick, too angry over the whole series of misfortunes to give it. Facing death on a brushy hillside was one thing; arguing to prove himself innocent was another. Her lack of faith hurt him like the sharp cut of a whip, and he was not flinching. Still sore with grief of his mother's and Jimmy's deaths, it was not in his make-up to defend himself. If she loved him, she would believe in him without explanation.

She whirled her horse and spurred off on the trail to Sanchez Peak. He frowned, watching her go. So they were posting women as lookouts, although the trail to the Sanchez held no danger and meant merely using field glasses to watch the flats and meadows that lay below High Creek rim.

He had lost the girl he loved along with his other losses. Losing Judy was something else to be added to his pain, added fuel to the flame of his desire to strike back at the Clauntons. He turned to take the trail back to his ranch. The place would be doubly lonely now, but he had no intention of staying there any longer than it would take to gather food and horses.

What he planned would take him into places even lonelier than Gallows Ranch. Over in Outlaw Canyon, in the old days, many a man had hidden from sheriffs and posses. Outlaw Canyon was on his range; he knew its little springs, its cliffs and caves. That canyon would be his headquarters. In it a man could stay indefinitely, to make a one-man campaign on the Clauntons.

The names his mother had given to him during her delirium were burned in him: Dud, Towner, and Gray Claunton, Lin Saugus, Sam Tovrey, and George Fitton. Six brutes who had shot a twelve-year-old boy as they would shoot down a deer.

He returned to his ranch, and on his way hazed down three of the best horses from his remuda. He was scheming coldly and laying his plans as he made a light pack of food, cartridges and a skimpy bedroll. It was dark when he rode out, with no intention of ever returning. Before he finished riding Gallows Mountains, he would return nowhere; he would be dead.

Dud Claunton had lived for years on a ranch at the far end of the Claunton range. A rawboned, husky man in his middle thirties, he regarded himself as chief warrior of the Clauntons, had acted as general in the warfare waged thus far. It suited Dud Claunton, sneaking around in the brush, stalking enemies.

It was breaking day when Dud awoke in the cabin where he batched and, dressing, stomped into his boots. He had a job that day. A trio of the Guards — young Gabe and Silver and Charlie — had been rounding up a bunch of cows in a distant pasture, throwing them into a trap. Then the Guards had ridden away. Sooner or later that day some of the Guards would come back for the cattle, and Dud was going to get one or more of them. It would be long-range shooting, but Dud had good eyes and long-range shots were his meat. He'd carve some more notches in his gun before sunset.

He yawned, clumped across the floor, swore at the empty wood box, and started for the wood pile. He'd make himself some coffee, fry meat and warm biscuits left over from supper, and then ride out. Might as well get water from the spring while he got wood. He picked up the bucket and stepped to the door, with no inkling of danger. His ranch was far back in Claunton territory and no Guards would dare ride in here. There were two rifles inside the house, one big buffalo gun his father had left him, and a smaller saddle gun, but he had not even a six-shooter on him as he headed across the yard.

He had taken but a few steps toward the pile of cedar wood that he had snaked down from the slope when someone rose up from behind the logs. Dud came to a dead stop and stood staring. He was staring at Rann Tate — the one man he most hated to find here, the most dangerous of the men in the Gallows Mountains. Uncle of the twelve-year-old boy that six Claunton riders had slaughtered. A rifle lay in the crook of Tate's arm. Dud expected a bullet from it the next instant.

"Damn you, Dud!" said Rann coldly. "You were in the bunch that killed the boy. Let's see what you can do against a man."

"I don't know a thing about it," gasped Dud.

His eyes were all but popping. He saw fading his plan on waiting in ambush on a warm slope for the Guard boys to come after their cows and calves. His mind was empty of all save the fact that he knew he was done for. His throat constricted; his lips grew white.

He could see himself lying on the ground, the water bucket rolling from him as he fell, blood oozing from a small hole in his head, while his legs kicked a little like those of a butchered animal. A few kicks of those legs, mocking signs of life that had gone, and that was the end of Dud Claunton. But what was Rann Tate saying?

"Turn around and walk into the house, Dud," Tate ordered. "Get you a gun and step out again . . . and come with it smoking!"

His ears must be playing him a trick, Dud thought, or maybe Tate wanted to shoot him in the back as Jimmy had been shot. The gesture of the rifle toward the door told him that he had heard rightly. He swung on his heels and, still holding his water pail, walked fast. Before the doorstep, he let the pail fall, and hardly breathed stepping over the threshold.

He had a chance, he thought exultantly. The odds were more than even in his favor. He'd jump behind the door, kick it shut, and blast that fool standing at the wood pile. Even if he could only keep Tate off until help came, he'd win.

He sprang for the saddle gun, clutching it hard, almost dropping it in his panicky haste. This was far different, he was finding, from waiting on a hillside to pot a hapless rider. He reached out a heel to kick the door shut and then froze.

At the window in the end wall of the house he saw a shadow. He guessed it then. Rann Tate had run noiselessly to the corner of the house and around it, guessing the treachery Dud would attempt. The shock paralyzed Dud. He swung the rifle without taking aim, and fired. His bullet hit the corner of the window frame, smashing out a pane of glass, and then the report of Tate's gun seemed to come as a clap of thunder in his ears, suddenly cut off short.

Dud spun around and, still clutching his rifle, took a stumbling step before he collapsed and fell through the door. His feet remained inside the house, his body lay stretched on the ground.

Two men came to Dud's cabin at about noon, a Claunton and George Fitton, the latter another one of the six killers of Jimmy. They were wondering why Dud had not shown up, and then they saw the figure lying before the doorway and raced their horses toward it. The plank door had swung partly to and was held ajar by the boots of the dead man. On the planks was a design in chalk. The pair stared at it uncomprehendingly for a moment. That crude sign was Rann Tate's Gallows brand, the standards and cross piece and the straight line dangling from the cross piece with a small circle to represent the loop.

Fear came to them then as they dismounted, looking back anxiously across the clearing. Rann Tate was standing waist-high in weeds in Dud's garden, a rifle in his hands. It was either fight or try to get to the house. They chose to fight.

Their hands swept down on their holsters. They, too, like Dud, had a better than even chance — two against one. Yet, as their hands went down, they must have realized that it was hopeless. Guns blasted the silence, the reports overlapping. George Fitton, who shared the guilt of a boy's murder, was the first to go down. His companion toppled and fell over Fitton's lifeless body. They didn't move again.

The warm air was tinged with the acrid odor of smoke. Deliberately Tate walked across the clearing and disappeared in the brush. Silence returned to the clearing. The horses, which had moved away at the roar of the guns, lowered their heads to crop grass.

Fear fell like a blight on the Clauntons when they found the three dead men the next day. They avoided each other's eyes, knowing they would read only a reflection of what was in their own — stark terror. They were up against a dangerous man, more dangerous than a small army. For Rann Tate knew this country, could travel through it, leaving little or no sign. He could wait for them along lonely trails in their own territory, riding swiftly, striking in deadly fashion now here, now there.

He disappeared for a week, and the Clauntons began to breathe easier. Maybe he had left the country. Maybe one of the three men, before they died, had planted a bullet in his body. For another week they rode warily and, then relieved, rode out again to resume their feud with the Guards. The pay of the hired gunmen was too great to keep them idle.

A week later three of them thought they had Rann Tate. Riding casually through the brush in lower Outlaw Canyon they saw a thin column of smoke. Approaching cautiously, they found one of Tate's horses staked out near the dying fire. He must have gone off somewhere to sleep. When he came back to that fire, they would get him. The trio took their places, hiding in the brush of the slope above the horse and campfire.

They waited all that night, stiffening in the cold, not daring to light a fire nor to smoke, or even to move about. At daybreak, as they stirred a little, a boulder came crashing down toward them from above. They turned to stare upward. Then Sam Tovrey, one of the six slayers of young Jimmy, whirled and saw a thatch of red curly hair behind him.

"You . . . you devil," he gasped, and swung his gun.

Tate's weapon crashed and Tovrey pitched forward, shot through the middle. Tate turned to meet the other two. Only one was staying to fight, a hired gunman. Firing at that shock of red hair, the gunman should have gotten Tate. And he would have, except for the cold that had slowed down his muscles. He went down, cursing, until a bloody spume came to his lips. The third ducked into the brush and, panting and whimpering, he fled afoot, leaving his horse.

It was a miracle to him that he got away at all and, not caring to strain his luck by staying to fight, he traveled to the nearest Claunton ranch. He realized now that the fire and the horse had been a trap for the three, not a trap for Rann Tate.

He brought eight men riding back to circle the camp cautiously. As they found the dead men on the slope above, another man gave a yell. There was blood on the ground where Tate had knelt behind a rock, a great pool of it. And there were splotches of dried blood all the way to his horse and a big one where he had mounted, evidently pulling himself into his saddle only after repeated attempts. Then they saw, on a flat stone, a chalk mark, the Gallows brand, waveringly made before he had left. They had him; he was heading back to one of the springs where outlaws had hidden in days gone by. They had him!

One who prided himself on his trailing ability led the gun-riders. It happened to be Towner Claunton, another of the six who had killed Jimmy. And Towner Claunton, in crossing an open space, found that being a bloodhound carried its penalties. He saw Tate just ahead of him but, as he jerked up his rifle, he knew he would never get to fire it. That red-headed devil was too fast.

Tate might have pulled down two or three more as they fled, but he did not. None of them belonged to the six men he had marked for death. The two only remained — Lin Saugus and Gray Claunton.

That Rann Tate had the brain of a devil; he had lured them on like damn fools, by making them think he was hard hit. The blood he had brought in a bottle from a butchered beef or deer, carrying it with him to use in some such deadfall. Three of the hired gunmen left that night without saying anything; they had had their bellies full of fighting in the Gallows Mountains. The red-headed rancher might not be a gunman, but he would do until one came along. When the Clauntons, in sheer desperation next day, sent their women to get Towner Claunton's body, they found the Gallows brand on a rock near it.

The two who remained of the six that had killed Jimmy stayed at their ranches, not daring to venture outdoors, letting their women-folk fetch water and chop wood. The Clauntons walked along a deadly pit whose brink crumbled beneath their feet. This was a wolf they fought, a killer wolf, whose teeth could tear across four hundred yards of space.

But even the wildest lobo could be trapped declared Gris Claunton, leader of he Claunton clan. They had to have help, however. This was too much for them. Hired gunmen would not do. And why not, asked Gris Claunton, let the Guards take the risk of pulling down that red-headed, two-legged walking death?

Since Tate's campaign had started, they had not ventured into Guard territory; the war had simmered down. The Guards apparently might be willing to let it drop; at least they would not come across to attack as long as they were left alone.

Between the two clans was a connection, a Guard rider who had married a Claunton girl. Through this woman who visited a sick sister at one of the Claunton ranches, going and coming unmolested, Gris Claunton knew that gossip could be passed along. Gris knew that the Guards had washed their hands of Rann Tate.

If he worked it right, through the Guards, he had a chance to get Rann Tate. First he'd have to persuade the Guards to help. And once they were brought in to help, he could persuade them to use bait that would catch a wolf. Bait that would trap even the most savage wolf. A bait as old as the race — a woman. Judy Guard!

☆ **III** ☆

BAIT FOR A WOLF

ris Claunton had come under a flag of truce to the ranch of Jep Guard. Gris, with his fox-like face and bulging blue eyes, was no fighter, but he was accounted the slickest of the Clauntons. So far his scheme had worked out. There had been a killing of one of the Guards — Lonny Guard — shot from ambush. By him had been left the brand of the Gallows chalked on a rock. That was Rann Tate's sign, the same he had left by the dead bodies of Clauntons.

"It's plain," Gris told Jep Guard, "that Tate's gone mad. Why would he have killed some of you and some of us? Plumb loco he is, but like many a crazy man his brain is sharper'n ordinary. Let him run loose in here and he'll kill every man in these mountains."

Jep Guard studied the ground. They were talking in front of his house. Five of the Guard riders had gathered to hear what Gris Claunton had to say. Judy Guard stood in the doorway behind the men, listening.

"He's probably crazy," Jep agreed. "Like a rabid wolf. I heard his mother died over north of here. Maybe that helped to drive him loco. He thought a heap of her."

"No one of us is safe until he's brung down," went on Gris Claunton. "None of the men, at least. Tate's in Outlaw Canyon, and a army couldn't git him outa there. Not unless you lured him out, same as green grass lures down the big mavericks in the spring." His pop eyes lighted on Judith Guard standing in the doorway behind them. The girl's eyes were fastened on Gris, watching his face as if trying to read something there.

"Us Clauntons has had enough of killing," whined Gris. "Likewise, I reckon you Guards has, too. We was both to blame for the start of it. Us more'n you folks, maybe, but we got young hot-heads on both sides. What's done is done, but we'll all be dead unless we pull that crazy killer down. We got to join forces to get rid of him, Jep. I know his kind. Red-heads like Rann Tate when they git on a rampage, they're hell-on-wheels. But I got a scheme." He moved closer to Guard and lowered his voice impressively. "By workin' together, we can git both his forefeet in a trap."

Judy Guard had moved closer to hear the mumbled words of Gris. She was the prettiest girl on Gallows Mountains, but qualities deeper than prettiness made her desirable. She had loyalty, courage, sympathy. And, too, there was a smart head on her shoulders. She did not trust Gris Claunton and his mumbling tongue. There was much that had to be explained, when she thought back over the bloody days. She knew, of course, that Rann's mother had died during that time when he had been absent from Gallows range. Maybe that explained his desertion. But it did not explain how Bronc Guard had ridden to his death when he was supposed to meet Rann.

"It needs bait to lure him out," Gris went on. "Bait for a wolf. He used to be sweet on Judy. . . ." His voice trailed off.

Jep Guard drew up his big shoulders and glared at Gris. "You mean to use . . . her?" he rumbled. "Damn you, Gris . . . risk my girl to do a man's work? Against a crazy man? What the hell you think I am?"

"He wouldn't hurt her," said Gris quickly. "He ain't that crazy. I bet he'd go down to her soon enough if she rode along the bottom of Outlaw Canyon. We could be keepin' outa sight, our guns ready."

Jep's hand fell to his Colt. "Git, Gris," he said. "Climb your saddle and ride."

Gris began a sidling movement toward the corrals. "No harm meant," he whined. "If we joined up. . . ." But Jep Guard's eyes continued hard, and Gris turned his back and walked rapidly toward his horse.

Judy Guard stepped up to her father. "Dad," she said, "there's something about all this that doesn't track. That chalk mark beside Lonny could have been put there by anyone. We never got Rann's side of his going away; he was too proud to give it. He never killed any of us. He's not crazy. Lonny was shot in the back, but those Clauntons that Rann shot were all shot from in front. All of them had guns in their hands, and they were facing Rann. He's no bushwhacker. Fall in with Gris's plan and I'll ride along to Outlaw Canyon. Rann won't hurt me."

"If he didn't, when we opened fire to get Tate, you'd likely be hit," pointed out Jep. "Or he'd kill you then, figgering you'd drag him into a trap."

"I'll risk that. I want to see him again."

"I won't allow it," said old Jep, but he groaned under his beard. This girl of his still loved Rann Tate, believed in him, even though Bronc Guard had come to his death through Tate.

"You pretend to join up with the Clauntons," ordered the girl. "I'll take care of myself. Each of you take ten men, and you make them hold their fire when they see Rann."

Before his daughter's sudden strong resolution, Jep Guard saw all of his objections being swept aside. Common sense was not a strong enough dam to stop the courage and daring of youth. If he did not go with her, the girl was capable of going alone to hunt Rann Tate.

He called after Gris Claunton, and the man rode back to hear the astonishing news that the Guards had taken up his proposition. Each family was to take ten men and no more; the two parties were to meet the next day at noon in upper Outlaw Canyon.

After he was gone, Jep Guard swore at himself for giving in to Judy. He was of a mind to go back on the agreement, but there was a positiveness about his daughter that kept him silent.

When they set out for Outlaw Canyon, she rode in a divided skirt and she wore her scarlet neckerchief and brown velour sombrero. Any rancher would know a mile away that the rider was Judy Guard but, to make it impossible to mistake her, she rode her black-and-white paint horse.

Gris Claunton and nine others met them in a side canyon. Gris's face was one triumphant leer. A pretty girl to bait a trap! It would work even better than he had hoped! Gris knew well enough that Tate was not crazy, that he only desired revenge for the merciless murder of his nephew.

From the meeting place Judy rode out alone, taking her lunch and a carbine in her saddle scabbard. The others followed her afoot, always keeping under cover. The approximate hiding place of Tate was known to the Clauntons, somewhere in the cliffs above a broad, fairly straight stretch of canyon. An army could have hidden in those slopes, broken by towering masses of rock and fallen cliffs. Somewhere among that giant playground lay Rann Tate.

A little shiver went through the girl as she rode on alone along the bottom of the canyon, but she shook off her fear. She was to bring in Rann Tate, and the Clauntons had agreed that no shots were to be fired. After they captured Rann, there would be an informal court. During that trial Judy was confident that Rann could prove that he had not killed Lonny Guard.

Her heart beat faster as she checked her horse and, firing three shots from her carbine, called Rann's name. Then she rode on a little distance and repeated it, dismounting from her horse and settling herself in the open to eat her lunch. As she waited there, her eyes swept the slope of the canyon opposite. If Tate were hiding far up toward the rim, it would take time for him to descend to her.

A half hour passed and the stillness of the canyon continued unbroken. Overhead an eagle, a small speck in the sky, circled. The spot of color on the slope not a hundred yards away caught her eye. A sombrero waved cautiously from a nest of rock pinnacles. And she knew that rusty black sombrero was Rann's.

She got to her feet. Leaving her horse with grounded reins, she pushed through brush and clambered over fallen fragments of cliff walls to come into a little cleared space. Here Rann Tate, unshaven, but with no maniacal light in his eyes certainly, met her.

"They sent you in here, did they?" he said harshly. "I saw men following you, although they were trying to keep under cover. They want you to bring me out into the open, I reckon. Sorry I can't oblige. I didn't think the Guards would be mixing in a man-hunt for me."

Her eyes met his in a level glance. "I want to apologize first of all," she stated. "I heard that you had lost your mother. That must have been why you forgot to send word that Bronc wasn't to meet you. The Clauntons stumbled onto Bronc by accident at your meeting place and killed him."

"Bronc didn't get word that I couldn't meet him that day!" he burst out. "I sent a letter by Cornwall to your father that I was leaving to take my mother away."

"Cornwall never showed up at any of our ranches," she returned. "He went to Tarrash where he told it around that you had been scared out of the country. And yet Cornwall surely wouldn't have told the Clauntons of that meeting you'd planned with Bronc."

"Maybe he did tell them," stated Tate. "Maybe they caught him and got that note off him or made him talk, and then turned him loose. But all that's water under a bridge now. What do you want with me?"

"They think you killed Lonny last week. They found your chalked Gallows brand on one of the rocks near Lonny, the same mark you've been leaving with the Clauntons you've killed."

"Six men killed Jimmy," he told her soberly. "So far I've got four of those six. I'm going to get the other two and I don't care how many others of the Clauntons. My mother saw them shoot Jimmy. She buried him without help and never told me a word then. But when I got home, she begged me to leave with her, to quit the country. I took her north to some friends. Before she died, she told of Jimmy's killing."

The color drained from the girl's face. "They did that!" she said in a low voice. "Killed a defenseless boy! And we ordered you away, when you came back." Quick tears of sympathy welled in the girl's blue eyes. "Rann, we didn't know. The

Clauntons arranged all this today as a trap. They gave their word to Dad that you were not to be shot, but they can't be trusted. Go back quick, wherever you're hiding out."

"They won't get me," stated Tate. "Not until my job is done. If I'm still alive then, this country will never see me again. I've no one here any more."

"You asked me to marry you once, Rann," said the girl. "Does that still hold good?"

"God knows it holds good," he said. "But I'm a killer now, branded the rest of my life. They'll be hanging me, if I'm not shot. There's no evidence that those six men murdered Jimmy. They'll believe that I got Lonny, too. And even if they don't, there's too much blood on my hands for me to ever marry a girl."

"I can face all that. There's no blood on your hands . . . not after they shot a boy. You've been too easy on them. Only get away, Rann. I'll go with you . . . to Mexico . . . anywhere. I love you, Rann Tate. And all this time I've been trying to make myself believe I didn't."

"You mean that?" he said huskily. "Even after those killings."

"Executions," she corrected him. "I've lived long enough in the West to know that where the law doesn't reach, a man is justified in enforcing his own laws. Those six men should have been hanged; you shouldn't have given them the chance that you. . . ."

The sharp whistle of a bullet, the sharp spat of the projectile on a rock, the rocking crack of a carbine, and the whirring off of the misshapen lead came all in a split second.

Tate whirled her down out of range. "That's part of the Claunton crew, the bunch that isn't with your father," he told her. "They're coming down from the rim to corner me. That shot wasn't for us. More like a signal."

"You've got to get out of here," she told him. "You. . . ."

A sudden heavy burst of fire from the canyon suddenly interrupted her.

"It sounds like a battle between your father's men and the Clauntons," exclaimed Tate. He crawled swiftly up the sloping face of a huge boulder and took a quick survey of the canyon bottom. Below, a group of men broke cover and raced across the broken rock and brush, heading toward Rann and Judy. Guard led them, and as they ran, they stopped occasionally to fire at the rifles that crashed back along the canyon.

"Clauntons jumped your father," Rann reported. "Gris Claunton must figure now that they've got you Guards and me both cornered. With one bunch of Clauntons above and one below, they'll move in to end us all."

Then he was calling to Jep Guard while his rifle crashed, helping to silence the Claunton weapons that sought to bring down the running men. The Guards had split into two groups. One group of three men was beleaguered in the mouth of a little side canyon. Covered by the guns of Jep's men, they came out now, plunging through the brush. One dropped to his knees, but managed to get up and hobble on. His two companions helped him along, until they finally reached the protected place where Jep Guard waited.

As Rann called to them, and Judy added her voice, the ten men, amid a hail of bullets, slid into the shelter that held the pair.

"Clauntons are figurin' on a clean-up in here," said Rann softly. "Which is queer, for that's just what I been figurin' on myself . . . a clean-up in here of the Clauntons!"

☆ **IV** ☆

BLOOD DESTINY

"Those buzzards turned on us," growled Jep as he reloaded his rifle. "But I was lookin' out for a trick."

The girl put her hand on her father's arm. "Dad, Rann never ended Lonny. The Clauntons did it and then left Rann's brand."

"I can well believe that," grunted Jep. "I kinda believed it before, else I'd never've let you go to meet him."

"Six of them shot little Jimmy when he rode home," the girl continued. "Rann wrote a note for Cornwall to bring to you, that he couldn't meet Bronc. Cornwall never brought it."

Jep eyed Rann Tate. "So that's the how of it," he muttered. "This has been a bloody mess, Rann. And they ended Jimmy? 'Tain't possible anybody could be that low . . . 'ceptin' the Clauntons. We was wrong, Rann, but no time to go into that now." The Claunton guns raised a thundering chorus that echoed heavily in the canyon. From the sound, a giant might have been beating the trunk of a huge pine against a cliff. "A bloody mess," repeated Jep harshly. "And it ain't done yet. How we goin' to git outa here?"

"We got to climb," answered Rann. "I know this canyon. There's a place above where they can't hurt us and there, if we want, we can hurt 'em plenty when they follow. I laid out a little sample room of hell against the time when they'd trail me up here. But they seemed a little spooked lately on followin' me anywhere."

"Can't blame 'em after all the misery you dealt 'em," grunted Jep, as he followed Tate and his daughter. The rest of the Guards trailed the three.

Ten minutes of steady climbing, and they stopped to breathe. The second Claunton group which had come down by way of the rimrock was dropping now into the canyon bottom hoping to press in on the Guards from one side while Gris Claunton's outfit came at them from the other. Tate, knowing every foot of this canyon slope, led his party through the line of men, alternately dodging and hiding. Below, the Claunton parties united and began climbing, fanning out over the canyon side like a pack of hounds trying to pick up a trail.

In another steep stage that left them gasping, Tate took his group upward, over little cliffs where the wounded man had to be carried, halting finally on a shelf, perhaps five hundred feet above the canyon bottom. Swinging to the left, Rann entered a narrow passageway that opened out on a side canyon heading in a series of stair-like cliffs. Ahead was a narrow ledge with a lariat strung along as a hand rail. Beyond this bridge, Tate took Judith in his arms and swung her across a chimney to the floor of a shallow cave.

Below them lay the bare trough of the side canyon, slanting steeply toward the bottom of the main canyon, and closed at the sides by precipitous walls. Above them the girl had a glimpse of high walls and pinnacles, and a huge cliff which was balanced on so narrow a base that it seemed ready to topple over at any moment. Tate knelt and emptied his gun for no other purpose, it seemed, than to save the Clauntons the job of hunting them.

The Guards noted that Tate had a camp in this little cave which was little more than a shallow shelf roofed by a slab of thick rock. There was a bedroll and a Dutch oven with a little stock of food in one corner of the cave. In another corner the Guards saw a small box, with a plunger projecting from it, one of the battery boxes used to explode dynamite from a distance. Two wires ran from the box up over the roof of the cave.

"They can come at this place from only one way," Tate told them. "From the little canyon below here. There's no chance of their finding their way along that rock passage I took you through. And if they come up that side canyon they walk into a trap. That's what the box is for. A week ago, I brought in a few sticks of dynamite and a few packloads of black powder. Sprung a hole up under that high cliff above us, and poured in enough powder to push that cliff down and let down a few hundred thousand tons of slide rock on top.

"Today, as soon as I saw the first signs of riders in the canyon, I hooked up my connections with the dynamite I planted with that pothole full of powder. I've been aiming to draw the whole tribe up this little canyon and then slide that cliff down on 'em. Enough rock above to bury an army ten foot deep. While I'd be here, sitting in a safe grandstand seat."

"You're a devil, Rann," exclaimed Jep Guard. "But they got it coming to 'em . . . anything you can hand 'em."

"I don't know about that," said Tate slowly. "There's two men in that bunch that helped dump little Jimmy out of his saddle. The rest may not be much better, but it's not for me to judge. I decided I couldn't use that little box. Getting those six was what I counted as justice, but burying a bunch of Clauntons and their gunmen alive would be slaughter. That sort of occurred to me after I talked to Judy. Men weren't made to be killed, anyways without a trial."

Jep, sore with the memory of his slain kinsmen, shook his head. "No room for that murderin' gang and us in these mountains," he stated. "But it would be slaughter, as you say. We'll have to fight 'em off. They think they got us and it'll be hard to make 'em believe they ain't." He raised his voice. "You, Gris! Listen to me!"

"I'm listenin'," came back Gris's voice mockingly from below. "Walk out and lay down your guns, you Guards, and we'll consider your case."

"We're considerin' yours, you skunks!!" returned Jep heatedly. "Clauntons, they ain't room enough in this range for both of us. There's been enough blood spilled here already to fertilize the grass. You're sellin' out to us, moving out of this country. We'll give you a fair price for your outfits."

Gris's scornful laughter came back, and the jeering yells of his followers. Shots hammered hard against the roof that overhung the cave.

"We'll either starve you out or shoot you out, it's all one to us!" shouted Gris.

"An easy way out," remarked Rann Tate, "would be to push down on the plunger of that battery box. The fools couldn't imagine that they're standing with a section of hell dangling over them. And they wouldn't believe it if we explained it. A little shove of that plunger and there'd be no more fighting but . . . I can't do it!"

The blood-madness that had possessed Rann Tate since he had listened to his mother babbling of the killing of Jimmy was gone. Four men had paid for that callous murder, and since he had talked to Judy Guard it seemed that there was no room in the world for sheer red killer-lust.

Until the girl had called to him, he'd been only a cold-blooded killing machine. Now for him the world was again a place where the great majority of men were decent, honest, where neighbors were friendly, helping each other in the work, sharing their joys and sorrows. He knew that his hand would never press that plunger.

He planned it out with Jep Guard. When darkness fell, Rann would lead the little party out of Outlaw Canyon, through the line of Claunton outposts. And they would ride down to Tarrash, place it all in the hands of the law, demand that the governor intervene, even if he had to send in a company of militia.

The firing died to an occasional shot. The Clauntons were coming up the canyon, working along the cliffs, trying to send angling shots. One of Jep's riders, Ben Tolman, who had worked for Jep from the time he had been old enough to wrangle horses, grew careless. As he leaned over to peer down into the little canyon, a gun held by a keen-eyed rifleman boomed from below. Tolman gave a choking cry, and took two stumbling steps.

"I think . . . I think. . . ," he gasped painfully and teetered for a moment on the very edge of the low cliff which dropped from the floor of the cave. Jep and Rann leaped forward to save the man but, before they could reach him, Tolman lurched back into the cave, and went staggering across the floor, toward the corner in which sat the battery box. As he fell, he put out his hands to break his fall and, when his lifeless body dropped forward, his hands dropped on the box with its raised plunger, sending it down to make contact.

"He's done it!" yelled Jep even before the man had touched the box. "Goddle-mighty, he's done it!"

A deafening grumble burst on the canyon, then a mighty blast of sound that made the cliffs tremble, booming from the base of the precariously-perched cliff above. With a succession of roars that were like claps of thunder, there came the crashing hammer of toppling rock masses, growing louder and louder until drowning out these prelimi-naries there came the deafening earth-shaking fall of the main cliff which Rann had undermined with powder.

From below, as the Clauntons beheld that sudden menace descending on them, came alarmed cries, penetrating faintly the rumble of moving rock masses. Only a few of the men were out of the path of the advancing storm and those few alone had a chance to escape. The rest were directly below the tumbling mass.

The advance army of the moving stream of rock hurtled over the overhang that sheltered the Guards. Then came the greater blocks of broken wall, and after them an unceasing stream of boulders and gravel and earth, blotting out the sky, roaring past like a gigantic Niagara. They could hear from below a few despairing cries of men caught in the torrent. Then these cries died away, and there was only the deafening cascade of stone growling and rumbling on down the canyon. Seconds only it must have lasted, but minutes and hours it seemed to the Guards before the river of rock and earth came to a stop. As the dust cleared, there were revealed a few uprooted cedars, raising their green arms above the rubble.

Not a word was spoken by the Guards. Judith, refusing to look below, stood with her red mouth a tight line, her eyes shut. The men could see in the moving ocean of rock slide only one sign of life, a Claunton who had thrown himself behind a tall pinnacle, and who now moved out slowly to descend the canyon. Under his feet the treacherous river again resumed its movement, and the man, losing his feet, rolled over and over, battling with the rumbling current until finally a greater wave than the rest overwhelmed him.

Silence descended finally. The girl was trembling and Rann lifted her in his arms for the return journey, crossing the ledge with the lariat hand-rail, retracing their way through the passageway and dropping to the canyon bottom.

Some of the Guards went to the slide, to make a vain search for survivors. Those few of the Clauntons who had escaped had already fled. There would be peace on the range that went by the grim name of the Gallows Mountains. Peace paid for with bloody coin. . . .

When, a month later, Judith Guard and Rann Tate were married in the big log house of Jep Guard, the people of Tarrash could no longer look on the mountain range and point out the symbol of the hard men who dealt in the Gallows range. Scaffold and rope and hanged man no longer were to be seen on the mountain flank.

Heavy rains had fallen and, nursed by warm autumn days, green things had sprung up to cover the cleft that made the dangling rope, while a green cloak had likewise been thrown over the black image of the hanged man. A symbol, Tarrash folk said, of peace, of good fortune.

GUNS FOR A PEACEMAKER

(1936)

———— ☆ ————

by LUKE SHORT

Luke Short was the pen name of Frederick Dilley Glidden. He was born in Kewanee, Illinois, and graduated in 1930 from the University of Missouri with a bachelor's degree in journalism. Glidden worked for a number of newspapers, but no job lasted very long. He spent two years trapping in northern Canada before he took a job as an archeologist's assistant in Santa Fe, New Mexico, and met Florence Elder of Grand Junction, Colorado, whom he married and nicknamed Butch. Fred read Dime Western *and* Star Western *and was convinced he could write a story as well as any he had read. Fred and Butch were renting two adjacent adobe houses in Santa Fe from Brian Boru Dunne, which they used as a combined unit. Fred asked Dunne if he knew of a literary agent. Dunne didn't, but he had another tenant who was a writer and who had a good one and he would ask him. That writer was T. T. Flynn. Marguerite E. Harper was the agent. In October, 1934 Fred sent Harper a story titled "Six-Gun Lawyer" and signed it F. D. Glidden. On April 17, 1935 Harper sold that story to* Cowboy Stories. *Harper told Fred she was concerned about his name. F. Orlin Tremaine, editor of* Cowboy Stories, *complained that it didn't sound very "Western." At first Fred thought of Lew Short—he wanted something "short" and memorable like Max Brand—and finally settled on Luke Short without realizing that this was the name of an actual gunman and gambler in the Old West.*

Although as a Harper client, Fred wrote his fair share of short stories for the magazine market, he preferred writing serials. Beyond this natural propensity, Fred probably realized he was not really the master of the short story and short novel the way Flynn was or, later, Fred's brother, Jon. In all, nine short novels by Luke Short were published in Star Western. *Of these, I have picked the one I feel to be his strongest and, at the same time, his most characteristic. The author was paid $120 for this story and it first appeared in the issue dated February, 1936.*

☆ | ☆

*L*arry Kehoe, a mild scowl on his face, stood reading the sign on the wall before him. A shotgun messenger was wanted for the Wickenburg run of the Wells Fargo Express Company. Any prospective guards should interview the company agent inside. As he read, he unconsciously rubbed a hand over the half dozen holes in his tattered shirt front, and with his other hand felt the holes in the pockets of his worn Levi's. He sighed a little.

"Nothin' but killer's jobs," he murmured.

He did not hear the two men come up behind him but, when one of them snickered, he looked over his shoulder at them, then stepped out of the way.

"I thought I was goin' to have to knock you out of the way, Kehoe," one of them growled. He was a ratty man, undersized, half drunk, but he wore heavy gun belts, something Larry did not carry.

"Just show your guns," the other man sneered openly. "An' he'll walk off."

Larry, from his six foot one, looked down at them with amused tolerance. His slate-gray eyes were gentle, unquestioning, and the broad, blunt hands on his hips neither clenched nor trembled. Even the muscles at his lean jaw-line did not cord, for he was untroubled. Only his shoulder muscles, broad and flat on their wide frame of bone, quivered a bit, as if about to act.

"What makes you think you could knock me down?" he said to the first speaker.

"You want to see me?" the little man hiccuped belligerently.

With a careless, almost lazy movement, Larry reached out, picked the speaker up by the shirt front, held him off the ground, flipped his guns from their holsters, and casually, indolently, slapped the man's face, twice. Then he set the man gently down on his feet.

"Don't get notions, little fella," Larry said evenly. "I don't wear guns, because I don't like to kill people. But I don't let pack rats pester me either."

He turned and strolled off down the boardwalk, his back to the two of them. Only when he was alone did he show his anger. His tanned face had drained of color, and he cursed softly to himself. Here it was again. Everywhere he went, word had got out that Larry Kehoe, once the toughest gunman in Arizona territory, had been licked by his three years in prison. He was yellow, now, people said. His spirit was gone. Any man could walk right up to him and insult him. He couldn't be rawhided into going for his guns, because he didn't wear any. Even the glory hunters, those cheap scavengers, could and did insult him.

Larry didn't expect to be understood. If asked, he would have said that he had learned his lesson in prison. There, for the first time in ten long years, he had known what peace was. No man had come hunting him. He could sleep easily; he could eat with his back to an open door, and he could look every man in the eye without wondering if the man were scheming to kill him. And there he had taken a vow. He would never wear guns again. Nothing in the world could ever make him kill another man. He would be known as a man of peace.

He had known it would be hard at first, and that he would have to take water time and again. But that didn't bother him. Every time a man taunted him and goaded him, Larry would think how easy it would be to kill the man. He never lost his temper. But even knowing this, he had not expected to find things the way they were. When word got out that he had quit fighting and killing, no man would hire him. He couldn't get the meanest job. Cowpunchers quit when he was hired. There wasn't a man in the whole of Arizona who would work with him.

"They want killers," Larry thought bitterly, as he swung up the steps of the Overland Hotel. "If I was a gunman, I could walk into Wells Fargo right now and get that job."

Inside, he looked around the lobby for old Phil Bisbee. Down at the livery stable, they had told him Phil would be in town this morning. Larry was going to hit him for a job, for old Phil Bisbee was a reformed gunman, and might understand. He would have to understand, for Larry was growing desperate. Rather than part with his saddle and his sorrel, Rusty, Larry had not eaten since yesterday. It was a job or starvation.

Off in the corner of the bare lobby, Larry saw a man and a girl sitting together. He walked over to the desk where a middle-aged, sour-faced clerk sat.

"Is that Phil Bisbee?" he asked the clerk.

The clerk stared at him hostilely for a moment. "Clear out, Kehoe. No bums is goin' to pester our cash customers."

"Thanks," Larry said dryly, but his face was flushed as he turned and walked over to the couple in the corner.

Bisbee stopped talking when Larry approached. He was a craggy man, big in black broadcloth, and his blue eyes were surprisingly gentle below fierce eyebrows. His head was massive, white-maned, and the room seemed utterly silent at the ceasing of his rumbling voice.

"Mister Bisbee?" Larry asked.

"Hello, Kehoe. Sit down," Bisbee growled.

Larry wondered how Bisbee knew his name, for he had never met or seen Bisbee.

"Oh, this is my daughter, Kate," Bisbee continued, nodding toward the girl. "This is Larry Kehoe, Kate. Sit down, son."

Larry yanked off his black and battered Stetson and bowed stiffly in the girl's direction. He was almost afraid to look at her, for he had felt the illimitable scorn of all women these past few months. But when he looked at her, he forgot all that. It was hard to imagine this slim, small-boned girl, dressed in a blue wool skirt and blouse, was the daughter of big, bluff Phil Bisbee. But there was no mistaking it. The peculiar greenish blue of her eyes was the same as Phil's, the straight flawless nose, and her chestnut hair just as wild and free and rank as old Phil's white shock.

She murmured something and Larry sat down uneasily on the edge of the chair Bisbee had indicated. The girl's cool, curious stare made him uncomfortable, and he resolved doggedly to get this over with and get out.

"If you knew my name, Bisbee, I reckon you know what I come to see you about."

"Work?"

"That's it. Any kind. It don't matter."

Bisbee's quiet, probing eyes looked searchingly over Larry, but there was no contempt in them.

"Have you had a job since you got out of jail?" he asked gently.

"Here and there. Nothin' steady," Larry told him.

"How come? You look able enough."

Here it was, and Larry spoke without a moment's hesitancy. "I won't wear guns, Bisbee. I'm through with it. I got sent to jail for killin' a man, and I learned my lesson. Now, people don't like it. I used to be somethin' of a gunman, and outlaw, and now they don't like the change, that's all."

Bisbee said nothing. Neither did the girl. It was the old awkward silence that was so familiar to him. He'd get out before they, too, called him spineless. He rose. "Well, I'm obliged, Bisbee. Good day, miss."

"Wait a minute," Bisbee cut in. "I never said I wouldn't hire you, did I?"

Larry waited.

"Do you know why I'm in town, Kehoe?" Bisbee asked bluntly. "I'm seein' my lawyer today. If I get the word from him I expect to get, then there's a range war certain, and it's goin' to break *pronto* between me and that coyote of a Lucas Petrie, that gunman killer and range hog. I've given him until today at noon to pay me for three water holes he's crowded me out of. It looks like he won't do it. If he don't, tomorrow I start movin' my stuff in on them water holes. Chances are, Lucas is goin' to fight." He shrugged and looked keenly at Larry. "You wouldn't fit in that very good, would you?"

"I reckon not," Larry said firmly. "Not for two reasons."

"What?"

"You know the first. And even if I was to carry a gun, I wouldn't fight other men's battles for them. And that's all any range war is. A pack of fools sellin' their guns and lives for money. I reckon you can't use a man that wants only common work and wages, Bisbee. Good day." He was half turned to leave when the girl spoke.

"And you don't believe in fighting your own battles either?"

Larry looked at her. There was no sarcasm in her question, no taunting, and he wondered if she was trying to understand him or merely trying to goad him into giving her a chance to vent her scorn and loathing on him.

"Not with a gun," he said evenly. "No argument is worth a man's life . . . not any." He turned to Bisbee. "That's why I wouldn't be much use to you, Bisbee. Much obliged, anyway."

"Hold on a minute," Bisbee said. "I think I can use you." His eyes were shrewd and bland as his gaze traveled from Larry's light, close-cropped hair clear down to his half boots. "If my men are all fightin', I'll need a water mason anyway. I can let the herds run, but they got to have water. You'll keep the springs open, the windmills repaired, and tote salt, for the Lord knows how long this thing will last. I'll give you thirty a month and keep . . . with no fightin'. Does that suit you?"

"Right down to the ground," Larry said fervently.

"Good." Bisbee extended his hand. "I think I know what you're buckin', Kehoe. It ain't easy. I've got the buckboard in town today. Throw in your warbag and start out for the spread. Tell Sisson, my foreman, I hired you."

They shook hands and Larry left. He was conscious as he walked out of the lobby that Kate Bisbee was watching him with her quiet, sober eyes, but he didn't care what she thought of him. He had a chance to work now. If Bisbee stuck to his word, then here was the chance to show him that a man of peace was as good as a man of war.

On his way to the livery stable, he passed the Wells Fargo sign. Glancing at it, he paused, and read a line which had been roughly penciled in below the signature.

Larry Kehoe wants the job if you'll promis not to cary a gun. It mite go off. Haw.

He read it over, his eyes stony. Then he took a stub of pencil from his shirt pocket and wrote just below the added message.

If whoever wrote the above has the guts to admit it to Larry Kehoe at Phil Bisbee's ranch, he'll get his neck broken by hand.

He signed his name, then turned down the street. For the first time in three months, he was whistling.

☆ II ☆
FISTS FOR A KILLER

*W*hen Larry rode in sight of the Slash B, he pulled up and looked it over. He had heard of the Bisbee spread, but he never dreamed it was so close to the ideal ranch. Set in cottonwoods, a stream flowing nearby, the house was low and rambling, made of 'dobe, a dozen different wildflowers scarring its dank shade of color. Off against a low, rocky hill close by lay the barns and corrals. The plank cook shack and 'dobe bunkhouse lay between the house and the hill.

Men clotted around the bunkhouse as he rode up. Obviously, they were waiting news from Saddlerock as to the outcome of Bisbee's business with Petrie. A short, hard-bitten, middle-aged man broke away from the group and hurried out to him.

Without any preliminaries, the man asked: "Come from Bisbee?"

"Yeah."

"Did he give you a message to Sisson?"

"Two of them," Larry replied. "One was that Petrie didn't show up. I left Bisbee buyin' out all the shells in the hardware store. The other. . . ."

But Sisson whirled, and called to the men. "Saddle up, boys. She's war!"

Then he turned back to Larry and Larry told him his business.

"What's your name?" Sisson asked.

"Kehoe. Larry Kehoe."

Sisson's eyes narrowed. Larry couldn't see his mouth under the full and ragged sandy mustache, but he saw the facial muscles settle the lips into a sneer. "Larry Kehoe, huh? You ain't tryin' to run a sandy on me, are you, about Bisbee? He really hired you?"

"There wouldn't be much of a chance of my stickin' if I lied, would there?" Larry drawled amiably.

"There ain't much chance of your stickin' even if you told the truth," Sisson said shortly. "Hell, what Phil needs is fighters." He shrugged contemptuously. "Unsaddle if you want to. I'll see you later."

With this contemptuous dismissal Sisson turned and headed for the big corral, where the men were already snaking out their horses for saddling. Larry's eyes narrowed a bit as Sisson walked away, and he checked the impulse to dismount, follow Sisson, and stretch him out on the ground with one good sledgehammer left. Instead, he smiled. Every time he let one of these rannies get his goat, it would be harder to take it the next time. He'd given in to his temper once today; that was enough.

He dismounted and walked Rusty over to the corral. He didn't want to put his horse away now when all the hands were in a rush to saddle up, so he took Rusty's saddle off, squatted against the corral and waited. Sisson had caught his black just inside the corral from Larry, and he was busy with deft fingers, clipping out instructions to the men as he worked.

"Frank, you and Johnny and Kimball go haze that Black Mesa herd over to that Salt Lick water hole. Mike, you and Parker pick up Sullivan and Billy at the Forks line camp and take that herd down to the Wells. Take it slow, so they'll be good and damn thirsty. That's where the trouble'll come. The rest of you jaspers throw in with either Frank or Mike, but drop back when you get near the water. I don't aim to let Petrie think we're crowdin' him especially. Tomorrow evenin' or the next mornin', the lid'll blow off. Keep them cattle there. If they tromp in the holes, to hell with it. We got a new water mason. He can dig 'em out." This last remark was intended for Larry, and he did not so much as turn his head. He was building a smoke and he continued to lick the paper, and light up.

"New water mason? Who?" someone asked.

"Gent outside the poles. Kehoe, by name. New hand."

The corral bars were down now and the hands were leading their horses out. All the friendly small talk dried up at Sisson's announcement, and Larry saw the men observing him, muttering to themselves. He looked them over with steady eyes. One or two of them he knew by sight from the old days, and he nodded, getting a cold stare in return. One of them was Blackie Murphy, a saddle bum up from the border towns. Larry knew him, and judged the man was working here only for a road stake. He had two of the hands in close conversation. Suddenly, all three looked at Larry. Murphy broke away and strode over to him.

He seemed a squat man. Yet he was tall, a saloon bully by nature, and a braggart by inclination. His broad purple-splotched face wore a perpetual sneer under its beard-stubble. He was unbuckling his belts and, when he reached Larry, he took them off.

"You workin' for Bisbee?" he demanded surlily.

Larry took a deep drag of his cigarette before he looked up and drawled: "Seems like I am, Murphy."

Murphy held out the gun belts. "Put 'em on. We're ridin' out to blast that Petrie clean out of the country."

"That's what I heard," Larry said amiably, paying no attention to the proffered guns.

Murphy glared at him. "If you're a Slash B hand, you're fightin' with us. Put on them belts!"

"I'm a Slash B hand, but I'm not fightin' with you . . . or anybody," Larry said evenly. "If I was you and I didn't want to fight while other men stayed home, I'd get my time, Murphy."

Murphy sneered. "Yellow, by God. It shows clean through to your belly."

Indolently, Larry rose to his feet, flipped his cigarette off, watched it drop. Then he hitched up his ragged pants and his calm gaze settled on the man before him.

"So a man's yellow if he ain't a killer. That's what you figger, is it?" he drawled.

"I say you're yellow!"

The last word was hardly completed before Larry lashed out with a short left to Murphy's midriff which teetered him off balance, so that he sat down abruptly and hard.

"Now stand up and take it, Big Mouth," Larry said coldly, his voice taut and flat. "I won't kill a man, but I'll come so danged close to killin' you that you'll wish I had!"

With a snarl of rage Murphy scrambled to his feet and rushed in. It was an even match on the face of it, with the weight of it slightly in Murphy's favor. The hands left their horses ground-haltered and gathered around in a loose circle. To a man, they were for Murphy. Larry gave way a little, letting Murphy ram into his rigid right arm. As the bigger man was stopped, yanked almost erect, Larry feinted with his right then brought in a left hook that seemed to mushroom Murphy's nose into a bloody blotch. He stood back, letting his arms drop, while Murphy shook his head, blinking unwelcome tears out of his eyes.

"This is fightin', Murphy," he drawled softly. "It's even. It don't depend on old man Colt, and how well you know him."

Murphy lunged in again, half insane with rage. Coolly, deftly, his head clear, but his will a white hot flame, Larry fought him. He watched his chances, met Murphy's flailing rushes, took them on his arms, then sank savage, telling blows in Murphy's face, in his heart, in his stomach. Time and again, he traded blows with Murphy, willing to take the punishment if he could land a crushing blow in return. All the pent-up rage and hate of months welled up in him, and he felt a savage joy in the fight. 'Round and 'round the circle they tramped, the hands giving way before them, then closing in again. Murphy was half crazed with the pain he suffered, but he fought like a maniac. He bit, kicked, gouged, snarled like a beast, ripped Larry's shirt to shreds, groped blindly for a hold that would enable him to crush Larry in his massive ape's arms. And Larry stood up to it all, slogging away, his blood exulting even in pain.

Murphy dove for a clinch, and Larry's blow was too feeble to stop him. Clinched, Murphy lifted a knee in Larry's groin, then rammed his crooked elbow in a savage, skin-tearing rake at Larry's face. The pain of it seemed to course through Larry's face like molten fire, and he fell away. He felt his arms heavy as logs, and he had to fight to keep his knees from buckling. Murphy wasn't licked yet; he was fighting on his guts, and his guts alone. He started another rush and, even as he did so, Larry knew he must finish the fight now, forever, or Murphy's sheer doggedness would conquer.

He gave way, rolling with Murphy's savage left, leading the heavier man farther and farther off balance. Then he saw his chance. He took a half step back to brace himself, but his spur caught on something, and he felt himself falling. Even as he bent backwards, he knew he had stumbled over his saddle. Then Murphy was on him.

He tried to cover up, to roll over, to protect his head, but the wild strength of the man on top of him beat him through his guard. Slowly, he felt the pain die away, felt his arms go numb, felt only the rocketing shock of the blows, none of the pain. Then blackness. . . .

When he came to, he was lying on his back, staring at the sky just washed over into night. He dragged himself to his knees and looked around. The place was deserted. He staggered to his feet, weaving unsteadily.

"You've taken a long time," a girl's voice said from somewhere near him. He whirled around. There, seated on the top rail of the corral, was Kate Bisbee. So still was her form against the background of the barn that he had not seen her.

"You . . . you saw?" Larry said, through swollen lips.

"Nothing. When Dad and I drove up, we found you lying alone here. Dad looked at you and said it would take some time for you to come around, but that you were all right. What happened?"

"I got beat up," Larry said, shaking his head to clear the hum and the dizziness in it.

"By whom? If one of the men bullied you, I'll see that Dad talks to him." Her voice was calm, almost sympathetic, without a trace of sarcasm. Larry looked up at her, but he could not see her face. Was she mocking him, making a more abject fool of him in her sight than he was now?

"I wouldn't," Larry said coldly. "It was a fair fight."

"Fight?" the girl echoed. She paused a full moment. "I . . . I thought you said you didn't fight."

"Not with guns. I'll fight any man with fists."

"Oh," said the girl quietly, and still there was nothing in what she said that Larry could call hostile. Rather, it was something he felt, as if this girl by her quiet womanly sympathy was trying to shame him.

"Where's your dad?" Larry asked.

"Quitting?" she countered.

"I reckon not," Larry said flatly.

"Then why did you ask?"

"I . . . I," he said, wondering why he had asked and could find no answer except that he wanted to change the subject, "I reckon I just said it to . . . well, just to be talkin'."

"He's out fighting," she said calmly. "With guns."

Larry felt the blood rise to his face. All of it, every single word of it, had been designed to shame him. And in this moment all the humiliation in these last months welled up in him bitter as only humiliation can be. He felt the impulse to pour out all his contempt, all his loathing for these blood-mad people on this girl, and to justify himself too, all in the same breath. Was it his fault if Murphy whipped him? He could truthfully say that Murphy took advantage of a brawling opportunity to conquer him. Was a man contemptible because he believed something with his heart and soul? Didn't it take courage, a finer courage than a killing courage, to stand up for what you believed was right?

But he knew with wry and hateful instinct that it would be useless. The girl couldn't see it. She had the blood of a killer in her veins. Why try to make her understand? And why stick here at all? The West was big. Surely somewhere he could find a quiet corner where his name was not known, and where he would be allowed to live in peace. But some dim stubbornness at the back of his mind told him that if he did not conquer this time, he was lost. He would be a beaten man forever after.

The girl was speaking. "I think Charley has your supper ready. The cook shack joins the bunkhouse."

She slipped down from the corral pole and started for the house, then paused. "If you want any bandages or anything, ask Charley. Oh, yes. Dad said to tell you that he wants those two springs in Sisters Canyon cleared tomorrow. The stock is moved out now, so you'll have the chance. I'm to ride up that way with you in the morning to show you the place. Good night."

"Good night," Larry answered dully. He watched her go into the house, then he turned toward the bunkhouse. There was a light in the cook shack, but he ignored it. All he wanted was to be alone and to sleep.

He was an outcast — beaten, defeated, despised. And for the first time since he had left jail, he wondered if it was all worth it. Could any one man hope to change all men around him? He was too tired to figure it out as he staggered into the bunkhouse, undressed, and tumbled into the first bunk he could find.

☆ **III** ☆

VISITORS TO HELL

*N*ext morning, Larry ate breakfast alone, for the ranch was deserted except for the two cooks, the girl, and himself. His face was a mass of livid bruises and Charley, the cook, regarded him curiously but without saying anything. He wolfed down his breakfast, then headed for the corrals.

He caught Rusty first, saddled him, then got a rope on the girl's roan. He was about to saddle it when Charley called to him.

"Leave him be, fella'. Kate ain't ridin' out this mornin'."

Larry looked at him. He had shed the khaki pants, soft shoes, and soiled apron of his kitchen, and now looked like any other cowpoke, with worn Levi's, soft black Stetson, and twin gun belts. He was a little man, grizzled, short-spoken, and his hair was generously shot with gray. Larry supposed him to be an old sidekick of Phil Bisbee's for Charley's every movement denoted that he thought he had plenty to say in the affairs of the Slash B.

"I'm ridin' out with you," Charley announced, as he let himself into the corral, not even looking at Larry. "The range ain't no place for a woman in these times."

Larry shrugged. He built his after-breakfast cigarette and watched Charley saddle up. He was just as glad that Kate Bisbee hadn't shown up. He wanted to be let alone and he knew old Charley would keep his own counsel. In fact, he knew exactly what Charley thought of him, for hadn't the old cook let him lie unconscious by the corral for three hours?

They rode out east toward the low foothills, neither of them talking. He caught Charley looking significantly at his waist — where guns should have been — but the old cook never spoke. By mid-morning they were out of the rolling grass country and entering the breaks and foothills. Twice that morning, Charley had reined up and listened a full minute, looking off to the north. Larry knew he was listening for gun-fire which would indicate Petrie's outfit had struck.

Then they headed into the canyons, where it would be impossible to hear gun-fire. Five miles or so of winding trail through a series of grassy *cienegas* and a labyrinth of cross-canyons and they reached a box canyon which showed the tracks of many cattle.

"Back there's the first spring," Charley said briefly, indicating the dead end of the canyon. The spring lay at the base of a wide sandstone shelf. It had been rocked up, so as to form a pool, with the sides about two feet high. Thirsty cattle, however, had tramped it down until nothing remained but a muddy puddle, the surrounding dirt scarred with a thousand hoof-marks. It would have to be cleaned out, then the wall built up again.

Larry dismounted, and looked at Charley. The old cook had a savagely bored expression on his face, as if to say that this was fine work to be doing while there was a range war on. Charley swung off his horse, but his foot had not touched the ground before a voice called out.

"Freeze, gents, and hoist 'em!"

Larry looked up. There, just behind the sandstone shelf above the spring, were two men, rising to their feet. They held twin Colts trained on the two men below them.

"Petrie's men, by God!" Charley growled.

While one man covered them, the other scrambled down the rocks to face them. The second man followed. They were cowpunchers, a little dirtier than the average, a little seedier looking, a little uglier in their laughing and cursing.

"We got a brainy boss," one of them drawled, the blonder of the two. "How's Bisbee goin' to like it when he finds all his water holes dynamited, Charley?"

Charley cursed them slowly, thoroughly, and the blond man laughed. His companion had a bundle wrapped in oilcloth, which he now laid down and started to unwrap. Occasionally, he glanced at Larry. Finally, he ceased his work and spoke to his partner.

"Ain't that *hombre* Larry Kehoe?"

The other man looked at Larry. A slow, ugly grin broke on his face. "Why, damned if it ain't. Larry Kehoe, the outlaw. Ain't you Larry Kehoe?"

Larry nodded and lowered his hands slowly.

"Keep 'em up!" the blond man commanded abruptly.

Larry continued to lower his hands. "You can see I haven't got a gun. I don't carry 'em."

"That's right," the second man jibed. "He's quit fightin'." To Larry he said: "What are you doin' ridin' for Bisbee? Didn't you know he wants gunmen now?"

"I'm not fightin' Bisbee's battles," Larry drawled evenly. "I hired out as a water mason. I aim to stay one."

"He's too proud to fight," the blond man said sneeringly. "I heard tell he won't slap leather with anyone. That right?"

"That's right," Larry said. He noticed that the other man had unwrapped three sticks of dynamite and six feet of fuse.

"You feel that way about it, Charley?" the blond man jeered. "You turned to preachin' too?"

"If I had a chance of gettin' these Colts clear of leather before you cut down on me, you'd damn soon see," Charley said bluntly.

"Oh, a tough guy?" the blond man sneered. "Just one of Bisbee's salty gunnies!" Charley didn't say anything. "Git that stuff in there," the man said curtly to his companion. He waited until his companion wedged the dynamite deep back in a crack of the sandstone shelf.

"Shall I touch her off?" his companion asked, when finished.

"In a minute," the blond man said, without turning his head. "Git our horses." He did not take his eyes off the two men before him, as his companion disappeared behind some giant boulders at the end of the canyon. When the other man returned with the horses, the blond man said, "Now light up."

Still he did not watch his companion as the man struck a match and the sputtering hiss of the fuse began.

"Still feel salty, Charley?" the blond man asked.

Charley had his mouth open to curse him, when the blond man's right gun exploded twice in quick succession. Charley staggered back, caught himself, then slowly his knees buckled. His hands were clawing at his holsters, then fell to his side as he pitched forward on his face. All Larry's horror changed to a red rage. He took a step forward, but the blond man's guns nosed up ominously at him.

"Take that back to Bisbee, Nellie," he jeered. "When you can grow up and carry a gun, I'll do the same thing to you if I see you."

"Come on!" the second man called sharply from his horse.

The blond man dived for Charley, flipped out his guns, rammed them in his belt. Still covering Larry, he ran to his horse, leaped astride it, and together the two men raced out of the canyon.

Larry looked at the crack where the dynamite was. It lay far back, for he had seen the man stick his arm clear in, then release it, and he had heard it roll another two feet. It couldn't be reached now, for the fuse had burned far inside the crack! He couldn't put it out with water, for the pool was too shallow to scoop up a Stetson full and douse it blindly down the crack. All this, he thought in a part of a second, then acted.

He raced over to Charley, picked him up, threw him over his horse's saddle, leaped on Rusty, seized the reins of Charley's horse, and tore toward the canyon mouth. He had not covered a third of the distance out before a rocketing, shattering blast seemed to lift him almost out of the saddle. Glancing back, he saw the tall pillar of rock and dirt geysering ominously overhead. He rammed in the hooks, holding tightly to the reins of Charley's horse.

In a few seconds, the shower of dirt and stones began. It beat him down into the saddle with shattering, bruising force, but he clung to the horn and spurred his horse savagely. Then it was over. He reined up at the mouth of the canyon and looked back. A heap of rubble, dust sifting over it, lay where the spring once had been.

Dismounting, Larry walked back to Charley's horse and gently lifted the old cook off the saddle and laid him on the ground. A quiet, murdering rage was coursing through his veins as he rolled Charley over and looked at him. Twin trickles of blood were runnelling out the corners of his mouth. His shirt was slowly blotting blood from a wound high up in the chest, and from another in his side. His eyes were open, pain-filled, and his jaw muscles were corded with the fight to keep from crying out.

"Hurt bad, old-timer?" Larry asked, ripping away the shirt.

"I . . . I can't breathe, son. Feels . . . like my lungs was filled . . . with lead."

Larry's jaw was set grimly as he washed out the wounds with water from his canteen, but he knew it was too late. Charley was strangling with his lungs full of blood. Mercifully, his eyes glazed over and he seemed to lose consciousness. Larry bent down to listen to his heart. It had stopped. The shock combined with the loss of blood had been too much for the old man.

Slowly, Larry rose to his feet, his gaze shuttling deliberately from Charley to the spring, then back to Charley. Something deep down in him told him that if he had been armed this day, this thing would never have happened. A good gunfighter would have called their bluff when ordered to hoist them. It would have been easy to streak up a gun, rolling out of the saddle at the same time, and blast them down.

But what was right? If, on the other hand, Charley had gone unharmed, if he had been a man of peace, they would not have shot him. What was right? In an agony of self-doubt, Larry went about his work, loading Charley's body on his horse and lashing him on the saddle. It was too late to do anything now. The murderers were safe from pursuit.

He started back for the spread, his heart heavy. He couldn't help but remind himself if it hadn't been for his refusal to fight, Charley would never have had to ride out with him this morning. Just outside the brakes he was jarred out of his moodiness by a dull explosion far off. For a moment he wondered, then he knew.

"They've blown another spring," he thought bitterly, helplessly. Charley dead and two priceless springs forever destroyed was the cost so far to Phil Bisbee for hiring him.

It was early afternoon when he topped the rise just to the east of the spread. He hated to look down at it, for he knew what it held for him. More scorn, more contempt, and another lost job. But looking, he reined up for an instant, blinking in surprise. The barns and outhouses had all been fired! They were a gutted mass of smoking ruins!

He spurred down the slope, noting that many men were gathered down in the corral lot and around the bunkhouse. Sisson came out to meet him, and Larry dismounted.

"What happened?" he asked slowly of the foreman. Sisson was staggering from fatigue, and his side was bandaged, his shirt bloody and torn.

"Did they get Charley?" Sisson asked hoarsely, ignoring Larry's question, while scorn and contempt colored his eyes.

"Two of 'em. Killed Charley and blew the spring in on top of us," he said harshly.

Without a word, Sisson turned on his heel and started for the bunkhouse. A blind rage rose up in Larry. He strode over to Sisson, grabbed him by the arm, and yanked him around.

"Damn you! I asked what happened!" he blazed.

Something in the cold, wintry eyes checked the oath on Sisson's lips. "They raided the spread, while we was gone," he said dully. "Fired everything they could, killed the other cook, and took Bisbee's girl. We was fightin' and raidin' all night and mornin'. Just got back."

Slowly Larry let go of Sisson's arm, and the foreman walked away. Larry stood rooted in his tracks, his eyes unseeing. Then he whirled and raced for the house.

Inside the low wall surrounding the house, he paused long enough to see Bisbee standing in a doorway that opened onto the patio. He strode over to him. Bisbee had grown years older in a night. He was hatless, coatless, his clothes stained and powder-grimed, and a raw scar gashed one cheek. He turned weary, frantic eyes on Larry.

"Bisbee, is it true they took your daughter?"

Bisbee nodded sadly. "Out of her room." He motioned inside with a helpless gesture.

Larry brushed past him into the room. The furniture and the rugs were awry, as if there had been a struggle. Curtains were pulled down, tables overturned, and the rug by the fireplace showed a bright stain of blood. In its rapid inspection, Larry's glance paused on one thing lying on the table by the bed. A spur! His spur, that had somehow been lost yesterday in his fight with Murphy! She thought of him! He saw it all now. Her goading him, her bitter shaming of him was not hatred. She had been trying to save him from a coward's brand. He turned sick inside. And now they had taken her, this helpless, brave girl, who had done her woman's best to save him, Larry Kehoe, from the mark of the craven.

He returned to Bisbee, who was gazing at him now with steely eyes, a sneer on his face. "She was s'posed to ride with you this mornin', Kehoe, because I thought you might be man enough to protect her. Why didn't she? Because she couldn't stomach them damned yellow coward's ways of yours?"

"She stayed here by choice. I rode out with Charley," Larry answered, trying to control something that was surging up in him.

"I see," Bisbee said, gesturing out to where Sisson was untying Charley. "Saved your own damned yellow skin and let Charley die. Or is he dead?"

Then something burst in Larry. He took three swift strides to Bisbee, and gathered the rancher's shirt front in a wad in his hand, yanked him up, and spoke, his face inches away from Bisbee's. "I'll remember that, Bisbee, and by God I'll ram it down your throat! You've been rawhidin' me to fight, to go gunnin'! All right, I will! I'll show you I can kill until you'll be yellin' for me to stop! *Give me those guns!*"

Bisbee hesitated in his surprise, and Larry reached out, unbuckled his gun belts, yanked them off, and lunged away, strapping the guns on as he ran. He saw it all now. It had taken Kate Bisbee to show him! If a man didn't fight for what he wanted, fight to the death, then he'd lose it. And he wanted Kate Bisbee more than anything in the world, right now. He wanted to fight for her, to kill for her, to spill oceans of blood for her, if need be. His vow was forgotten. No man could live that oath!

Now he knew that he had been sick these last few months, not afraid, but sick! All good men hated shedding blood but, when it was necessary, they did it! The fittest survived!

His anger made him wildly exultant as he raced for Rusty. He stroked the butts of the guns, and the old thrill of their solid coolness warmed him again. He was even smiling as he met up with Sisson, who was unstrapping Charley from the saddle. Larry didn't hear the words Sisson spoke — but he caught the sneer. He picked up Rusty's reins and laughed wildly. "What did you say, Sisson? No, don't tell me! I don't give a damn. I'm off to show you tin-horn gunmen how to fight! You understand, you ratty old mossback? *I said fight!*"

"Where you goin'?" Sisson asked slowly.

"Goin'? I'm goin' to ride over to Petrie's and take that gal from him! From him and his whole gang! You damned old women stay here. I'll tell you about it!" With one motion, he was on Rusty and riding.

Sisson stared wearily at him and slowly a smile creased his face. "Lord, Lord, it's the old Larry Kehoe! Get ready, hell, here's where you have visitors."

☆ IV ☆
GUNMAN WIPEOUT!

*a*nd it was the old Larry Kehoe. Even Rusty knew it, for he stretched out muscles that his horse sense had forgotten long ago, and he liked it. Petrie's C Bar P spread lay eight miles to the north, well into the rocky hills of the Las Cordilleras. Larry knew the entrance would be guarded, for even if Petrie had been fighting all night and morning, he would be cagey enough not to leave his spread unguarded.

When the country started to tilt up into the foothills, he knew he should go warily, but for some reason he did not check Rusty. This day, he felt invincible.

He was in thick piñons now, racing between low close hills, when he heard the warning shots — first the whine of the bullet overhead, then the far-off blast of the explosion a second later. Then the fusillade started. It came from off to the right, and from ahead, on a little crown hill just off the road.

He knew that, head on, Rusty was a deceptive target as he flashed in and out of the piñons, and Larry resolved to stay on him until Rusty was shot down, or was close enough so that he would be in the shelter of the thick piñons at the base of the hill. The firing was getting hotter, but he stuck to Rusty until he was sixty yards from the hill, then he rolled out of the saddle into the shelter of a tree. Rusty stopped.

He was on his feet instantly, starting his calculated, foolhardy zigzag up the hill, using every bit of rock and brush for cover. He blazed away with one gun until it was empty, then used the other, cramming in fresh loads as he ran. And he saw that the very daring of it would win. The guards on the hill, two of them, were getting panicky, shooting quickly and wildly, harried by his amazingly accurate snap-shots.

The old feel of a Colt was coming back to him. Each shot he threw at the hill was kicking up dust close to a telltale Stetson. The guards had counted on a long distance rifle duel. Now he was carrying war into their own camp!

A shallow step of rimrock, perhaps seven feet high, atop the hill formed the rampart of the guards. It was well chosen, for twenty feet of utterly bare ground lay between it and the last shelter, a stubby piñon. Larry dived for this piñon, and paused. If he waited, they would nail him, but they were scared. They were both down now. He drew a deep breath. He'd have to get one of them from here.

As he thought it, he saw a rifle barrel appear on the rimrock, then the crown of a Stetson edged up, paused, then edged higher. Larry stepped out from behind the piñon, inviting a shot.

"Watch out!" he yelled.

The rifle barrel whipped down in a swift arc. Larry's Colts nosed up, blasted in chattering, scorching fire. He moved up swiftly, shooting as he ran. When he saw the Stetson sweep off the guard's head, when he heard the shriek, he knew one guard was hit. Then, reckless with the old thrill of battle, he leaped for the rimrock, both guns in his hands.

As he raised himself up, he looked into the barrel of a Winchester, looming big as a keg, so close he could see the rifling. He lashed out with his gun, sweeping it away, as it exploded almost in his face. The explosion seemed to suck all hearing out of his head.

The guard, with no time to lever his Winchester, dropped it, fell back on his haunches, and streaked for his guns. Larry blurred up his Colts. Once, three times he fired, then let the guns sag, and crawled up the rock.

The man had been blasted over backwards. His hands were clawing at his chest, then they settled limply. The other man was dead, too.

"Blood," Larry muttered, looking at them. They deserved death.

He dropped off the rimrock and hurried down the hill. On Rusty again, he lifted him into a wild gallop and, reins in teeth, loaded both his guns. The rifle blast had made him temporarily deaf, and he did not hear the riders coming upon him until Sisson drew up beside him and reached out for Rusty's reins. The two of them stopped in a moil of dust, as a dozen more Slash B riders, including old Bisbee, slammed to a halt beside them.

Bisbee was yelling something, but Larry could hear only the pounding in his ears.

He raised a hand and Bisbee stopped talking. "I can't hear you, Bisbee. I don't want to. Go home! I'll get your daughter!" he jeered.

Bisbee shouted that they were riding to certain death this way.

Larry pretended to listen, grinning, then he laughed wildly. "To hell with you! To hell with all of you! You asked for blood and you'll get it!"

He roweled Rusty into a rear which scattered the horses before him. Then he dashed on, already in a full gallop. Rusty rounded a bend and Larry found himself in the cleared space where the buildings of the Petrie spread lay.

He sized up the layout in a second. Off a little to the left, ahead of him, was Petrie's *casa grande*. It was a right-angled building, shaped like a wide wedge, the open part almost facing him. A *portale*, shading many windows, ran the whole of its length. Directly on his left was the bunkhouse. Between the two was a giant cottonwood.

And Larry noted, with a veteran's eye, that the end of the *casa grande* was window-less, blank. Just around the corner from it was a window, small, and high up in the wall. He swerved Rusty toward the cottonwood, lying low in the saddle, like an Indian. If he could make the cottonwood, he might have a chance.

He did. He made it, rode under it, headed for the end of the buildings, when he felt Rusty falter. He whipped his feet out of the stirrups just as Rusty went down. Then he raced for the end of the building, only a few yards off. He felt something smash his arm, and he was whirled half around, but doggedly he ran.

The last two yards he dived, and skidded in the dust to safety. Before he could rise, Bisbee's horsemen swung into sight, and headed for the bunkhouse under the swell of gunfire. Now was the time to act, while they were trying to drive Bisbee off. Larry tried his arm. He could use it, for it was only a flesh wound.

He edged around the corner of the building. He was in plain sight of Petrie's guns, but the defenders were intent on Bisbee. They had forgotten him. Two feet over his head was the small, square window. He leaped for the sill, pulled himself half up, slugged out the glass, his back crawling coldly. He was a dead shot for the man who spotted him. Frantically, he hoisted himself up, and in.

Half in, he saw that the window let onto a small, musty storeroom. Then he saw the door slam open and a man, shotgun in hand, blundered in. If he dropped back again, he would be killed surely. He'd have to go on!

But his guns were holstered, and he was lying on them! Even as the man's shotgun tilted up, Larry wrenched off his Stetson and sailed it across the eight feet of space at the man's head, pulling himself through the window with a mighty heave at the same time. Even as he was dropping the six feet to the floor, the shotgun blasted deafen-ingly, and a slab of plaster from the wall above the window crashed down.

"Nailed," the man muttered, seeing the window empty.

Larry, gasping for breath, rolled over on his side and whipped up a gun that exploded almost before the echo of the shotgun died. The man dropped the shotgun, teetered back on his heels through the door, and Larry heard him slide down the corridor wall to the floor.

Larry stepped out into the corridor and walked swiftly down the hall. The first door he came to, he paused. Inside the room men were shooting. Larry tried the knob, and eased the door open gently. Four men were hunkered down below the sill of the two windows. Larry swung the door open with a kick. Twin Colts rested in blunt palms.

"Drop it!" Larry snarled.

The four men whirled to face him.

"Kehoe," one of them muttered softly.

"The old Kehoe," Larry said silkily. "If you don't believe me, hold that gun five seconds longer and I'll show you!"

Not a man moved.

"There's four of you," he continued. "If you got the guts, make your play!"

Swiftly, the four rifles clattered to the floor, and hands were hoisted.

"Now chuck them out the. . . ." He paused, and took a step nearer, peering at one of the men. Then he straightened up, and a cold smile creased his face.

"Blondy," he said softly. "The tough guy." It was Charley's murderer.

"I. . . ," Blondy began, but Larry cut in: "Your Colt's loaded, Blondy?"

"No," the man said swiftly.

Larry tossed him one of his Colts, and it landed on the floor at the man's feet. "Pick that up and holster it," he said.

The man did not move.

"You'd rather have me kill you like you killed Charley?" Larry drawled. "I'm givin' you an even break, *hombre*. I'll kill you anyway, but you're gettin' a chance. Don't you want it?"

Haltingly, his terrified glance glued to the gun Larry held, the man knelt to pick up the gun on the floor.

"Touch that hammer and I'll let this thing off," Larry jeered quietly. "I want you to holster it. Savvy? Holster it!"

Blondy picked up the gun by the base of the butt, and dropped it in his holster.

Larry straightened up. "I'm holsterin' mine now, gunnie. Make your play . . . all of you or any of you . . . when my hand leaves the gun butt."

Blondy's gaze shuttled to his companions, and his eyes pleaded for life and help. But the eyes of the other three men could not meet his. They had deserted him, and he knew it. Seven guns against one, but they would not take the chance.

"Listen, Kehoe. . . ," Blondy began.

"Any time," Larry cut in frostily.

A last glance at his companions, and Blondy looked at Larry. His face was contorted with fear, and with the image of death confronting him. With a small, pleading cry, he streaked for his gun, as the other three men dived away from him. Larry's big hand blurred down, up, and his gun crashed in the same motion. His hand still traveling to his gun, Blondy's head whipped back into a scream. He was slammed back against the window, a neat hole in his forehead.

A shot from Bisbee's alert men now in the bunkhouse caught him in the back, checked him, drove him forward. His knees buckled, and he pitched on his face, and lay still.

Larry drew a deep breath, his gun, four loads left, trained on the other three. "Anyone else?" he drawled quietly.

"I've quit, Kehoe," one man blurted out in sheer terror. "For God's sake. . . !"

"Then throw those six-guns down."

The men complied.

"Now wave a handkerchief out that window, then crawl through it, go around to the end of the house, and sit there."

"Hell, they'll. . . ," a man started to say.

"They'll let you live, damn you!" Larry snarled. "Bisbee don't hire sure-thing killers. Clear out now!"

He waited until they signaled surrender. As he predicted, Bisbee withheld fire at this room, although the steady racket of firing at the rest of the house never ceased. Two men piled out the window and raced for the end of the house. The third, Larry stopped.

"Where's Bisbee's girl?"

"Petrie's got her," the man answered. "In the house somewhere."

Larry nosed his gun up. "Maybe a little lead would help you remember."

"You can shoot if you want, Kehoe," the man said dazedly. "That's all I know. There's a big room in the center of the house and some rooms in the other wing of it. But the girl, I dunno where he's got her."

"Clear out!" Larry snarled, and strode into the corridor again.

Should he try every room, running the chance each time of being cut down and letting Petrie escape with Kate? No. The rooms on the left were full of killers. Those on the right, toward the back of the house, were the safest. Perhaps Petrie had her in one of these. He tried the first, a bedroom; it was empty.

At the door of the second, he paused. It was directly across the hall from a room where the blast of gun-fire was a continuous roar. If Petrie was in here, and cried for help, he could never be heard. Larry smiled, and swung the door open. A man was standing in the center of a richly furnished room, his back to Larry. Against the far wall, Kate Bisbee was huddled on a deep leather sofa. As Larry opened the door, letting in the swell of the gun-fire, the man turned his head a little, but did not look around.

"Has Bisbee hightailed it yet?"

"No, not yet," Larry drawled back.

The man whirled. Kate rushed past him into Larry's arms, between his guns.

"Larry!" she cried, throwing her arms around his neck. Larry wanted to look at her, to kiss her, to whisper all his thanks to her, but he knew if he took his eyes from Petrie, the man would go for his guns.

"Darlin'," Larry muttered huskily, his eyes watching the man before him, one arm around the girl he would die for.

"I knew you'd come! I knew you'd find yourself, Larry!"

Suddenly, the man in the center of the room smiled. "Now, Kehoe, if you'll let my wife, Missus Petrie, go, we'll talk," he drawled.

Larry stared at him. Was this a trick to get him off his guard?

"Wife?" he asked dully.

"My wife, the former Kate Bisbee," Petrie said. "Married two hours ago."

"Is it true?" Larry muttered hoarsely to the girl. He would have given his life at that moment to look into her eyes, but he did not dare. Petrie's hands were poised like a snake ready to strike.

"It's true! He's had a greasy Mexican Justice of the Peace up from the border for a week, waiting for this. Larry, he's my husband!"

"Do you love him?" Larry asked, his voice almost a whisper.

"I loathe him!" the girl cried.

"Then . . . then why did you give your consent?" Larry stammered. His face was drained of color, his lips gray, and the gun in his hand was trembling.

"Oh, Larry, I was tortured into it!" Kate moaned. "He claimed he had set a charge of dynamite under our house last night and that he would blow it up on Dad if I didn't give in! He beat me, too. Look! See the bruises."

Larry's jaw clamped shut with a click. Only the dim snarl of gun-fire could be heard in the room.

Petrie laughed easily. "You can't beat a marriage, Kehoe. Get out! I'm not interested in fighting you."

Slowly, Larry raised one hand, gently removed Kate's arm from his neck, then moved her out of the way. "Wait, girl," he murmured. "Get out of the way." Kate drew slowly to one side of him. "No, I can't beat a marriage, Petrie," Larry said softly. "Not even that kind of a one. But there's no law that says I can't love and marry a man's widow."

Petrie laughed again. "Oh no, Kehoe. I know you, know all about you. You give every man an even break for his guns. You'll give me one . . . and I'll kill you. I've got fighter's guts. You haven't."

"When you find out that's a lie," Larry drawled, "you won't care. You'll be dead."

Quick as thought, he holstered his guns, and let his hands fall. And so they stood, one man, a drawling giant in tatters who was winning back his manhood, the other a cool, daring killing machine, nerveless and arrogant.

"You make the play," Larry said.

Petrie shifted his feet a little bit. Larry hunched his broad shoulders, leaned his weight a little forward on the balls of his feet. There was a calm smile on his face. His muscles felt loose, ready.

He saw Petrie's light eyes slam into sharp focus. Then, fast, Larry's hands streaked, slapped up to gun butts, swiveled Colts up in a precision arc against his hip-bones. His guns rocked, danced, bucked, in their infernal chatter of death. Petrie, his guns just cleared of leather but unfired, was driven back step by step, shot by shot, across the room. His fighting doggedness kept his feet for him, but he was a dead man walking. On the last shot, he sagged onto the sofa. There was nothing on his face except a quiet, still-eyed look of surprise.

"Larry!" Kate cried. And before the wisping gunsmoke had a chance to smart Larry's eyes, she was in his arms.

"Like it should be," Larry murmured. He heard steps in the hall, but they did not register on his consciousness. He held Kate at arm's length, and looked into her fine, fighter's eyes. "You were tryin' to tell me how to get back my guts, weren't you?"

She nodded and smiled. "You never lost them, Larry. You were always a fighter. But what you didn't see is that sometimes death is the only way to life. You can't make the world choose your weapons. You've got to use the world's weapons. And if they are guns that spell death, then you must make them yours."

"I know," Larry said. "I've made 'em mine, and they'll always fight for peace. And I'll make you mine and *we'll* always fight for peace."

The door opened behind him and Bisbee stood there. Cagey old gunfighter that he was, he had outsmarted and outfought his enemy. Petrie's men had surrendered. And now the grizzled old man, guns still hot, stood in the doorway, smiling.

He had seen Larry. He knew it was the old Larry Kehoe, and he knew that dim scheme he had thought up back in the hotel had come to fruition. He had made Larry assert his manhood.

"Well, what does this mean?" he asked.

Kate ran to him, kissed him.

"It means the Slash B has to change its brand. From now on, its the K Slash B, Dad. K, for Kehoe, your daughter's new husband."

BOOMERANG BOUNTY

(1937)

⎯⎯⎯⎯⎯ ☆ ⎯⎯⎯⎯⎯

by PETER DAWSON

Peter Dawson was the pen name of Jonathan Hurff Glidden who was born in Kewanee, Illinois. He graduated from the University of Illinois with a degree in English literature and begun to write Western fiction at prompting from his brother. In his career as a Western writer, Jon published sixteen Western novels and over 120 Western short novels and short stories for the magazine market. From the beginning, he was a dedicated craftsman who revised and polished his fiction until it shone as a fine gem. His Peter Dawson novels are noted for their adept plotting, interesting and well developed characters, their authentically researched historical backgrounds, and stylistic flair.

Jon's first novel, The Crimson Horseshoe, *won the Dodd, Mead Prize as the best Western of the year 1941 and ran serially in Street & Smith's* Western Story Magazine *prior to book publication. After the war, the Peter Dawson novels were frequently serialized in* The Saturday Evening Post. *One of Jon Glidden's finest techniques was his ability after the fashion of Charles Dickens and Leo Tolstoy to tell his stories via a series of dramatic vignettes which focus on a wide assortment of different characters, all tending to develop their own lives, situations, and predicaments, while at the same time propelling the general plot of the story toward a suspenseful conclusion. Jon's model had always been Ernest Haycox among Western authors and he began early on to experiment with character and narrative technique in a fashion his younger brother never did.* Rattlesnake Mesa *(Circle Ⓥ Westerns, 1996) and* Dark Riders of Doom *(Five Star Westerns, 1997), a story collection, are among his most recent book publications. Jon Glidden published nine short novels in* Star Western. *This story was his third.*

☆ **I** ☆

He was medium tall and thin, and his eyes were a cold gray, deep-set in a lean, bronzed face. He wore a black Stetson, a dark gray vest over a gray shirt, waist overalls tucked into soft high-heeled boots. His guns were a pair of horn-handled, silver-mounted Colt .38s riding low in open holsters at his thighs. Chiefly, it was the eyes and the guns that you noticed.

From across the cowtown street a cowpuncher and a girl watched him dismount and throw the reins of his sleek, straight-legged dun stallion over the tie-rail in front the bank.

"Who is he, Ed?" the girl asked.

She was too far away to see the stranger's eyes, but she had caught the white reflected sun-glint from his weapons. That, plus her long familiarity with this country, made the presence disturbing. She was frowning as she gazed up at her companion;

but, even with the frown, a softness touched her glance which heightened her good looks and made it at once obvious that this was the man of her choice.

"I wouldn't know," Ed answered. "But I'd like to have the hardware he's packin'. It'd pay up a good share of the interest on my note this fall." He was well set up, broad-shouldered and tall. Even a close observer would have overlooked the shabbiness of his outfit, for it was clean and fit him well.

No one in the bank knew the stranger. But they all saw him enter and, when he sauntered back and asked the teller in the last cage if he might speak to Tade Wardow, the president, he was given the respectful answer: "Yes, sir. I'll call him."

"Never mind. I'll do the callin'."

Before the teller could protest, the stranger had walked around the end of the counter and was crossing to the glass-paneled door which was lettered, "President."

He didn't knock at the door; he pushed it open and stood looking in as it swung back. Tade Wardow glanced up from where he sat behind his polished mahogany desk. A belligerent frown gathered on his round plump face: "I'm busy," he snapped. "You'll have to wait outside."

"I'm Lonesome Barkley," the stranger drawled in soft tones that were meant only for Wardow's ears.

His words seemed to put sudden fear into the banker's steel-blue eyes. With an attempt at affability, Wardow managed to get out: "Come in. Come in, and take a chair."

The stranger stepped in and let the door swing shut behind him. But he made no move toward the chair Wardow indicated. Instead, he leaned indolently against the wall and hooked his thumbs in his belt.

"Talk Wardow," he said.

Tade Wardow's manner now was somehow ridiculous compared to his blunt arrogance of a moment ago. He opened his mouth to speak, closed it again, and swallowed with difficulty — as though his mouth was full of cotton. He was a big man, young, dark, and handsome in a well-fed way. His black coat and spotlessly clean white shirt fit his thick chest and shoulders faultlessly.

The banker's glance dropped down to take in the stranger's guns. Finally he got out: "Don't be proddy, Lonesome. No one else knows."

"Go on."

"It's like I said in my letter," Wardow explained hastily. "I'm the only one Jim Hogan talked to. He sent for me before he died. We were alone. I'm the only one who knows about it."

"What?"

"About . . . about. . . ." The banker was having difficulty with his throat just then.

"About the stage robbery up at Tentpole?" Lonesome prompted.

Wardow nodded stiffly. "That's it."

"All right. You know that Jim and I did it."

"Get this straight, Lonesome. I wouldn't go to the law with what I know. I'd. . . ."

"You'd know better."

The words were soft-spoken, spaced deliberately, but Wardow cringed visibly at the threat of them. Lonesome laughed softly, unpleasantly, seeing the banker shrink down into his chair. His two blunt hands clutched the chair arms until the skin on his knuckles showed a dead white,

"I swear to God I wouldn't!" Wardow breathed hoarsely. "I brought you down here for something else . . . something with money in it."

"I'm still listenin'."

"There's a mine payroll due here this afternoon," Wardow said. "It's to be stored in this vault overnight . . . eleven thousand dollars. It's covered by insurance . . . if . . . if anything should happen to it."

Lonesome Barkley's expression altered imperceptibly as he listened; his lean features hardened, and two bright red spots crept in under the tan of his skin, high up on his cheekbones. Seeing it, a doctor would have suspected that Lonesome was a sick man and that something beyond a violent inner emotion caused that heightening of color. Wardow was no doctor and, besides, he was too blind with fear to notice. But he could have had his warning then of what was coming.

"It's a perfect layout," the banker went on, heartened by Lonesome's silence. "I'll give you the combination to the vault and you can do the job tonight. There won't be any risk." He leaned back from his desk and reached down into a drawer at his side.

As he moved, Lonesome shoved out from the wall. Seeing this and understanding it, Wardow added hastily: "It's not a gun, Lonesome. Only the combination. I've written it down."

He extended his hand and opened it. A small white card lay in his palm, with two lines of numbers written on it in a neatly-penciled hand. On the card lay a plain six-pointed spur-rowel.

"What's that?" Lonesome asked.

"The rowel?" Wardow shrugged. "I want this left in the vault after you do the job."

Lonesome came over to the desk and picked the steel crescent off Wardow's green blotter. He looked at it, then at Wardow, and asked quietly: "A frame up?"

"You can call it that."

Lonesome waited until the silence lengthened awkwardly. "So you think I can handle it?"

A measure of the banker's confidence returned. He shrugged his sloping shoulders carelessly in answer, saying: "Why not? Who'd ever suspect Lonesome Jim Barkley, the famous hell-town marshal?" He chuckled and a look of admiration crept into the glance he focused on his visitor. "You've been slick, Lonesome, accordin' to what Jim Hogan told me. First it was that Tentpole job with Jim sidin' you. Then you went on alone to Benson, then Granite City. Maybe that's why they call you Lonesome."

"Maybe it is."

"You did a good job tamin' those towns, made your name with guns while you wore a marshal's badge. It's none of my business what else besides law-making you did in those places."

The color on Lonesome's cheeks heightened. "Supposin' I told you that the Tentpole job was the only one, Wardow?"

"Supposin' you did? If that's your story, stick to it. Your secret's safe with. . . ."

The flashing down-swing of Lonesome's right arm clipped off the words. Tade Wardow lunged up out of his chair, his eyes dilated in stark horror as Lonesome swiveled up the blunt snout of his .38. The weapon rose and fell in a swift chopping stroke that caught the banker high above the right temple. The blow drove him to his knees, so that his solid bulk hit the carpeted floor with a jarring thud. He fell backward, knocking the chair aside, then lay there without moving.

Lonesome Barkley stared down at the inert figure for five seconds; he was breathing hard from the exertion, with a rising flush mounting to his face. All at once he put a hand to his mouth and coughed; it was a deep, hollow-chested rattle that made him stoop over in pain. He coughed again, and again the pain-spasm doubled him up. Half a minute later he straightened once more, drew a deep breath, and the tide of color gradually receded from his face.

He wasn't thinking of Wardow then; he was remembering Harry Quinn, the tin-horn gambler in the saloon up in Granite City who had cashed in with a cough like his own. Harry had looked more like a mummy than a man who had lived and breathed and bet his roll on the turn of a card.

Lonesome hadn't been to a doctor about his lungs; he was afraid to hear the truth. Now, as always when these coughing fits hit him, he was wondering how much longer he had; it might take years, like it had with Quinn, or it might be over in a few short months.

He looked down at Wardow dispassionately, knowing this breed of man and hating it. Not many had earned Lonesome Barkley's hatred and lived; some had met a swift and violent death in facing the lead slugs of his .38s; a few had known the man they faced and ridden out of his life. Jim Hogan was one of the latter.

So Jim had talked! And, as a result, the one dishonest act of Lonesome's life was striking back at him! He should have killed Hogan that night on the road near Tentpole, killed him instead of losing his head and cutting down on the stage driver. That was years ago, when Lonesome's youthful pride had turned more to demonstrating his uncanny swiftness with a gun than to realizing what would come out of the unbridled use of it.

Hogan's dare that night had made Lonesome side him; what had happened made a man of him overnight. Since then his guns had backed the law, and had earned him a deep-seated respect from the Rio Grande to the Platte, from the Rockies to the Missouri.

Wardow's letter telling of Hogan's death had brought him here; he had ridden in with a vague foreboding of what was to come. This was it, then — he was face to face with the greatest problem of his life. He eased back onto the desk and sat there, considering what Wardow had said. He would kill this man. But how?

Beneath him he felt the prod of the spur-rowel; he reached down and took it in his hand. "It'll build a rope necktie for some poor jasper," he mused. "Jim, you snake-belly, you brought me into something here." Then, idly, his mind toyed with the idea of going through with the thing. That thought inspired another, until finally a wry smile wreathed his features.

A hint of that same smile still lingered five minutes later when Tade Wardow opened his eyes and stared up at him blankly. The banker's first instinctive gesture was to raise a hand to ease the pain in his head. When he recognized Lonesome, a sneer twisted his features into ugliness.

"I looked for this," he snarled. "A week ago I gave Sheriff Mays an envelope. Jim Hogan's confession is sealed up in it. If anything happens to me, Mays opens it."

"So there's a reward still out for the Tentpole killin'?" Lonesome asked levelly.

"Three thousand, and what Mays has will put every lawman in Arizona on the prod for you." He came stiffly to his feet as he spoke, glaring defiantly. "Take it or leave it, Barkley. Do this my way, and you clear out of here with eleven thousand. Do it yours . . . and you'll hang!"

Strangely enough, Lonesome smiled and shrugged. "I'm listenin', Wardow. Only I didn't like what you said a while back. You know too much."

"I've said you're safe with me. Play along on this and you'll come off a free man."

Lonesome didn't answer. Wardow waited a brief moment, then asked: "Are you in with me?"

"What about the envelope you gave your lawman?"

The banker smiled smugly: "He keeps that. Something could happen to me later on." He was no longer afraid, believing himself safe so long as he possessed this evidence against Lonesome.

"That's a tough bargain, Wardow."

"Take it or leave it," the banker repeated.

Lonesome looked down at the spur-rowel resting in his palm and seemed to consider what Wardow has said. At length, he drawled: "What do I do?"

"Come to my place, the white house out at the east end of the street, at nine tonight. I'll give you enough dynamite to touch off so that it'll look like a real job. You'll find the money in sacks on the floor at the back of the vault. Leave the money sacks and the rowel on the floor, inside. Close the vault door, don't lock it, set the dynamite, and ride away from here. And you never saw me, Lonesome."

"But why do I leave this?" Lonesome indicated the pointed bit of steel in his palm.

"There's a thing or two in this world money won't buy. That's going to get me one of 'em."

If Wardow had known his man, he would have been suspicious when Lonesome reached back to take the card from the desk and put it and the spur-rowel in his pocket, saying meekly: "I'll be there at nine."

The banker's arrogant smile returned as the door swung shut behind Lonesome, and the light of a full confidence crept back into his eyes. He was once more his old self.

☆ II ☆

BRANDED FOR DEATH

From where he stood under the sidewalk awning, Lonesome looked across the street and up to the second-story window, lettered DR. SILAS HOYER. Yet it was a good five minutes before he finally went across and climbed the stairs to the doctor's office. Inside, he found a portly, gray-haired man drowsing in a swivel-chair. His worn boots were propped on an untidy desk.

Doc Hoyer opened his eyes at the sound of the closing door, glanced at his visitor, and muttered gruffly: "You don't look sick."

"I reckon I don't. But I've got a cough, Doc. Tell me what to do for it."

The sawbones swiveled around and dropped his feet to the floor. "A pint of Red-eye Barton's bourbon is the best thing for a cough. Let's hear it once."

Lonesome coughed, gently. Even so, Hoyer's eyes narrowed in studied inscrutability. He shrugged and stood up, saying casually: "Peel off your shirt and I'll have a look."

He went over Lonesome's chest, laying his palm flat against it and tapping the fingers of that hand with the stiff third finger of his other. Finally he stepped back and looked at his patient: "Like I told you, a pint of liquor's what you need. Hell, you big strappin' cusses come in here if you cut your finger. It'll cost you two dollars this time, stranger." His tone was gruff but now there was a softness behind the look in his honest brown eyes that he couldn't hide. Lonesome caught it, and in it had his answer.

"How much longer will you give me, Doc? A year?" he asked quietly.

Hoyer's expression hardened. "You're talkin' like a damn fool. Your lungs are sound, man. A good rest might not hurt. Plenty of eggs and milk and good food, and you'll be here to bounce your grandchildren on your knee."

Lonesome only half heard what Hoyer was saying. He was staring vacantly out the window and down onto the street. It was what he expected. His answer lay in Hoyer's look, and now he felt strangely relieved for the certainty it gave him. Perhaps it was because he'd known it for so long that he could feel no regret. His life had been like his name: he was a lonesome man. Beyond a very few real friends, he had no one to make it hard to face what was coming . . . no woman he loved, no family. There was one man, had he lived, a young cowboy from Wyoming who had ridden with Lonesome into the death which was pounding madly in a thundering stampede. The youngster never came out again; Lonesome did, and owed him for his life that wild night of storm. How many years ago had that been?

His glance shuttled on up to the street to the brick front of the bank, and his thoughts for the moment centered on the bank, on Tade Wardow, and on the part each was to play in what was planned. Thinking of the man, it surprised him to see Wardow step out of the bank entrance at that very moment and turn to come down the opposite walk toward him.

Lonesome watched the banker, feeling again a deep-rooted hatred toward him. He watched until Wardow, almost directly across the street now, stopped, and tipped his low-crowned hat to a girl coming down the walk. It was the girl who took Lonesome's eye then. She wore a brown skirt, a bright yellow blouse, and was hatless. Frankly studying her, Lonesome was instantly aware of the subtle beauty of her slim figure and tawny hair and light, creamy skin.

"Who is she?" he asked, aloud. "Looks sort of like I'd seen her before." And yet he knew he couldn't have.

"Who?" Hoyer asked, coming to stand alongside Lonesome. "Oh, Mary Latrobe? She's a good friend of mine. And she's talkin' to the biggest skunk that ever walked on his hind legs."

Lonesome waited for more, surprised and interested at the doctor's blunt outburst. But Hoyer stood there in a frowning silence, glaring at Tade Wardow and the girl.

"Sounds like you don't take to him," Lonesome offered.

"No. I know him better than most. He owns half the town and the county and is tryin' awful hard to get the other half. Like I said before, Tade Wardow's a prime polecat. Not that it would interest you."

"What about the girl, Mary Latrobe? Is she his, too?"

"Not by a damned sight! He'd like to have her, but Ed Hardy has something to say about that."

"Who's Ed Hardy?"

Hoyer looked up at him, his glance faintly quizzical. "There's no reason why I should be runnin' off at the mouth to a stranger. Who's Ed Hardy? He's a poor, busted, hard-workin' devil who's in love with that girl over there. She's in love with him too, but they can't get spliced. Ed's got a mortgage on his outfit . . . couple of thousand dollars . . . and stands a good chance of spendin' the rest of his life workin' it off. They say he'll lose his shirt this fall. I wouldn't know for sure."

"Now don't tell me that this ranny across here . . . Wardow . . . holds the mortgage."

"How did you know?" Hoyer asked, chuckling grimly. "Wardow's the banker here. Yes, he holds the mortgage. And he'd be the first one to close out on Ed."

The two of them stood there in silence, watching Tade Wardow as he once more tipped his hat to Mary Latrobe and stepped to one side to let her walk on past him and up the street. So Mary Latrobe was what Wardow's money couldn't buy! It was almost as if fate had blazed his path into this town. Again the memory of that night, years ago, came to him when a young cowpuncher named Red Latrobe had gone down under the thousand knife-sharp hoofs of that mad herd. Gone to die so that Lonesome Barkley might live.

Piece by piece Lonesome was fitting together the puzzle that had come out of his visit to the bank. He was thinking of the spur-rowel too, thinking that a spur is a thing that pretty accurately labels a man. There were exceptions, of course, but ordinarily a man with money would wear something better on a pair of fine boots than the plain piece of steel Wardow had given him. This rowel fit a spur a man could buy at a dollar and a half a pair at any hardware store. It was plain and worn and hardly one to be one used by a particular man.

Dipping a hand into his pocket for the money he owed the doctor, he felt the cold chill of the steel. And suddenly he knew what Tade Wardow was trying to do. It was Ed Hardy who was being framed — framed because he loved the girl Tade Wardow wanted.

"Here's your money, Doc. Maybe this Ed Hardy won't lose out after all."

"You're wrong about that," was Hoyer's grim answer. "Anyone who bucks Wardow loses out. It'll take time, but Mary Latrobe will be Missus Wardow one of these days, and Ed'll be movin' away to try the grass on some other range. It's a hell of a world!"

"Would you trade places with me?"

Hoyer's grizzled countenance flushed a trifle. He smiled thinly: "You aren't so bad off, stranger. You aren't so bad off."

At three that afternoon, a loquacious oldster down at the livery-stable pointed out Ed Hardy to the stranger without knowing he'd done it. At five Lonesome saw Hardy go in through the swing-doors of Red-Eye Barton's saloon. By six-thirty he had finished a leisurely supper and was standing at the bar in Red-Eye's place.

Lonesome stood there twenty minutes, took three drinks of bourbon straight, and then sauntered back to look in on the poker game at the back table. Ed Hardy was in the game; so was Doc Hoyer. Ten minutes later Hoyer turned and looked up to see who was standing behind his chair. He smiled pleasantly as he recognized his patient.

"Want to sit in, stranger? It's penny-ante. We don't lose much and we don't win much."

"Suits me," Lonesome answered. "I'll stay till I use up this dollar."

He went around the table and took a chair backed by the wall. At any other time the force of the long habit would have prompted him to do this, but now he did it because it put him directly across the table from Ed Hardy. The fog of tobacco smoke that hung over the table bit into Lonesome's lungs and made him cough several times. Once he caught Hoyer's pointed scrutiny. The sawbones' eyes abruptly shifted when they met his, and Lonesome smiled, knowing what the other was thinking.

Doc Hoyer was the oldest man at the table. The three others were men of Hardy's age, young and clean-looking and obviously playing for the enjoyment of the low-stake game. In all Lonesome's experience he had never found a thing that so quickly and accurately mirrors a man's character as a game of poker. For that reason he watched how Ed Hardy played his cards. When it was his own turn to deal, he invariably called for a hand of stud. A man showed more at stud than he did at draw.

In less than half an hour he learned that Hardy's game was a conservative one, balanced with an occasional bluff-hand that would have made him dangerous at high stakes. On one hand of draw, Hardy stole a pot against Doc Hoyer, betting the limit each raise until the sawbones threw down his three kings, face up, growling: "You've got 'em or you wouldn't bet. If you'd only play Mary that way, Ed! You don't have a damned thing to lose!"

Hardy smiled, a smile that would have been mirthless but for his open friendliness toward Hoyer. He reached out and raked in the stack of chips, saying: "Nothing to lose? No, I reckon I haven't, Doc. But she has. A two-bit cow-nurse like me doesn't have much to offer."

Hoyer snorted. "In my day a man didn't let things like that bother him. It's your deal, stranger."

Lonesome had the feeling that Hoyer had mentioned this to remind him of their conversation that morning. Regardless of Hoyer's motives, he had prompted an answer from Ed Hardy that was pregnant in its meaning — an answer that somehow settled things in Lonesome's mind. He watched Hardy closely after that, seeing the hint of a worried frown that wrinkled the man's high forehead under his sandy hair. Mention of Mary Latrobe had put that frown there and, when it didn't disappear with Hardy's winning several hands, Lonesome knew that the worry was so deep-rooted within the man that it would eventually become a part of his makeup.

At eight-thirty his mind was made up. He tilted back in his chair, drawling: "Cash me in, gents. I may be back later on." He had lost sixty-seven cents and had enjoyed the game as much as any he could remember.

Outside, Lonesome walked on up the street to a point beyond the lighted store windows before he cut across and into an alley and started back toward the center of town. It lacked half an hour of the time Tade Wardow had set for their meeting. He didn't know what lay ahead, and for that reason he hurried now, walking silently in the deep shadows as the looming bulk of the back brick wall of the bank rose out of the darkness ahead.

"The door should be open," he mused, half aloud. "He wants to make it easy for me."

His guess was borne out a moment later as he tried the knob on the door. It swung in soundlessly on well-oiled hinges and he stepped quickly in and closed it behind him, one of his six-shooters in a hand planted at his hip. He stepped noiselessly to one side of the door and stood there a full minute, listening and identifying the sounds that came to him. Somewhere up front a clock ticked slowly. He waited until his hearing became accustomed to the sound, until he could hear beyond it. Then there was nothing but dead silence.

He moved on in, stepping around the end of the counter. He could pick out the cobalt rectangle of the vault door against the lighter shade of the tan wall. His glance shuttled over each subject in the cleared space behind the cages, identifying it, searching the shadows. Finally he was satisfied, and dropped his weapon back into its holster.

Putting his head close to the dial on the vault door, he vaguely made out the numbers on it. That afternoon he had memorized the combination Wardow had given him, and then had burned the card. Now he spun the dial carefully, knowing that a mistake would cost him precious seconds. When he caught the faint sound of the tumbler-click that told him the lock was open, he felt a wave of relief surge through him. Wardow might be framing a man, but he was playing straight with Lonesome Barkley.

He put his weight against the thick handle of the vault door and felt it give under the pressure. The massive steel panel was heavy and it took a good bit of his strength to swing it open. The exertion brought on that feeling of constriction in his lungs, and he coughed twice, softly, muffling the sound with his bandanna held at his mouth.

With the door closed behind him, he lit a match. In the sudden flood of light he saw the money sacks piled on the floor against the rear wall of the vault.

"Eleven thousand. A man could buy a nice layout for that. He could take things easy for a few years," Lonesome thought.

The temptation was undeniably there, but he stifled it down as he set to work in the darkness. He emptied the sacks, piling the bundles of crisp banknotes onto the floor behind him. Once he went out of the vault and spent two full minutes hunting until he found an empty ledger box. He brought it back inside and piled the money into it. Then, carrying the box, he came out again and shut the vault door.

He made his exit soundlessly; but this time he walked down the alley in the direction opposite the way he had come, carrying the box. Five minutes later he came within sight of a large white frame house at the end of the street, looking gray under the starlight. Here, behind the house and close to him, lay the sprawled outline of a shed.

It was what he wanted. He went inside, with a gun in one hand and the box under his other arm. After setting the box down, he risked lighting a match, flicking it out when he'd glimpsed the shiny new buggy standing to one side, ahead of two vacant stalls. He crossed over to the buggy and lifted the seat-cushion. Beneath it his groping hand ran around an empty locker. Five seconds later he had hefted the box into the compartment and put the seat-cushion back into place, so that the box was hidden beneath it. This would have to do. It was an even better hiding place than he had hoped.

Outside once more, he made a wide circle of the house, keeping out of sight in the darkness until he came to the street. When he approached it again, he came along the front walk, moving at a slow easy pace, and made no attempt to hide his coming.

Wardow answered his knock, opening the door stealthily on an unlighted room so that his well-fed, plump figure showed only for an instant before he stepped back onto the shadow. Lonesome went in, heard the door close softly behind him, and felt Wardow's hand on his arm as he was led toward the back of the house.

They went through an inner door. Wardow's hold relaxed and he said: "Wait. I'll get a light."

In another moment a match flared in his hand. He touched the flame to the wick of a lamp, and immediately Lonesome saw that he was in a high-ceilinged kitchen. The shades were drawn tight down over the two windows. The precautions Wardow was taking brought a twisted smile to Lonesome's thin lips.

"You're spooky, tonight, Wardow."

"Careful is all," the banker answered. His full, round face had a measure of that same paleness Lonesome had seen that morning. When he moved now, he did so with the jerky motions of a pent-up nervousness. He pointed to a bundle of three wrapped sticks of dynamite and a four-foot length of fuse lying on the table in the center of the room. "Set that off at the base of the vault door. The fuse is long enough to give you a five minute start. The back door of the bank's open. You won't have any trouble."

Lonesome nodded, his glance holding a faint hint of intolerance. "Is there anything else?"

"Remember what you're leavin' on the floor with those money sacks."

Again Lonesome nodded.

Apparently his studied calmness bolstered Wardow's courage. For a fleeting moment all trace of fear went out of the banker's eyes. "I won't forget this, Lonesome," he said.

"Neither will I. Eleven thousand is a lot of money. I come out the best on this deal."

The smile that crossed Wardow's countenance meant more than he intended. He faced the table and handed Lonesome the dynamite, reaching back again to turn down the lamp. Then he crossed to the door, inched it open, and said: "Take the alley. It leads to the bank."

"In twenty minutes I'll be a mile out on the trail into the hills," Lonesome told him as he went out. "You can time it if you want."

It took him only three minutes to reach the bank again. He moved surely this time, putting the dynamite at the base of the vault door as Wardow had directed. It took him little more than a minute to be sure everything was just so. Then he lit the fuse.

As the powder-flame hissed across the dead silence, he stood there watching it. He waited until it had burned for better than a foot of its length, leaving a charred black ash. Then, carefully, he smothered the flame beneath his boot-sole and waited for a full half minute longer, making sure that it had died.

☆ III ☆

LONESOME PAYS OFF

heriff John Mays looked up as the door to his office opened. The stranger he had seen riding in on the dun stallion that morning stood there. He took his pipe out of his mouth and said: " 'Evenin', stranger."

Lonesome nodded an answer to the greeting, then asked abruptly: "Should anyone be in the bank at this time of night, Sheriff?"

Mays frowned, puzzled. "No. Why?"

"I went over there to look in at the clock a few minutes ago, and saw a man movin' around back by the vault. I thought you ought to know about it."

The lawman's spare figure lunged up out of his swivel chair. He reached for his gun-belt, swung it off his desk and around his waist. "Why didn't you holler? He's probably gone now, with the mine payroll."

"I did better than that," Lonesome told him. "I waited in the alley out back until he came out. I followed him to a big white house at the edge of town. He carried a box away with him."

Mays sat down abruptly, sighing his relief. All the tension had suddenly left him. He laughed softly: "Goddlemighty, but you had me scared, stranger! The man you saw was Tade Wardow, president of the bank. He lives in that big house at the end of the street. He was probably workin' late at his office."

"But what was he carryin,?" Lonesome asked, his expression bewildered.

"Books . . . ledgers, probably. He carts 'em home 'most every night."

Lonesome grinned guiltily, shrugged, and turned to the door. "My mistake," he said. Then a frown crossed his face, as though he had thought of something. "You'd better tell this Wardow to be more careful, Sheriff. He left the back door of the bank open. I know, because I tried it on my way back here."

"That's not like Tade," Mays muttered, rising again. "I'd better go take a look. Want to come along?"

Lonesome shook his head: "It probably won't amount to much. I'm due back in a game of draw across the street."

He walked with the lawman to a point opposite Barton's and left him, crossing the street and waiting there until the other had disappeared into the opening between the bank and the adjoining building. Once the sheriff was out of sight, he went on unhurriedly up the street. Beyond the stores, his pace quickened. He recrossed the street to a vacant lot, cut through it and back to the alley once more. He'd hide in the shed in back of Tade Wardow's and wait there for the sheriff.

With the shed in sight once more — a black squat shape showing against the lighter shade of the yard surrounding it — Lonesome stopped for a few brief seconds to listen. The night sounds were strangely magnified. Somewhere in the distance a dog howled mournfully; he plainly heard the hoof-pound of a trotting horse far down the street, and even the sound of his own breathing was loud in his ears.

He was tuned to a high-pitched wariness as he walked on toward the shed. The hinged double-door was as he had left it, standing open a good three feet so that he could walk through without having to move it. Inside, the darkness was impenetrable. Trying to remember what he had seen in the brief glow of the match on his first visit, he was about to move out of the door when an indefinable sound shuttled across the stillness ahead.

"Hold it, Lonesome!"

It was Tade Wardow's low voice!

Lonesome froze where he stood, instinctively realizing that he was outlined by the faint light of the open door behind. The hackles rose along the back of his neck. It wasn't fear he felt, but a tense expectancy of the blast of Tade Wardow's gun, for the man must have a gun lined at him.

"Shuck out your hardware," came Wardow's ominous words. "And take it slow!"

There was no choice. Lonesome lifted his two .38s out of the holsters and dropped them so that they thudded hollowly against the rough planking of the floor. He timed his motions to an awkward slowness, remembering the makeup of the man who stood there ahead of him in the darkness.

"So you'd double-cross me, would you?" Wardow asked softly. "It was a good hunch . . . coming out here to watch after you'd gone." He paused there, until the silence suspended unbearably. Then: "How did you frame me?"

"Mays is on his way here."

He spoke with a grim purpose backing the words. He was trying to rouse Wardow's anger.

"That means I'll have to get rid of you both," said Wardow, his words edged with a faintly recognizable panic. "It'll look like the two of you shot it out."

"It won't work. Mays will come to the house . . . the front."

"It will work. When I cut loose on you, he'll come back here."

Lonesome was staring in the direction of the voice, his perceptions keyed to an alertness that caught every hint of sound. The slight scraping of one of Wardow's boots on the floor helped along with the voice. He knew where the man stood now; the buggy's front wheel-hub would be directly behind him.

"And the bank? What about that?"

"I'll find the money and take it back. You must have brought. . . ."

Before the words were completed, Lonesome lunged in a rolling dive. A blasting explosion ripped across the silence, and Lonesome felt the air-rush of the bullet as it whipped past his face. And then he was slamming into Wardow's yielding body.

As they crashed together to the floor the purple-flamed thunder of the gun cut loose again. And with that inferno of sound Lonesome felt the tensed muscles of Wardow's body beneath him jerk once in a writhing spasm. Wardow choked out a stifled groan and went suddenly limp. And when Lonesome pushed himself to his knees and reached for a match and lit it, he saw the answer.

The banker's right elbow had slammed against the wheel-hub of the buggy as he fell, twisting the six-gun into his side. The blow had knocked his thumb from the hammer of the weapon. A wisp of smoke curled up from the torn, blood-soaked cloth of Wardow's coat. He was dead.

It was while he knelt there that he heard the pounding of boots in the gravel outside. Up front, behind one of the stalls, he had seen a narrow door. He smothered the match in his hand, came to his feet, and made for that door. He was none too soon, for as he stepped through the door and eased it shut again he heard Mays's strident challenge from the alley out back.

Lonesome tried to move soundlessly, as he crossed the strip of yard in back of the house and turned the corner to put himself out of sight of the shed. All the while a growing, insistent constriction in his overworked lungs made him want to cough. He choked it back until he had crossed the road out front. There, he gave in to it, once more muffling his deep hacking with the bandanna pressed to his lips.

He waited there a long quarter minute before he moved on. No sounds came from behind the house. Mays was being quiet about his discovery. He wasn't to learn the reason until later.

Going back to Barton's saloon, Lonesome skirted the rear of the houses that flanked the street. He passed the stores, and went beyond them before he returned to the board walk. When he entered the saloon, he had come from the direction opposite to that of Tade Wardow's house.

"Back to make a cleanin'?" Doc Hoyer grinned as Lonesome sauntered up to the table and took the chair he had vacated earlier.

Lonesome nodded, throwing a silver dollar onto the green-felted table. Hoyer was banker, and counted him out his chips, asking: "Did you hear a couple shots out there a while back?"

"Must have been someone out beyond town takin' a lick at a coyote," Lonesome answered.

He won the first hand, and he won the second. His expression was sober as he looked at his cards, belying the tumult of expectancy within him. He was waiting for Ed Hardy's turn at the deal, thinking of the three thousand dollar reward still out for the stage robbery at Tentpole, thinking that three thousand would mean a lot to a man trying to make a go of a small outfit.

It was Ed Hardy's deal. A perfect calm settled through Lonesome Barkley as he watched Hardy gather in the cards and shuffle the deck. It was as though he had never left the game, as though the happenings of the last forty minutes had not been shaped for these next few seconds. Suddenly he heard Doc Hoyer say: "Here comes John Mays. He looks like trouble."

Mays was already half way between the door up front and the table. They looked at him with a rising curiosity at the worried expression of the lawman's grizzled face. One of them, Lonesome, looked up with bitter disappointment overriding every other emotion. He had planned this, planned it carefully, but Mays had come in a little too soon.

Mays stopped, standing behind Ed Hardy. Seeing that the sheriff's glance had settled on him, Lonesome lost all hope. Mays knew. He had been to his office and read Jim Hogan's confession.

Then Mays was speaking to him: "You were right, stranger. The bank was held up. But I was right, too. Tade Wardow was the man you saw. I went out to see him and he heard me comin' and shot himself. Blew a hole through his side. I found the money hid in his buggy out in the shed behind the house."

Mays went on, speaking to the others now, leaning down over the table and talking quietly so that those at the bar up front wouldn't hear. He didn't want the news to get out, he said, until he'd had time to see the bank directors in the morning. People were liable to be spooky and think something was wrong about the bank. It might stir up trouble if they found out tonight. He told about discovering the dynamite and the fuse that Tade Wardow had lit. Still unable to believe that was Wardow, he'd gone out to his house to see him and heard the shots as he was coming along the alley.

"But why?" Doc Hoyer asked as the lawman finished, "why would Tade do a thing like that?"

Mays shrugged and threw out his hands in an unknown gesture. "That's what I can't figure. Insurance, maybe. He came to me a couple of weeks ago and gave me a sealed envelope. Told me to open it if anything happened to him, that he was expectin' trouble. This must be what he meant. I'm goin' over now to open it and see what's inside. You go ahead with the game and don't let on anything's happened. Above all, I don't want this to get out."

He turned and walked across the room and out the door. Lonesome, his hopes alive once more, said briefly: "It's your deal, Hardy."

They were all silent as Ed Hardy shuffled the cards and passed the deck to Doc Hoyer for the cut. The news that Mays had brought had left them stunned. Ed Hardy moved his hands automatically, and Hoyer cursed softly time and again as though unable to comprehend what he'd heard. Hardy dealt a hand of draw. Doc Hoyer opened, and Lonesome and Ed Hardy and one of the others covered his bet. Hardy filled in the other hands, raked in the discards, and then dealt himself two cards. As he laid the deck on the table, Lonesome lunged up out of his chair, kicked it from behind him so that it crashed into the wall, and drawled: "Hold it, Hardy! You palmed that last card!"

Five pairs of eyes swiveled up to stare at Lonesome in hard disbelief. He stood there glaring across at Hardy, whose face took in a quick flush at the insult.

"You're loco, stranger," he said. "I wouldn't know how to palm a card."

"Will you get onto your feet, or do I have to blow out your guts where you sit?"

Every muscle in Ed Hardy's body came taut. The words hit him like a blow in the face. He started up out of his chair, and shook off the hand Doc Hoyer put out to stop him. Lonesome Barkley cleared his throat and coughed, gently, as though the words he had just spoken had torn something loose inside him. He hunched over a little, his flat chest rising and falling noticeably as he caught his breath.

Then they were moving, Hardy clawing at his holstered .45 in a frantic haste, and Lonesome's hand streaking to his own weapon in a blur of practiced speed. His six-shooter had cleared leather when another coughing spasm hit him. A deep-chested hacking doubled him up, broke the smooth flow of his gun-arm. Ed Hardy's .45 nosed up and darted flame in a blasting roar. Lonesome's Colt thundered an answer but, stooped over as he was, his aim was wide. They saw the bullet hit, jerking Lonesome backwards so that he fell into the wall and slid slowly to the floor as his knees buckled. The expression on his face held no trace of surprise as Doc Hoyer came around the table and looked down at him. The others stepped in beside Ed Hardy and took his gun away from him.

Hoyer had one look at the blood that flecked Lonesome's lips, at the red smear that crept out across his shirt-front, and gazed up at the others, and shook his head slowly. Then he leaned down and asked: "Why did you do it, stranger? Ed Hardy never cheated at anything."

"Maybe I didn't see right," came Lonesome's whispered answer. "I wanted to win that hand."

"A fifty-cent hand?"

"Lay off, Doc. Come closer." When Doc's ear was close to his mouth, Lonesome said, "There's three thousand on my head. Is that enough?"

Silas Hoyer's tough old face softened. He glanced obliquely at Ed Hardy and then back at Lonesome. "It's plenty," he said huskily. "Plenty."

Lonesome closed his eyes and smiled. It would be enough, too, to square a debt to the kid sister of a young cowboy called Red Latrobe who had died one night, years ago, in the Bar X stampede. And even after the rise and fall of his flat chest had ceased, the smile still held. . . .

SUNDOWN CORRAL

(1938)

⭐
---

by ALAN (BROWN) LeMAY

Alan (Brown) LeMay was born in Indianapolis, Indiana, and attended Stetson University in DeLand, Florida. Following his military service, he completed his education at the University of Chicago. His short story, "Hullabaloo," appeared the month of his graduation in Adventure *(6/30/22). He was a prolific contributor to the magazine markets in the mid-1920s. In 1929, two years before Ernest Haycox, LeMay broke into the pages of* Collier's *(2/23/29) with the story, "Loan of a Gun." During the next decade LeMay wanted nothing more than to be a gentleman rancher and his income from writing was intended to supplement the income generated by raising livestock on his ranch outside Santee, California. In the late 1930s he was plunged into debt because of a divorce and turned next to screenwriting, early attaching himself to Cecil B. DeMille's unit at Paramount Pictures. LeMay continued to write original screenplays through the 1940s, and on one occasion even directed the film based on his screenplay.*

The Searchers *(Harper, 1954) is regarded by many as LeMay's masterpiece. It possesses a graphic sense of place; it etches deeply the feats of human endurance which LeMay tended to admire in the American spirit; and it has that characteristic suggestiveness of tremendous depths and untold stories developed in his long apprenticeship writing short stories and quite a few "short, short" stories for* Collier's. *A subtext often rides on a snatch of dialogue or flashes in a laconic observation. The following narrative is one of the short short stories LeMay wrote for* Collier's.

*H*idecamp cowboys liked to tell about what they called the fight at the Sundown Corral; but they get most of it wrong, because the Sundown Corral was no corral at all, but just a hitch rack back of Kelly's, and the fight wasn't there anyway, but all over the town. And they can't tell you why the fight changed Torch Breen as it did, because they didn't know.

Torch Breen was a big, hulking figure with a bush of wiry red-gold hair, hardly ever cut; long horse-bowed legs from nearly twenty years, man and boy, spent in the saddle; and the swift, sure judgment of a well-advanced, boy of seven. When he was half drunk the red blaze of his hair was matched in his eyes. There was a sort of angry glory about the arrogance of Torch Breen in liquor.

But after his fight with the Kettlesons he hung up his gun, drank seldom and sparingly, and brawled with no one. Later he even married. He married a girl from the East who worked in the kitchen of Kelly's restaurant, had a kid of her own, and called herself a Mrs. Smith. The cowboys, in their innocence of mind, supposed the kid to be Torch's, since both Torch and the kid had red hair. This was untrue. But, anyway, Torch built a cabin on a section of land, and became a thing of the past completely.

His aggrieved friends felt that the Kettleson fight hardly explained it. It was true that throughout the fight Torch Breen had chiefly shown an inflexible determination to get away. Yet even in retreat he had done so much damage, against odds so great, as to make a name for being poison to fool with. No sense in his coming out of it spirit-broke, like that.

Without knowing just how it started, everybody knew that Torch Breen and the Kettlesons were openly on the gun. Still, both sides avoided meeting — until that smoky twilight when Torch Breen, along with Shanty Simms, walked square into the Kettlesons, all six of them, clamped along the rail of the Point-of-Rocks Bar.

Breen's gun jumped into his hand, and there was a mighty long minute of quiet while Torch waited for them to make their play. They made no play.

Torch said, "Come on, Shanty." He kept his gun on the Kettlesons while the two backed out of there. Once outside, Torch and Shanty made a dive for Hawk's store, next door. Just as they made it Guy Kettleson sprang to the door of the Point-of-Rocks; his gun spoke and Breen's answered.

Torch Breen's shot smashed Guy's arm, but Torch and Shanty didn't know that. Shanty shouted, "Every man for himself . . . there's a million of 'em!" And both ran out of the back of Hawk's store, meaning to cut north behind the buildings to the Sundown Corral — that unfenced hitch rack back of Kelly's restaurant — where their ponies were. It was the worst thing they could have done. Buck and Willie Kettleson were waiting for them back there, barricaded behind a pile of whiskey kegs. There was a swift fusillade; Buck got a busted leg from a slug that somehow filtered through the barrels, and Willie got his face cut by a jumping splinter. Willie always was easily satisfied.

"Gee!" Shanty whimpered, "we're surrounded!" He and Torch dived into the back end of the Muleskinner Saloon and ran through to the front.

Wham! Dee Kettleson had swung himself up onto the roofs, where he could command front and rear, and as Torch and Shanty appeared in the street he fired over Hawk's false-front parapet.

Both Torch and Shanty returned his fire. As their shots crashed through the flimsy clapboards, Dee Kettleson jerked straight upright, pitched forward over the parapet, and rolled down the wooden awning to fall heavily into the street.

"We're done for!" Shanty Simms moaned. "They're everywheres!" Four Kettlesons were out of action now, but Dee Kettleson was the only one Torch had seen fall. Where the other five were he had no clear idea. They ducked back through the line of buildings and turned north again, yearning for the Sundown Corral and their waiting horses.

Boom! Another miracle as Lloyd Kettleson missed. Lloyd, guessing where their ponies were, had placed himself while Torch and Shanty were settling Dee in the street, and now blazed away from cover of a wagon shed. One of Torch's answering bullets ricocheted off Lloyd's gun, breaking three bones in Lloyd's hand. Five Kettlesons out of action! But —

"We're headed off!" Shanty gasped. "Torch, we got to fight through this solid wall of Kettlesons! It's our only hope!"

So they charged straight on this time, from time to time tossing a shot in this direction or that, picking off imaginary Kettlesons. They reached the Sundown Corral, all right.

But Torch Breen went berserk now. He wheeled, facing back the way they had come, and he wasn't in a hurry any more. His eyes had a crazy red blaze as they swept the ramshackle backs of the wood buildings. Nothing moved there at first, anywhere.

Then, in a pile of boxes behind Kelly's restaurant, Torch saw one big packing case move, as if someone stealthily had crept forward to its cover from the corner of the unpainted wall.

Torch Breen blasted a bullet through the box at twenty yards, and would have fired again, but the hammer snapped upon an empty shell. Torch snarled crazily and charged, immune to sense, immune to fear. He snatched the big packing case aside, and his gun barrel flashed up for a skull-cracking hand-to-hand smash. It would have been suicide, and the end of him, if a Kettleson had been there.

Nobody was behind the box. Torch hesitated, swearing futilely. He started to turn away. Then Shanty Simms saw him freeze. Breen stood motionless, caught in mid-step, almost.

Shanty kept gibbering for Torch to come on; and, when Torch still stood there, seemingly unable to hear, Shanty spurred his pony over to Torch, meaning to drag him bodily away. But Shanty also froze when he looked down into the box, forgetting their situation.

In the bottom corner of the box — overturned there when the box overturned — huddled a little girl perhaps three years old. Both thumbs were in her mouth, and she rolled her eyes up at Torch Breen without moving anything else — too scared to move, too scared to cry. Her hair was red, like Breen's, only brighter; and a fingerbreath above the shine of that hair they could see the forty-five caliber hole Breen's shot had made in the thin wood.

After a couple of moments a woman ran out of the back door of the restaurant. It was the woman who called herself Mrs. Smith. She was young, but she was pitifully thin, and she always had a hunted look; and now she looked scared to death too, so that she looked fifteen years beyond her age. She caught up the child, and for just half a second stared at Breen with eyes full of repugnance and terror, then ran back inside.

Torch Breen still stood there, his face the color of something from under a board, so that he looked like a dead man stood up. Even his gun looked dead, dangling in his hand with the look of a lead gun, not meant to be fired; and the hand that held it looked dead, as if unable to lift it, even to put it away. Only his hair looked alive, shining like something burning, in the failing light.

THE BLOCK K RIDES TONIGHT!

(1939)

—————☆—————

by WALT(ER JOHN) COBURN

Walt(er John) Coburn was born in White Sulphur Springs, Montana territory. He was once called "King of the Pulps" by Fred Gipson and promoted by Fiction House as "The Cowboy Author." He was the son of cattleman Robert Coburn, owner of the Circle C ranch on Beaver Creek within sight of the Little Rockies. Following his enlistment in the U. S. Army during World War I, Coburn tried writing and for a year and a half he wrote and wrote, earning endless rejection slips. Then one day Bob Davis at Argosy-All Story *accepted Coburn's short story, "The Peace Treaty of the Seven Up." From then on Coburn would try to write at least 2,000 words a day, never rewriting, six days a week, with Sundays off, never working more than four or five hours a day but also never taking a vacation of longer than two or three days once a story was completed.*

It would be daunting to list Walt Coburn's contributions to Star Western *since he had a story in almost every issue for nearly a decade and a half. On the whole, though, Coburn's early fiction from his Golden Age, 1924–1940, is his best. In these stories, like Charles M. Russell and Eugene Manlove Rhodes, two men Coburn had known and admired in life, he captured the cow country and recreated it when it had already passed from sight. "Pat," as Walt called his wife Mina, was the inspiration for many of his heroines, including Kathleen Mavourneen Kilgore in this story which also served as the basis for* The Return of Wild Bill *(Columbia, 1940), the first of a series of "B" Westerns starring Bill Elliott in the role of Wild Bill Hickok.*

☆ **I** ☆

RETURN OF A FEUDIST

Old Mitch was drunk when he set the shotgun trap at his big pole gate. If the old rascal had been sober and hadn't whiskey-fumbled the contraption, Cole Griffin's head would have been torn off by its double charge of buckshot as he leaned from his saddle and yanked out the long wooden gate pin. The string that was tied to the gate pin was attached to the triggers of the double-barrel shotgun.

The roar and flash of the ten-gauge shot was terrific. The heavy buckshot tore through the air a few feet above Cole's head. He was off balance, his weight all in his left stirrup, the twenty-inch gate pin gripped in his right hand, bridle reins held loosely in his left hand. Cole's big bay horse whirled, twisted, and pitched. He was thrown heavily, landing on one shoulder, his head hitting the hard ground with a thud.

Cole was dazed, scared, and bewildered. For a moment he lay there on the ground.

Then instinct worked swifter than any actual coordination of mind and muscle. He rolled over and over, landed in a patch of sagebrush, clawing for his six-shooter. He threw the gate pin away with a muttered curse and pulled his gun.

In the moonlight he saw the door of the log cabin open and someone run outside. He crouched behind the patch of sagebrush and thumbed back the hammer. His horse had quit bucking and was standing stiff-legged, facing the swinging gate. The spooked horse was whistling through widened nostrils. The running figure looked more like a boy than a man, small and slight.

"Pull up, you would-be murderin' son!" Cole shouted. "Reach for the moon, or I'll gut-shoot you!"

"Oh!"

The running figure halted abruptly. A pair of arms reached high. In one hand a long-barreled six-shooter was pointed straight up at he stars.

"Drop that gun!" Cole rasped.

The big six-shooter dropped to the ground. The hammer must have struck a rock, for the gun exploded with a roar, its recoil sending it spinning through the air. And its loud echo was stabbed by a woman's shrill scream. The lifted hands dropped with a womanish gesture to cover her eyes.

Cole swore softly and grinned. "You kin take your hands away from your eyes, lady. Nobody's hurt."

From inside the lighted cabin sounded a man's bellowing voice. "Lemme up! Lemme outa here! What in hell's tarnation's a-goin' on out there? Git me outa this mess, Sammy Lou, and gimme my gun!"

Cole looked around. Save for the girl, dressed in overalls, shirt, and boots, standing there now with her hands raised to the level of her shoulders, nobody was in sight. And the bellowing man in the cabin seemed to be the only other human on this little ranch. Cole stood up, his gun in hand, still shaken and hot with seething anger. He stared hard at the girl.

The man's voice inside the cabin was cursing thickly, but the girl didn't seem to hear. Her face was white and her eyes were wide with fear. Her hair was a thick mop of black curls that had been cut off like a boy's for convenience rather than any attempt to set a style. She might have been fourteen, or she could have been half a dozen years older. But she still looked like a small, slim boy who was badly scared. She was staring at Cole, her eyes searching for some sign of gunshot wounds.

"Are you hurt?" she asked in a small, scared voice.

"No. I'm not hurt!" Cole shouted. "But that ain't your fault, nor his. Tell him to stop that roarin' and cussin'. You'd think he'd have more respect for a female. Tell him to dry up, or I'll bend a gun barrel acrost his murderin' head."

"Sammy Lou! Dagnation, gal, why don't you. . . ?"

"I'm all right, Mitch!" the girl called. "I'm comin'!"

"Who's shot? Who got 'er, Sammy Lou? If it's Jake Kilgore, let 'im lay there. Git these ropes off me an' I'll tend to his carcass!"

"Mitch," the girl said to Cole, "is gettin' over a bad 'un. I always tie him up till he quits seein' things. I'd better get back to the cabin before he goes hog wild. Put up your horse, mister. You're sure you're not hurt?"

"I'm not hurt. And before you go runnin' back to the cabin, let's git one or two things straightened out." Cole's searching eyes had discovered the sawed-off shotgun trap. He walked over to and kicked down the ten-gauge. "Are you alone here? Don't lie to me, young lady. I ain't in any humor for lies or any more gun jokes. Who else is hid out around here?"

"Nobody. Old Mitch is there in his cabin. I rode over to get him sobered up. If you weren't a plumb stranger, you'd know that without askin'."

Cole caught the note of bitterness in the girl's voice. Her features were far from beautiful. Her nose was too short, and her red-lipped mouth was a trifle too large. Her chin was firm and slightly cleft, and her smile was as infectious as a small boy's. She smiled at him now, her dark eyes crinkling almost shut. Her strong white teeth showed for a second or two.

"I'd better take Mitch his six-shooter . . . if you'll let me pick it up."

"And let him finish the job that his shotgun trap bungled?"

"Don't worry about it. He probably set it for Jake Kilgore. They've been at it for years."

"Been at what?"

"This gun business . . . feudin'. It started before I was born, back in the old vigilante days here in Montana. My daddy was mixed up in it. He was killed. So were some others. If you crossed the Missouri River at Rocky Point or Cow Island, you must have heard tell of it."

Cole Griffin nodded. He picked up the big six-shooter and handed it to the girl. "So you stay here and ride herd on that old warthog, Mitch, while he's soberin' up after a big drunk. Some job for a girl, that is! I'm takin' you up on that invitation to stay over night. What was it he called you?" Cole nodded towards the cabin where old Mitch's voice was subdued now to unintelligible mutterings.

"Sammy Lou Sorrels." Her tone was defiant.

"Then your father, like as not, was Sam Sorrels."

"Yes. The vigilantes hung him for horse stealing and murder. See that big lightning-blasted cottonwood down in the lower pasture? That's the tree he was hung from. They strung up five from the same tree. Mitch was the man who cut 'em down and buried 'em. Jake Kilgore and another man rode up on him. Mitch shot Jake Kilgore's gun-arm off and killed the other man. That's the story, if you haven't heard it before." The tremor was gone from her voice now.

"I heard it for the first time only a few months ago, down in Texas. I'll put up my horse and go on to the cabin. If your friend Mitch is able to savvy what you're sayin', tell him Hank Griffin's son sprung his shotgun trap. I'll be along directly."

The girl's dark eyes stared hard at him now. "Hank Griffin was one of the men. . . ."

"Hung from the same tree with Sam Sorrels about eighteen years ago. But you don't look old enough to have been livin' then."

"I was three months old. Then your name is Cole. Mitch made you a saddle for your sixth birthday. Your mother took you and disappeared. She left the country with Grant Kilgore."

"You shore know your history." Cole's faint smile was grim and his eyes were icy blue in the white moonlight.

"It's all I do know," she told him. "I've been raised right here on the banks of the Missouri River in the badlands . . . the orphaned kid of a hanged outlaw. Figure it out for yourself, what kind of a chance I've ever had to become a lady. My mother was a half-breed Sioux. She'd gone to the government school and taught me to read and write. I sent off for books. All the books I could get. A captain on one of the riverboats always stops at our place to load on cordwood for his steam engine. He brings me books. He left me a trunk full of his daughter's clothes last summer. I wore the prettiest dress to the Christmas dance at Rocky Point, and Kate Kilgore laughed at me. I grabbed a butcher knife and tried to kill her. Then I rode back to the ranch and bawled like a kid. And I'm not ashamed of it!

"I'm a river 'breed, and my father was hung for a rustler. The man who hung him and Hank Griffin and three other men was Grant Kilgore. He was head of the gang of murderers who disguised themselves as vigilantes. Your mother ran off with Grant Kilgore. You were raised as Grant Kilgore's son. Your name was changed to Cole Kilgore, wasn't it?" Her dark eyes blazed hotly. Her voice was a little shrill with hatred and contempt.

"Wasn't it?" she repeated, her hand gripping the big six-shooter.

Cole's face had whitened under its deep coating of tan. His ice-blue eyes matched hers for cold fury. "You know too much," he told her, holding his voice steady. "You know a couple of facts, and then you make your own story to fit 'em."

"Your mother ran off with Grant Kilgore. She was ashamed to let her son keep his real father's name. Your mother was a white woman. They called her the most beautiful girl in Montana. But she was. . . ."

Cole's hand was across her mouth. His other hand gripped her slim shoulder, shaking her roughly. "Leave my mother's name alone." His fingers tightened on her shoulder.

The girl winced; her white teeth bit his hand. He jerked it away, blood trickling from his thumb. "It's too bad," she panted, twisting out of his grip, "that Mitch's shotgun missed. Damn you, ride on to the Kilgore ranch where you belong!" She twisted away and ran back to the cabin.

Cole saw the door bang shut. He stood there, breathing hard, scowling. Then he suddenly relaxed. He looked at his bloodstained hand and grinned. "The little wampus-cat!" he muttered, and walked over to his big bay horse.

As he picked up the bridle reins, he heard the clatter of shod hoofs. His right hand dropped to the butt of his six-shooter and he stood there in the gateway waiting for the three riders to ride up.

The man riding slightly in the lead of the other two had a heavy gray mustache and square-cut beard. His left arm was a stub with the heavy flannel sleeve cut off and sewed shut. The rider at his right had a drooping black mustache. The third, several years younger, was clean shaven, but both had the same hawk beaked nose and the high cheek bones of the older man. They were, Cole guessed rightly, Jake Kilgore and his two sons, Bart and Sid. They pulled their horses to a halt, the two sons with their hands on their guns. Jake Kilgore acted as spokesman.

"We heard shootin'. What was it about, and who are you?"

"Old Mitch was shootin' at snakes, but he didn't kill any. Ketch me over on your Block K range and mebbyso you'll have a right to ask questions. But this place belongs to Mitch. I don't figure that my name is any of your particular business tonight."

"I've seen you before," said Jake Kilgore, leaning across his saddle horn, his bleak eyes studying Cole's face.

"Yes?" Cole's tone was flat.

"Yeah. I don't fergit a face."

"Me'n Sid," said Bart Kilgore, "could make the feller talk. For a stranger in a strange land, he's acts too high an' mighty. If me'n Sid was to. . . ."

"Dry up," snapped the elder Kilgore. "I'll recollect where I've seen this jasper's sign."

Cole wondered if he resembled his dead father. Perhaps that was what was giving Jake Kilgore the notion they had met before. Cole's hat was pulled down to throw the shadow of his hatbrim across his eyes. If old Jake Kilgore recognized him as Hank Griffin's son, he might make a gun-play.

Mitch's double-barrel shotgun lay behind the sagebrush within easy reach. The gun was empty, but they had no way of knowing that. A sawed-off double-barrel shotgun at close range is a weapon that few men will tackle. Cole took a step toward the sagebrush and stooped over with deliberate unconcern. When he straightened up, the sawed-off shotgun was covering the three Kilgores. The twin hammers clicked back under the pressure of his thumb.

"I'm tellin' you peacefully to ride on down the road. If any of you claws a gun, both barrels of this scatter-gun is goin' to explode. I ain't aimin' to miss. Now git goin'."

"He might mean it," said Sid. "Hell, let's git away from here. Let 'im alone, Paw. We'll take care of 'im another time."

"Dry up," snapped Jake Kilgore. "You figger on hangin' around these parts, mister?"

"I aim to locate here. Are you goin' now or are you stallin' to ketch me off guard?"

"Not with that thing pointin' at us. Come along, boys. We'll take care of this gent some other night."

Jake Kilgore and his two sons rode on, and Cole Griffin watched them out of sight.

Sammy Lou Sorrels came suddenly into view from a patch of willows. She carried Mitch's six-shooter. "I slipped back when I saw 'em coming down the road. I heard everything you all said. I saw you run that bluff on 'em with the empty shotgun. I was going to do something about it, if the bluff didn't work."

"Somethin' like shootin' me in the back?" grinned Cole, ejecting the empty shells from the shotgun.

"We didn't part exactly friends, did we? I'd like to hope I was all wrong about . . . about your mother."

"You were," said Cole. "I didn't know that was how people like Mitch or you felt about the way she left Montana. Up until a few months ago I didn't know my father had been hung, as a horse thief and cattle rustler. That's what fetched me back to Montana. I came to learn the truth about my father, to find out the things Grant Kilgore left untold when he died."

"Grant Kilgore . . . dead?"

"I killed Grant Kilgore at El Paso, four weeks ago." Cole said flatly.

☆ **II** ☆

A COYOTE DODGES THE WOLF PACK

Old Mitch was a huge man, powerful in spite of his years. When he was sober, his gray blue eyes were as clear as the Montana sky after a spring rain has washed the alkali dust from the air. His hair was thick and white and a drooping white mustache hid the humorous, firm, square-cornered mouth. He was somewhere around seventy, but his big white teeth were as intact as those of a youth. His surname was probably Mitchell, and no doubt he had a given name of some sort, but his given name had been lost during the years, and the Mitchell had been whittled down to Mitch.

He had a standing bet that he could fist-whip or rassle down any man along that strip of the Missouri River badlands. He made the best corn whiskey in that part of the country, but he never sold a drop of it. He drank it himself, averaging a quart a day, and gave it to his friends. Mitch was a rip-snorting, profane old hellion with a heart as big as a bucket. Loyal to the men he called friend, he was bitter in his hatred for men who had incurred his enmity.

Sammy Lou had him tied down to his bunk. The sight of the huge bulk of a man with arms and legs spread-eagled and tied with ropes to the four heavy pine posts of his bunk reminded Cole of a picture he had once seen in some child's book of the giant Gulliver tied down. Sammy Lou looked very small as she stood beside the bunk. Cole closed the door behind him and stood there, a slow grin spreading his lips.

Mitch's bloodshot eyes stared hard at the tall cowpuncher. A stubble of sand-colored whiskers marred the clean blunt line of Cole's jaw. His straw-colored hair needed a barber's shears. Dust powdered his tanned skin. His eyes were as blue as clear ice. His grin widened and Mitch broke the tense silence.

"You got her hair but that grin and them eyes is Hank Griffin's. Sammy Lou tells me you run off the Kilgores. That'll help wipe out the Kilgore name you bin a-usin'. See if you kin untie the knots the young 'un put in these ropes. She wet 'em like I told her, and they're tighter'n a miser's wallet strings. She used two ketch ropes, and I don't want 'em cut. I always git her to hog-tie me thisaway when I'm gittin' over a bad 'un. Because once when I was locoed drunk she got in my way and I slapped her. Like to kill her, savvy? I'd sooner have a whole herd of Kilgores a-standin' over me and hackin' at me with dull knives than to hurt that young 'un, understand?

"Untie them knots, young Cole Griffin. We'll have a snort of the best likker that ever washed the dust out of a man's windpipe. Sammy Lou says you're all right to tie to. Your daddy and Sam Sorrels was as good friends as I've ever had. They died a-fightin', and the vigilantes under Grant Kilgore strung 'em up to my big cottonwood as a warnin' to scare me outa the country. But I shot the gizzard outa the Kilgore top gunman, and I shot the gun arm off Jake Kilgore. Git me untied quick, young Cole Griffin. This talkin' gits a man's tongue dry. Did you come back to whup the men that hung your daddy?"

"Somethin' like that," said Cole, untying the last knot.

"Sammy Lou tells me," said Mitch, swinging his big legs over the side of the bunk and flexing his stiffened muscles, "that you killed Grant Kilgore. The news ain't reached this far yet."

"It will," prophesied Cole grimly. "Grant Kilgore was goin' under another name at the time I shot 'im. He called himself Jake Grant."

"Usin' his brother Jake's name." Mitch reached under the bunk and brought out a jug. The girl was making fresh coffee and biscuits.

Cole said, "There were three of the Kilgore brothers. Grant was the oldest. Then Seth, then Jake. I heard Seth was shot down on the street in Fort Benton. That left Grant and Jake."

"Drink?" Mitch asked.

"I'll wait for the coffee," said Cole. "I'm scared of whiskey."

Mitch nodded and tipped up the jug.

"Take it easy, Mitch," said Sammy Lou. "Hungry, Cole?"

"I shouldn't be," grinned Cole. "I ate yesterday."

Mitch chuckled. Sammy Lou smiled and shoved the pan of biscuits in the oven of the little sheet iron stove. Then she began slicing thick steaks from a large chunk of loin beef. Cole saw that the hands of the battered alarm clock on a shelf above the bunk pointed to midnight.

"What fetches the Kilgores out this time of night?" he asked.

"They might be after cattle. Of a moonlight night they might pick up a few head of wild stuff that bush up in the daytime and slip down outa the brakes to water at night. Them cattle is wilder'n blacktail deer. Some is in the Kilgore's Block K iron. Some belongs to other men. The Kilgores claim Hank Griffin's old HG brand. They got Joe Colter's Figger 8 iron. Likewise Pete Master's Triangle brand and the J B that belonged to Jim Blake. After them fellers was hung, the Kilgores grabbed their ranches and what livestock they had. Hank Griffin's widder had done gone down the Missouri River on a steamboat with Grant Kilgore. I wonder how she cleaned her conscience when that steamboat passed my place where Grant Kilgore and his vigilantes had hung pore Hank."

Cole's face went white. His hand dropped to his gun. He faced Mitch who sat on the edge of his bunk with the wicker covered demijohn.

"My mother was the finest woman that ever lived. Don't talk that way about her unless you back it up with a gun. She was in Fort Benton when my father was hung. Grant Kilgore told her that the vigilantes were goin' to kill her and her small boy. That was me. Grant Kilgore did a lot of smooth lyin'. The newspaper at Fort Benton printed the story that Hank Griffin and the others were an organized band of rustlers and killers. My mother and father had quarreled a year before. Separated. She had been a singer in a river show boat company when my father married her. For a year she had been earning her own living singing and acting with a troupe at the Fort Benton Opera House. Grant Kilgore was a big, handsome, smooth-talking man. He had money and posed as a government cattle and horse buyer.

"She didn't find out he was a tin-horn gambler until long after she married him at St. Louis. When she found out the truth, she left him. Just before she died she told me that he had headed the vigilantes who hung my father. I had my own cow outfit on the Rio Grande in Texas. I sold out and picked up Grant Kilgore's cold trail. I cut his sign in an El Paso gamblin' house. He recognized me and shot first. His bullet parted my hair. Mine tore out his black heart. That's the story. I'll kill the man who says anything against my mother. Is that plain?"

"It's plenty plain, young Cole Griffin. And I'm proud to hear you clear the name of the purtiest woman I ever laid eyes on. You're right. She wasn't meant for ranch life. Her and Hank both made a big mistake when they married. They was never happy together here on the river. They agreed to call it quits. That's when Hank Griffin begun drinkin' hard. Whiskey was rank poison to Hank. You got a right to be scared of the stuff. Me, I'm different. I git snakes in my boots when I'm gittin' over a big 'un. But outside uh that, likker is food an' drink. I make my own likker and I drink. Look sharp, young feller. Somebody's a-comin'. Bar the door an' put out the light, Sammy Lou, and git into the cellar. If that's the Kilgores a-comin', me'n young Cole Griffin will deal 'em misery."

"Mitch!" called a voice from outside the cabin. "Open the door, Mitch! You gotta hide us!"

"It's Frank!" cried the girl. "He's in trouble, Mitch!"

"Let the young 'breed coyote in," growled Mitch, cussing softly as he shoved the demijohn back under the bunk.

Sammy Lou shoved back the heavy wooden bar and opened the door. She gave a startled little gasp as a tall girl in leather divided shirt, beaded buckskin blouse, and tawny braids stumbled into the cabin. Behind her, shoving her inside, stood a tall, handsome, black-haired young cowboy wearing bearskin chaps and a buckskin shirt. His face was tense and grayish under its natural swarthy color. He had a six-shooter in his hand. His eyes were a yellowish gray. He shut the door behind him and stood with his back against it, breathing hard.

The girl with the yellow hair was looking at Cole. She had fair skin that was freckled across her aquiline, thin-nostriled nose. Her lips twisted in a forced smile. The look of fear left her eyes slowly as she smiled faintly at Cole. He flushed a little under her bold scrutiny.

"Jake and Bart and Sid are huntin' us!" panted the tall cowboy who was obviously part Indian. "We gave 'em the slip but if they pick up our sign. . . ."

"They'll shoot you down fer a coyote," growled old Mitch, "and if I had my say, they'd shoot *her* before she gits any more damn, fools killed along this river. Damned if I'm a-runnin' any hide-out fer Jake Kilgore's she-whelp and her sheep-brained fellers! Clear out, Frank Sorrels. Your daddy must be a-turnin' over in his grave right now. His son a-gallivantin' with Jake Kilgore's. . . ."

Sammy Lou's hand was across Mitch's mouth.

"Look out he don't bite," Cole could not help but say, holding up his left hand that was crusted with dried blood.

"If the Kilgores are hunting her," said Sammy Lou, ignoring Cole's grin, "they'll never look for her here. Frank's my brother, Mitch. I've helped you. You've got to hide him and Kate in the cellar!"

"Hide him?" said Kate Kilgore, her large eyes still looking at Cole. "Coyotes always hunt a hole when a wolf shows up. I'd rather be horsewhipped than stay in this whiskey shack. It was his notion, not mine, that fetched us here."

Her hands, covered with Indian-tanned buckskin gauntlets, coiled the heavy plaited braids that came below the level of her beaded belt. She bunched the braids in a coil knot at the nape of her white neck and put on her wide-brimmed black hat. She was by far the handsomest girl Cole Griffin had ever seen in his life. Even her throaty, husky voice had a charm that made a man shiver a little. She possessed that indescribable magnetism that is given to few women, and she knew how to use it.

Her straight height dwarfed little Sammy Lou and her white-skinned, tawny beauty made the little quarter-breed girl look shabby and uncouth. She had courage and vanity and selfish pride. She was made to wear silks and velvets and jewels.

"Take good care of the coyote," she said, opening the door. "The wolves are on the prowl tonight." Then she looked boldly at Cole.

"Why don't *you* ride on to the Block K ranch with me? Or are you also afraid of wolves?"

"Is that an invitation or a challenge?" Cole had difficulty in keeping his voice steady under the direct gaze of her long-lashed yellow eyes. Cole, his eyes on Kate Kilgore, was unprepared for Frank Sorrel's swift attack. He felt a hard fist crash against his jaw and saw the glitter of a long knife blade. He was thrown against the wall. The knife missed his throat by a scant inch as he ducked. Then Cole swung a vicious, looping left into the distorted face of Frank Sorrels. He followed it with hard, smashing rights and lefts that drove the quarter-breed backwards. A swing that had all his weight behind it dropped Sammy Lou's brother in a limp, battered, bloody heap at her feet.

"The next time you pull that pig-sticker on me, you damned 'breed, I'll carve my name in your yellow hide!"

Sammy Lou, her face white with rage, stooped to grab the hunting knife from her brother's limp hand. Cole pulled her back and picked up the knife. Mitch took Sammy Lou in his big, powerful hands and held her as she kicked and fought like a little wildcat.

"Git that buckskin-maned Kilgore female off the ranch," growled Mitch at Cole. "I'll have the young 'un cooled down by the time you git back. Git 'er off the place, Cole! Take your time a-comin' back. Looks like you done broke Frank's neck."

☆ III ☆

AT THE HANGMAN'S TREE

*C*ole had a white man's loathing for a knife and a contempt for the man who would pull one in a fight. The swift, blinding rage, that sears a man's brain when he kills, was slow to cool. That anger now included the sister of the man who lay as if dead on the cabin floor. She was trying to fight free. Cole saw her blazing eyes flick a sidelong glance at the butcher knife she had been using to slice the steaks. He still had her brother's handled hunting knife. He drove the blade deep into the log wall and snapped it off at the brass hilt, tossing the bladeless handle on the floor. Even the drunken Mitch was included in his blind anger.

"Shotgun traps and knife-fighters!" He grinned twistedly at Sammy Lou and big Mitch. "Mebby you were right when you said I belonged with the Kilgores. At least they pack their guns in their hands and they don't jump on a man's back with a knife. Your damn' right I'll take my time comin' back. I still don't know where *you* was, Mitch, when the vigilantes hung Hank Griffin."

"You better clear out," said Mitch, the whiskey now firing his blood. "You're crowdin' your luck. Me and Sammy Lou has got along plenty many years while Hank Griffin's son was wearin' the Kilgore name. You string your bets with them and yourn will be just one more Block K hide to hang on the fence. Take that yaller-eyed Kilgore wench an' git off my place!"

Cole backed out the door and closed it. He hardly glanced at Kate Kilgore as she mounted her horse. A few minutes later he had saddled his horse and rode off into the night. Kate Kilgore, riding alongside him, was wise enough not to break the silence. She was smiling faintly, her yellow eyes covertly watching him.

"I hope," she said, "that old Mitch will send for you and bury the hatchet when he gets sobered up. You may need him for a friend if you stay in this part of the country."

"What makes you say that?"

"Paw and my brothers were not at the ranch today when one of the hands fetched the mail from Rocky Point. There was a letter that had an El Paso postmark and the return address was marked the sheriff's office. Female cat curiosity prompted me to open it. It was a sort of formal routine notice that said my father's brother, Grant Kilgore, had been shot and killed by Cole Griffin, alias Cole Kilgore."

Cole shifted his weight to one stirrup, turning in his saddle to look squarely at the girl who rode alongside him. When he spoke, his voice was firm. "I shot Grant Kilgore. I only wish I'd gotten the job done many years ago. But I was too little then to aim a gun. Grant Kilgore was a snake. He needed killing plenty."

"So I've heard my father say. But blood is, as the saying goes, thicker than water. Jake Kilgore won't be pinning any leather medals on your shirt for killing his blackleg brother, Grant. If you have any real common horse sense, you'll keep right on riding till you're out of this part of the cow country. The name Kilgore should be spelled with two 'l's. They run this country around here."

"Are you tryin' to throw a scare into me?"

"Perhaps I am. I don't want to see you killed. I got you into a mess back yonder. I lost you a friend . . . two friends, if you count the little 'breed girl. Maybe you killed Frank Sorrels on my account. He dropped like a shot beef. But if you didn't kill him, you made a bad enemy. Drunk or sober, Frank's treacherous. I got you into that mess. I'm trying to keep you from tangling with my father and brothers. This is not safe range for the man who killed Grant Kilgore. You just left the only place where you'd find a safe hide-out from the Block K outfit. The Rocky Point Crossing on the Missouri is only a few miles up the river. The horse I'm riding is fresh and he's as good a horse as you'll find in Montana. Let's swap horses here. Go back to Texas or wherever you came from. Or better yet, take me with you. I'll go down the trail to Texas with you, Cole Griffin."

Kate Kilgore's husky voice was steady. Her yellow eyes shone like smoldering lights in the moonlight. She was looking at him squarely, the smile wiped from her lips.

"I don't understand. Go to Texas with me? Why?"

"Why? Because it would be adventure, danger, excitement. I'd be riding with a man who would fight to keep the love I could give him. What is there here for me, shut in by the same skyline day after day and night after night? Listening to the same talk day in and night out. Women slaving over stoves and wash tubs, wearing cheap cotton dresses they get from mail-order houses. Men smelling of stale sweat and barn stalls asking you to waltz to the squeak of a two-bit fiddle. Listening to the Kilgore men brag about their toughness. Watching the river steamers go by on their way back to St. Louis where there are lights and music and white table cloths and real silver. In my room at the ranch is an old theater poster. It has the picture of one woman who ran away from here because she felt the same thing stifling her heart. That woman was your mother. Grant Kilgore was a blackguard and a gambler, but he had been to big cities and he had a college education. Grant Kilgore offered her an escape from the slow suicide of ranch life here in the badlands. She was billed at the Fort Benton Opera House as Kathleen Mavourneen. My mother named me after her. Kathleen Mavourneen Kilgore . . . Kate Kilgore.

"I don't love you any more than you love me. But I could learn to worship the man who took me away from here. You're different from any man I have ever met. You'd never be content to bury yourself in this God-forgotten place. Would you be sheep-brained enough to slave away the finest years of your life building up a cow outfit here? Fighting the heat and mosquitoes in the summer. Snowed in from November till May? Take me with you. I'll share every hardship along the trail. I'll sleep on the ground with a saddle blanket for cover. I'll go hungry and thirsty. I'll take a gun and help you fight. I'll go through hell with the man who will take me down the long trail and I'll help him fight to get the things that can make us both happy. I'd help him rob trains or hold up banks and win a South America stake to live in a city like Buenos Aires. We can get fresh horses at the Block K horse camp across the river. I'll go down the outlaw trail with you, Cole Griffin. If they trap us, I'll die fighting beside you!"

They had pulled up now, off the road and in the shadow of a giant cottonwood. Overhead was the moon. The stars were like millions of white diamonds in a black velvet sky. Cole's blood was pounding hard in his veins. He knew that there was no other woman on earth like this white-skinned girl whose eyes were golden pools in the shadow of long, thick, black lashes. Her husky voice thrilled him until his nerves tingled. She had taken off one of her buckskin gauntlets and her long-fingered hand was on his arm. Their stirrups touched.

Some wild thing in the brush made a noise and Cole's head turned quickly. His eyes, still a little hypnotized by hers, saw five grassy mounds marked by five weather-beaten wooden slabs. This was the Hangman's Tree. One of those graves was that of Hank Griffin. The answer that he had been about to give the daughter of Jake Kilgore died unspoken. He took hold of the white hand that was on his arm, gripping it tightly.

"My father was hung from this tree. He's buried in one of those graves. I'd never find happiness anywhere if I ran off now like a coyote in the night. I rode up the trail from Texas to fight it out with the men who hung Hank Griffin."

Two drops of scarlet blood showed on her under lip that she had caught between her white teeth. Her golden eyes were almost black now. She jerked her hand free and pulled on her glove with a vicious jerk.

"You're no better than the Kilgore men!" Her voice was almost a whispered snarl. "You're no better than that drunken beast back there in his cabin. I thought I had found a real man, but instead I've been wasting breath on a stupid clod. I hope the Kilgores hang you, like Grant Kilgore hung the man who made a prisoner of your mother!"

She swung her rawhide quirt down on the rump of her big black horse and was gone before Cole could find any word or gesture to stop her. Something white had fluttered from her skirt pocket and lay now on the ground. It was a large envelope folded in the middle.

Cole Griffin swung from his saddle. His hand was a little unsteady as he picked up the envelope. It was addressed to Jake Kilgore and in the upper left hand corner was printed, *Sheriff's Office, El Paso, Texas.* He read the brief notice of Grant Kilgore's death and shoved the letter and its envelope into the pocket of his chaps.

He walked over to the five graves. He found the slab with Hank Griffin's name burned deep into the pine wood with a branding iron. His hat in hand Cole Griffin stood there in the shadow of the giant cottonwood that had been struck by lightning and remained now with a charred rip up the base of its heavy trunk, its thick branches leafless, like the fleshless arms of a skeleton.

"I was a long time gettin' here," he said aloud. "I'll pay off your debt or die a-tryin'."

He got on his horse and rode off alone into the black shadows of the broken badlands.

☆ IV ☆

THE MIDNIGHT BRANDING

*T*here must have been fifty head of cattle in the bunch that milled in the two corrals that were connected by a short chute and a squeezer gate. Three steers were held in the chute. A fourth was held in the pressure of the big, flat-sided squeezer. There was a branding fire that heated half a dozen irons. Some gunnysacks soaked in a wooden trough near the branding chute.

Bart Kilgore and Sid were doing the branding. The gray-bearded, one-armed Jake was bossing the job.

"Wring that sack more dry, Sid. Damn it all, won't you never learn nothin'? Git a sack too wet and all it does is cool off the iron. It's gotta scorch plumb through. Through the sack and onto the critter's hide. Now bear down, Bart. Shove that iron hard and steady. Git that brand on right or I'll peel your hide off with a jackknife. *Hard,* dammit! Put your weight ag'in it!"

Sid held the damp sacking against the steer's hide. Bart shoved the bar iron hard. There was the hiss and white cloud of steam. Then the smoke of burning, wet hair. Bart, hat pulled slanting across his eyes, leaned his weight against the branding iron.

"Take it away!" snapped old Jake.

Bart stepped back, holding the iron. Sid jerked the sack away. There was a four inch strip burned out of it.

Jake Kilgore brushed the altered brand on the steer's hide with one gloved hand, leaned closely to examine the job. He straightened up, then bent over and picked up a handful of loose dirt, rubbing it over the brand. He nodded curtly to Sid and Bart.

"That makes that Slash steer one of our Triangles," he snapped. "Let 'im go."

Sid released the long pole that held the squeezer. Old Jake swung open the little chute gate. Bart prodded the steer with its newly altered brand into the far corral that held about half the cattle the Kilgores penned at their hidden corrals.

The chute gate shut. The next steer was prodded into the squeezer and Sid fastened the long pole with a rope. Jake climbed the corral and mounting a saddle horse inside, crowded the cattle against the opening of the chute until another steer was reluctantly crowded into it. Bart closed the gate at its rump. The chute again held four steers, one of them gripped fast by the squeezer. Another wet sack. The steer wore a big S brand. Bart picked up a cherry red quarter circle branding iron. Jake cussed him.

" 'Tain't hot enough. White-red, I told you so many damned times you orter sing a song about it. Make a clean lookin' Figger 8 outa that S or I'll take a blacksnake to your back. Damn it all, Sid, use a fresh sack. They cost two-bits, that's all they cost, unless you stole 'em fer nothin'. And a blotched brand costs us mebbyso a stretch in the pen. That Wyoming buyer is gittin' spooky about blotched brands. You heered him say he was turnin' back everything that was blotched or new lookin'. I kin learn Kate to do a neater job than you two done on some of that last bunch we turned out."

"Kate, hell!" snapped Sid, hotly. "She's moonlightin' right now with that damn Frank Sorrels 'breed."

"You're damn tootin' she is," snarled the gray-whiskered Jake. "Them's her orders. She's keepin' that quarter-breed away from here and scarin' the guts outa him by makin' him think we might ketch her with him. Kate's got more brains than a corral full of things like you. And another night soon she'll be holdin' hands with that Wyoming cattle buyer, Dude Krebbs, down on the Little Big Horn."

"And holdin' out one of her lily white hands," put in Bart sourly, "for a share of the money we git for these cattle."

"She earns it, just as much as you two whelps earn yourn," snarled Jake Kilgore. "And she banks it. She don't go blowin' it fer booze er losin' it to tin-horn gamblers. She's buildin' herself a stake."

"Yeah. A gitaway stake," snarled Sid. "The high toned lady! She'll wind up in a St. Louis honky-tonk. . . ."

Old Jake Kilgore reached his younger son in two long-legged strides. There was a short prod pole in his hand. It struck Sid alongside the head with a dull, sickening crack. Sid's long legs buckled at the knees and he went down, the wet sack slipping from his hands.

"You hadn't oughta done that," muttered Bart, stepping away from his one-armed father. "You mighta killed him."

"Slap him alive with a wet sack," growled the elder Kilgore. "He's too ornery to die natural, thataway. It'll learn him an' you both to treat your sister fer what she is. A lady, by grab, and don't you ferget it!"

Cole Griffin slipped further back into the black shadows of the brush. He worked his way back cautiously to where he had left his horse. He had seen all that he needed to learn about the hidden corral he had located by the bawling of cattle. His horse needed rest and feed. He was half starved himself and needed some sleep. He had a sack of salt and a butcher knife in his saddle pocket. He would rope and butcher a calf and build a fire after daylight in some remote part of the badlands. The Kilgores were delivering their bunch of worked branded cattle down near the Wyoming line on the Little Big Horn river. With a pair of horse clippers he would erase the wet sack brands they were sweating and losing sleep to make. He would have a law officer with him when he rode up while the Kilgores were making delivery to their crooked cattle buyer. Rustling was punishable by a long prison term.

Cole Griffin had used a gun on Grant Kilgore, and now he was smashing the Block

K outfit. He'd send Bart and Sid to the pen and buy their outfits that would be confiscated and put on the auction block at a sheriff's sale. Cole Griffin's job here in the badlands was finished for the present. He was going to Fort Benton next to have a talk with the sheriff and the cattlemen who were forming a Livestock Association, tell them what he knew.

Before daylight Cole butchered a Block K calf and hung the meat to cool. He dared not risk building a campfire until after daybreak. The light of a fire might attract unwanted visitors. He was camped at the head of a little creek not more than a mile above the deserted old Hank Griffin ranch, that the Kilgores now used for a winter line camp. He staked out his horse and tried to sleep, but his eyes would not close. He lay on his back and watched the moon. He kept thinking of the little quarter-breed Sammy Lou, who had only once worn a woman's dress. Of Kathleen Mavourneen Kilgore who had a picture of Cole's mother in her room at the Block K ranch. Kate Kilgore helped her father and brothers rustle cattle by making dupes out of men like Frank Sorrels and the Wyoming buyer. She was banking her money to build up a getaway stake.

Cole wondered if Kate Kilgore had told her father and brothers about the letter from the El Paso sheriff. She had been plenty mad when she had left him sitting his horse by the lightning-blasted Hangman's Tree. If she had the sort of vindictive nature that would nurse a grudge, she'd tell Jake Kilgore about the lost letter and put the Kilgores on his trail. On the other hand, she might be playing a more clever and subtle game. Kathleen Mavourneen Kilgore had brains and a daring brand of courage. She had a contempt for her father and the two gun-toting brothers whose lives were bound by the badlands horizon. From what she had said and the things she had left untold for him to figure out, she parried and blocked their uncouth, clumsy abuse with a sharp-edged, stabbing wit and intolerance that galled her brothers and won the secret admiration of her cattle-stealing, hard-bitten father.

Kate Kilgore had opened and read the letter from El Paso. News of that shooting of Grant Kilgore would be slow to travel this far north. The sheriff down yonder had fulfilled his duty by informing the closest relative of the dead gambler. Only by accident would further notice or information concerning Grant Kilgore's death get to Jake and his two sons. But Kate Kilgore knew. And if she kept her secret, she was armed with a weapon she could use on Cole Griffin if he stayed in this part of the country. Cole reckoned that it would be more in keeping with her nature and temperament to keep her secret. She was not done yet with the man who had humiliated her, hurt her pride and vanity.

She had bared her heart and soul to him. Certain of her beauty and her strange power over men, she had offered herself to a man she had known less than an hour. And he had refused to take her. That must have hurt her far worse than anything she had ever suffered at the hands of any man. She had not been playing with him as she did with fools like Frank Sorrels. She had been hurt badly enough to have killed him. And she was not going to let any man wound her pride and vanity like that and get away unhurt. She was a Kilgore. If she had chosen any other spot than that Hangman's Tree, Cole might have yielded to the seductive beauty of the yellow-eyed, tawny-haired adventuress. But she had halted there in the shadow of that stark tree. She must have purposely chosen that place. She was too clever to make a big blunder.

She had gambled on her charms being stronger than any feud code that bound

Cole Griffin to his hanged father. There was something a little splendid about Kate Kilgore's courage. She wanted no weakling for a mate. She wanted a man who was willing to make a big sacrifice for her. She was not selling herself cheaply. She had stacked the odds against herself and then made her splendid play. Kate Kilgore had lost, but she would get her revenge.

Even now, as the day began to brighten, the memory of her beauty quickened Cole's pulse. His life had been packed with danger, adventure, excitement. He, too, felt all the impulses Kate Kilgore had in her heart. But he was a cowpuncher. No big city could ever hold him longer than a few days or a few weeks at the longest. He needed the freedom of open ranges, the untainted air of mountains and deserts and rolling prairies. Cities like St. Louis were all right for a week or two — a cowpuncher's spree in town, lights and music and gaiety for a few nights. Then he had to ride away from it and get back out to the cow country he loved.

Kate Kilgore was willing to risk the rigors and dangers of the outlaw trail. But not for long. At the end must be that dazzling goal of some big city. She was the most beautiful and fascinating woman Cole Griffin had ever met, ever hoped to meet. He did not fool himself by pretending that he was not sorely tempted to find her again, and ride away with her. He had gotten a good price for his outfit down on the Mexican border. He did not need to rob banks or hold up trains to get a South America stake. He could give Kate Kilgore all those things that meant so much to her. But he could not share that gay city life with her and find happiness. Their dreams of high adventure were much the same, but their ultimate goals lay in opposite directions.

Cole wanted to meet Kate Kilgore again. He wanted, somehow, to heal the wound he had made in her woman's heart. He wanted to tell her that she was the most beautiful woman in the world, the bravest girl he had ever known. He wanted to hold her in his arms and tell her that. Then he wanted to say good-bye forever. He hoped that he had the strength to do that. But he was more than a little afraid of himself.

He broiled strips of fresh veal over a little fire and ate until the gnawing pain in the pit of his stomach was gone. He let his horse graze at the end of a picket rope while he bathed in the creek and shaved the heavy stubble of whiskers from his jaw. He spent the day lazing in the shade, his saddle cinched loosely on his horse, always alert and ready for flight or a gun fight if he was attacked. Because he felt half ashamed of his hot-tempered break with old Mitch, he made up his mind to ride back there and make peace with the old cowhand who had been his father's friend. He hoped, for Sammy Lou's sake, that he hadn't broken her brother's neck. He felt sorry for little Sammy Lou who thought herself just a little river 'breed and whose only friend was whiskey-soaked old Mitch.

☆ V ☆

COLE RIDES OUT

At the Cow Island Crossing Cole had heard about old Mitch. Men called him a dangerous old rascal who openly defied the big Kilgore outfit, butchered Block K beef when he needed meat, and let all manner of renegade outlaws use his place for a way station along their dim trail to nowhere. Mitch was a tough old son, they said, the last of the little ranchers who had been wiped out by Jake and Grant Kilgore. Since his five partners had been hanged, Mitch had carried on a single-handed war against the Kilgores.

"Ol' Mitch," said the man who had a little trading post at the Cow Island Crossing on the Missouri River, "has them Kilgores ridin' in bunches. They none of 'em has the guts to ride alone past Mitch's ranch, day or night, drunk or sober."

Old Mitch had plenty of courage. They let him alone. Even tough old Jake Kilgore with one arm shot off, had respect for the old rannahan. Cole had taunted him with the question about where he had been the night Grant and Jake Kilgore and a bunch of so-called vigilantes had hung Mitch's five partners. It had been an unfair question and Cole was heartily ashamed of it. He'd had no right to hint that Mitch had hid out somewhere, afraid to fight. He was going to ride back there and make peace with old Mitch. And he was going to tell that little Sammy Lou that he didn't think of her as a moccasin 'breed. He hoped he hadn't killed Frank Sorrels even if the young knife-slinger did deserve killing.

It was dusk when he kicked dirt on his little fire and tightened his saddle cinch. He headed along a dim trail that would meet the river road just below Mitch's ranch. The trail took him through rough, broken country. He rode down a little canyon toward the river. Then the ugly whine of a rifle bullet jerked him out of his musing. The bullet nicked the crown of his hat, struck a rock, glancing off with a pinging whistle. Cole jerked at his saddle gun as he jumped his horse off the trail and into a patch of buckbrush. He saw the telltale puff of gun smoke on a rimrock two hundred yards above him. The echoes of the shot crashed in the little canyon. The would-be bush-whacker kept shooting. Bullets droned like hornets, clipping the branches of the thick brush. The man on the rimrock was hidden from sight as he lay flat on his belly and sent down his deadly hail of bullets.

Cole and his horse were hidden by the thick brush. There was no sense in wasting bullets shooting at the man on the rimrock. The smoke of Cole's carbine would give away his exact position. In half an hour it would be dark enough down here in the canyon to make a run for it. Cole swung from his saddle and stood crouched, his carbine ready for a snap-shot if the bushwhacker on the rimrock moved into sight. Then, booming through the echoes of the rifle up on the rimrock, came the roar of a heavier calibered gun. There was a quick movement up on the rimrock. The roar of the big calibered rifle crashed again. And behind its echoes came the bellow of old Mitch's voice, hurling profanity.

"The next time, you bushwhackin' snake, I won't be shootin' to scare you! I'll blow the briskit plumb outa your damn hide!"

Mitch's voice and the roar of his gun came from somewhere not far down the canyon. Cole got back on his horse. He still had his carbine in his hand and now, as he sat on his horse, he caught sight of the man Mitch's bullets had driven from the rimrock ledge above. Cole's carbine raised to his shoulder with a swift, unbroken movement. His sights were lined on a man wearing a black hat, riding a bay and white pinto horse.

It was an easy shot for as good a marksman as Cole Griffin. The spotted horse had to travel at a walk on a narrow strip of trail that skirted the side of the rimrock. Cole had seen that paint horse the night before at Mitch's place. It was Frank Sorrels's horse. Sorrels had worn a big black hat and his neck had not been broken. The big young quarter-breed had made a bushwhacker try at revenge.

Cole lowered the carbine, letting down the hammer with his thumb. He worked the gun lever to drop the cartridge out of the barrel into the palm of his hand. He shoved the cartridge into his chaps pocket and slid the carbine into its saddle scabbard. Emptying his gun-barrel of a loaded cartridge was a safety precaution that any man but a greenhorn always took. But quite another motive prompted him to put the brass cartridge in his chaps pocket rather than shove it back in the gun's magazine. A faint grin twisted the corners of his mouth. Then he rode on down the canyon. When he had traveled a little way, he pulled and raised his voice to a cautious shout.

"Hi, there, Mitch! This is Cole Griffin! How about. . . ?"

"You needn't be hollerin' your name to the wide world." Mitch's big voice sounded so close that Cole jumped a little. Mitch came from behind a patch of heavy chokecherry brush, a long-barreled .45–70 rifle in the crook of his arm. "I figgered it might be you," said Mitch, "that Block K bushwhacker was a-foggin'. I hoped to cut your sign. I bin up here in the canyon runnin' off the last of the drippin's from as purty a batch of sour mash corn as ever was 'stilled. Sammy Lou's a-cookin' us a son-of-a-gun in the sack. And I'm tellin' you, son, you never tasted a real son-of-a-gun till you've throwed your lip over a bait of hern. We might as well git on down to the ranch."

That was old Mitch's way of letting Cole know that he was holding no grudge. Cole grinned and took the cartridge from the pocket of his fringed, round-legged shotgun chaps. He held it in the palm of his hand.

"This cartridge was in my gun barrel and the hammer was cocked, Mitch, when I lined my sights back yonder on Frank Sorrels."

"I kinda hoped you'd believe me when I let on that it was a Block K man that was shootin' at you. Not on his ornery account. He's a bad 'un. The sooner somebody kills him off, the better. But don't judge little Sammy Lou by her brother. Her heart's as white as yourn. The Injun in her is good Injun. Frank got his bad streak from travelin' with bad company and drinkin' the wrong brand of likker. Though even good whiskey is bad medicine to any Injun or 'breed I ever knowed. Injun blood and hard likker don't mix. There's no sense in lettin' Sammy Lou know that Frank was layin' up on that rimrock."

"That's right, Mitch." Cole shoved the cartridge into the magazine of his saddle gun. "I'm pullin' out for Fort Benton. I want to have a medicine talk with the sheriff. I spent half the night watchin' the Kilgores workin' the brands on some big three- and four-year-old steers they're deliverin' to some gent named Dude Krebbs."

"The hell you say! You mean you wasn't moon-ridin' with that buckskin-maned Kate Kilgore?"

Cole felt his face grow hot, and he was glad that it was dusk and old Mitch couldn't notice. He went on quickly, giving Mitch no time to express his vitriolic opinion of Kate Kilgore. "They were sack-brandin' stuff into the Figure 8, Triangle, and J B irons."

"Them's the remnant brands they still use. They're almighty keerful not to mess with Jake's Block K. Them remnant brands is registered in Bart's and Sid's names. So if there's any slip-up, it'll be the boys, not old man Jake, that gits jailed. That ol' he-wolf is plumb cautious thataway."

"They work the S iron into a Figure 8," said Cole. "The Slash brand goes into the Triangle iron. They make their J B connected out of some gent's Pot-hook."

"The S is the Sorrels's brand," said Mitch. "The Slash belongs to Bob Means on Telegraph Creek. The Pot-hook is owned by a dude feller named Parkes over on Beaver Creek. Except for the S stuff, them steers has come from a long ways. Strays that the Block K cowhands has bin throwin' back where the Kilgores kin pick 'em up handy. You watched 'em brand out them steers?"

"I heard cattle bawlin' and cold-trailed 'em to some brandin' corrals back in the badlands. From the way they talked, it was the last bunch they had to brand. They're holdin' a herd somewheres across the river and they start trailin' 'em for the Wyoming line tonight."

"Sellin' the cattle to Dude Krebbs, you say?"

Cole nodded. "Know him?" he asked curiously.

"Plenty. Dude is Kate Kilgore's fancy man. One of them blackleg college fellers that was sent out West. Remittance man. He got out of Fort Benton on account of a crooked beef contract him and an Army officer was workin'. The Army officer blowed his brains out. Dude Krebbs hightailed it before they could git enough on him to send him to the federal pen. He's smart as a fox and a bad man in a gun scrape. One of them range dudes that has a squaw sew a buckskin seat in his britches. Packs a white-handled gun and curls his mustache. Krebbs ain't his real name. His old man is some big toad in the Washington puddle, they say. He'd be a hell of a lot fu'ther away than Wyoming if he wasn't plumb stuck on Kate Kilgore. Dude Krebbs sided me once in a bad tight. Supposin', Cole, we leave the Fort Benton sheriff outa this deal? I bin fightin' the Kilgores a long, long time and I ain't never asked fer no law help yet."

"Just as you say, Mitch."

"If Dude is mixed up in this," said Mitch, "it's on account of Kate Kilgore. And the pen is a hell of a place to send even a man like Dude Krebbs. I seen one of them tigers once that was locked up in a cage. One of them zoo places at St. Louis. I stood there a long time, watchin' that tiger walk back and forth, staring through them steel bars. As handsome a wild thing as ever I seen. I stood it as long as I could. Then I slid my six-shooter out and shot that tiger square between the eyes. It cost me all the drinkin' money I'd fetched along to paint St. Louis red. But I'd want a man to do the same fer me if I was locked behind jail bars. I reckon Dude Krebbs would feel likewise."

"We'll keep the law out of it," said Cole.

They mounted. Mitch broke the short silence as they reached the wagon road and were riding side by side. "Me'n you kin handle the Kilgores," he said simply, and Cole smiled faintly at the old hellion's confidence in himself and the son of Hank Griffin.

"They'll have cowpunchers helpin' 'em with the cattle," said Cole, weighing possible odds they'd be up against, "and there's Dude Krebbs to handle."

"That don't sound much like Hank Griffin a-talkin'," growled Mitch.

"Hank Griffin got hung," Cole reminded him grimly.

"None of them five would have got hung if they'd done what I told 'em to do. They was drinkin' rot-gut whiskey . . . not my likker. Grant and Jake Kilgore and their hired gun-toters they called vigilantes had all the bulge on Hank and Sam Sorrels and the others when they jumped 'em. But them gun-slingers that Grant had hired around Fort Benton is dead or quit the country years ago. Jake will have his two sons,

Bart an' Sid, a-backin' him. Two-three cowpunchers, mebby. Most mebby, though, there'll be just the Kilgores handlin' them cattle. Jake don't trust nobody outside his own kin when he's handlin' stolen cattle. Like as not Kate will be ridin' up on the point with Jake. She's as good a cowhand as Bart or Sid. Dude ain't takin' up no gunfight fer the Kilgores. I tell you, son, me'n you is men enough to git the bulge on 'em and whup 'em."

"All right, Mitch." Cole let it go at that.

They rode on in silence, each busy with his own thoughts. Cole was dreading this meeting with Sammy Lou. He was relieved when they reached Mitch's place and no light showed at the cabin.

Sammy Lou was not there. The son-of-a-gun in a sack, no more or less than a tallow pudding cooked in a flour sack, stood on the back of the stove. But the fire in the stove was almost cold. Mitch looked in a crevice between the logs, lifted out a piece of wooden chinking and reached into a small cavity behind where it had been. He took out a folded piece of paper and scowled over the note she had left him.

"She's pulled out," Mitch said, his voice edged with worry and anger. "That no-account brother of hern has bin here again. She's gone off with him somewheres. It would have bin better all around if you'd broke his damn' neck last night."

"What does the note say, Mitch?"

Mitch reluctantly handed Cole the note. The rounded letters on paper stood out accusingly at him.

Good-bye for a while, Mitch, he read. *Frank needs me worse than you do now. I can straighten him out. Take care if yourself. Don't trust that Cole Griffin. Kate Kilgore put the Block K brand on him last night. Sammy Lou.*

"She slipped off early this mornin'," said Mitch, "and rode off to the Sorrels's ranch before breakfast, then come back to my place. I rode past the Sorrels's place on my way to the still. She'd burned up that trunk of fancy clothes the river captain give her."

"Got any idea where she went?"

"No. She's gone off into the hills with her brother. He must have took the short trail here after he quit the rimrock. No tellin' what kind of a whiskey lie he told her. He's bad medicine. He was all right till rot-gut whiskey an' the Kilgore gal made a plumb fool outa him. There's no use in tryin' to locate 'em now. They know every hide-out in the badlands. Only thing to do is fergit her till she shows up again."

But Cole knew that old Mitch was worried. They ate supper in silence. Mitch lit a blackened corncob pipe and pulled slowly at the tooth-scarred stem, exhaling blue clouds of strong smoke.

Cole kept thinking of Sammy Lou's burning up the trunkful of clothes. White woman's clothes. The dress she had worn to the Christmas dance with moccasins instead of high-heeled slippers to match. The poor little kid. Cole reckoned he'd hurt her a lot more than his fists had hurt her brother, Frank, when he had called Frank Sorrels a knife-slinging 'breed. It made Cole feel almighty cheap and cowardly. Finally he got a sheet of paper from the writing tablet Sammy Lou kept at Mitch's cabin when she did her written lessons from her school books. He whittled the lead of a rifle cartridge to a point and used it for a pencil. It took half an hour and he wasted several sheets of paper before he got a note composed. It was a clumsy effort, but it was the best he could do. He read it over, frowning:

Sammy Lou,

    It was just plain childish of you to burn up your pretty clothes. Don't ever let anybody or anything make you feel like you don't belong in those kind of clothes. You're not a common little river 'breed. It looks like I'll have to get you a new outfit and take you to the next dance to prove it. How about a red silk dress and slippers to match it? Unless a better man beats me to it, I'm taking you to the next Christmas dance. You've got to believe that I am your friend.

Cole Griffin

He gave it to old Mitch to read. Mitch nodded his approval and Cole felt a lot better.

"Put it in behind the hunk of loose chinkin', Mitch." Cole took his hat and saddle gun from the deer antlers above the door.

"Where you goin'?" questioned old Mitch.

Cole grinned faintly. "The Kilgores don't know who I am or where I come from. I'm ridin' over to the Block K outfit and hirin' out to Jake Kilgore for a tough hand. That note of Sammy Lou's gave me the idea. Unless my luck spoils I'll be ridin' on the point or slappin' the drags with my rope when that cattle drive reaches the Little Big Horn on the Wyoming line."

Mitch could find no argument to stop him. When the old rannahan found out that Cole was determined to throw in with the Kilgores, they made their plans accordingly.

"But unless you got a trick up your sleeve, son, you're a gone goslin'. You're bluffin' with a bobtailed flush."

"Mebbyso I've got the joker buried, Mitch. I'm gamblin' on my hole-card bein' the right color."

"That hole card," guessed Mitch shrewdly, "wouldn't have yaller hair, by any chance?"

"By any chance," grinned Cole, his face flushing a little under the older man's keen scrutiny, "she just might."

"Then you'll find that Dude Krebbs is twice as dangerous as any one of the Kilgores. He's a coiled rattler."

"I'll be keepin' that in mind," said Cole.

"I'll be cold-trailin' you," Mitch reminded him. "You know how to signal me. I won't be too far off."

Cole left old Mitch cussing softly, there at the barn, and rode alone down the river. He had a good idea where he would overtake the Kilgores and the drive of stolen cattle. He was gambling that Kate had kept her secret about the letter from the Sheriff at El Paso.

☆ VI ☆
SIGNED ON TO DIE

*T*he Kilgores were traveling with a pack outfit and a small remuda of top horses. The outfit was eating a daybreak breakfast when Cole Griffin rode up. Sid Kilgore was with the herd. The remuda was penned in a rope corral. Jake Kilgore, Bart, and Kate were squatted around the little campfire, their plates loaded, their coffee cups filled.

Cole rode up, whistling the dismal tune of the "Cowboy's Lament." He kept his hands clear of his guns. Bart's six-shooter covered him. Jake's big hand was on the cedar butt of his long-barreled Colt and his bleak eyes were sharp with suspicion.

Cole looked hard at Kate Kilgore. She smiled faintly and lifted her big tin cup of coffee in a sort of salute. Cole's nerves relaxed a little. He knew that she had kept her secret about his identity and the killing of Grant Kilgore.

"I sighted your camp," said Cole, "and remembered I was hungry. I've been ridin' all night."

"Then supposin' you keep right on ridin'," said Jake Kilgore. "I'm particular who eats at my camp."

"Or fill your hand with a gun," said Bart Kilgore who was on his feet now. "The last time we cut your sign, you had a shotgun in it."

"Dry up," snapped old Jake Kilgore, getting slowly to his feet. "We don't want no killin's along the trail. Keep a-driftin', mister."

Kate Kilgore put down her coffee cup and deliberately walked between Cole and the two Kilgore men. "Did I get you in bad with old Mitch? I didn't get a chance to thank you before, mister, for taking my part. Get down and rest your saddle." Kate turned to her father, ignoring Bart's ugly scowl. "I didn't tell you, Dad, because I didn't want to get you all in a lather. Frank Sorrels spooked the other night and made me run with him to old Mitch's place. This man was there. Mitch was drunk and ugly. Frank was showing the coyote. This man took my part. Frank Sorrels tried to knife him and he beat the 'breed senseless and dropped him at old Mitch's feet. Then he cussed Mitch out and got me away from there. He rode a mile to two with me to see me safely on my way. He's some man who was riding the outlaw trail and using Mitch's ranch for a stopping place along the way. If he got into a ruckus with you at Mitch's ranch, I reckon it was because he didn't want strange company bothering him there. He got me out of an ugly tight. If he's not welcome here, then neither am I. If this man rides on, I'm riding with him."

"Another of her fancy men," sneered Bart. "She's. . . ."

"Dry up, Bart," said Jake Kilgore. "If you guessed right as many times as Kate does, you'd amount to somethin'. You and Sid said you sighted Frank Sorrels at the Cow Island whiskey camp and his face looked like he'd tackled a grizzly. Fill that mouth of yourn with grub, then git out to the herd and relieve Sid." He looked hard at his daughter. "You mighta told me about the ruckus at Mitch's place."

"And have you and that drunken old hellion locking horns? We've got these cattle to move. We're short-handed as it is, without you gettin' laid up and calling a doctor to pick buckshot out of your hide."

Jake Kilgore grinned. "Long-headed and close-mouthed. If you'd bin born a boy, I'd have had a son to brag about. If you say this jasper helped you out of a tight, then I reckon he's worth feedin', anyhow. Git down, mister. I've cut this feller's sign somewhere before we run into him at Mitch's. I'd give a purty if I could place 'im. Did Mitch call him by name?"

"Now I remember," said Kate Kilgore, her golden yellow eyes looking at Cole with tantalizing mockery, "I think Mitch did have a name for him."

Cole's right hand was near his gun as he dismounted, putting his horse between him and Jake Kilgore. Bart had mounted his horse and spurred off at an angry lope, leaving his breakfast half eaten on his tin plate.

"Mitch called him Cole," she said, her husky voice almost purring, "Henry Cole."

Jake Kilgore's hard eyes stared at Cole. "Never heard of him. But a man's name is easier to change than his looks. Tie into some grub, mister."

Cole was riding his horse with a hackamore instead of a bridle. He led the horse to where the grass was tall and loosened the saddle cinch, removing his carbine from its saddle scabbard. "Just in case he takes a notion to roll," he explained, leaning the gun against a rawhide-covered kiack box. "I had the stock broke off a saddle gun thataway once." Cole filled a plate with steak and fried potatoes and dutch-oven biscuits and filled a tin cup with strong black coffee. He sat on the ground between Kate Kilgore and her father, and began eating.

"Which way were you headed," asked Kate, "when you sighted our camp?"

"South. Mexico is south, accordin' to my geography."

"Traveling light," she went on, her eyes challenging him. "Are you in any particular rush?"

"There's nobody hot-trailin' me, if that's what you mean." Cole met her challenge with a fine grin. "Unless it's that 'breed gent. He took a bushwhacker shot at me yesterday evenin'. The light was kinda bad and mebby he was too drunk to shoot straight. Anyhow, he missed."

"Did you?"

"I let him get away. There was no sense in clutterin' up my back trail with a killin'."

"And besides," smiled Kate, "Frank's sister is a mighty pretty girl, for a 'breed."

"I reckon mebbyso that did have somethin' to do with it," Cole agreed frankly.

"That damn 'breed Frank Sorrels," put in Jake Kilgore, "must have gone on the warpath plenty. He shot one of my men at the Cow Island whiskey camp early yesterday mornin'. Crippled him in one laig."

"And left us short-handed," said Kate. "I was coming to that. Cole could ride his string, Dad. We'd make better time with the drive. Nobody's crowding his trail."

"I'd have to talk it over with the boys. Bart don't like him. He'll rib Sid. Nope. Can't put on a stranger, nohow."

"Better a stranger than some home range cowboy that gets loose-tongued the first saloon he finds. Bart and Sid can't tell a real hand from a range tramp. It was one of their side-kickers that got shot by Frank Sorrels. I saw Cole take a knife away from Frank and wipe up the cabin with him, then challenge Mitch. That's more than any of your Block K men would tackle."

"Sounds like your dead set on hirin' this Cole feller."

"You're a smart man, Jake Kilgore," she smiled at her father. Then she looked squarely at Cole. It was a direct challenge. "There's a job for you, Cole, if you have the nerve to tackle it."

"You've hired a cow hand." Cole's eyes were icy blue, belying his easy grin.

So Cole Griffin was firmly, dangerously established in the camp of his enemy. It would need but a word from Kate Kilgore to wipe him out with a deadly hail of bullets. Bart and Sid were open in their enmity and suspicion. And Cole was a good enough judge of men to know that old Jake Kilgore was more dangerous than his sons because he was disguising his suspicion behind what seemed to be a gruff tolerance of a man who had pleased his daughter's fancy.

Sid's attitude was insolent and Bart's was surly, as they broke camp. The remuda and pack horses were trailed along with the cattle. Kate and her father rode up on the point, on opposite sides of the strung-out cattle. Jake put Cole in the swing across from Bart. Sid was bringing up the drags and cussing his job.

When the cattle were strung out, Kate Kilgore dropped back to where Cole was riding. "Whatever your name is," she said, her voice no longer soft, "it's not going to win you anything but a lonely grave."

"You said you hoped I'd hang. I'm obliged to you for not telling Jake Kilgore my right name. For not mentioning the letter."

"Perhaps I'm not quite as obvious as your little 'breed girl. But don't forget, even in your sleep, mister, that I'm what the old saying calls 'a woman scorned.' You followed us. You knew whose camp it was you were riding into. Perhaps I'm clever enough to know that you gambled on getting this job I gave you. I'm wondering if you're fool enough to think I'm going to swallow any other excuse for your being with this drive of cattle. I was fool enough to throw myself at your head the other night. Now I wouldn't marry you for all the gold and diamonds on earth. So don't waste time playing any love games."

"You didn't need to remind me of that, Kathleen. I rode away from that Hangman's Tree just as badly hurt as you were. I don't ask you to believe that, but it's the truth. If I made love to you, I'd mean it. If you were fool enough to marry me, we'd bust up quicker than my mother and Hank Griffin did. I'm a cowpuncher. I'll never be anything else."

"A cowpuncher," she caught him up quickly, "is supposed to be loyal to his outfit. That's part of a real cowpuncher's code. Only a low-down snake breaks his own code. You just hired out to the Block K."

"I hired out to Kate Kilgore. I intend being as loyal as I know how to be. You're my boss. I never had one I'd sooner fight for. I'm not goin' to let you down."

"Save the rest of it till tonight when the herd is bedded down. You'll go on guard with me at midnight. I'm curious to hear just what's in this speech you've been rehearsing to yourself. Bart looks like he might take a shot at you, herd or no herd. Better drop back to the drags and send Sid up on the swing. I can't tell you how thrilling it is to have Cole Griffin riding with this drive of stolen cattle. It breaks the monotony of the trail. And don't let Sid get you on the prod. He's just a mouthy kid. Keep your hand off your gun or you'll be acting out the lead role in that song you were whistling, about 'bury me not on the lone prairieeee.'"

☆ VII ☆
BUSHWHACKER'S SHOWDOWN

*S*id and Bart Kilgore were planning to crowd Cole into going for his gun. Sid was the worst with his ugly taunts that hinted Cole was Kate's lover. When they got too nasty, old Jake would stop it with his wolfish, *"Dry up!"*

Kate would sit cross-legged, her yellow eyes watching the dangerous play. Once or twice, when she saw Cole's jaw muscles quiver with the effort to keep cool, she had gotten between him and her brothers. Her eyes would silence even the loud-mouthed Sid.

Five days and nights of it had worn Cole Griffin's nerves raw. He wanted to ride away from the outfit, or signal to old Mitch who was cold-trailing them. Bart was letting up some the past day or two, a fact that made Sid even more antagonistic and ugly. Cole wondered if he could stand it much longer. His hands ached to get at Sid's throat.

Now and then, during the day, Cole sighted a lone rider somewhere along the distant skyline, sometimes behind, sometimes ahead of the herd. Yesterday he had sighted three riders. He reckoned that Mitch had located Sammy Lou and her brother, Frank. Because Mitch mistrusted Frank and loved Sammy Lou, he was keeping them with him.

If Jake Kilgore and his two sons suspicioned that they were being followed and watched, they gave no outward sign. But Kate Kilgore, standing night guard with Cole, taunted him about it openly.

"I might have known you weren't playing it lone-handed. Is it that whiskey-soaked Mitch and a couple of his beef-butchering neighbors that you have trailing us, or did you soften up and call on the law to help you hamstring the Kilgores? I forgot to tell you that I know you watched some of these steers get branded. I was trailing you when you located the branding corrals that first night we met and you spurned my brazen hussy advances. I was curious to see if you'd go back to Mitch's cabin. You didn't. You heard cattle bawling and watched my dad and brothers do a little fancy brand work. I don't blame you for getting help on this job. You'll need it if you call for a showdown, if you live long enough to make your big play. You're not wearing a law badge pinned to your undershirt, by any chance?"

"No."

"It wouldn't do you much good, anyhow. The Kilgores haven't the proper respect for the law. A tin badge don't mean a thing to Jake Kilgore. As for Bart and Sid, it would make them that much more ornery. You've taken just about all you can stand from them, haven't you?"

"I can stand it," said Cole grimly.

"We camp tomorrow evening on the Little Big Horn. That's where Dude Krebbs takes delivery. I thought maybe you'd like to know. Bart and Sid are getting spooky. I'm not the only Kilgore that's caught sight of those skyline riders. I wouldn't buy your chances, mister, for a lead dollar. Why don't you ride away from this herd right now?"

"With you?" grinned Cole.

"Not with me, cowboy. I gave you your chance back at the Hangman's Tree on the Missouri. If you were playing a lone-handed game, I might be tempted. But you're just the monkey that's going to try to pull the hot chestnuts out of the fire for old Mitch. I tell you, Bart and Sid are going to crowd you tomorrow night at supper. Nobody can get there in time to side you when they make you pull your gun. Please, for my sake, Cole, ride away from here right now!" Kate's voice was soft, husky, vibrant.

"For *your* sake?"

"If you're killed, I'd feel like your murderer."

"Your brothers call me your lover. It's when Sid starts dirtying your name that I can hardly stand it. It's goin' to be a pleasure to tromp the head off that young sidewinder. He's as mangy a whelp as ever I've had the bad luck to meet. Tomorrow night can't come too quick to suit me."

"I thought it was Jake Kilgore you were after. The boys were too young to have any part in the hanging of Hank Griffin."

"Compared to Sid," said Cole, "Jake Kilgore is a gentleman."

"It was Jake Kilgore," said Kate, "who told me to get rid of you tonight. He told me that Bart and Sid were going to jump you tomorrow night at supper. After his own fashion, he thinks a lot of me. He shares the boys' opinion that I'm in love with you. He told me to get rid of you, even if I had to run off with you."

"Your father knocked Sid down at the branding corrals for an ugly crack the young whelp made about you. I've watched him when Sid was draggin' your name in the mud to git a rise outa me. I got the notion he might even side me in a gun-tight."

"You're wrong. Blood is thicker than water. Jake Kilgore's not siding Hank Griffin's son against his own two boys."

"But Jake Kilgore," smiled Cole, "doesn't know I'm Hank Griffin's son."

"No? You're a little stupid. He's known it for two days. When he got me off to one side to warn me, I told him I'd known it from the start. He turned gray. You'd have thought I'd stuck a dull knife in his heart. You think you were in danger when Sid and Bart crowded you. You were never closer to death than you were at camp night before last when I told Jake that I'd known your name was Cole Griffin. I thought he was going to kill us both."

"What stopped him?" Cole's throat felt as dry as dusty flannel.

"I lied to him. I told him you followed me here because you loved me. I told him he'd better kill us both. I didn't think I'd lie that much for any man. That's why, tonight, I hate you. Can you understand, Cole Griffin, that I hate you?"

"You told Jake Kilgore that I loved you and that you were in love with me," said Cole. His face was almost as white as hers in the white moonlight. His voice was no more than a croaking whisper.

"I lied!" Her lips barely moved and her voice was so low-pitched that he sensed, rather than heard, her words. "I hate you!"

Cole Griffin leaned sideways in his saddle. His arms were around her, locking her in an embrace she could not break. She fought wildly for a minute, then her mouth was against his and her arms were around his neck.

Neither of them saw or heard the approach of the tall, black-mustached man who rode up behind them. His voice, deadly calm, tore them from each other's arms.

"I thought Frank Sorrels was lying when he told me I'd ride up on something like this. Mitch tells me your Hank Griffin's son. Your father ain't alive to play his hand.

I'd turn the job over to Mitch if you weren't trying to steal something I claimed. You're either double-crossing Mitch or you're playing a damned blackguard trick on Kate Kilgore. In either case, mister, you're a sneaking, yellow cur-hound. We'll meet over in that cut coulee. Have your gun in your hand when I sight you."

He reined his horse around and ride off at a lope. Cole and Kate Kilgore stared after him. They looked at each other, both still dazed. Then Cole Griffin laughed as heartily as if he had just watched some comedy trick on the stage.

Kate Kilgore smiled. Cole edged his horse closer and reached for her hand. His laughter faded to an easy grin. He dropped his bridle reins over the saddle horn and his free hand groped in his pocket. He brought out a little buckskin sack, loosened its string with his teeth, and took out a rather heavy gold ring set with a large emerald. He slid it slowly down over the third finger of her left hand.

"It belonged to my mother, Kathleen. The only bit of jewelry she ever wore on the stage. She'd want you to have it. I wanted to give it to you that first night, there at he Hangman's Tree. No matter what happens, I want you to wear it, always."

Tears welled to Kate Kilgore's golden yellow eyes as she leaned from her saddle and kissed Cole. Then she read something else in his eyes and her arms tightened around his neck. "Cole! You're not going to shoot it out with Dude Krebbs!"

"So that's Dude Krebbs! I thought so, from the way he talked about claimin' you. I've got to knock his horns off. You wouldn't be proud of a man that'd take a cussin' like that. For four days and nights I've gritted my teeth and grinned when I wanted to knock the heads of your two brothers together till they cracked and rattled like gourds. This purty gent is no kin of yours. He prodded me where it hurt. He's half way right about my double-crossin' of Mitch, and not playin' out Hank Griffin's hand."

"But he lied when he said he had any claim on me," Kate said slowly. "You're the only man I've ever kissed in my life!"

"And I'll come back to claim you for keeps. The shootin' will spook the cattle, so watch out. I reckon this is goin' to spoil the sale of these steers, so you might as well let 'em scatter and drift. I'll meet you at camp. I've got to talk to Jake . . . tell him I'm marryin' you. Then I'll give Bart and Sid a fist-whumpin' they'll remember, and have a showdown with Mitch. My night's chores are shore laid out. I'm commencin' right now with Dude Krebbs!"

Cole rode off, his six-shooter in his hand. He knew now what old Mitch had done. The old rascal had ridden ahead and contacted Dude Krebbs. He had made some kind of a dicker with the crooked cattle-buyer. Krebbs had mentioned Frank Sorrels. Frank and Sammy Lou were with Mitch.

Ahead, not more than two hundred yards, was the cut coulee. Its black shadows hid Dude Krebbs from sight. But Cole would be plainly skylighted against the moon. Dude Krebbs was a killer. He was in love with Kate Kilgore. Cole knew the breed of swaggering gun-slingers well enough to feel sure that the blackleg Dude was going to take any advantage that came his way. Cole pulled his hat down across his eyes and gripped his gun tighter.

His teeth bared in a mirthless grin, he raked the big Block K horse with his spurs. He topped the rim of the cut coulee with his horse at a run. From the shadows below he saw the flash of a gun. A bullet nicked his shoulder. He shot at the gun blaze as the running horse went down the steep slant. He saw other guns blaze swiftly. One to his right, the other ahead and below. It looked like he had ridden square into an ambush.

The thought came to him that old Mitch and the quarter-breed Frank Sorrels were siding with Dude Krebbs.

Cole was going down the slope with the breakneck, reckless speed of a Pony Express rider carrying the mail. He shot at the gun flash on his left, threw a second shot toward the shadowy outline of a rider to his right, and rode headlong at the blaze of the gun ahead and below him.

"You yellow-backed, bushwhackin' coward! If there's any guts in you, Dude Krebbs, ride out in the open!"

Dude Krebbs spurred his horse from behind the shadow of some buckbrush. Krebbs was shouting something Cole couldn't make out. Their guns blazing, the cattle-buyer could not get out of Cole's path quickly enough, and the two horses and men piled up in a wild tangle.

Cole jerked his feet free of the stirrups and let himself get catapulted through the air. He landed in the heavy buckbrush which broke his fall. Shaken, his face and shirt ripped, he scrambled to his feet. He saw the two horses untangle themselves. He made a leaping lunge at Dude Krebbs's horse when he saw that Dude, limp as a sack, dead, perhaps, had a foot caught in the stirrup. He grabbed the bridle reins of the lunging, rearing horse.

Old Mitch came up, his horse on a run. Cole clung to the reins of the frightened horse with his left hand. His gun swung toward old Mitch. "Throw away your gun, you bushwhackin' old son, or I'll shoot the bell off you. Your pardner's foot's hung in the stirrup. His neck should be hung in a rope. Yours likewise. Get 'im loose!"

"Loco!" growled Mitch, quitting his horse with a speed that was almost miraculous for a man of his age and heavy build. Mitch got Dude Krebbs's foot free of the stirrup, laid the limp form on the ground, and bent over him.

"Shot twice," he muttered, "neither wound bad enough to hurt. Knocked his head on a rock or got kicked by a horse. He's a hell of a long ways from dead, to my way of thinkin'."

Old Mitch looked up. Cole's six-shooter was covering him. The young cowpuncher's eyes were blue ice.

"You had to bushwhack me. Dude Krebbs wasn't man enough to play a lone hand. He had to have you and his 'breed pardner side him. You got a gun in your hand, you old hellion. Stand up and use it like a man!"

Old Mitch dropped his cedar-handled six-shooter as if it was the wrong end of a hot branding iron. He straightened slowly, his hands in the air. "You ain't gone loco, have you, young Cole? I was acrost the ridge and heard shootin'. That was the signal me'n you fixed that was to fetch me with my gun in my hand. I find you swingin' onto Dude's horse and a-cussin' me. I ain't fired a shot tonight. I found Sammy Lou an' Frank afore I left home. Kep' 'em with me. I located Dude this evenin' and we made medicine. Dude said he might scout the Kilgore camp some. I wake up and find I'm alone. Dude ain't come back. Frank's gone. Sammy Lou's gone. I swaller me an eye-opener and fork my horse. I hear shootin' and come a-foggin'. But my gun ain't bin fired . . . yet!"

"Three men were shootin' at me when I rode down off the rim." Cole's hot temper was cooling quickly. There was no doubting the truth of old Mitch's words. Mitch, for all his shortcomings, was no liar. "Pick up your gun, Mitch. I'm wrong and plumb sorry. Somewhere in this coulee is two bushwhackers. Krebbs is comin' alive."

Mitch picked up his gun. Cole found Dude Krebbs's white-handled six-shooter. As Dude sat up dazedly, Cole tossed the gun towards him.

"Just you and me this time, mister. When your eyes and brain are clear, pick up your gun. I want to see how tough you are."

☆ VIII ☆

FEUD TRAIL'S END

Old Mitch stooped and grabbed the white-handled gun. His growl was like that of an old, cranky grizzly. "Cool off, you two young roosters! There's bin too much of this damn nonsense a'ready. Cole just saved you from bein' drug to death, Dude. And what's this about you and two more gents bushwhackin' Cole?"

Dude Krebbs got to his feet. He wiped the blood and dirt from his bruised face. His left arm was wounded and a trickle of blood came from a bullet nick along his ribs. "I suppose it did look like a trap," he said. "But it wasn't. I rode back here to wait for Cole Griffin. I saw Frank Sorrels ride into the coulee. He must have followed me. Then, before I could send him away, I sighted another rider. It looked like Sid Kilgore. Just as Cole Griffin topped the rim and came down the slope like a bat out of hell, Frank and Sid sighted one another and opened up. They were shooting at each other, not at Cole Griffin. Griffin rode through their line of fire and came at me. We were shooting at each other when he rode me down. I'm no bushwhacker, Griffin. Give me my gun, Mitch."

"And let you shoot a man that just saved you from gittin' your head kicked off? I'll whup you both, directly, if you don't git some sense. It's that yaller-eyed, buckskin-maned. . . ."

"You're talkin' about the girl that's goin' to marry me, Mitch," said Cole hotly.

"Keep her out of it, Mitch," added Dude Krebbs. "That girl is aces. Looks like you win there, Griffin. I'd be a cheap sort of sport if I couldn't wish you both luck. You can give me back my gun, Mitch. I'll need it to side Cole Griffin when he breaks the news to the Kilgores that Hank Griffin's son is marryin' Kate. You and Kate would be wise to hightail it right now, Griffin. Mitch and I will take the news to old Jake."

Mitch was staring hard at Cole. He talked as if he were musing aloud. "Looks like I might have bin wrong about her, all along. There ain't a weak point about either of you gents. You couldn't both be plumb wrong about her. She's got nerve. She's got more nerve than any one of the Kilgores. Dude's right, young Cole. Let me take this hunk of news to that ornery Jake."

"Jake Kilgore knows about it already."

"The hell!" Old Mitch's voice lost its mirth. "Me'n Dude will go along, anyhow. You seen anything of Sammy Lou, Dude?"

"Didn't she stay back at camp?"

"She was gone when I woke up from a leetle dozin' spell. Let's git goin'. No tellin' what she's got into."

They got on their horses. They saw two riderless horses on the slope of the coulee. Frank Sorrels and Sid Kilgore were both dead. The two had fought out a lifelong enmity and died with their boots on and their guns smoking. They laid the dead enemies side by side and covered their faces. Then they rode on toward the Kilgore camp.

Jake looked up, his bleak eyes fixed on old Mitch. A faint, grim smile twitched the bearded corners of his mouth. "Git down. Kate, it looks like you'll have to patch up Cole and Dude. Git off your horse, Mitch. And don't git gun-jumpy. I'll handle Bart an' Sid when they show up. This coffee won't poison you, Mitch, no more than the Block K beef you bin eatin' fer years."

Old Mitch untied a bulky sack from his saddle and produced a jug. He grinned as Kate put her arms around Cole and kissed him. "Reckon you need somethin' stronger'n coffee to stand that, you ornery ol' hellion," he chuckled.

"And you'll need a jolt of forty-rod when you read this." Jake Kilgore set down his cup and brought a piece of folded wrapping paper from his pocket. He handed it to Mitch who took it warily and unfolded it as Jake emptied half the coffee from his tin cup and filled it with whiskey. He read the penciled scrawl and cussed softly. Then he glared at Jake Kilgore.

"How long has this bin goin' on?"

"That's the first I heard of it. Bart wrote that note an' left it in one of my boots sometime durin' the night. It kinda accounts for times that Bart rode off from the ranch alone."

"And fer the times Sammy Lou pulled out and never said where she had bin keepin' herself."

"The note says they're ridin' to the nearest town to find a preacher, and when they come back it'll be too late fer me to do a damn thing about it," said Jake. "Says they'd have got hitched long ago, except fer you ridin' herd on Sammy Lou."

The twinkle came back into old Mitch's eyes. "I knowed Sammy Lou wouldn't run off without leavin' some kind of word."

"I don't know," said Jake Kilgore, "how Frank Sorrels and Sid will take it."

"Frank," said old Mitch, "is dead. So is Sid. They locked horns tonight."

Jake Kilgore took a stiff drink of his coffee and whiskey. Kate knelt beside him and put her arms around him.

"Bart will come back," Kate told her father. "And if you need me, Dad, I'll come back."

Jake Kilgore nodded. He got to his feet and the bleakness was gone from his pale gray eyes. He was looking at old Mitch. "Mitch, I always aimed to tell you, that time when me and Black Jack rode up on you when you was diggin' them five graves. You killed Black Jack and shot my arm off. And after that the grudge between us was too deep to git acrost. I had no part in the shootin' and hangin' of Hank Griffin or the rest! Me and Grant Kilgore split fer keeps before Grant organized what he called them vigilantes. I heard about the hangin' of the five men. I got it outa Black Jack. I made him go along with me to your place to have him tell you I had no part in it. I aimed to do the right thing. You never give me the chance, and I never quit hatin' you fer it. Not till right this minute.

"I was waitin' here to tell Cole Griffin what I just told you. I wanted him and Kate to know, so they'd be happy together. I was tellin' Kate about it when you fellers rode up. Tellin' her I'd swore to kill my half-brother, Grant Kilgore, on sight if ever I cut his sign again. She told me that Cole had killed Grant Kilgore. I hold no grudge ag'in Cole Griffin. Him and Kate will always be welcome at my place."

Old Mitch picked up the wicker-covered demijohn in his left hand. His right was held out toward Jake Kilgore. "I never figgered this time would come, Jake. But now that it's happened, I'll be damned if I ain't almighty glad. It's bin twenty-five years since me and you got drunk together. That was afore me and your other half-brother, Seth, shot 'er out at Fort Benton and started the feud between the Kilgores and us other fellers. And up till now I never admitted it to no man that there was times when it was almighty hard to keep on a-hatin' you. I'd kill a Block K veal and then leave a big keg of good likker where I knowed you'd find it." He turned to Cole. "And that shotgun-trap that you rode into, Cole. Wasn't there a sign nailed to the post gate warnin' the Kilgores and anybody else who come past that there was a scatter-gun trap planted inside the gate?"

"Frank Sorrels tore the sign down right after you put it up," said Kate.

"Frank," said old Mitch, "was ornery. Sammy Lou's got all the good Injun there was in that family. Kate, I bin shore wrong about many things. Sizin' you up wrong was the worst mistake of 'em all. And it's no time now to be askin' favors. But if you and Cole have a weddin' here, if you'd sort of ask Sammy Lou, and make her wear a dress and slippers. . . ."

"I'll dress that youngster up till she'll be the best looking girl there," Kate said. "Dude, will you dance with her?"

"Every dance that I can take away from Bart and Cole Griffin. And I hope it's at Fort Benton. I've paid off my debt there . . . down to the last dollar. Cleared Major Smith's record, to boot. Perhaps I robbed Peter to pay Paul," he added with a faint grin.

"Let's me'n you," said old Mitch to Jake, "take along the jug and gather them cattle. If we sell 'em under the right brands, mebbyso Honest Dude'll take 'em off our hands." Jake Kilgore was about to agree when he saw Mitch pick up the short handled camp shovel. They had two graves to dig.

Kate, fixing strips of bandages and heating hot water, saw Jake and Mitch ride off with the demijohn and the shovel. Tears stung her eyes. She had never loved Sid as a sister should but, now that he was dead, sorrow pinched her heart. She was remembering the tune Cole Griffin had been whistling when he rode up to the Kilgore camp. "The Cowboy's Lament." It had seemed prophetic then, and now a verse of the old trail song came back to her. "For I'm a wild cowboy, and I know I've done wrong. . . ." Kathleen Mavourneen Kilgore was to sing it at sunrise as she stood by the two open graves and tarpaulin wrapped forms. She was destined to sing her songs where the lights shone with extravagant brilliance, standing alone on a raised platform; but Cole was to hear her sing more often as they rode, side by side, around their own beef herds that were bedded down on the wide prairie under a canopy of stars. Because Kate Kilgore loved the lonesomeness of the big cattle country she had been born to, even more than she could love the false gaiety of the crowded cities. Kathleen Mavourneen and Kate. Cole Griffin was marrying them both.

BULLET REQUIEM FOR LEN SIRINGO

(1940)

☆

by W(ALTER) RYERSON JOHNSON

W(alter) Ryerson Johnson was born in Divernon, Illinois. "Pulp fiction," he once commented, was "a never-never land that existed only in the glowing imagination of the writer and the transient 'suspension of disbelief' of the reader. Bigger than life. Adult fairy stories." The impulse toward adventure was already in him as a teenager when, having "listened to trains go banging through town" for so many years, one night he climbed atop one of them and "went west." He traveled more than 20,000 miles across the United States and Canada. After four years at the College of Commerce in the University of Illinois, Johnson took a story-writing class as an elective. The result was "The Squeeze." He sold it to Adventure *where it appeared in the issue dated 3/20/26. His stories after that were published in a wide variety of magazines,* Top-Notch, Western Story Magazine, Cowboy Stories, Short Stories, West, Ace-High Magazine, *and* Louis L'Amour Western Magazine, *among them. He wrote only two Western novels,* South to Sonora *(Samuel Curl, 1946) and* Barb Wire *(Arcadia House, 1947), but they are well worth reading. A collection of his Western stories recently appeared in a trade paperback edition from Barricade Books. In 1939 Johnson created one of his most popular and enduring series characters, Len Siringo, range detective and master of disguises. He wrote twenty stories in all about Siringo in the years 1939–1943. With the exception of his third Siringo story, which appeared in* Ace-High Western Stories, *the others were all published in* Star Western. *The Len Siringo story included here is his fifth published adventure.*

☆ | ☆

HURRY — CALL FOR LEN SIRINGO

Spring roundup was approaching, but old Rip Andrews took time out to ride two hundred and twenty miles to mail a letter. At Creosote Falls he delivered the letter personally into the hands of the stage driver whom he knew and trusted. The letter was enclosed in a homemade envelope, which was wider on one end than the other; but it was constructed of strong brown paper and it was serviceable. It was addressed to:

> *Len Siringo, Town-Tamer*
> *Somewhere West of the 98th Meridian*

Old Rip rode back to Las Flores Valley, fierce triumph showing on his wrinkled saddle-leather face. He stopped at the head of the divide where a sprawling cluster of shacks on Crazy Creek passed for a town. Travel sore, dusty — and dry — he eased his creaking frame from saddle and hitched in front of Big-Foot Jimson's saloon.

Inside he threw down silver on the bar. "Somethin' cold and foamin'," he ordered. Old Rip's voice trembled from awareness of his secret knowledge. He had risked a bullet in the back to mail this letter to Len Siringo. Because of the letter, the pall of dread which hung over Las Flores valley would lift, and honest ranchers again could breathe freely.

The bartender obliged with the beer, looking at old Rip in an oddly expectant sort of way. Four men playing poker at a table near the door suddenly lost interest in their game. They continued betting their cards, but silently, mechanically, each kept more than half an eye on old Rip.

Old Rip — the first cowman of them all to run a brand in Las Flores valley — wasn't aware of the tension his appearance had created. He was still blinking the outside sunlight from his eyes as he hoisted the beer in thirsty anticipation. Then, with the cool brew half way to his lips, he stared violently. His hand trembled, and he whacked his unsalted beer down so hard that he splashed foam across the bar.

Suds Halloran, the barman, was watching him from behind the spigots. "What's the matter with the beer?" he asked sourly. His mouth didn't move as he put the question.

Old Rip's head jutted forward on his corded neck, his eyes bulged wide with disbelief. He raised an unsteady finger. "That there envelope you got stuck in the bar mirror — leave me see it closer."

"Sure," the bartender said. His eyes had a hard gleam as he took the envelope between wet puffy fingers and put it down in front of Rip.

Rip's kindly face, as he stared at the envelope, turned a pasty gray, something near the color of bleached leather. The envelope was a crude affair of brown paper, and it was addressed to —

"Len Siringo, somewhere west of the ninety-eighth," the bartender intoned. "The envelope interest you, Rip?"

Rip's stringy throat muscles jerked as he tried to push out the words. He was remembering that two other men before him had tried to do something about bringing the hell-gunning range detective, Len Siringo, to Las Flores valley, and that both those men were four-foot under now, covered with a gravel blanket in boothill. Both of them with bullets in their backs.

Rip's mouth cracked open as he waved the envelope. "Where'd you get this here?"

"What's it to you?" Suds Halloran wanted to know.

Again the words choked in old Rip Andrews's throat. He was remembering what Big-Foot Jimson had said. Big-Foot liked things the way they were in the valley.

"Len Siringo, the way he pokes his gun into other folks business, would plumb crowd things here," Big-Foot had asserted. And then Lafe McNaughton, who had defiantly penned the first appeal to Len Siringo, had been gunned down from behind. Sugar Scott, the stage driver who had picked Lafe's letter up from the depot here in Crazy Creek, was the second.

"What's it to you, Rip?" the bartender demanded again.

"Huh? Oh, nothin' . . . nothin'," Rip disclaimed. "Curious, that's all, the way a fella is."

"It's been opened," the bartender said. "If you're so curious, you can read it."

There was nothing for Rip to do but play out the cruel game. A single glance behind him had informed him that one of the men at the poker table was Big-Foot Jimson, himself. The men were still playing lazily, betting the cards around, but all of them, old Rip felt, were paying more attention to bullet space between his shoulder blades. Old Rip stood there bracing himself for the bullet, and read the letter that he himself had written and carried two hundred and twenty miles for safe mailing.

"Guard her with your life," he had told Whip Daggert, the stage driver and Rip's lifelong friend. "It means life to more'n one in Las Flores valley."

"It'll be over my dead body that anyone gets it," the driver had promised.

Old Rip wondered now if Whip, too, was crowding gravel with Big-Foot's lead brand on his back. It was a hot day, but cold sweat beaded out on Rip's face as he stood there. The letter was short. It read:

Mister Siringo, we've all heard how you hate gun-rule and injustice worse'n sidewinders. And how you range around puttin' a lead finish to same. Mister Siringo, there is more gun-rule and injustice to the square mile in Las Flores valley than anywhere outside of hell. Mr. Siringo, wherever you are lone-ranging, drop everything for God's sake and get here quick!

The letter was signed boldly, "*Rip Andrews.*" There was a scrawled postscript which said, "*Get here before roundup or it'll be forever too late. Big-Foot Jimson's the biggest owner around here and he'll be the one to appoint the roundup boss, like he done last year. You know what that means. Last year all of us come out of the roundup crippled. This year will be our finish.*"

Suds Halloran was leaning with one fleshy elbow on the bar. "Makes interestin' readin', huh?"

"Yeah," old Rip said hoarsely. He turned away slowly. Something was spinning, spinning inside his head and, for a moment, he felt weak.

The bartender's voice went hard. "Wait a minute, feller. I got orders from the chief to hold anyone who comes in here and asks to see this envelope."

"The hell you preach!" Old Rip wheeled around to face the four at the poker table. "All right, Big-Foot, you got me! What you expect me to do, get on my knees and whine?"

With a single jerk of his hand, old Rip tore open his flannel shirt front. "Now blast, damn you!"

Big-Foot Jimson pushed back from the table, rose heavily to his size-sixteen feet. Most everything else about Big-Foot was large in proportion. Everything except his head. It was small. "Like an apple on a beer barrel," someone had described him once. Big-Foot wasn't as half-witted as he looked, though. At least he packed enough brains in his pint-sized skull to gun-rod Las Flores valley. He had come in late, started in easy, and then, by dint of crookedness and cruelty, he and his gun-hands had spread out from the saloon until now they black-shadowed the whole valley. Big-Foot hitched at his gun-belt. There was a hard gleam in his little eyes as he moved toward Rip with a truculent swagger. In close, he pulled his gun and jabbed it into Rip's stomach. But he didn't trigger lead.

"I'm leavin' you live, you old fool," he said, "on account you're more good to me alive than dead. You know now better'n anybody else in the valley that it's no good tryin' to buck Big-Foot Jimson. Hell, I had a man on your trail from the time you left here to mail the letter." Big-Foot teetered back on his heels, looking very pleased with himself. He jabbed old Rip again with the gun. "Your word carries some weight with the ranchers. I'm dependin' on you to tell 'em it's the smart thing to quit fightin'. It'll make it a mite easier for me . . . and it'll save your life."

"And if we don't fight," old Rip snorted, "you'll end up ownin' the valley, and we'll end up in the dust without even a horse to ride."

"And if you do fight," Big-Foot reminded, "you'll end up the same way . . . except more of you'll be *under* the dust instead of in it."

Rip Andrews's shoulders sagged. "All right," he said wearily. "Looks like you win." Then he bucked up to ask a single tight-lipped question. "Where'd you get hold of my letter?"

"That's easy," Big-Foot said. He tossed a glance at one of the men at the card table. "Cue-ball Baile found it where someone stuck up the stage not more'n three miles outside Creosote Falls. He brung the letter back ahead of you. We been waitin' for you."

"So, Cue-ball *found* the letter, huh?" old Rip snarled. "On Whip Daggert's dead body, I reckon, after Cue-ball blasted him!"

Big-Foot Jimson shrugged.

"Did Cue-ball kill Whip Daggert?" Rip demanded.

Big-Foot screwed his little head around on his ponderous shoulders, made sure there were only his men in the place, then came out into the open. "I dunno if he did or not, Rip. I didn't ask him." He threw an inquiring glance at his flat-faced, bald-headed gunman. "Rip wants to know, did you kill his pal when you took the letter?"

Cue-ball Baile seeped smoke from his tight lips. "Appeared right dead to me, chief."

☆ **II** ☆

ENTER DISHWATER DAN — HELL-COOK

n the days following Rip Andrews's return to the valley, Las Flores ranchers were busy making plans for the annual calf roundup. But gloom hung heavily over the range. The preparations lacked the old fire and fervor which had always characterized roundup time before Big-Foot Jimson starting crowding the territory with his Diamond 88 brand. The Diamond 88 was a thirsty brand. It worked like this: Big-Foot Jim took the trouble to obtain a land grant on a slice of open range on Crazy Creek. Naturally nobody took that kind of ownership seriously. But it became apparent soon enough that it was more than a coincidence that Big-Foot's land grant took in the only range where it was safe to water cattle.

All in a single day, ranchers who had lived in harmony through two generations in the valley, awoke to find barb-wire, and a keep-out sign, and hard-mouthed, cold-eyed strangers barring the way. Big-Foot called a meeting then, gun-guarded by his imported hardcases. Every rancher in the valley was represented. Big-Foot Jim said, "I'm puttin' it to you cold. The barb-wire stays."

"But it's the only strip o' range all up and down the crick where a man can water his critters," old Rip Andrews had blazed. "The rest is all quicksand or too high and rocky. . . ."

"Now ain't that too bad," Big-Foot had cut in. His little mouth in his little head was grinning, and his hulking shoulders were weaving restlessly. "Well, I won't be hard on you, boys. You can use my water. Sure. But at a price!"

So Big-Foot had named his price. And they'd all been paying off ever since. It was extortion, pure and simple. But Big-Foot had the jump on everybody from the first. He had the gunmen, the scruples of a hungry wolf — and he got away with it. Now and then a man reared up, tried to break the stranglehold, and Big-Foot had him gunned down.

It was during roundup that Big-Foot really put on heavy pressure. As the largest rancher in the valley, he was the one who appointed the roundup boss and the tally man. With a combination like that to beat, the ranchers didn't have a chance. Most of them wouldn't be able to weather another roundup that Jimson directed. That was why old Rip had put the postscript to the letter he had written to Len Siringo, urging that free-cruising gunman to come quickly.

The day before the roundup saw the valley ranchers ride in with their remudas from all over the range. Big-Foot supplied the cook, and the chuck wagon groaning under its weight of food and bedding. He supplied the hoodlum wagon too, with its water barrel, fire wood, and branding irons. The men might have been gathering for a funeral to judge from their long faces, muttered salutations. And in a sense, it was a funeral — to independent ranching in Las Flores valley.

That night at supper one of the cowboys sounded off — about Big-Foot's cook. "Last cook was bad enough. This'n's plumb poison!"

Others joined in the denunciation. It wasn't good-natured growling. It was an expression of their hatred of Big-Foot, blown off at one of Big-Foot's menials.

"Right sorry my cook ain't pleasin' you, boys," Big-Foot smirked. "My old one got drunk and took a run-out. This long, sad, cat-whiskered Dishwater Dan come along and he was all there was and I hired him."

The name of Dishwater Dan caught on. Men muttered it back at Big-Foot and the gun-boss said, "Tell you what I'll do. I'll bring him out here on a charge of attempted poisonin' and we'll hold a kangaroo court."

A couple of Big-Foot's gun-uglies went around behind the chuck wagon to get the cook. They went around swaggering — but they came back running so fast they wobbled, the air behind them filled with blue-forked profanity and flung dishwater. One of the men caught a high boot-heel in a piece of loose rope and fell sprawling. The dishwater showered over him. He got up, drenched, and pawing for his gun.

"Hey, you can't kill my cook!" Big-Foot Jim bawled. "Bad as he is, he's better'n none."

The way it turned out, Big-Foot didn't need to worry about his cook. Tonka Glidden was the gunnie who had fallen and got the dishwater bath. Enraged, he jerked his gun clear of leather and started leveling down. Then from the night shadows in back of the chuck wagon sounded a whir and, twirling into sight, glinting in the fire light, came a fearful looking weapon.

"Look out," a stricken voice shouted. "He's throwed the meat-axe!"

The warning wasn't soon enough. The weapon chawked into Tonka Glidden's arm and knocked the six-gun from his grasp. Tonka stood there stunned, afraid to look at his arm. From the force of the blow, he thought it must be half cut off.

Then a hoarse laugh sounded. "Hell, he only throwed the fryin' pan!"

Stalking into the fire light came the cook. He had fire in his eyes and a meat cleaver in his hand.

"Yeah, it's only the fry pan," he said, in a voice like the rumble of dirt on a coffin lid. "But I can follow it up with the meat-axe if I'm urged." He stood there glaring, as though hoping to be urged. The fire light played over his long, angular frame, putting a satanic look on his face. He was only the camp cook, but he had thrown a frying pan and knocked a gun from a man's hand. "Pick up my fry pan," he ordered Tonka Glidden, in that deep, oddly stirring voice.

Tonka took one look at the meat-axe in the cook's hand and another look at his own six-gun where it lay in the dust. The meat-axe was closer than the gun. So Tonka, scowling, picked up the frying pan.

The incident was a welcome diversion to most everybody except Tonka Glidden. It started them talking about cranky cooks they had known. But that was only on the surface. The sullen, angry knowledge remained in the minds of all that, with the morning, Big-Foot Jimson would start his drive for the final extermination of independent ranching in Las Flores valley. The little grass and hide empires which men had created through the years with their own hands and the sweat of their brows were tottering.

Those ranchers weren't gunfighters, and they didn't have the money to hire any. The only gunfighter they knew who would have worked for them for nothing was Len Siringo. Men had been killed trying to reach him, and the letter which Rip Andrews had penned reposed even now on the bar mirror in Big-Foot Jimson's saloon.

It was "early to bed" that night, and before dawn the cowmen roped and saddled and moved out in prearranged groups separating fanwise, each group covering a section of rangeland; and it wasn't long before the tally man, back at camp, was working his pencil stub, making marks on his tally sheet and droning out, "Bar 80, one calf, Box R, one calf. . . ."

Ordinarily the tally man at roundup was chosen for certain well-defined qualifications such as honesty and accuracy with the tallybooks. In this case the tally man was chosen by Big-Foot Jimson because he was Big-Foot's bartender and not very handy on a horse. Big-Foot himself had instructed Suds Halloran in the job the night before. It was going to be a matter of professional pride for the pink-skinned bartender to swing as many extra calves to Big-Foot Jimson with his pencil stub, as Big-Foot's riders could do with a branding iron.

As the morning wore on, Big-Foot Jimson put the squeeze on the other ranchers in a dozen different ways. The tension increased, and tempers shortened to a point where only the presence of Big-Foot's gunners kept it from spilling over. But eventually the gunners weren't enough. Suds Halloran looked at a calf and announced "Rafter 33" and made an entry in his book. The Rafter 33 was Rip Andrews's brand. Rip wasn't riding. He was hugging the fire, watching like a hawk. The men had his calf down, putting the brand to it when suddenly Rip howled.

"Leave me see that brand!"

Tarp Baxter, the roundup boss, happened to be on deck at the moment. Tarp was Big-Foot's man, of course. He had a shifty, half-wild look in his eyes, and his hair shagged long over his ears. He looked like he had just come down from the hills, and there were those who claimed that he had. He wore his gun low, and on what would have been the wrong side for most men. It was generally believed in the valley that on the owlhoot this same Tarp Baxter, roundup boss, was none other than the notorious rustler and killer, Kid Lefty.

The roundup boss snarled at old Rip Andrews, "It's your own Rafter brand, you old fool."

Old Rip had elbowed in close and was down on his knees with his hands on the calf hide. "Sure, it's my brand," he yelled in shrill triumph. "Hair brand!"

"You locoed old. . . ." The roundup boss drew back his fist.

Rip Andrews held his ground. "You run it on me last year, and this time I been waitin'. Yes, sir. Caught you dead to rights. Your men usin' the iron so easy that the hair's burned away without scarrin' the skin."

Rip was so excited by this time that he was letting his tongue run away from him. Disregarding warning glances from some of the other ranchers, he talked on, bringing the whole ugly business into the open. "It's my Rafter 33 brand you've hair-branded on, sure; but the first chance you get, you'll blot it into the Diamond 88, with no man able to prove you've swiped my beef. . . ."

"What you said is fightin' words and you're plumb old enough to know it!" the roundup boss roared. "Pull 'em smokin', or. . . ." Baxter suddenly gave the sign to Tonka Glidden.

The words sobered old Rip with a jerk. He realized all at once that he had given the wolf pack all the encouragement it needed. Another man was going to be weighted down with the blasted lead as an object lesson to the other ranchers. And that man was going to be Rip. . . .

He could see Tonka Glidden's hand go down and rest on his gun-butt. He could see the bald, slick-faced Cue-ball Baile standing there with his death's-head grin.

"You been a thorn in our trigger-fingers long enough," the roundup boss cut in again. "Big-Foot's give you plenty breaks, but you don't appreciate 'em. Come up smokin', you old buzzard. It's your last warnin'."

Old Rip looked helplessly about. And then the roundup boss gave the final sign to Tonka Glidden. Tonka came all the way up with his gun. His eyes blazed and his lips were tight in a cold, relentless line. A few men cried out hoarsely. Those whose eyes remained drawn to the scene observed something which at first they didn't comprehend. They had been looking at a man about to die.

Suddenly, cleaving through the smoke from the branding fire, came a twirling object, glinting in the sun.

One man, more nerveless than the others, called it. "Fryin' pan!"

But it wasn't the frying pan this time. It was the meat-axe.

Once again Tonka Glidden had a gun knocked from his grasp, as the axe smacked into his fist. Tonka knew it was an axe. His arm hung numb from his shoulder. At first he was afraid to look at his hand — afraid there might be blood — and no hand! Then, through glazed eyes, he saw the meat-axe where it had fallen into the fire. There was no blood on the blade. He looked up and saw the cook watching him. That long lank passel of bones called Dishwater Dan was standing just outside the ring of men about the fire. He was puffing fast on another long stogy which jutted, as always, straight out from his steel-trap mouth. In his hand he clutched a short-bladed butcher knife. Glittering eyes shifted back and forth.

"I could just as well've took your hand with the axe if I'd been minded to," he announced in his doom-cracking voice. "And I could just as easy put this knife to your heart. Jerk that axe out of the fire and bring it to me. I got meat to trim for dinner."

Tonka Glidden moved like a man hypnotized. There was something about the deep sonorous tone of the cook's voice, something about the disturbing accuracy of his throw. Or was it accuracy? If a man threw an axe and claimed he could just as well have connected with the blade as with the handle, he was likely bluffing wasn't he? No bluff, though, about the fact that Tonka Glidden had had two guns knocked from his hand. Muttering, glaring bloody murder, Tonka snaked the axe from the fire, handed it to the cook.

☆ **III** ☆

HOT GRUB FOR A KILLER PACK!

*A*fter things had settled down, the roundup boss muttered to anyone who wanted to listen, "Crankiest old pot-walloper I ever see. We got to eat, and he knows it. So he sounds off in a way that would get any other man shot off his feet. Wait till after roundup and watch me take the starch out of him."

With the question of the cook disposed of, the men went on with the branding. The Diamond 88 kept up its reputation for skullduggery. The roundup boss called Tonka Glidden out of hearing of the others and there, in the shadow of the chuck wagon, said, "They're gettin' too independent. Big-Foot'll want this nipped fast. Take Comanche and put him watchin' Harry Zeeland. You hang on to old Rip. Shadow 'em all day if you have to, but don't come back in to supper till you've gunned 'em down. Don't take no damn fool chance. A slug in the back kills just as quick."

"It'll be a pleasure," Tonka said.

So he hunted up a *mestizo* renegade known only as Comanche — and when Harry Zeeland of the SO next rode out on the range, Comanche disappeared soon afterwards. No one missed him, not even Tonka Glidden, because Tonka was already gun-shadowing old Rip Andrews.

Tempers were short that night as men swarmed down on the chuck wagon bellowing for food. They were late in getting in, and they cursed and grumbled, from Big-Foot's gunners on down. All of them except Rip Andrews and Harry Zeeland and the two of Big-Foot's men who had gone gunning for them. The four weren't missed at first, as the men fell on the barbecued steak and beans that Dishwater Dan was putting out.

"It's about time," Big-Foot grumbled, between mouthfuls. "Stick to your pots and pans after this, instead of sashayin' around the range."

Dishwater Dan was touchy, as always. "Can't cook without fire. Had to roundup some mesquite roots."

It wasn't until the men had taken the edge off their hunger that they began to miss Rip Andrews and Harry Zeeland.

"And where's Tonka Glidden?" someone asked.

The question of Tonka was answered first. A distant hoof-drumming welled close.

A horse, hard-ridden, came into the circle of fire light. A man leaped out of saddle. It was Cue-ball Baile. He strode forward, sombrero pushed far back on his bald head. The fire light glinted from his smooth head and face. A little short of the chuck wagon, he stopped.

"Come here," he said harshly to Big-Foot.

"Huh?" Big-Foot grunted, his mouth dripping bean juice. "Come here yourself."

"All right, you asked for it. Thought maybe you'd want it in private. It's about Tonka Glidden. He's dead! One bullet through the heart did the business!"

"The hell!"

"And, chief. . . ."

"Yeah?"

"The bullet wasn't fired from behind."

There was heavy silence while they all digested that one.

"Tonka's gun was out. He'd fired one shot . . . into the ground."

Big-Foot's little head was peering around and his huge shoulders were weaving. "You mean," he jabbered incredulously, "Tonka shot it out with someone and lost? There ain't a man in the valley with guts enough to take on Tonka face to face and, if there was, there wouldn't be anyone fast enough to beat him, unless it was one of my own men." He swept his gunnies with glaring eyes. "Any you wolves havin' a private feud?"

No one knew anything about a feud. But while they were all talking about it, another of Big-Foot's men rode in. He didn't spend time with preliminaries, just moved in and announced, "Somebody killed Comanche."

"Huh?" Big-Foot gasped.

"Yeah. I run across him shot up in Wagon Wheel Canyon."

"One bullet?" Big-Foot asked tightly. "From the front?"

"Yeah. How'd you know? One bullet . . . through the heart."

"And Comanche had his gun out?"

"Yeah. Looked like a showdown fight and Comanche was slow. Didn't much more'n clear leather. He put one shot . . . in the ground."

A buzz of excited talk sprang up. An unseen killer stalking Big-Foot's men! Was it possible? Or was there some more ordinary explanation? A fierce, exultant hope sounded in the guarded words of Las Flores valley ranchers. Uneasiness lay in the words of Big-Foot's gunners, and glaring suspicion was in their eyes.

"Is that all you know?" Big-Foot demanded of the man who had brought the news.

"One other thing, chief. I wasn't goin' to mention it. . . ."

"Why not?"

"Some kind of a joke I reckon. Didn't see no call to worry you."

"Worry me about what?" Big-Foot's voice was getting hoarse.

The man shifted nervously. "There was a note stuck in Comanche's gun barrel."

"All right, what'd it say?"

"Mebbe you better read it."

Big-Foot took the note and read. So did several others who were looking over his shoulder. It said:

> *How do you like the sample, Big-Foot?*
>
> *Len Siringo*

Big-Foot let out a bellow. "What the hell is all this?"

"Someone playin' a joke, chief," the man said quickly. "Couldn't be Len Siringo, on account we stopped the letter to him. I say find Rip Andrews and Harry Zeeland."

Bob Morningside, from the Two Bar I spoke up, "Big-Foot here just admitted that no one from the valley could stand up to Tonka's guns."

"*Somebody* stood up to 'em," Big-Foot said hoarsely. He turned to Tarp Baxter. "You're roundup boss here. You're responsible for deliverin' the carcasses of Rip Andrews and Harry Zeeland to this brandin' fire, dead or alive, by tomorrow mornin'. Now feed your faces everybody." He raised his voice. "You, Dishwater Dan, these beans is cold. Trot me out some hot ones."

"Keep your shirt on," the booming voice of the cook sounded from the direction of the chuck wagon. There was an interval of silence, then suddenly what appeared to be a raving maniac came tearing around the end of the wagon.

It was Dishwater Dan. His sharp elbows and knees were punching air in a way comical to behold. He had lost the black sombrero that he wore, in ludicrous contrast to his soiled apron. He came on, and he didn't stop until he was in the middle of things. He tried to talk, but his jaws must have been clamped so tightly on his half-burned stogy as to be wedged shut. He fluttered his long disjointed fingers and pointed. Then he got he words out — hoarse words.

"I quit! A cook expect some jokes, but not this kind. Dammit, I quit!"

Big-Foot scratched in exasperation at his little round head. "More jokes? What the hell you hollerin' about?"

"I'm hollerin' about quittin'. It's enough to cook for an outfit of killers, without I got to fish dead men out of my bean pot! I quit!"

Big-Foot grabbed the cook and shook him. "Talk sense!"

"Come here and look," Dishwater Dan yelled.

Big-Foot went with him behind the chuck wagon where, over an individual fire, the supper beans simmered in a huge iron caldron. Everyone else went too. It was probably the most interrupted range supper on record.

"Look!" Dishwater Dan proclaimed, with a sweep of his bony hand.

But he didn't have to tell them. They were looking — at the body of a man jack-knifed inside the steaming bean kettle!

Who is it?" Big-Foot demanded.

"How do I know?" Dishwater Dan started tearing off his apron. "I quit!"

The men moved close. Stabbing apprehension cut through the valley ranchers. They were certain that they had discovered either old Rip Andrews or Harry Zeeland. But their fears were misplaced. It was one of Big-Foot Jimson's new gunners that they fished from the caldron, dead from a stab wound.

Big-Foot was scratching his head with both hands now, and eyeing his cook murderously.

"Don't look at me like that," Dishwater Dan shouted. "It's none of my doin's. I'm in the chuck wagon when you holler for beans. I come over here to get 'em and I find this dead man sittin' in 'em. I quit!"

They were all thinking the same thing. Three men dead, and nothing to show for it. Nobody had seen anything or heard anything. But Big-Foot Jimson's men, from the way they rested their hands on gun-butts and scanned the shadows, looked as though they expected to any second. The wind crept in from the prairie, making a dry rustle in the sagebrush — something like the rustling sound a man might have made, with air escaping from his lungs through a stab wound.

"Somethin' is in his mouth," a man muttered.

They looked into the dead man's mouth, and sure enough there was. Piece of paper. Big-Foot himself pried the jaws open and gouged the paper out with his thick finger.

There was writing on the paper. The same scrawled handwriting as on the note which had been found in Comanche's gun barrel.

The note said: *It won't be long, Big-Foot, till someone'll be taking one of these out of your mouth.* It was signed the same as the other, "*Len Siringo.*"

Big-Foot didn't say anything this time. Nobody did. Not right then. They all stood listening, and looking into the shadows. Len Siringo! And all at once the night about them was clothed in menace. It wasn't just reasonable to believe that the crusading gunner could be here. And yet. . . . here were three dead men. And Len Siringo was known as an avenger who came as stealthily as the wind, who struck as ruthlessly as that same blast whipping down from the high ranges.

Again the wind whimpered in from the prairie, and suddenly a man said starkly, "Look!"

They strained their eyes in the darkness, and finally they saw it — a dim shadow shape that rose up from behind a bulking mesquite thicket, lurched forward, and dropped to the ground. A dozen hands slapped at holster leather.

"Wait!" Big-Foot Jimson snapped. "Out of the light everybody. He's only one, and he can't hurt us if we're watchin'. I want this slinker wolf alive, whoever he is."

Down on the ground they waited, gulping air in quick, hard breaths, six-guns tight-gripped and ready. The shadow shape, in erratic fits and starts, came closer.

Big-Foot Jimson let it get well within the outside rim of fire light, then he blared, "Throw up your hands and come in slow. We got you covered."

The shadow shape said nothing at all. It kept coming. Something peculiar about the way it moved. If it was stalking the camp. . . .

"I'm a mangy coyote's uncle!" Big-Foot exploded. "If it ain't my old cook! Drunk as a cockroach!"

Men pulled to their feet, swearing sheepishly, with tension easing off all over the place. The incoming shadow shape went down again, reared up, and staggered forward almost into Big-Foot's arms.

"Here I am, Big-Foot. I come to get my old job back. I walked all day. . . ."

The man became aware of Dishwater Dan standing there with an apron over his arm. "That's the man that got me drunk," he charged excitedly. "That's him, right there. He got me drunk so's he could get my job. I'm the best cook this side of the St. Joe . . . and the soberest when I'm not drinkin'. I want my job back"

"You can have it," Dishwater Dan told him. "Dead men in the beans! I quit!"

"Not until you've done some explainin', you don't," Big-Foot came back at him. "You go to a lot of trouble to get my cook drunk and get his job. You can't cook nohow. And now you want to quit. Sounds loco to me. And three of my men was killed. Are you a spy in my camp, Dishwater Dan? Are you frontin' for the killer? Do some fancy talkin' *pronto,* or get dressed down with lead."

Dishwater Dan stood there, uncertainly, with the cook's apron still draped over his arm. Somehow he had managed to maneuver around until now he stood with his back to the chuck wagon. "I dunno what you're talkin' about," he said. "All I know's I don't like it here and I quit."

Big-Foot's temper, already strained to breaking point, gave way. "On the end of a lead slug you quit!" His hand jerked out toward his gunners. "Weight him down, boys."

There were three close enough in to have clear shooting at the cook. Their hands moved for their guns. Not fast. The way they figured it, there wasn't any danger. They might as well make this last. At the end however they moved fast. That was because the cook went into a crouch suddenly with a yell like a Sioux brave and, bursting through the apron held over his arm, came a fan of saffron gun-flame and roaring lead.

Two of Big-Foot's men never did complete their draw. They caught the first two of the cook's bullets through their hands. The third man, cursing, drew — and died. Died with his gun still unfired. Died from a bullet through the heart in precisely the way that murderous pair, Tonka Glidden and Comanche, had died. By this time men were falling back in all directions and more men had a chance to line on the gun-blasting cook.

"Get that dog!" Big-Foot howled.

They did what they could, close-thundering their lead at that strange crouched figure. They riddled the chuck wagon, sent wood splinters whanging, and a cry went up as they saw Dishwater Dan go down.

"We got him!" Big-Foot raged — and then he raged some more as a fresh burst of firing from the cook brought snarling lead close.

It was plain to them all that this incredible cook had foreseen the possibilities of gun action and had cached another six-gun in the grass behind the wagon wheel. They couldn't stomach his kind of close-in gun-play. They scattered backward, firing wildly. And Dishwater Dan took advantage of the confusion to disappear behind the wagon.

At the same instant Cue-ball Baile and another gunner, urged on by Big-Foot, flanked the wagon on the run, guns blazing. They were met with another Indian whoop of Dishwater Dan's — and with an actual pan of dirty dishwater which caught them both as they rounded the wagon end, drenching them to the skin. The cook threw the dishpan too. Cue-ball Baile went down with the upturned pan ringing his bald head, and his gunning sidekick tripped over him.

A quick thud of hoofs beat through the night as Dishwater Dan slammed into the saddle of a bronc ground-hitched close by, and rode away, holding low and firing back at booming muzzle flares.

☆ IV ☆
LAST STAND OF LAS FLORES COWMEN

*T*he amazing interlude was over as quickly as it had started, except that Big-Foot Jimson was still bellowing around like a wild bull. While the hoof beats of the cook were still drumming through the night, he rounded up half his crew and personally led them in breakneck pursuit. The rest of his men he left behind under direction of his roundup boss, Tarp Baxter.

"And watch that none of the valley men gets big ideas," he pounded out his final instructions. "Keep 'em close gun-herded till we get back with this locoed cook's hide."

The sound of Big-Foot's posse grew dim with distance, and disappeared. Once again there was only the fitful prairie wind, and somewhere far off the disturbing wail of a coyote. The men who were left behind huddled close about the fires, bringing crude first-aid relief to the cook's bullet-punched victims, and trying not to look too often at the three pairs of boots sticking out from under the covering blanket — boots that would walk no more.

"That cook must of gone plumb crazy in the head," Tarp Baxter muttered.

"Shootin' awful straight for a crazy man," a gunner pointed out.

"Hey, what's that white?"

"Where?"

"There on the ground, near the wagon wheel where the cook had his second gun cached."

The man nearest stooped and picked up a piece of paper wedged in under the wheel.

"Looks like another them damn notes!"

He read it aloud, while they listened tensely. "*I'll be back, boys,*" the note said. And, like the others, it was signed "*Len Siringo.*"

The silence was thick enough to cut, until men voiced their fears and their hopes.

"It was Len Siringo. . . ."

". . . masqueradin' as Dishwater Dan!"

"Now I believe everything I've heard about that gunman!"

"How'd he know enough to come here?"

" 'I'll be back,' he said. . . ."

"Yeah, he'll be back," the roundup boss cut in sharply. "Chopped into hamburger by our slugs. With ten men gunnin' for him, how can he get away?"

It was a persuasive argument. Len Siringo was good, but there were limits to even that famous range detective's magic. Black as the brooding night, the future pressed in on the valley ranchers.

Tarp Baxter didn't brighten it any by his next words: "When Big-Foot gets back, there'll be some more of you come in for personal attention," he threatened.

Suddenly they froze, every man of them, as a voice which sounded as though it came from a tomb, called out, "Speakin' of personal attention, you're gettin' it now, Baxter. Don't a man move!"

They recognized that deep resonant voice. It was that of Len Siringo, alias Dishwater Dan. The voice sounded from somewhere close, within the shadows of the chuck wagon. In another moment they were making him out, the glint of fire light on his six-shooter as he stepped a little forward, covering them.

"I . . . I thought. . . ," Tarp Baxter began hoarsely.

"You thought I went away," Len Siringo finished for him. "I did. But not far. I left my bronc and came back. Now you're goin' away, you and Big-Foot and all your gun-scum, away from Las Flores valley forever."

"Big talk," the roundup boss scoffed.

"There's dead men to prove it. It's up to you how many more will have to die."

"What do you mean?"

"I'll show you." He sought out Bob Morningside with his eyes. "Bob, you and the other ranchers and your men start backin' away. After you get separated, detail three men to defang these sidewinders. Detail two more to rummage around in back of my chuck wagon. I got a young arsenal stowed away in there under the beans and bacon. Step lively. Big-Foot'll find my bronc with the empty saddle, and he'll come back here. We'll be waitin' for him."

The ranchers started moving, new hope making their eyes bright and their hearts beat faster.

"You can't get away with it," Tarp Baxter raged, and he looked around at his men. They met his glance stony-eyed. None of them wanted to be the first to jar lead from Len Siringo's gun. So Len held them under his weapon and kept on getting away with it.

For a long minute there it looked as though all the troubles of Las Flores cowmen were wrapped up in one tight bundle, subject to Len Siringo's disposition. While the ranchers were still making the gun transfers, the sound of Big-Foot's returning posse beat loud on the air.

"Make it fast," Len Siringo warned.

They did what they could. But the minutes were against them. Made bold by the nearing of Big-Foot and the other gunnies, one of Tarp Baxter's men dropped to the ground and threw a snap-shot at Len Siringo.

But he made a miscalculation on that. There wasn't any second shot. Not from his gun. On the echoing roar of his first bullet, Len Siringo put in return lead. He silenced the gunner, but the harm was done. Everyone of Tarp Baxter's men who hadn't yet been disarmed pulled guns and started firing.

"Back at 'em, men," Len Siringo roared, and he stood his ground, gun blasting in livid flame, right and left.

The cowmen joined him, their guns crashing with thunder roar on the prairie. They were doing all right too, pushing the hired gunners back, forcing some of them to turn and hunt cover. But the flashing guns and roaring lead acted as a spur to Big-Foot Jimson and his returning pack, of course. They came storming in, leaning low in saddle, shooting as they rode, boring their way through the night with their own bullets. Tarp Baxter's men rallied.

Outnumbered, put at a terrific disadvantage by the mounted gunners, Len Siringo's men fought desperately, but hopelessly.

Siringo ranged among them. Then suddenly his commanding voice rang out. "To your horses. Follow me!"

The lone-ranging trouble-gunner, whose only creed was justice, was the last to fill a saddle. He took the brunt of Big-Foot's attack on his own shoulders, fighting Indian fashion, firing and moving, maneuvering toward the horses. At the last he joined the others in full gallop, retreating into the rangeland darkness. His plan for deliverance of the oppressed ranchers had misfired by such a little.

Big-Foot tarried long enough to organize his scattered forces. By the time he had wrangled horses all around for his men, Len Siringo and the ranchers had made good their escape.

But it was a hollow victory. Bob Morningside expressed the way they all felt. Len Siringo had marshaled them in a greasewood draw to take stock and do some fast planning. "We go away with our hides . . . whatever they're worth!" Bob said. "But you can bet yer shirts Big-Foot won't take this lyin' down."

"They're worth whatever price you put on 'em," Len Siringo said fiercely.

There, under the rangeland stars, the rancher spread his hands palm up in a gesture of helplessness. "What can we do? Any minute now, Big-Foot'll come gunnin' down on us. We're outnumbered two to one, and they can shoot circles around any of us."

"All except Mister Siringo here," a hard-bitten waddy from the Two Bar I chipped in.

"Lots of time," Len said, his deep voice reverberating, "a man can do what he has to do." The quiet confidence of the famous man, the memory of what he had already accomplished alone today, worked wonders in patching their broken spirits. "I can't fight your battles for you," Len continued. "But I can help you fight 'em yourself."

"What about that man in the beans, Mister Siringo?" a man asked curiously.

"He ran across my cache of guns," Len informed him, "and got almighty nosy. It came to a showdown between us, and I did what I had to do. Watched my chance while everyone was eatin' supper."

"Then *you* stuck him in the bean kettle yourself!"

"Yeah."

"And throwed off suspicion by bein' the one to discover him."

"Somethin' like that."

They gazed at the eccentric range detective in open admiration. They had been hearing about his exploits — a hundred different stories — now they were watching him work.

"What about old Rip Andrews and Harry Zeeland?" someone asked quickly.

"I was hangin' close to the roundup boss," Len supplied. "And I heard him hand out dry-gulchin' assignments on those two." He smiled grimly. "That's why supper was a little late. I had to take time out to get Tonka Glidden and Comanche before they got in their bullets to the back."

"Then Rip and Harry are safe?"

"Yeah." Len smiled again. "I give 'em a man-sized chore to do. They're likely tireder tonight than they ever were in their lives." He raised his voice. "If you're all with me on buckin' Big-Foot tonight, call in the men and we'll be movin'."

Now they followed Len without question. Bulking sagebrush, greasewood, and mesquite loomed before them. The reached the high cliffs of Crazy Creek, and turned left, following the canyon rim. Far below they could catch occasional glimpses of the precious water where it was silvered by moon glimmer, that water that couldn't be reached except at one place in the valley. The water that should have been free to all, but which Big-Foot Jimson was doling out at ruinous prices.

They kept on riding until the land started grading down to the creek crossing. They came upon the posts which Big-Foot had sunk to string his barb wire on when he first started levying water tariff. There was no one guarding the drinking privileges. Big-Foot had the ranchers trained now to where they paid off without much prodding.

"It's the water hold-up that beat us," a rancher mumbled. "The rustlin' and such was bad enough, but month in and month out payin' Big-Foot for good, clean water that the Almighty meant to be free to everyone. . . ."

"I been hearin' about it," Len said. He raised his voice to shout across the creek.

An answering hail came back in the darkness.

"That's old Rip!" someone said.

They all splashed across the ford. On the opposite shore they were met enthusiastically by old Rip Andrews and Harry Zeeland.

"Everything under control?" Len asked, enigmatically.

"Yup," old Rip said. "And I'm so dang tired I could sleep on nails."

"Listen," Harry Zeeland cut in.

They listened. Clearly, through the night, they could hear the sounds of approaching horses. The drumming hoofs were like the sound of muffled thunder.

"Big-Foot and his gunnies!"

"Rip," Len Siringo directed, "you and Harry get along. The rest of you come on with me."

Rip Andrews and Harry Zeeland started riding upcreek. Len led the others in a gallop away from the creek. They rode on, with the sound of Big-Foot's riders growing constantly louder.

"Hold your shots," Len warned, "and follow me. Head for the bottom of the draw. On the other side we'll take cover in the rocks. We may as well make our stand there."

Spurred by Big-Foot's approach, they galloped into the draw. The grade leveled off some at the bottom, then climbed abruptly. Presently Len gave the order to drop out of the saddle.

"Scatter out all along the ridge and find cover and watch out for yourselves," he barked.

This draw had been Two Bar I territory since the earliest days of ranching in the valley, and it was more or less familiar ground to them all. From behind the shelter of rocks, they started blazing lead as Big-Foot and his pack rode in below. With guns blazing all along the steep slope, Big-Foot's men had clear targets at last. They fired up at the muzzle flashes, but Big-Foot's bullets splayed against the rounded sides of boulders.

"Pour it into 'em!" came Len Siringo's booming command.

☆ V ☆

BULLETS BUY WATER!

Big-Foot's voice could be heard below, cursing, ordering his men back. They retreated in confusion, and the ranchers took the opportunity to scramble around and better their firing positions. It was lucky they did. Big-Foot brought his army back in a bull-like rush, and they didn't stop at the bottom of the grade this time.

"In among 'em!" Big-Foot howled. "Earn your fightin' money!"

They earned it, all right. Under Big-Foot's bellowing, they came on, shaking the ground under their horses' thudding hoofs. Straight into the ranchers' belching guns they rode, slamming out their own lead. The valley ranchers fought valiantly. With Len Siringo raging among them, an avenging scourge in the night, they laced the darkness with gun-flame. But it was a losing fight. Heavily outnumbered by professional gunners, the ranchers were forced to fall back. They took up other positions higher on the slope, and Big-Foot's men bored on relentlessly.

"Don't leave one of 'em alive," Big-Foot howled.

"I'll bring you back a scalp," Tarp Baxter promised Big-Foot.

The roundup boss jumped from his horse and, in the covering darkness, worked his way through the boulders till he came out behind big Bob Morningside. He had his knife out and ready before the rancher was aware of his danger. But Bob turned, deflecting the first downstroke of the murderous knife with his six-gun barrel. For the next few seconds they were locked in silent, desperate battle. A rock turned under Bob's foot and they went down, his gun spinning from his hand. Tarp Baxter, with a death yell, pitched on top of him, his knife raised high, ready for the kill.

Assistance came, amazingly, from out of the night. Bob Morningside didn't understand it at first. He only knew that Tarp Baxter dropped his knife at the last split second and slumped on the ground. His body rolled over and brought up against a rock twenty feet down slope. Bob Morningside gave silent thanks to whatever gods had directed that bullet. He found his six-gun and got back into the general fight.

He was none too soon. With Len Siringo blasting the night wide open with his famous .45, and the ranchers backing him to the limit, every gun was still needed. They turned the tide there at last.

"Back down, you sons!" Big-Foot's voice blared above the gunfire.

And once again the charging gunnies left the battlefield, retreating to the bottom of the draw.

"They'll be back," a rancher predicted tragically, "and they'll have learned somethin' from their first two trips. We'll never hold 'em off another time."

Men waited desperately for the next charge; but hope was gone. Even the leadership of Len Siringo hadn't been enough. Gun echoes cut off the ranchers' low-pitched talk. But amazingly, the sounds didn't come from where Big-Foot was holding a final confab with his killers. The sound came from high above on the canyon rim — three quick blasts fired straight into the air, judging from the spouting muzzle-flame.

"Big-Foot's got in back of us!" a cowboy gasped. "We'll be wiped out without a chance! We're surrounded!"

"Keep your shirts on," Len said calmly. "I sent one of our own men up there to make them shots in case we could push Big-Foot and his pack down the hill. . . ."

Again Len was interrupted, this time by a booming muffled roar that was like thunder from the sky. And as though a gigantic bolt had struck the earth, they felt the ground beneath them tremble. The echoes rolled away, reverberating in the canyon. White-faced, wide-eyed, the embattled ranchers looked at Len Siringo.

"Listen," Len said.

In the brooding hush of the night they stood there, and as the thunderous echoes rolled away, a new sound came to take their place. A softer roaring, more imminent in its terror, growing louder by the second. Then, striking through the gathering roar, came frightened shouts from Big-Foot's men below — high, piercing, stricken shouts.

"Get ready to receive prisoners," Len said tersely.

The shouts of Big-Foot's men were swallowed suddenly by the roaring which welled close. A wall of water, frothing white in the moonglow, was sweeping in along the ridge, swallowing scrub trees and cabin-size boulders. The water fanned out on the broad floor below, cutting off escape for Big-Foot and his men. There was but one way that they could go, and they took it.

Disorganized, terrified before that rushing wall of water, they dropped their guns and climbed up the ridge slope — straight into the waiting arms of Len Siringo and Las Flores valley ranchers. Two of them didn't make it. The water cut them down. The choked scream of a horse added to the terror. Exhausted, bruised, and lacerated from their scramble for life, Big-Foot and the others were easy game for the waiting ranchers. Under the ranchers' guns they waited — and watched while the wave of water passed on, sucking along the side of the ridge.

Len Siringo chuckled. "I did a little prowlin' around here while I was cookin' for Big-Foot," he explained. "I figure this was the original stream bed for Crazy Creek in old times. All day I had old Rip Andrews and Harry Zeeland busy luggin' dynamite and sinkin' it downcreek, where an explosion would divert the water back into this old channel."

It took them a moment to grasp the importance of his words.

"This is Two Bar I property," someone said.

"And there is no more water in Big-Foot's loop of the creek."

"We're back in the free-water days, men!" Bob Morningside shouted.

"Leave me make a suggestion," Len Siringo urged.

"We're listenin'," voices shouted.

"It would be right cruel to Big-Foot's cows not to let 'em drink. Maybe you better let 'em drink . . . for a price."

"But we can't afford to have Big-Foot in the valley," a cowman made fighting answer. "He'd be crowdin' us out again."

"I said, 'at a price,' " Len answered. "And here's the price: You let Big-Foot's cows drink just this once. In return for which he signs over his Las Flores valley property complete, to be pro-rated among you, 'accordin' to the degrees he's robbed each rancher. He'll still be owin' you money, but this is the best settlement I can think of. How does it sound?"

While they were jubilating, old Rip and Harry Zeeland stumbled in, and their arrival was the signal for more shouting. Somebody put the question then to Len Siringo that had puzzled them all from the first.

"If you didn't get old Rip's letter, how'd you know we so needed help, Mister Siringo?"

Old Rip answered that one himself. "Len's already told me. Whip Daggert, who drives the stage out of Creosote Falls, sent for him. I'd told Whip what was in my letter, of course. After Whip's coach was robbed and Whip come out from under the bullet shock enough to hold a pencil, he wrote a letter of his own to Len tellin' him to come."

The prisoners were trussed up, ready to be delivered to the law. But Big-Foot's little eyes glared defiantly. "Somethin' I'd like to know myself," he said to Len Siringo. "Back at the camp you made the brag that you could sling a meat-axe so it hit with either the blade or the handle. You may be good with your gun Siringo, but me an' the boys think that you was runnin' a windy that time!"

Len's mournful face lit up with a sadly inscrutable smile. He turned to big Bob Morningside. "Did an act of God pry you out from under Tarp Baxter's scalpin' knife a while ago?"

Bob looked startled. "Yeah. I thought it was a stray bullet caught him. Was it you?"

Len pointed downslope. "That's his body caved in ag'in the rock. Take a look, anybody that's interested."

A man worked his way down and lit a match. The body of the renegade roundup boss was revealed with a short-bladed cleaver piercing his neck.

Big-Foot shuddered. "That's plenty. I'm plumb convinced."

Len Siringo sighed. "You'll have to admit, boys, I held off on killin' as long as I could. But you crowded me, and I done what I had to. . . . This is the last blood-shed Las Flores valley will see for a long time to come." And Len spoke the truth.

THE WAGES OF SIN
(1941)

———— ☆ ————

by DAY KEENE

Day Keene was the nom de plume *of Gunard Hjertstedt who was born on the south side of Chicago. In the 1930s he began writing scripts for radio soap operas, first in Chicago and then in Florida. In 1940 he started contributing to pulp magazines specializing in crime and detective fiction. His first stories were published in* Ace G-Man Stories *and* Dime Mystery *and later he graduated to* Black Mask *and* Dime Detective. *He made the transition readily in the early 1950s from the waning magazine markets to writing original paperback crime novels for imprints like Fawcett Gold Medal, Graphic, and Ace Publishing. His one Western novel,* Guns Along the Brazos *(Signet, 1967), came relatively late in his professional career, but it still repays reading. "The Wages of Sin" in* Star Western *(1/41) was the fourth story he published and his first Western story. It would also be his only Western story until nearly the end of the decade when "One More Hill to Hell" appeared in* Fifteen Western Tales *(7/48). In all he would write only a dozen or so magazine stories set in the American West, but a Day Keene Western story has about it the same qualities that are so attractive in his crime stories: a sure sense of forward pacing and narrative momentum. The years spent writing for the radio allowed him to develop to a fine art the skill of telling a story that grips the reader's attention from the very beginning and retains it to the end.*

☆ **I** ☆

GUILTY AS HELL

Purple evening shadows were sliding down on the Big Lost River range to clothe the rainbow-hued obsidian monstrosities of the Crater of the Moon in their somber robes of night, when the jury in the case of the State versus Black Margo came finally to a verdict. For hours the silver-white thunderheads had bombarded the naked peaks with lightning. Now it began to rain.

At first it rained softly. Then in huge splattering drops. But Ah Sin didn't heed it. He stood, a forlorn Chinese boy, six thousand miles from home, his pigtail coiled beneath his wide-brimmed, flat black hat, and his capable yellow hands tucked into the sleeves of his best alpaca coat, staring with approving eyes at the gallows erected at one end of Red Knob's main and only street.

It was an ugly thing of rough pine planks, unpainted. But to Ah Sin it was beautiful. From a sturdy cross-bar a business-like manila rope terminated in a dangling noose, swaying slightly in the wind. A noose that soon would hold a man's struggling body for a few brief seconds before a yawning trap door would drop him down into hell where he belonged, his broken neck twisted grotesquely to one side. It was just the thing for Black Margo!

Ah Sin reached out and patted the wet, rough pine of the trap door. "Nice. Much velly nice. Soon boss-man go much hot place an' Ah Sin go home China."

He continued to stand, despite the rain and the darkening shadows, beaming at the gallows with approving eyes. Lawyer Bender had promised him that if Black Margo hung, his estate would have to pay the wages due Ah Sin. Wages, which as Ah Sin had computed laboriously on the beads of his swanpan during many a night, now amounted to thirty-six "Amelican" months times thirty "Amelican" dollars, a grand total of one thousand and eighty silver dollars — a *grand* total in China, or in Red Knob, for that matter.

That Black Margo would hang was almost certain. Ace Pointdexter of the Silver Horn was giving five to two. Sheriff Wyndott was so certain of the verdict of the jury he had already had the gallows built at which Ah Sin was staring. Ah Sin was so hopeful he had bet the only thing that he had left — the clothes upon his back.

"Nice. Much velly nice," Ah Sin repeated.

He stiffened at a fusillade of shots across the street in the Last Chance Bar, then crouched low in the mud against a possible stray wasp of lead. The shooting ended as suddenly as it began. Ah Sin watched with placid eyes a man stagger through the swinging doors to fall an awkward heap of buzzard bait upon the walk. A cluster of men, Lawyer Bender blowing the smoke from his pistol and Sheriff Wyndott among them, followed.

"No need to worry, Tom," the sheriff opined. "It was a clear case of self defense an' we all seen it." He nudged the body with his foot. "Shoshone plumb asked for it, oratin' off fer Black the way he did." He stuffed a great piece of twist into his mouth. "Well, we kin plant him after the hangin'. We'd best git down to the courthouse. They say the jury's just about comin' in."

Ignoring the body on the walk, the group of men followed the sheriff. Ah Sin continued to crouch in the mud, his sloe eyes thoughtful.

"Amelica velly stlange place," he shook his head. The intricate niceties of American six-gun jurisprudence were difficult for a boy to keep straight in his head.

An excited squeal followed by a torrent of river-junk Chinese brought him to his feet. Low Lung, the only other Chinese boy in Red Knob, was dancing excitedly on the walk and pointing angrily at his pants.

"You makee my pants all dirtly!"

Ah Sin strode toward the high board walk with stiff kneed dignity, the effect marred a trifle by the fact that the mud was ankle deep and he had to stop three times to retrieve his slippers.

"Still my pants," he said stiffly. "Allee soon Boss man hung, len you owe me."

Low Lung smiled craftily. He had been in Red Knob longer than Ah Sin and knew Black Margo's way with juries.

"Hey, you, Sin." Sash Margo stood in the doorway of the Painted Lady wiping froth from his long black mustache with the back of his hand. "Betteh come on along down to the courthouse with me. They say the jury's comin' in."

Reluctantly, with a last fond look at the gallows, Ah Sin joined his boss-man's cousin. Low Lung, he noticed disdainfully, followed a respectful distance behind them. In voice, looks, and size, Sash Margo was as alike his cousin as the southern profile of two black geldings headed north. But there the resemblance stopped. Black was a killer and a bully. Sash was a rabbit who took orders.

"Think they'll dare to hang him?" Sash made conversation.

Ah Sin shrugged politely. "Can do." Sash being the boss-man's cousin, it didn't seem polite to add that he fervently hoped they would. The fall winds on the Big Lost River range were cold — and a China boy's hide was thin.

"Yeah, they kin do it. But they hadn't betteh," Sash warned grimly. "Black is right powerful cross when he's aroused."

Shag Stingo joined them on the courthouse steps.

"Indian Pete ain't heah?" Sash asked.

"Pete's busy." Stingo grinned, exposing tobacco-stained yellow fangs. "An' I jist took me two hundred dollars of thet five to two thet Ace is givin'."

Sash Margo spat moodily. "Hit's a gamble. But I'da done me some bettin' if Black had given me a rightful cut of the money I got comin', 'most four thousand dollars."

Ah Sin sighed. He hadn't seen more than one single dollar at a time since the boss-contractor had paid him off in Ogden. That had been four years before, when the Central Pacific, laying track out of Sacramento with coolie labor, had married the Union Pacific westbound from some heathen "Amelican" place called Omaha. That had been a celebration to remember. He hadn't known quite what it was all about, but it had seemed like a good idea at the time, and Ah Sin had gone mad with the others.

He groaned mentally in remembrance. When he had come to his right Chinese senses, all he had left was a headache his ancestors might have envied, a hazy recollection of a ten-thousand-legged torchlight parade, not unlike the feast of a thousand dragons, an empty whiskey flask, and a picture of a bearded man with friendly eyes whom a bull-voiced freighter had told him was Ulysses S. Grant, the top-boss of all "Amelica." And he had somehow got to Red Knob.

Ah Sin sighed more deeply. He was just a simple Chinese boy a long, long way from home — and China growing farther away every year.

Together the three men entered the crowded courthouse, but the best they could make was the threshold of the building. They stood there as isolated as three skunks in the milling crowd that had come to hear Black Margo sentenced to be hanged.

Ah Sin looked around him, hurt. He was a genial man and thought well of his neighbor's good opinion. He hadn't known the Margo spread for what it was when he had signed on as its cook. But since he had, he meant to stay until he had collected the wages duly worked for and owed him.

The courtroom was small and lighted with flickering yellow lanterns. It smelled of rain-soaked clothes and unwashed bodies, of stale tobacco and of rancid grease. It smelled terrible. Ah Sin breathed deeply in ecstatic bliss. His eyes closed in a nostalgic twinge. With his eyes shut a boy could almost imagine he was home in Canton.

Then the door of the jury room opened. The jurors filed in slowly and took their chairs. Two or three looked flushed and angry. All looked hungry and hollow eyed. They had been out for eighteen hours.

Black Margo was brought in handcuffed to the sheriff. He was a big man with a black mustache and he wore his hair long after fashion of Buffalo Bill, the top boss-hunter of the Union Pacific, whom Ah Sin had admired no little bit at the wedding of the East and West in Ogden.

Shag Stingo took advantage of the natural hunching forward of chairs and scuffing of feet to whisper," If it's guilty, git ready to fork your hosses an' git out of heah. I got our broncs tied right outside. If the boys give Black the rope, they're like to include us in."

Sash Margo nodded, his eyes on the inscrutable faces of the jurors.

Ah Sin turned to Low Lung behind him. "Still my pants," he beamed.

Stingo nudged him into silence. Old Judge Convers was peering at the jury through his tobacco-stained, bushy white whiskers. Then he banged on his desk with his gavel.

"This-yere Superior Court of District Number Forty of this-yere territory is now reconvened. There will be silence in the courtroom." The scuffing of feet and murmur of voices stopped. "You fellows there," he indicated the jury, "have heard the evidence of how the prisoner before the bar has climaxed a long and indecent career of sluice-box robbin', rustlin', stagecoach holdin' uppin', and what-not, by feloniously shootin' down Bud Handler of the Cross Bar O in the Painted Lady dance hall, Bud bein' armed with nothin' more deadly at the time than three aces an' a pair of queens. Has the jury come to a verdict?"

Young Tom McLain, foreman of the Cross Bar O and of the jury as well, stood up. His bronzed face was flushed. "Yes, your honor. We have."

Judge Convers cleared his throat. "You will read the verdict to the court."

Young McLain wiped his lips nervously, looking over at the scowling prisoner, then down at the slip of paper in his hand. An expectant hush filled the courtroom.

"We, the jury in the case of the people versus Black Margo," young McLain read quietly, "hereby find the defendant" — his voice trailed off almost to a whisper — "not guilty."

For a moment there was a shocked silence in the courtroom. Ah Sin felt an unfriendly, appraising pat on the seat of his trousers. Then hell broke loose. The county prosecutor demanded angrily that the jury be polled. Judge Convers banged frantically on his desk. Sheriff Wyndott and his deputies stood unwilling guard over Margo. A bunch of shouting Cross Bar O boys started to storm the sheriff and his prisoner, their poised hands aching just above their gun butts. A few shots were fired into the air.

"Let him alone now, boys," the sheriff shouted them down. "I don't like the verdict no better'n you do. But the law's done took its course."

"It's course, nothin'," Ruby of the Painted Lady shouted. "Black Margo either bought or skeered thet jury. He's guilty as hell!"

The crowd in the courtroom surged forward, stopped as Shag Stingo and Sash Margo, a gun in each hand, stepped into the circle of deputies guarding Black. Black Margo merely grinned.

Twenty minutes later, in front of the sheriff's office, Sheriff Wyndott handed Black Margo back his gun belts. "If I was you, Black," he said curtly, "I think I'd light out of town right sudden."

. Black Margo grinned, wiped the rain from his drooping mustaches, and buckled on his belts. "I aim to." His grin widened. "But I ain't lettin' this skeer me off none. I'll be seein' you."

"I," Sheriff Wyndott said coldly, "wouldn't be none at all surprised." He stepped back in his office and banged the pine door shut.

Sash Margo tugged nervously at his cousin's sleeve. "Let's ride Black."

Stingo had brought their horses from the courthouse hitching rail and a party of

Cross Bar O boys were drifting slowly down the street. Black Margo eyed them coldly, checked his party. "We all heah?"

"All but Indian Pete," Sash told him. "I ain't see him since this noon."

"Pete's busy," Black said curtly. "We'll meet him up the trail a piece." He swung lightly into his saddle, stared at the ancient, sway-backed brood mare still standing at the hitching rail. "Where's Ah Sin?"

"Me here," a small voice answered meekly from behind the broad side of the mare.

"Then git on your hoss," Black ordered. A hatless head showed over the far side of the mare, then a yellow face with wide, black, embarrassed eyes.

"Ah Sin think he go back to lanch," the head announced.

"You'd betteh," Black Margo told him grimly. "I used you fer to bribe thet jury. I had Indian Pete kidnap Tom McLain's twin girl an' boy. Then I sent word to Tom thet if the verdict didn't favor me, thet you an' Pete was aimin' fer to torture the kids, China fashion."

Sash and Stingo howled. Black was a hot one. Ah Sin sighed deeply and swung up into his saddle. His bare, yellow rump smacked emphatically as it made contact with the rain-soaked leather.

Black Margo stared, incredulous. But for the leather thong with which his queue was tied, Ah Sin was as naked as he had been on the day that he was born. Black Margo gulped so hard he almost swallowed his tobacco. "Where the hell are your clothes?" he demanded.

"Me bet 'um," Ah Sin admitted in the same small voice. "Me lost," he added superfluously.

In a growing gale of laughter that left strong men leaning weakly up against the store fronts, the "ondecent" little cavalcade moved up the street.

☆ II ☆

WAYS THAT ARE DARK

For some time the country itself had puzzled him. But Ah Sin had finally solved the problem to his own satisfaction. First the great Lord Buddha had made China, then he had made the United States. Then he had made the Seven Celestial Heavens for good Chinese boys to go to. Then he had made Hell. But when he had finished with the latter task he found he had a lot of molten slag and lava left over so he made the Crater of the Moon country so that bad boys might know just what they could expect.

There was no other explanation. For some seventy-five to eighty miles in a westerly direction and some one hundred and twenty-eight miles running southward down toward the border of the Utah territory, it was hell on earth but for the one green fertile plateau where the Margo hide-out ranch now stood.

Weirdly shaped beasts and birds painted with a lavish hand in every known color of the rainbow stood side by side with agonized, twisted, snake-like formations of obsidian. As far as the eye could see, there were spluttering bubble holes, water holes that had no bottom, still-smoking volcanic craters.

Red Knob was on the edge of it, twenty miles away. Much closer, by nineteen and

a half miles horizontally and almost a half mile vertically was the new spur of the
Union Pacific that ran up from the mainland at Ogden through Preston and Blackfoot
to dead end at Red Knob. In fact the new spur passed through the sheer walls of a
natural canyon a hundred feet directly below the rim of the flat rock on which Ah Sin
sat kneading bread dough in a dish pan.

Ah Sin paused in his kneading to look alternately along the faint trail in the lava
that led to the distant black speck that was Red Knob, and at the smoke belching steel
hog pulling its tail of brawling cattle cars through the canyon below him. His usually
impassive face beamed with delight.

"Can do," he decided.

Perhaps a China boy might get home after all. Kneading the dough industriously
with one hand, he banged noisy time against the tin dishpan with his free hand and
began to sing. It was a song he had picked up from discharged Union soldiers who had
drifted west after the war to earn a stake in the track gangs before starting out to
prospect on their own. The words didn't make good Chinese sense, but he liked the
tune.

> Mine eyes have seen the comin' of the gloly of the Lold,
> He is tlampling out the vintage whe'e the glape of w'ath are sto'ed.
> He hath loosed the fateful lightning of His tellible swift swo'd,
> His tluth is malching on.

Then he came to the part he really liked and he roared it out.

> Gloly! Gloly! Hallelujah! Gloly! Gloly! Hal. . . .

He stopped short at the scuff of a boot heel. Sash Margo stood looking down at
him sarcastically.

"Thet all you got to do, set heah an' sing?" he asked.

Ah Sin rolled back a slipping sleeve of his over-size, borrowed shirt and pointed
one dough-covered finger to his dishpan. "Ah Sin making blead." He studied the other
man's face intently, then nodded his approval. "You look velly nice, long hail. Look
almost twice so much like Black."

Sash Margo squatted down on his haunches beside him. His squinty black eyes
were avaricious. His voice lowered confidentially. "Look. What's on your mind, Ah
Sin? You told me thet ef I let my ha'r grow long, you could put me onto a way of
gittin' my rightful cut from Black." He brushed his long, coarse black hair back from
his forehead. "Well, I've done 'er."

The Chinese studied the other man's face thoughtfully. With his hair worn long
and the same type of black mustache Sash Margo looked as like his cousin as two one
yen black pepper devils ready for the sacrifice fire. "You pay me wages?" Ah Sin
demanded. He calculated swiftly on his fingers. It had been two months and eleven
days since Black Margo had inconsiderately refused to become an estate, and Ah Sin's
wages now stood increased by that much. "You pay me one thousand, one hundred
and fifteen dollal?"

"Shore. Shore I'll pay you," Sash promised. He chuckled. "Black woulda paid you
long ago, but yo're the best cook we ever had, an' he's afraid you'd quit."

"You pay me?" Ah Sin repeated.

"Said I would, didn't I," Sash nodded. "You jist tell me how to git my hands on my rightful share of the money Black has cached an' I'll pay you." He dropped his voice. "But how's it done?"

Ah Sin beamed. "Velly, velly simple."

For a full hour the Chinese talked excitedly, intently, pointing occasionally to Red Knob and occasionally to the recently-built spur of the U. P. below them as he brought home a point of procedure. Sash Margo listened in silence. But when Ah Sin had finished, he got slowly to his feet, a twisted grin on his lips.

"Why you Celestial son-of-a-witch!" he admired. "You got somethin' thar; you shore have." His slouched shoulders straightened and his perspiring palms caressed the black butts of his low-slung Colts as he stared at the rambling ranch house and corrals that comprised the Margo spread. "Yes, siree! Why I'd be the head snortin' bull o' the hull shebang."

Ah Sin looked up intently. "Will do?"

"Will do," Sash Margo agreed. His face clouded in an experimental imitation of Black Margo's scowl. Then he grinned. "Schucks. Why, I'd be a fool if I didn't Ah Sin, you're a smart Chink!"

Ah Sin sighed audibly in relief. It might just be that a China boy could not only regain his face but get home after all. He chalked down a mental reminder, however, to burn a few joss sticks to the gods in the morning in respectful petition that the top "Amelican" boss-man be restrained from holding any more torchlight processions not unlike the feast of a thousand dragons until a boy could get safely on a boat with his wages in his pocket.

The Margo home spread complement of riders wasn't large. Just Black Margo himself, his cousin Sash, Shag Stingo, and Indian Pete. Black could always pick up extra gun-rannies whenever they were needed.

Ah Sin served supper in silence, as usual. And, as usual, the four men ate in silence until the heaping platters of biscuits, fried venison, baked beans, and huge slabs of dried apple pie had disappeared. Then Black Margo uncorked a fresh bottle of whiskey and washed down the last of his supper with half a pint of forty-rod.

"Think we betteh take them spring beeves into Red Knob in the mornin'," he announced.

Shag Stingo nodded. "Mout as well. I got a few bets to collect from Ace, too, on account o' you wasn't hanged."

Indian Pete merely grunted and held out his hand for the bottle.

"You think it's safe fer you to show up in Red Knob so soon?" Sash Margo asked meekly.

Black Margo scowled his contempt. "They ain't got ary a thing again' me down thar. The law acquitted me free an' square. An' ain't nothin' to worry fer 'bout them beeves. I ain't never sold a blotted brand in Red Knob, an' you know it."

The others nodded. Black Margo was a thief, but he wasn't a fool. Changed and blotted brands had hung too many men. He was content with selling the drop of the cattle he rustled around Red Knob. Besides, rustling was just a side line. There were too many gold-laden stages pounding down the trails from Coeur d'Alene country to allow a man to risk his neck for pennies when there were double eagles to be had for the taking.

Stingo got out a greasy pack of cards for their evening game.

"Cyards?" he asked as was a nightly ritual.

"Mout play a few hands," Black agreed.

Indian Pete grunted and swept the dishes from in front of him. "Dealer's choice."

Ah Sin cleared the dishes from the table, then came back ostensibly to wipe the table and sweep the crumbs and leavings from the floor.

"You playin', Sash?" Black demanded.

"Hain't got no money," Sash poor-mouthed. "You don't give me nowhere near a square cut, nohow. An' what you do give me," he added bitterly, "you win right back from me at cyards."

His cousin hitched his gun belt slightly and grinned across the table at him. "Well, you know what you kin do if you don't like it."

"I've been studyin' on it," Sash admitted. "You don't need me nohow. Might be I mean to leave heah."

"Jist talkin'?" Black demanded.

Sash Margo shook his head. "Been studyin' on it fer some time. If you'll give me my rightful cut of what you've been savin' fer me in your belt, might be I'd ride the cyars out from Red Knob in the mornin'. Might be I'll sashay south some down Virginia City way."

The two other men looked mildly curious. Black Margo grinned. "Sashay ahead."

"But, Black," Sash Margo protested, "you know that hain't fair. When we four joined up, you promised me a four-way cut."

His cousin eyed him coldly, his thumbs hooked lightly in his slanted gun belts. "Want to take on about it?"

"No," Sash admitted, "I don't."

"But now you've spoken your piece," Black told him, "you're leavin' heah anyhow. You help us haze those beeves down to Red Knob in the mornin', and mout be I'll give you a piece of money to ride the cyars."

He leaned across the table and deliberately slapped the other man across the lips. "You've been gittin' too big for your boots fer some time now. But wearin' your hair an' mustache to look like me don't make you the man I am. You know what I'd do to a man who did to me what I jist did to you. I'd shoot him daid, thet's what I'd do."

Sash Margo's lips twitched but he said nothing. He could afford to wait.

"Dang!" Shag Shinto exploded mildly his eyes searching the floor around him. "There's one of these yere cyards is missin'." He tore up the deck and threw it on the floor. "Git me a fresh pack outen my war sack, Sin."

"I get," Sin beamed.

He returned with an unopened packet and placed it at Stingo's elbow. The squat, yellow-fanged outlaw broke the seal with his thumb nail, slid out the cards, and slapped them on the table. "Shuffle an' cut for deal," he said.

"Deal," Indian Pete grunted.

"Table stakes, dealer's choice?" Stingo asked as he took a handful of gold pieces from his money belt and stacked them on the table before him.

Black nodded, yawned.

As card players, the three men were about evenly matched. And while the nightly stakes ran high, at the end of the season the runs of luck usually evened up and the game was little more expensive on their individual purses than if they had been playing penny ante. In the present run of luck, however, Shag Stingo was some few thousands ahead and Ah Sin had taken that into careful consideration before he had steamed open the seal on the pack of cards in Stingo's saddle bag and added two extraneous aces after painstakingly stacking the deck. He breathed a deep sigh of relief as Indian Pete waved the cut for deal away and Stingo picked up the cards.

His lemon-tinted face impassive, Ah Sin wiped an imaginary crumb from the table in front of Pete. "Mist' Stingo pletty lucky, uh?" he prodded. "Mebbe so play bette' pokel as you."

The Indian, scowling, said nothing.

"Straight poker," Stingo announced. "You kin bet what you got on the table. Ten dollar ante."

"Deal me out," Sash said. He got up from the table and sat in a corner of the room reading, or pretending to read, a six-month-old Boston paper.

Stingo anted a gold piece, dealt the three hands swiftly, and put the balance of the deck down on the table.

"Jacks or betteh to open."

"Open," Indian Pete nodded, his heavy-lidded eyes narrowing slightly. He took five of the ten-dollar gold pieces in front of him and stacked them in the center of the table. "Open for fifty dollars."

Black Margo tossed in his cards and took another pull at the bottle. "Too steep for me without a pair."

Shag Stingo grinned at the Indian. "Looks like we gotten us a tanglin' hand yere, Pete. I'll stay an' up you fifty more."

The Indian pushed in five more gold pieces without comment.

Stingo picked up the deck. "Cyards?" The Indian discarded a card. "One." He rapped the table once.

"An', two to the dealer," Stingo announced. He dealt the cards and looked at his hand. "Check to the one cyard draw."

"Fifty dollars," the Indian bet.

Shag Stingo grinned. "An' up you a hundred, Pete. You walked right into thet one."

The Indian scowled. "You're bluffin'." He saw the raise and upped it fifty more. Stingo saw the raise and raised again. The Indian called. "All red," he exposed his cards.

"No good," Stingo grinned. "I got me four aces."

The Indian scowled. "Nice hand," was Black's comment.

Then it happened. Ah Sin, still wiping the far edge of the table, reached over in front of Stingo to mop up one last crumb and somehow got his long sleeve caught in the unused portion of the deck. It turned face up, exposing two more aces.

Shag Stingo's face turned white. "Now listen Pete," he began. "I never. . . ." His hand streaked for his gun.

The two gunshots rocked the cabin. Ah Sin crouched on the floor in fear. He was afraid both men hadn't died. But they had. Indian Pete had gotten Stingo squarely through his left nipple as Stingo's gun swept up to send a heavy slug crashing through the half-breed's temple.

Black sat looking at the cards. "Now what the hell do you know 'bout that?" he said. "No wonder Shag's been winnin'."

Ah Sin got up wide-eyed off the floor, looked from one dead gunman to the other. "He cheat?" he asked.

"Looks like," Black said tersely. "Damn. They was both prime top hands an' this leaves me short as hell." As he spoke, he gathered up the gold pieces from the table, then felt under each of the dead men's shirts and removed their money belts.

"I think," Sash protested from his corner, "thet I should have a cut of thet thar money, Black."

The outlaw snorted. "The hell you say." He jerked his head toward the door. "You an' Sin git these bodies out of heah. Drop 'em in one of them bubble holes back of the corral. I'll pick me up a couple of more gun-rannies in Red Knob in the mornin'."

Ah Sin approached the bodies with obvious distaste. "But me aflaid of blood," he protested. Then offered tentatively, "Mebbe so you pay me wages I no be aflaid no more."

The outlaw kicked at him savagely and caught him in the stomach. The Chinese boy's face went gray, but he said nothing. His expression was as impassive as ever.

"I said, drop 'em in a bubble hole," Black ordered curtly. He turned to Sash. "Then you git back in heah an' git some sleep. We're proddin' them spring beeves down to Red Knob jist the same come mornin'."

Sash Margo picked up Stingo's feet and Ah Sin took his arms. Neither man spoke until they were safely back of the corral and Shag Stingo's body had been heaved into a steaming hole to bubble up grotesquely several times then disappear forever in the boiling mass.

"Hell an' Maria, but thet was slick," Sash admired. "Do you reckon I kin git Black thet easy, come tomorrow? Shore it's all set?"

Ah Sin nodded solemnly. He was a peaceful China boy and he was sick of blood and bloodshed.

"Can do," he said through gray lips. "You keep plomise? You pay me back-up wages?"

"Sure, sure I'll pay you," Sash Margo promised. "Hell. With what he just tooken off of Pete an' Shag, Black must have twenty, thirty thousand dollars cached away. C'mon. Let's git back fer thet other body."

Ah Sin followed slowly, his eyes on a brawling white yearling inside of the stock corral. Perhaps Sash would pay him. And again, perhaps he might not. It might be well for a helpless China boy a long, long way from home to have a little insurance. As soon as he had helped Sash dispose of the other body and the hide-out ranch had settled down for the night, he'd burn a few joss sticks to the gods and ask their advice on the matter.

☆ III ☆

TRICKS THAT ARE VAIN

*I*t was early evening when Black Margo, riding point, prodded the fifty foot-sore beeves that gave him a claim to being a legitimate ranchman into the railroad corral in Red Knob. The lava trail had cut their hoofs and dew claws to bloody shreds as it always did, but that didn't matter to him. They were merely his yearly bid for the bedraggled cloak of respectability.

Sash Margo, riding drag, slipped his neck cloth from his mouth and swung the corral gate shut. "Ain't forgittin' you promised me a piece of money for to ride the cyars on, have you, Black?"

His cousin shook his head. "You'll git your cut." He coughed. "But we'd best git up to the Silver Horn an' irrigate this dust."

The two men swaggered side by side up the almost deserted boardwalk. They looked like a man and his scarecrow. Black had shed his leather chaps and his well-cut gabardine trousers fit snugly into his boot tops. His shirt was silk. Anyone who knew hats could tell at a glance the high-crowned, broad-brimmed beaver cocked over one scowling eye had cost no less than five double eagles laid down on the barrel head. His gun belts were embossed Spanish leather, his Colts pearl-handled. Sash looked the poor and meek relation that he was. His boots were run over and patched. He still wore his rock-snagged chaps and his pants were coarse, rough homespun. His black alpaca sweat-stained shirt looked like it hadn't been washed in a year. His hat was cheap and so was the single gun belt and the serviceable black-butted Colt that bumped his thigh.

"You ain't aimin' to come back?" Black asked.

"Nope. Ain't aimin'," Sash said briefly.

"Thet's good," was Black's curt comment. "You always was a yellow-bellied no 'count."

Sheriff Wyndott stepped out of his office as they passed. "Lookin' fer trouble, Black?" he asked.

The outlaw shook his head. "Nope. Not ary. Jist come in to sell my beeves. Any objections?"

"Not if they're your beeves," the sheriff told him pointedly.

Black Margo grinned, took off his buckskin gloves, and tucked them in his belt. "Take a look at 'em, if you want. I'll eat any of 'em, hide an' all, thet you find a blotted brand on."

The sheriff nodded curtly. "Stay out of trouble, Black. It's a good thing none of the Cross Bar O boys is in town t'day. They don't feel kindly toward you after thet trick you pulled on Tom."

"His kids weren't hurt none, were they?" Margo scowled.

Sheriff Wyndott shook his head. "No. But you're like to be, if you pull another stunt like that."

Black Margo's scowl deepened. "You're talkin' pretty big fer a tin-star sheriff, Jim." His scowl faded and he laughed. "But you've done the community some good. You've skeered Sash heah into leavin'. He's goin' out t'night on the cyars."

The outlaw turned his back deliberately and strode on. Sash followed admiringly. He might, he admitted grudgingly to himself, step into his cousin's boots, but he would never be the man that Black was. Sash heard the night combination coach and cattle train whistle at the loading platform while he was downing his third drink. He tugged at his cousin's sleeve.

"Might be you'd give me my cut of thet money now, Black. The cyars is fixin' to leave.

Black Margo turned from the young and admiring ranny to whom he had been talking. "Might be," he scowled. "But I ain't aimin' to. If you're goin', git goin'. You kin ride a box car jist as easy as you kin the plush."

"But, Black. . . ," his cousin protested.

The other man slapped him smartly across the face with his gloves, then pushed him, still half blinded, sprawling toward the door. "Git goin', you nit-witted, lob-sided saddle-bum afore I smoke you out. Right heah an' now I disclaim all kinship to you. Now, git. You kin go to Virginia City, or you kin go to hell, for all I care."

Sash crawled slowly to the door while the long bar rocked with laughter. His hand itched for his gun-butt, but he knew before he touched it that he would be dead. Then he remembered Ah Sin's words of caution served with the morning flapjacks. He could afford to wait.

"All right. I'm goin'," he said. "An' I ain't never comin' back heah no more."

Black Margo grinned and tossed several four-bit pieces at his feet. "Never is a long time, cousin. Might be thet you'll need a few bits to eat on."

Sash Margo ignored the coins and stumbled out the door, raucous laughter trailing after him like a can tied to the tail of a hound. When he reached the loading platform, the train had begun to move. He stabbed inexpertly at the open door of the first empty car that passed and pulled himself inside. For a moment he crouched, panting in the darkness. Then he remembered what Ah Sin had told him, and he stood erect in the open doorway.

Sheriff Wyndott, sitting on the top rail of the stock corral, waved, not unfriendly, as the train pulled past him. Sash waved back at him.

The track passed not five hundred feet from the Silver Horn and Black Margo and several admiring cronies were standing in the door to watch the train go by. Black cupped his hands and yelled derisively. "When you git down to Utah territory, why don't you turn Mormon, Sash. Might be you could git three or four wives to support you in the style an' comfort thet I have."

Then the first of the foothills rising steeply behind the Painted Lady shut off the Silver Horn. Sash had one quick glimpse of the still-standing, unused gallows before Red Knob faded back into the night. He sat down in the doorway of the car to wait. Half of Red Knob had seen him leave. All of Red Knob would know within the next half hour that he was gone, headed south with the train's first stop a hundred miles away at Blackfoot. He grinned admiringly.

"Dawgone if thet China boy ain't smart, at thet." He considered the matter. "Yes, sir. Might be I might give him some of the wages due him, after all."

He settled back for the long, tedious, upgrade ride. In the distance, black against the early moon, he could see a dark mass he knew was the sheer side of the canyon that marked the Margo spread. He would have to be careful getting off. The canyon was narrow; the rock was hard; one misstep would mean death.

Forty minutes later, his breath whistling between his teeth, he stood in the doorway of the car and eyed the sheer wall sliding by, rapidly increasing speed as the panting engine made the grade and started down the other side. Then he saw a yellow light atop the cliff. That was the lantern that Ah Sin had promised.

He shut his eyes, took a deep breath, and jumped. He landed running awkwardly in his high-heeled boots. For a few wild paces he kept his balance then one of his heels twisted on a piece of rock and he fell face forward toward the canyon wall, shielding his head with his arms. When he looked up, the red light of the caboose was rounding the farthest bend and the click of the rail joints was growing faint; then it faded away entirely. He sat up and felt himself all over cautiously. There were no bones broken.

"You all light?" Ah Sin's voice reached him faintly.

"All right," he called. "Let down thet rope, now, Ah Sin." He looked up the sheer canyon wall and shuddered. "An' for God's sake hang on tight to it."

A moment later, a long, spliced rope flicked snake-like down the cliff and dangled at his feet. Sash Margo tied it securely underneath his arms, tugged at it tentatively. The whole Margo spread was his if he had nerve enough to claim it. He gritted his teeth against his fear, sought a starting handhold in the rock. "I'm startin' up," he called. "You keep a strain against the rope."

Ah Sin didn't answer. Instead he chirruped and Sash Margo felt himself being drawn up steadily and easily without the slightest effort on his part.

"I make imployvement," Ah Sin beamed when Sash had reached the top of the canyon wall and hung dangling over space. "I take hay pulley out of barn and cow pony out of collal. I make noise like kiss, he pull like hell."

The rope cutting him in two, Sash Margo nodded. "Damn smart, Ah Sin. But git me in from heah."

"You pay me wages?"

"Shore, shore," Sash grunted. "Jist as soon as I kill Black."

Ah Sin tugged the big man up onto the rock, chirruped to the pony who eased the strain so the rope could be untied.

Sash Margo just lay on the rock breathing hard. Then he got to his feet and walked shakily to the ranch house. For hours, Sash Margo sat drinking steadily, practicing Black Margo's scowl, and roaring commands at the delighted Ah Sin. It was he who heard the hoof-beats first. He took Black Margo's carbine from the wall and handed it to Sash.

"He come, now."

Sash Margo listened. "It's him all right. An' Black's drunk as a fool the way he's ridin'." He paused in fear. "But how do we know thet he's alone."

"He be 'lone," Ah Sin promised. "Don't be 'flaid now."

They crouched in the shadow of the porch until the lone rider came thundering up the trail. Sash, the carbine leveled across the rail, waited until the panting rider had flung himself from his sweat-lathered horse. Then all he said was, "Black!"

Black Margo stopped.

"Sash!" he gasped. Then he saw the leveled carbine in the moonlight. "No! Wait! I. . . ."

The carbine roared, flame streaked through the moonlight, and a heavy slug slapped soddenly at Margo's forehead. The outlaw fell slowly forward. Sash shot him four times more as he fell.

The Chinese boy kicked the dead man's expensive beaver hat away from the rapidly spreading pool of blood. Then he began to undress the dead man carefully.

"Ah Sin peaceful man," he explained. "No likee blood and boom-boom."

The dead man's cousin pushed him roughly to one side and stripped the corpse. Then he dressed in Black Margo's clothes, his whole nature changing with each garment that he donned. The whining, sniveling rabbit had become the mountain lion. "Hell," he stormed, tugging Black's expensive beaver down over his scowling eyes, "this hain't all his money. Black's got more'n this cached around."

"We find," Ah Sin soothed him patiently. "But better so we put old clothes an' dead boss-man down in bubble hole."

Together they carried the dead outlaw to the same hole of molten lava that already held two of his riders and watched the body bubble up and then sink out of sight. Ah Sin brushed his hands together lightly. It was time for a boy to start for China.

"You pay me wages now?" he asked.

"Wait, wait," Sash Margo temporized. "Let's find the rest of Black's money first. Hell, you ain't goin' nowhere."

Ah Sin sighed deeply. That was what he was beginning to be afraid of.

They searched for hours. It was almost dawn when Ah Sin found it. It was behind a loose stone in the fireplace. There was thirty thousand dollars in gold. Sash Margo dumped it on the table. He ran his fingers through it like a miser. He counted it in glittering piles. Then he added to it all but a few hundred dollars of the money that Black had been carrying in his belt and returned the whole to its hiding place behind the stone.

Ah Sin watched him apprehensively. "You no pay me wages yet," he reminded.

"Will you quit botherin' me, you pigtailed, yelluh heathen," he roared. "I'll pay you your wages when I git damn' good an' ready."

"Lat's," Ah Sin admitted, "what I aflaid of." He turned and walked out of the room to burn a few more joss sticks.

When a China boy was young and simple, and guileless, it was fortunate that he had gods to turn to — practical gods who advised a boy that, while to trust may be divine, it's nice to have insurance.

☆ IV ☆

THE HEATHEN CHINEE IS PECULIAR

*D*awn was breaking, gray and obscene among the weird creations of the Crater of the Moon when Sash Margo came out of his stupor. His throat was parched and his head ached dully. He listened and could hear Ah Sin's untroubled snores from the lean-to.

His eyes as red as Black's had ever been, Sash strode to the door and looked out. Black's twisted scowl came naturally to his brow. All that he saw was his. He wasn't Sash Margo the rabbit any more. He was Black Margo, whose reputation was enough for most men. By coasting on that reputation, he could live for years without ever raising a finger. He wondered idly why Black had been riding so fast, yawned, then stretched.

"Thet's good. Hold thet picture, Black!" Sheriff Wyndott's voice warned from out of the gray.

Sash shook his head to clear it, started to lower his arms. The sharp crack of a gun made the voice official. A slug bit into the door jamb just above his head.

"You ain't hearin' things, Black," Sheriff Wyndott warned. "There's at least thirty of us out heah. Me an' my deputies, an' 'bout twenty of the Cross Bar O boys, includin' Tom McLain."

Cold sweat beaded his forehead. "What . . . what you boys want of me?"

"No use you playin' dumb, Black," Tom McLain's voice called out coldly. "We got you dead to rights this time. Betteh tell them gun-rannies of yours to start smokin' if they're goin' to."

Sash started to say that they were dead, then changed it to they'd gone away.

"So the rats run out on you, eh, Black?" the sheriff taunted. "I thought you were smart. Hell. You're nothin' but a saddle-bum!"

Voices began to materialize into shadowy gray figures that in turn grew into grim-faced, hard-eyed men. Sheriff Wyndott lifted Black Margo's pearl-handled Colts from their embossed holsters. Then he called. "It's all right, boys. I got his teeth." He handcuffed the man in the doorway to his wrist and dragged him back into the cabin. "I thought shore thet you'd light out fer parts unknown after I called you in the Silver Horn, an' you had to shoot your way out of town."

Ah Sin appeared, shining-faced and excited in the doorway. "You allee come fo' bleakfast?" he demanded.

Lawyer Bender chuckled. "Hell, no, Ah Sin. We come to make you a present. Looks like you're goin' to collect from Black's estate, after all."

"Bettee so you stay fo' bleakfast," he persisted. "Got coffee made an' flapjackee mixed. Quick fly bacon."

"By gum if he ain't!" a Cross Bar O rider called from the cook shed lean-to. "He's got enough flapjack batter mixed up here for to feed an army!"

No one thought to ask Ah Sin how he had happened to prepare so much. They were soon all too busy eating. All but Sash Margo. He sat at Black's table, handcuffed to the sheriff's wrist until the sheriff and the boys had had their fill. They talked constantly of hanging. But for what? Sash Margo's rat-like mind ferreted into every corner and could find no out. The law had acquitted Black of the murder of Bud Handler. Sheriff Wyndott admitted openly that he, Black, hadn't killed anyone in Red Knob on the day before. Sash strove desperately to catch the eyes of Ah Sin. But Ah Sin was always busy.

"Well, what with the election celebration t'night an' all, we'd best git goin'." Sheriff Wyndott rose from the table, dragging Sash by one hand while the wiped his mustache with the other. The sheriff ran his free hand around his prisoner's middle and pulled out Black Margo's money belt. "How much you say thet this skonk owes you, Sin?"

"With today, one thousand, one hunled an' sixteen dolla," Ah Sin computed.

"That's a shame." The sheriff counted the money in the belt. "There ain't but a leetle over four hundred in his belt." He tossed it to Ah Sin. "But you take thet, an' the hull blamed ranch heah fer the balance if you want it."

Ah Sin eyes grew wide. "Me take hull lanch?" he gasped.

"Sure. An' every daggone thing in it," the sheriff grinned. "Black ain't got no heirs an' there's someone got to collect." He nudged his prisoner up on a waiting horse. "Up you go, Black. Time to git along to thet gallows I had built fer you some months ago."

"But what . . . what are you hangin' me fer?" Sash panted. "I ain't done nothin'."

"No?" Tom McLain of the Cross Bar O said coldly. He took a fresh steer hide from a pack horse and spread it on the ground. The unmistakable Cross Bar O brand had been burned deeply into the white hair and hide with a running iron. McLain looked up at the prisoner on the horse. "There was four like this in thet bunch of beeves thet you brung down. An' mebbe you are so tough thet we cain't hang you fer murder, Black, but we shore as shootin' kin hang you for rustlin' your neighbor's cows."

Sash tried to speak and couldn't. He looked frantically at Ah Sin. Ah Sin beamed back cheerfully.

"But I tell you this is a frame, boys," Sash managed to stammer finally. "I tell you I ain't Black Margo. I'm his cousin, Sash."

"Oh hesh your mouth," the sheriff said. "You cain't pull thet dodge on us. Come on. Git ridin', boys."

"You tell 'em, you tell 'em, Sin," Sash Margo panted, wild with fear. "You tell 'em who I am."

Ah Sin looked at him, his face inscrutable. "Why you Black Ma'go. Sash Ma'go he go away on tlain."

"I seen him myself," the sheriff said. He prodded his prisoner's horse and roweled his own. "C'mon. Hit your last trail, Black. You're long overdue fer hangin'."

The little procession filed slowly out of the ranch yard. Only Lawyer Bender stayed behind. "Best come on down to Red Knob, Sin," he tempted. "We're goin' to have big doin's. Goin' to hang Black this afternoon an' celebrate Grant gittin' a second term t'night."

Ah Sin's eyes grew wide. "Mist' Glant . . . you have big tolch-light palade?"

"Yes, I reckon we'll have a torch-light parade," the lawyer chuckled. "A lot of us old Army men feel mighty proud to think thet. . . ." But he was talking to air. Ah Sin had already gone to saddle his trusty pony.

He would, Ah Sin decided, just take the four hundred dollars with him. That should be enough for a poor China boy to celebrate respectfully. And perhaps, he decided, as he fumbled a saddle awkwardly on the bored and patient pony, he wouldn't go back to China at all. A boy with as much money as he had behind the loose stone in the fireplace could send for a beautiful picture bride and settle right down here on the lovely "lanch" that Black Margo's estate had given him. He could raise cows that didn't give milk and a lot of fat "Chinese-Melican" boys to march in torch-light parades for nice, bearded "Mist' Glant."

For after all, he forced himself to admit, there were some features of the feast of the thousand dragons that admittedly were better than a "Mist' Glant tolch-light palade." But there had never been a feast of the thousand dragons in all of China that had been so profitable to a poor China boy six thousand miles from home, as the last torch-light parade in which he had marched in Ogden, and from which he'd awakened in Red Knob. Why, there was no telling what might happen to a boy.

"Nice, velly nice," he nodded solemnly. He swung his leg up and hit leather, winced slightly as the bridle reins cut into the palm of his hand where the running iron had burned it, and jogged, smiling, out of the corral to join Lawyer Bender.

"Nice, velly nice," he repeated. "But velly stlange countly, lis Amelica!"

FAITHFULLY, JUDITH

(1942)

★

by ERNEST HAYCOX

Ernest Haycox during his lifetime was considered the dean among authors of Western fiction. When the Western Writers of America was first organized in 1953, what became the Golden Spur Award for outstanding achievement in writing Western fiction was first going to be called the "Erny" in homage to Haycox. He was born in Portland, Oregon. While still an undergraduate at the University of Oregon in Eugene, he sold his first short story to Sea Stories. *His name, however, soon became established in all the leading Western pulp magazines of the day, including Street & Smith's* Western Story Magazine *and Doubleday's* West. *His first novel was* Free Grass *(Doubleday, Doran, 1929). In 1931 he broke into the pages of* Collier's *and from that time on was regularly featured in this magazine, either with a short story or a serial that was later published as a novel. In the 1940s his serials began appearing in* The Saturday Evening Post *and it was there that modern classics such as* Bugles in the Afternoon *(Little, Brown, 1944) and* Canyon Passage *(Little, Brown, 1945) were first published. Both of these novels were also made into major motion pictures although, perhaps, the film most loved and remembered is* Stagecoach *(United Artists, 1939) directed by John Ford and starring John Wayne, based on Haycox's short story "Stage to Lordsburg." No history of the Western story in the 20th Century would be possible without reference to Haycox's fiction and his tremendous influence on other writers of stature such as Peter Dawson, Frank Bonham, Wayne D. Overholser, and Luke Short, among many. He almost always has an involving story to tell and one in which there is something not so readily definable that raises it above its time, an image possibly, a turn of phrase, or even a sensation, the smell of dust after rain or the solitude of an Arizona night. "Faithfully, Judith" first appeared in* Collier's *(4/11/42).*

Judith Murray stepped from the train into a great wind beating off the prairie. Wind struck harder as soon as the train pulled away, driving her back to the wall of the small station house, pressing her clothes on her body until she felt indecently exposed. This town, Virgil, was a single street of frame buildings against which the wind rushed, crying through every thin projection, straining at walls, slamming and slatting among movable things, rushing on with a soft roar of its own. A buckboard and two horses ran forward on the street, ripping up the gray-yellow dust. The driver yelled "Heyii!" and turned and halted the buckboard hard by the station's platform. He dropped to the ground and gave her half a glance; then his hands went automatically toward the tobacco pocket of his shirt. "You're Judith Murray, the new schoolteacher for Ingrid?"

"Yes," she said. "My trunk's down there on the express cart."

He was a spare young man with black hair and gray eyes and he kept his eyes on the cigarette forming in his fingers. He wore a pair of gray trousers, sharp-heeled boots, a thin cotton shirt that was no protection at all from the wind's sharp bite, and a wide-brimmed hat. He lighted the cigarette, which was a deft trick in this wind, said, "I'm Charley Graves," and gave her a hand up to the rig's seat. He went on for the trunk and brought it back to dump it in the buckboard's bed, thereafter taking his place beside her. He looked upon the horizon as he spoke: "Three-hour ride ahead of us. You warm enough?"

"Yes."

He wheeled the buckboard into the main street and stopped before a store and went in, presently reappearing with a sack of mail and a blanket. He tossed the mail sack at his feet; the blanket he spread over Judith Murray's lap. "You might get cold. Air's thin out here. Heyii!" The next moment she was flung against him as the team lunged into a full run. Charley Graves seemed drunk with the wind. He hallooed at a friend on the boardwalk; he rushed by a lumber wagon, hub almost touching hub; the buckboard bounced through the ruts at the end of the street and left Virgil behind a violent pall of dust. "May be rough," he explained. "Long ride . . . can't go slow."

Before and to either side of them the prairie's horizons were a-mist with ragged, fast-driven clouds of dust and that dust hurt her face with its gritty stinging; she felt it in her throat, in her clothes and in her hair. Tumbleweed rolled in great, growing balls and the sun was a dull round spot in the sky, its heat blown out of the world by the wind which went crying on into space.

"You'll board at Missus Rand's hotel in Ingrid," he said. "Wasn't anything out on the flats four months ago. Then Teddy Roosevelt opened the reservation to homesteadin' and five hundred people filled it in a week. Big argument on the school. Some wanted it, some didn't."

"How could anybody not want a school?"

"This country," he said, "requires a strong back and a weak mind. Not that I'm prejudiced. Never had schoolin' myself, but maybe it's necessary. World's changin'."

"Do you have a homestead?"

He shook his head. "Man like me wouldn't like a hundred and sixty acres after chasin' cows all his life. I'll be movin' on one day, away from the barb wire. Fences and houses close together ain't natural." He dragged the team to a stop, shouting "Who-aa!" He tucked the loose blanket more securely around her and sent the horses on again with a yip and a yell. In the forward distance dots of dust showed in the haze and at the end of an hour they began to pass wagons full-loaded with household goods and families.

"The weak ones give up," pointed out Charley Graves. "They came for somethin' free, figurin' to get rich. But it's a year until crop time and winter's comin' and there's considerable work and starvin' to go through. People wantin' things free never have the sand to stick. These kind have been leavin' for a month. What's left now are the tough . . . good tough and bad tough."

A great woolly grayness raced across the sky as soon as sunset came and the rustle and roar of the wind was all about them. They began to run by wagons loaded with wood, these moving toward the blur of a settlement in the distance. Three hours exactly after leaving Virgil the buckboard came into Ingrid, which was a half a dozen houses on the prairie, and wheeled before Mrs. Rand's hotel. Mrs. Rand, young and soft-faced and pretty, stood at the door. "I'm glad you're here," she told Judith. "It is always a tiresome ride. Charley, take the trunk to the corner room upstairs."

Judith entered a living room warmed by a huge central stove. Mrs. Rand lighted an extra lamp, and Charley Graves, having carried the trunk upstairs, came down and paused by the stove. Judith noticed that he was ordinarily a shy man but when he smiled, as he did now, the devil flickered in his eyes. "Feel the house shake? That's the way it is out here . . . bend or break." He went on out of the house.

Mrs. Rand showed Judith to her room and departed. Wind jolted the house like a giant hand and this motion added its uneasiness to the ride on the buckboard and gave Judith a moment's seasick feeling. She freshened up and she stood still in her room, tired and now depressed by the rawness about her. "I'll never keep clean," she thought, and went down to supper.

Afterward some of the settlement people came in to meet her. The elderly Adam Brewerton and his wife appeared, with their daughter, Letty, who was a fair, serene girl of Judith's own age. Charley Graves came by and stopped, warming his back at the stove. The Swensons, both beyond sixty, dropped in. The plump and jolly young girl who had waited on table was Ingrid Berg, for whom the settlement was named; and a big and very capable man later entered and was introduced to her as Tom Kertcher. They were all friendly people and they all had the air of being agreeable and this lasted until one more man came to the hotel — thin and somewhat dry of face and with a disagreeable pair of eyes. He was, Mrs. Rand said in her soft voice, Clyde Jacks.

Clyde Jacks gave Judith a civil, careful stare and made it plain how he stood on the school. "I was . . . and am . . . against such fool waste of money." As long as he remained in the room there was definitely less friendliness; these other people clearly disliked him and he knew it and showed his bristles, and then departed.

Judith was very tired and presently made her excuses and returned to her room. She wrapped herself in a robe, found her writing materials and drew a chair before the bureau to compose a letter:

Dear Harry:

I have arrived and this is the first night. I had thought of the West as being mountainous but there is nothing here but distance stretched out as flat as the floor of Charpenter's hall as far as you can see. The wind is blowing and the hotel shakes. I think I mind the dust most of all. There isn't much here to remind me of the neat, white houses and the green lanes of Salem.

She wished to add that she missed him, that she was afraid, and that his presence was her greatest desire. But they were really not yet engaged and so she ended it by writing, *Faithfully, Judith,* sealed the note into an envelope and addressed the envelope to Harrison Gurdon, Salem, Massachusetts. This was her first year of teaching and perhaps it had been foolish of her to wish to venture so far from home. It had seemed an exciting thought at the time; something like the far voyaging of her earlier sea-captain ancestors sailing around the world. Now she was afraid.

Swenson and his wife moved homeward through the rough wind. Swenson steadied his wife with his gentle old man's voice: "Lean against me, Anna. Turn your face from the wind. Hold my arm."

"Winter's coming," she said. "We have eleven dollars. It will be a whole year before we can see a garden. It will be hard, Nils."

"Very hard," he said. "If I were a younger man. . . ."

"You should not speak of that."

Their shanty lay a half mile down the road on one of the flat's best homestead quarters. Swenson led his wife inside and moved around to light a lamp. "I would be easier in my mind," he said, "if there was wood. But at four dollars the cord. . . ."

The shanty was two rooms and a shed thrown together of raw pine lumber and sealed with roofing paper. Mrs. Swenson had made neatness of all this with curtains at the windows and a calendar picture here and there. In the kitchen was a big wood stove, a table, and a couple of chairs built by Swenson and a huge cupboard with bins and shelves and drawers and dish racks. There was no fire in the stove.

They were an aging, gentle pair who had joined the land rush in the hope of finding a last home, and had been lucky in drawing a good quarter section. But Swenson was older than he liked to admit and there was a fear in him which he held from his wife; and Mrs. Swenson knew it and would not let him see that she knew it.

"I will build a little fire," said Swenson.

"No. We will go to bed and save the wood."

Somebody knocked and opened the door without waiting an answer. Clyde Jacks came in, bulky-shaped inside his fleece-lined storm breaker, his long nose reddened by the wind. He had a lantern with him and carefully dimmed it to save oil. "I been noticin'," he said, "you ain't got your wood yet."

"No," said Swenson, "we have not. Have a chair."

Jacks ignored the invitation. "You're shy of money. We all are. But you ain't goin' to get through the winter without ten-twenty cords of wood."

"You may be right," agreed Swenson courteously. He did not like this man, but he would not let himself show it. "Momma," he said, "I will light a fire and you will make Clyde some coffee."

"Even if you had wood," said Jacks in his dry, pressing voice, "how you goin' to plow and plant and how you goin' to fence, and how you goin' to harvest?"

"Those things are to be considered when they come," said Swenson.

"Consider them now," said Jacks. "When time comes to prove up and take title, you got to have your improvements made and you got to pay the government five dollars an acre. You ain't goin' to do it. You're broke and you'll freeze if you stay. You'll lose this quarter except you get help. Now listen, I will stake you to twenty cords of wood and I will give you money enough to keep grub. When time comes to get title, I'll advance enough for you to pay the government's fee. Then you deed the quarter to me and I will throw in another five hundred dollars for you."

"The government says I cannot do that," said Swenson.

"The government won't allow a deal to be made before you get a deed. After that you can sell where you please. You got my word and I got yours and we say nothin' to nobody. What's the difference? Half the folks on the flat will be doin' the same thing."

"It was my wish," said Swenson slowly, "to make a nice place of this. We're not young, and movin' around is not good now. Five hundred is not much for this nice land."

"You're broke," pointed out Jacks, "and you will lose it."

Swenson murmured, "That is probably right," and fell silent. His wife had moved into the other room, out of sight. Swenson sighed and dipped his head and had his thoughts, and knew that every word spoken by Jacks was wholly true; it had been a problem in his mind since the beginning. Suddenly he hated Jacks, but he thought of his wife and he came to his hard conclusion. "I will accept the bargain," he said.

Jacks gave Swenson a sharp, sly look. "None of this is on paper. You could do me, but I take you for a man of your word, or I wouldn't be botherin'. Say nothing about it to people." He went out into the brawling night.

Nils Swenson stood in the cold small room, knowing the last and greatest of many defeats; and he wanted the support and nearness of his wife but he would not go to her, thinking she would be feeling worse than he felt. Then he heard her voice behind him as she came out of the little bedroom, loving as it had always been: "It is nothing, Nils. We are together. That is enough."

Judith dreaded failure. Now, looking out upon the sixteen youngsters seated in the dull light of late afternoon, she knew she was failing. The long rough wind, ceaselessly blowing since her arrival ten days before, shook the flimsy schoolhouse, and the sound of it made the youngsters nervous; they turned in their seats and scraped their feet along the floor and whispered and would not keep their attention on lessons. Tara was at the moment reading aloud from the fifth-grade book, her voice indistinct. The end of the hardest day so far was at hand and the cordwood piled around the schoolhouse half covered the windows, so that the light, never very good, was now almost gray. Kurt Dyckman made a fugitive motion with his hand under the desk and the restless youngsters began to titter.

"Kurt," Judith said, "straighten on your seat and be still."

That boy, she realized at last, was the cause of her trouble. He was not a boy at all, but an eighteen-year-old giant as large as two ordinary men, with a dim, sly mind which would never grow big enough to grasp seventh-grade work. The school could do nothing for him and he did not belong in it; he was a mountainous shape above the other little figures of her class and his furtive rebellion ran among them and ruined all her efforts at discipline.

She said, "That will be all, Tara." She sat at the desk before them, slim and straight, her gray eyes very serious, her small shoulders squared. The children were on the edge of their seats ready to bolt at her word of dismissal. Kurt Dyckman stretched both legs into the aisle, knowing she disliked this. Each day his impudence increased. She said, "School is out. Kurt, I wish to see you."

The youngsters made a scurrying storm down the aisles; they went crying and shouting into the wind. Kurt Dyckman lifted his huge bulk and walked deliberately away. Judith Murray waited until he had reached the door before speaking again. "Kurt," she said, "just a moment."

He went through the doorway and turned and sent back his dull grin. Judith Murray stiffly checked her anger and rose and crossed the room, going into the yard to face him.

"Kurt," she said, "I know it is difficult for you to be among children. After all, you are a man. I need a man to help me with some of the chores. I'd like to count on you."

He listened to her with his head lowered. He was slow-minded, and therefore suspicious. He laboriously turned the proposition over in his mind and looked up with his unpleasant grin. "I got chores enough at home." He came half a step nearer, made bold from knowing she could not control him. "You're a mighty pretty woman," he murmured, and walked away from her. Some of the youngsters had stayed in the background. Now they ran on, knowing she had failed to control Kurt. It had not helped discipline at all.

She was angered enough to cry and she thought, "That meanness should be beaten out of him." She put the thought away as unworthy — and lifted her head to see Charley Graves sitting on his horse twenty yards off. She wheeled into the school-house, hating to have him witness her distress.

When she at last closed the school door behind her, Charley Graves was still waiting, smoking a cigarette, one leg tossed across the saddle horn. The wind whipped color into his face and he wore no coat and time seemed to mean nothing to him. He dismounted and fell into step behind her, leading his horse down the rutty road toward Ingrid.

"Why," she asked, "did they pile the wood against the windows?"

"Come a good windstorm, it sort of anchors the shebang. That shack ain't stout."

"It is a cheap, flimsy thing."

"Folks," he said in his easy way, "don't have much to work with out here. Not much money and not much time from their own chores."

She was rebuked and knew it, so she kept still, involved in her own troubles as she marched along the up-and-down-ruts of the road with the wind beating at her face.

"Everything all right?" he asked. "Havin' any trouble at school?"

"No," she said. "Charley, when will this wind stop?"

"Maybe in an hour. Maybe not for a month." He cast his quick, direct glance at her. She felt its bite, its force. Then he looked away, idly saying: "You got to learn to bend with it, or you'll bust. Kind of hard on educated folks."

"The way you speak," she said, "it sounds as though an education is a handicap."

"The way I figure, education ought to make a person see more and feel more. That's all to the good, except that if you're strong on feelin', you're goin' to be more miserable in bad times. It ain't the dumb folks that go crazy when the wind blows. It's the ones that feel too much."

She felt a small glow of surprise. He had little learning of the kind she taught and yet now and then his observations dug deep. Harry Gurdon, so wise and sometimes so prematurely weary with his culture, could not have said it better. She felt slightly disloyal for making the comparison, and then her own troubles returned and she grappled with them as far as the small shanty of the Swensons. Clyde Jacks was at the moment unloading wood beside the house, bending and lifting with a kind of me-chanical regularity. Mrs. Swenson stood at the door, beckoning.

Judith noticed the narrow way Charley Graves looked upon Clyde Jacks. She said, "The Swensons seem lonely. I'll drop in for a moment." She wanted to thank him for walking with her, but suddenly she was embarrassed and turned quite abruptly from him. Mrs. Swenson waited for her at the doorway with an old woman's vague and beaming smile. "Coffee is ready for you," said Mrs. Swenson. "It is cold today."

Charley Graves rode back toward the schoolhouse. Wind shredded out his cigarette at once and wind lifted loose earth from the plowed lands and darkened the air. He thought, "There goes the soil, hell-bent for China." There never had been any excuse in his language for the plowing under of this beautiful grass; but he had had some reservations lately. Maybe it wouldn't do to judge too soon. People had to farm somewhere. Past the school house he saw youngsters dotting the distant horizon, homeward bound; and he saw Kurt Dyckman's big-lumped shape forward on the road. He narrowed his eyes on Kurt and rode up to him.

"Wait a minute," he said, and got down. The giant boy's face looked upon him and showed insolence; he was a full head taller than Charley and a natural bully. Charley considered him with a grave thought, and got down. There wasn't any use of explaining anything; only way to break a bad horse was to beat him humble. He was taking some chances, considering Kurt's plain animal strength.

He went at Kurt the same way he chopped trees, one lick at a time. He beat him on the soft flesh under his jaw, he dug at Kurt's flanks. They went ambling down the road as they fought and once Kurt got in a wild swing and jarred Charley clear to his boots. Charley ducked his head, and took a chance on his knuckles with a full flush punch on Kurt's chin. Kurt went to his knees.

Like all animals, he was all through when something stronger came along; there wasn't any pride to make him fight after he was hurt. He looked up at Charley and shook his head. His lips were bleeding and he put a hand on them and saw the blood, and a thin point of fear glittered in his eyes. "Cut it out. Cut it out."

Charley Graves swung up to his saddle. The kid was a mountain of butter, a bully turned into a yellow pup. Charley said, "Your education's all over . . . don't ever go near that school again," slanting his hat over his forehead, and loped away.

Judith drank Mrs. Swenson's strong Scandinavian coffee brew and felt considerably improved, and meanwhile observed how little the Swensons had. There were these two rooms, sealed in with building paper, and a shed built on behind. The shed had a floor and a window and tarpaper walls.

"It's nice," she said, "that you have your wood."

Mrs. Swenson was a guileless soul and her smile simply faded and she sat with her eyes pointed to the door. "Yes," she said, without heart, "that's nice enough."

"Where's Mister Swenson?"

"Helpin' Mister Carney build a barn." Mrs. Swenson shook her head. "Even for two dollars a day he is too old for that. Maybe he's on top of the roof and this wind blows him off. If it wasn't for the wood, he wouldn't feel so small." Mrs. Swenson drew up the edges of her apron to her face and began to cry. Not with much sound, the tears rolled along her smooth, flushed, girl-like face, into the waiting apron, and presently she sighed and ceased to cry. "You know how that is?" she asked and then, needing to tell this to someone, she related the whole story of the homestead and Clyde Jacks to Judith. "You mustn't say nothing. Swenson promised, and when he promises a thing he will do it."

"If the government doesn't permit agreements like that," said Judith, "then the promise needn't be kept. He's taking advantage of you."

"Poor people cannot choose."

Judith said, "Right is right," and looked at the bare walls and the neatness of Mrs. Swenson's kitchen cupboard. She moved to the end of the room and looked into the shed. "You should talk to Jacks. Make him see what is fair."

"You are still a girl. Things in this world are not all straight."

Judith said, "Thank you for the coffee," and left the cabin, marching across the rolling Swenson quarter section toward Ingrid's buildings a mile distant. Wind slapped her and dust rolled like smoke around her. She bowed her head, thinking of the Swensons and knowing for the first time their desperate poverty. Then she thought,

"Perhaps others here are equally poor," and was appalled at the quick suspicion that her pay of fifty dollars a month caused somebody privation.

She stopped at the Brewertons' for her expected letter from Harry Gurdon and went on to the hotel. She read the letter in her room, its serious lines, its little sallies of humor, and she saw Harry as he wrote it, a tall man, leisurely and whimsical, with a character that produced actions always right and never unexpected. He was a comfortable man. She saw him; yet as she brought his face before her mind's eye there was a vagueness that was strange, as though distance dimmed what he was.

She had her dinner and returned to the room and began her letter to Harry. She sat long still, thinking of her own troubles at school, feeling the cold dread of failure; and the problem of the Swensons never was out of her mind. Presently she sighed and went to bed, the letter unfinished. There had to be some way of waking Kurt Dyckman's good instincts. That was the purpose of education.

When she faced the class the next morning and saw he was missing, she felt an enormous relief, and immediately afterward was reproached by her conscience. He did not appear after lunch hour and this day was her best day until, when school was out, young Reeves Pownder brought the news.

"Kurt ain't comin' back any more. Charley Graves beat the tar outa him last night and told him to stay away."

She was glad it was gray enough in the room to conceal her blush. All the youngsters rushed at the doorway, leaving her to struggle with the information. She was relieved to hear Kurt was gone; but this relief shocked her conscience and she grew slowly angry and the anger remained as she marched against the endless wind. Charley had done something for her which she should have done herself. Moreover, everybody would know at once about it and speculate on her attitude toward Charley Graves. She was in a grim frame of mind when she turned in at the Swenson house. Mrs. Swenson had the coffee already poured.

"I must move from the hotel to a place nearer to school," said Judith. "Your house is the closest. If you will put a bed in the shed, it will make a very satisfactory room. Twenty dollars a month is what I would be charged elsewhere. Is that all right?"

Daughter," said Mrs. Swenson, "it will be cold."

"We have wood, haven't we? And perhaps later we can get a little stove." She saw that Mrs. Swenson was about to cry and so hurried on with her brisk tone. "You will have rent money enough to pay Clyde Jacks for the wood. You must go to him and ask him to release you from your promise. Do it tonight, if you possibly can. I'll see about the bed today and perhaps I can move over tomorrow." She carried the talk rapidly to the end and left the house at once and moved across the quarter section toward Ingrid. When she reached the road near the settlement, she saw Charley Graves riding forward. She stopped in the dust, waiting for him. When he rode up and prepared to dismount, she pitched into him.

"You stay right there. I'm angry with you. I'm ashamed of you. What gave you the notion to interfere in my affairs? Everybody will laugh at me for needing a man to straighten out my troubles. What made you think it would be any good to knock Kurt down and scare him away from school? That's just force. It doesn't settle a thing. Do you know what I am going to do? I'm going to tell him to come back to school. I've got to find a better answer than yours. Education isn't violence."

He looked down at her, not smiling but close to a smile; and the admiration in his eyes further irritated her. He said: "The lad's a dumb brute and the only kind of education he savvies is a punch in the beak. I reckon I was a pretty good teacher." He rolled in the saddle, perfectly self-contained. "You can invite him back but, if he comes, I'll wail him again, which he knows. So he won't come back."

"Charley Graves, you stay out of my business! There's too much violence out here. You have taught him something wrong."

"I taught him that bein' balky will bring him a beautiful punch in the nose. That's education in any language."

"Fighting," she said, "settles nothing at all."

"Maybe not," he said, "but it sure does a lot of mind-changin'."

She went by him with her outrage. "How can you reason with a man like that?" she asked herself. She stepped into Solomon's store and priced a bed and a mattress and bedding and made arrangements to have it taken to the Swensons the following day. In her room she seated herself at the bureau before the unfinished letter to Harry Gurdon, but could write nothing. He was far away, and vague, and her problems here were too real to bring the memory of him before her. She sat quite still and felt the shock of knowing he was not uppermost in her mind; and at last went down to supper.

She hated to tell Mrs. Rand of her decision to move, but Mrs. Rand, the most understanding woman, seemed pleased. "The Swensons," she said, "need help badly, and this is the nicest possible way. You are kind to think of it. I will lend you sheets and pillow slips."

There was a deep feeling of neighborly obligation among them, the close tie of people all in a common lot, and that came upon Judith with its goodness. Later, when the usual group dropped in, Mrs. Rand spoke of the move, and Judith felt the approval of their eyes. She had done something which placed her within the group; it was the first time she had sensed this. Charley Graves stood with his back to the stove, his head bent over the manufacture of a cigarette; he lighted it and his glance struck over the edge of his cupped hands, grave and searching. Tom Kertcher came in, looking puzzled.

"Swensons just walked into Clyde Jacks's place. Now I wonder."

Judith remembered a question she had in her mind and now asked it: "What is a quarter section worth after it has been patented?"

"Depends," said Kertcher, "where it is. Anything within two-three miles of here is worth five thousand dollars of anybody's money."

Charley Graves casually murmured: "Any particular claim in mind, Judith?"

She shook her head, but all these people were watching her and she felt they knew why she had asked. They were sharp and wise in many things; not in things that came from books, but in the knowledge of people and the common troubles of people — the close and small and always pressing items of living. She thought of the Swensons and worry came upon her and she looked over the room and went out into the windy darkness. She stood there and in a little while she saw the Swensons leave Clyde Jacks's house and walk forward, very slowly. When they came to the hotel, they paused and Mrs. Swenson said: "It was a nice thing of you, but Clyde said it was a promise. So, if we gave our word and he will not give it back to us, we will keep it."

She watched them go on, shadows moving slowly into the beat of the steady wind; and she was outraged again, and this outrage made up her mind for her. She walked straight down the road, past the store and Brewerton's place, toward Clyde Jacks's

window light, and she walked with the inflammatory sense of justice of all her ancestors seething inside her, and she was shocked at the vigor of her hatred. People, she
thought, shouldn't let themselves go so freely, but she still felt all this, and knocked on
Clyde Jacks's door with firm knuckles.

When he opened the door — a long, slack man who seldom bothered to shave —
she walked into the room, past him, and waited for him to turn about. It was a queer
room, more like a woodshed than anything else, filled with gunnysacks and bits of wire
and rope and empty bottles and pieces of harness. A stove stood at one end and there
was a table made out of packing boxes and a bed in the corner with dirty quilts on it.
Then she was aware of Clyde Jacks's narrow, scarcely civil stare.

"If you want anything of me," he said, "you ain't goin' to get it. Everybody wants
somethin'. Just because I'm thrifty and work hard is no sign I got to share with them
that ain't got push enough to keep from starvin'."

"The Swensons can pay for their wood. That should be enough for you."

"They would have starved or froze if they stayed. If they left, they'd've lost the
place. I made a fair deal and I expect 'em to keep it."

"They can pay now."

"They couldn't when we dickered. A deal is a deal."

"You can't keep a bargain that's against the law."

He gave her a narrower stare. "Ain't you got enough to do without interferin'?
Half the folks out here will sell as soon as they get deeds."

"But they can't make agreements to sell before they own," she pointed out.

He shrugged his shoulders. "Amounts to the same thing."

"No, it doesn't. If I told the land office, you'd have trouble."

"You got nothin' to prove it," he said. Then he grinned when he saw he had her.
"The Swensons ain't the kind to talk after they promise somethin'."

This grew worse and worse. He was a sharp man, trading on other people's
honesty and he was amused at her foolishness. When she thought of the Swensons, the
whole thing became unbearable. "You think," she said very distinctly, "you're safe,
don't you?" She looked around her and her eyes fell upon a yard-long piece of harness
strap with a metal buckle at one end. She stopped and she seized it and she said, "I'll
show you how to be unfair," and slashed him across the face with the leather, its
buckle taking him on the mouth. He backed and jumped aside, and came in and
seized the strap. She held it with one arm and slapped him across the face and then he
seized her and shook her until she grew dizzy. After that she felt cold air pour into the
room and Clyde Jacks had jumped away from her. Charley Graves and Tom Kertcher
were in the doorway.

Jacks said in a changed voice, "This wasn't anything I started."

Both men stared at Jacks in a way that made her afraid. They were solid men but
now they were dangerous; there wasn't any mercy in them at all. Kertcher said, "Well,
Charley, you want to do it, or do you want me to?"

Jacks backed to the far end of the room and stood sallow and sullen, deeply afraid.
She put a hand up to her disturbed hair and was calm. Now she knew how this would
be. "The wood is four dollars a cord," she said. "Ten cords is forty dollars. They will
pay you ten dollars a month."

"All right," Jacks agreed quickly. "That's all right." Charley Graves had started across the room at him. Judith put out a hand and stopped Charley. "Then," she said, "that ends the Swensons' promise to you?"

"All right," said Jacks and kept his eyes on Charley Graves.

Judith said, "You hear that, Charley? He doesn't hold the Swensons to any promise." She was still a little afraid for Jacks's safety. These two big men were pretty definite in what they thought; she caught Charley's arm and turned him around, feeling his unwillingness, and drew him toward the door. She said, "I brought it on . . . I had to hit him to make him reasonable." She took Tom Kertcher's arm also and got both men outside the door. As a matter of safety she reached back and shut the door on Jacks, seized the arms of the men again, and led them toward the hotel.

They didn't say a word all the way to the hotel. She stopped there, and Tom Kertcher started to turn in. He looked back, suddenly smiling. "Kind of a tough citizen here, Charley," he murmured, and went on into the hotel.

"Charley," she said, "I know what you're thinking. But this was much different."

"Ahuh," said Charley Graves. He was a very deliberate man and he took his own time to build and light a cigarette. The match-light flickered in his eyes and went out; then he said, coolly, tantalizingly, "Still, it was violence in my book. Mighty shocking. Can't imagine the example you're settin' young children."

She had nothing to say. She watched the glow of the cigarette make its shine on his long, dark cheeks. He pondered the situation deeply and she waited, not knowing why she should. Wind ripped across the flats, bringing its dust and its curt chill; she swung a little, coming into the shelter of his tall body.

"You know," he said, "if I was a farmin' man, I wouldn't homestead on this side of the river."

"Wouldn't you, Charley?"

"I'd go across the river and lease a chunk of that good land from the Indians. Foolish of me to think of such a thing, though."

"Is it?" she said. "Good night, Charley."

She went inside and straight up the stairs to her room. She lighted the lamp and stood still. She saw herself in the mirror, her shaken hair and the smudge of dust on her face, and she was rather proud of what had happened. Was sin always this pleasant? She sighed and sat down to the unfinished letter, still conscious of the beat of the wind; but it didn't trouble her at all. It had become a familiar sound and she got to thinking of herself as one of the group — one of the slow and steady people making their fight against this new land. She took up her pen, well knowing she could say nothing of these events to Harry. What was there left to say to him?

She thought of it for a long while, wrote a few sentences, and prepared to add her usual *Faithfully, Judith.* But before she did she brought the image of Harry Gurdon forward and looked at his face a long while, and saw it slip backward into the mists. She realized then it would never again come forward clearly to her; and she knew also that sometime during the day Salem had ceased to be her home. How strange this was. She signed her letter simply, *Judith Murray,* and turned it over on the bureau and rose to leave the room. She heard the group talking below her and she wanted to join that warm and comfortable circle. She hoped Charley was there.

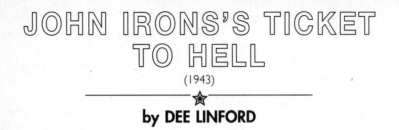

JOHN IRONS'S TICKET
TO HELL
(1943)

☆

by DEE LINFORD

Dee Linford *was born on a cattle ranch in western Wyoming, the product of three generations of pioneers in Wyoming, Idaho, and Utah. He attended Utah State Agricultural College and was graduated from the University of Wyoming. For many years he served as the editor of* Wyoming Wild Life, *the conservation magazine published by the Wyoming Game and Fish Commission. He had a lifelong interest in fundamental issues like the use of public lands and the need to protect the environment and habitat of wildlife. These are basic themes in his only novel,* Man Without a Star *(Morrow, 1952), which was later successfully filmed.*

Linford began publishing Western stories in 1940 when Mike Tilden introduced him to readers in a story titled (by Mike Tilden) "The Gunsmoke Saddle-Bum" in Star Western *(2/40). Linford went on to contribute nearly a hundred Western stories to magazines. His agent was Captain Joseph T. Shaw, once editor of* Black Mask Magazine *and also agent among Western writers for Thomas Thompson and Frank Bonham. Thus Linford paid two debts when he dedicated his novel: "To Mike Tilden and Joseph T. Shaw." Sudden John Irons made his debut in "Way-Station for Horse-Thieves" in* Dime Western *(4/40) and went on to become one of the most popular series characters in Western magazines published by Popular Publications. The environmental theme of the story that follows is unforgettable and reminds us that it was possible to do this in pulp magazines in 1943 precisely because they did not depend on advertising revenue.*

☆ **|** ☆

TRAIN TO TEN TREES

𝓘n the dust covered archives of the Western Anti-Horse and Cow Theft Association — the only existing authentic chronicle of the wanderings of Sudden John Irons — there rests a musty, dog-eared manila folder across which has been scrawled the legend, "Case unclosed." Then, evidence that the writer had at some later date changed his mind, these words were crossed out, and "Case closed" is written in the same vigorous hand below. The correction is initialed "R. McD.," signifying, of course, Oregon Rob McDade, Western Anti's two-fisted secretary and nemesis of stock thieves from the Pecos to the Platte.

The folder is entitled laconically, "The Case of the Cobblestone Pool." But John Irons called it "The *Curse* of the Cobblestone Pool" the night he heard the ugly story in McDade's Cheyenne office.

Oregon Rob had smiled his deceptive, cherubic smile. "You kin call it what you want," he'd said, and his voice was as deceivingly soft as his smile, "jest so you call it closed, time I see your homely face in town ag'in."

John Irons lifted one eyebrow in wary surprise. "You said Fronce Ryan was lookin' after Western Anti, up in the Ten Trees Hills."

McDade's mud-brown eyes caught and held his assistant's steady gray gaze, and his thick finger tapped a telegram on the desk between them. "Fronce Ryan is dead," he said, his voice rattling in his throat like wind under dead leaves. "Fronce was picked up a couple of days ago, on the Cobblestone Range. He was shot in the back . . . an' three weeks dead!"

John Irons sat up sharply on his straight-backed chair, and his hands brushed the grips of his guns without his knowing it. There was a saying in the rangeland that Western Anti always got its man. And when one of its representatives lost his life in the line of duty, there was no rest, no easing up or even any sleep for any man in the organization until the murderer was brought to justice. It was a tradition, and a prideful and useful one. John Irons could see where the bee was falling this time, and he was proud and thankful that it was so.

Fronce Ryan for many years had been his colleague in the organization, and there had been a bond between them which had gone deeper than mere affection. Fronce Ryan had saved John Irons's life more than once, and vice versa. Each had long been pledged to see the other through in case of something like this. A big question remained in John Irons's mind. But before he could speak it, Oregon Rob rattled the cowbell on the desk between them, and Mike Howe, Association handyman, poked his bald head into the room like a dog to his master's whistle.

"A Denver and Western freight is leavin' town t'night," McDade said, "on accommodation run to Ten Trees. John here will be on that freight. An', beginnin' now, you kin charge his time an' expense to the Case o' the . . . uh . . . the *Curse* o' the Cobblestone Pool."

Then, whipping his brown eyes back at his lean inspector-at-large, Oregon Rob in eight words supplied the answer to the question which still burned in John Irons's mind. "John, I want that Cobblestone war stopped. An' I want Jim Chilcote . . . *dead or alive!*"

There were other questions on John Irons's tongue. But something in the executive secretary's bulldog face hinted that the interview was over. Anyhow, he knew what he needed to know worst. He could learn the rest himself, first hand.

"I'll be on that train, Rob," he said. "An' I'll bring in Jim Chilcote, dead or alive!"

Twenty minutes after leaving McDade's office, John Irons had his bedroll spread on the spare bunk in the caboose at the rear of the long puddle-jumper freight. The conductor, a bilious, one-eyed man, was not given to talk, and the only other passenger was a tow-haired cowboy already asleep on one of the bunks, so John Irons stretched out on his own bed and closed his eyes. But sleep was impossible on the hard, crow-hopping bench and, as the night wore on, he had ample time to reflect on what he'd heard that evening concerning the job that awaited him, in the war-torn Ten Trees Hills.

The Cobblestone affair, it appeared, was another case of a small-scale rancher getting big ideas and going all-hog-or-none against his neighbors. Old Chandler Chilcote, John Irons knew, had long been a trusted and highly respected leader on the Cobblestone Range in the Ten Trees Hills. Chan Chilcote had organized the small

Cobblestone ranchers like himself into a militant association to hold the grass-rich Cobblestone Range for their joint use. And the Cobblestone Pool had long stood as a monument to the workability and fairness of the pool system. Then, unexpectedly, this Chilcote and his wild-haired son, Jim, had gone hog-wild and turned on their neighbors like curly wolves.

The Chilcotes, father and son, had started by dynamiting Barrel Spring, principal water hole on Cobblestone Range, closing half of that rich grassland to cattle grazing. They had been caught in the act and read out of the Pool. But old Chan had drag enough in the association he'd founded to take a part of the members out with him, and to split the Pool wide open.

The Chilcote faction, it seemed, had been strong enough to hold its half of the Cobblestone Range — the watered half — at gun-point. The remaining ranchers, deprived of water and therefore of range, had been closed out, and the Chilcote crowd had come out on top. Then, just when these were congratulating themselves for having picked a winner, the powerhouse squeeze was turned mercilessly against themselves, and they'd found themselves out in the cold.

The Chilcote crowd had been building a barb-wire barrier to protect their range from ruined neighbors when one of the post-holes filled up, mysteriously, with oil. Word had gotten around, and the resulting stampede of wildcat oilmen and get-rich speculators had ruined the surviving members of the Cobblestone Pool — all but the Chilcotes. The latter seemed to have seen the catastrophe coming. They had cut down operations before disaster struck. The Chilcotes had squeezed through, while their less fortunate associates went down fighting to hold their range against the government-backed oil leases.

When the whole of the Cobblestone Range lay under lease, it was found that the "strike" was processed petroleum from a Casper refinery. And when the bubble had burst, the Chilcotes had set about buying up the worthless leases cheap. Within a year, the Chilcotes' Anchor Ox controlled all the ground formerly grazed by the Cobblestone Pool. The Chilcotes, father and son, were on the make! But then, as if Fate itself had taken a hand, a bona-fide oil strike was made on the Cobblestone Range. The government, in selling the oil-leased land to the Anchor Ox, had wisely withheld oil and mineral rights, and the Chilcotes at last were left holding the bag.

The Chilcotes, caught like coyotes in their own trap, had imported gunmen from south of the Platte to hold their rangeland against the money-mad boomers. But the vengeful Cobblestone Pool had grabbed off the best active leases, and the Chilcotes had already taught the Poolers to fight. The Pool had imported its own gunmen, and the Anchor Ox had been doomed from the first. Old Chan Chilcote himself had died under the guns of the Pool's regulators and young Jim, refusing to admit defeat, had taken to the Ten Trees Hills with the remnants of his curly wolf crew to continue the fight from there.

"What's it got to do with Western Anti?" John Irons had demanded of McDade. "We're a *stockman's* protective league. Why we got to pull a oil company's peanuts outa the fire?"

Oregon Rob had looked troubled and grave. "This here Sam Blazzard that's headin' the Pool now is canny," he'd explained. "The Cobblestone Pool's a oil company, open an' shut. But Blazzard was long-headed enough to keep it incorporated as a stockman's pool. An' he's dug up the Pool's life membership in Western Anti. Now that Jim Chilcote is raidin' outa the Ten Trees Hills like a crazy Injun, burnin' rigs an' dynamitin' wells, Sam Blazzard needs help. An' he's makin' us live up to our pledge o' protection. I'm 'feared to renege, John. It would cost us many a payin' member."

John Irons still hadn't been convinced at that point. But, learning that Fronce Ryan had already ridden up to give Sam Blazzard the protection he demanded and learning that Ryan had already been shot in the back, John Irons was converted. It was Western Anti's fight now, all right. It was *his* — John Irons's — fight, too. He would bring his colleague's murderer to justice, or he would die trying.

John Irons must have slept without knowing it. For he was aroused from a bad dream by the screech of braked locomotive wheels on the iron rails and a solid push that ran backward through the long string of cars — a shove that popped the light caboose at the rear in the way that an artful whacker could pop the snapper at the end of his long mulewhip. Invisible hands picked John Irons up off his bunk and slammed him to the floor. The grunting conductor lit crosswise of his head in the dark, then got to his feet, muttering apologies and deprecations at the lantern he could not find.

Finding it at last, he got it lighted and stepped out into the night to investigate the reason behind the sudden stop. But before he left, plunging the interior of the small railroad caboose into darkness once more, John Irons had a glimpse of the tow-headed cowboy sitting upright on his bunk, dragging a Winchester from his saddle pack.

Harsh voices sounded outside then, and John Irons knew there was trouble brewing along the railroad that night. Then the cowboy spoke, confirming his hunch.

"Better fade, stranger," the tow-head said, calmly as if asking for a smoke. "It's me they want, an' I got no chance. They'd shoot me like a rabbit if I tried to jump. But that ain't nothin' to do with you. You better get out while you can."

John Irons did not comprehend. But he smelled trouble smoking right under his long nose, and the smell was not an alien one. Getting to his feet, he groped his way to his bunk and buckled on his heavy gun belts. The voices outside were nearer now, more threatening and ominous in their tone. A line of light glowed beneath the caboose door, and he saw the cowboy had spoken the truth. If he were going to get out, he hadn't much time. Shrugging faintly in the blackness, he opened the caboose door and looked out. The sight that met his eyes was not a pleasant one.

☆ II ☆

MEN WITHOUT FACES

pwards of a dozen ghoulish figures stood in a wide semicircle about the rear of the caboose. Two of them carried lighted lanterns, and in the yellowish light John Irons could see they were all heavily armed. Then he saw what was so strange in their appearance. They had no faces! All wore flour sacks over their heads, with holes cut for their eyes and mouths. The eyes behind the sack cloth reflected the lantern light like live fires.

"Get out!" the cowboy whispered hoarsely, "an' shut that door!"

John Irons obeyed and, as he stepped onto the caboose platform, rough hands seized him and pulled him over the railing to the ground. He struggled to free himself, and a pistol barrel slammed against his head. The ring of faceless men gyrated, and the lanterns made a complete circle of fire around him. When things steadied again, his arms were pinioned, and one of the masked figures was holding a light close to his face. This man towered above the others, and seemed to be leader of the band. And if John Irons ever saw murder in a pair of eyes, he saw it in the eyes that burned behind the mask.

"This ain't him!" the faceless man growled, as if the sin were John Irons's own. Then he stepped behind the Association man, shoved a gun into his back, and marched him down the road grade to the bar-pit.

"Lissen, fella," the big man growled, halting him under the Cheyenne-Casper telegraph wires that paralleled the tracks, "them wires run south . . . to Cheyenne an' Denver an' as much farther as you wanna go. Stay under 'em, an' keep walkin' till you're outa this country. Stop this side o' Cheyenne, an' you're a-goin' to wish you'd a-died when you was a pup. Now git. An' don't look back!"

John Irons still had his guns — either by reason of his captors' oversight or overconfidence — and he obeyed the command without hesitation or retort, thinking only to get out of sight before the masked man changed his mind and disarmed him. The railroad and the paralleling wires curved around the point of a low hill within a hundred yards, and John Irons stretched his legs toward that point.

Once around that point and out of sight of the caboose, he left the wires and doubled back through the brush on the hillside. He could see, on pushing his head cautiously above the rise, what had stopped the train so abruptly. A big fire had been kindled between the rails ahead of the locomotive, and this was still burning. Then the caboose was in sight again, and he hunkered down to watch.

The big night raider, it was plain, had already forgotten him. He was back now at the caboose, directing operations against the lone man imprisoned inside the rickety railroad crummy. His gun was still in his hand, and sulphurous invective flowed from his mouth.

"You comin' out?" he demanded of the caboose, "or do we got to come for you?"

The trapped cowboy fired through the caboose door for answer, and one of the hooded men spun half way around, clawing at his shoulder. The big man signaled a rush up the platform steps. But the Winchester inside stuttered and crashed, and three more masked men went down before they'd touched the platform steps. Falling back, the others opened fire on the caboose. Their lead made a sieve of the old box-on-wheels. But the rifle inside would not be silenced.

Then the big man's voice boomed above the raving clamor of the guns. "Part of you keep the door covered. Rest of you gather brush an' pile it along the box. We'll smoke him outa there like a polecat!"

"You can't burn the train!" one of the band objected.

But the leader waved the objection aside. "Train, hell! We'll burn it an' all the tracks b'tween here n' Ten Trees, if we have to. He ain't goin' to slip through our fingers ag'in!"

John Irons heard the name Ten Trees with surprise. It told him that he must already be on Cobblestone Pool range. And it told him something else, something which followed indisputably from the other. The faceless, ghoulish raiders who conspired to burn the trapped cowboy alive in the caboose would be Jim Chilcote's

Anchor Ox night riders. The big man would be young Chilcote in person, directing another murder.

The probability became a certainty as he considered it, and the blood coursed a little faster in his veins. Before him, behind those unsightly white masks, stood the men — the *man*, at least — who had murdered Fronce Ryan! Fate had crossed their trails early in the game. But all in the same thought, he realized the hopelessness of his position. He still had his guns, but the odds if he opened the pot would be a dozen to one against him. He might kill Jim Chilcote, all right. But he would be certain to die himself. And the game cowhand inside the caboose would die also.

Suddenly, saving the life of the plucky tow-haired cowboy who had in some way incurred the wrath of the Anchor Ox had become more immediately important to John Irons than the taking of Chilcote. There'd be time later to deal with the outlaw. But, for the game cowboy who had ordered John Irons out of the trap set for him time was running out. Half a dozen raiders were pumping lead through the caboose door to keep the tow-head inside, while the others collected brush and heaped it high against the old box-on-wheels.

John Irons considered circling ahead to the locomotive and warning the engineer what was up, so that the hogshead could throw the train in reverse and move the cowboy back to safety. But then he saw the train crew had been taken prisoner, and was being held under heavy guard beside the wheezing engine. But the plan, in dying, suggested another. The train had been stopped on a steep upgrade. The gradient was sufficient that, if the caboose were to be cut loose from the cars, it would roll backward under its own weight!

Keeping low, taking advantage of every rock and brush clump, John Irons circled the caboose and cut back toward the train, midway up the line of cars. It was a dangerous maneuver, but weeds and brush grew thick over the right-of-way and, wriggling and writhing snake-like through the shallow cover, he gained the shelter of the cars undetected. The needle-sharp boiler cinders cut and slashed his elbows and knees as he dragged himself back toward the caboose, under the cars. Twice, discovery seemed inescapable, and he stopped and lay low, his hands gripping his guns, determined to make a fight of it. But luck was with him. Anyhow, the raiders had forgotten him and expected no interference — not, at least, from under the train. And, after what seemed an eternity, he reached the end of the last car.

The gap between the car and the trailing caboose was, to his immense relief, well-screened now by the brush piles on either side. But even as he congratulated himself, the big man's voice boomed a command, and the brush on both sides of him was ignited. The tinder-dry sward crackled and popped as it took fire, and the flames rose quickly on both sides, licking hungrily at the incendiary sage and greasewood. For an instant he felt like a rabbit trapped in a burning box. Then he heard the raiders retreat to a safe distance, and he came up crouching beside the iron car coupling.

He could see the coupling plainly in the glow from the mounting fire, and triumph surged wild inside him. The union was of an old-fashioned cast, consisting simply of a sandwich joint secured by a heavy iron pin. The hookup was worn and loosely fitted, and the impact of the sudden stop had knocked the joiner pin half way up out of the union. The entire weight of the caboose seemed to be resting against the cocked pin bolt, but it came out readily when he tugged at it.

And then he could see why. The crummy was cut loose from the train now. But it didn't move. One of the wheels, John Irons guessed, might have been flattened slightly by the abrupt stop. And John Irons was trapped, along with the tow-headed cowboy! Full realization of his predicament was staggering. The roaring flames on both sides of him were leaping skyward now, licking at the sides of the caboose and the car ahead, reaching for Sudden John himself with darting, whip-pointed tongues. The smoke was blinding, and the heat seared his flesh. If he stayed where he was another five minutes, he'd be barbecued. If he jumped through the flames to safety, he'd meet death from the raiders' guns.

He was struggling mightily with himself to keep a level head when his hurting eyes focused suddenly on a crack in the caboose wall. It was an inch wide and must extend clear through the thin box, inside. An idea slashed into his desperately devising brain, and he pressed his mouth to the crack.

"Don't shoot me through this crack, cowboy," he called, loud enough to be heard inside the box but not by the raiders beyond the flames. "I'm your friend. Open the door like you was goin' to make a break. Don't show yourself. Just start a fuss that'll draw 'em to that end o' the caboose. An' maybe we'll get outa this!"

There was only silence from inside the crummy, and John Irons feared he was too late — that the cowboy was dead. Then he heard boots scrape the floor inside, and the door screaked open. The cowboy yelled, a wild Indian yell, and the Winchester was crashing as fast as the tow-head could work it.

John Irons grinned, in spite of the pain from the searing flames. The tow-head was one to ride the river with! Then he heard the big man's voice, directing attention to the caboose door, and he knew his moment had come. Standing upright and holding his breath, to avoid breathing in the lethal smoke and flames, he placed his back against the car ahead, and straightened, slowly. He knew later that under ordinary circumstances he could not have done it. But just then, with the fire licking at his clothes and flesh, every tortured muscle and sinew had the strength of ten. Slowly but surely, the caboose moved backward. The gap between it and the stationary car widened until John Irons fell flat to his back upon the cinder-strewn grade. And the flaming brush tumbled in on him from either side.

The cowboy's diversion must have worked well, or else the raiders, seeing a man spring up from the very heart of the fire, could not believe their eyes. For John Irons bounded up. And, in full view of them all, he caught the near side of the metal ladder running up the near side of the caboose and swung himself aboard the moving car — without drawing a shot!

Only when he was lying flat, face down on the roof of the shack-on-wheels, did the surprised raiders come to life. Even then they didn't shoot. Instead, they surged forward as one man to halt the runaway caboose. But John Irons had anticipated such a maneuver and was ready for it. He had a gun in either hand and cut loose with a sudden thunderous fire. His guns were trained at the ground, but the whining slugs kicked cinders and ash in the pursuers' faces, and they took the hint. They were yelling when they abandoned the chase and scattered for cover.

Once safely in the brush, the raiders opened a murderous fire. Lead riddled the caboose's thin shell and filled the air above John Irons's head with a vicious, spiteful *whurr*. But the cowboy was on the platform, firing his Winchester again, and the bonfire on the tracks was receding rapidly as this runaway car gathered momentum.

Soon the caboose had lumbered around the curve which had shielded John Irons once before that evening, and they were in the clear.

The raiders pursued them beyond the turn. But by now the runaway caboose was out of all but rifle range, and in the space of a minute they had completely lost the faceless men and the bonfire. By then, the speed of the unwieldy car had become a fear-inspiring thing. It had lurched abruptly in rounding an invisible curve, and almost hurled John Irons into space. Taking thought for the first time in several seconds, he holstered his guns and clawed at the brake wheel, screwing it down as fast as he could, hoping to stop, or at least to reduce, the breath-taking speed of the lumbering car.

There was no way of telling how fast the loose caboose was moving, but it was plainly far out of control. Already, John Irons had the brake-wheel screwed down as far as it would go, and was holding it down by main strength. But his efforts seemed to have no effect. He could smell the overheated brake shoes, and the wheels were throwing scintillant streams of sparks out into the black night. The grade seemed to fall away sharper and sharper beneath the wheels, and the vehicle seemed to run faster instead of slower.

How many miles were covered in the crazy flight, John Irons was never to know. Crouching there beside the brake wheel and peering futilely into the black void ahead, he knew only that he had traded one form of sure death for another. The free-running car had become a witless, fire-show monster, roaring madly and blindly to destruction. There would have to come another curve in the invisible tracks soon, and John Irons knew the rickety old vehicle would never negotiate it. Not at its present speed. And the effort of holding the brake shoes against the raving wheels was becoming too great for his aching arms to endure. Soon he'd have to turn the runaway caboose loose entirely, and then the infernal chariot wouldn't need a curve to fly the track. It would soar sky-high of its own accord, and smash itself to matchwood on the rocks.

He heard the cowboy on the platform yelling faintly, and he tried to call back. But the rushing blackness tore his lips apart and snatched his words from his mouth and hurled them into oblivion. He didn't even hear himself. And then, just as he was wondering how much longer it could go on, he felt the car violently lurch and cant. He knew then the cowboy's shout had been one of warning. The cowboy knew the road. He knew the curve had come — that the car was leaving the tracks and turning over. From the second of his realization until the world was obliterated, John Irons's mind was a whirling chaos. His ears were filled with a shriek and grind of tortured steel. Then something stuck his head, and his hold on the brake wheel was broken. He seemed to soar high, almost lazily through space . . . through pitch-black, plushy space that had no meaning and no end.

☆ **III** ☆

WAR-CAMP IN THE HILLS

*J*ohn Irons came out of it slowly, knowing that his mind had been blank for a long time. His first thought, as memory returned of his wild flight atop of the runaway caboose, was that he was still down on the railroad grade, and he looked around for sight of the old car and the cowboy. But what he saw brought a grunt of surprise from his bruised lips.

He wasn't down on the grade. He was up in the hills — in what appeared, at first glance, to be a roundup camp. But there was no chuck wagon, and no sign or sound of cattle. He could hear running water and the blurred hum of voices, and that was all.

He was lying on an outspread bedroll in a patch of shade cast by a woven-willow sun-shelter, and the barren conical humps of the hills about him told him he was in the Ten Trees hills. When he moved, he was surprised to find he felt no pain. His arms and legs all worked and, when he sat up, his head was clear. His hat, gun belts, and the wallet which contained his papers lay together on the ground, just out of reach. Beyond them stood the tow-headed cowboy of the train, smiling.

"Glad to see you comin' 'round, John Irons," the cowboy said, almost merrily. "Me an' the boys here was startin' to worry. You been out like a light since las' night. . . ."

Sudden John saw "the boys" then, and they were a hardy crew. Their hair was long, their faces weathered and unshaven. All were heavily armed, and they carried their guns as did men who were well accustomed to the extra weight. And around them all over the camp were open-mouthed pack panniers containing crated dynamite and ammunition. John Irons knew then why he had heard no cattle. This was no roundup outfit. It was a guerrilla war camp!

It struck him strange, belatedly, that the tow-head should call him by name. He mentioned the fact, and the tow-head indicated his wallet, on the ground beside him.

"It ain't often I go through a man's possibles, without his say-so, John. But one o' me boys recognized you, after we'd packed you up here. I had to make shore. An' I had to find out what you was up to, here on Cobblestone Range."

John Irons grunted. "An' now you know?"

The tow-head nodded. "Now I know. An' it's a cryin' shame."

"How you figger, cowboy?"

The cowhand laughed. "You know who I am?"

John Irons had an inkling then, but he couldn't quite believe it. He wagged his head. The cowboy watched him, bemused. "I don't believe you do," he said softly, as if to himself. "An' I was hopin' you did. This means the fun is over, for us both. An' it *was* fun, sidin' you in a fight. *I'm* Jim Chilcote!"

Sudden John had suspected it, after seeing the war-like appearance of that hill camp. But it hadn't seemed possible. He liked this game youngster, intuitively. It was hard to conceive of him as the curly wolf whelp of the Cobblestone Range — as the man who had murdered Fronce Ryan.

"Then who," he demanded, hoping his surprise was in some measure concealed, "was that buzzard pack that held up the train?"

The tow-head's voice was bitter. "That was Lute Poage an' his Cobblestone Pool regulators. I'd been out of the country on business, an' they found out somehow I was in that caboose. My boys here got wind they aimed to stop the train an' take me off, but they didn't know where the holdup would be staged. They didn't find us till they heard the shootin' an' the crash o' the caboose. They picked us both up an' brought us up here."

The tow-head smiled suddenly. "Hey, I'm gettin' it now, John Irons. This here's a purty fine joke . . . on somebody. An' I reckon it's on you. You didn't know me.

You thought Poage's pack was my outfit. That's why you took a hand, an' pulled me outa that crack. You kind've got off on the wrong foot, didn't you?"

The outlaw's words suggested he understood completely the nature of John Irons's pilgrimage to the Ten Trees Hills. Sudden John glanced at his wallet again, and the cowboy nodded.

"That's right. I saw your warrant for me, an' your orders. '*Dead or alive,*' Oregon Rob says. That's strong talk, John."

It had been dark in the caboose the night before, and John Irons hadn't gotten a full look at the outlaw then. Likewise his mind, so far that morning, had been too confused and too busy to take adequate measure of the man. He took that measure now, deliberately, allowing the minutes to pass in silence. He had no fear of silence, in the camp of the enemy. He was the law, waiting, certain of himself, inexorable as iron. He had come to the Cobblestone Range with the conviction he'd have a bitter fight to take Jim Chilcote. He still expected that fight. But he no longer looked forward to it with his relish of the day before.

The tow-head's boyish, slight appearance was, he saw, deceptive. Chilcote was almost as tall as John Irons himself, and clean-cut as a wedge. But it was the eyes that caught and riveted John Iron's attention. They were the kind of eyes John Irons liked in a friend, and hated to find in an enemy. They were bright and bluish gray, like polished steel in sunlight — frank and open, but harboring potential danger. There was no hostility in them for the man who had come to take him to justice. Nor did John Irons's professional lawman's attitude bother him. The eyes were smiling and friendly and curious, like the eyes of a boy taking in a hero of boyhood dreams.

Had the outlaw abused him and threatened him with immediate death, John Irons would have felt more comfortable. It upset his hard self-assurance to have the man he was taking to the hangrope treat him with that warm and easy camaraderie. And Jim Chilcote was laughing at him! Laughing because John Irons, summoned by the Cobblestone Pool to help corner him, had begun by snatching him out of the Pool's hands. Laughing because John Irons, out to capture him, had — himself — been captured!

"This here's complicated, John," the cowboy went on, drawing additional enjoyment from the situation. "You got to kill me, after savin' my life, 'cause I won't never be took alive. I got to kill you . . . or be killed. But I can't, 'cause I owe you for my life, already. Now what the hell am *I* going to do?"

"Maybe it would be easier," John Irons suggested softly, "if you done it to my back. *Like you done Fronce Ryan!*"

Then he saw the blue-gray eyes change. The blue drained out of them completely; the gray went hard and cold as ice. Yet they still contained no threat to him. There was hate — deep-seated vehement hate — the kind that leads to killing. But that hatred seemed general and unfocused. At least, it was not directed toward John Irons.

"So that's the way the wind blows." The outlaw's voice lacked its former vibrancy and good will. "Be no good, I reckon, to tell you I didn't kill Ryan?"

John Irons wagged his head. "Not 'less you could tell me that you an' your pa didn't plot to take over the Cobblestone Range for your Anchor Ox. Not 'less you could tell me you didn't blow Barrel Spring to stop its flow an' split the Pool, then plant that refinery oil to start a stampede an' ruin the ones that had sided you in the Pool fight . . . so's you could take them over too!"

For a minute, Chilcote didn't answer. His gray eyes looked through John Irons as if he hadn't been there. "I can't tell you we *didn't* blow the spring," he said at length, his voice as toneless and gray as his eyes. "But we didn't plant that post-hole full of oil. An' we didn't aim to bust the Pool. We blowed that spring to try and *save* the Pool. The others wanted to make it a fight — afterwards. We had no chance."

"How would blowin' the spring have saved the Pool?"

Jim Chilcote appeared to reach a decision inside his head. He took a long breath, and his gray eyes focused again on Sudden John. "I'll tell you the truth . . . all of it. Not that you'll believe me. You're too smart, but you're on the level. I know that, an' I want you to hear my side of it, before I have to fight you. Why'd we blow that spring? I can see now it was a blunder. But we didn't think so, then. Pa an' me was cleanin' the thing out that mornin' to increase the flow. We dug too deep, I guess. We increased the flow all right. But it wasn't all water. Part of it was oil . . . thick an' black an' stinkin' as Sam Blazzard's heart!"

"Yeah?" John Irons's voice was incredulous, and Chilcote shouted at the disbelief mirrored in the Association man's eyes.

"That's what happened! I yelled like I was crazy. I thought we'd struck 'er rich. An' I reckon we had. But Pa set me down on the grass there, an' told me what happened to a country when oil was found in it. Told me about Cy Iba in Casper, when Cy made the Salt Creek strike. Cy was a rancher, an' a good 'un. But his place went to hell when it was overrun by wildcatters, grease-monkeys, an' thieves that filled Casper up after the strike. Cy didn't mind at first. He thought he was goin' to get rich quick, with the rest. He let ranchin' go, an' played the oil game. But he couldn't play poker with the big thieves. He lost his shirt to speculators an' shysters, an' then his ranch was gone. Cy died on the grub-line!"

The outlaw's voice was low and vibrant, and the strength of his emotion was mirrored in the flush of his face. "Pa told me it would be the end o' ranchin' here, if word o' the oil got around. He told me the Chilcotes would make their own above-board, with cows an' grass . . . not rootin' like hawgs in the ground, for muck! He made me promise to say nothin' about the strike, an' I lived up to my word. Then we talked 'er over. We knew there was others in the Pool that would want to play the oil, no matter what it done to the cow range. So we decided to keep it dark. We decided to blow the water hole an' shut the whole thing off.

"That's what we done, John Irons. We rode back to the Anchor Ox an' got dynamite, an' blowed it. We expected trouble, but nothin' like we run into. We couldn't explain *why* we'd done it, you see, an' Sam Blazzard had us read outa the Pool. But some o' the old bunch stood by Pa, trustin' him. An' when Blazzard crowded a fight on us, we accepted it. I know we been accused o' plantin' oil in that post-hole . . . to start a rush an' ruin the Poolers that stood with us . . . so we could take them over. But that's a lie. Hell, you think we'd have *faked* a' oil-rush, right while we was tryin' to *cover up* a real strike?"

The outlaw's story was convincing, and his appeal to be believed was a disturbing thing. But John Irons was cautious. All evidence was against him. It couldn't all be wrong. "What," he asked, drawing tighter the net he thought would trap the outlaw, "about the way your Anchor Ox turned on the Poolers that sided you, after the fake strike? Didn't you save yourselves, then take the others over . . . after they'd gone to hell an' back for you, during the Pool war?"

The outlaw's face clouded. "We saved ourselves, yes, shore! Who wouldn't? But we didn't sell the others out. We offered 'em a hand; they spit in it! We thought the fake strike was the McCoy, an' we got ready for a stampede. We cut down our herds an' went on tame feed, to get by without the Cobblestone Range. We tried to get the others to do the same. But they had the oil bug. They let ranchin' go, an' went a-wildcattin'. They all got mortgaged, neck-deep, to a tall Injun to develop their leases. When the bubble busted, the banks owned the boots they wore. The Anchor Ox picked up their leases . . . from the banks . . . because we still aimed to see that the Cobblestone stayed cow country! It was hell on them that had sided us . . . shore it was! It was hell on us too. But we tried to save 'em, an' they wouldn't let us. An' if a man's goin' to start feelin' sorry for all the damn fools in the world, he's got no business tryin' to ranch!"

John Irons was puzzled by the whole picture. "Who besides you would have filled that post-hole with oil? Who else would have killed Fronce Ryan?"

The cowboy shrugged. "I can't answer that. But I got my ideas. Yet, if I made law charges without a scrap o' proof, I'd be bad as them that set you onto me for killin' Ryan. The evidence is good enough to satisfy me. I'm actin' on it. An' I'm clearin' my range o' the stinkin' oil holes that kill my grass an' poison my springs!"

John Irons wagged his head. "Yo're a fool, Jimmy. You can't. . . ."

"I know where I stand, John Irons," the other snapped. "I know I'm damned, whichever way it goes now. But I'm certain-shore that I know who killed my dad an' Fronce Ryan, an' why. An' I'm out to make 'em pay. That's all. After that, if I'm still alive, I'll ride down the long trail to where I ain't known. But till the job's done, I'm stickin' to my guns . . . whether you or the Pinkertons or the whole U.S. Army comes again' me. Wouldn't you do the same?'

John Irons, a critical judge of men, completed his judgment of Jim Chilcote in that moment. He saw he might as well oppose the wind as try to deter the outlawed and broken-hearted youth from his chosen course. He knew that a man caught in a passion as strong as Chilcote's would not fear anything on earth — not even the law. And the prospect of a fight to the death with an antagonist in whom he was matched — perhaps even overmatched — brought a familiar old thrill into his blood.

"I'd do the same as yo're doin', Chilcote," he admitted. "An' I reckon you'd do the same as I've got to. You know the law, an' you know my orders. I got to stop this fuss, an' I got to take you in dead or alive! I aim to do both, Jimmy. An' that, I reckon, brings us down to earth. You got me, like a snake in a forked stick. Question is, what *you* aim to do with *me?*"

"I'm beholded to you," the outlaw replied, "for saving my life. But even if I wasn't, you'd be welcome to stay in this camp or to leave, as an' when you want . . . long as you didn't try to make good your brag an' take me along. I ain't afraid of you, John Irons. I wouldn't be in a fight . . . I don't believe. But we won't fight. Time you've looked into this thing, you'll be on my side o' the fence, I know that. I'm not worried."

Chilcote's voice was level and unexcited. He was confident, sure of himself. His eyes had deepened to a friendly blue again, and once more he was smiling. But John Irons did not misinterpret that fact. He knew Jim Chilcote would continue to smile, even when it came to a fight to the death between them. And John Irons respected a smiling fighter.

"If I don't side you, Jim?"

Their eyes met on a dead level, and the quiet gleam in the still friendly blue answered before the outlaw spoke. "Then my lettin' you go now will have squared my debt to you, Sudden John. Then it'll be a fight to the finish . . . with no holds barred!"

"No holds barred!" John Irons returned the other's smile, knowing it would not be misinterpreted, either. "Not even the strangle hold, Chilcote . . . on the end of a rope! An' now, if I can have my guns an' purse an' a horse to ride, I'll head for Ten Trees. I'll look into this thing, like you recommended."

The horse was brought, and saddled and bridled at the outlaw's command, and his guns and wallet were returned. John Irons mounted.

"You can leave the horse at Jimson's livery barn," Chilcote told him. "One o' the boys will pick him up, sometime. An' John, to even up for the loan o' the horse an' keep us even on favors, you can run a' errand for me. There's a girl behind the counter at the Warbonnet Cafe. Her name is Nellie, an' she's got eyes like a columbine an' hair like wild flax. Drop in an' tell her you seen me, will you? Tell her I'm all right?"

John Irons looked closely, to see if he were being hoorawed. He saw the outlaw was in dead earnest — and a little bothered in front of his grinning crew. John Irons nodded gravely and, on impulse, offered the outlaw his hand. Chilcote took it eagerly, and the grip of the sinewy fingers made John Irons realize what a deadly hold that hand could take — on a man's throat as well as his fingers.

So were the rules drawn for the coming fight. No holds would be barred. . . .

☆ IV ☆

GUN-BOSS OF HELLTOWN

*I*t was nearing evening when John Irons's borrowed horse climbed the arid flats where Ten Trees, metropolis of the Cobblestone Range, shouldered out from the turgid Greenhorn River. And Sudden John's face registered sharp distaste as he squinted at the old cow town through the bright luminous haze of the afternoon.

Ten Trees, he saw, was puffing up like a poisoned pup and it was about as attractive. The half block of cabins and false-fronts he had known had suddenly lengthened into an unsightly serpentine maze a mile long. New brick and clapboard buildings stood starkly above all else, with black smokestacks belching black filth into the air. Monuments, John Irons reflected dourly, to what men called civilization. He spat.

The ten stately cottonwoods — only trees for fifty miles in any direction, and the landmarks for which the hills and the town had been named — were gone now, hacked down for firewood or green lumber for some man's shack. The dwellings on the town's outer fringe were squalid, miserable, and filthy. There were tents and shacks and dugouts where whole families lived underground, like rodents. Dirty, starved-looking children played listlessly in the white dust. And the stench that boiled up from ugly, weather-blistered black storage tanks was appalling.

Down in the heart of town, prosperity was more in evidence. The business buildings — some of them — were imposing and new. Every place had its hitching rail in front, and the longest and strongest were before the bars and honkatonks. Of the old Ten Trees John Irons had known, everything was gone, except an occasional cabin dwelling or small false-front cowman's shop, shouldered into oblivion by the new town. Ten Trees was gone. In its place was a boom town — a town John Irons didn't know, sheltering a population he didn't know. A town of wildcatters and riggers and shyster lawyers manipulating laws and leases for their private gain. Sam Blazzard's town!

This, John Irons thought grimly, was the thing Jim Chilcote was fighting. And he felt another bond of sympathy with the game young outlaw. It was a hopeless fight, he knew. But he'd have given his left arm to have been able to side the cowboy in it.

A hand-lettered sign announced the location of the unimposing Warbonnet Cafe, reminding John Irons of the errand he had to perform. He had dismounted before the place and was anchoring his horse to the tie rail, when a shadow fell across him from behind. It was the shadow of a powerful man. And the man held a gun in his hand.

"Leavin', stranger?" a grating voice asked, "or jest comin'?"

John Irons turned slowly to face his inquisitor. The man was of his own approximate height, but was much heavier through the shoulders — a surly, leering hulk of a man with icy, colorless eyes and a big Colt pistol in his hand. The gun was trained on John Irons's chest.

"I ain't decided . . . yet," the Association man replied, entirely frank. "What you think?"

"You're stayin'!" the big man said, emphatically. "You're stayin' a long time! That's an Anchor Ox horse you're ridin'. An' ridin' Anchor Ox horses jest now ain't a healthy pastime. Not in this town!"

The big man flashed a badge as he spoke — a tarnished silver shield showing the words, "Regulator, Cobblestone Pool." And then John Irons recognized this man. Something had turned over in the back of his head when first he'd heard the voice. Now he had the man pigeonholed. It was the masked man who had led the raid on the Ten Trees accommodation train. Lute Poage, Chilcote had called him.

"I ain't ridin' the horse by choice, friend," John Irons eased. "I was on a train. That train was stopped an' set fire to, an' I was booted off in the middle o' the night. I was headed this way, an' it was a long ways to walk. I was offered this horse to ride. An' I wasn't fussy."

The regulator's heavy jaw dropped. He looked at John Irons intently, out of his small pig-eyes. Then recognition lighted his face. "So it's *you!* Wal, I'll be go-to-hell! Brother, I was prayin' I'd meet you ag'in some time. But this here is too much! Say, Sam Blazzard's goin' to be glad to see you! Unbuckle your guns, an' let 'em drop!"

John Irons knew he could have the bully crawling, simply by making his identity known. But his experience with the regulator on the train, plus the man's present overbearing manner, aroused in him a contrary streak which oft-times before had gotten him in trouble. He preferred to make the regulator crawl without divulging his name.

"You plumb shore you're doin' right?" he asked, never winking.

The regulator nodded, profoundly. "I'm takin' you to Sam Blazzard. *Unbuckle them belts!*"

John Irons gambled that the man wouldn't shoot. He shrugged, faintly. "If you want my guns," he said softly — too softly, if the regulator had but known it — "you got to take 'em."

Lute Poage snarled and did what John Irons figured he'd do. He lunged forward in what he thought would be a surprise maneuver, his pistol barrel upraised to club down the cold-eyed stranger. But the surprise maneuver came from Sudden John. He was waiting, his eyes measuring. And when the gun muzzle was uplifted, no longer trained upon him, he reacted as if propelled by a suddenly released internal spring. His left arm knocked the descending gun to one side, his right hand straightened in a drive so blindingly fast that it was doubtful the regulator knew what hit him. He sat down, blank-eyed, in the dust.

Poage still held his gun, but John Irons kicked it from his hand and then shoved it into his own belt. He grabbed the regulator by the shirt and pulled him erect. Supporting the dazed man with one hand, he slapped his face sharply with the flat of the other. Awareness came back into the little eyes. But Lute Poage made no effort to strike back.

"Now," John Irons said, his voice as cordial as it would ever be for Lute Poage, "if Blazzard is spoilin' to see me, it ain't right we should keep him waitin'. Turn around slow an' take me to 'im. But don't try nothin', or I'll knock a grunt outa you as long as a sleigh-track!"

The regulator turned, snarling, and started across the street, weaving like a drunken sheepherder. John Irons followed, aware then of the crowd that had formed over on the sidewalk. If occurred to him that some of the regulator's henchmen must be present, and a glance behind confirmed his hunch. Half a dozen armed men were tagging along. But Lute Poage had reached the opposite side of the dusty street and was entering an ornate clapboard building lettered "Cobblestone Pool, Inc." John Irons followed, gun in hand, ignoring those behind him.

Lute Poage strode straight through a big outer office filled with clerks and secretaries, straight toward an oaken door marked "Samuel H. Blazzard, President." The desk workers looked up casually from their tasks as the head regulator stalked through, and the sharp intake of their breath, when they saw John Irons with the gun in Poage's back, was audible throughout the room. But no one spoke and no one interfered.

Poage opened the oak door and passed through it. John Irons followed, closing the door behind him.

In the president's office John Irons was simultaneously aware of three things. One was a polished mahogany desk, as big as a dance hall, against the far side of the room. The second was the man behind that desk — a heavy man with iron-gray hair and a weathered outdoorsman's face that looked ludicrous and out of place behind a desk so lavish. The third was another man — an older man with stooped shoulders, a drooping walrus mustache, and a city marshal's badge on his stringy vest. Their entrance had, it was plain, interrupted a conference of importance. The red-faced man behind the desk turned white with sudden anger.

"What you mean, bulling in here when I'm busy without knockin'? By the Lord, I'll. . . ."

The red-faced man saw the discolored egg on his henchman's forehead, and his eyes whipped over to Sudden John, and to the gun in the Association man's hand. His voice gave out, and he sank back in his chair. His anger seemed to give way to amazement and curiosity.

John Irons advanced and laid the gun upon the desk. The red-faced man's hand jerked toward a open drawer in front of him. John Irons looked at the hand, and it stopped as if it had encountered a red-hot object. For Irons had placed the gun with its muzzle trained carelessly in the man's direction. His fingers had not yet released the grips.

"It was my idee," Sudden John said, almost pleasantly. "Lute didn't have no choice. He said you was eager to see me, though. An' I kind o' wanted to see you. I wanted to tell you to call off your dawgs, Blazzard. I'm gettin' tired o' them houndin' me. I got job enough here, without havin' to regulate your regulators."

Sam Blazzard, oil king of the Cobblestone Range, looked puzzled.

Lute Poage bristled, defensively. "He's the long-nosed buzzard that we mixed with, on the train!" the regulator blurted. "He helped Chilcote to escape. An' he shows up in town now, ridin' an Anchor Ox horse. I jumped him. But I was alone . . . which I won't be when I go after him ag'in. An' you kin see the lovin' he give me. If he's anybody you know, Sam, git him outa town. 'Cause I aim to skin him alive, an' wear his hide for gloves!"

Sam Blazzard looked at John Irons intently, appraisingly. There was respect and apprehension in his eyes. "Who are you, man? What game you playin', on my range?"

John Irons fumbled in his wallet and handed over his credentials — including the warrant for Chilcote's arrest which the outlaw hadn't bothered to remove while the Association man was unconscious. The oil king scanned the papers, looked up to glance quickly from John to the regulator. Then he burst into a humorless, belly-shaking laugh.

"Lute," he told his henchman, "you better think o' somethin' that'll keep you outa town a week or so. When you find out who you've braced against, your hair's a-going to turn snow white. Lute, I'll make you 'cquainted with Sudden John Irons. Lute Poage."

" *John Ir. . . .*" The big regulator's voice failed him, and he blinked like a light-blinded owl. "An' I said . . . said I was goin' to skin him alive!" Lute Poage forced a laugh, but it was plain he saw nothing very funny.

John Irons let him pass it like a joke, however, and the hulking man backed out of the door, with no effort to get back his captured gun. The stoop-shouldered man got up and followed the regulator, timidly giving John Irons a wide swing.

Sam Blazzard's fog-horn voice halted him in his tracks. "Don't rabbit, Marshal. You'll want to hear this, too. John, meet Chet Sombers, town marshal. You can say anything in front o' Chet you'd say to me alone. Now, where you got him?"

"Got who?"

"Why, Jim Chilcote." Sam Blazzard wiped the laugh-tears from his eyes with the back of a bear-paw hand. "You'll have to make allowance for Lute. Lute ain't too quick to see things. But you ain't fooled me, any. I can see you used Lute an' his boys to get yourself in solid with Chilcote, so's you could catch him off-guard. Well, that's no hide off my back. I'd as leave hand you the reward money as the next 'un. Where is he?"

"Last I seen him," said John Irons, distinctly, "he was at his camp, up in the Ten Trees Hills. He lent me a horse to ride in on."

The oil man stared. "You didn't bring him in?"

John Irons nodded. "That's right. I didn't. I ain't chasin' any reward up here, Blazzard. An' I ain't here to kill your snakes. I got two jobs here . . . to end this war an' to find the man that killed Fronce Ryan. An' that's about my limit."

"But you owe us protection, man. We have a lifetime membership in your Association. . . ."

"We're a cowman's outfit," John Irons reminded him. "We ain't runnin' competition to the Pinkertons. If we'd been called in while this was still a cowman's range fight, we might have took a hand. But we ain't catspaw for your oil company."

The good humor drained out of the oil man's face. "It isn't my funeral, if Oregon Rob wants to renege on a contract. That'll hurt him, not me. But let's understand each other, John Irons. Up here, you either stand with me or again' me. An' you ain't leavin' me much doubt, which."

"I stand for Western Anti," John Irons told him, and a plan was born inside his restless mind. "I stand for bringin' in the man that killed Fronce Ryan an' for endin' the war here. With you or against you, Blazzard, makes no difference to me. I reckon you'll benefit much as any, though, if I can put the lid on this fuss here. So I got a proposition. I'd like to set down with you an' Chilcote both, an' thrash out an item or two."

The oil man started. "Bring Chilcote in *here?*"

"I'd have to have your word," John Irons replied, "that you wouldn't try to hold him."

He watched Blazzard carefully as he spoke. But the oil man's eyes were veiled, taking everything in, letting nothing out. "It might be all right," he said. "Good might come of it." But John Irons couldn't be sure what he was thinking.

"Then I got your word?"

Blazzard nodded. "When do I look for 'im?"

John Irons was purposely vague. "I'll let you know when."

Leaving the oil office, Sudden John crossed to where his horse was tied. Turning suddenly, he started back across the street, and met two men he'd seen in Blazzard's outer office. He knew he was being shadowed, and the knowledge increased his dislike and distrust of the oil king, both of which had been instantaneous and intense. It was evident Blazzard aimed to have him followed, to learn the location of Chilcote's camp. Blazzard had not promised the outlaw amnesty out there.

Changing his plan, Sudden John turned into the Warbonnet Cafe, and took a stool along the counter. Soon the door from the kitchen opened, admitting a host of tantalizing smells and a girl with eyes like columbines and hair like wild flax.

"I seen a cowboy today, out in the hills," he told the girl, abruptly, when she'd paused to take his order. "He asked me to tell you he was all right."

The girl, beautiful before, was suddenly radiant. And John Irons had another point in favor of the cowboy outlaw. If Chilcote were as bad as he had been painted, he would not be loved by a girl so pretty and nice as this one.

"I have to get in touch with Jim," he told the uncommunicative girl. "And I can't ride out to him, myself. Certain folks in this town are expecting me to do just that, so's they can follow and spot his camp. Now I rode an Anchor Ox horse in town today. Jim told me to leave it at Jimson's barn. The horse'll be there tonight, when it's dark. If you know somebody who'd ride that horse to Jim's camp and give him my message, I would be obliged. And Jim, I reckon, would be ahead."

The girl was watching him intently. "I know someone who might ride out," she said, guardedly. And John Irons was both cheered and distressed. Jim Chilcote had loyal, intelligent friends.

"Tell . . . have the party that goes . . . tell Jim to be in town tomorrow night.

Tell him it's important. He's to come alone, and John Irons will guarantee his safety while he's here. Tell him I'll meet him at Jimson's barn."

Leaving the place half an hour later, his envy of Chilcote heightened by the cooking he had eaten. John Irons delivered the horse to the livery barn, as appointed. Then, as evening wore on, he made himself conspicuous about the bars and gaming houses, to divert attention from the barn. At last, satisfied that the girl with the columbine eyes would be well on her way to the Ten Trees Hills, he went to the railroad ticket office and scribbled a telegram to McDade's assistant in Cheyenne, requesting he check the ownership of Barrel Springs at the territorial land office.

"Tap this out on your brass key," he told the freight agent, playing out a hunch born inside Blazzard's office hours before. "It's for Mike Howe, in Cheyenne."

The agent peered at him skeptically through the grill and inched toward the sawed-off shotgun, kept handy for emergencies. Then Sudden John pulled a fresh new fifty dollar bill from his wallet, tore it exactly in half, and pushed one segment under the iron grilling.

"That wire's important," he remarked. "And I want the answer, quick as it comes through. I'll be somewhere in town, and you can look me up. Take this half of bill now. And the other's yours when you give me the answer."

☆ **V** ☆

THE TEN TREES GUNFIGHT

*I*t was late the next night when John Irons found Sam Blazzard in the palatial Black Gold Palace, drinking with his wizened city marshal. Lute Poage was not in sight. John Irons did not like that angle. But Jim Chilcote had complied with his request, and every minute the outlaw was in town his life was in mortal danger. John Irons couldn't keep him waiting. He made for the oil king. And Blazzard turned, seeing him in the mirror.

"Have a drink," the oil man invited.

John Irons declined. Drinking with a man was — in Sudden John's code — a pledge of lasting friendship. And he was not yet ready to make Sam Blazzard such a pledge. "Maybe later, thanks. Right now there is a big game in the back room of the Stockman's Bar. I thought you might be interested."

Blazzard's eyes were alert. "Big game, eh? What are the stakes?"

"Control of Cobblestone oil range," John Irons said. "An' the loser hangs for the murder of Fronce Ryan. Might say the sky's the limit."

Minutes passed in silence with Blazzard's narrow eyes boring into John Irons's gaze, as if peering into the inside of his mind. Then he seemed to reach a decision. Turning his attention to his drink, he drank his chaser, poured his straight whiskey down on top of it, and never noticed the difference.

"I wouldn't mind buyin' chips in a game like that," he said.

John Irons was certain the marshal had overheard the conversation. And he didn't mean to leave the man behind to inform the regulators where their chief had gone. "Better string along, Marshal," he invited. "Sometimes it helps to have the law handy, in a game where all the chips are blue."

The lawman started to decline. But something in John Irons's eyes changed his mind. He drank his drink and wiped his handlebar mustache on the back of his hand. "Don't mind of I do string along," he said agreeably. "An' watch."

The Stockman's Bar was small and modest — a relic of the Ten Trees John Irons had known before the coming of the oil. Only the old-timers patronized it, and John Irons had no fear that any of the regulators would be present. Indeed, it was for that reason that Jim Chilcote had selected the place as scene for the coming conference. But there was a chance they would be followed, so he took a devious, roundabout path to the unlighted backdoor and he knocked before entering.

They found Jim Chilcote seated alone at the table in the center of the small room. He didn't get up when the others entered. He only looked at Sam Blazzard. And John Irons sincerely hoped that no man ever looked at him so.

The Association man bolted the door they had entered, and crossed the room to bolt the door leading to the barroom. Then he looked the room over very carefully. The only window was unblinded. But it was small, and too high off the ground, for anyone to see in from the outside.

"Gentlemen, set," he said, graciously, "an' be sociable. We might be here a long time. Nobody is leavin', till I know who killed Fronce Ryan. And why!"

The two men standing accepted the invitation, but they gave no further indication they'd heard him. Blazzard and Chilcote were sitting on opposite sides of the table, their eyes locked in icy stare. Chilcote's hands gripped the edge of the hardwood board, just above the butts of his holstered guns. Blazzard's right hand was below the table level, near the gun he carried belted in front. The mustached marshal sat alone at the table's far end. The tips of his right-hand fingers were lost under the left lapel of his clawhammer coat. His eyes were vacant as an Indian's.

"I never thought, Blazzard," Chilcote was saying, "that I'd set this close to you with a gun under my hand, an' not shoot your coyotes' eyes out!"

The oil man stiffened on his chair, and his cold eyes hurled a challenge. "You can try it," he said, "any time you feel lucky."

The showdown in the Cobblestone feud, John Irons could see, was coming — and prematurely. Nor was it to his liking. He had gotten Blazzard and Chilcote together in the hope that he could in that way drag or scare the truth out of one of them. But the situation had gotten out of hand. And dead men, he knew, told no tales. He was casting about a way of stalling off the crisis when a knock sounded at the door leading into the barroom.

"Telegram," a throaty voice called. "For John Irons!"

"Slide it under the door," John Irons replied, and under it came. Then Irons slid the second half of the torn bill the way the telegram had come, picked up the wire, and read it through. It was from Oregon Rob, and it read:

Original filing on Barrel Spring in Chan Chilcote's name. What's wrong with that water hole? Fronce Ryan wired to find out same before he was shot.

Coldly, John Irons lifted his eyes to Sam Blazzard. "You like a chaser with bad news?" he inquired. "Or can you take it straight?"

Blazzard looked toward the telegram, and John Irons handed it over. Blazzard read it then handed it back, his face expressionless. "Bad news is right, John Irons, if it's true."

John Irons shifted his position to where he could watch the oil man and the crooked marshal at once. "It's worse'n you know, Sam. You're under arrest . . . for murder. You killed Chan Chilcote and Fronce Ryan, and you've tried to kill Jim here, too. All because of what that telegram says!"

Blazzard sneered. "You've lost your mind, *hombre.* . . ?"

John Irons's voice filled the room, cutting him off. It wasn't a pleasant sound. "It's no good Sam. You're done. I know just about everything, and what I don't know I can guess. You came up on Barrel Spring that day three months ago while Chan and Jim Chilcote were gone back to the Anchor Ox for dynamite to. blow it with. You saw it flowing oil, and you saw the Chilcotes coming back, so you hid out there-abouts to watch. You saw 'em blow the hole, and you guessed what they were up to.

"You took the next train for Cheyenne, Blazzard, to file on that spring section yourself, figuring to open up that oil pocket. But you found Chan had beat you to it by a couple of days. So you had to run Chan off the range, to get it back. You let it out you'd seem 'em blow the spring, and you got the Anchor Ox read out of the Pool. When that didn't put Chan out of business, you planted that refinery oil in the post-hole . . . not on ground where there *was* oil, but on ground Chan was using for range . . . to stampede his cow pasture and ruin him.

"Chan knew what you were up to," the Association man went on, the jigsaw segments falling together to complete the pattern as he spoke. "But he couldn't bring the law on you without letting the cat out about the real oil, and he knew what that would do to his cow range. So he fought you the only way he could . . . with a gun. And he played square into your hand, 'cause that give you an excuse to kill him and get him out of the way, permanently.

"With Chan dead, you were sitting pretty, Blazzard. But young Jim was Chan's heir and rightful owner of the spring section. You had to kill Jim, too, before you were all in the clear. You were well on your way to getting that done, too. But you slipped badly when you called Western Anti in to do your killing. And you caught your neck in a noose!"

The oil man smiled, confidently. "You're nuts, John Irons. You're barkin' up the wrong tree. Ain't a court in the land would touch me."

"There's one court that will," John Irons promised. "Blazzard, the only jury you'll see will be the men you've hoodwinked, and ruined. They'll touch you, once I've told 'em what I know. They'll turn on you like curly wolves. Blazzard, you won't live tomorrow out in this town, once I've spilt!"

"You've spilt now, John Irons!" the oil man snarled, and Sudden John could see he'd jabbed where the oiler was touchy. "You ain't tellin' nothing more around this town. An' Barrel Springs will still be mine, because Jim Chilcote won't be around to claim it. My filin' will stand, John Irons. An' you're going to die. . . ."

"Like Fronce died," John Irons cut in, "when he got into your game. That it, Sam?"

The oil king nodded, and smiled, recalling. "Like Fronce died, John, for stickin' his long nose into things that didn't concern him. Don't move, either of you. John Irons, don't even blink your damned cat's eyes. You're covered! Lute Poage is outside that window right now, on a stepladder, an' his carbine's got its ears back. First of you that wiggles his ears will die first, the other one second. Don't nobody crowd now, 'cause you'll all git your turn!"

John Irons heard glass tinkle behind him, and the look on Jim Chilcote's face told him Blazzard wasn't bluffing. He was covered, all right. He swore at himself for a fool, for walking into such a trap. Then, unexpectedly, guns crashed outside the saloon, and a shout went up — two shouts, in fact. One was a rousing triumphant yell of vengeance, the other a snarling, savage whine of men caught and trapped by certain death. At the same time Lute Poage's bullet-riddled body smashed through the window and fell into the room. And what happened then broke fast.

Sam Blazzard came to his feet in a backward leap that upset his chair, and his right hand clawed for the gun in the holster under his Prince Albert coat. The crooked marshal didn't bother to stand, but snaked the gun from his shoulder carrier, and started shooting from his chair.

John Irons's own guns were out, and he fired rapidly, backing away from the open window. He played the marshal first, because that man's lead was already snarling near his head. He got the lawman's range. Two crimson rosettes flowered as if by magic on the florid waistcoat. The marshal slumped face-down upon the table. His gun was silent.

John Irons turned his guns quickly at Sam Blazzard. But he didn't shoot. He didn't have to. Jim Chilcote, his eyes blazing with a lethal hate, had beaten Blazzard by a hair to a fair draw. He had almost emptied the cylinder of his gun into the big man's barrel chest. But the oil king of the Cobblestone Range was dying as hard as he had lived. His heart must have been shot to shreds, but he wouldn't give in. Not so long as a man he hated as he hated Chilcote still lived.

Sam Blazzard stood on widespread feet, swaying like a mortally wounded buffalo bull that refused to go down. It took both his hands to lift and steady the pistol in his hand. But he lifted it, steadied it, and shot. The bullet went wild, however, and the punctured heart in the big chest seemed to burst under the strain of that final effort. Sam Blazzard teetered forward, following his falling gun to the floor.

The raving clamor of the guns outside ceased as suddenly as did the firing inside the smoke-filled room, and the stark silence was as unnerving as the fury of sound had been. As John Irons wondered about that shooting outside, a man's anxious voice called through the locked door. "Hey, Jim! You all right? You an' that long-barreled, ranniky badger with you?"

"All right enough!" the outlaw shouted back. "You boys keep after 'em out there. Don't stop till there ain't a regulator left this side o' the Greenhorn. The country'll get by without 'em."

Chilcote caught John Irons's inquiring look, and he explained. "I figgered Sam for a play like this, trappin' us in here from outside. So I rigged up a rannicaboo of my own. My boys strung along tonight, an' I posted 'em around this bar where they could do the most good . . . while you went for Blazzard."

"An' a damn' good job you did!" the Association man admitted.

"But nothin' like the job you pulled," the cowboy said, "runnin' that bluff about Pa filin' on Barrel spring an' ownin' the oil! Sam shore swallowed that! It was rich. . . ."

John Irons nodded. He could see a squall brewing, and he acted to head it off. "Shore he swallered it. And Jimmy, you better start chewing on it yourself. 'Cause it's the fact. I guessed it, when you told me about you and Chan finding that oil last spring. I knew Chan was a cowman before anything else, and he'd fight to the last ditch to hold his grass. But he had a head for business, too. I knew he wouldn't turn his back on a oil strike, leaving it for someone else to file on. That would have been asking for the very thing to happen that did. I sent a wire to Oregon Rob, asking him to check filing records in Cheyenne. This here is what I got back."

He gave Chilcote the telegram, saw amazement and stubborn rebellion flare in the blue-gray eyes. "This is one o' your tricks, John Irons!" the cowboy blazed. "Pa wouldn't have dirtied his hands in that stinkin' grease. He told me so! An' if he had owned it, why'n't he come inta the open an' claim it, after the trouble broke?"

"Your pa didn't *want* to dirty his hands in it . . . without he had to," John Irons said, choosing his words with care. "But he was a smart man. Which you aren't. He saw if that oil was ever found, all hell and hot water couldn't hold the wildcatters off the Cobblestone range. He saw that if that brand of hell was going to be let loose up here, why he'd better be in shape to keep a check rein on it. So he filed on the land. He didn't say anything at first, because he wasn't shore that oil in the post-hole was the real McCoy, and he was still trying to cover up that real strike. Then when Blazzard brought out the big strike, Chan was dead and couldn't say anything."

But the cowboy saw a ray of hope. "The filin' won't stand, though. The gov'ment is holdin' back oil an' mineral rights on this ground!"

"*Since* that fake strike was made," John Irons amended. "But Chan filed on Barrel Spring before the government dreamed there was oil in this country. Your rights are good, Jimmy. You own the Cobblestone oil fields. She's all yours!"

Rebellion flared brighter in the hard blue-gray eyes. "I don't want it, John Irons! I'll never claim it. I won't be another Sam Blazzard 'round here!"

John Irons's temper slipped a notch. "You won't need to be a Sam Blazzard. I'm only trying to show you how you can keep Blazzard's kind out of control here . . . by taking over yourself. You could even bring ranching back, maybe, and help the Poolers that deserve help back on their feet . . . with your take from the oil. I was thinking if you'd do that, why I'd see to it Western Anti would get the law charges against you smashed. Then you could settle down with that blue-eyed gal and do the things your pa would've done."

Jim Chilcote was quiet a long time. Then his slow smile broke again. "I never fancied oil-ranchin' much, John," he said. "But it looks like your mind is made up. And I oughta know better'n to fight you. I'll take over. Your war's over, too. Now I better find Nellie."

Three days later, John Irons faced Oregon Rob again, back in Western Anti's Cheyenne office. McDade had read newspaper accounts of Sam Blazzard's death, at Jim Chilcote's hands. He had seen where Jim Chilcote was now oil king of the Cobblestone Range. He had seen no word or mention of John Irons. He had drawn his own conclusions and had marked the Cobblestone case "unclosed." Impatiently, he'd awaited the return of his inspector at large. And even after he'd heard John Irons's story, Oregon Rob was skeptical. "I never knew you to fall down on a case, John," he growled. "But this time I ain't shore. I'd sorta counted on hangin' Chilcote, an' mebbe you jumped at conclusions . . . an' missed. I can't hardly b'lieve it was Blazzard behind that powerhouse grab. Not after the fuss he put up to keep Chilcote from takin' over the Cobblestone Range. Seems funny that he was plottin' to do the same. . . ."

John Irons yawned. " 'Tain't so funny, Rob, when you look at it. You ever see two hound dogs chase a rabbit? Didn't you ever notice it's the one falling behind that does the yapping?"

A moment passed in silence, with Oregon Rob looking at his gaunt inspector out of beady, bright eyes. Then he crossed out the words "unclosed" and wrote "closed" to the Cobblestone Case. "It must have been a dry ride back," he remarked, civilly. "You use a bit of somethin' to take the edge off the heat? I'll buy!"

SIX-GUN SNARE

(1944)

☆

by LES SAVAGE, JR.

Les Savage, Jr. was an extremely gifted writer who was born in Alhambra, California, but grew up in Los Angeles. His first story was "Bullets and Bullwhips," published in Street & Smith's Western Story Magazine. *Almost ninety more magazine stories followed, many of them published in Fiction House magazines such as* Frontier Stories *and* Lariat Story Magazine *where Savage became a superstar with his name on many covers. Such noteworthy Savage titles as* Silver Street Woman *(Hanover House, 1954) and* Return to Warbow *(Dell First Edition, 1956) are classics of the Western story. Due to his preference for historical accuracy, Savage often ran into problems with book editors in the 1950s who were concerned about marriages between his protagonists and women of different races—commonplace on the real frontier but not in much Western fiction in that decade. As a result of the censorship imposed on many of his works, only now have they been fully restored by returning to the author's original manuscripts.* Table Rock, *Savage's last book, was even suppressed by his agent in part because of its depiction of Chinese on the frontier. It has now been published as he wrote it by Walker and Company in the United States and Robert Hale, Ltd., in the United Kingdom.* Six-Gun Bride of the Teton Bunch *(Barricade Books, 1995) is the title of a Western story collection and among his most recently published novels are* Fire Dance at Spider Rock *(Five Star Westerns, 1995) and* The Legend of Señorita Scorpion *(Circle Ⓥ Westerns, 1996). Savage wrote five short novels for* Star Western. *Mike Tilden changed the title of this story to "Water Rights—Bought In Hell!" when it appeared.*

☆ **I** ☆

THE KILLER COMES HOME

𝕯irk Hood stood on the curb where the Caldwell-San Antone stage had deposited him, for a moment unaware of the strange hush that had settled over Caprock. It had been four years since he'd stood here on Second Street, with the white alkali dust sifting up from beneath his boots and filling his mouth with that familiar gritty taste — as acrid and bitter as all the hate and fighting and killing that had swept this town from its beginnings.

There were young things about Dirk Hood, standing there, and old things. The skin across the high plane of his cheek was pale from some long confinement, and smooth. But his mouth was drawn too thin for youth, and his eyes held a cautious, almost secretive look. His black hair was beginning to grow long again beneath an ancient flat-topped Stetson. He had a good breadth to his shoulders beneath the faded gray coat, and his legs fitted the brass-riveted Levi's with a slight horse-collar bow.

He carried a denim warsack under one arm, filled with his few belongings. It was the only thing Caprock had seen him take with him four years ago; it was the only thing Caprock would see him bring back. The other things he had taken away and had brought back were deep inside him, and he meant to keep them there.

Mickey Walker's spotted hound trotted across the intersection of Second and Mesa, half a block east of Dirk, disappearing into Kruger's Barns on the northwest corner. The movement drew Dirk's attention to the strange quietude lying over the town. He felt a sudden catch at his throat that wasn't the dust. He knew that stillness. There was something special about it.

The same silence had gripped Caprock four years ago, when Dirk had stood across the street by Kruger's big frame barns, waiting for Hugh Glendenning to step out of the covered stairway that led down from the second story of the red brick bank on this side. Waiting with a gun, because that was how Hugh Glendenning had told him to come.

The snort of a horse turned Dirk's head. They had escaped his notice, standing at the corner of Hammer's bank, so they could see all four ways from the intersection. There were three men, sitting horses with the Keyhole brand showing dimly on dusty rumps, holding two empty horses. Dirk Hood squinted his eyes to recognize Lige Glendenning.

Then the covered stairway leading down the south wall of the bank from the land office above trembled to the hard-heeled descent of two men. They stepped onto the sidewalk one after the other, swept Second with a swift glance, and moved toward the horses.

The one leading was Lige's father, Orson Glendenning. He owned the Keyhole outfit. Hugh Glendenning had been his only brother. He was a tall man, Orson, with the long square jaw of one who might be hard to put off his single-track once he got going on it. His black Mormon set squarely on iron-gray hair that was cropped short on his bony skull. The six-gun that drew its bulge beneath his town coat held its own ominous significance; he was known as a man who never wore a gun unless he meant to use it.

He spoke to his son before he reached the corner and, in the silence, the words carried plainly to Dirk. "I told you Hammer wouldn't give us the loan, Lige. He's Kruger's man now, just like all the rest."

Then Orson must have seen how intently Lige was looking past him down Second. He stopped speaking, and turned to follow his son's gaze down beyond the bank to where Dirk Hood stood in front of the stage office. Dirk saw the slow stiffening of his gaunt body. Then Orson Glendenning turned around and began to come back toward Dirk; the Keyhole hand who had accompanied him followed. Lige said something to the pair of mounted men, climbed off his horse, and came after his father. Their boots made a hollow rattle on the plank walk. It was the only sound.

Dirk shifted his warsack beneath his arm. He knew what was coming. Part of it was that the Glendennings led the South Fork faction, and that four years ago Dirk Hood had ridden for the North Fork bunch, and that it had always been this way between the two factions when they met in Caprock. Most of it was that Hugh Glendenning had been Orson's brother, and Lige's uncle.

Orson Glendenning stopped in front of Dirk, leaning forward tensely when he spoke, disbelief in his voice. "Dirk Hood. I thought you were sent up for life."

Dirk didn't answer. There was nothing for him to say. Orson Glendenning spoke again, anger sweeping away the surprised sound in his voice. "You were paroled," he stated. "Kruger finally swung it."

Dirk nodded, still not speaking, feeling the clammy sweat forming beneath his armpits. He could see thin hate twisting into Lige's face.

"And you can come back here," said Lige venomously. "You can come back here and stand in the very street you stood in to murder my uncle."

Dirk felt his own anger rising. "Lige. . . ."

"He was your friend," said Lige, taking a vicious step forward. "Hugh was the only decent man you ever called your friend in your life, Dirk Hood, and you murdered him."

"Shut up!" Dirk's voice seemed to explode from him. "I didn't come back to talk about it. What do you suppose I've been thinking about the last four years? Talking like that doesn't help now. I know what I did!"

Lige moved in till his face wasn't a foot from Dirk's. "I told you never to let me see you in Caprock again, Hood."

Orson grabbed at his son's arm. "Wait a minute son. How do you know Kruger didn't put Hood out here for just this purpose?"

Lige shook his father's hand off and reached out to grab Dirk by the lapels, yanking him off balance. "Maybe he did. I hope so. Things might as well finish here and now."

"Take your hands off me," said Dirk Hood.

"You're leaving, Hood!" said Lige Glendenning in a gusty voice. "You turn around and march out of Caprock and don't ever come back, or by God I'll give you the worst pistol-whipping Texas ever watched."

He gasped suddenly. Dirk's hand was closed on his wrist, tearing his fingers from the coat lapel. With a harsh curse, Lige jerked backward and tried to yank his arm free. Dirk flung Lige's wrist down and away from him.

"Lige," yelled Orson, jumping at them.

Lige's face twisted savagely as he whipped one of his Colts out and above his head, lunging back at Dirk. Hood bent forward suddenly, swinging his warsack from beneath his arm and jamming it upward. Lige was plunging in and couldn't stop the down-swinging gun from thudding into the denim sack where Dirk held it above his head.

Dirk felt the warsack thud against his shoulder from the force of the blow. He let go of it and hit Lige in the stomach. Then Orson's weight crashed in from one side and the Keyhole hand struck him from the other.

In a moment Dirk was the center of the struggling mass. His head rocked as Lige struck again with his gun. He gasped as the Keyhole rider came in with a knee lifted into his belly. Then Dirk lurched on forward into Lige and caught him in the stomach, knocking him off the curb. Whirling, Dirk grabbed Orson about his spare middle and jerked him around into the cowhand. He lowered his shoulder against Orson and shoved him and the rider off the curb and into Lige who was just getting up, and they all went down in a heap.

Dirk was on his feet like a cat, kicking free of Lige's clawing hand, turning sharply from one man to the other, panting, bent forward a little with his arms out. Orson jumped backward and shoved his coat away from his gun. Lige drew his second Colt and lifted it without trying to rise. A mounted Keyhole man fought his rearing horse around to aim his Winchester at Dirk.

"That'll do, damn you, that'll do!"

Dirk saw Lige's Colt stop coming up, saw Orson halt with his coat held back from a weapon half drawn. Dirk turned toward the intersection, from where the booming voice had come. Sheriff Mickey Walker shook the earth as he descended from the high curb to the rutted street and walked down to them. The sheriff had a big Peacemaker in his horny fist. His eyes blazed like a ringy bull's from the apoplectic red of his face, and every time he took a step his snow-white goatee bobbed in rhythm to the angry quiver of his paunch. He reached the group and planted his size-twelve Hyers in the ground like post-oaks. He shoved his ten-gallon back on a mane of white hair.

"Lige Glendenning," he thundered, "you and your whole clan get on those horses and race back to the Keyhole, or I'll throw you in the calabozo for disturbing the peace. Dirk Hood's here on parole and I'm responsible for his conduct. No herring-gutted South Fork man's going to cause any trouble with him!"

Lige picked up the gun he had dropped and stood there a moment, trembling with rage. Breathing heavily, Orson walked over to him. The older man drew his son toward the horses. Lige mounted his dish-faced mare; he swung it so he faced Dirk from the saddle.

"All right," he said. "Don't think this'll help, Hood. Don't think you're staying here . . . you or Kruger or Kruger's fat tin-badge. You're all going! Just remember that, Hood."

Sheriff Mickey Walker stood there in the dusty street, watching the five horsemen turn the corner at Mesa and lift a cloud of dust southward toward the Keyhole. Finally the lawman turned to Dirk. "Tarnation, son," he said. "How do you expect to stay out of jail on good behavior when the first thing you do back in town is start a ruckus?"

"I didn't want it that way, Mick," said Dirk heavily. "But it was bound to happen. How did you swing the parole? I thought Orson was fighting it."

"Things have changed in Caprock, Dirk," said Walker, putting his gun away. "When you rode for Jess Kruger, he was the underdog, and Glendenning sat the saddle here. But the cinch has busted under Orson. The South Fork's drying up."

Dirk had bent to pick up his warsack. He straightened, a strange tight look on his face. South Fork drying up? That was incomprehensible. Twenty miles west of the townsite, the Rio Cabezon forked into two branches, the South Fork running below Caprock, the North Fork turning above. Dirk Hood's father had pioneered here with Hugh Glendenning, Orson's brother. From their original quarter sections, both men had spread out, until John Hood's Keyhole outfit and Glendenning's H Bar H controlled all the water of the South Fork.

Whatever newcomers arrived after that had to be satisfied with the grass and water of the North Fork, which was already showing signs of drying up. One of these newcomers had been Jess Kruger. Kruger's refusal to submit to the stronger South Fork group had started a feud that grew until Caprock was known from Oklahoma to Mexico as a town where a man would find lead pushing his breakfast out backwards if he so much as struck a match on the wrong side of Second Street. And throughout that long bitter war, it had always been Jess Kruger fighting from the bottom. Now. . . .

Walker saw the look in Dirk's eyes, and he nodded. "With the South Fork drying up, Orson and his bunch don't swing any more rope than Jess Kruger. Just as many of their cattle died this summer as Jess's did; just as many of them have first and second mortgages on their spreads. You saw how Orson went out. It's Kruger's town now; he ain't the underdog anymore. I think that's partly why you rode for him; you was always a kind to pull for the underdog."

"Partly," said Dirk. "Mostly because I thought I hated Hugh Glendenning more than any man on earth. He and Dad built this country together, Mick. For sixteen years I thought Hugh was the best friend Dad and I had. How could he turn on me that way when Dad died, Mick?"

The sheriff dropped his hand on Dirk's shoulder. "You've got to remember none of your friends could help you that time, Dirk. Hugh was in the same fix as everybody else, Dirk. He didn't have a dime left after that winter."

Dirk shook his head. "I believed Hugh at first, when I went to him for help and he told me he couldn't do anything. Then Orson Glendenning came from Chicago and brought the Keyhole at bank sale. Not six months after I'd lost it because Hugh said he couldn't help me. What else could it look like?"

"You didn't let it look like anything else," said Mick, not meeting his eyes. "I can't say as I blame you. On the surface it did look like he sold you out. There was other folks thought the same thing for a long time afterward. I guess it made you pretty mad. Did you think you'd get even with Hugh, signing up with Kruger that way?"

Dirk drew a heavy breath. "I don't know, Mick. I was all mixed up. Maybe Uncle El was right. He tried to make me stay out of the feud. He said it took a stronger man to stay in the middle than it took to take sides. He said I'd end up regretting what I did, whichever side I rode for. I'm telling him that now, Mick. I'm telling him that he was right."

Dirk felt the sheriff's hand tighten on his shoulder. "Kid," said Walker, "your Uncle El . . . your uncle's dead."

Dirk stood there a long moment, a heavy constriction in his chest. Abstractedly, he was aware that the town had come to life again. A group of Jess Kruger's Long Shank riders had moved out of the hardware store on the northeast corner of Second and Mesa, were standing on the sidewalk beneath the overhang, holding Winchesters. A man crossed from Kruger's Barns to the bank, looking southward down Mesa after the Keyhole bunch. The shock was gone now, and Dirk felt the first grief.

"When did he die?" he asked, almost inaudibly.

"Just after you were sent up," said Mick. "Almost four years ago. We found him in his barn with his head knocked in. . . ." He cut off as Dirk's pale face jerked up; there was a sharp, twisted look to the boy's mouth. Mick nodded. "We don't know who did it. They used one of his own hammers."

"But why?" almost whispered Dirk.

Why? An old man like that, without an enemy in the world!

"My uncle's things," said Dirk suddenly. "Where are they?"

Mick opened his mouth a little. "His what?"

"His things," repeated Dirk harshly. "His tools, his forge. I told you how it was going to be. I came back to tell Uncle El he'd been right, and to live in this town the way he wanted me to. I didn't come back to shoot anybody."

Mick's eyes widened beneath shaggy white brows. "Listen, kid, we all know how you feel about Hugh Glendenning. We don't blame you for what happened, even for sending him that note. . . ."

"I didn't send any note," said Dirk hotly. "I got one from him, saying to meet him at Second and Mesa, two o'clock that day, with my gun out."

"Okay, okay," said Mickey Walker, tightening the hand on his shoulder. "It doesn't matter. But you can't let it affect you this way, kid. None of us blame you for what happened. He sent you a note saying to meet him that way. What else could you do when you saw him step out of Slagel's stairway and saw his hand move. If your shot hadn't killed Hugh, Seeco Smith's would have, or some other Long Shanker's. You know how the fireworks started the minute you pulled your gun."

"He was unarmed, Mick," said Dirk hoarsely. "He was just raising his hand and I thought he was drawing and I murdered him."

"You didn't know that," said Mick.

Dirk's face was white and set. "Did you ever stay awake most of the night, night after night, for four years, knowing you'd killed a man who'd been your best friend as long as you'd lived? Do you think I'd pack a gun for Jess Kruger again?"

"But Jess sprung you," said the sheriff tightly. "You can't buck him. You know what'll happen if you try it. He owns Caprock, and he'll get rid of you just as fast as he would a South Forker."

"Or my uncle?" said Dirk, and felt Mick's hand slide from his arm, saw Mick's face turn suddenly pale. "*Where are my uncles things, Mick?*"

☆ **II** ☆

DEAD MAN ON THE FENCE

Clyde Slagel's office was on the second story of Hammer's red-brick bank. It was a comfortable, furnished room, its sagging leather armchairs and huge littered desk reflecting Slagel's easy-going disposition. Slagel himself sat with his swivel chair tilted back, feet propped up on the desk. He wore a blue Prince Albert and pin-striped trousers. His hair was graying at the temples, giving him a mildly distinguished look. He was smiling beneath a small, clipped mustache.

"Sheriff Walker was right, Dirk," he said pleasantly. "I handled El Hood's estate. There was no kin to do it, with your father dead, an you, ah, upstate. El had some debts and his barn and lot went for them. There was some old equipment, along with his personal effects, that I couldn't get rid of. You'll find them stored in the rear end of Kruger's Barns."

From where he stood, Dirk could read the sign on the glass of the window. Clyde Slagel, United States Land Office. Beyond that, across Second, was the two-story, paint-peeled side wall of Kruger's Barns. Clyde Slagel's black crow hopped across the desk, fluttering through the mess of papers.

"There's something more, Mister Slagel," said Dirk. "About Uncle El."

Clyde Slagel's smile faded a little. "I suppose you want my ideas?"

"Not unless you want to give them," said Dirk stiffly.

Slagel shrugged. "I have none, Dirk. He was found dead some weeks after you were sent up. That's all I know."

Dirk's face hardened. "I understand how it is. You and my uncle were about the only men in town who didn't belong to one side or the other."

Slagel took some breadcrumbs from a drawer and began to feed the crow. "And now I'm the only one left, is that what you meant? I'm not afraid of Jess Kruger, Dirk. If I had any ideas, you'd be first to hear them. But I haven't. There wasn't any reason to kill your uncle. You find me a reason and maybe I'll find some ideas. Isn't that right, Edgar?"

"Nevermore," rasped the crow.

Slagel laughed softly again, then turned to his son who lounged in one of the leather chairs. "Victor, you take Dirk over and unlock that storeroom of Kruger's."

Victor Slagel had none of his father's refinement. He was a big, top-heavy man in his middle twenties, with heavy black hair that fell unbrushed over a low forehead. He wore a smith's apron over the knotty bulge of his shoulders. The hand he jerked at Dirk was callused and grimed from the forge.

"You aren't going to let him. . . ," he began.

"Victor," said Clyde Slagel, feeding his crow another crumb, "we owe Dirk what help we can give him. If he's going to stay out of the fight like his Uncle El did, it makes him one of us. Just because you work at Kruger's forge doesn't mean you're Kruger's man. I thought we had that out a time back. If you don't like real estate, that's all right with me. But don't you get to thinking like a Kruger man. A town should be a place where you can live as you want and think as you want and do as you want. Don't you agree, Edgar?"

"Nevermore," croaked the crow.

"Thanks, Mister Slagel," said Dirk. "How about a place to set up in? I got ten dollars when they released me. It'd do for a first month's rent till I got started."

Slagel pursed his lips. "Kruger owns more of Caprock than he used to, Dirk. Whatever I hold is rented."

"Who holds that vacant lot?"

Victor's mouth sagged. "Across from Kruger's?"

Clyde Slagel began to laugh, then he got up. "Yes, Victor, across from Kruger's. What other kind of boy did you think Dirk Hood was? The vacant lot across from Kruger's. I hold it, Dirk. And if you want to set up there, you go right ahead."

His soft laugh followed them out the door and down the stairs, and Dirk didn't know whether he liked it or not.

Sullenly, Victor went with Dirk across the street and into Kruger's. Dirk followed him down the lane between the stalls to where several Long Shank riders lounged around the forges at the rear of the big frame barns. Seeco Smith sat on an unused anvil. When Dirk had begun to ride for Kruger, it had been Seeco who taught the boy gun-savvy. And when the time came for the meeting between Dirk Hood and Hugh Glendenning, Seeco's teaching had turned Dirk's draw into an instinctive reaction that he didn't even have to think about — until it was too late to think.

Seeco's flannel shirt hung loose on a slat-limbed torso, tucked into the tight waistband of rawhide *chivarras* that served him for pants. There was nothing fancy about the way he wore his wooden-handled Remington; the only thing that marked his talent was the myriad of faint scars across the top part of his worn holster, which might have come from the constant scrape of fingernails over the leather.

"Hello, Dirk," he said without smiling. "I hear you're going to watch the roundup from the fence."

The towering blacksmith had stopped working his bellows. A silence had settled over the barns. The other Kruger men were watching Dirk intently. From up front a horse snorted.

The hand Seeco Smith rubbed across his sandy three-day growth of whiskers did not show any rope burns. "It hits men that way sometimes. Maybe you remember I told you that. Shoot their first man and they lose their guts. I wouldn't have wasted my time on you if I'd've thought you were that kind."

Kirk took a small, jerky step toward him. Seeco didn't move. His pale blue eyes were old and wise behind their wind-wrinkled lids. Dirk took a heavy breath; then he turned to Victor, jerking his head. Victor went on past the forge, and Dirk followed. Behind him he heard the hollow puffing sound of the bellows start up again. He could feel the nails of his closed fingers digging into the flesh of his palms.

El Hood's old anvil stood beside his pile of rusting tools in the storeroom at the very rear. Dirk picked up a hoof chisel, toed at some corroded nail-nippers. Beneath them lay a strange three-pronged object in the form of a Y, with a torn buckskin sack on the end of one prong. The leather of the sack looked slick and gummy, as if it had been pitched to make it water-proof.

"That isn't Uncle El's," said Dirk.

"That's Clyde's," said Victor, picking it up swiftly. "Since the South Fork started drying up, Orson Glendenning's been hunting for a dome of water underground. Figures it must be somewhere around here because the Rio Cabezon rises from underground. Clyde's been using this water-witch to help him locate it."

"Found any water?"

"No," said Victor, almost defensively, "but I've seen it work. You hold the two forks in your hand with the sack full of water hanging toward the ground. They use it the same way to find a dome of oil, or minerals . . . except they fill the sack with oil, or put in a silver dollar or gold piece on the bottom prong. When you get directly over the water or oil, the witch begins shaking like a spooked horse. I've seen it happen."

"Not around here, though," muttered Dirk, squatting to sort through the tools. "Where's the tin box?"

Victor Slagel seemed to hesitate. "What tin box?"

Dirk stood up, turning to him. "Uncle El had a tin box of personals. Locked. He told me some of Dad's stuff was in it. Said Dad had left me something they couldn't take away with all the mortgages in Texas. Said I'd get it when I was of age."

Victor was sullen. "We didn't find no tin box."

Dirk moved toward him. "Don't lie to me, Victor."

"Listen," said Victor, "call me a liar again and you won't even get this much. Now take your junk and get out."

For a moment they stood face to face. Close up, Dirk saw how big a man Victor really was. He stood a head above Dirk, and his work at the forge had filled out his shoulders and chest until their tremendous bulk appeared almost grotesque, even above his broad hips and solid legs. Dirk felt his lips draw back against his teeth; the anger in him settled to a slow dull burn.

He spoke with difficulty. "I'll need a wagon for the forge."

Victor nodded to a buckboard with a horse already in its hitch up ahead of them. "Clyde's rig. I've been shoeing his dun."

Jess Kruger had several hoists for loading his feed and lifting his sick horses — heavy chains suspended from runners that worked in steel tracks along the rafters. Dirk went over to the nearest one and began pulling it across to the forge.

"You're wasting a lot of time," growled Victor. "If you don't get out of here before Kruger comes, you'll have trouble."

He moved deliberately to the large forge. It took a moment for Dirk to realize the man's intention. Slagel bent and put his thick-fingered hands carefully under the two ends of the forge. He set his legs close together; his sweat-stained shirt suddenly drew taut about the muscle humping up across his shoulders. He lifted the forge.

Dirk realized he had let his jaw sag slightly; he clamped it shut. He had never seen anyone lift a forge single-handed like that, and he had seen plenty of smiths proud of their strength. The buckboard shuddered and settled as Slagel heaved the ponderous mass of iron over its tailgate. He turned, wiping sweat from his low forehead, mouth still twisted sullenly. Dirk put in the smaller anvils and dumped the tools under the seat. He turned and gigged the dun forward past Seeco Smith and the others, toward the door. A man came in from outside, silhouetted by the light at first so that Dirk didn't recognize him.

"Where do you think you're going with that rig?" he asked.

It was Jess Kruger. Dirk stopped the buckboard, squinting his eyes to see the owner of the Long Shank against the light. He was a big black-haired man, Kruger, as solid and beefy as the Polled Angus bulls he ran on his North Fork spread. The ruthlessness of the man was evident in his atavistic beak of a nose, jutting sharply from beneath a brow that was shaped like one of the granite crags in Yellow Horse Canyon. He stood with his black tailcoat hanging over a hand stuffed in his right pants pocket; with his other hand he removed the cold stogie from thin, hard lips.

"Dirk," he said. "Didn't recognize you. I wondered where you disappeared to after that ruckus in the street. Wanted to welcome you back."

"Thanks, Jess" said Dirk. "I heard you were responsible for my parole."

"I told you I'd spring you if I ever got the chance, kid," said Kruger, spitting and putting his cigar back in his mouth. "Glendenning brought pressure to bear whenever I tried it before. But his political pull is gone now, without any water to back him. You saw what happened this morning. It was his last bid. He's sold everything but his saddle for money to sink those wells, and he hasn't found that underground reservoir yet. We expected Orson to blow up when Hammer refused him another loan today. Maybe he would have, too. He came in with his gun. I'm not saying you stopped him, but you sure snubbed his dally enough to interrupt him. Going riding?"

"These are Uncle El's things," said Dirk. "I'm taking them."

Kruger nodded, took out his cigar, and studied it a moment. "Too bad about your uncle, Dirk. Nobody could figure who'd do a low-down thing like that. We'll try and make it up to you. There's a bunk waiting for you in my rooming house over the hardware, and any horse in my string is yours. I'm glad you're back. Orson Glendenning is through, and he knows it, but he isn't going out without a fight. It just depends on whose fork goes bone-dry first. Either way, you'll see a war that'll make the past ten years' fighting look like a sick dogie. I'll need a man who can handle his guns like you. . . ."

He broke off suddenly, still holding his stogie, and looked up at Dirk with a strange expression. Seeco Smith had drifted up from the rear; he was watching Kruger intently. Dirk sensed the shift of other Long Shank riders behind him. He tightened his reins a little.

"Where did you say you were going with El's stuff?" asked Kruger.

Seeco Smith stood beside the wagon now. He held his right fist up against his chest. It was a sign men who know Seeco Smith could read well enough. Dirk knew Seeco Smith.

"I tried to explain it to Mick this morning, Jess," Dirk said, "but he didn't understand. I know you won't. Nobody can understand until they've been through it themselves. I won't try to tell you why. I just didn't come back to ride for you, that's all. I'm setting up for myself."

Kruger didn't seem surprised. He looked at his cigar a long time. The two Long Shank cowpunchers had come up to stand beside Seeco Smith now. Victor Slagel had come around the tailgate with the other blacksmith. Kruger put his cigar back into his thin lips and clamped them shut.

"Yeah," he said finally. "Yeah. Mick told me about that a few minutes ago. Orson, then?"

"No," said Dirk, "I didn't come back to ride for him either."

"Your uncle tried that, kid," said Kruger. "It can't be done. There are only two sides in Caprock. A man's either with me or with Orson Glendenning. I sprung you Dirk. . . ."

"You sprung me all right," said Dirk, "to use me. Maybe you used me in the first place to get rid of Hugh. I came back thinking I owed you something, Jess. I'm beginning to wonder."

Kruger flushed. He took his hand from his pocket, seeming to control himself with an effort. "If you want to be a smith, you can have a job at my forge."

Dirk shook his head. "What's the difference, riding your horse or working your bellows? I'd be your man."

The anger Kruger had been holding suddenly trembled through him. He took his cigar out, stabbing it at Dirk.

"Then get off that wagon. You aren't taking anything out of my barns."

"They're my things, and this is Slagel's wagon," said Dirk, blood beginning to pound in him.

Seeco had a strange, taut look to his narrow face; the fist held against his chest was white at the knuckles. Kruger grabbed the dun's bridle, half shouting.

"Dirk, if you don't get off that rig, we'll take you off!"

Dirk was surprised at how quiet his voice sounded. "Jess, don't do that, don't try to stop me."

"Take him off," Kruger yelled hoarsely. "Drag him off there!"

Dirk was already bending sideways as the men surged forward. In a blur, he saw Seeco's white fist flash down toward that Remington as he leaped toward the wagon — saw the twisted faces of the Long Shank riders behind Seeco — felt the buckboard shudder and tilt as the blacksmith swung over its side farther back.

Then Dirk was standing erect suddenly, and the sun coming in through the big double doors glinted across the metal of one of El Hood's tools.

"You ever been hit in the head by a hoof hammer?" he yelled.

Seeco hadn't quite freed his gun. The surprise twisting his face was almost ludi-crous. Instinctively, he recoiled, dropping his hand from the springs of the wagon seat and taking a step back into the Long Shank 'punchers, knocking them away. For that moment, Dirk's lean tense young figure, standing rigid above them with that hammer, held the men.

The sudden pound of boots across Mesa Street from outside broke the spell.

"It's Doc Alcott," a young man shouted from out there. "His mare's run away with him again. She's coming down Second. She'll take the turn sure. He'll be killed this time."

From the doorway, Dirk could see the black buggy clattering suddenly into view down Second Street. Doctor Alcott was thrown back from the seat, with his feet kicking air helplessly, and the reins were dropped into the doubletree. A rider was lashing his cowpony into the mare and leaning out to grab the harness. But Doc Alcott's house was up at First and Mesa, and at the corner of Second, the mare took its habitual turn. The man on the cowpony was slammed away from the mare's flank. The careening buggy struck him and knocked his horse aside and he jumped free as the cowpony stumbled and went down.

"The buggy'll drag her," shouted Victor Slagel. "She'll never make that full turn. She'll smash right in on us."

The men around Dirk scattered back into the barn yelling. Dirk dropped the hoof hammer. He jumped out of the buckboard and ran into the street. The mare was pounding around Kruger's Hardware on the opposite corner, buggy tilting crazily on one rear wheel. But already the drag was evident. The animal would never make a complete turn.

Dirk cut down the front wall of the barns to the corner across from the hardware. By the time he reached the end of the wall, the mare was fully into Mesa, heading diagonally across toward the barns, unable to turn farther with the buggy crashing around behind on one wheel and pulling on it. Dirk was south of the line the horse would take when he turned away from the barns. He quartered in on the animal, allowing her to come on his flank, flinging himself toward her from the side. For one blind moment he felt the slap of gritty dust in his face and the sound of thundering hoofs shaking the ground beneath him and the terrific impact of the brute's sweaty shoulder against his chest. Then his hand clutched the mane, and his other arm hooked around the neck. He jumped into the air with his grip acting as a lever upon which the mare's momentum, added to his own, swung him up and over onto her.

With his left foot on one tree and his right leg kicking over the horse, he grabbed blindly for the off-rein. He was dimly aware of the big-frame barns looming up ahead, rushing toward him. He found the rein, and the horse's head jerked to his sudden pull. The buggy shuddered behind them, tilting crazily over onto its left wheel again as the horse spun under Dirk's desperate rein. The boy fought on over the animal, kept pulling savagely on the ribbon. The barns were directly ahead and he got a blurred impression of the towering, paint-peeled walls and the buckboard standing in the gloom of the doorway and the shouts of the men farther back inside. Slagel's dun whinnied and reared as the mare came charging at it.

Gasping, Dirk yanked for the last savage time on the off-rein. The horse turned on farther up Mesa, dragging the buggy and all, and the barns were suddenly on their flank instead of ahead. Dirk's left leg was almost torn off as the horse followed the building wall down, ripping a board out with the end of the left tree.

The mare's rump slammed against the wall as Dirk pulled it out and away. The buggy crashed against the building behind them, and the collision knocked it upright again. The mare jumped the corner wildly, and the buggy crashed across the planks behind them, wheels popping and screeching.

Dirk lay limply on the mare, feet hooked into the trees. He heard the buggy dragging behind them and knew it had dished a wheel going over the sidewalk. The quivering animal hauled the wrecked outfit clear across the street, and wouldn't be stopped till she reached the white picket fence surrounding Alcott's big house up near First.

There was already a crowd around the horse when Dirk slid off. The buggy's whole left side was a mess of ripped black leather and broken hoops. The left wheel had collapsed and some men were helping Alcott out of the buggy where it had dragged to a stop. Doc Alcott's housekeeper, a big motherly lady with her gray hair in a bun, wouldn't allow anybody inside but the doctor and Dirk Hood. She plumped Alcott down on the living-room couch and fussed around.

"Woman," said the doctor peevishly, "I'm all right. Just shaken up a bit. You go and put something on the stove."

She stood back from him, hands on her ample hips. "Put what on the stove?"

Alcott was a rotund little man, brows forming a fuzzy line above round blue eyes set in a pink face. He wore an archaic fustian with a huge silver watch-chain across his white waistcoat. He waved his hand vaguely.

"Coffee, tea, anything. I don't care. Just put it on the stove."

"I declare," she said, turning to Dirk, "this is a fine homecoming for you. I certainly ain't going to waste my time making coffee. What you need is some horse liniment and hot water, both of you."

She flounced off through the sliding doors leading to the dining room, muttering to herself. Doc Alcott straightened with a heavy breath.

"That woman," he chuckled, shaking his head. Then his smile faded and he looked up. "So you came back, Dirk Hood?"

Dirk nodded, rubbing a bruised elbow, feeling as if a herd of whitefaces had run over him all night. Alcott rose suddenly, grunting with the effort. He went to the mantle and stood there a long time, faced away from Dirk. Through Mrs. Fowler's starched curtains on the big front window, Dirk could see some Long Shank riders trying to unhitch the excited mare from the wrecked tree.

"You saved my life, boy, but I guess you know that."

Alcott's voice startled Dirk. He turned. "I just. . . ."

"You saved my life," said the doctor almost angrily, waving a pink hand at the couch. "Sit down, Dirk. I've got something I want to tell you. It's preyed on me four years now. Millie's dead. She was a good wife, and she died two years ago."

Dirk's eyes darkened in sympathy. "I'm sorry. . . ."

Alcott nodded. "It won't be long for me now, boy. Things have changed in four years. Millie's gone. I'm on my way. And you saved my life. I don't know why you just didn't let me crash right into Kruger's Barns and break my worthless old cranium wide open."

"Don't talk crazy, Doc."

"I'm not talking crazy," said Alcott, brushing dust from his coat absently. "I'm talking straight for the first time in four years. I had Millie before, Dirk. You've got to understand that. I was Jess Kruger's man and I knew what would happen if I said the wrong thing. Just like your uncle. . . ."

Dirk stood suddenly. "You think Kruger . . . ?"

Alcott drew a heavy breath. "I don't know. You can't be neutral in this town. I don't know why El Hood was killed or by whom. I just know I would have gotten the same thing if I'd talked wrong. More than that, I was afraid for Millie. You know Kruger. You've got to understand."

Dirk grabbed his arm. "What are you trying to tell me?"

"As the doctor attending when you had the run-in with Hugh Glendenning," said Alcott, "I was called on to testify at the trial. I said that death had come instantly from the only bullet that struck him."

"I never blamed you," said Dirk. "It was a simple statement of facts."

"Not all the facts," said Alcott, breath suddenly coming faster. "I testified that the bullet struck his head. But there was more than that. I didn't tell the jury that the bullet had entered the top part of Hugh Glendenning's frontalis and passed through his brain to lodge in the axis vertebra. If it had gone out, I couldn't have gotten away with it. But there was no point of exit and a layman couldn't tell the direction of that slug's passage. I could. Frontalis to axis, Dirk. . . ." He stopped, turning toward the two men who had come in through the front door. Jess Kruger and Clyde Slagel.

"Heard about the excitement, Doc," said Clyde Slagel, smiling. "Thought I'd drop in and see how you were. What's that about a frontalis?"

☆ **III** ☆

HAMMER OF DEATH

*T*he leather had rotted off El Hood's old bellows, and Dirk set about sewing new hide onto the frame that next morning, hunkered down in the shade of the willows at the back end of Slagel's lot between Alcott's white house and Kruger's Hardware. Jess Kruger had still been at the doctor's with Slagel when Dirk had left, and most of the Long Shank riders were still trying to get the horse extricated from the smashed tree without any more damage. Only Seeco Smith and Victor Slagel were in the doorway of the barns when Dirk went back to get the buckboard with his forge and tools.

He was finishing the rawhide stitching on his bellows when a sudden shriek jerked his head up. Jess Kruger had offices on the second story of his barns across Mesa. Dirk saw that one of the windows had made that sound, being shoved up. Kruger stood there looking southward down Mesa, cigar clamped in his mouth. Mick Walker came out of the courthouse up at First and Mesa, his boots making a resounding clatter on the plank sidewalk. In front of the Jaykay Saloon he stopped suddenly, looking open-mouthed on down the street. In the sudden silence, his voice carried clearly to Dirk.

"Tarnation," he said. "Terry Glendenning!"

Dirk moved to the front end of the lot where he could see south down Mesa Street. Orson Glendenning's daughter, Terry, was coming up from the south. She was trotting her pinto up the center of the street, looking neither to right nor left. And she was coming alone. The girl sat straight in the saddle, a slim figure in a flannel shirt and cream-colored cowhide vest, her hat shoved off her head and bobbing against her back, held there by the tie-thongs around her neck. She reached the vacant lot and turned in. Once, before Orson had bought the Keyhole, there had been things between Dirk and this girl that were brought back to him now, by the way the sunlight played through her wind-blown hair, turning the deep chestnut color to flickering gold.

"Terry," he said. "Are you crazy, coming into town alone?"

She swung down. "You're here, aren't you? Alone. I understand you're going to take up your uncle's trade. My pinto needs shoes, Dirk."

He didn't understand it for a moment; he held out his hand. "But you . . . you're a Glendenning . . . you. . . ."

"I should hate you, like Lige, and Dad?" she supplied. "You know I never could, Dirk. Maybe for the first few days after it happened. Not any longer. And there were so many odd things about it. Those notes. It isn't logical that two men, neither of them knowing what the other was doing, should each write the other a note naming an identical place and time for a meeting like that."

"How many times do you think I tried to tell them that at the trial?" he said, and glanced at Kruger's Barns, with the open window of the office above.

She caught the glance, "Dirk, you don't think somebody. . . ."

"If Hugh Glendenning got a note," said Dirk, "somebody else besides me sent it. I don't know who or why. I've tried to figure it out, but nothing adds up. Nobody stood to gain anything by getting Hugh out of the way. It wouldn't waken the South Fork bunch any. Your dad just took the lead with Hugh gone. But it isn't that troubling me most, Terry. . . ."

He bent to get the pinto's reins. When he straightened, his glance met the girl's. He realized suddenly that she understood what he had gone through the past four years, knowing he had killed a man who'd been as close a friend as Hugh. It was in her eyes. Maybe he couldn't explain it to Mick, or the others, but he didn't have to explain it to Terry.

He hitched the horse to the tree, then lifted a hoof. "You should know better than to let a horse go this long without refitting, Terry. Look at those sidebones."

"All our horses are that way, Dirk," she said. "You Uncle El did all our refitting. When he died, Kruger's Barns was the only place left. You know what a chance we had there. Dad wouldn't even ask Kruger. We tried to do our own refitting. It might have worked on grassland, but not in the Caprock country. The horses began throwing those homemade shoes right away. We need an experienced farrier, Dirk. Another week or so and we won't have any horses to ride. They're all crippled up like this."

Dirk bent to cut the heads of the nails from the old shoe with the clinch cutters. He said, "Uncle El had some screw-caulked shoes in his kit. They're used, but they're still better than these you've got."

"Dirk," she said huskily, "if we don't get our whole string refitted, we're through. It won't matter whether we have water or not. Without horses, we're through. I promise Lige won't cause any trouble."

He nodded, not meeting her eyes. "I have sent to San Antone for some new shoes. The day they arrive on the stage I'll be out at your spread."

"Dirk," she almost whispered.

He turned to set up the bellows, smiling faintly. It had been a long time since he'd heard his name said like that. The puff of hot air and the ring of steel on the anvil were welcome, and he settled into shaping the old metal with sweat running down his face. She came around the horse and stood nearby, studying Dirk.

"We tried to explain to you at the time," she said, finally, "but you were blind mad and you wouldn't see it. Uncle Hugh never sold you out. You must realize that now. When you went to him for help, he was on the verge of bankruptcy. He had written that to us, that's why we came out. Dad helped him back on his feet and, by the time we decided to settle here, your Keyhole had been in Hammer's hands almost six months. It was next to the H Bar H, and being held at sale price by the bank. It was only natural for Dad to take advantage of that."

He nodded. "Four years cools a man down, Terry. Maybe I would have seen it that way sooner if I hadn't started riding for Kruger. Being with the North Forkers that way just naturally kept me all whipped up inside against Hugh and his gang. Let's not talk about any of it any more. I'm tired. I want to forget it. I hear you went to school while I was away."

She nodded. "I wasn't able to finish. The South Fork began to go and Dad had to pull in his horns."

"Nursing?" he said. "Isn't that what Mick told me? Would you know what a frontalis is?"

"Yes, it was nursing," she said, and tapped her forehead, "a frontalis is this. The front of your head."

"And the axis vertebra?"

She smiled. "That's the base of your neck. . . ." She trailed off at the sudden look in his eyes. He slipped his hoof hammer into his belt without knowing it. He was staring at Doctor Alcott's white house, and he didn't see it.

"And something entering the top part of the frontalis," he said in a hollow voice, "and passing through the brain to lodge against the axis vertebra, would be coming. . . ."

"From somewhere above," said Terry. "Why?"

The girl had left, and it was almost dark when Dirk put a tarp over his forges and went down Mesa toward the stage office. He hadn't answered the girl's question; he didn't know the answer.

Mick Walker's spotted hound cut across from the hardware and disappeared into Kruger's Barns. It drew Dirk's glance to the darkened upper windows where Jess Kruger had his offices. He shook his head, eyes swinging back to the building ahead of him, on his side of Mesa — the false-fronted two-story building with Kruger's Hardware on the bottom floor and rooms above for whatever of Kruger's riders were in town, and for a few paying roomers.

Across Second Street from the hardware, someone lit a cigarette in front of Acto's Dry Goods Emporium, the glow a red pinpoint in the dusk. Acto's was two-storied also. Hugh Glendenning had kept offices on its top floor before his death.

The soft click of Hammer's clerk locking the bank doors for the night came to Dirk, and he was drawn to look from the drygoods store to the bank on the southwest corner of the intersection. The clatter of the clerk's shoes down the sidewalk on

Second diminished past the covered stairway leading up to Clyde Slagel's land office above.

There they were, then. Four years, Dirk thought. Four years the thought that he had murdered Hugh Glendenning had galled him like a sore that would never heal, haunting him at night, oppressing him during the day. And now. . . .

He realized suddenly that the movement in the barns across Mesa had not been Mick's dog coming back out. He could see the man's form now, cutting across the street toward his side of the intersection ahead. Kruger had three blacksmiths working for him; only one of them possessed the breadth of shoulder this man showed. He reached the middle of Mesa about the time Dirk came to the north side of the hardware. He seemed to be carrying something on his shoulder. Dirk caught the turn of the man's head.

"Dirk?"

"You know it is, Victor," said Dirk.

There was a certain deliberate purpose in Victor Slagel's walk, and Dirk suddenly saw what it was he carried on his shoulder. But Clyde Slagel had said. . . . What did it matter what Clyde had said? Victor worked for Kruger; he was Kruger's man.

"I hear you're going to do some work for the Glendennings," called Victor, still moving diagonally across so he would reach the corner of Mesa and Second about the same time Dirk did.

"That's right," said Dirk.

There was no stopping now. His boots made a steady pound on the walk. His hands slipped down to the twelve-pound hoof hammer he carried in his belt.

"You're making a mistake, kid," said Victor Slagel.

Dirk suddenly turned off the walk and into the street directly toward the man. The change of direction seemed to surprise Slagel; he turned, still walking, and shifted the huge sledgehammer on his shoulder a little. Dirk was remembering how he had seen the man lift the forge in Kruger's Barns.

"I'm making no mistake," said Dirk, and stepped over a wheel rut. "I'll shoe Glendenning's horses if he asks me. I'll shoe Kruger's horses. I'm a blacksmith. I'm not Kruger's man or Glendenning's man. And I'm not making any mistake."

The long-handled sledge must have weighed thirty pounds. Slagel lowered it from his shoulder without any apparent effort and held it in both hands across his belly as he stopped walking and turned there in the middle of the street to face Dirk. The man was close enough to see the sullen twist in the boy's mouth. He stepped across another rut, coming forward steadily.

"You could set up shop in any town from here to Montana," said Slagel. "You could take tomorrow's stage north and set up any place you picked."

"Is that Kruger's offer?" said Dirk. "Tell him I'm staying here."

Slagel's voice sounded strained. "I'm giving you a chance, kid. You're making a mistake."

"I'm making no mistake," said Dirk, and took the last step.

His head was turned up and his eyes were wide open. He heard Slagel's tremendous grunt; he saw the sledge swing up over Slagel's head. The man's body was a blur in front of him, lunging forward.

Dirk's boots made a sudden scraping shuffle and he threw himself to one side, lashing out with the hoof hammer at the same time. The sledge crashed down where he had stood a moment before and struck the ground with a shuddering impact. Victor yelled hoarsely as Dirk's hammer struck his arm.

The big man spun, whipping his sledge up and around with that grunting sound. Dirk struck hard with the hammer again, jumping back. The sledge caught at his shirt and tore it from his pants, going on around, its momentum carrying Slagel with it. Before the man could recover, Dirk leaped in, hacking at him. Slagel screamed. He stopped his hammer with a tremendous effort and jerked it back toward Dirk without raising it. The whole length of the sledge's handle slammed into Dirk, knocking him away. He rolled to the ground, pain paralyzing his right side.

With a savage cry, Slagel leaped at him. Dirk saw the sledge coming down. He was still rolling and he jerked his legs desperately into a jackknife, feeling the ground shudder beneath him as the sledge missed his bootheels by inches and thudded into the earth. Dirk rolled on over and dove at Slagel, as the man jerked the sledge up. He caught Slagel across the knees with the hoof hammer.

"Goddamn," sobbed Victor Slagel, and tried to fight away from the vicious little hammer.

Dirk stumbled on forward and kept beating at the man's legs. Cursing with pain, Slagel swung his sledge from the side. It struck Dirk's left shoulder. Slammed to the ground, Dirk heard his own shout of agony. Crying hoarsely, uncontrollably, he caught hold of the sledge before Slagel could lift it again. He climbed half way up it, slugging at the man's legs. Slagel tried to jerk away. Grunting, Dirk hacked stubbornly at him with the hoof hammer. Slagel gasped sharply and went to his knees, finally managing to jerk the sledge free. He whipped it around behind him.

Dirk sprawled over Slagel and caught the sledge, and they both went flat to the ground. Dirk struck savagely, blindly. He heard the dull crunch of metal on bone. Slagel stiffened beneath him, then went limp.

It took a long time for Dirk to get his hands and knees above the man. He was crying without shame now, and he didn't think he could stand the pain in his left shoulder much longer. Slagel had rolled over and was lying on his belly, holding his head, moaning softly. He didn't try to rise.

"Next time," sobbed Dirk hoarsely, "use a bigger hammer."

Twenty-five years before, John Hood had staked his claim beside Hugh Glendenning's on a small creek feeding into the South Fork of the Rio Cabezon. Their old cottonwood cabin still stood in the little fold of crumpled hills above the creek that had been dry since Dirk was five.

The boy halted the horse and mule he had borrowed from Acto in front of the rotting structures. He swung down, glancing at the mule behind him which carried the new shoes from San Antone, and a portable forge. He was on his way to the Keyhole as he had promised, but he had detoured to see this cabin. He was in a sullen, vindictive mood, and he shoved the sagging door in impatiently.

Why did it have to be that way? That was what he kept asking himself. First his Uncle El Hood, now Doctor Alcott. Why?

The doctor's housekeeper said she had heard the crash from inside the house. She told everyone who would listen that she had warned the doctor a thousand times not to lean back that way in his chair. But he had been sitting out on the porch, tilting his chair back with his feet up on the railing and his pipe glowing, watching the night settle over Caprock like that for fifteen years. Somehow Dirk couldn't believe he had fallen. His neck was broken, and he was dead, and Dirk had attended the funeral this morning, but somehow he didn't think the doctor had fallen by himself.

He kept remembering that it had been fear of crossing Jess Kruger which had kept Doc Alcott from telling the true facts about the bullet causing Hugh Glendenning's death; he kept remembering that Jess Kruger had been the other man who walked into the doctor's parlor when Alcott had finally unburdened himself of the thing that had plagued him those four years, and Clyde Slagel had asked, " 'What's that about the frontalis, Doc?' "

Dirk kicked up the puncheon flooring of the old cabin methodically. He didn't know what he expected to find. But there was a nameless connection in his mind between Hugh Glendenning's death, and Doctor Alcott's. And there was that tin box of El Hood's which had contained something John Hood had left his son. Dirk finished in the cabin, finding nothing but some old newspapers and rotting clothes and a rusty knife. When he went outside, his horse and mule were gone.

He stood there a moment, a vagrant wind whipping at his old gray coat. Then he started looking for signs. There were no other marks beside the animals' own tracks; they had drifted. He followed the trail for a mile down through the gullies that furrowed the roll of hills, coming into a level stretch of caprock. Both animals were standing there, noses muzzling the dry earth.

Dirk went over to them, tired and angry, jerking their heads up. Then he saw the hole that had been sunk in the ground. It was about two inches in diameter. There was another one farther off. Both holes had been refilled with earth. Dirk remembered Orson Glendenning had been sinking wells to find water.

"Your head ought to be bored for the holler horn," he growled at the horse, mounting stiffly. "You know there hasn't been any water around here since that creek dried up."

Grabbing the mule's lead rope, he turned around and headed back toward the cabin. He was riding from the mouth of the gully leading into the creek when his horse whinnied suddenly. There was an answering neigh from the rising ground across the creek, then a sudden scraping sound.

Dirk was pulling his reins when the shot slapped out. Lead whined viciously past him. Tossing its head, the horse took the bit and headed straight down into the bottoms. The horse bolted through scraggly mesquite in the dry creek-bed, and nothing Dirk could do would stop it. He threw himself from the saddle as the next shot rang out, followed by another and another. He hit running but was going too fast to keep his balance. The mesquite rattled and cracked and tore at him as he rolled into it, trying to keep off the shoulder Victor Slagel had broken with the sledge. He stopped finally, and lay there panting, hearing his crazed horse crash up on the other bank. Then someone shouted.

"Lige, Lige. Stop it. I told you he was coming. Lige!"

"You stay there," yelled Lige Glendenning. "That's Dirk Hood and I'm going in after him."

Dirk caught the scraping sound again. He raised himself and saw Lige Glendenning coming down the bank into the bottoms with both guns out. There were two more Keyhole hands clattering down the rising ground from the cabin. Dirk recognized Terry Glendenning's voice now.

"Lige, stop. Please. I won't let you."

Dirk couldn't see the girl. Lige reached the sandy bottom and plunged into the brush. Dirk squirmed around to cut away down the creek from them. He realized what they meant to do, and he was unarmed. Lige must have seen his movement. Both the man's guns began roaring, and he came on in, shouting something. Lead clattered through the mesquite. A bullet clipped Dirk's hat off. Another stung his hand. He turned from one side to the other, stricken with the panic of a trapped animal.

"Lige. . . !" called Terry Glendenning once more, and then through the sound of Lige's bellowing guns another shot, harder, sharper. It was the last one. For a long moment Dirk stood crouched there, listening. There was no other sound. Finally, someone came sliding down the bank.

"Dirk," called the girl. "Come out."

He stood straight and could see them. Lige was in the mesquite, half way between the bank and Dirk. He was holding one gun, looking at his left hand. It was covered with blood, empty. The other gun lay at his feet. There was a surprised, blank expression in his eyes.

Terry came through the mesquite, holding a .30–30 across her stomach with both hands. A thin trickle of smoke spiraled from its bore. "I promised him you wouldn't cause any trouble," she told her brother, face pale and set. "I meant it."

Dirk broke through the mesquite toward them, feeling a dull throbbing pain in his broken shoulder from the jarring he had taken. Orson Glendenning wheeled a big black into view on the bank, spoke to one of the dismounted Keyhole hands up there. He put the horse down the barranca on its hocks and urged it through the brush to Dirk and Lige. There was a thin sound to his voice, and a hurt look in his gaunt face as he spoke to Lige.

"I never hoped to see a son of mine do a thing like that."

Lige jerked his head to his father. He opened his mouth to say something, waving his right hand vaguely toward Terry. Then he turned without speaking and walked stiffly toward the bank. Orson looked for a long moment past Dirk to where the mule had stopped and was placidly cropping mesquite, unaffected by the gunfire. Then he looked at Dirk's left arm, bent into the sling Mrs. Fowler had made from a black bandanna; his eyes dropped to Dirk's waist, unspanned by a gun belt. Finally he took a deep breath.

"One of our hands spotted you crossing the South Fork," he said heavily. "Lige got out ahead of us. Terry told me about it, but I didn't think you'd do it, Dirk. I didn't think you'd come."

"I'm a blacksmith," said Dirk. "If your horses need refitting, I'll do it."

Orson didn't speak again till a Keyhole hand came down the bank with Dirk's horse. Dirk mounted and got his mule. They headed toward the Keyhole house.

"What was Hugh doing in Slagel's office that day?" asked Dirk

Orson turned toward him. "Slagel said at the trial that he'd collared Hugh and taken him to his land office, tried to stop him meeting you. But Hugh's wife says he went to the land office of his own accord."

"You own Dad's old homestead site?" said Dirk.

"Of course," said Orson. "Your dad's original homestead was state land. He built the rest of his spread by buying out smaller spreads and hooking onto county land.

The original survey was sort of complicated. Clyde Slagel cleared the title for us and made a new survey when he handled the deal through Hammer's bank."

"It was Clyde helping you try to locate that underground water too, with that witch of his," said Dirk absently. "You sink any shafts over by Dad's homestead site?"

"No," said Orson. "We didn't."

"Somebody did," said Dirk.

☆ IV ☆

WATER RIGHTS — IN HELL

*T*he courthouse was a big white frame building, colonial style, with faded brown shutters. It was set back from the street on the corner of First and Mesa, directly across from Doctor Alcott's house. The sheriff had his office at the rear of the musty old building, down the hall past the courtroom. Mick Walker was in prodigious repose in his padded swivel chair, boots resting on the scarred roll top desk. He jerked up sharply, as if he had been dozing, when Dirk came in.

"Seeco said you wanted to see me," said Dirk.

Mick shoved his hat back on his white mane, clearing his throat. "Dirk, you're letting yourself in for it, going out like you did yesterday and shoeing those Keyhole horses. And that fight with Victor Slagel. It could well constitute a violation of your parole."

"Is that why you asked me in?" said Dirk. "If Victor cracks my skull, that's all right. If I crack his, I violate my parole."

Mick swung slowly around in his swivel chair till he was looking out the window. "Jess told me he didn't send Victor out there, Dirk."

"Told *you?*" said Dirk. "Why should he bother telling *you?* You're his man."

"That's the point," said Mick. "Jess Kruger always shows me his cards. He lets me take care of this end, and I let him take care of his, and we don't interfere with one another. But I already know what's in his warsack before he pulls it out. And he knows what's in mine. If Jess had sent Victor out that night, I would have known it. I'm giving you that straight, Dirk."

Dirk moved to sit on the desk, staring past Mick out the window. "I'll take it straight, Mick. You never lied to me before. Maybe . . . there's been only two sides in this town for so long it just doesn't occur to us there could be a third. Somehow, I couldn't see anyone else doing it but Kruger. Mick, does a man convicted of man-slaughter lose his rights of inheritance?"

"What inheritance?"

"Land."

"Didn't know you had any land."

"Supposing I did," said Dirk. "A hundred and sixty acres. A quarter-section."

"Homestead?" said Mick, turning around. "In the case of state land like that, you'd lose it by abandonment if you went to jail."

"And it would revert back to the state," said Dirk. "And anybody who wanted to could file on it. What about the original patent? Would it have to be in evidence?"

"If the new party filing on it couldn't produce the first deed," said Mick, "they'd have to go through a lot of red tape before they could get the quarter-section. What are you driving at?"

"What was in the tin box Uncle El had, for instance," said Dirk, and then turned toward the slap of boots from the outer hall. Terry Glendenning shoved open the door and ran on in, panting.

"You've got to come quick," she said, grabbing Mick Walker. "Lige just got a note from Seeco Smith to meet him on Mesa Street with his gun."

Dirk jerked off the desk, pulling her around. "Terry. . . ?"

"Yes, Dirk," she gasped, faced toward him. "The same thing all over again. You know how hot-headed Lige is. Dad couldn't stop him. I got out of the house ahead of them, but they're right behind me, Dad and Lige and the whole crew and others of the South Fork bunch. Lige'll be killed just like Hugh, and that'll only be the start of it."

Walker hoisted himself from his chair with a grunt, and the floor shook beneath his pounding weight as he went out the door. Dirk and the girl were right behind him. As soon as he reached the door behind the sheriff, Dirk could see down Mesa to where the haze of dust crawled above the cavalcade of South Forkers, just crossing Fifth Street and coming on up through the residence section. From Fifth on up to Second, Mesa Street was empty and silent. The sudden sound of Jess Kruger's shoving through the batwings of his Jaykay Saloon was startling. Behind Jess came Victor Slagel, head bandaged, walking with a painful limp.

"Jess," shouted Mickey Walker, "what's this about Seeco?"

Kruger turned a moment. "Seeco got a note from Lige Glendenning to meet him at Mesa and Second. This is it, Mick."

Mickey and Dirk and the girl had reached Kruger by then. The sheriff shoved back his hat, voice swift. "Jess, there just isn't any use in this. Glendenning's through as it is. The minute Seeco and Lige cut loose the lid'll blow. You know how it was with Dirk and Hugh. You help me stop Seeco."

Kruger looked at him, lips clamped around his cold cigar. "I thought you rode in my wagon."

Mick flushed. "You know I do. But I say there isn't any use in this. You don't have to do it to finish the South Fork bunch."

Kruger jabbed his stogie at the sheriff. "If this is the way they want it done up, that's all right by me. You handle your own team, Mick."

He turned and stamped down the sidewalk. Victor Slagel looked sullenly at Dirk a moment, hate black in his eyes; then he turned and went back into the Jaykay. The sharp clatter of Kruger's boots turned to a dull thud as he left the sidewalk and moved across the dirt in front of his barns. Seeco Smith was a dim bulk in the dusk, coming from the big double doors of the building. Mick started running after Kruger, toward Seeco.

A gust of wind eddied, sifting white dust up out of the ruts in the street, and slapped it against the curbing. It passed on down the street, and the dust settled again. Seeco Smith kept walking out toward the middle of the street. He held his fist up against his chest. Terry Glendenning had seen that before, and Dirk heard her sharp indrawn breath beside him.

"Seeco," called Dirk.

Smith stopped, half turning. They had been friends once, Seeco and Dirk, and the older man had taught the boy all he knew. "You aren't trying to stop me?" he asked.

"I know I can't," said Dirk. "Just tell me one thing. Did you write a note to Lige?"

"No," said Seeco, and said something else before he turned back down Mesa. "This sort of thing has always got to be done alone, Dirk, but I sort of wish you were backing me. When you went to meet Hugh Glendenning, I was backing you."

Then he turned around and moved out to the middle of Mesa and headed southward. With a curse, Mick followed him, grabbing his arm. Seeco shook him off and kept going. The dog reached the barn and turned around and around in one spot, whining softly. A pair of Kruger's Long Shank riders came out of the barn and went across Mesa behind Seeco to the hardware, taking their stand in the doorway there.

Dirk saw Lige Glendenning get off his horse at Third and Mesa. Orson leaned out of his saddle and said something to his son. Ignoring his father, Lige began walking north toward Second. Orson dismounted with a jerk, and the Keyhole crew swung down and the other South Forkers who had come. Most of them carried saddle guns. They lined out behind Lige Glendenning, moving up after him, spreading the silence before them like a rock spreading ripples in a pool.

Someone shoved up a window above the hardware. It made a shrieking sound. Kruger came out of the barns with his two blacksmiths and, when he saw the sheriff still arguing with Seeco, called after him angrily.

"Mick, I told you. . . ."

Dirk was looking up at the window of Kruger's offices on the second floor of the barns. They were bright squares of yellow light in gathering darkness. Then he looked at Hammer's bank across the street. It showed no light, top or bottom. And suddenly he knew . . . he knew!

"I'm backing you, Seeco," he breathed.

"Dirk," called the girl.

Kruger turned sharply toward him as Dirk ran past. Then he was on the other side of Second, running down past the bank to where the San Antone Stage Company office and sheds were. He rounded the stage office to the yard behind. A solid pack-pole fence enclosed the compound, and the stables were backed up against the bank. Dirk hoisted himself over the fence with his good arm, dropped off into the compound, ran the rail till he found a coil of hemp on the middle bar. From the top rail he reached the slanting roof. He almost slid off and had to catch the edge with his left arm. The stabbing pain drew a grunt from him.

The stable roof hit the wall of the bank some four feet below the top. It cost him more agony, using his left arm to get onto the bank's roof. He kicked his boots off and ran across the tarred roof-top with the rope slung on one arm. He reached the opposite parapet.

Peering north through the dusk, he could see Seeco Smith crossing Second. Southward, Terry Glendenning was struggling with her brother. She must have run down there while Dirk was getting on the bank's roof. He heard Orson say something, and one of the Keyhole crew grabbed the girl and pulled her over to the sidewalk.

All the time he was watching them, Dirk had been bent over the parapet. When his glance was drawn to the scraping sound to the right and below him, he held his breath. The faint dark line edging away from the brick wall might have been a gun barrel. It shifted southward, toward the Glendennings. Dirk had spotted the ventilating pipes behind him. With a swift, skilled throw he snaked the hemp around one, pulled it taut, tested it. He waited an instant longer. Seeco and Lige were less than half a block apart now, much less. And Lige spoke.

"Seeco?" he asked, and in the silence Dirk heard it plainly. He climbed onto the parapet.

"Lige," said Seeco.

Dirk knew it was the time, and his voice rang out in a violent yell as he swung down off the parapet on the rope. "Seeco!" Then his boots crashed into the rifle barrel beneath him and struck it aside just as it exploded. As he smashed on it through the partly opened window, he caught a last glimpse of Lige and Seeco standing with hands gripping on their half-drawn guns, faces turned up toward his shout and the sound of the shot.

Dirk plunged feet first into the darkened room. He struck the body of a man and crashed to the floor with glass shattering all over him, cutting at his face and neck. The man cursed beneath him, struggling to get from beneath his rolling body. Agony numbing his broken shoulder, Dirk clawed for the rifle with his good hand. The man struck at him with the rifle, gasping. Over the sharp hard scuffle, Dirk heard a rasping voice.

"Nevermore, nevermore. . . ."

The man swung the rifle again, trying to knock Dirk's weight off him, and it grazed Dirk's face. Head rocking from the blow, Dirk heard someone running down the hall outside. The door shook under a man's fist.

"Unlock it," a voice shouted. "You missed. Something went wrong and they're coming up. Unlock the door."

Dirk fought to keep on top of the struggling man beneath him. He beat blindly at him with his right fist, heard a smothered yell of pain. The rifle swung up from the side and hit him directly across the face this time, knocking him off. He felt the man scrambling away from him, heard the sharp dry sound of another shell being pumped into the chamber. Dirk threw himself upward, smashing the man back into a big square desk.

The door shook again, as if someone had thrown his body against it from the outside. The gun went off above Dirk as he fought for it, and he jerked spasmodically to the bite of hot lead across his skull. Blinded, stunned, he got a desperate grip on the barrel. Heedless of the agony in his shoulder, he held the rifle with both hands and jammed it back into the man. He heard a sharp grunt, and shoved again, bending the man backward over the desk. The door buckled as the man outside threw himself at it a second time, and staggered into the room.

With a gasp, Dirk brought the rifle down square. The body collapsed beneath him, sliding off the desk to the floor. Unable to see the man who burst in, Dirk whirled, reversing the rifle to claw at the pump. The man shifted into the dim light from the door until half of him was silhouetted, and Dirk saw the bulk of a six-shooter in his hand, and saw the gun coming up.

"That you, Dad?" the man asked harshly.

Dirk cocked the gun without answering. The hammering detonation of both weapons filled the room.

For a long moment Dirk stood there, watching the man's body melt into the blackness of the floor. He felt the blood from his creased skull leaking down over his forehead, but that was his only wound. By the time Mickey Walker came thundering down the hall, Dirk had a lamp lit. Victor Slagel lay just within the doorway where he had taken the rifle slug. Mick stood pop-eyed there, looking at the other man where he lay unconscious by the desk.

"Tarnation," gasped the sheriff, "Clyde Slagel."

"It's been Clyde Slagel all along," explained Dirk, after the rest of them had come up, and two Long Shank riders had carried Victor Slagel's body away. "When the North Fork began to go dry, Clyde must have realized the South Fork would go, too. He was using that water-witch a long time before Orson Glendenning came and started hunting for the underground reservoir.

"No telling how many years before Dad's death it was that Clyde found the dome of water which rose beneath Dad's original homestead. Clyde sunk the shafts to verify his find. It's uncanny how thirsty animals smell water; that's what my horse and mule did out there, even though Clyde had refilled his two shafts, trying to hide them. He knew whoever owned that quarter-section would have the whip hand when the other water went."

"But your dad owned it," said Lige, impatiently.

"There's always ways, with a man like Clyde," said Dirk. "When I lost the Keyhole after Dad's death, everybody took it for granted that Dad had mortgaged his original homestead along with the rest of the spread. When Clyde handled the deal, he saw on the original survey that the homestead had not been mortgaged. He cleared the title and made a new survey when Orson bought the Keyhole, and on that new survey, he included the homestead site in Orson's purchase, thus covering the fact that it should have been inherited by me."

"That must have been what Hugh came to this office about, the day he was killed," said Orson. "Just a week before, I'd asked him about putting a new fence on that quarter-section. It was the first time since I'd bought the Keyhole that we'd discussed that part of it. Hugh seemed surprised I had it. He said he didn't think John Hood would have mortgaged his original homestead under any circumstances."

Dirk nodded. "How about it, Slagel?"

Clyde Slagel sat at his desk under the watchful eye of Mick Walker; he toyed with an inkwell, nodding sullenly. "When Hugh found the homestead site was in Orson's name, he came up here asking to see the original survey. I put him off and he got suspicious. Said the next time he came he wanted it cleared up, or he'd cause trouble."

"So you sent him a note, and me a note, and waited up in your office with a rifle to make sure Hugh died whether my bullet killed him or not," said Dirk grimly. "Which it didn't."

"Two birds with one stone," said Mick Walker angrily. "Hugh dead so he couldn't spread Clyde's secret about the water. And Dirk in the pen, so Clyde could reveal his supposed mistake on the survey whenever he wanted, and have the quarter-section declared abandoned by Dirk, reverting back to the state."

"And Clyde could file on it, and have the only water in the county," said Dirk. "Only you wouldn't want a lot of red tape and investigation. You had to get the original patent. Is that what was in Uncle El's tin box?"

Slagel nodded dully. "Your father's deed and papers to the homestead. Victor had found them when your uncle came in on him."

"And Doc Alcott didn't fall off his chair by himself," said Dirk. "Did Victor take care of that too? Because you overheard the doc tell me about a frontalis? But why this, today?"

"When Hammer refused Orson the loan," said Slagel, "Orson came up here and told me it was the finish, said to have everything straightened out for whatever would happen to his Keyhole. The homestead was still under his name, and I couldn't afford to straighten anything out or clear the papers on the Keyhole until I'd gained legal possession of that quarter-section. If Orson died, it would give me time to get the homestead site and cover what I'd done before the Keyhole was disposed of. Orson's an older man with a cooler head. If I'd sent the note to him, he might have stopped to think. I sent it to Lige, knowing Orson would come with him."

"If Dirk's bullet didn't kill Hugh," said Mick Walker, "then he was sent up on false charges and didn't legally abandon his homestead. It's yours, Dirk."

"No." said Dirk, and he was looking at Terry. "It's Caprock's, Mick. There's enough water for all of us if we use it right. As long as I've been alive, there's been fighting and hate and killing in this town over water. There won't be any more."

Clyde Slagel's crow rustled through the papers on the desk in front of its master's blank gaze.

"Nevermore," it croaked. "Nevermore."

HELL'S HIGH-GRADERS

(1945)

★

by (ALFONSO) CLIFF(ORD) FARRELL

(Alfonso) Cliff(ord) Farrell was born in Zanesville, Ohio, where earlier Zane Grey had been born. Following graduation from high school, Farrell became a newspaper reporter. Over the next decade, he worked his way west by means of a string of newspaper jobs. He would claim later that he began writing for pulp magazines because he grew bored with journalism. His first Western stories were written for Cowboy Stories *in 1926. His byline was A. Clifford Farrell. Clayton publications like* Cowboy Stories, Ranch Romances *and* Ace-High Magazine *remained his principal market in the 1920s, but by 1928 his byline was abbreviated to Cliff Farrell and this it remained through more than 500 short stories and short novels and over twenty hardcover Western novels. While Farrell had contributed stories to* Western Rangers *from Popular Publications in 1931, he was covering auto racing for the* Los Angeles Examiner *and writing racing car stories for* Short Stories *in 1933 when Rogers Terrill invited him to contribute a story to the first issue of* Dime Western. *Farrell became a regular contributor to this magazine and in 1934 to* Star Western *as well. In fact, many months he would have a short novel in both magazines. Henry Steeger confided to him that the only author whose stories he would take home to read at night for his own pleasure were those Cliff had written. Farrell became such a staple at Popular Publications that by the end of the 1930s he was contributing as much as 400,000 words a year to their various Western magazines. His earliest Western fiction tended to stress action and gunplay, but increasingly his stories began to focus on characters in historical situations and the problems they faced.*

☆ I ☆

BLOOD-RANSOM

*T*he big cake bore twenty-four candles, and said "Happy Birthday" in red jelly-beans set in its thick pink icing. Britt Burnett found the cake sitting on the table in his cabin in Lodestone when he came in just after dark.

Cap'n Kidd, the big red and green parrot, who shared the cabin with Britt, screeched a raucous welcome from his cage. "Many happy returns, dammit!" Cap'n Kidd squawked. "Many happy returns, dammittohell!"

"You old devil," Britt remonstrated. "Nettie Lang taught you the first part of that greeting, but the cuss words are your own idea. If you disgrace us by using any of that bull-whacking lingo while she's here, I'll give you a bar of harness soap to chaw on."

"How 'bout a slug o' brandy?" the parrot squawled.

Hard-rock miners and powder men had been the bird's tutors. They had also taught him to drink brandy. Cap'n Kidd had a reputation as an incorrigible sot. Britt poured a few drops of brandy in his cup, and the parrot dipped his beak joyously.

Britt looked at the cake and thought of Nettie Lang's lively brown eyes and winsome beauty. He wondered if she really knew how much this day meant to him. This was more than the mere passing of a milestone for Britt Burnett. Tonight would mark the end, for him, of six months' self-imposed probation during which he had placed his pride on trial for public verdict. He lighted the candles and stood there, wondering what to wish for. There were so many things.

He thought of Nettie's father, Big Tom Lang, who was hitting tough luck at his Sweet Julia mine. And he thought of his brother, Luke, missing six months and wanted for murder and robbery. Britt looked a lot like Luke, who was six years his senior. Both of the Burnetts were dark-haired, dark-eyed men, long-legged, with solid jaws, and the deep brawn of hard-rock miners. Now Luke was outlawed, wanted by the sheriff.

"This is my last trick on a treasure car," Britt told the parrot. "Six months is long enough to prove my point. Folks are beginning to forget, beginning to look at me like a man instead of a freak. Big Tom needs me at the Sweet Julia. I'm quittin' after tonight's run."

"Hellsbellsdamnation!" said Cap'n Kidd.

Through the distant thunder of the stamp mills Britt heard the cautious scuff of boots approach the rear of his cabin. A hand furtively tapped at the kitchen door.

Britt frowned. He blew out the birthday candles, opened the door. He stonily eyed the two men in miners' garb who stood there, avoiding the streaming lamplight.

"Kin we come in?" one asked in a half whisper.

Britt hesitated, then nodded. They pushed quickly in, shoving the door closed. One, named Gotch Stover, was burly, with sloping shoulders and long arms. A stubble of black beard filmed his underslung jaw, and his eyes were like little dull pieces of coal. The other, Whitey Meech, was a spindle-legged, milky, pallid miner who looked like a consumptive.

Stover and Meech were shift bosses at the Montezuma mine, a rich diggings operated by Park Quimby. These two men had testified at a coroner's inquest that Britt's older brother had murdered a mine guard, and escaped with the Montezuma monthly gold clean-up one stormy night half a year in the past.

"Pull down them blinds, Burnett," Gotch Stover rasped.

"Afraid of something?" Britt asked quietly.

"Maybe," Stover shrugged. "There's reasons why it ain't best for us to be seen together tonight. We got a little proposition to make."

"Start talking," Britt said curtly.

"Me'n Whitey has got a chance to earn five thousand dollars tonight," Stover said. "Thet's the price Park Quimby, our boss at the Montezuma, has offered fer the delivery of a certain party to the law . . . dead or alive. We kin make the delivery right on the hoof, but figgered we'd talk it over with you first."

Britt felt the impact of that drive through him. He knew what they meant. His brother was charged with killing a mine guard named Coke Barrett, and fleeing into the mountains with a bullion clean-up worth more than twenty thousand dollars. Gotch Stover and Whitey Meech had told of trading shots with Luke as he escaped into a howling blizzard.

No word had ever come back from Luke, but Park Quimby, the Montezuma owner, still had a five thousand dollar reward posted for his capture. Britt did not believe that reward would ever be collected. He had been mighty close to his older brother. He was more than half convinced that Luke was dead. Otherwise he believed Luke would have got word to him, somehow, of his whereabouts.

Britt stood there remembering the hell he had lived through after the Montezuma holdup. As the brother of an outlawed killer, he was a marked man, and under suspicion. To his own surprise, and to the indignation of the mining camp, he had been offered a job as shotgun guard on the express company treasure cars which carried the mine clean-ups from Lodestone to Denver.

Shocked citizens had flooded the express company with protest, predicting the same outlaw strain that cropped out in Luke would show up in Britt also. Britt knew that Big Tom Lang was back of his being hired for such a responsible position. Big Tom, who had made and lost two fortunes in mining ventures, had powerful friends, and some of them no doubt were connected with the express company.

Britt and Luke had saved Big Tom's life more than a year in the past when a premature explosion had trapped the mine owner in a drift. They had performed miracles with dynamite and drills, getting to him before he suffocated, risking their lives in the rescue. Big Tom had never forgotten.

Having Britt named as express guard was Big Tom's way of showing his faith, and of smashing the tide of public opinion that might have driven Britt into the wolf pack out of sheer desperation. Britt had acted as gun guard in express cars for six months. Three times a week he made the round trip to Denver, standing watch over money and bullion consigned to the banks or mint. No treasure safe in his custody had ever been robbed. When he wasn't riding guard, he was spending what time he could working in Big Tom's Sweet Julia mine, helping fight a discouraging series of cave-ins that were threatening to bankrupt the owner.

Now he stood there staring at Gotch Stover, shaken by the veiled hint that Luke was alive.

"Luke is dead," he blurted out.

"He's alive," Gotch Stover sneered. "An' he ain't fur away. We got him. We was tipped off not long ago thet a chap answerin' Luke Burnett's description was workin' fer a freightin' outfit up in Wyoming. Me'n Whitey took a pasear up there a few days ago by train. It was Luke all right. We done the job ourselves, because we didn't aim to split the reward with nobody. We sneaked him back home, an' put him on ice where we kin lay our hands on him ag'in in a hurry."

"All right," Britt said icily. "Let's see your hole card."

"Five thousand dollars ain't such a bad stake if we turn Luke in," Stover drawled. "Then ag'in, we said to ourselves, maybe Britt Burnett, bein' Luke's brother, might want to tilt the ante if we let Luke go loose an' forget we ever cut his trail."

"How would I go about tiltin' this ante?" Britt jeered. "Do I shake the money out of my sleeve?"

"Maybe you could shake it out of an express company safe tonight," Stover grinned.

The room was silent. Through that silence Britt could hear the harsh thud of his pulse. He tried to laugh scornfully. "You don't expect me to really believe you've got Luke a prisoner."

Whitey Meech extended a hand, opening it so Britt could see what lay in the palm.

Britt stared at the hammered gold finger ring, adorned with a carved buffalo head. Luke had worn that ring always. Britt had one just like it. In case of a life-or-death crisis, the brother in trouble would send the other his ring, if he could, as a sign that he needed help.

Britt took a long breath. He believed them now. "Where is he?" he asked huskily.

Stover's attitude became menacing. "Don't git any notions you kin find him. We'll turn him loose on one condition, mister. You're ridin' guard tonight aboard Number Sixteen. The Montezuma clean-up is bein' shipped to the mint on that train, and it amounts to a nice jag of bullion. We ought to know, 'cause we delivered it to the express office this afternoon. We're fed up workin' fer day wages for Park Quimby. Number Sixteen always stops at the Summit Station water tank at ten-fifteen. We kin git to Summit in time by saddlepack over the pack trail if we start right now."

Stover studied Britt for a moment, then added, "Unlock the door on the express car when you hit Summit Station tonight. Have the safe unlocked. We'll do the rest. It's a cinch, ain't it?"

Again that silence fell. Britt's mouth was a bitter, thin line. "Luke'll swing shore, if we fetch him in," Stover prodded.

A vast emptiness was in Britt. He thought of the faith Big Tom Lang had shown him, and of Nettie's loyalty. This was to have been the last night of his probation, and now. . . . He couldn't let Luke go to the gallows. Guilty or not, it just wasn't in his blood to let that happen. "The door will be unlocked at Summit," he said wearily. "The safe will be open."

☆ II ☆

DEATH AT THE SWEET JULIA

*T*riumph showed in the hard eyes of the two men. "See thet you don't change your mind," Gotch Stover warned. "Don't forget we got Luke where we kin make things miserable fer him."

"When you head for Summit take along a fast horse for me," Britt said. "You don't think I'm going to take your word that you'll turn him loose, do you? I'm staying with you until I see Luke alive . . . see him with my own eyes." Then he added with blazing bitterness, "Don't you savvy that I've got to ride? I'll be an outlaw myself, after tonight."

They glanced at each other. Then Stover nodded. "It's a deal. We'll have a horse fer you. And you'll see Luke all right."

They opened the door and slipped out. The rumble of the stamp mills beat a dismal refrain to Britt's thoughts. He heard the bell of the switch engine in the distant railroad yards, and the clash of couplings. Number 16, the night train to Denver, was scheduled to pull out within an hour, and he would be riding in the express car, as usual. Summit Station was only about ten miles from camp by way of mountain trails, but the distance by rail was more than double that because of the grade that had to be conquered.

Britt shaved, changed to a dark, sack suit, and soft white shirt. He got down a sawed-off shotgun and a rifle from the rack, made sure their bores were clean, and loaded them. He laid a holstered six-shooter on the table alongside the heavier guns.

A rider pulled up before the cabin. Light, crisp heels approached, and a hand tapped the door. It was Nettie Lang, wearing a riding skirt in the fashion of the day. Her roan gelding, which was tied to a sapling pine before the cabin, bore a sidesaddle.

"Happy Birthday, Britt," she smiled.

"Thanks for the cake, Nettie," Britt answered, trying to put life in his voice. "How about a sample?"

"How 'bout a slug o' brandy?" Cap'n Kidd screeched.

Nettie wagged a reproving finger at the parrot. "Keep a decent tongue in your head, you nasty old pirate," she admonished. She covered the cage with a cloth, consigning the parrot to a darkness that silenced him. "That's safer," she chuckled. "You've simply go to teach him better manners, Britt."

Her rich, dark hair was piled in a big coil at the back of her head. A tiny bonnet was perched forward on her head. She was shapely and vitally feminine, but Britt had seen her on hunting trips riding hell-for-leather on that sidesaddle through rough country that had stopped more than one man. She was an expert wingshot with a quail gun and could handle a rifle and a six-shooter.

She looked at the guns on the table. "The last night as a guard, eh, Britt? I'm glad."

"The last night, Nettie," Britt nodded. His voice was wooden. There was no life in him, none of the old response this girl had always aroused in him. Britt had never spoken of love to Nettie, but she had understood that he was only waiting until his self-imposed probation was over.

His mood subdued her now, frightening her. "It'll be a blessing to Dad when you can give full time to the mine," she said slowly. "Dad needs you. He's hit nothing but grief lately."

"I know," Britt said tonelessly.

Grief was a mild term for what Big Tom Lang was bucking. His mine, which was named after Nettie's dead mother, was the discovery prospect in these diggings. Big Tom had hit pay ore two years ago, and that strike had created Lodestone. Half a dozen other paying mines were in operation in the district now. The railroad had been built into the camp to help develop the country. But mining was always a gamble. The Sweet Julia vein had faulted, and Big Tom had sunk most of his previous profits driving exploratory drifts in an attempt to pick it up again. He was confident that he had never really struck the true bonanza, and believed the mother lode lay somewhere beneath his property.

After months of heavy expense Big Tom's patience had been rewarded. Thanks to the sagacity of Luke Burnett, a thin stringer of ore had been picked up. That trace had showed promise of widening into something sensational as it was followed deeper into the mountain. Then misfortune hit Big Tom again, dealing him a series of paralyzing blows. Dynamite being carried in ore cars into the main shaft had let go, bringing down an enormous cave-in. A pump engine had broken down, flooding the diggings. Another cave-in had followed. The climax came with the robbery at the neighboring Montezuma mine, which cost Big Tom the services of Luke Burnett, his shaft boss on whom he had come to lean heavily.

Britt had stepped into Luke's shoes as best he could, helping direct the crew that was battling to reopen the mine. The job had taken months, but was now nearing success. Another week or two would see the shaft cleared. Then they could begin trailing that stringer of ore again, hoping it would soon lead them to the bonanza Big Tom was confident lay near at hand.

Nettie watched Britt, a shadow in her eyes. He had not cut the birthday cake. He seemed to have forgotten it. She began pulling on her gloves to leave. A deep jar ran through the earth, and Britt felt the cabin lift to the tremor. The report of a heavy explosion rolled over Lodestone with whip-lash violence.

He and Nettie rushed into the open. The camp was aroused. Men and women poured into the straggling length of the street. Above camp the lights of three of the mines showed against the face of the mountain, with rock dumps spilling down the slants in giant fan-shapes.

"It's the Sweet Julia!" Nettie gasped.

A plume of dust was mushrooming above the face of the mine, dimming the stars. Britt tossed the girl on the sidesaddle, mounted double behind her. They crowded the horse up the grade. The dust was clearing, and Britt saw that the shaft house at the mouth of the Sweet Julia tunnel had been blown into fragments. The donkey engine had been hurled off the platform, and the boiler was gone, except for a few jagged fragments.

Big Tom Lang's gaunt figure and shaggy thatch of gray hair loomed up as they reached the scene. Nettie uttered a sob of relief.

"Boiler exploded," Big Tom said dully. "I was in the shaft at the time. Shorty Wills is dead. Old Nelse Anderson got a broken laig. It could have been worse. The night shift had just gone down the shaft, or they'd have been wiped out."

Big Tom stood with sagging shoulders, watching them load the victims in an ambulance. Britt climbed to the face of the mine, and spent many minutes peering around. That hadn't sounded like a boiler blast to him. The explosion showed all the characteristics of dynamite. Still there was no way of being sure. He kept his own counsel as he descended to where Big Tom and Nettie stood. This was another body blow to Big Tom. Work would now be held up again for days and weeks until new machinery was brought in.

A thick-set man with a bulbous nose and loose, moist lips came up and shook hands with Big Tom. "Hard luck, Lang," he said. "If there's anythin' I kin do, any help I kin give you, jest say the word."

The arrival was Park Quimby, owner of the Montezuma, whose property abutted on Big Tom's discovery claim. Park Quimby had operated on a shoestring, sinking his shaft as close to discovery as mining law permitted. He had produced only low-grade ore for months. Then suddenly the Montezuma had hit it rich. Quimby was the man who had posted a five-thousand-dollar reward for Luke Burnett's capture, dead or alive. It was his bullion Luke was charged with stealing that January night.

The man ignored Britt. He had never relented in his opinion that Lodestone would be better off if it got rid of Luke Burnett's kin. He had bitterly opposed Britt's appointment as express car guard. Quimby beamed upon Nettie Lang. He wore expensive jewelry and tailored clothing, but he was marked by hard drinking, and he was gross and hard-tongued. He lived in a big, new house and maintained a stable of Thoroughbreds now that he was in the money. He was getting rich at the Montezuma, but he was held in contempt by real hard-rock men because of his methods. Quimby had imported two score of Chinese coolies from San Francisco to labor in his shaft.

Nettie Lang turned her back on Park Quimby. She had always distrusted the man.

☆ **III** ☆

LONG RIDER

Britt accompanied Big Tom and Nettie back to camp. Big Tom was silent, wrapped in his gloomy thoughts. It was nearing train time. The realization that this would be his final parting with Big Tom and this girl hit Britt now.

"*¡Adios!*" he said. "You'll look after Cap'n Kidd tomorrow, Nettie?"

She peered at him. "Of course. I always do when you're gone overnight to Denver. Is . . . is there anything wrong, Britt?"

"No, Nettie. Nothing wrong."

He went to his cabin, got his guns. He lifted the cloth from Cap'n Kidd's cage. "You'll have a new owner tomorrow, Cap'n," he whispered. "Be good to her."

Britt went out, closing the door softly behind him. He had in his pockets what few valuables he cherished. One was a picture of Nettie.

Cap'n Kidd uttered a single plaintive squawk as he went away. It was as though the bird understood. Cap'n Kidd had originally belonged to Luke. The night of the Montezuma holdup the parrot had sat in a corner of its cage, moaning and uttering heart-broken sounds. He had refused to eat for days afterward, and had nearly died. Cap'n Kidd had grieved like a human for a loved one. The strange part of it was that the parrot had started mourning for Luke even before word of the robbery had reached Britt. Some wild instinct that humans could not understand had warned Cap'n Kidd. That was why Britt had given up Luke as dead, that and the fact Luke had never sent back any word — until today.

Carrying his guns, Britt walked to the railroad station. Number 16, consisting of a combination express and mail car, a baggage car, and three coaches was just pulling in.

Britt headed for the express office, which occupied the far end of the building. The station platform was deserted in that vicinity. Britt halted a pace before he reached the lighted door of the express office, which stood open. The hiss of steam from the arriving locomotive had wiped out the sound of his approach. Then it had stopped suddenly, in time for him to hear his name mentioned inside the office.

He identified the voices of Big Tom Lang and Charlie Andrews, manager of the Lodestone express office. He started to turn away, not caring to eavesdrop. Then he heard the express manager say, ". . . that's a heavy jag of bullion going out tonight, Tom. If anything happened to it through any fault of Britt Burnett, you'd have to make good on that bond. Fifty thousand dollars is a heap of money."

Britt halted, listening.

"I'm good for it, ain't I?" Big Tom challenged.

The answer came dubiously. "Just about. I checked up on you this afternoon. It's part of my job to keep an eye on bondsmen. You was good for a quarter-of-a-million six months ago when the Sweet Julia was in pay ore. But not any longer, Tom. The mine would still bring a fair price. But if anything happened to Burnett, the express company would have to throw you into court to make good on that bond. You'd lose your mine, your home . . . everything. They'd clean you down to the clothes on your back."

"Hell!" Big Tom snorted. "Britt's guarded bigger shipments than this one."

"I'm bankin' on Britt too," Charlie Andrews agreed. "But, bein' a friend of yours too, I figured I'd better mention it."

Britt tiptoed away. He had always wondered why the express company had given him such a responsibility in view of the charges against his brother. He had known that Big Tom had a hand in it, but had never been told that Big Tom had signed as his bondsman. To go through with this pact with Stover and Meech would mean Big Tom's ruination.

Britt waited until Big Tom had left he express office. He entered then, reporting for duty. The bullion was in the office safe in two sealed express boxes. It was from Park Quimby's mine.

"Quimby's hittin' it rich for a fact," Charlie Andrews gossiped as he and Britt stood gun-guard while baggage men muscled the heavy treasure boxes into the express car and shoved them in the safe. "This is the biggest clean-up he's made."

Charlie Andrews locked the safe, and attached the company seal. Britt knew the combination. Only his hand would open the safe when the shipment reached Denver.

Britt closed and barred the car door after the agent had left. The forward third of the car was a mail compartment, separated from the express section by a steel wall, pierced by a door, which had a little round glass port for observation. That door was locked on both the mail and express side of the steel coach.

Pop Dillon, the railway mail clerk, was busy over mail sacks, distributing letters. Pop, spectacled, gray-haired, and a family man, saw Britt peering through the glass port, and waved a friendly greeting.

Britt was alone in the express section, with ten minutes still remaining before the train pulled out. Ten minutes in which to weigh his brother's fate against his loyalty to Big Tom and Nettie Lang. . . .

Presently the conductor bellowed, "All aboard!" The engine bell clanged, steam hissed. Number 16 was rolling.

Britt watched the lights of Lodestone fade, listened to the staccato beat of the exhaust from the engine as it fought to build up momentum before hitting the up-grades. Rock cuts echoed back the roar of the train. Britt peered from the barred side windows. The moon was dragging itself clear of the mountain rims to the east. It was a clear, silvery June moon that flooded the land with white mystery, a night for love-making and romance. Britt tried to keep Nettie Lang's memory out of his mind.

He marked off the familiar landmarks. The spidery network of cattle chutes at the L K ranch roared by. He noted the lights of a sheep ranch as the train thundered across Boiling Fork bridge below Five-Mile Gorge, and hit the last tortuous grade to the summit. Presently the whistle wailed in triumph as the panting locomotive crawled over the crest of the grade. Britt went to the safe, and opened it. Brakes clamped, and the train ground to a stop at the water tank.

Britt unbarred the door on the side away from the tank, shoved it back on its track. Two masked figures instantly came running out of the moonlight and entered the car. Gotch Stover and Whitey Meech wore padded slickers that altered their appearance. They had covered their hands with white gloves. Bandannas were wrapped over their faces and their hair. Gunnysacks concealed their boots. Only their eyes showed. They had cocked six-shooters in their hands. Britt saw old Pop Dillon staring, startled, through the port.

Gotch Stover cursed and swung his gun around to shoot through the glass, but Britt pushed the weapon down.

"That's only the mail clerk. He can't interfere if you work fast. That door is locked. The safe is open. Fetch up the horses."

Britt helped drag the two heavy treasure boxes to the door. Whitey Meech brought up three saddled horses and a pack mule equipped with a cross-buck packsaddle. It was the work of seconds to load the steel boxes on the mule, and swing into the saddle. Pop Dillon was still standing there, staring through that port as they spurred away into the night.

Stover and Meech lashed the mule ahead. They were well out of gunshot, spurring through rocks and brush when the locomotive whistle began screeching an alarm. Pop Dillon had given the warning of the robbery.

"What kin they do?" Gotch Stover exulted. "They can't chase us acrost country with a railroad train. An' they got no horses. It'll be two hours before a posse kin git on the job. Here's Blue Crick. We'll cool our trail in the stream until we hit the Spanish Duke ore road. Jerkline teams travel that road all night, an' will wipe out any sign we leave."

"First," Britt said, "we go to where you say you got Luke on ice."

He had his cocked six-shooter in his hand. Gotch Stover scowled at the gun. "Keep your hair on," he snarled. "We're headin' thetaway."

☆ IV ☆

THE LIVING DEAD

They left the stream where the mine road forded, and followed that dusty route. The direction was toward Lodestone, and once they pulled off into the brush to let an empty ore wagon and jerkline string pass by, bound back to the Spanish Duke mine. Britt stayed close at the heels of the two men who had now removed their masks and slickers. In the bright moonlight he never let his eyes wander away from them, ready to shoot at the first suspicious move they might make.

But they rode steadily ahead. Britt sighted the lights of Lodestone through a notch in the hills down the mountain, no more than two or three miles away. Gotch Stover looked back as they turned off the ore trail. They crossed a mountain meadow, then dismounted. Leaving their horses tethered, they moved ahead through brush. Boiling Fork Creek coiled through the meadow to the right, and just below the meadow it plunged through the series of rapids known as Five-Mile Gorge. Britt could hear the faint hum of the rapids.

There was an abandoned prospect hole nearby, and an old dugout some miner had occupied in the past. Britt had come upon the place while hunting. Pushing through the brush, the dim outline of the dugout entrance lay before them in the moonlight.

Stover spoke. "He's in there, Burnett."

Britt motioned with his gun. "You two go in first."

"You're a suspicious cuss," Stover snorted.

But he and Meech descended into the dugout, bending low to clear the sagging doorway to the place. Britt followed closely at their heels, his gun ready. Stover scratched a match and in its brief, first flare Britt saw the shadowy shape of a man lying on the ground with ropes around his feet and ankles.

"Luke!" Britt exclaimed, and abruptly leaped ahead.

The ropes around the man's wrists fell aside. His hands jerked the six-shooter from Britt's fingers, and then clamped on his arms, holding him tight. In the faint light Britt found himself looking into the face of Park Quimby, the bulbous-nosed owner of the Montezuma mine!

"Bust him one!" Park Quimby barked.

Britt tried to wrest free, but Quimby, exerting his strength, held him helpless for the instant it required for Stover to leap upon him. The muzzle of Stover's six-shooter crashed down on the back of Britt's neck, and he sagged limply forward across Park Quimby's legs.

The blackness that engulfed Britt seemed suddenly to explode into agonizing flame in his head. He had a horrible sensation of suffocation, and then one of slowly freezing. His stunned mind told him that he was under water — drowning. He considered that with remote detachment for a space. Then the shock of complete return to consciousness drove through him, and with it came the will to live. Instinctively he began to struggle for his life.

His head emerged. Half strangled he finally got a breath of reviving air into his lungs. He had been pitched into Boiling Fork Creek. With a gasp of horror he realized that the sullen rumble in his ears was the echo of the rapids where the stream left the meadows and began its descent of the mountain through the rocky Five-Mile Gorge.

He was no more than fifty yards above the gorge and was being swept with increasing speed toward the brink of the first rapids. He struck out frenziedly for shore, but the current was too strong for him and he was carried inexorably toward where the stream narrowed between big, spray-wet boulders to start its plunge. He managed to reach one boulder that joined with solid land, but his desperate fingers slipped from its water-slimed face. He drifted to the brink of the falls and had a terrifying glimpse of foaming, spray-torn white water below.

Then his legs hit something solid, just beneath the surface. It was a long tree trunk, wedged across the lip of the descent, caught between big boulders. He wrapped an arm around it. The drag of the stream threatened momentarily to snatch him away, but he finally inched along it into quieter backwater near shore. He fought his way to dry land and fell, gasping and spent.

After minutes he got to his feet. He was chilled to the marrow by the icy mountain stream. His head throbbed. That blow from Stover's gun numbed his nerves, but immersion in the stream had revived him. There was no sign of the three men who had tricked him. He looked down at himself in sudden wonder. He was barefoot. In place of his own clothes he was now clad in the ragged, soaked garb of a Chinese coolie. The finger ring he had been wearing — the companion ring to the one Luke had — was gone.

Britt suddenly turned, staring with a vast and grim horror down the rapids where spume drifted in the moonlight.

"Luke!" he said despairingly.

The removal of his own ring by his assailants, and the recollection that Stover was in possession of his brother's ring and the other personal belongings, were too significant to be mere coincidences. It brought vividly to his mind another incident. A month in the past a prospector had found the partial skeleton of a human being lodged in driftwood below Five-Mile Gorge. There were only a few human bones that had survived the battering of the stream. Clinging to them were shreds of rough, cotton cloth of the type of material the coolies at the Montezuma mine used for their smocks. There was a bullet hole in the shoulder of the smock. The coroner had ventured the opinion that the victim might have been a white man, though the evidence of the scraps of cotton cloth indicated that it was more likely the remains were that of one of Park Quimby's Chinese miners.

Britt looked down at his own garb now. Quimby and his two conspirators had consigned him to Five-Mile Gorge, with all identification marks removed, dressed as a Chinese. The parallel was obvious.

Suddenly Britt knew in his heart that Luke was dead. He had been thrown into the stream, and it was only by chance that any clue to his disappearance had ever been found. But why? Why had he been murdered? Britt stood there, thinking hard. He mentally recounted every incident of his brother's disappearance, everything that happened since.

Then, suddenly, he began climbing away from the stream. He scouted the dugout where he had stepped into Park Quimby's trap. It was silent, deserted. The pack mule and saddle horses were gone from where they had been tethered.

Britt headed toward Lodestone by way of the ore trail. He suddenly ducked into the brush, hearing riders coming. Crouching there, he watched six armed men streaming by, heading toward the summit. A deputy sheriff was in the lead. It was a posse. Word of the train robbery had reached Lodestone. Britt knew that every trail and pass in the mountains would be guarded as fast as the law could spread manhunters through the region.

He resumed his own way down the mountain, avoiding the road. Rocks and thorns gave his bare feet hell, but he hurried ahead. He came out on the open mountainside not far above the mouth of the Sweet Julia diggings. The mine was dark, unlighted. Because of the explosion, all work had been brought to a standstill. Big Tom had laid off his crew.

Britt crossed a ridge into a small gulch. Park Quimby's Montezuma tunnel entered the mountainside on the flank of this gulch just below him. The Montezuma shaft house was lighted, the donkey engine puffing. He saw mules dragging ore cars to the waste dump. The squalid shacks where the Chinese lived were scattered in the barren gulch bottom not far from the foot of the waste dump.

Britt descended and cautiously scouted the odorous colony. He crept to the wall of one of the hovels. The sour tang of opium smoke assailed him, and he heard faint, sing-song voices. He moved to another shack. It was silent. He opened the crooked door. Its occupants evidently were on shift at the mine. Searching around he found a pair of ragged, rope-soled sandals which he donned.

He had to search three more hovels before he came upon one of the round, bowl-shaped straw hats the coolies wore. It was a final addition to his disguise, and it served as an effective shield for his face. In this shack he also made a find he had hardly dared hope for. A six-shooter and a box of shells lay in plain sight on a shelf. Hiding them in his sleeves, Britt left the coolie colony.

Keeping to cover, he climbed to the level where the track for ore cars operated to the dump. The donkey engine in the shaft house was laboring, and he heard the whine of the cable. A string of six ore cars crawled from the slanting tunnel, loaded with waste rock. Mules were hooked to the cars. Driven by two coolies, the cars came squeaking to the dumping point. Britt waited in hiding as the string of cars approached. They halted, and were spilled one by one, sending rock rattling down the slant.

Britt arose, grasped the side of one of the cars, and began to slide over its side toward a hiding place in the bottom. As he did so, he glanced ahead to make sure the coolies were not in sight. He was startled to see another figure clambering into the farthest car ahead. Like himself this furtive passenger wore the flapping garb of a Chinese, and a dishpan hat. But the hat toppled, and its wearer reached out and grabbed it before it fell to the ground. Then that shadowy figure slid out of sight into the bottom of the empty ore car. Stunned, Britt stared for an instant. He had glimpsed a thick, braided coil of lustrous dark hair, such as no pig-tailed coolie had ever owned. It was Nettie Lang, disguised as a Chinese! Like himself she was bent on secretly entering the Montezuma shaft.

Then the ore cars were rolling back toward the main tunnel. Britt glimpsed a gun-guard, and was forced to crouch out of sight. The mules were unhooked; the engine cable was attached; and the cars began moving with increasing speed down the slanting shaft of the Montezuma diggings. Britt wanted to join the girl, but he could not leave his present position now, for the Montezuma tunnel was big enough only to accommodate the cars. To lift his head now meant being crushed.

Britt's eyes were grim. He had his own reasons for this secret trip into the Montezuma. He wondered if Nettie Lang had the same purpose in mind.

☆ V ☆

UNDERGROUND DEATH

*N*o visitor had ever been allowed in the Montezuma. Park Quimby kept a gun-guard always on duty at the shaft house to enforce that rule. But Britt had a hunch at least one other intruder had been down in the Montezuma in the past. That man was Luke, his brother. And Luke had never come out of the Montezuma alive.

Faint light appeared, and increased. The string of cars jolted to a stop. Britt chanced a cautious glimpse. They had reached a sizable stope, lighted by a dusty overhead acetylene. The underground stable for burros was located here, and this chamber was the central point for galleries and drift tunnels that opened out in various directions.

A faint, cheerless smile pulled at Britt's lips as he noted the direction of one of those drifts. From far away in that tunnel came the faint sound of mining operations. The two other drifts were silent, and it was evident they were not being worked. He glimpsed Nellie Lang wriggling from her hiding place, sliding over the side of the car into the shadows. He followed suit. A coolie had hooked a tandem team of burros to the string of cars, and now led them away into the drift that was being worked. That heading was where Park Quimby was hitting the pay ore that was making him rich.

Britt and the girl were alone in the low, dimly lighted chamber. Water dripped from the timbers overhead. The faint crash of jack hammers on drills echoed from the drift along with the receding rumble of the heavily laden ore cars. The girl, small and shapeless in her coolie costume, discovered him. She turned her back, started walking casually toward that south tunnel. She had taken it for granted he was a Chinese. Britt strode to overtake her. She heard him and whirled, and he found himself looking into the muzzle of a cocked six-shooter.

"Lift you hands!" she ordered tersely. "Do you understand English? If so, do what I say, and. . . ." Then she recognized him, and the gun sagged. The girl stared, white-faced, grim-eyed. "So it's you, Britt. Well, I suppose this is as good a place to hide as any."

"Get out of this mine, Nettie," Britt burst out. "Are you loco? If Park Quimby catches you here, he'll. . . ."

"Why did you do it, Britt?" she asked lifelessly. "I know about the train robbery. Didn't you know this means the end of everything for Dad? He had signed your bond. He'll lose the Sweet Julia . . . lose everything."

"What are you doing here?" Britt demanded.

"I imagine you can guess. I've had a hunch for a long time all Dad's bad luck wasn't accidental. That explosion at the shaft house tonight convinced me I was right. It wasn't a boiler explosion. That was done by dynamite . . . deliberately. I began to figure things out. So I came down here to see if my hunch was right. I don't have to go any farther to know that I had added everything up and got the right answer." She pointed to the south tunnel. "That drift where Quimby is hitting his pay ore heads right under Dad's Sweet Julia property, and from the sounds I'd say Quimby is working ground at least five hundred feet or more inside our claim. He had tapped the mother lode that Dad always knew was there . . . but it isn't his, legally. He's looting our claim.

"That's why Quimby uses Chinese who can't talk English, and keeps them supplied with opium," she went on, breathlessly. "That's the reason the Sweet Julia has had all those cave-ins and explosions. Quimby, and the ruffians who are in on the deal with him, have been dynamiting the Sweet Julia shaft to keep Dad from finding the pay ore, while they work it from the Montezuma diggings."

She kept the gun rigidly on him now, her finger on the trigger as she spoke. "I . . . I saw Gotch Stover and Whitey Meech sneaking away from your cabin earlier tonight," she continued haltingly. "I refused to think anything wrong about you then. But when I heard the train had been robbed, and that you. . . ." She burst into tears. Britt's lips were ashen. She had every reason to believe he was in on this scheme to loot the Sweet Julia property.

The rattle of an ore car, descending from the surface, aroused him. Britt reached out, pushing Nettie's gun down. Taking her arm, he hurried her into one of the deserted drifts. She was still shaken by heart-broken sobs. He pulled her beside him into a crevice between timbers, squeezing into a narrow space barely big enough for their bodies. From that hiding place he had a partial view into the main stope.

The ore car rolled into view and stopped. Britt felt the girl's body grow tense. Her sobbing ended as they watched Park Quimby clamber from the car, followed by Gotch

Stover and Whitey Meech. Meech lifted out an opened dynamite case. Working fast, they began pulling out wired bundles of explosives, half a dozen sticks in each bundle. The three men busied themselves capping the dynamite, and attaching long coils of fuse.

"Maybe we ought to let them Chinks out before . . . before we. . . ." Whitey Meech looked pallid in the dim light.

Quimby cursed him with explosive violence. "You goin' yella? You know damned well it wouldn't look right if the night shift was on the surface. People would guess we had blown the Montezuma in on purpose. Then they might figure out the rest of it."

Gotch Stover was also scowling at the spindly man. "You're in this to the finish, Whitey," he gritted. "Don't go belly-up now . . . it's too late. And don't forget it was you that shot Luke Burnett in the back after we ketched him here in the mine. An' you helped git rid of his brother tonight the same way we took care o' Luke's body six months ago. You want a trip down Five-Mile Gorge?"

Meech swallowed hard. "Hell, I'm stickin'," he declared. "I didn't mean nothin'. You figure you kin buy the Sweet Julia, Park?"

"It's a sure thing," Quimby declared. "We'll use Big Tom's own money. The express company will sell him into bankruptcy to meet that bond he put up for Britt Burnett. Charlie Andrews told me about that bond a month ago. Thet's why I figgered out this stunt tonight."

"Britt Burnett was gittin' a little curious anyway," Stover said. "I seen him lookin' over that shaft house tonight after we blowed it up. He knew damned well it was a dynamite job. He'd soon've been figgerin' out things, like his brother did."

"It's time we covered our tracks," Quimby nodded. "We'll soon be working that lode from the Sweet Julia, and it will be done legally. The law can't touch us. The express company will pay us fer that bullion we took off the train. Someday we'll dig them boxes up from where we cached 'em. Thet's what you call eatin your cake an' havin' it too. We'll have to pay something for the Sweet Julia when it's auctioned off, but it'll be cheap at the price."

"Plenty cheap," Stover gloated. "There's a couple o' million still to be dug out of that block of ore, or I miss my guess. We ain't more'n scratched the surface."

They had finished capping the dynamite, and now began placing the charges around the stope, and in the drift that led beneath Sweet Julia's property. They were going to blow in the mine, and entomb a dozen or more Chinese who were in the heading.

A match flared, and the first string of explosives was alive. Nettie Lang uttered a little gasp. She had been poised tensely in that cramped position, her feet on loose rock that had accumulated against the timbers. The rubble was giving way beneath her feet. Her fingers clutched at the wet timbers, slipped. She staggered, lost balance, and was forced to take a step out into plain sight.

Park Quimby heard that faint sound as he finished a second fuse. He came to his feet with an oath, peering at the figure he glimpsed dimly a score of feet down that tunnel.

"What the hell!" he exclaimed. "Pinch them fuses a minute, boys. There's a Chink down there. . . ."

Discovery was inevitable. Britt reached out, pulled the girl back into shelter. He snatched the six-shooter from her hand. Then, armed with two guns, he leaped out into view. He moved into the lighted stope, knowing what was coming, but determined to draw gunfire away from the girl's position. The two fuses that had been touched off were sputtering, but they had a long way to burn, for Quimby had allowed plenty of time for himself and his partners to get to the open.

"Reach!" Britt snapped at the staring trio.

That was the mistake he made — giving them that chance.

Park Quimby leaped aside, drawing. His six-shooter blasted as he moved. Stover and Meech chimed in and the stope was lighted by flickering, vicious spurts of gun-flame. Britt's six-shooters were blasting in response. He felt one slug tug at his ragged garb, but he was moving, leaping around as he fired. Their bullets were bracketing him, thudding into the timber around him, but they didn't down him with that first burst.

He caught Whitey Meech in his sights, sent a slug through the man's chest, and saw him fall. But he realized in the next instant that the odds were still great against him in this lighted stope. He shifted his aim, fired, and the acetylene lamp was shattered by the slug. The mine was plunged into darkness. Then the sputtering, tiny glare from the two lighted fuses made itself felt. That faint light was enough to betray any man who moved between it and a watching opponent.

A momentary, breathless silence came. Britt flattened himself against the damp timbers. He had three slugs left in one gun, two in the other. He could hear the others breathing heavily. Then a gun blared twice, the double wink of flame etching out the scene in brief brilliance. It was Quimby who fired. Britt saw Stover outlined against the black background of a drift and triggered instantly with both guns. He heard the slugs tear through flesh, then the deep sighing sound of a man dying.

"It's you and me now, Quimby," Britt challenged.

Quimby fired at the sound of his voice, but the slug was wide, for sounds were distorted in this echoing stope.

"Throw your gun down, Quimby," Britt spoke flatly. "Light a match so I can see you . . . and move fast. Those two fuses won't burn forever. They can't have more than two, three minutes to go."

His answer was another shot that had no better luck than Quimby's previous attempt. Britt tried to remember how many times Quimby had fired. He wondered if the man's gun was empty. It was evident Quimby, knowing he would hang anyway, meant to die here when that dynamite let go, rather than surrender.

Britt heard a faint, metallic sound. It was the sound of a man trying to reload his gun. It might be a trick, but Britt had to take that chance, for those fuses must now be perilously short. He charged across the black stope. He heard Quimby pull a quick, involuntary breath into his lungs as the big mine owner awaited that oncoming rush. That sound helped Britt. He barged into his quarry in the darkness. He swung with a gun muzzle, missed, and heard the swish of Quimby's return blow as it grazed his ear.

He was off balance. He twisted around, emptying his two guns, sweeping the area around him with three slugs. He heard one of those bullets register. Quimby, who was no more than arm's length from him in the darkness, groaned, and then fell against him.

Britt lowered the limp body to the floor, then leaped toward the fuses. He fell over the ore tracks, arose, and hurled himself on the sputtering snakes, stamping them out.

"Britt!" It was Nettie's voice, hoarse with anxiety.

"Yes, Nettie," Britt said. Then he found her, in the darkness. He held her tight against him, his lips pressed against her hair until her hysterical sobbing began to fade.

"I . . . I was afraid it would be someone else who would answer," she sobbed. "Oh, Britt! I love you, and yet I doubted you. Forgive me."

Together they climbed up the slanting main shaft to the surface. Quimby's gun-guard was on duty there, peering around uneasily. He stared at their Chinese garb, then found himself looking into Britt's gun.

The rest was easy. An hour later a score of men from Lodestone were in the Montezuma mine, listening to Britt's story as they looked at the evidence. They had found Park Quimby still alive. He would live to hang. Whitey Meech and Gotch Stover were dead.

Big Tom Lang stood with his arms around his daughter, his lined face somber as he listened.

"My brother must have scented this scheme last winter and sneaked into the Montezuma for a look-see," Britt told them. "They discovered him. There must have been a gun fight in which he killed one of them, but they got him in the back finally. Then they framed the story of that holdup to explain Luke's disappearance and the killing of their pal. They dressed Luke in Chinese clothes, and threw his body into Five-Mile Gorge, the same place they tried to get rid of me tonight. They thought I was dead, too, I reckon."

The sheriff was present. He stepped up to Britt. "I reckon the jury will be lenient with you, Burnett," he said. "You pulled that robbery under duress and threat. Loyalty to your brother will be considered. But the bullion is gone. You heard Quimby say they cached the treasure boxes. These mountains are mighty big. Chances are the gold will never be found. I'm sorry, son, but you'll have to stand trial for robbery."

Britt looked at Nettie, grinning. "That bullion should be just about in Denver now," he said, "aboard the same express car in which it left Lodestone. I opened the safe before the train pulled out of Lodestone last night, opened the express boxes, and hid the bars of bullion back of some trunks and crates that were being shipped in the car. I climbed out the other door long enough to toss aboard some fish plates and railroad spikes that were on a section car of the siding. Then I filled the treasure boxes with scrap iron. Quimby must have cached the boxes without even taking time to open 'em. They're not worth the trouble of looking for. Wire the mint at Denver . . . they'll find the bullion when Number Sixteen pulls in."

Nettie rushed to him. "I'll never doubt you again, Britt," she said contritely.

Britt kissed her. "You never really doubted me," he chuckled. "You let me push that gun away when you were holding it on me. You never really believed in your heart I was a train robber."

Her arms tightened around his neck. Britt looked at Big Tom. The big man's gaunt face was suddenly alight with triumph. Big Tom glared around at the bystanders challengingly. He had been vindicated in his faith, and he wanted them to know it.

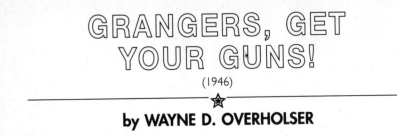

GRANGERS, GET YOUR GUNS!

(1946)

☆

by WAYNE D. OVERHOLSER

Wayne D. Overholser won four Golden Spur awards from the Western Writers of America and has a long list of fine Western titles to his credit. He was born in Pomeroy, Washington, and attended the University of Montana, University of Oregon, and the University of Southern California before becoming a public school teacher and principal in various Oregon communities. He began writing for Western pulp magazines in 1936 and within a couple of years was a regular contributor to Street & Smith's Western Story Magazine *and Fiction House's* Lariat Story Magazine. Buckaroo's Code *(Macmillan, 1948) was his first Western novel and remains one of his best. In the 1950s and 1960s, having retired from academic work to concentrate on writing, he would publish as many as four books a year under his own name or a pseudonym, most prominently as Joseph Wayne and Lee Leighton.* The Violent Land *(Macmillan, 1954),* The Lone Deputy *(Macmillan, 1957), and* The Bitter Night *(Macmillan, 1961) are among the finest Overholser titles. Many of his novels are first person narratives, a technique that tends to bring an added dimension of vividness to the frontier experiences of his narrators and frequently, as in* Cast a Long Shadow *(Macmillan, 1955), the female characters one encounters are among the most memorable. Almost invariably, his stories weave a spell of their own with their scenes and images of social and economic forces often in conflict and the diverse ways of life and personalities that made the frontier so unique a time and place in human history.*

☆ **I** ☆

GUN-SLINGER'S PAST

Ed Rawlins carried a sack of flour out of the Mercantile, dumped it into his wagon, and straightened his lank body, looked across the street squarely into the eyes of Bal Tilse. It had been a long time since he'd seen Tilse. He rutted back into his memory. Five years. . . ? No, six — and he'd have been happier if it had been another six. His first impulse was to run, an impulse that died the instant it was born, for Ed Rawlins was not one to duck an issue.

It was not that he had anything against Tilse, for at one time the man had been his best friend. It was simply a case of Rawlins's smoky past being brought back to him in the form of Bal Tilse, a past that ran through the years like a frayed and tarnished ribbon. Rawlins, watching Tilse cross the street to him, thought grimly that Tilse was the last man he wanted to see. He thought, too, with a sharp stab of regret, that a man's past is always with him, always haunting him and casting its long shadow across his future.

"Ed, you old, long-legged, smoke-eating son of sin," Tilse shouted, and held out a hand. "Sure is good to see you."

"It's good to see you," Rawlins lied, and shook Tilse's hand. "What are you doing here in Sills City?"

"Looking for a job . . . and for you. Heard you were here."

"You get a job?" Rawlins asked, and felt his stomach muscles knot. There was only one man in Sills City who would hire a gun-slinger like Bal Tilse, and Rawlins knew the answer to his question before he asked it.

Tilse nodded. "Hired out to Ira Sills."

"Yeah, I know him," Rawlins murmured, and let it go at that.

Tilse cuffed his Stetson back, and stared at Rawlins, and Rawlins felt the disappointment and then the contempt that was in the man.

"You look like a farmer," Tilse said. "That don't make sense for a gent who had the fastest gun hand of any *hombre* I ever sided in a showdown."

"It don't make sense for a fact," agreed Rawlins mildly.

There was silence for a moment, both thinking of the years they had been together, and of that last ride through the blackness of an Arizona night with a dozen men not more than a jump behind them. They had parted in the desert while the pursuit thundered on past, and Rawlins had not heard of Tilse from that moment to this. Now, clad in the heavy shoes, the overalls, cotton work shirt, and straw hat of a farmer, Rawlins felt suddenly ashamed.

"It's damn funny," Tilse said, his green eyes narrowing. "I remember how I used to cuss a gunfighter's life, claiming I'd like to settle down on a farm and watch things grow. And all the time you said I was a damned fool."

"I was a crazy kid," Rawlins murmured, "and you were old enough to know what you wanted."

"And now you're digging in the dirt, and I'm still drawing down gun-slinger's pay." Tilse shook his head as if he couldn't believe this thing he saw.

"I'm just one of fifty farmers, Bal," Rawlins said, "who settled here on Purgatory Creek and took land under Sills's ditch. I'd like to remain that."

"Hell, you got nothing to be ashamed of," Tilse said sharply. "No use hiding your talents." He paused, eyes again narrowing thoughtfully, as if his mind was trying to probe the mystery of this change in Rawlins. Bitterness came to him then. "I've been the fool, Ed, keeping on the dark trails half the time and wasting my life. I'm forty. Damned near ready to be an old man."

"I'm not so young, either, Bal. Well, I'll see you again."

Rawlins crawled into the wagon seat and picked up the lines. Tilse stared up at him, eyes still questioning. He asked softly, "You say this is Sills's land?"

Rawlins nodded. "State got it from the government under the Carey Act, and Sills had to put water on it."

"You get it free?"

"Not quite." Rawlins lips tightened. "Fifteen dollars an acre."

"What the hell does he need gun-slingers for?" Tilse demanded. "I figgered he was having a scrap over water rights."

"No."

Tilse laid his hands on the front wheel, the sourness in him whetting an edge to his words. "I sure need a job, Ed, but I didn't figger that coming here would put us on opposite sides."

"Funny thing," Rawlins said, and clicked to his team.

Bal Tilse stood there in the street, staring after him, dark face still sour and a little puzzled.

It was strange what a man would do for a dream, Ed Rawlins told himself as he drove home. He thought now about his smoky years as he had not thought about them for a long time: empty years, filled with riding and shooting and killing, years when he'd earned big pay and spent it as fast as he'd earned it. Then there had been another job after he'd left Tilse, and another fight, and he's been shot to pieces. It had been the weeks in a hospital bed that had changed him. He hadn't buckled on his guns since that time, hadn't fought with a man since then. He'd worked, and saved his money, and now he was making a try for his own land here on the Purgatory.

It wasn't the land, exactly, that was his dream. He drove into his farm yard and past the house to his barn, looking at the buildings, critically now, and weighing them against the possessions that Bal Tilse's life had brought him. They weren't much: the house was a one-room, tar-paper shack; the barn was made of pine logs he'd brought down from the Cascades; his garden was just coming up and was nothing but a promise. He thought grimly of that. A promise? Nothing more and, unless Sills fixed the ditches so that he'd have more water than he'd had last year, it was a promise that would not be kept.

Rawlins put away his team, carried his groceries into the house, and cooked dinner; but his mind was still on the past, still considering the forces that had made him what he was. It was partly the pain and nearness to death while he'd been in the hospital, but it was mostly Trudy Gilder, and what she meant to him. That was the dream: her love, a home, children. Those were the things that gave a solitude to life, a feeling of depth, a value to the bare struggle of living. And Trudy Gilder did not approve of fighting. She would give him back his ring if she knew what his past had been. Shock came to Rawlins with that thought. If Tilse told, and the story spread along Purgatory Creek, Trudy would hear.

Ed Rawlins was not a man to give way to panic. He fought it now, telling himself it wouldn't happen, that Tilse wouldn't tell. Yet he couldn't be sure, and the worry was still in him that afternoon when he was working on his mower and saw Jack Kelton and Lew Dosso ride in from the county road.

At first the sight of Ira Sills's two men did not mean anything to Rawlins. He straightened, laid the monkey wrench on the mower seat, and reached into his pocket for pipe and tobacco. He called an amiable, "Howdy, gents. Light down and rest your saddles."

They dismounted, and came toward him, neither speaking and both, he saw, were a little drunk. Officially they were supposed to be some kind of construction men for the irrigation company but Rawlins, who understood these things better than most of the folks along the Purgatory, knew that their real job was to smash opposition to Sills. Kelton was a big, thick-shouldered man with sharp, black eyes that were surprisingly small for so large a face. Dosso was thin and stooped, with a huge beak of a nose and long-fingered hands that were deadly fast with the six-guns he wore. They made a good pair for Ira Sills and were the principal reason why none of the farmers had seriously kicked about the small and inadequate ditch system.

Rawlins wondered why neither spoke, but he didn't see their intent until they were close, and Kelton said, "We thought you were just a farmer, Rawlins . . . just a plain, ordinary, mud farmer."

Bal Tilse had wasted no time about his past. That was the first thought that came into Rawlins's mind as he slid the tobacco can back into his pocket and held a match to his pipe. Then a second thought struck him: this was trouble with a capital T and he wished his guns were on his hips instead of in the house. "That's all I am," Rawlins said coolly, taking the pipe out of his mouth. "Just a farmer." He wondered why he'd thought about his guns and, remembering Trudy Gilder, knew he must meet this threat without his guns.

"I hear different," Kelton said. "I hear you used to be a gunfighter, a regular ring-tailed wowser. A real curly wolf from the forks of Bitter Crick!"

"Who have you been listening to?" Rawlins asked.

"Don't make no never-mind about that," Kelton snarled. "The point is, we don't want no trouble. You take fifty crazy mud farmers, get 'em heated up some, and you've got trouble. We ain't gonna have that, Rawlins."

"All right," Rawlins said, "we ain't gonna have trouble."

Lew Dosso had cocked his head, hard blue eyes on Rawlins. He said, "He could be a tough hand, Jack. Look at them gray eyes. And them long fingers. That quick way he's got of moving. Put a gun on his hip, and he could be hell on little red wheels."

"Rawlins, it don't make no sense for a gent who's been a gun-slinger to come here and take up land and act like a farmer." Kelton gestured with a meaty hand. "You're playing some kind of smart game. What is it?"

Rawlins's pipe had gone dead in his mouth. He tamped the tobacco down with a forefinger, eyes on Kelton and then Dosso, and held a match flame to it. He knew men like these two, knew that the only things they respected were a man's fists or the gun he carried. He blew out a cloud of smoke that hung for a moment in the still air. Then he said, "To hell with you. There's no smart game about it. I want to farm and be let alone. That's all."

But Jack Kelton had not ridden out here from Sills City to let him alone. He snarled, "I think you're taking the farmers' pay and, when the time's right, you'll buckle on your hoglegs and start raising hell."

"I haven't worn my guns for a long time, Kelton. Now suppose you mount up and git."

"Not yet, mister. I came out here to show you you'd better stay a farmer. Now I'm gonna show you."

Kelton lowered his head and came at Rawlins, great fists lashing out at Rawlins's face. It might have surprised a man who had less understanding of the caliber of those with whom he was dealing, but it did not surprise Ed Rawlins. He had laid his pipe down on the mower seat beside the monkey wrench. Now he stepped to one side, and struck Kelton a jarring blow on the side of his head.

Kelton let out a bellow that held more surprise than pain, wheeled, and rushed Rawlins again. This time Rawlins held his ground. They came together, hard, Rawlins punching savagely at Kelton's stomach; but weight was with Kelton, and he forced Rawlins back. They moved toward the mower, Kelton lashing at Rawlins's face. Rawlins, seeing that it was Kelton's intention to back him against it and batter him into submission, suddenly swung away and brought a vicious right to the side of the man's face. Kelton went on, carried by his own impetus and the force of Rawlins's blow, and fell headlong against the mower, his head cracking sharply against the wheel.

Rawlins stepped back, bruised lips stretched in a grin. He asked, "What was that you was going to show me, Kelton?" It was then that Lew Dosso's gun barrel cracked against Rawlins's head and he spilled forward into the litter of the barn yard.

☆ II ☆

FRIEND — OR TRAITOR

Ed Rawlins was still lying beside the mower when Trudy Gilder rode into the barn yard and found him. She was cradling his head on her lap when he came to. He stared into her face, shut his eyes and, when he opened them again, she was still there. He murmured, "No harps. I always thought there was harp music in heaven."

"I'm no angel," Trudy said softly, "but I thought for a minute you were. What happened?"

He told her as his fogged memory cleared. Then he said, "You said once you hated men who settled trouble with guns."

She made no answer and, when he looked at her, there was a small smile in the corner of her lips. She was a pretty girl, this Trudy Gilder, with the darkest brown eyes Rawlins had ever seen, and hair as black as a crow's wing. Rawlins had seen pretty girls before, but he had never seen one like Trudy. He had often wondered what there was about her that set her apart from other women, and he had never been sure. He had always noted the great pride that she possessed, a sort of hewing-to-the-line quality that was in her and now, looking up at her face, he wondered if that was it.

Rawlins sat up rubbing his aching head and then got to his feet. He reeled uncertainly for a moment, his head whirling, and grabbed at the mower seat to steady himself. He said, "I guess you're the kind of a person who never goes back on what she says, and it wouldn't be fair of me to go ahead letting you think I'm something I'm not. You're bound to hear it sometime anyhow."

"Don't tell me, Ed." She was on her feet now, facing him and there was a softness about her he had never seen before. "We're having a settlers' meeting tonight. Dad says it's important. That's what I came to tell you and I'm not interested in what you were. I'm only interested in what you are."

She kissed him then, a quick kiss that left a feeling of uncertainty in Rawlins and, turning from him, swiftly mounted and galloped away, a slim, lithe figure who rode gracefully and well. Rawlins didn't stir until she had disappeared into the junipers. Then he walked to the house, still a little dizzy, and sitting down on his front steps stared at the long skyline of the Cascades.

A week ago or even this morning, Rawlins would not have wished for his guns as he had when Kelton and Dosso rode up. He did not understand it. He had thought that life was entirely behind him, and Trudy had promised to marry him in the fall.

"One good crop," he had told her, "and we can build another room."

Now everything was different. Bal Tilse had done that to him; the contempt in the man's eyes was a stinging nettle across his brain. He got up and went into the house. He stared at the trunk that held his guns, walked around the room, and came back to the trunk. He had asked Tilse not to tell about his past, but Tilse had told. Ira Sills had sent his men out to make threats when talk became a little too strong against the irrigation company, but this was the first time they had gone beyond the making of threats.

Lifting the lid of the trunk, Rawlins took out the gun belts. He buckled them around him, and the weight of them on his hips was good. He lifted each gun from holster, practiced the draw, and finally slid them back into their casings, smiling in satisfaction. Gun magic, once learned as Ed Rawlins had learned it, was not easily forgotten.

Reluctantly Rawlins unbuckled the gun belts and put them back into the trunk. They weren't the way. Not yet. He fed his chickens and pigs, milked his cow, cooked supper, and shaved. He didn't know what the settlers' meeting was about, and he didn't know what Ira Sills had in mind, but he knew one thing. He wanted to lay his hands on Bal Tilse. He saddled his horse, anger slowly rising in him until it had reached the boiling point by the time he rode into Sills City.

The sun lay just above the Cascades when Rawlins tied his horse in front of he Jubilee Bar. He shouldered through the batwings, thinking that the saloon was the most likely place to find Tilse and seeing in one quick glance that he'd been right. Bal Tilse stood half way along the bar talking to Ira Sills and, except for the barkeep, they were the only men in the saloon. Rawlins came quickly along the bar, laid a hand on Tilse's shoulder, and brought him around, hard.

"It's a hell of a thing," Rawlins said, anger honing a sharpness to his voice, "when you see an old friend for the first time in six years and that friend rushes off as fast as his legs can carry him to blat all he knows."

"Hell, Ed," Tilse said defensively, "I told you there was nothing to be ashamed of."

"No, I'm not ashamed of anything I did then, Bal, and I'm not ashamed of what I'm doing now. But mebbe you're ashamed of your double-jointed tongue that got me a beating."

"What are you talking about?" Tilse demanded.

Rawlins told him, and added, "Sills, I'd like to know what you had in mind when you sent that pair of quick-triggering saddle bums to my place."

Ira Sills was small and shrewd and smooth. He had a way of making people trust him, and he had somehow been able to duck trouble the summer before when there hadn't been a farmer on the creek whose crops had had enough water. He studied Rawlins a moment before he answered, his dark eyes hooded. Then, with unexpected frankness, he answered: "When a gunman moves into this project, I feel better when I know he's on my side. I don't want trouble, Rawlins, and I'm hoping the sample the boys showed you this afternoon will encourage you to move . . . or at least to watch your step."

"You don't know me very well, Sills."

The promoter shrugged. "There are other ways of handling a difficult situation, Rawlins. It strikes me that a man with your background would not be here posing as a farmer unless there was something in the wind."

"You wouldn't understand a man wanting to settle down, would you, Sills?"

"No, not your kind of a man," Ira Sills said.

Rawlins swung back to face Tilse. "Now you can talk, Bal, and you'd better make it good. Why did you run off at the mouth about me?"

"Don't start talking tough to me," Tilse said with sudden anger.

"I am talking tough, mister . . . and I'm still waiting to hear why you gabbed to Sills."

"When I hire out to a man," Tilse snarled, "I give him more than my gun. I thought Sills ought to know who you were, and I'm like him. I smell something that ain't in the open, and before we're done I'm gonna find out what it is."

Of all the men Rawlins had known, he had once liked Bal Tilse best. Now, looking at the gunman, he saw that there was nothing of the old feeling left. What had been a fine and strong friendship lay between them as shriveled and useless as a brown autumn leaf. Tilse was as much his enemy, now, as Lew Dosso or Jack Kelton.

"You think that a man like Sills deserves your loyalty more than a man who once fought beside you?"

"Hell, yes," Tilse snapped. "I like a man to be open and above board. You're not. I said I would find out what kind of sneaking game you're up to, and by God. . . ."

Rawlins hit him then, a short, powerful blow that caught Tilse on the side of the face and knocked him flat on his back. Tilse lay there a moment, eyes staring up at Rawlins as if not understanding this.

"A man doesn't have to take that," Sills said.

Slowly Tilse's hand came up to his cheek and touched the spot where Rawlins's fist had hit him. Then, his face scarlet, he raised himself up on his left elbow, his right hand yanking his gun.

"You've gone down a long ways, Bal," Rawlins said, "when you'll draw on a man who isn't packing a gun."

The gun was leveled in Tilse's hand. It stayed that way for a long moment, Tilse's lips twitching with the struggle that was going on in him.

Sills, moving cautiously out of the line of fire, said, "Go ahead and drill him, Tilse. Be no witnesses but me and the barkeep, and we'll tell the right story for you."

Slowly Tilse came to his feet, the gun still in his hand, the decision not yet made. Rawlins laughed softly. "You're a better man than you think you are, Bal. You're so good that you won't be working long for a man of Sills's caliber."

It was then that Sills's office man parted the batwings, and called, "They're out here, Boss."

"All right." Sills moved away, thrusting a raucous glance at Rawlins. "I've got a lot at stake in this thing, Rawlins, and I won't let it go up in smoke. I'm hoping you won't be a damned fool and throw your life away on a fight you don't have to make."

Excitement stabbed through Ed Rawlins. The grin that broke across his bronzed, bony face held a cold challenge. "I haven't been in a fight for a long time, Sills, but I'm in this one . . . right up to my ears."

"If you aim to fight, you better start packing those guns you're supposed to be so good with," Sills retorted. "And you'd better be damned sure you have them before you meet up with Tilse again." With that, Sills motioned curtly to Tilse, and left the saloon.

A heavy sigh came out of the barkeep as the batwings flapped shut behind Sills and

Tilse. He said, "Ed, I know Ira Sills pretty well. I know how far he will go . . . and, in case you don't know it, you're in trouble."

"What do you mean?"

The barkeep began mopping the mahogany, his lips compressed. He said, "I own this saloon, Ed, and it's a town where I'd like to spend the rest of my life. I think the future of this country depends on farmers who are making a good living here, and not on a bunch of them a promoter like Sills brings in because he's got a lot of land he wants settled. That's all I'm gonna say, except for one thing. Watch your back."

☆ **III** ☆

PILGRIM'S CHOICE

*W*hen Rawlins left the saloon, he saw the hack with a load of men in it pulling away from in front of the hotel and taking the road that led to the lower creek country. His farm was there, and so was Walt Gilder's, and half a dozen others that were the best kept and most prosperous farms along the Purgatory.

Bal Tilse was driving the hack and Ira Sills was in the back seat. The other men in it were strangers who had probably just come in from Cassburg. Rawlins stood thoughtfully loading his pipe, and watched the hack until it disappeared. The sun was half way down behind the Cascades now, and there was little of the day left by which these strangers could see the country; but Ira Sills, good talker that he was, didn't need much daylight to show these men what he wanted them to see along the Purgatory, and get them signed up for eighty acres of land apiece.

Rawlins crossed the street and went into the hotel. He sat down, feet cocked up on a chair in front of him and, pulling steadily at his pipe, gave thought to this thing as he saw it now. He had shirked his responsibility, and shame was in him because if it. He had not gone to any of the settlers' meetings; he had paid little attention to Ira Sills's moves and, except for exchanging a little work with Walt Gilder and courting Trudy, he had lived within himself almost entirely.

It had been wrong, all wrong, and he saw it now as he had not seen it before. He had the choice of running, which was what Sills wanted him to do, or of staying and conducting a one-man fight against Sills. His chances of winning that fight were close to zero. He had been through too many not to take cognizance of the odds. He needed help but, whether the farmers would listen to him and whether they'd fight if they did listen was something he seriously doubted.

Rawlins was still in the hotel lobby when darkness came, and lights bloomed along the street. The hack stopped in front of the hotel, and the strangers got down, talked for a long time with Sills, and then came in while the hack wheeled away. Rawlins stepped in front of them, and asked, "Are you men thinking of taking land here?"

They were farmers, blunt-fingered men with faces weathered by wind and sun. They were much like other settlers who lived along the Purgatory, big-muscled men who felt a little cramped in their store clothes.

"That's right," one of them answered. "We're from Wagontown, on the other side of the hump. We figgered it was time we quit renting and started in owning our land."

"Has anybody told you we didn't get the water we needed last year?" Rawlins asked.

The men exchanged quick glances and nodded, as if expecting this. The spokesman said, "I don't know why men who live here now would try to discourage further settlement, but I'm telling you something, mister. All the big talk you put out won't stop us. More than that, it won't stop a thousand others from crossing the mountains to live here. We like the looks of this country, and we're staying."

They started around him as if satisfied that he'd been told enough, but Rawlins wasn't finished. He stepped in front of them again, and said, "You owe it to yourselves to come to the settlers' meeting tonight."

"It would be a waste of time," one of the men said sullenly. "We were told by Mister Sills that there is a group of settlers here who want to hog this whole segregation, and are doing all they can to buck him and discourage others who want to come. Well, we'll have no part of it. Now if you'll step aside, we'll go to our rooms."

Rawlins watched them go up the stairs and muttered, "Fools! Damned, stubborn fools!"

"With their life savings in their pockets and bent on spending it," a man behind Rawlins said. As Rawlins turned, the man held out his hand. "The name's McCann. Sam McCann from Portland."

"Ed Rawlins," Rawlins said, as he shook hands. "I guess I've got a talent for sticking my nose into other men's business. Only thing is the more of those yahoos who come in, the less water there is for the rest of us."

McCann was a tall, lantern-jawed man with corn-colored hair that successfully pointed in several directions. He had a pencil thrust behind one ear; several sheets of paper were stuffed into a coat pocket; and his general appearance was that of an animated scarecrow. He studied Rawlins for a moment. Finally he said, "I've heard of you. You're the farmer who's had quite a past as a gun-slinger, aren't you?"

"That's right," Rawlins answered. "That story seems to have traveled."

"Sounds like a good story," McCann said. "I'm a reporter, Rawlins, and I've always got my ears open for something that's good. It strikes me this is good."

"There's nothing about my life that would make a good story," Rawlins murmured and, moving toward the door, went through it and turned toward the school house.

"All right," McCann said, catching up with Rawlins, "we'll let your life story go, but I think you'll help me do the job I'm down here for. You know, of course, that these irrigation projects around Cassburg make up a huge amount of acreage and will furnish homes for thousands of people if properly operated."

"Which this one isn't," Rawlins snapped.

"I was wondering," McCann persisted, "about that very thing. Now around Cassburg everything seems to be in order, but it's Ira Sills who does most of the advertising, and I expect a thousand families to move in here before fall."

"Look, McCann." Rawlins paused, and faced the reporter. "How can a thousand families make a living here when we didn't get enough water last summer?"

"Perhaps they won't, but they're like these men you just talked to. They have some money saved, and they want to own their land. That money will go into Ira Sills's hands, and their starving is not a problem that will worry Mister Sills."

"I guess you've about got it," Rawlins agreed sourly. He told McCann about

Kelton and Dosso visiting him that afternoon, and added, "I guess that was Sills's way of trying to get me out of the country."

"Rawlins, it looks like the beginning of a story here. If I had a good one, I'd splash it across the front page of my paper, and it would be read all over the Northwest. That's the only way I know to stop these people from believing Sills's advertising."

"You want a good story, do you, McCann?" Rawlins said softly. "All right, I'll give you one, but you may not live long enough to print it. Come along. We'll go see what this settlers' meeting is all about."

The school house was jammed. Rawlins, pushing his way through the crowd that stood just inside the door, saw that most of the fifty settlers living along Purgatory Creek were here. They were a somber-faced lot, the women and children filling the seats, the men standing around the back of the room and along the sides.

Walt Gilder, president of the Purgatory Creek Settlers' Association, pounded on the desk in front of the room, and Rawlins, jostled to one side by the late-comers, saw Lew Dosso and Jack Kelton on one side of him, and Bal Tilse on the other. Sills's office man was there, but Sills was not. Gilder told the secretary to read the minutes of the last meeting and, after he'd sat down, Gilder asked if there was any new business to be brought up. The crowd shifted, shuffling feet, and the ripple of talk made a restlessness in the room. Gilder pounded for order, and tried to glower, but a successful glower was not in Walt Gilder. He was a little, red-cheeked man who looked more like Santa Claus than he did a farmer, but the spirit of resistance was in him, and it was Rawlins's feeling that Gilder was one of the few in the room who could be counted on if it came to a finish fight.

"Well," Gilder said, "this here meeting was called for a definite purpose, and the sooner we get to discussing it, the better. We 'bout starved last summer, and things don't look too good this year. A sink hole showed up on the other side of the butte so the settlers on the lateral didn't get water for a week. The company was too busy to fix it, so some of us took a day off and did it ourselves. Seeing as this project is supposed to be supervised by the state, it appears to me that it's time for us to make a kick to the right people. Now I'd like to hear some discussion."

Again there was that shifting of bodies and scraping of feet, but no one wanted to talk. Rawlins looked at the crowd, saw there would be no determined resistance from them.

"Most of you come quite a piece to get here," Gilder said testily. "You gonna sit here like a bunch of wooden heads just 'cause you're scared of Ira Sills's toughs?"

A man jumped up. "We shouldn't talk that way in meeting, Walt. Mebbe we just better wait through the summer, and see what kind of service we'll get."

"The ditches aren't any bigger than they were last summer," Gilder snapped, "and they didn't carry enough water then."

Jack Kelton grinned broadly and nudged Lew Dosso. On the other side of the room, Bal Tilse watched Rawlins. Sam McCann growled an oath in Rawlins's ear, and said, "They're scared to open their mouths."

"All right," Gilder said in disgust, "might as well adjourn the meeting. But at least go home and think about it. Mebbe you figger you can hang on till hell freezes over, but I can't. I've got to have a crop if me and my girl are gonna eat."

"Walt," Rawlins said, and stepped forward, "I've got something to say."

Walt Gilder grinned. "Go ahead," he said. "You sure got the floor in this meeting."

The women and children turned to see who it was, and for the first time Rawlins saw that Trudy was there. Indecision halted him for a minute. Trudy wouldn't like what he was going to say. Then he gritted his teeth, put his hands on the back of the seat in front of him, and began to talk.

"The way I see this thing," he began, "it isn't so much a proposition of enlarging the ditches and telling the state about what's going on as it is informing the people who might be settlers here that there just ain't enough water in Purgatory Creek to go around. There's four men at the hotel who were taken out to see some farms by Ira Sills this afternoon. Now they want to settle here. What's more, they got sore because I told them we didn't get the water we were supposed to last summer. They said there'd be a thousand others crossing the mountains to settle here. I'm asking you men just where would we or Ira Sills or anybody else find water to irrigate the thirty thousand acres that Sills has in this segregation?"

"There never was that much water in Purgatory Creek," Gilder nodded.

"Sills knows that," Rawlins went on. "A while ago somebody said we shouldn't talk about Sills's toughs. Now mebbe we oughta be scared out of our shirts. I oughta be, because they came out to my place and beat me up today. I'm scared, all right, but I'm gonna make my holler just the same. I'm gonna holler so loud that these suckers coming in are going to find out this valley ain't just what Ira Sills tells 'em it is."

The issue that faced the settlers had never been put into words the way Ed Rawlins had just put it, and Ira Sills's name had never been publicly mentioned before. It seemed to all the settlers except Walt Gilder that it was something like treason to talk this way, and for a long moment there was only silence, tight, tense, and filled with a grim foreboding.

Jack Kelton wasn't grinning now. He made a step toward Rawlins, but Lew Dosso whispered something in his ear, and the two of them pushed their way through the crowd and left the school house. Bal Tilse still watched Rawlins, his lean face puzzled and uncertain.

"Anybody else got something to say?" Gilder demanded. "When you got a man with Ed Rawlins's spunk in the crowd, there oughta be somebody else who's got guts enough to back him."

"I don't call it spunk," a man shouted. "He's a gunfighter . . . a killer. We all got that word today, and I'm thinking he's here for some purpose that ain't good. I never seen him at a settlers' meeting before."

"Neither did I," another called out.

"Gunfighters thrive on trouble," a third man yelled. "Might be his way of getting a job. We've got wives and kids, but Ed Rawlins ain't."

"You're a bunch of old women," Walt Gilder roared. "Damn' yellow-backed old women who are sacred of your shadow! I'm resigning this here job you gave me. I think I'm a man, and I know danged well I don't want no office in an outfit that. . . ."

A gun blazed outside, the slug slapping through a window. Again it roared. The two wall lamps winked out. A flame leaped ceilingward, caught a curtain, and seemed to explode.

Fire! The cry came out of the men, shrill and scared, and panic was upon them as they broke for the door. Some thought of their families, some only of themselves. Rawlins knocked a man down with his fist who plunged for the door. At the same instant he shouted; "Keep that door clear, you fools! Let the women and children out first."

But Ed Rawlins might as well have tried to stop a stampede.

☆ **IV** ☆

GUN-GUARD FOR A REPORTER

Men had jammed into the doorway, wedged tightly, and now could not move. Bal Tilse, cursing and swinging his gun barrel, battered men out of the way and somehow cleared the doorway. Rawlins, McCann and Gilder got to the windows on the side away from the fire, kicked glass from the frames, and helped the children and the women through. Within a matter of minutes the school house was empty, and barely in time. Rawlins stood in the fringe of light, an arm around Trudy, and watched the walls cave in, a great column of sparks and flames rising skyward.

"Awful lucky," Sam McCann muttered.

"Won't be no school for our kids this winter," a man said.

"We'll build another one," Walt Gilder shouted.

"You donate the labor, and I'll put up the money." It was Ira Sills standing there, not ten feet from Ed Rawlins. "Education for our children is the most important thing we have. Whatever happens, we must not let it go."

A smart move, Rawlins thought, the sort of move that could be expected from Sills and one that would make it doubly hard to get any cooperation from the settlers. Whether Dosso and Kelton had fired the shots upon Sills's orders, or whether it had been their own notion, was something Rawlins would never know; but he had a hunch that the idea was to plunge the school house into darkness and produce a panic for the purpose of stopping the discussion Gilder and Rawlins had started. Probably the fire was a result they had not foreseen but, in any case, Sills had cleverly turned it to his advantage.

"If your gun-slingers hadn't started the fire, Sills," Rawlins said, "you wouldn't have to put up the money."

"Can you prove who fired those shots?" Sills demanded.

"No, but Dosso and Kelton left the school house just before the shots were fired."

Sills laughed scornfully. "That proves nothing! As a matter of fact, they came over to my office to report about this sink hole we failed to fix. I'm sorry about that, but we were busy at the time. We'll see it doesn't happen again, even if we have to double our maintenance crew."

"You'd better keep your mouth shut, Rawlins," a man cried. "We've got kids to go to school, and you ain't. I think that's a fine offer Mister Sills has just made."

Rawlins said softly, "Come along McCann. You, too, Walt," and, holding Trudy's arm, he beat a path for her through the crowd toward the hotel. Always before Rawlins had fought for pay, and the men who had hired him and those who fought beside him had given him complete cooperation. He was not fighting for pay now; it was a common fight where all the interests were the same, and yet there was no cooperation at all. There was even resentment among the settlers because he wanted to fight.

"You can't get those men to fight, Rawlins," McCann said. "They don't understand."

"The damned fools!" Gilder said heatedly.

They were in front of the hotel, the light from the window falling across Trudy's face, and pride came into Ed Rawlins then. He was proud of this girl who had promised to marry him, proud of their dreams.

He asked, "Are you mad, Trudy?"

"No," she answered quickly, "but what are you going to do now?"

"What I do depends on McCann." He motioned to the reporter. "He said he would spread our story all over the front page of his paper, if it was a good one. What about it, McCann?"

"It's a good one, Rawlins." The reporter grinned. "A damned good one, and that fire was what made it extra good. I'm hiring a rig to take me to Cassburg in the morning so I can catch the stage to Shaniko." He pulled the pencil down from his ear and reached for the paper in his pocket. "Right now I want a few facts about the total acreage in the segregation, the size of the present farms, the amount of water in the Purgatory, and so on."

"Walt can give that to you," Rawlins said. "Trudy, let's go home. Where's your horse?"

"In front of the Mercantile."

"I'm glad to have met you, Rawlins." McCann shook Rawlins's hand. "It's a funny thing in this state. On the other side of the Cascades life goes on just about as it has for generations. Over here it's new and tough and damned near primitive. That's why these folks who come from there are a little slow seeing that they have to do their own fighting. Give them time, Rawlins. Meanwhile, I'll give you a story that'll put a crimp in Mister Sills's plans."

"Thanks, McCann," Rawlins said, and crossed the street to his horse.

There was little talk between Rawlins and Trudy on the way home but, after her horse had been put away, they faced each other in front of her house, her face a pale oval in the darkness.

Rawlins said, "I wanted to tell you this afternoon what I'd been, but now you know. Does it make any difference?"

"I told you then it's what you are now that counts, Ed," the girl said softly, "not what you were when you rode with Bal Tilse. I'm proud of you and what you did tonight."

"It may not be over," Rawlins said somberly. "Sills is afraid of me or he wouldn't have sent Kelton and Dosso after me. After what I said tonight, he'll have to get me. I know about men like him, Trudy. I know how they work. They have to keep going, have to keep folks iced into line, or they're done."

She was silent a moment as if thinking about it, and then she said, "I guess I've felt the way I do because of Dad. We've been through these things before, and he always fights just like he's fighting now. He'll get killed, Ed. And if you die, too, then there'll be nothing left. I lost a brother three years ago. He was shot in the back and left in the sagebrush to die. It was like this. I can't stand to go through it again."

"But is there any sense in losing the things you've dreamed about and worked for just because you won't fight for them?" he asked roughly.

"Forty years ago people out here had to do these things. It was fight or die. That was the life people lived, and they knew it and understood it. It's different now. If I'm going to have your children, Ed, I want them growing up in a world that can give them security."

"They'll never have security on the Purgatory if we don't fight for it now," he said stubbornly.

She started to say something, and whirled away instead and ran into the house. Rawlins waited until he heard the door slam, and then mounted and rode away, the feeling in him that a man has when he sees his life's treasure slipping out of his hand and is powerless to hold it.

Rawlins made his bed outside that night, his guns loaded and beside him on the ground. Sills's next move would be fast and ruthless, and there was no sense in dying in his shack like a trapped rat. The settlers would not fight now, but they would if driven far enough, and another crop failure might touch off the dynamite.

It was dawn when Rawlins awoke, and the thought that had been in his mind when he went to sleep was still there, and with it was another thought. Sills would kill Walt Gilder. Rawlins swore he had been so sure Sills would strike at him first that he had forgotten Walt completely. He latched his belts around him, saddled his horse, and started back toward Gilder's place, cursing himself for not having foreseen Sills's move sooner. Rawlins did not hold the settlers' trust; Walt Gilder did, and for that reason Gilder was more dangerous in the long run to Ira Sills's plans.

The light was still thin when Rawlins, topping a ridge north of his farm, saw the vague form of a rider, then heard the muffled thud of fast-traveling hoofs in the sandy soil. Rawlins reined off the road and pulled a gun, despair, then cold fury rising in him. He had been too late! That was his first thought. The rider had killed Walt Gilder, and was coming on after him.

Rawlins waited a full five minutes until the rider was within fifty feet of him. Then he reined into the road, his gun cocked, and called, "Pull up!"

It was Bal Tilse who yanked his horse to a stop. He said, "Easy on that trigger, Ed," and made no move for his gun.

"What are you doing here?" Rawlins asked.

Tilse laid a steady gaze on Rawlins's face. "I'm a fool, Ed, the damnedest, most muddle-headed fool that ever walked this earth! I figgered when I heard you was here that you were holding down some gun-slinging job, and I had an idea to get you to throw in with me and we'd do a little bounty chasing. Then I got here, and found out you wasn't even packing a gun, you were just a farmer, and I got sore. I guess I wasn't so sore at you as I was at myself. You were doing the thing I'd always wanted to, Ed, and I'm so damned small I pretended to think you'd gone plumb to the bottom."

Bal Tilse wasn't lying. Rawlins saw that, and he asked softly, "What set you straight?"

"It's like you said in the Jubilee. I'm too good a man to be working for a skunk like Sills. I lost my head after you walloped me, and pulled my gun. Sills wanted me to smoke you down. I guess that started it. Then that business of burning the school house. A lot of people might have got burned to death, and what Sills is after ain't worth it. Sills was up all night thinking what he was gonna do. He got me and Dosso and Kelton up about an hour ago and gave us our orders. I was supposed to come out here and bushwhack Walt Gilder, then get you. Ed, I've done some killing, but by hell I never bushwhacked a man in my life, and Ira Sills don't have enough money to get me to."

"What about Dosso and Kelton?"

"Dosso heard what you and Gilder and McCann said in front of the hotel. He'd told Sills, and Sills says the one thing that can beat him is for a big daily like McCann's paper to run that story. Kelton is to drive the rig with McCann aboard this morning, and he'll have a team that ain't broke. About the same time they get to the top of the grade on the other side of the Purgatory, Dosso will cut loose with a few shots, and scare the team. Kelton makes a jump, and the rig will go over the grade with McCann inside."

"When are they pulling out?"

"They're probably gone by now."

"Bal, how are you playing this game from here on in?"

"Son, I'm right behind you! And when this is all buttoned up, if you want a partner who don't know nothing but trigger-pulling, I'm with you."

"You're signed up, Bal." Rawlins held out his hand, and Tilse shook it. "If we ride straight for the creek, we'll probably beat Kelton's rig to the foot of the grade. Chances are Dosso is forted up behind a lava pile that's just north of where the road comes over the rim. If you can get McCann out of that buggy, I'll handle Dosso."

"I'll do it," Tilse promised.

They stayed together until they reached the creek, and Rawlins said, "You better hit for the road, Bal. Good luck."

Tilse grinned, and swung upstream. Rawlins rode as nearly straight up the east wall of the canyon as he could, angling among boulders, and gradually working downstream to where an ancient tributary had worn a passage through the rimrock that lifted a sheer thirty feet above Rawlins.

It brought Rawlins to the plateau above the Purgatory about two miles downstream from where Lew Dosso would be holed up, a long way around but the only way because if he had tried to come up the road he'd have been shot out of his saddle by Dosso before he reached the plateau, and there was no other break through the sheer cliffs on the east side of the Purgatory for ten miles.

Rawlins paused to blow his horse, and saw the buggy cross the creek and start up the grade. Bal Tilse was not in sight, and for a moment Rawlins felt doubt break across his mind. Ira Sills might have set up a bushwhack trap, using Bal Tilse to lure Rawlins into it. Then he put that from his mind. He had gone too far now to doubt Tilse.

Making a swing into the junipers away from the rim, Rawlins came presently to the road and turned toward the Purgatory, his gun palmed. It was then that gunfire blasted apart the morning quiet, and Rawlins thought he was too late. He saw Dosso the same instant the gunman saw him, and they fired together. He made a high target in the saddle, and there was only Dosso's head and shoulders above the lava but Dosso, surprised by Rawlins's sudden appearance and the firing from the canyon, missed his first shot and paid the penalty for having missed. His second shot was nothing more than a finger twitching in death, the slug burying itself in the dirt below him. Rawlins's bullet had caught him between the eyes.

There was no more firing from the road below Rawlins, but he heard the run of horses, and he put spurs to his own mount. He came around the first bend in the grade, saw the approaching team running hard, Kelton hanging onto the lines and weaving drunkenly in the seat. Rawlins reined his mount toward the bank, and then a cry came from him, for the team swung too near the edge, loose dirt giving way under them, and then plunged off into space, Kelton's scream riding above the roar of land-sliding rocks and dirt.

Bal Tilse came into sight, his cocked gun in his hand, saw Rawlins looking over the edge, and called, "What happened?"

"Dosso's dead, and Kelton just went off. It ain't a pretty sight, Bal. A hell of a way to die, even for Jack Kelton."

"He had one of my slugs in him," Tilse said. "I beat 'em to the foot of the grade, came part way up, and pulled in behind a pile of rocks. When they got close, I rode out and covered Kelton, telling McCann to jump. McCann jumped, but Kelton allowed he'd smoke it out with me. I reckon he was shot so bad he couldn't hang onto his team."

McCann was waiting for them in the road, puzzled and angry and, when he saw Rawlins, he shouted, "Life over here isn't primitive, Rawlins. It's just plain savage. By the time I get done writing my story, there won't be anybody but tough hands who'd want to live over here."

"You still figger you've got a good story?" Rawlins asked.

A grin spread across McCann's dusty face. "Mister, I had enough of a story last night, but it gets better all the time. Fact is, I don't think I'd live long if it got any better than it is now."

"You're lucky you're alive this long," Rawlins said dryly. "You ride my horse, McCann, or you won't get to Cassburg in time to catch the stage. Bal, you'd better ride with him. Tell the deputy in Cassburg what happened."

"I ain't stopping in Cassburg, Ed," Tilse said. "I'm going to Portland with this gent, and I'm not coming back until I've got a copy of the paper with this story in headlines a foot high."

"You'll get them," McCann promised.

It was late that afternoon when Rawlins stopped at the Gilder farm. Trudy was making a strawberry pie, and there was a patch of flour across her forehead that made Rawlins grin and hand her a towel and call her "dirty face."

"Stay for supper," Trudy said, "and, while you're waiting, tell me what happened."

"You're sure something's happened?"

"It's written all over you," she said. "Go on."

He told her, then, and added: "I had a little talk with Sills when I came through town. I never saw him scared before but, when he found out that Dosso and Kelton were dead, he was plenty scared. Then I topped that off by telling him that Tilse will repeat what he planned for me and your dad, and Sills started begging. He may go to jail before it's over, but he's sure going to sell out here."

"If Tilse hadn't been the man he was," Trudy mused, "you and Dad would have been murdered."

"That's right but, after I hit Bal yesterday, Sills figgered he'd enjoy beefing me. It goes to prove that there's different levels of honor in all occupations, which same is true with gunfighting like everything else. I knew about Tilse, but I wasn't sure when he'd find it out." He came to her then, and took her hand in his. Her eyes went down to his guns and when they lifted to his face, he asked, "What's the answer, Trudy?"

"You're right," she said simply. "I didn't see it until you said last night that if our children were to have security here, we had to fight for it . . . now. I'm proud of you, Ed."

He kissed her then. "Maybe we'd better not wait for that room," he grinned.

She smiled. "I'll be ready, Ed . . . tomorrow."

DEATH-SONG ON THE SINGING WIRES

(1947)

☆

by FRANK BONHAM

Frank Bonham made significant contributions to the Western story in a career that spanned five decades. By 1941 his fiction was already headlining Street & Smith's Western Story Magazine and by the end of the decade his Western novels were being serialized in The Saturday Evening Post. "I have tried to avoid," Bonham once confessed, "the conventional cowboy story, but I think it was probably a mistake. That is like trying to avoid crime in writing a mystery book. I just happened to be more interested in stagecoaching, mining, railroading. . . ." He was highly knowledgeable in the technical aspects of transportation and communication in the nineteenth-century American West. In introducing these backgrounds into his narratives, especially when combined with his firm grasp of idiomatic Spanish spoken by many of his Mexican characters, his stories and novels are elevated to a higher plane in which the historical sense of the period is always very much in the forefront. On even the shortest list of the finest Western novels ever written would have to be included Snaketrack (Simon & Schuster, 1952), Night Raid (Ballantine, 1954), and The Eye of the Hunter (M. Evans, 1989). One Ride Too Many is the title of a Bonham Western short story collection reprinted by Barricade Books in 1995 and The Canyon of Maverick Brands (Circle Ⓥ Westerns, 1996) has recently made its first appearance in book form. Mike Tilden told Captain Joseph T. Shaw, Bonham's agent, that he would publish any Western story Frank would be willing to write. In the decade from 1942 to 1951, Bonham had a dozen stories published in Star Western. *The one that follows is collected here for the first time.*

☆ **|** ☆

FIRST COMMAND

ＬＩ ieutenant Thatcher's detail broke camp an hour after dawn, while the air was still crisp. The sun hung notched by the piñon-stippled hills, casting long and ungainly shadows from the signal men moving about on the valley floor. It brought to shimmering life the thread of copper wire flashing back into the distance. Outside camp reeled a spindly line of new poles.

Thatcher gave close attention to the loading of the mess wagon and ambulances. He made sure the fire had been covered with earth. While he performed these duties, he was conscious of the sidelong glance of the sergeant and the mock gravity of the other enlisted men.

First command. . . . Thatcher had heard older officers joke about their first commands, about how scared they were, how bungling and stiff with dignity. Twenty years from now it perhaps would seem funny to Ross Thatcher that he had hardly slept in two weeks, for worrying if he was stretching the wire too tight or too slack about how much discipline he should exact from his men on an informal detail, and about the possibility of Indian trouble.

At the Point they told you how to set security guards, load a wagon, and feed your men. But they didn't tell you how to convince troopers with twenty years' service on their sleeves that you knew more about soldiering than they did. The ambulance drivers were waiting the order to stretch out. Private Moriarity had tapped in at the base of the last wired pole. He glanced up as the lieutenant stopped beside him.

"Can't raise him, sir," Moriarity said.

They had left Corporal Bruff at the raw adobe station five miles back. It was the lieutenant's privilege to guess what was wrong. None of the silent, seasoned men standing about was going to help.

Thatcher checked to see that his knife was in. "Maybe he's getting wood. Keep trying."

He mounted and gave the order to move on. The six ambulances with their gleaming rolls of wire lumbered up the slope. From the last wagon, wire spun smoothly off a creaking drum. Poles had already been set by the timber crews several miles ahead.

Sergeant Hicks came hurrying up. "Still can't raise him, Lieutenant. Reckon there's been trouble?" Hicks was a lean, tough old Army man. He was a born sergeant, reliable as a mule — if he liked you. He was in his middle forties; the story was that he'd refused a commission because he didn't want the responsibility. He was thin as a rake, with dry, sallow features, and peppery sideburns.

"I doubt it," Thatcher said. "He may have overslept with the switch out. I'll ride back and find out. Take over."

"Think it's wise to leave the command, sir? It's Indian country, you know."

Thatcher spoke sharply, mainly because he knew the sergeant was right. "There's been no trouble for six months. I'll go myself. Unless you don't feel competent to handle the job?"

"I had a little experience in the war, sir. I'll risk it."

The lieutenant hesitated, eyeing the sergeant angrily. "I want to check the poles on that ridge, anyway. It may be we should have used guys." He swung his pony and jogged down the shallow valley through the hills. He was disgusted with himself for having let the man take the conversation into channels where sarcasm lay ready. But, as he rode, he felt confidence return. He was a dark man who wore his brass without flourish. His face had taken the imprint of the elements as the land itself had — sunburned, roughened by the wind. He knew how each detail of his job should be handled — according to the book. It was only when he let himself be drawn into an argument that he got into difficulty. He made a note to be as aloof with Hicks hereafter as the Great Stone Face.

The air grew warmer, though at six thousand feet it seldom grew uncomfortably hot in this lonely corner of Arizona territory. Where the wind stroked the yellow grass of a high ridge, the signal man dismounted. He was thinking that in February the wind probably shrieked across this hogback like a bereaved squaw. With a coating of ice, the wire could damn well snap. There would have to be guys. They broke a man like a matchstick for blunders like that.

Suddenly, as he rode on, he felt a cool finger of anxiety slip down his spine. He didn't know why. It was nothing he had seen or heard. But his intuition had caught a scent. All at once he looked up. The wire above his head was loose. Gently it sagged from cross-arm to cross-arm in easy loops. That meant a break somewhere.

The dry scrape of Sergeant Hicks's voice recurred: *Think it's wise to leave the command, sir? It's Indian country, you know!*

Thatcher drew his carbine, casually, trying to persuade himself he wasn't frightened. For himself, he wasn't. But if his command was wiped out because the sergeant failed to put out security guards, the blame would be his own. Now that he had come this far, he felt he must go on. The operator might be in trouble. As he rode, his head turned continually. In the quiet of the morning he felt menace. He halted at the top of a rise. Below him, the land sloped away in great troughs, valley and ridge, valley and ridge, with the mountains in the distance. A half mile away he saw the break.

In ten minutes he reached the spot. Maybe an eagle had dropped a rabbit on the wire. That had happened before. Maybe a splice had broken. As he looked up at the pole, the full impact of the disaster struck him. A hundred-foot length had been cut out of the line and carried away. Apaches did that. You couldn't splice a gap.

As he sat there, trying to comprehend it, a puff of dust kicked up on the ground ahead of his horse. He heard the ball wail in a short arc across the hilltop. The sound of the rifle came an instant later. By that time, Thatcher was riding.

The operator's shack was a mile ahead — if it still stood. He heard the unshod hoofs of the Indians' ponies behind him. He glanced back to see four paints sweeping across the dry summer grass. The riders were small brown humps on the horses' backs. The ponies carried no saddles, no saddle bags, no rolls of wire. They were closing in.

Ross Thatcher reached back and let his emergency roll of wire drop. He tried to loosen the coat-straps and failed. He bent across the low swell of the McClellan and let his dime-size spur rowels cut the pony. The horse began to reach. Across the second ridge he sighted the shack. *Thank God!* he thought. There was no sign of smoke at the adobe.

He fired a shot to attract Corporal Bruff's attention. Down there on the bench a man appeared in the adobe's portal. Thatcher saw him running from the cabin to the horse picketed a short distance away. He pulled the picket-pin from the ground and hurriedly led the horse through the door into the cabin. The lieutenant heard a ball snap past him with the sound of a popped neckerchief. The drumming of hoofs was close; the sweat of fear was on Thatcher's face. He hit the ground before the cabin.

Bruff's gun roared. Thatcher dove through the doorway and the horses swerved. Then he heard a hard animal cry and the sound of a man striking the ground.

"Damned stinking devils!" Bruff panted.

Thatcher braced himself against the jamb and pulled a bead on one of the Apaches. He held his shot. The target was already out of effective range. His eyes snapped to where the downed man was dragging himself after the others. Bruff took slow aim.

Thatcher said, "Hold it! They'll hang around to recover the body if we kill him. He's out of the fight anyway."

The Indians pulled off to the fringe of a motte of scrub oak. One of them had recaptured the wounded man's pony. When he was a hundred yards away from the cabin, another warrior rode out to assist him. The signal men allowed them to draw away. They disappeared into the oaks.

After an hour Bruff saddled, rode out, captured the lieutenant's horse, and returned to the shack. The key began to clatter. They looked at each other.

"That'll be the post, Lieutenant," Bruff said. His thick fingers began to take down the message with a stub pencil.

This was Thatcher's big moment, his chance to say, "Send fifty-man patrol at once. Signs of Indian uprising."

It would also be the chance for older officers to grin and say, "Poor Thatcher! I'll bet he saw a wild turkey and decided it was Geronimo! He won't last a month out there even if he did go to the Point."

But if there *was* trouble, and he hadn't taken adequate steps to protect his command. . . .

Bruff looked up. "They're wanting to know why the morning report hasn't gone in."

Thatcher started. "Tell them a splice broke," he said. "I'll want the usual amount of wire and spikes. Expect to reach Benton's Store by night." He hesitated. "Say a small bunch of Apaches was seen, apparently a raiding party. I want three men sent out to each station to stand twenty-four hour guard."

Bruff looked relieved. He began to tap out the message. Thatcher went out. He heard the key still chattering when he rode off.

☆ II ☆

BENTON'S STORE

*T*hatcher rejoined his detail with no comment as to his skirmish with the Apaches. The country was flattening out. In this dry land of few creeks and no trees, John Benton's place was an oasis. Thatcher had spent two days at Benton's Store, on Bitter Creek, last spring, checking the route he was to follow. Benton had come here twenty years ago with a wagon train of immigrants. The farmer was impressed with the way dry soil responded to water. He stayed on at Bitter Creek, digging irrigation ditches and putting Mexicans to farming the land for him. In his big, cool adobe trading post, he sold everything the cowboy, trapper or traveler might want.

Poles had stepped across the valley where Benton's farms lay and eastward for ten miles. The pole camp rested here. At sunset Thatcher brought the wire to a point two hundred yards north of the trading post. They made camp and he and Sergeant Hicks rode on to the post. As they racked their horses, they heard a girl's laughter. Recollection threw a thin, bright ray across Thatcher's gloomy thoughts. He had almost forgotten the Benton girls.

The interior of the store was a wilderness of smells and goods, everything that could be stacked, hung or shelved. Strings of red chilies, coffee and hams made the big room fragrant. Crates and heaps of merchandise formed islands about the floor. A girl sat on a counter near the door, a stack of Indian blankets beside her. The man who sat alongside looked up. He was a big, bald-headed American in a buckskin shirt and Army trousers.

The girl recognized Thatcher. "If we'd just known you were coming, Lieutenant, we'd have called out the color guard. Did I hear you pounding stakes down there?"

"Unfortunately, you will hear us pounding them up here in the morning," Thatcher said. "Is your father here, Miss Jean?"

Jean Benton pouted. "I thought you'd come to see me." She jumped down, a lithe, full-bosomed girl with dark hair and fair skin. There were no pastels about John Benton's older daughter. Her lips were red, her eyes dark blue.

Thatcher smiled. "Just an excuse," he said. "As a further excuse, I'm dragging seventy miles of wire behind me. I'd like to replace a few things in the mess wagon before we go on."

"This the new line to Fort Grant?" the man on the counter asked.

"In that general direction," Thatcher said.

Jean led him around the mounds of merchandise to a door at the rear. She opened it and went through. Thatcher waited. He heard John Benton's voice, the voice of an invalid. "Well, send him in!"

When Jean came back, she was smiling. "You could really give me your order," she said, "but Dad would scalp me. It's not every day he gets to yarn with an Army man."

She went back to where Sergeant Hicks and the man in the buckskin shirt were talking.

Thatcher moved into Benton's room. He was on the point of closing the door when Benton, from his chair by the window, said curtly, "Leave it open, Lieutenant . . . I like to see. Particularly when government beef contractors are in the store. They'll steal anything from your tobacco to your daughter."

Benton was a long, wasted figure in the armchair, a blanket across his knees. Despite his tartness, Thatcher liked him. He had a big nose, a thin Scotch mouth, brushy brows, and eyes cold as a December sky.

Thatcher shook hands. For a few minutes they talked of the weather, crops, politics. Behind the trader's eyes was a mind as sharp as a skinning knife. He asked the same question the beef contractor had. "I suppose you're heading for Fort Grant?"

Thatcher smiled. "The fewer people who know where I'm heading, the less trouble I'll have."

Benton shrugged. "Your first command, isn't it?"

Thatcher hesitated. "How did you know?"

The trader's dry lips smiled. "You've got the look on you. You're carrying your dignity like a basket of eggs. Relax, Lieutenant. There won't be any trouble. If there is, you'll know how to handle it when it happens."

"As a matter of fact. . . ." Thatcher halted. He stopped himself from telling Benton of the morning's ruckus. It had been merely a bunch of bronco warriors out for some hell; the less he made of it before a veteran frontiersman, the better.

"We ought to have a quiet enough time, at that," Thatcher said.

"Haven't heard of any trouble," Benton agreed. He nodded toward the front. "Except from Jim Shepley. He gets around, all over the reservation. He hears talk before you men ever do. He says some of them are getting pretty damn restless about trespassing."

"They'll get over it."

The silver music of Jean's laughter came to them. Benton frowned and his fist rapped the chair-arm several times. He ended the conversation abruptly. "You might as well be getting fixed up. My other girl will help you. Jean's supposed to be taking care of Shepley." He called, "Sharon!"

A door opened and Thatcher remembered her, though she had stayed in his mind less vividly than her sister. She was blonde, shorter than Jean. Where Jean was bold, Sharon was reserved.

"Help the lieutenant to whatever he wants, Daughter. That's in cash, Lieutenant?"

"Gold."

Jean was lighting lamps about the store. Gloom gathered mustily in corners. Sharon kept track of purchases while Thatcher and Sergeant Hicks carried the goods to the porch. Shepley spoke to Thatcher as he set down a sack of cornmeal.

"Got my wagon right over yonder, Lieutenant. Be glad to haul your doin's up to camp for you. Save bringing an ambulance down."

Thatcher thanked him. "We'd appreciate it."

Shepley stuffed coarse tobacco in a stained meerschaum pipe. When he lighted it, the hard planes of his face came into relief; his lips were wide and hard, the brows strong. There was fathomless confidence in the face.

"Came off all right in that little scrape this morning, I hear." He said it casually, as though remarking on something he had read in the paper.

Thatcher blinked. Hicks couldn't have told him; Hicks didn't know. "You weren't riding a paint horse without a saddle this morning, by any chance?" he asked.

Shepley laughed. "You may be working for the Great White Father, but Jim Shepley's the Apaches' uncle. I heard about it on the way up today. I'm going north now to sell a little beef and bring back some hides and blankets. I heard that four anxious bucks had their ears knocked down by Gray Horse for cutting a telegraph line."

Thatcher regarded him closely. "I hope so. You don't think there'll be a repetition?"

"Probably not. Not until the line is complete. You can understand how they feel. Uncle Sam gives them the land. But he reserves the right to build telegraph lines across it, send troopers over it, start forest fires, and pinch their squaws' rumps if they feel like it. It ain't right."

"We're interested in nothing but getting across this country the quickest way."

Shepley shrugged. "If you're just going to cut across the southeast corner of the reservation, like you're doing, it's probably all right. But if you mean to swing northeast, why. . . ."

"Where I swing is government business. Gray Horse will have to like it."

"Bet he don't," Shepley said. He picked up the meal sack and carried it to his wagon.

Jean and Sharon were talking with the sergeant when Thatcher went inside. Sharon said, "Father wants you and the sergeant to have dinner with us, Lieutenant. If you'd sleep in the store tonight, too, we'd be happy."

"Think the men will be all right?" Thatcher asked the sergeant.

Hicks grinned. "They can look out for theirselves, any time we get a chance to eat civilized chuck and sleep under a roof."

In a large, low-ceilinged room hung with Indian blankets, they stuffed themselves with the kind of a meal soldiers dream about. Corn-and-chili dish, golden *camotes* with fresh butter. There were steaks to make a man let his belt out. Jean and Sharon sat down after all the men had been served. Hicks ate like a hungry dog. Shepley ate slowly, deliberately, stopping once to compliment the cooks. Benton had Thatcher sit next to him and kept talking steadily.

After dinner, Thatcher excused himself. "I'll have to ride up to camp and see that they haven't built the cook fire under the mess wagon."

Benton spoke quickly as he left the table. "Jean, why don't you walk up with him and see how Feliciano is?"

"All right, Dad."

They walked up the road in the still, cool darkness. On the bed of the valley lay a faint river-mist; beside the river a collection of Indian hogans was revealed by the light of supper fires. They stopped while Jean inquired after a workman who had been injured. Afterward, they walked on to the signal camp. The presence of this dark, vivacious girl set up a tingling in the lieutenant. She had a hundred questions to ask about army life.

One of the men was singing when they reached the camp. As they moved close enough to hear the words, Thatcher felt the blood surge to his cheeks. It was a bawdy barracks song. He glanced down at Jean, seeing a puzzled expression on her face. For a moment he had hoped that it had been so rank she did not understand it. Then she said faintly, "Maybe I'll wait here."

Thatcher strode ahead. Despite his embarrassment, he knew it was his own fault for having brought her here without warning. The men were sitting about the fire. Private Moriarity was the singer; Corporal Faitz was accompanying him on a Jew's harp. One of the other men was taking a pull at a bottle. He lowered it and passed it to Moriarity.

Faitz saw him first. The nasal twang of the Jew's harp died. He scrambled to his feet. "'Tensh- *hut!*"

They found their feet hurriedly, though two didn't stand too steadily. Moriarity glanced at the lieutenant and raised the bottle. He took a drink and set the bottle down carefully. He got up and reached in his shirt pocket for tobacco.

Thatcher snapped, "The command was attention."

Moriarity said, "Excuse me, sir." His teeth bit a generous corner off the black navy plug. He didn't hurry about replacing the tobacco.

Thatcher walked over and took the plug out of his hand. He threw it in the fire. Moriarity's bluff Irish face darkened. "Look here, now, Lieutenant!" he complained. "We ain't going to have brass poisoning in camp are we?"

Thatcher kicked the bottle. "Pour that stuff out."

Moriarity met his stare. He had had enough whiskey to lose his inhibitions, not enough to be good-natured. "Sir," he said, "the Articles of War forbid cruel and unusual punishments."

Someone snickered. Thatcher glanced at the faces about him. They were sober, except for the eyes. They were the faces of men seeing someone in a tough spot and wondering if he had the cleverness to get out of it.

The lieutenant picked the bottle up, then slammed it against a rock. To the other men, he said, "At ease." He told Moriarity, "Walk over there beyond the mules." He removed his tunic and followed.

They confronted each other, away from the light of the fire. Moriarity appeared sullen but nervous. Slowly, his palms rubbed his thighs.

"We're a long way from a stockade," Thatcher said. "I'll have to improvise a punishment in keeping with the offense. I don't think you'll find it cruel or unusual. On the other hand, if you still want to apologize. . . ."

"Is this man to man," Moriarity asked, "or will I be shot for striking an officer after we go back?"

"I'm wearing no insignia," Thatcher said.

Moriarity said: "Ah!" and smashed a right to the officer's face. It struck Thatcher on the cheekbone hard.

Moriarity stepped in. He was a shorter man, built like a draft horse: blunt, solid, close to the ground. His fists carried the weight of his shoulders. As he fought, he snorted, his teeth shining faintly in the dark.

Thatcher found he could no more stop all those blows than he could have dodged a handful of corn. He got his chance when the trooper threw a haymaker that missed. Moriarity was off-balance. Thatcher's fist came down like a hand-axe. Blood came in a dark gush from the other's nose. He floundered away, blindly, his hands before him as he searched for his opponent.

The lieutenant followed, slamming lefts and rights to Moriarity's head. It was like hitting rock. Thatcher fired one at his belly, but the Irishman's arms doubled across his middle and he took the blow on an elbow. Then he came recklessly back at Thatcher. A solid, punishing smash on the ear that sent the officer down. The private stood above him, staring down at his slowly stirring body.

The concussion was a ringing blackness in Thatcher's head. He found himself trying to get up, resting on hands and knees. Vaguely he realized Moriarity was coming in again, his foot swinging at his head. He knew this, but lacked the force to evade it. Then he heard Moriarity swear, saw him stumble.

Jean Benton said angrily. "Indian fighter, are you! You fight more like an Apache than a trooper!"

Moriarity hesitated. While he was trying to digest her sarcasm, Thatcher got up. He came in again, viciously. Thatcher went back four steps while Moriarity threw blows from every corner. The instant he slowed, Thatcher shot one at the fourth button of his shirt. It connected and the soldier gasped. Moriarity doubled up, stumbling into Thatcher. Then he slumped to his knees and fell forward.

Thatcher waited until the private was able to get up again, sick and shaky. Moriarity stood swaying before him. Thatcher said, "No more liquor, Moriarity. No more tobacco-chewing when the command is attention. Agreed?"

Moriarity's eyes closed slowly and opened again. "Stand corrected, sir." His eyes stood uncorrected. They were saying, *Will you be as much of a man when the arrows are as thick in the air as cottonwood down?*

Thatcher was wondering the same thing.

✩ **III** ✩

NIGHT VISIT

They started back to the trading post. Jean looked up at him and stopped. "You've got a cut on your face." He let her dab at his cheek with her handkerchief.

"I'd have worse than that," he said, "if you hadn't pushed him."

"I like a fight," Jean said, "but I like it fair. You had him whipped, up to then." She was silent for a moment, and they walked on. Then: "Ever been in an Indian fight, Ross?"

He liked her using his first name. He liked her taking his arm. "Once, on the way out here. It wasn't very much of a fight."

"They used to raid us about once a month, until Dad got them civilized. I think," she said, "I'd like the army. Travel, excitement. I wasn't made to stay in one place very long."

"The way to fix that up," said Thatcher, "is to marry an army man." He caught her quick, quizzical look. Her eyes had the soft sheen of moonlighted water; her throat, above the Mexican bodice, was satin smooth.

"No army man's ever asked me," Jean said.

Thatcher turned her to him, holding her by the arms. "I'll bet you've said that to a dozen of them," he told her. "And I'll bet this is what they've done!" He pulled her close, let his arm catch her firmly, and kissed her. Her lips were smooth and warm; her perfume swirled through his head.

It was an effort to release her and say, ". . . And then I'll bet they've said, 'Will you marry me Miss Jean?' Only I've had girls before, and I know you're the kind that always says she isn't quite ready. So I'm not going to make a fool of myself."

Jean looked a little stunned. She, too, had been playing; but her face was sober now. Then the dark eyes grew angry. "If I were a cat," she said, "you'd have scratches all over you face. If a man's not willing to take that risk, he oughtn't to kiss a girl. Good night!"

She ran up the steps to the store. Thatcher felt as though he had stood too close to a whirlwind. His emotions had been given a spin.

Benton's voice called out to him as he went into the store where, now, only one lamp burned. He went back to the man's room.

The trader squinted at him. "Ain't been scrapping with enlisted men, I hope?"

"I've been disciplining one."

Benton grunted. Then: "Play chess?" He had a chessboard already set up.

"Used to. Spot me a rook and a bishop and I'll take you on."

They played for an hour. Benton won three games straight. As he was replacing the pieces in a box, he said off-handedly, "Have a nice walk with Jean?"

For an instant, Thatcher thought Jean must have told the old man about the scrap. Yet he knew that would have been out of character for her. He said, "I did that. She's a fine girl."

"She's a little bit of a worry," Benton remarked. "She's not a quiet girl like her sister."

"A long way from it."

Benton had finished packing the chessmen, but he kept fussing with the box, moving it about on the table, frowning, fumbling. "I'd like to see her well married someday, Lieutenant. She's too quick to play. Someday, God forbid, she'll play with the wrong man and get burned." He stared at Thatcher.

Thatcher's chuckle was strained. "Oh, I wouldn't worry about that, sir. She's a good girl."

"You never know what even a good one will get into sometimes. You, Lieutenant," Benton said, his eyes coming up quickly, "you ever thought about how much a good wife can mean to a man?"

Thatcher had been no more stunned when Moriarity hit him. "Why, not exactly. I haven't given it much thought."

"Should. In the army a man's wife is as much responsible for his promotions as the man himself. Jean," he said, "is the army type. Likes people. Mixes well. You could do a lot worse."

Thatcher's color was high. "I'm sure I could. But. . . ."

Benton waved a skinny hand. "Not trying to sell you anything, Lieutenant. But you'll be back this way one day. Think about it. Marriage wouldn't hurt either of you a bit." He added brusquely, "Your room is the one behind the hardware. There's a candle burning in it. Good night."

Thatcher lay there in the small room a long time, half amused, half worried. It had happened too quickly to evaluate it properly. He liked Jean. There was no mistake about that; but he liked her sister, too. And he didn't think he was ready to tie himself down. He could see the trader's point, but he'd be damned if he'd plunge into matrimony so that John Benton could sleep nights. Then he began to imagine himself married. Jean filled the requirements for an army man, all right. But how long would one man interest her? She was too damned wild. If she hadn't been, she wouldn't have let him kiss her.

Sharon would be as faithful as an old hunting dog. When you talked to her, you had glimpses of deep, exciting currents under the surface. But would she try to put down roots every time the wagon slowed? There was one other point he could not get out of his mind. As an officer, he was still on trial. He was still a junior, suspected by the older men, not deemed worthy of a really important duty. He didn't intend to take a wife into that kind of a setup. . . .

Small things will wake a man trained to sleep on a hair-trigger. In Ross Thatcher's case, it was odor. He found himself dreaming of the apple-blossom fragrance of Jean's perfume; then he realized he was not dreaming. It was in the room.

Something fell softly to the floor and Thatcher put his legs over the side of the cot. "Jean?"

The door closed gently and footsteps retreated through the deserted, unlighted store.

Thatcher pulled on his trousers and thrust his feet into his boots. He lit the candle. By its light he saw his tunic lying on the floor near the threshold. He picked it up, but he knew immediately what would be missing. His orders. The papers setting down the route he would follow across the reservation!

He strode into the big hardware room. It was a wilderness of shadowy mounds, heaps and counters. He saw nothing at first. Then he realized someone was standing in the center of the floor, watching him. He walked deliberately to her. She started to back off, but he seized her around the waist. "So you're getting even for tonight, are you? Too high and mighty for a mere lieutenant to kiss. . . ."

All at once he knew his blunder. The hair of this girl was blond. It was Sharon.

The girl stepped back. "I . . . I don't understand. I heard someone in the store and came out to see who it was." Her eyes were large and frightened.

It occurred to Thatcher that he had been only half wrong. There was a breath of sachet about Sharon. It was the same scent Jean used. He said, "Someone has just stolen orders from my tunic. I thought at first it was your sister. I recognized her perfume. Now I see that you both use the same."

She was less frightened now. He saw more spirit in her face than he had thought she possessed. "If you're accusing me of stealing them, Lieutenant, you're at liberty to search me." She stood there in a ruffled nightgown and a blue flannel robe.

Thatcher was silent for a moment. Then: "I'm sorry. I thought it must have been you or Jean."

She pressed her lips firmly together. "You don't think it possible you could have imagined it? Why would either of us want your papers?"

Thatcher hadn't reasoned that far ahead. "Someone did," he said lamely.

Sharon drew her robe about her. "It's just possible you missed them. If you don't find them, I'm sure we can in the morning. Or perhaps you lost them in your little scuffle with Private Moriarity."

She left him. Thatcher went back and closed the door. He made a search of the room and his clothes, but the orders were gone. It hadn't occurred to him before that he might have lost them during the fight with Moriarity. It was evident that Jean had brought home a report of the night's doings.

The whole thing was illogical: that either of the girls had wanted the papers, or that one of them had actually broken into his room. As he got back in bed he sniffed the air thoroughly. There was no odor at all but the rancid smell of the smoking candle.

The detail left shortly after dawn. Thatcher had been unable to find the papers on the ground where he and Moriarity had fought, or in the store. He was convinced that they had been stolen when Jean brought them to him, saying she had found them in a keg of nails.

He remembered Jim Shepley's interest in his route. It occurred to him that the bald-headed man might be operating some kind of game on the reservation which he did not want reported. Government contractors had an unsavory reputation in the territory. They were inclined to charge the government forty thousand dollars for nine-thousand-dollar school houses. Their beef was disposed to stringiness, though they received top price for it. Then he noticed the men standing in the shade of one wagon. There was something ominous about their attitudes. Thatcher understood it when he saw the man stretched out on a blanket on the ground.

☆ **IV** ☆

BADLANDS GUIDE

*H*icks was flushed and tight-lipped. "It's Bowers, the scout," he told the lieutenant. "I rode ahead with him to spot the stakes. We were in Icehouse Canyon when they jumped us. Must've been a dozen bucks. Two of 'em had carbines. They weren't out for scalps or we wouldn't've got out."

Thatcher knelt beside the wounded man. His eyes were closed and death was on his face. The ball had gone into his shoulder. Private Reevis sat by him with a canteen.

"That ball ought to come out," Reevis said dully. "He might have a chance if it was out."

Hicks asked, "You any good at cutting, Lieutenant? I seen Captain Rice take a man's leg off at the knee, once, after a wagon run over it. This man ought to be took care of."

And if you're worth a damn, his eyes said, *you'll take care of him.* Thatcher felt the sweat come out on his upper lip. But he took his knife out of his pocket. "Does someone have a stone?"

Private Reevis carried the knife off to the tool wagon. Thatcher unbuttoned Bowers's shirt and pulled his boots off. He noticed the rowel of one of his spurs. It was clotted with slate-colored clay, not a usual type of earth in this country. Reevis brought the knife back, razor-sharp.

Thatcher found the blackish hole where the bullet had gone in. For just an instant he thought he would not be able to cut. The knife hovered. Then the point dropped. He probed deeply, finding nothing. He was marveling at the slight flow of blood when the blade touched metal. The significance of it did not come home until he had worked the scarred ball of lead from the hole. It was someone else who voiced it.

"He's quit."

Jean went off and stood by herself while they buried the scout. Thatcher stood stolidly beside a wagon, sickness turning clammily in his stomach. He had laid the slug and knife on the wagon tailgate. He glanced at them and wondered vaguely how a carbine happened to be firing a small-caliber bullet.

Sergeant Hicks came up, leading their horses. "Sir," he said, "something's got to be done about this."

Thatcher was silent, his eyes on Hicks's lean face. "What would you suggest?"

Hicks slapped his thigh with his gauntlets. "That's for you to say, Lieutenant. But I'm damned if I'd take a detail into hostile country with no more protection than we've got."

"You seem pretty sure it's hostile country."

Hicks stared at him. "If you've got to see scalps to be convinced, I reckon you won't have long to wait."

"I know this," Thatcher said, "Trader Benton and the scouts I talked to before we left the post assured me there was nothing to worry about. I know that if I take the outfit back with our job unfinished, I'll be hooted out of camp." Hicks's mouth tightened. He did not reply. "So I'm going ahead by myself," Thatcher said, "to read sign on these Indians of yours. I have a suspicion the only war dance they did before setting out this morning was over a pile of silver dollars. You'll return immediately to the other detail, Sergeant."

Hicks pulled a brisk salute. "Yes, sir. But I'd advise you to be careful."

Thatcher walked to where his and Jean's horses stood. "You may as well ride back as far as the wire camp with the sergeant."

Jean was looking up at the mountains. "You don't know those canyons, do you?"

"I've got a map."

She swung into the saddle. "You've better than that . . . a guide."

The girl spurred across the mesa and he mounted hastily and followed. He got as far in arguing with her as he expected to. She had made up her mind to accompany him to Icehouse Canyon, and not all the lieutenants in the Signal Corps could dissuade her. Through growths of piñon and incense cedar they ascended to a high country of larger trees and rougher canyons. Thatcher saw no trail, but Jean seemed to know where she was going. They crossed three minor ranges, to pause above a long, twisting defile at the base of a chain of jagged peaks.

"There's Icehouse Canyon." Jean pointed down.

Thatcher experienced a crawling sensation along his spine. According to the map, the attack should have taken place directly below this point. His eyes searched the pines cloaking both sides of the deep gorge. The warm, pitchy air carried no sound but the distant rush of white water. In all the acres spread out beneath them there was no visible movement.

Jean started down. Suddenly, across the canyon, Thatcher sighted a white scar in the underbrush. It was several moments before he recognized the long, tapering apron of a mine dump. Jean saw it too.

"That's funny," she said. "I've never heard of any mine in this section. Let's have a look."

It was near the bottom, on the opposite side of the canyon, so that they had to cross the shallow stream. Thatcher was not surprised, this time, when he discovered wagon tracks stamped deeply into the earth. The tracks led down the canyon. He knelt to examine them. His forefinger tapped the earth beside the sharp rut cut by an iron tire. Some of the dirt fell into the rut. When he stood up, he had a little better understanding of what happened to Scout Bowers.

Jean, standing near the maw of the mine, was excited. "Why, this thing's new, Ross! It can't be over a year old. I thought it must be an old Spanish mine. You don't suppose . . . ?"

Something stirred in the dark tunnel. It could have been a frog plopping into the stagnant water which had collected on the footwall, except that frogs did not whistle as they passed. A moment later the echoes of a rifle shot poured down the canyon.

Thatcher pushed Jean and she stumbled away to fall on a boulder. The lieutenant, his navy pistol coming up, pivoted to search the brush beside the creek. He saw the smoke in a wolf-willow, and fired. If they were facing Apaches, he preferred to make a run for it. Indians had unpleasant ways of getting people out of caves. If they were whites, he could fort-up in the tunnel and hope the men got around to searching for them in a couple of days.

Jean settled it by darting toward the horses. "Let's get out of here!"

He followed her, firing again into the brush as he heard a bullet whine off the ground between them. They hit the saddle as the brush moved. Thatcher had a glimpse of a gray shirt; he sent another shot at it and there was a chaotic threshing in the brush. The gunman was down. But there was no way of telling whether he had been alone. As they went down the trail there was another shot and then silence drifted over the canyon. For ten minutes Jean kept her pony at a lope. She crossed the stream and took a zigzag route up the mountain. She didn't pull the horse in until they had gained the ridge.

Thatcher said reflectively, "No danger at all, just like you said. The Indians in these parts won't do any worse than kill you."

"Those weren't Indians," the girl snapped. "If they had been, we'd have been cooked. We'd never have known what hit us." She rode on.

Night was gathering in the pockets of the range as they neared the pole camp. After the trouble in Icehouse Canyon, neither of them had any notion of trying to ride back to the post by night. Thatcher had the ambulance cleared and installed Jean in it.

Breakfast was sizzling over the cook fire when Jean Benton showed up in the morning. She had somehow contrived to make herself look as fresh as ever. Here, Thatcher reflected, was a girl who could take the jolts of army life without breaking down. John Benton's suggestion didn't seem so ridiculous, now. And yet between him and anything like that lay a wide gulf. He had come to a point where he must force ahead through the mountains or turn back. What happened in the next few hours would either prove him an officer capable of handling a tough assignment, or a soldier whose fights would be made from behind the rampart of a desk.

Thatcher instructed the corporal in charge of the detail to hold it where it was until further orders. They started back to the wire camp. The sun was high and hot when they arrived. A crew of men was hauling back on the shining copper strand while the man on the pole made it fast to the insulator. Moriarity sat on the tailgate of a wagon. As Thatcher approached, he stood up with no great show of sprightliness. Thatcher returned his salute.

"Where is Sergeant Hicks?"

Private Moriarity looked surprised. "We reckoned he was with you, sir."

"I sent him back yesterday noon."

The soldier blinked but ventured no guesses. Desertion was a serious matter. Thatcher hesitated a moment. There were only five saddles in camp and each must be filled by a competent, loyal trooper for what lay ahead. How loyal would a man be who had suffered a whipping at his hands?

"Saddle one of the horses and draw fifty rounds of ammunition," he told the private abruptly. "We're going back to look for Hicks."

The Irishman rubbed his jaw. "The desert's a big place, Lieutenant."

He said: "Not when you know where to look. I'm banking he's gone back to Benton's Store. Bowers, the scout, was murdered yesterday. Sergeant Hicks said he was shot by Indians." He brought the scarred pellet of lead from his pocket. "I took this out of Bowers's shoulder. Hicks said whoever was shooting carried a .32 caliber gun."

Private Moriarity stared at the slug. He seemed to be recalling that Sergeant Hicks carried a .32 caliber gun. "I don't see why he'd. . . ."

"Neither do I, but we're going to find out."

With Moriarity and four others, he and Jean moved back toward Benton's Store. They made the ten-mile ride in three hours, arriving in the middle of the afternoon.

Indians were working in the fields where the irrigation ditches were rich, dark stripes across the earth. A train of wagons was drawn up before the post. Jim Shepley, the beef contractor, was back from his trading trip to the villages.

Shepley was on the porch when they drew up. His bald head was beaded with sweat; he held a cup of water he had dipped from an *olla*. He squinted at Thatcher's horsemen. "Not going back, Thatcher?" he exclaimed.

The lieutenant cuffed dust from his cap. "I'm not a man to die for false principles," he said. "It begins to look like you were right. One of my scouts was murdered in Icehouse Canyon."

Shepley wagged his head. He drank part of the water and threw the rest on the ground. "Miss Jean ought to have known better than that, even if you didn't. What'll you do now?"

"Go back. I've wired the post to send out fifty men to escort my materials back. We'll meet them here."

Shepley nodded. "It's hard going. But you'll get farther in the army with only a retreat against your name than a massacre."

"On your way back, Jim?" Jean asked Shepley.

"Tucson. You caught us just in time. Told the old man to put my jug of rum to the back of the shelf for me."

He went down the steps and the skinners climbed the great wheels of the wagons. They were massive six-mule freight wagons with tarps lashed across their loads. Shepley went down the line, checking ropes. Thatcher called after him. "Haven't seen my sergeant, have you?"

"No. Lost him?"

"Looks that way. These regulars are good for about two years. Then they have to break away for a little fuffooraw. But I'll have some skin off this one's hide."

☆ **V** ☆

FORBIDDEN SILVER

*T*he wagons rattled down the valley, their dust drifting across the broken hills as they sloped west for Tucson. Jean was staring at Thatcher. "What did you mean, you're going back? You didn't tell me."

Moriarity was regarding him with frowning wonder.

"I didn't tell the post either," Thatcher said. "But I'm not discussing my business with every trader who crosses our trail. We're going to have a damn good look around for Hicks."

He went into the post. John Benton had seen nothing of the non-com. Jean disappeared for a moment. It was the opportunity Thatcher had been looking for. He strode back through the big, dim room. He didn't want Shepley to get too far away. There were a few things he had left unsaid because, if the beef contractor took exception to them, some innocent people might be hurt really badly.

He was on the threshold when Sharon called his name. Blonde and slender, she hurried through the sprawling heaps of merchandise. When she reached him, she did not seem to know how to begin.

"I . . . I lied to you the other night, Ross."

Thatcher smiled. "I know. And you hid my orders in a keg of nails after you'd copied them."

Her eyes widened. "But if you knew. . . ."

"I didn't. Not until Jean told me where she'd found them. Who told you to do it?"

She bit her lip. "Jim Shepley. I thought I was doing right, Ross, and now I'm not sure. He said you were leading your men to death, that if he could just find out where you intended to go, he might be able to turn you aside, use his influence with the men he knows at the fort, or something like that."

"He went to a lot of trouble for a dozen army men," Thatcher said. "I'm glad you told me. It makes me certain of something I was guessing at before."

As they rode, Thatcher figured. Shepley counted eleven men, two to each wagon. If there was trouble, the odds would not be good. They were close enough now that the dust of the wagons still lingered in the air. He pulled in beside Moriarity. Moriarity was stiff and silent.

"How are you in a scrap?" Thatcher asked him.

Moriarity's head turned. "I don't know that six men against one could be counted a scrap, sir."

"How about six against twelve? You know what we're going to find in those wagons, don't you? Silver ore. Probably the richest in Arizona. Shepley's hauling it all the way to the reducers at Tombstone, so it must assay high."

The soldier blinked. "But they say he's hauling hides and blankets and such-like."

"He's hauling ore from the mine I found in Icehouse Canyon. It's in Indian territory that's not open to mining. Sergeant Hicks killed the scout because he'd discovered it. I figure Shepley bought the sergeant the night we were here."

Moriarity pondered it. "Then you think the Injun trouble was rigged up?"

"I think Shepley sicced a few bronco Apaches on me the other day to scare us off. In about five minutes we'll know."

Moriarity did not look too certain. In his dogged mind lingered a barb of resentment. But if any convincing remained to be done, Thatcher decided, it would have to be done in action. He rode back to the head of the small column.

The hills here were low and rough, dotted with brush. It was good stalking country. Thatcher took a steep hillside and gained a rocky bump. A half mile ahead, the dust of Shepley's wagon train hung in the winding pass. Through a notch, he saw a span of laboring horses move by.

He rode faster now, picking his spot and riding for it. He kept behind the higher hills until they struck the arroyo he had spotted. Down the dry wash they rode at a lope. They reached a point a hundred feet from the mouth of it. Thatcher reined in. On the hot, dry air vibrated the tinkling of harness belts. He took the men ahead. Behind a screen of brush, they waited.

The wagons came into view. Four of them passed. Jim Shepley came last, riding alongside the last wagon. Seated on the tarp was Sergeant Hicks. He was mopping his face with a neckerchief. "By God," he was saying, "I ain't sweated so much since we crossed the Jornado! It's a plain sweat-box under that tarp!"

Shepley muttered, "It's going to be hotter if anybody spots you. I'm a-warnin' you. . . ."

Hicks ignored it. "I'm going to like seevilian life, Shep. Eighteen years in the army and what do I get? Eighteen dollars a month! You ain't forgetting," he reminded the other, "I'm to get a cut o' this?"

It was the proper moment for six blue-clad horsemen to swing casually from the mouth of the canyon. They split up, each man moving in to cover a wagon. Moriarity and the lieutenant taking the last one. Shepley's brain was not sluggish. His gun was suddenly in his hand. Thatcher's finger was already tight on the trigger when he realized the contractor was covering Sergeant Hicks.

"Yes, sir!" Shepley said loudly. "We got your man, Lieutenant! Where do you think he was? Under the tarp! Must've crawled in last night, where we laid over. The heat smoked him out."

Hicks's face wore a stricken look. Then it congested. "You carrion-eatin' son-of-a. . . . You can put me in irons, Lieutenant, but so help me. . . ."

Shepley's gun leveled. Down the line of wagons, teamsters were turning startled faces. Thatcher said quickly, "I'm putting you both in irons. It's the end of the line, Shepley."

Shepley saw that. He saw, too, that he had nothing to lose by fighting. He spurred his horse. As the animal bucked, he slipped from the saddle, sprawled in the dirt, and rolled under the wagon. At the head of the caravan a carbine cracked, a teamster went to his knees, and fell woodenly under the wheels of his wagon. Other wagons broke out of line as their drivers ducked and began to fire.

Big Jim Shepley's Colt roared. The shot slapped past Ross Thatcher. Then he heard Moriarity's saddle gun crash. Shepley hunched against the ground and slowly relaxed. Sergeant Hicks and the driver of the wagon were both standing, guns lining down on the lieutenant. Thatcher swung his horse and, in the same instant, he fired.

The bullet took the sergeant in the left arm. It dangled as he went to his knees. Thatcher heard the skinner's revolver bark. The bullet tore through the low swell of the saddle and struck him in the thigh. Pain was a swirling blackness before his eyes. He tried to fire again at the sergeant. He heard the gun roar but he didn't feel the recoil. As he started to fall he was aware of Private Moriarity spurring in to catch him. . . .

It was hot when he awoke, though he lay in the shade of a wagon. Moriarity was sitting beside him. He held a canteen to Thatcher's lips. The lieutenant drank and the giddiness in his head retreated. He sat up and shook his head.

Moriarity said with concern, "Easy, now Lieutenant. The ball went right through the muscle, but you got to be careful. I've got you plugged up and I reckon you're going to be all right."

"Did any of the men. . . ?"

"Tully got himself an ear shot off. Otherwise we're a hundred percent. The young lady from the store was out here a minute ago," he said casually. "She's gone back for a wagon."

"Maybe I'll surprise her," Thatcher said. "I'm going to ride in." Moriarity objected, but the lieutenant grinned. "You can't kill a greenhorn, Moriarity. Get my horse."

"Only you ain't a greenhorn," the trooper contended. "For a man with his first command, you've made out right well." The soldier grinned.

Thatcher rode back toward the store. He felt better than he had in days. First command. . . . It was just a shadow you fought with. It had no more reality than you gave it. When you stopped fighting it, it disappeared.

He decided he must have a long talk with Trader Benton about army wives. Seemed to him the old man had the subject figured out just about right. This time, he didn't think Jean would have any objection to the way he took his cues.

WHO RULES DEAD MAN'S RANGE?

(1948)

☆

by THOMAS THOMPSON

Thomas Thompson was born in Dixon, California. His stepfather was an avid reader of Western pulp magazines and Tommy "adopted" all the discarded issues. He was working in the furniture business in Los Angeles and studying writing in his spare time when he was introduced to Harry F. Olmsted and James Charles Lynch. Lynch was the chief writer in Olmsted's syndicate at the time, supplying stories for pulp magazines published under the Olmsted byline. Tommy started writing stories for Olmsted and by this means he learned his craft. But it was Jimmy Lynch who offered to work word for word with Thompson to show him how a story was constructed. Their first collaboration was published under the James Charles Lynch byline. Before long, Thompson was writing Western stories on his own. Captain Joseph T. Shaw became his agent, and he moved to Portland, Oregon, where he lived for many years. Tommy evidently lost his fascination with back issues, since he kept track of his own pulp stories by tearing the covers off the issues and pasting them on his wastepaper basket. He wrote close to 300 stories for the magazine market and fifteen novels. For many years he was story editor for the "Bonanza" television series before he founded a newspaper for mobile home owners which he co-edited with Barry Cord. Thomas Thompson never wrote a story or novel that is less than good and many are very good indeed — something that made my selection process far from easy! Windy McCloud was one of Tommy's most popular characters in Popular Publications' Western magazines.

☆ **I** ☆

SHOT-IN-THE-BACK ACE

*I*t was a terrain of miles and grass, a place of tightly-drawn, cloudless skies and wind-puckered, summer-browned land, a country of many cattle, few fences and no railroads. It was a place where even a dead man could be lonesome and Windy McCloud, misplaced son of the Trans-Pecos, thought of this as he stood by his horse and tried to take his eyes away from the face of the man whose head had stopped a bullet.

Windy didn't know the dead man nor did he know who might have killed him, for McCloud was only passing through on his way somewhere. If the cards fell right he might look in on Pete Conners, that amiable old four-flushing renegade who, rumor had it, was sheriff in these parts. Windy had found a soft chuckle in that rumor, for if that old ex-confidence man and land swindler was mixed up in the law it probably wouldn't be with a badge on his vest.

307

Mostly Windy had come this way because he liked the feeling of space at his elbows. The distance between cows was a more comforting thing to contemplate than was the breath-confining closeness of timber there across the mountain range at his back, where Mt. Hood stood ice-tipped and disdainful, shrugging forests from its shoulders.

But death is a serious thing, even to a man who had seen it before. The corpse that lay there, face half turned, work-knotted fingers twisted into stubby bunch grass as if trying to pull life from the roots, reached out of this enormous silence and held the saddle-weary Texan as surely as if it had spoken. So in time he did the only thing he could do — loaded the body across his saddle and started leading his horse to he didn't know where. Somehow this man, unarmed, had died here with a bullet in the back of his head. The scatter of sage, the misplaced and bewildered pieces of lava rock, and the dry brown grass knew how it had happened. It was a secret that had perhaps been picked up by the wind that moved in slow, shifting eddies. And the wind might take it to the mountains where in time it would become part of the constant enigmatic sigh and moan that dwelt forever in the spruce and fir on the slopes of the Cascades. It was, McCloud told himself, no particular business of his, and yet he was getting mixed up in it.

The dusk was not far from the horizon and the Wallowas were blue with distance when Windy came into the deep gash of the dry coulee and saw the band of riders, not more than a mile ahead, coming in his direction. At any other time Windy would have welcomed the chance of company, for it had been a long ride and McCloud was a man who liked to talk. But if by any chance talk wasn't what the riders wanted, there was a cedar butt .44 in a well-worn holster nestled on the lanky redhead's hip. Men who knew said that gun had put more than one period at the end of McCloud's conversations.

Now with the blue dusk hovering closer and the fall wind testing the burn of winter's first ice, Windy felt more than the chill of the weather rippling the skin on his back. It was the dead man, back there across the saddle. A man he didn't know. Although he hadn't considered it in that light before, a man takes on added stature once he is dead. There was no telling what part this corpse had once played in the lives of those riders. It was senseless to try to avoid the meeting. If he left the floor of the long straight coulee, he would stand out like a shadow picture on a white sheet there on the flat, brush-hummocked plain. If he stayed here in the wash, he could not help meeting them. So he walked on, leading the horse with its grisly burden, but before he did he let his gun belt out one notch, and without knowing he had done it lifted his gun free of its holster and let it drop back into place.

The riders stopped, but only for a second, as if they were not in the habit of taking long to make up their minds. And when they came on one man rode in the lead — a tall, heavy-set, rawboned man. He had taken a rifle from his saddle boot and now carried it easily across his pommel. The others, a dozen of them, rode with an easy indolence that marked them as men having no worry about meeting a lone stranger who walked and led his horse. The big man stepped out of the saddle and the rifle fell naturally into the crook of his arm. Windy stood there flat-footed, his blue eyes puckered, and with his tongue he flicked off a particle of tobacco that had been clinging to his tightly-drawn lips.

In the way he had of appraising a man, Windy had marked this rider down as big, tough, probably gun-handy and able to use his fists. Now he saw he had underestimated the man all the way down the line. The man was bigger than he had appeared in the saddle; he was six foot six if he was an inch, and he had the muscle and meat to go with his height. That certain flatness to the bridge of his nose told that he had tried his fists more than once, and the way his holster was tied indicated that he didn't pack a gun for show. But what Windy hadn't been able to see before was the mental stature of the man. Here was a man who had every physical attribute he needed, but in addition he had the swift-moving brain of a fox. It showed up as soon as he smiled and it lurked in his tone when he said, "My name is Wyatt Grinnel. Folks hereabouts usually ask me before they go riding around loose. What have you got there on the horse?"

Windy didn't shift his weight. He said, "From the size of the hole in the back of his head I'd say it was a dead man. He looked lonesome out there where I found him. I figured somebody might want to know about it."

The smile had never left Grinnel's face. He said, "Sometimes it's best to leave dead men alone." He jerked his head slightly and a man directly behind him dismounted and took two steps forward and stood there leering at Windy. He hadn't drawn his gun and his attitude seemed to say that he didn't need a drawn gun to meet any man — that there'd be plenty of time when the need arose. Wyatt Grinnel moved over to Windy's horse and lifted the blanket from the dead man's face. He held it up for a few seconds and then let it drop back into place.

The short, bow-legged, beard-stubbled man who stood in front of Windy said, "Jeb?"

"It's Jeb Parker, all right," Wyatt Grinnel said. "He's gonna be dead a long time."

The bearded puncher let his lips pull back from his teeth. He said, "I didn't figger he'd walk away after I left him."

Wyatt Grinnel moved slowly and easily and, when he was a foot away, his fist shot out and clipped the bearded puncher on the side of the chin. The short man went down hard, hit the dust, and rolled. Then he raised on one elbow, his hand reaching back toward his gun. Wyatt Grinnel, his voice still soft, said, "You talk too damn much, Reb."

There was a deep, crackling silence in which Windy thought he could hear the other men swallow. Grinnel said, "We'll take over, stranger. That's Jeb Parker. Owned the J P Cross. He was sort of a business partner of mine. Got anything to say about it?"

"It's none of my affair how a man dissolves a partnership," Windy said.

Grinnel's face lost some of its color. He turned and faced the Texan and his upper lip curled slightly away from the left corner of his mouth. He said, "You want to say that in some other way?"

Eleven saddles complained slightly. They stood there facing each other, Windy McCloud and Wyatt Grinnel, and the dusk came on across the flat plains and lurked in blue puddles around the squat clumps of stunted sage. From out of that silence came a warning yell from one of the riders. Windy caught the move, threw himself to one side, dropped to his right knee. His left hand shot out and caught Wyatt Grinnel around the ankles, jerking the big man off his feet. There behind him the short, squat, bearded puncher called Reb, blood trickling from one corner of his mouth, had rolled over. His gun was in his hand. He fired once, and the bullet went harmlessly over

Grinnel's falling body. The gun swiveled toward Windy, but it never had a chance to blast.

The Texan felt his finger curl surely around the trigger. There was a sharp recoil, no sound, particularly, that he could hear. Then the blue-biting smoke of his own gun was pressing against Windy's nostrils. Reb got to both knees, tried to raise his gun again, and then fell over, and was still.

Grinnel got to his feet and before he spoke he took time to brush the dust from his clothes. Then he offered his hand and said, "Thanks, stranger. That was fast work."

Another of Grinnel's men had dismounted. A tall, lanky, pinch-faced man with huge-knuckled hands and sleeves too short for his arms. When he spoke, he left his mouth partly open. He said, "That man you just killed was a friend of mine, stranger."

Before Windy could answer Wyatt Grinnel said, "You would have let him shoot me in the back, wouldn't you, Crash?"

Crash said, "I always figgered you was big enough to take care of yourself, Wyatt. I was talkin' to the stranger here."

"The name is Windy McCloud," Windy said quietly. "Seems your friend had a habit of shooting at men's backs." He tipped his head slightly toward the body on his horse, making his meaning clear. "I never took to that pastime."

Windy hadn't seen the move but Grinnel had a gun in his hand. He said, "Pull in your horns, Crash, and get the hell back on your horse." To Windy he said, "I like the cut of your britches, stranger. Lookin' for a job? I think I could fix you up."

"A meal at least," Windy said.

To his men in general Grinnel said, "Dig a hole and cover Reb up so that coyotes don't get at him. Put Jeb Parker's carcass on Reb's horse and we'll take him into town. You, McCloud, ride along with me. I'm always in the market for a good hand who ain't too anxious to shoot me in the back."

☆ II ☆

HANGTREES ARE DAMN HANDY

*T*here was something strange about Wyatt Grinnel's Walking W spread. As Windy thought at the time, "It's all bunkhouse and saddles and damn little ground." Yet in spite of that there was a feeling of wealth and power about the place. The horses Windy saw in the fenced pasture near the barn were as good a string as he had laid eyes on in some time. It was mostly quarter-horse stock; they were all in top shape and looked as if they were ready to go someplace in a hurry.

The ranch house itself, though sparsely furnished inside, had a fresh coat of paint. It was two stories high and the huge square posts that supported the half porch over the front door gave the whole place an air of domineering elegance. There was a Chinaman cooking in the beautifully equipped kitchen. The dining room could seat and handle twenty men. The part of the living room that was directly in front of the yawning native stone fireplace was furnished with comfortable chairs; the balance of the room was bare. The rest of the house echoed with emptiness, except where packing cases were tossed around without much reason or planning. Wyatt Grinnel, Windy decided, was a bachelor.

The man called Crash — Yonkers was his last name — had come into the house with Grinnel and Windy. Now he stood in front of the fireplace, his big-knuckled, freckled-splotched hands behind him. He looked at Windy, not trying to hide the hatred in his eyes. His gaze drifted to Grinnel and he said, "What you aim to do now?"

"How'd it look in town?" Grinnel countered.

"Hornet's nest," Yonkers said. "Manten would have been lynched by now if he hadn't got out. Lucky for me Funeral seen him make the break. Manten was comin' after me right enough. I winged him, I know for sure. I seen him fall down and roll over once and then he just disappeared into no place. I had the boys circulate around and do some talkin' and now folks figure for sure he's guilty . . . even some of them that was stringin' along with him are sayin' that if he busted out of jail he must be guilty. Maybe you're worryin' about nothin', him gettin' out. If he keeps runnin', what the hell . . . we're shet of him. If he comes back, they'll lynch him sure as hell."

"I want him brought in and lynched now, so people will remember it and not be so anxious to listen to the next one that starts shootin' off his face," Grinnel said flatly. "We'll take Jeb's body into town. That'll get 'em stirred up again. If we find Manten, I want the sheriff to take him in. Everything has got to be legal-like."

Yonkers didn't try to hide the grin that curled his lips and Windy hoped that he himself hadn't shown the interest that pricked him at mention of the sheriff. Yonkers said, "Sure, boss. We'll keep it legal-like." Then, half worried: "The sheriff's been balkin' some, Wyatt. That damn niece of his is plenty sweet on Larry Manten. . . ."

Windy didn't miss the hot spread of color that touched Grinnel's high cheekbones, nor did he miss the mention of the lawman's niece. As far as he knew that double-dealing old warhorse, Pete Conners, had no relatives. Grinnel upset it by snapping, "I've handled Conners for five years, haven't I? You saying you don't like the way I'm running things?"

Yonkers pushed himself away from the fireplace and shrugged. "Take it easy, boss! Take it easy! I didn't mean to mention your lady love."

"You're gettin' damn free with your remarks, Yonkers," Grinnel said softly.

"Forget it," Yonkers said. With his right hand at the back of his head he tilted his hat forward over his eyes and left the room.

Grinnel stood there, watching the door close behind Yonkers. Then, speaking as if to himself: "Yonkers, there, is my ramrod. There'll be an opening around here one of these days for a smart man. You a pretty smart man, McCloud?"

"Depends on what it takes to be smart," McCloud said.

Grinnel took a cigar from his vest pocket. He snipped off the end with a small knife, applied a match, drew deeply, and expelled the smoke. He said, "It takes guts, like you showed me back there in the coulee. Most of all it takes a man who can listen to orders and keep his mouth shut."

"I'm pretty talkative," Windy said. He wanted to stretch this out if he could, hoping to find out more about Conners. "Talkin' is where I got my first name."

Wyatt Grinnel eyed the Texan for a long time. When he started speaking, Windy knew the man was probing for reactions. Grinnel paced back and forth in front of the fireplace while he talked, but it was not the action of a nervous man. He said, "That dead man you picked up back there . . . Jeb Parker. I told you he was a sort of partner of mine. He was, in a way. He owned the J P Cross, one of the biggest outfits in this part of the country. Mostly leased land. I'm sort of a speculator myself . . . deal in local politics, too. I buy up cattle here and there, at times. No railroads in this part of the country and some of the little outfits don't figure it's worthwhile to trail. They'd just as soon sell here. They always took the lead from old Jeb because he was the big operator. Whatever he said the price was, that's what they took or they didn't take nothing. I bought up their stock, combined it with the J P Cross stuff, and trailed it to the railroad. Me and Jeb had it so it worked out pretty good."

"Ever get any complaints on the prices you paid?" Windy asked. His voice didn't say whether he cared or not.

The smile hesitated on Grinnel's lips. He said, "Once in a while some small rancher would get his back up. Always turned out to be somebody who was rustlin' J P Cross stock, too. We got a damned good sheriff here, McCloud. He ain't never missed gettin' one of them rustlers yet. The sheriff and me see eye to eye on a lot of things."

Windy couldn't tell whether that was a threat or additional sales talk, and at the moment he didn't care. He was trying to picture old white-headed Pete Conners working as a sell-out sheriff. Until now the worst the old man had ever done was take a few thousand dollars away from some wealthy widow on the pretext of buying a wedding present. Windy looked at Grinnel and said, "I've sometimes had trouble making the law see eye to eye with me."

Grinnel let the smile develop now. "This is bad country to let that happen in," he said. "Know what an Oregon boot is?"

"Suppose you tell me," Windy prompted.

Grinnel laughed openly now. He said, "You know what it is all right."

"Let's have the proposition," Windy said. He relaxed and let his eyes stay on Grinnel's face.

"There's a boy called Larry Manten," Grinnel said.

"Sounded to me like you had that pretty well taken care of."

Grinnel ignored the interruption. "This Manten is a left-handed adopted relative of Jeb Parker's. Him and Jeb never could get along. Manten didn't like the way me and Jeb ran our business. Manten's a funny boy. Says what he thinks and has a way of making some people listen to him and believe him."

"Looks to me like the wrong man got shot in the back of the head," Windy said dryly. He felt suddenly that he needed to do something with his hands so he started rolling a cigarette.

Wyatt Grinnel's shrewdness was in his eyes now. He said, "Ever hear of a martyr, McCloud? If a man gets killed just when he's beginning to get people to listen to him, they call him a martyr. A martyr is dangerous as hell a long time after he's dead. Folks are still fightin' over Abe Lincoln." He stopped, his gray-green eyes full on Windy's face. Taking a deep drag off his cigar he said, "On the other hand, if a man who's had so much to say about good and evil turns out to be a dirty, back-shootin' dry-gulcher and gets hung for it. . . ." Grinnel shrugged. "People sort of lose faith then and they're easy to handle."

"So," Windy supplied, "this Manten shot his uncle, or whatever he was, in the back of the head so he could get his hands on the J P Cross. But with Manten caught and hung about the only one with money enough left to buy up the Cross would be maybe you?"

"I figured you were smart, McCloud," Grinnel said softly. "I'm seldom wrong in judging a man."

Windy lifted the cigarette he had made and inhaled deeply. "So where do I come in?"

"This Sheriff Pete Conners I was telling you about," Grinnel said, "he seems to have a funny idea that maybe Larry Manten didn't kill Jeb Parker. Seems to me it's time the sheriff has a deputy to help him with his thinking."

"And that deputy's job would be to find Manten?" Windy tried to conceal the tickle of excitement that was playing along his spine.

Grinnel shook his head. "Me and my boys will do that," he said. "We know this country a lot better than you do. We'll bring him in and turn him over to the law so that folks who have been getting the wrong impression of me can see I'm willing to do everything legal."

Windy nodded. "And it would be a deputy's job to see that Manten stays in jail this time, that it?" He looked at Grinnel, his face betraying no emotion, and he added, "Of course, if a lynch mob came and took him away from me. . . ."

Grinnel said, "I keep a bottle there in that cupboard behind you. It's special stuff that I save for men who are smart enough to drink with. Care to have one with me, McCloud?"

☆ **III** ☆

THE RANGE OF BROKEN MEN

*T*he place called Crawford was more a collection of buildings than a town. Houses stood undecided, some facing each other directly, others half turned as if not knowing whether or not they would stay. There were two saloons and an Oddfellows hall on one street, which could have made it the main drag except that there were two saloons and a low squat courthouse on another dusty road that angled off dejectedly and stopped suddenly. It didn't seem a likely place to pick up a loose nickel, but Windy had learned from Wyatt Grinnel that Crawford was a trading center for a vast area and was more of a town than could be found elsewhere in this sparsely settled country.

He knew more about the town, too. Such as where he could find Funeral, the man who ran what passed as a furniture store but did better at undertaking and was well satisfied with his salary as county coroner. He too, it seemed, saw eye to eye with Wyatt Grinnel as did a certain judge and some county supervisors that Grinnel had mentioned in an off-hand way. It sounded like a pretty handy setup and Windy was sorry that Pete Conners had ever become a part of it.

He rode directly to the furniture store, leading the pack horse with the canvas-shrouded body of Jeb Parker behind him. Dismounting, he looped his horse's reins through the ring in the only iron post in town, batted the dust from his Levi's with his hat, and then went on into the dark shambles of the store. A small bell tinkled twice as the door closed behind him.

The man who came from behind the counter was small and bullet-headed. A green eyeshade threw a sickly cast across his pasty features and his hairless head glistened where it caught the light that trickled through the dusty windows. He kept rubbing his hands together with a dry, rasping sound. Windy matched up the description Grinnel had given him and said, "I got a customer outside for you, Funeral."

Funeral's expression was one of trained sympathy and wariness. He said, "Not someone close, I trust?" Then, motioning with his hand as if trying to rake an elusive memory out of the air: "I don't seem to recall. . . ."

"Name's Windy McCloud," Windy said. "You can let down now. It's Jeb Parker I got out there. Wyatt told me to bring him in."

Funeral was still smart. He said, "Wyatt? Oh, yes, Mister Grinnel, of course. Poor Mister Parker. Isn't it a terrible thing?"

"Turn off the tears," Windy said dryly. "Wyatt wants you to fix him up pretty and give him the best funeral the town's ever had. Says you got a special box back there in the storeroom with a lid that slides back so folks can get a last look. Wants you to dig up every flower you can get hold of and dust out them silk ribbons that say 'To my lifelong friend' and all that."

Funeral's voice had lost all of its practiced honey. He said, "Where do you fit into this, McCloud?"

"Stick to your buryin' business!" Windy snapped, letting his hand drop to his gun butt. "My orders from Wyatt don't include answerin' your damn' questions." He turned on his heel and walked out abruptly, hoping he had been successful in leaving the impression that he was a new hardcase hired for his gun.

He mounted his horse and rode out toward the edge of town, noting as he did at least four buildings on which Grinnel's name was prominently displayed, including the livery stable at the end of the street. He left the Walking W pack horse and his own there with no more than a curt "Howdy" for the old man who took them. Then, pulling his hat low over his eyes and taking a hitch in his gun belt, he sauntered down the street toward the dusty stone courthouse that seemed strangely lost among the frame buildings.

Across the front of the courthouse a black sign with deeply indented gold letters, some ten years weathered, said CRAWFORD COUNTY COURTHOUSE — 1871. At the near corner of the building was a window, battered green shade drawn now to cut out the morning glare. On an iron bracket jutting from the stone another sign made a squeaky complaint as it swayed in the wind that seemed to whip constantly around the corner of the building. The runny letters proclaimed that this was the sheriff's office.

Windy shook his head, went up the stone steps, and kicked open the door without knocking. The single occupant of the room jumped from behind the desk in a cloud of wounded dignity, puffed his mustache like a turkey gobbler inflating his wattles, collapsed suddenly, sat down and said, "I don't believe it."

All morning on the ride in from the Walking W Windy had planned exactly what he would say to Sheriff Pete Conners. Now, face to face with the old man, the well-rehearsed lashing was promptly forgotten and Windy grinned. That warm feeling that comes from liking a man a long time seeped through him and mixed itself with the tone of his voice. He said, "You was gonna show me how to work them educated walnuts shells of yours, Pete. You left town before I got a chance to learn."

Pete Conners spanned the years as if they were seconds. He said, "Ah, yes. That widow. An unreasonable woman, Windy. Completely unreasonable. If you heard any malicious gossip. . . ." Then, as if realizing for the first time who his visitor was, he got up from behind the desk and came walking out slowly, both arms extended. "Windy, my boy! It's good to see you! Just passing through?"

"Nope," Windy said, sitting down and hooking a heel over the rung of the chair. He blew on the back of his fingernails. "Stayin' right here. Got a job."

"You? A job?" Pete Conners laughed. "Same old Windy." Then, as if worried: "What kind of job?"

"Helping you."

"Crazy as ever," Pete Conners said. "Windy, it's good. . . . Doing *what*?"

"Helping you. Starting now."

Conners went back to his desk and sat down. He was a man who could look extremely busy doing nothing and develop a tremendous amount of dignity in the process. He pushed two papers aside on his desk, put them back together, picked them up, and evened them precisely. There was an inkwell which he moved to the left. "Don't think I couldn't use a deputy at times," he said officiously. "Big county but little money in the budget. Windy, to think I can't find a job for you, of all people." He snapped his fingers as if suddenly struck with a brilliant idea. "Can you stick around for a couple of months? Board of supervisors will be meeting. . . ."

"Cut it out, Pete," Windy said. "Wyatt Grinnel told me you needed a deputy. He don't like the way you're handling Larry Manten."

Conners was an old man. Ordinarily it was not apparent. It was now. Unmasked by surprise his cherub-like pink-and-white face showed the dozens of worry wrinkles that gathered at the corners of his innocent blue eyes. His amazing wavy mane of white hair was the hair of a man past sixty-five and it was easy to see that the straight firm set of his shoulders was a practiced gesture. They sagged some now.

But he was a man who had lived long by his wits. He recovered quickly. He said, "Yes. The Manten case." He reshuffled the two papers on his desk. "Had something on that right here. I've done a lot of work on it."

"Look, Pete," Windy said softly, "remember how come you and me got to be friends? Dodge City, wasn't it? I was running a faro bank. You had a loaded wheel, three walnut shells, and a fake Arapahoe buck selling snake oil on the side."

Pete Conners locked his well-kept hands over his comfortable middle. He chuckled silently and the ripples of his laughter followed the white piping of his checkered vest. "Chief Bear Who Walks Like A Man," he reminisced. "Mud-Foot Charley was his real name. Half-breed." He slipped easily into the well-rehearsed trick of leading the conversation out of dangerous ground. "Ever tell you about Mud-Foot, Windy? Met that boy. . . ."

"We decided to play a little poker that night, you and me," Windy said, as if he hadn't heard. "It broke up right sudden when we both came up with four deuces at the same time, remember? We shook hands then and decided that from there on out we'd keep our cards on the table, face up."

Windy was leaning across the desk now, his eyes holding those of Sheriff Pete Conners. After a while Pete could no longer meet the gaze. His shoulders drooped again and he became an old man who was saddled with more trouble than he could comfortably handle. His voice sounded tired, but it was the tiredness of worry rather than fatigue. He said, "I guess we did decide that, Windy."

"All right, Pete," Windy said softly, "let's have 'em that way. Out on the table. Face up."

Windy had not known that a man could age so much in the span of a few seconds. All dignity and erectness were gone from Pete Conners's body now and he slumped there behind his desk, whipped and broken. It was not a pleasant thing to watch. When he looked up, there was pallor in his face. He said, "Windy, I've made a hell of a mess of things. How much do you know?"

"Only that a yahoo called Grinnel runs this county, including you. An ugly-lookin' jigger named Reb did a good job of blowing the back of Jeb Parker's head off and they're tryin' to hang it on somebody called Larry Manten. Suppose you take it from there, Pete."

Conners took a deep breath and wiped his face with a 'kerchief. He said, "You've got it straight enough, as far as it goes. How come you to get mixed up in this?"

Windy used few words in telling it. Then: "I might put the same question to you, Pete."

"Mine's a longer story," Conners said wearily. "Suppose we just say I put the wrong lies in the letters I wrote to a sister of mine. She died a few years back and I got caught with the job of raising a niece."

"I'd say the shell game and snake oil was a better deal than this," Windy said dryly.

Pete Conners shrugged. "Ever see a mess of little coyote puppies?" he asked. "Woolly and cute and soft and innocent-looking. It's not until they grow up and start killing sheep that you realize what you got on your hands. It was the first chance I ever had at a respectable job and I wanted it for Violet, my niece." He waved down Windy's objections. "Sure, I knew there were angles . . . stuffed ballot boxes and things like that. What the hell, Windy, you can find that every place. This Jeb Parker and Wyatt Grinnel ran things together and I did as I was told. Maybe it wasn't all exactly according to Hoyle, but I drew my pay and nobody got hurt. There wasn't any killings or anything like that. Believe me, Windy, when I tell you that. I was gradually working things around to where we were going to have a respectable county."

"How about this Larry Manten?"

"He's the finest boy that ever drew the breath of life, Windy. He was the adopted son of Jeb Parker's brother. Never knew Parker's brother . . . lived back East some-place. Seems he put Jeb in the cow business and it's all legal and set that when Parker dies the J P Cross passes on to Larry Manten."

"And Manten don't see eye to eye with Grinnel, that it?" Windy asked, using Grinnel's pet phrase.

"That's putting it pretty mild," Conners said. "It only took Larry about a month to see through the setup here and then he started telling everybody who'd listen just how he felt. In the short time he's been here he's raised more stink than this country's seen since the Indians left it. Besides that he's got himself engaged to marry my niece."

"Did you let him out of jail?" Windy asked.

"Well, I wouldn't exactly put it that way," the sheriff said, hedging. "I got a little careless with my keys and I guess maybe Violet found them. Next thing I know Larry was out. Violet wanted him to make a run for it. She'd come to him wherever he was. That's the way I thought it would be, but Larry, he don't play that way. He knew Crash Yonkers was in town and he started to get him. They were laying for Larry and the kid got pretty badly shot up." The old man's face was white. He said, "Windy, if that kid had been killed, it would been just as if it was me that shot him. Do you see that?"

"I reckon I do, Pete," Windy said softly. Then: "How come you didn't run in this Reb if you knew it was actually him that did the killin'?"

The old man spread his hands hopelessly. "Windy, I can find you twenty-five men who will swear on the Bible that Reb and Crash Yonkers haven't left town in over two weeks. You can't beat that kind of a setup. Not when you couple it with a judge who's paid to listen to only one side of the testimony."

"And now the whole county figgers for sure Larry Manten is guilty, that it?" Windy prompted.

"With the exception of five or six small ranchers, yes," Pete admitted. "Wyatt Grinnel has got enough men right here in town to make up a big enough mob that, if Larry shows his face, he'll be decorating a cottonwood before anybody can do anything about it."

"You know where Larry is?" Windy asked.

The sheriff fumbled with the papers on his desk a long time before answering. He nodded and said, "Yes, I know where he is. I reckon Wyatt is beginning to suspect I know, too. That's why he wanted you around here to keep an eye on me. Unless I miss my guess, pretty soon I'll get a hurry-up call to go chase somebody that branded the wrong cow and I accidentally won't come back." He shrugged his shoulders and the hopelessness was bright in his eyes. "There they are, Windy. Just the way you asked for them . . . out on the table, face up. I check it to you."

Windy had moved over to the window and raised the shade. He turned now and said, "It looks like the boss is coming to see how things are shapin' up. Dig out one of them deputy tin-star badges and pin it on my shirt."

☆ IV ☆

BARROOM BLOW-OFF

𝖂yatt Grinnel made no pretense or cover-up when he came into Sheriff Pete Conners's office. He sat down in the sheriff's chair, put his fancy-tooled, handmade boots on the desk, and lit one of his expensive cigars. Expelling the smoke noisily he said, "You saw eye to eye with me on hiring a deputy, did you, Pete?"

Windy gave the sheriff a scowling wink and a quick negative shake of the head and Conners said, "If that's the way you want it, Wyatt, it's all right with me. I could sure use some help."

"From what I can see this country needs a little more rawhide law and a little less pussyfootin'," Windy broke in. "I was just tellin' the sheriff here if you hang 'em quick enough, they don't get a chance to make a jail break."

Grinnel let that crooked smile trickle out of the left corner of his mouth. He said, "Maybe you and me are gonna get along all right, McCloud. Seen the town yet?"

"Ain't had a chance," Windy said, rubbing his sleeve across the new deputy badge on his shirt. "Suppose you and me take a look at it."

Grinnel took his feet off the desk and let them drop to the floor. "Go on over to the Bull's Head and have a drink on the house," he said. "It's just down the street a piece. I'll join you there in a little while. There's a few things I want to take up with the sheriff."

Windy hesitated, not sure whether he should leave Pete here alone. Then he decided that Grinnel wouldn't be fool enough to try anything so openly. He nodded curtly and went out.

The sun lay hot and thick on the sprawling town and there was no shade in the east-west street. The interior of the Bull's Head was a welcome relief of coolness when Windy batted aside the doors and went in. There was a long bar down one side of the room, a small dance floor at the back, and a scatter of poker tables took up the rest of the floor space. There were half a dozen men widely spaced at the bar and the single bartender stood waiting for Windy to pick his spot. At the far end of the bar two men were in a lively conversation. Windy gave them a scant glance, stepped up to the bar, and motioned for whiskey and a glass.

He had a quick drink and saw a third man move down as if to get into the argument that seemed to be growing hotter. Pouring a second drink he heard one man, younger than the others, say, "The whole damn bunch of you are yellow, that's the trouble. A week ago you were agreeing with everything Manten said. Now you're just as quick to want to put a rope around his neck."

Windy picked up his bottle and glass and moved closer to where he could hear more. He kept his body half turned so that the law badge on his shirt didn't show. A fourth man moved into the argument and said, "It's all right to be loyal, Kimball, but you haven't got a damn leg to stand on. You saw Larry and his uncle have it out right here in this bar and you heard Larry tell old Jeb he'd see him in jail if need be. You're forgettin', Kimball, that Jeb wasn't Larry's real uncle. There wasn't no blood tie there to keep Larry from shootin' him in the back of the head. Hell, if he got away with it, he'd own the biggest spread in this county."

The younger rancher called Kimball broke in, his voice loud and raw-edged. "And suppose he don't come into the J P Cross? Suppose we convict him with a bought-off judge and a paid jury and hang him, then what the hell happens? Are there any of you got money enough to buy the J P Cross? By God I haven't, what with the price of beef the way Grinnel and Parker been settin' it the last few years."

The doors opened, throwing a momentary shaft of light into the room. The three men tried to motion the vociferous Kimball to silence by jerking their heads toward the door where Grinnel stood, thumbs hooked in his belt.

Kimball turned, his face red with anger. He said, "Why in the hell should I be quiet just because Grinnel's listening? Who does he think he is, God Almighty? It's about time somebody told him what they thought. That's why he's so damn set on hanging this killing on Manten. Larry had the guts to say what he thought!"

There was a broad smile on Wyatt Grinnel's face. He walked forward slowly and stopped at Windy McCloud's elbow. Out of the corner of his mouth he said, "Kimball there is sort of a trouble-maker, McCloud."

Windy thought swiftly. If he was going to get himself in solid with Wyatt Grinnel, this was as quick and harmless a way to do it as any. Without answering he walked down the bar, took Kimball by the elbow, whirled him around, and said, "You talk pretty loud, fellow."

Kimball stopped, his mouth open, taken off guard by the sudden interruption. Slowly his eyes went to the law badge on Windy's shirt, then drifted on to the gun that hung on the redhead's hip. With an open sneer he said, "So, we got some new gun law in town, have we? What jail did Grinnel get you out of?"

Windy didn't want to hit the man. He liked his spunk and the rancher's sentiments too closely paralleled his own. But McCloud had his eye on bigger game. Without warning he lashed out and his fist cracked against the point of Kimball's chin. The rancher went over backwards and sprawled on the floor and before he could get to his feet Windy had his gun out in an exhibition of smoothness that was good enough for even Grinnel. He said, "Get the hell out of town, Kimball, and don't come back until you learn to handle your likker better. I'm not puttin' up with any drunks at this hour of the morning."

He reached down with his left hand and jerked Kimball to his feet. Prodding him with his gun, Windy hurried the rancher to the door and shoved him outside. Holstering his gun then, he went back to the bar and poured himself another drink. Wyatt Grinnel held his glass in both hands, turning it slowly. He had his eyes fixed on his own reflection in the backbar mirror. His voice unable to conceal the pleasure he felt, he said, "Windy, you're gonna do all right. You might even become sheriff some day. You can try it on for size for a while, anyway. I'm sending Pete out to investigate some missing horses of mine."

Windy felt a chill touch his spine. He said casually, "That so? When's he leavin'?"

"Right now," Grinnel said. "I told him to get on it right away. Can't have horse stealin' going on."

Windy flexed his shoulders and yawned, as if it meant nothing to him at all. He said, "Reckon I'll ride along with him. It'll give me a chance to look over some of the country."

"There's no need of it," Grinnel said. "It's a one-man job."

"Think I'll go along anyhow," Windy said.

Grinnel had turned now and that hard shrewdness was back in his eyes. He said, "You better stay here in town and keep an eye on things, McCloud."

"Look, Grinnel," Windy said easily, "up to now you and me been gettin' along fine. That idea of me becomin' sheriff some day sort of appeals to me. That Pete Conners don't strike me as a man who's any too careful. He meets up with them rustlers who stole your horses he might get himself shot or something. Guess that would make the sheriff's job open right sudden, wouldn't it?"

Grinnel looked at McCloud a long time, as if he were trying to see every recess of the Texan's mind. After a while that slow smile came to his lips. He said, "You're a cold-blooded son, ain't you, Windy?"

"Somebody told me once that when opportunity knocks you should open the door," Windy said, his eyes never leaving Grinnel's face.

Grinnel said, "That's the way I've always played it. When you come to them twin rocks on the north trail, maybe you better lag back a hundred yards or so. There's a good view from there. After you get back from this ride, you and me ought to understand each other pretty good."

Windy said, "Yeah, Wyatt, I reckon we should."

He walked out of the saloon and he could feel Grinnel's hard eyes boring into his back. He couldn't tell whether Grinnel had suspected him and was calling his bluff or whether this was a piece of showmanship designed to show Windy who was boss in

Crawford County. Of one thing he was certain. This little trip had been destined to be Sheriff Pete Conners's last ride.

He hurried back to the sheriff's office as quickly as possible without being too obvious, saw that Pete was not there, then went on to the livery stable where he had left his horse. He spotted Conners, mounted on a grulla dun, surrounded by six men. He recognized them all as men he had seen at Grinnel's ranch; the one who was doing the most talking was Crash Yonkers. As Windy came into the building, he heard Yonkers say, "Better go get Wyatt, Dally." The man called Dally started up the street.

Conners was sweating profusely, but he was managing to maintain his dignity. He said, "When I ask for a posse around here, I'm supposed to get it. If you boys are afraid to go after Larry Manten, I'll go myself."

"We're not afraid, Sheriff," Crash Yonkers said softly, touching his gun. "It's just that it's a hot day for a wild goose chase."

"I tell you. . . ."

"Save it for Wyatt," Yonkers snapped. "He'll be here directly."

"If there's a posse formin', I reckon I ought to be in on it," Windy drawled, "seein' as how I'm part of the law."

Conners didn't meet the Texan's gaze. He said, "You stay here in town and keep an eye on things. I'll handle this alone."

There was a broken scatter of conversation while the men waited and from it Windy knew Pete Conners had admitted he was hiding Larry Manten but that he was now ready to bring him in. He puzzled over this until he decided that Manten must be hiding here in town and this was Pete's way of giving the kid a chance to make a break for it. He caught Pete's eye then and shook his head. Wyatt Grinnel would bluff just so long. As soon as he found out what Pete was up to. . . . The men stepped aside as Grinnel came into the stable. He had a broad smile on his face. He said, "Getting smart again, Pete?"

"I'm not anxious for any of that bushwhack lead you had lined up for me," Conners said.

"It's getting so it's hard to trust you, Pete," the boss said softly. "Why a posse? If you know where Manten is, why don't you go bring him in alone? We know he's shot up some."

Windy was proud of the way Conners stared down Grinnel. The old man said, "Let's quit fooling each other, Wyatt. I want you boys where I can see you. I'm trading my skin for Manten's. I don't want to get shorted on the deal."

"You're beginning to sound smarter, Pete," Grinnel said. He was still smiling. "I'll compromise with you. Me and half the boys will go along with you. If we find Manten, like you say, you'll come back all in one piece. Crash, you and McCloud take the rest of the boys and stay here in town . . . just in case." Grinnel's smile was broad now, as if he realized he had called the old man's bluff. He said, "I'll be ready to ride in a minute, Pete. You better know where you're going."

☆ **V** ☆

DEATH WATCH

*T*here was a feeling of death hanging over the group of six riders that left town that noon. Pete Conners had looked like a man who was desperately sick as he rode out with Wyatt Grinnel keeping close to his stirrup. The other four in the group, all Grinnel men, rode as if they cared little one way or the other. Windy watched them go and the sweat ran down the crease of his back and moistened the palms of his hands. Behind him Crash Yonkers said, "Reckon you'll be full sheriff tomorrow, McCloud. It won't make me like you none better."

Windy turned swiftly. "I'll watch my back, Yonkers," he promised. Then: "You and the boys go on over and have a drink if you want. I'm gonna go see what that gal of Pete's has to say. Which house they live in?"

"That white one at the end of the street," Crash said. "But I wouldn't do it if I was you. The boss sort of has an eye on that girl. He don't like to have her bothered."

"The boss ain't here," Windy reminded sharply. "I'll make the decisions."

"Go ahead," Yonkers said, shrugging his thin shoulders. "You can't get in no trouble. Wyatt said to keep a couple of the boys watchin' you. Maybe you ain't ridin' so damn high as you think, McCloud."

Yonkers and two of the other men sauntered off toward the Bull's Head, but the remaining two stayed, leaning against the sun-warped wall of the stable, their thumbs hooked in gun belts, grinning openly at the lanky Texan. He turned his back on them and started toward the cottage at the end of the street and he knew that they had fallen in behind him.

Half way there Funeral came out into the street and stopped him. The bullet-headed little man said, "Wyatt expects me to do the impossible. I got a dozen questions I wanted to ask him and he won't even to talk to me. Look, McCloud, about that. . . ?"

"Get the hell out of my way!" Windy snapped.

"I can't get flowers where no flowers grow," the undertaker whined. "I got to ask you. . . ."

"You smell like a dead man!" Windy said. "Leave me alone!"

The undertaker stepped aside, complaining bitterly. Behind him Windy knew the two gunmen had spread out some, one on either side of him, watching every move he made. He felt his heart hammering against his ribs and he took a deep breath and expelled it. That helped some.

He didn't know what kind of a girl Violet would be. He didn't even know for sure he would find her at the house. But it was the only chance he had of putting his finger on anything. Conners had made a desperate attempt to get Grinnel and his men out of town and that could mean only one thing, as far as Windy could see it. Manten must be here and this was intended as a break, so that he could get away. But Pete had failed and any move Manten would make would have to be stopped. It was only logical to assume that Violet, the one most concerned, would be in on it. He came to the gate in the picket fence, opened it, and went up the walk. The door didn't open to his knock but a voice from inside said, "Who is it?"

"Windy McCloud. Friend of your uncle. Let me talk to you, Violet. There's something I got to tell you."

There was a long silence and then the girl's voice strained. "I'm dressing now. You'll have to come back later."

"Look, you little fool," Windy said, his voice close to the panel, "it's about Larry. Pete's plans went wrong. Crash Yonkers and four men are watching things here. Let me in, will you?"

Again there was that long, exasperating silence in which Windy felt the sweat ooze from his pores. The two Grinnel gunmen were directly across the street from him now. He looked toward town and saw Funeral still standing undecided in the middle of the street. The little man saw Windy there on the porch and started up the street in that direction. Windy said, "For God's sake, open that door!"

He heard the bolt slide then and the door opened slightly. Pulling open the screen door, Windy thrust his foot inside the house and hunched the heavy door open with his shoulder. It made him enter the room sideways and, when he turned and saw the girl standing there, she had a six-shooter in her hand and the hammer was back.

His first thought was to knock the gun aside, but as he shifted his weight a voice said, "No you don't, stranger. I'm not so far gone I can't pull a trigger." Turning his head slightly, he saw the bandage-swathed figure propped in a chair at the far end of the room.

The wounded man in the chair must have been badly hit. There was no color in his handsome face. Only in his eyes was there any life; they were the eyes of a man who doesn't change his mind once he's made it up. It wasn't hard to guess that this was the Larry Manten who had rebelled against Parker and Grinnel and had had guts enough to say why. Windy forced a grin and said, "You can put down that gun, Manten. I'm on your side of the fence in this thing."

"I'll decide that," Manten said. "Start talking."

It was to the girl that Windy did his talking and before he had gone very far with his story he found he was having some difficulty putting his words together. A beautiful woman always did that to him. After a while he saw that he was convincing her, but that made it even worse now because there was a lot of softness coming into those wide blue eyes and when her lips parted slightly they looked like lips that were made to be kissed. He felt the color crawling into his cheeks and he blundered, "Well, that's the way it is, damn it! Me and Pete been friends a long time."

"It's all right, Larry," the girl said, and it was the kind of voice a man hears sometimes in a pine tree when the sun is warm and the spring grass scent is in the air. It left a little shiver in Windy McCloud. She laid the gun on the table and came forward and took Windy's right hand in both of hers. "I've heard Uncle Pete talk about you. You were a banker, weren't you?"

Windy coughed over that one, decided a faro dealer could be called that all right, and said, "Yes, ma'am. Your uncle was in the medical business at that time."

Larry Manten said, "Are you sure, Violet?"

There was a deep stain of worry in the girl's face but a hint of relief found its way into her eyes. She said, "I'm sure. He fibs as fast as Uncle does."

Larry Manten still didn't lower the gun that protruded from under the blanket drawn across his lap. He said, "I can't take any chances, McCloud. What's the play?"

"If you figured on making a break for it, you better hold off," Windy said tersely. "Crash Yonkers and four others are in town. They're keeping an eye on the house."

"But Uncle Pete said they were all going to the ranch for a couple of days. We've got a buckboard out back and we were going to Kimball's place."

"Wait a minute, McCloud," Manten said softly, "I thought it sounded too easy. What kind of cock-and-bull story did Pete give me, anyway? He said he had called Grinnel's bluff and Grinnel was backing down."

"How about this Kimball and some of the other ranchers?" Windy cut in. "Can you depend on them?"

The girl's eyes had gone wide with sudden fear. "Uncle Pete's in trouble?"

"Don't worry about that now," Windy snapped. "Take the buckboard and get to Kimball's place as fast as you can. Tell Kimball to get hold of all the men he can and head out on the north trail. Pete can stall for a while but as soon as Grinnel finds out he's on a false lead. . . ."

Manten had pulled himself up out of the chair and he stood there, swaying unsteadily, his face white with pain. "Get me a horse, McCloud," he said.

"Don't be a fool," Windy snapped. "You'd be in the way."

The girl had started toward the back door when they heard the creak of hinges and the movement of air on their backs. They turned quickly and there framed in the doorway was the misshapen body of Funeral. The little man started to say, "I got to talk to you, McCloud. . . ." Then his eyes focused on Manten. He gave a squeal of terror and bolted back across the porch and down the walk. Windy sent a shot crashing over the undertaker's head, yelling for him to stop. But Funeral had turned and was running down the street. They could hear his high-pitched voice yelling, "Larry Manten's in there!"

Farther down the street Windy saw the gaunt frame of Crash Yonkers come out on the sidewalk, pause, then duck into the nearest building. Windy slammed the door and bolted it. With one swift movement he shoved Larry Manten's chair near a window. To the girl he said, "Drive like you never drove before. Me and Larry got a little job to do here. We'll be along directly!"

☆ VI ☆
SIEGE

*I*n the next few minutes Larry Manten showed the stuff he was made of. Windy helped him into the chair in front of the window and pain spouted silvery-beaded perspiration across the kid's forehead each time he moved. Gritting his teeth, he said: "The old man keeps shells in that table drawer there. Get me a couple of boxes and go see that Violet gets started all right. If Yonkers wants trouble, I'll handle him from here."

Windy hurried out the back door and found Violet had already led the team out from under the shed. She was on the buckboard seat, the lines gripped in her hands.

"You all right?" Windy asked. Her face set, the girl nodded, took the whip, and braced her feet against the floor board. "Once you start, don't look back," he warned. "Regardless of what happens. Drive 'em until they drop, if need be, but get Kimball and all the men he can scrape up out on that north trail."

She turned toward him and her eyes were bright with tears. Her lips barely moved when she said, "You take care of Larry. Promise me that." She raised the whip and lashed it across the rumps of the well-kept team. The horses stretched out and the buckboard lurched crazily as she swung around the corner of the house and slid into the street. Windy ran out into the open and called, "Hey, Yonkers! Over here!"

Two men ran out toward the buggy and Yonkers's voice snapped, "The hell with it! Let her go."

Windy tried to find the man's hiding place from the sound of his voice. He failed, so he ducked back into the house. Larry Manten was staring out the window, his hand gripped tightly around the butt of a cocked .44. Without looking at Windy, he said, "If they had touched that team, I'd have killed them both."

Again Yonkers's voice called, "Can you hear me, McCloud?"

"I hear you all right," Windy yelled.

"What's goin' on over there?" Yonkers wanted to know. "Have you got Manten?"

"I've got him."

"Then bring him on out here and let's get it over with. I already sent one of the boys after Wyatt."

"I'll keep him here, Yonkers."

There was a long silence, and now the town was beginning to breathe with excitement as the word passed along that Manten had been found and was at bay in the Conners's house. Men came out on the street but kept at a safe distance. Women disappeared and a deathly silence settled over the nearest houses. Crash Yonkers's words were clear enough to carry a distance when he called, "Is this a double-cross, McCloud?"

"You figger it out," Windy called back. "I don't need help in handling one prisoner. When you and your lynch-crazy crew get out of town, I'll bring him out. Not before."

Again there was that long, nerve-sapping silence. A man came out of the house across the street and walked hurriedly toward where a crowd had gathered in front of the Bull's Head. After a while he came back and there were six more men with him, lagging along behind as if they didn't want to come. They went into the house and after what seemed hours Crash Yonkers voiced their decision. He said, "I reckon we don't trust you, McCloud. We're coming over after Manten."

"Come ahead," Windy said flatly, "but I'm warning you now that will be interference with the law and I'll shoot the first man who steps into the street!"

He scanned the room quickly then, found a shotgun and a rifle, and these he stood by his side before kneeling down under the front window. He had no false hopes about Crash Yonkers's holding off. Yonkers had been slipping in Grinnel's favor and he must have known it, just as he must have known that there was a chance of Windy McCloud's moving into his place. Here was his chance to reinstate himself in the eyes of his boss. He wouldn't be likely to pass up such an opportunity. But more than this Windy thought of old Pete Conners riding out there with Grinnel and those others at his back, making a desperate and hopeless attempt to lead these killers off Larry Manten's trail. They'd been gone over an hour now. In another hour they'd be into rough brakes and canyons. After that it was only a matter of how long Pete could stall. Grinnel was no fool. He'd see through it quickly enough, and even if Pete, with that particular talent of his, could pull the wool over Wyatt's eyes, it would blow up in his face when the man Crash Yonkers had dispatched got there. Windy's mouth was dry and hot when he thought of it. He said, "How far is it to Kimball's place?"

"Take her about a half hour," Larry Manten said. Apparently his thoughts had been paralleling Windy's. He didn't look at the redhead when he spoke now. He said, "You go after Pete. I'll be all right here."

Windy looked at the kid who seemed to be using every ounce of strength he had just to hold that gun in his hand. He said, "Yeah, you'd do fine."

Manten turned, his eyes hot with anger. He said, "The only reason you're here is because you're too damn' yellow to get out there and face Grinnel."

"Good try, Manten," Windy said, grinning. "From what I've heard around, you're what this country needs. I reckon Pete would want me to keep as much of you in one piece as I can."

It was another five minutes, and it seemed like five hours, and then across the street a rifle smacked and the glass shattered in the window above Larry Manten's head. Crash Yonkers called, "That's a warning, McCloud. This is your last chance."

"Come ahead," Windy invited.

A dozen guns answered his challenge. The glass cracked out and rifle bullets ripped through the front door. Grabbing the large oak table that stood in the middle of the room, Windy tipped it over and pulled Larry's chair behind it, making an additional shield for the wounded man's body. "Hold your fire," Windy ordered. "They might figger they got us with that blast and come out in the open where we can get a shot at 'em."

His strategy proved partly correct a few minutes later when four men come edging around the corner of the house across the street. Windy waited until the men were even with the end of the porch, standing there partially screened by shrubbery, guns drawn. Then Windy said softly, "Now!"

Manten's gun and Windy's spoke at the same time. Two men came tumbling out into the open as if they had been clubbed from behind. The other two made wild dives for cover. Windy fired again, and only one man got back into the shelter of the house.

Again that solid blast of gunfire ripped the front of Conners's dwelling and stray lead smashed lamps inside the room and buried itself with soggy thuds in the opposite wall. "Hold it!" Windy ordered again, and again they waited.

Only two men came out this time. Forewarned, they came from opposite sides of the house and made for the cover of the huge cottonwoods that lined that side of the street. For a while they were lost from sight, and then risking a look Windy saw one running across the street a block away.

"Figger on comin' in behind us," he told Manten tersely. "Hold your fire. Get down on the floor and play dead, and make it convincin'. I'll try to get 'em out back. If they get through, take 'em when they bend over to look at you."

He went into the kitchen and stood behind the open door, straining his ears for any sound he could hear. After a while he heard them moving cautiously and he could tell where they were from the sounds. The dry leaves were across the driveway. The hard solid step was the driveway itself. Then the soft yielding sound and that would be the flower beds where the pinks and cosmos grew. He held his breath after that and he thought he could hear one of them moving around the side of the house. He had visions of them going to the front door. He had been so sure they would try this back way.

More movement outside and then whispers. "I can see one of them in there. Looks dead enough. Manten. I'll take a look. Back me up."

There was a creak of boards as the man put his weight on the back steps. The slight hinge complained as the screen opened. And then Windy knew that the man was in the room, not over four inches away from him. Still he waited, wanting them both inside before he made a move. He could not see, but he knew that the man was moving cautiously across the kitchen, keeping his back flattened against the wall. And then the second man tested his weight on the steps and came into the room.

Every muscle taut Windy kicked the door closed and barked his order. "Drop 'em!"

The man who had entered the room first did as he was told, but the second man, being closer to the entrance and slightly behind Windy, made a try. His gun blasted and the lead ripped across Windy's side. Windy fired once and saw the man go over backwards, his flailing body crashing into the closed door. The first man had dropped to the floor and was clawing frantically for his gun. Windy jumped, his boot heels grinding viciously into the man's hand. There was a scream of pain, and then Windy had his fingers locked in the man's collar and was jerking him to his feet. Windy recognized him as the one Crash Yonkers had called Dally, back there at the livery stable. He said, "Keep your mouth shut, Dally, and do as I say or this gun's gonna go off damned sudden."

Windy rammed the barrel of the six-shooter hard against Dally's spine and kicked him into the front room. Larry Manten tried to get to his feet and couldn't make it. Keeping the gun centered on Dally, Windy reached down with his left hand and gave Larry a lift. The kid slid into his chair, shaking violently. He licked his lips and said, "The hell with me, Windy. Go help Pete!"

Windy said, "Hold your fire and keep quiet. They'll be wantin' to know what happened to Dally and his gun-handy sidekick."

It was five minutes, maybe, before Crash Yonkers, unable to stand the strain any longer, called out, "Beckett! Dally! You all right?"

McCloud's lips curled away from his teeth. He stuck his gun into Dally's back. "Open that door and stand there in full sight," he ordered. "Tell 'em it's all right and they can come on over. One slip and you're gonna know what it's like to get your backbone cut in two with a bullet."

Dally's voice was weak, but his standing there in full sight made it sound convincing enough. In a moment the front door across the street opened and six men came out, walked through the yard, and started across to the Conners's place. Windy McCloud picked up the shotgun and took his place at the window. He looked at Larry Manten to motion for him to get ready. The pain and exertion had been too much and the kid was out. Dally stood in the doorway, his knees knocking together, while Crash Yonkers and his five men came across the street in a tight body. When they were at Conners's gate, Dally gave way. Throwing himself headlong off the porch, he screamed, "It's a trap! Scatter!"

Windy McCloud let loose with both barrels of the shotgun.

☆ VII ☆
GUNS OF HELL

*T*he double charge of buckshot caught the tightly-grouped men and exploded among them, scattering them as if a cannonball had been dropped in their midst. Windy could see one man crawling on all fours; another lay there, still in the dust; a third took two running steps, fell, got to his feet, and fell again. The other three made headlong dives for the protection of the porch where they were joined by Dally. Windy put the shotgun aside and took up his six-shooter. He could hear Yonkers yelling for the men to spread out. One man got up and tried to run around the end of the porch and Windy drove him back with two shots. Further up the street a silence had settled over the group of townsmen grouped there, watching the battle.

Lead ripped through the shattered window and cut across Windy's left arm, leaving an ugly flesh wound. He crawled over behind the table where Manten was beginning to stir. He took time to rip off a piece of his shirt and tie it around the wound. Manten's eyes opened. He smiled weakly and tried to raise his gun. "Take it easy, kid," Windy said, "We got 'em on the run."

The interval had given Yonkers time to spread his men and a bullet came ripping in from a side window and plowed splinters out of the floor, inches from where Windy hunkered down. He swiveled his gun that way, fired twice, but knew he had hit nothing. A face appeared at the window in front of Manten. Larry yelled a feeble warning, got his gun lined, and fired. The face disappeared.

But they had the house surrounded now, one man on each end of the long living room, Crash Yonkers himself pouring a deadly fire through those front windows. There was nothing Windy could do about it, for if he raised his head to where he could get a shot, three guns could pick him off. Manten's pain-racked voice: "Make a run for it out the back way, Windy."

"You go to hell!" Windy said.

Windy became obsessed with the idea of Crash Yonkers then and in his mind he could see that pinched, bone-heavy face, the huge freckle-splotched hands with their prominent knuckles. He felt if he could get Yonkers out of the way, he would have accomplished something.

The front door was standing open where Dally had gone out and Windy kept eyeing it, calculating the distance between the table that protected him and that open door. Another bullet from a side window cut close to his feet, making the decision for him. He hunched his legs under him, threw himself out from behind the protection, rolled across the floor, and came to his feet standing fully exposed in the open doorway. Crash Yonkers, hunched down for protection by the porch steps, was caught by surprise. Windy fired and missed. He saw the corner of the porch step chip off a half inch from Yonkers's face. Yonkers's gun blasted back, knocking Windy's gun from his hand.

Yonkers was calm now. All he had to do was aim his gun and fire again. He took his time, determined to make his shot, and in that he made his mistake. For he had miscalculated the Texan's swiftness. Windy made a headlong dive and, as Crash's gun exploded in his face, his shoulder hit Yonkers in the chest. They went down together and their hands clawed with the strength of men locked in the death struggle. From inside the house Manten's gun barked once. Windy got one hand free and sank a fist into Crash's middle. The gunman coughed with pain, rolled back, and ripped his fingernails across Windy's face.

Fists were not Crash Yonkers's weapons. He kept trying for the gun that had been knocked out of his hand and, each time he'd reach for it, Windy's fist would crack against that bony chin. The blows seemed to have no effect. They rolled again and Yonkers was on top, clawing at Windy's throat with his left hand, still reaching out for the gun that lay in the dust two feet away. Windy brought his knee up sharply and caught Yonkers in the groin. The gunman stiffened with pain, and Windy kneed him again. Gasping for breath, Yonkers threw himself free and his hand closed around the six-shooter's butt. Windy lunged toward the man's legs, trying to pull him down. Crash side-stepped and even in the confusion Windy could hear the hammer of the six-shooter come back.

He saw the gun line on his face and the bore of it was like a sinister black eye that held his gaze. Again he lunged at Yonkers's legs and again Yonkers was ready and side-stepped. The gun was close to his face and Windy closed his eyes and braced himself for the impact of the lead. The concussion of the gun slapped against his clothes, but there was no hammering drive of the lead. It had only been the smallest fraction of a second and, when he opened his eyes, Yonkers was standing there, a foolish expression on his face. Windy realized that the man was turning slowly as if he were going to walk away. Then he swayed sideways, still gripping that gun, still swinging it toward Windy. There was another shot. Yonkers's body jerked away from the lead and from the broken front window smoke trickled from the muzzle of Manten's gun.

Windy scooped up his own gun from the dirt, vaulted onto the porch, and ducked back inside the house. Larry Manten was standing there by the front window, his body braced against the sill, holding himself erect with every ounce of strength he had. He looked at Windy, grinned and said, "I thought he never would stand up where I could get a good shot at him." Then the kid's knees went out from under him.

From the left side of the house another shot crashed through the window, followed by the sound of running feet. Stepping out on the porch, Windy saw the gunman angling across the street for the protection of the cottonwoods. Windy fired once, missed, and then the sudden surge of screams, the wailing of voices, the curses of men told him that this had all been but a matter of seconds. Now it was over and Yonkers and his crew were through.

There was a biting wound across Windy's ribs. The pain in his arm was beginning to be a pounding thing that tormented him and kept him from thinking straight. He tried to figure his next move but old Pete Conners and his niece Violet, the rancher Kimball and the crusading Larry Manten, kept getting mixed up with one another in his thoughts. He couldn't leave Larry here alone for there was no way of telling how many more of Grinnel's paid agitators were in the town and he couldn't leave Pete out there alone any longer, either. As long as Wyatt Grinnel was alive, this thing was not over.

In the street he heard the babble of voices, the voice of a mob without a leader, a mob with opinions yet unformed. He reloaded his six-shooter, dropped it into its holster, and then went and picked up the broken body of Larry Manten in his arms. Packing the hundred-and-sixty pounds of Manten as if he weighed half that, McCloud stepped out onto the bullet-riddled porch of the Conners's home. He knew that blood was running down his arm now and that blood had stained his shirt. His face was ripped from the gouging of Crash Yonkers's fingernails. His clothes were matted with dirt where he had rolled in the dust. Holding Manten in his arms, he looked out at the wide-eyed, fear-crazed crowd that stood in the street.

"Until Pete Conners gets back, I'm the law in this town!" he bawled. "I'm putting Manten in jail and I mean for him to stay there until he's had an honest and proper trial. The first man who gets within half a block of that jail has got me to deal with."

He walked off the porch then, turned his back on the crowd, and went down the middle of the street. Any man there could have shot him in the back. No one made a move.

He took Larry inside the jail, made him as comfortable as he could on a cot; then, leaving the door open, he went back outside and called to the crowd that had followed him at a block's distance. "If there's a doctor in this town, I want him. Now!"

There was a hesitation, a buzz of voices, before a thin, dark-suited man with a derby hat came timidly out of the crowd and started walking down the street. "You've got nothing to worry about, doc," Windy told the medic as he approached, "so long as you see that kid in there don't die."

"I'll do my best, Deputy," the doctor said.

"You're stayin' right with him until I get back," Windy said. He led the doctor to the cell where Larry lay, white-faced and still, and closed the door behind them and snapped the lock.

He replenished his ammunition belt from a stock he found in the sheriff's desk, then he went toward the livery stable at the head of the street where he had left his horse. He was half way there when he saw the cavalcade led by Pete Conners coming in from the north trail. For a second Windy stood there, shaking his head as if unable to believe what he saw. Then all the strength went out of him and he turned around and headed back toward the courthouse. Behind him he heard old Pete Conners calling his name. He didn't even stop to answer.

Kimball was in the crowd that rode back with Pete Conners. He had four men of his own and there were six other small ranchers, each with a couple of hands. The men rode grim-faced and silent, and yet there was a sort of victorious elation in their bearings. Three of Grinnel's men were dead. Grinnel himself was tied in his saddle. The town boss rode erect, defiant, arrogant. A towering hulk of a man, a sneer curling the corners of his mouth. The girl was there, too. She asked one single question and Windy handed her the key to the cell and nodded toward the jail.

The crowd was still in the street, waiting for one word that would give them an inkling of what their decision should be. They were still touched by the years of corrupt dictatorship imposed by Grinnel, wavering now as they saw Kimball and the other small ranchers who had dared to back the fire-spouting Manten. Windy said, "You better make the speeches, Pete. Just pretend you're back in Dodge, selling snake oil. Only you got something better to sell this time. Give 'em the truth."

While Sheriff Pete Conners, his head erect, the soft wind rippling his snow-white mane, convinced the citizens of Crawford that an end had come to Grinnel and his machine politics, that now a man could sell his own cattle on an open market at a fair market price, Kimball offered his hand to Windy McCloud. The two of them led Grinnel into the sheriff's office.

Grinnel stood there, saying nothing. Unarmed, his hands tied, he was still a giant of a man who was not whipped. Along the wall was a rack of rifles and shotguns. On the desk, where Kimball had put it, was Grinnel's own six-shooter. Windy stepped forward and untied Grinnel's hands. Softly he said, "I remember you telling me Oregon was a bad state to get caught in, Grinnel." He motioned his head toward the open door.

Grinnel moved with the swiftness of a striking snake. His fist caught Windy a glancing blow on the side of the head, spilling him backwards. His elbow jerked back and jabbed into the unsuspecting Kimball's stomach. His hand scooped up the six-shooter from the desk.

Windy's hand dipped toward his holster as Grinnel fired. But Kimball had recovered enough to lunge his body against the man and spoil his aim. Again Grinnel's gun lined on McCloud. But Windy was ready now. He fired once, and Grinnel stumbled backwards, caught himself against the wall. The man's arms spread out and he slid slowly down the wall. Windy walked out into the bright sunshine of the street.

It was late afternoon when Windy, his wounds bandaged by Violet, came out on the street and saw that there was no longer any doubt in the minds of the citizens of Crawford County. There was a commotion there in front of the Bull's Head and, when he got there, he saw that Funeral was the center of it. Two men held up a fence rail. Two others picked Funeral up and set him astride the rail, tying his feet beneath him.

Windy heard other voices stirring, too. There was a lathered horse in front of the saloon and a young rancher talking excitedly. Someone was remarking, "He says Supervisor McNeil is packed up and leavin' sudden." There was a roar of good-natured laughter. "They'll be others takin' a trip, I reckon!" And then Windy remembered suddenly that Pete Conners, too, had been a part of this machine.

He went back to the jail, for they hadn't moved Larry yet. He went walking straight in, head down, and then he stopped, coughing and spluttering. Larry Manten was better, it seemed. Well enough at least to get his one good arm around Violet's neck and pull her down to where he could kiss her. Windy hadn't realized a man could kiss a woman so long. Finally they came back to earth and they looked up and saw him. Manten's voice was weak and trembly, but maybe it wasn't all from the pain. He said, "I'm glad you came by, Windy. I was just talking to the sheriff. He wants you to stay on as his deputy."

Windy fumbled. "You mean you'll be wanting Pete to stay on as sheriff?"

Manten smiled. "This is a big country, Windy" he said. "Folks admire a man for what's really inside him. If it takes a lot of years for that real good to show up, folks don't hold it against a man, just so they know for sure the good is there."

Windy looked at the kid and then into the shiny eyes of Violet. She got up suddenly, came forward, and kissed Windy on the mouth. Windy stepped back quickly, sniffed and rubbed his nose vigorously with his forefinger, then tugged his hat a little more solidly on his head. He said, "That being the case, I reckon I'll just drift along in the direction I was going. I wouldn't want to spoil Pete's chance for election and I wouldn't want you gettin' jealous of me and Violet."

He got his horse and for the first mile and a half he rode fast, putting distance between himself and the town of Crawford. He hadn't bothered to say good-bye to old Pete Conners, nor had he planned to. Pete was such a soft and sentimental old cuss he might have made a scene.

FAIR EXCHANGE

(1949)

by TOM W. BLACKBURN

Tom W. Blackburn was born on the T. O. Ranch near Raton, New Mexico, where his father was employed as an engineer. The T. O., which controlled such a vast domain it had its own internal railroad system, was later used as the setting for Blackburn's novel, Raton Pass *(Doubleday, 1950). Tom eventually moved with his family to southern California where he attended Glendale Junior College and then UCLA. He first began writing Western stories for pulp magazines in 1938 through syndicates operated by Harry F. Olmsted and Ed Earl Repp, but by 1939, like Thomas Thompson, he was writing in collaboration with James Charles Lynch or under his own name. In the decade between 1939 and 1948 he contributed over 300 stories of varying lengths to such magazines as* Dime Western, Star Western, Lariat Story Magazine, *and* Western Story. *Also during the 1940s he worked as a screenwriter for various Hollywood studios, a circumstance which prepared him to adapt his own Western novels as screenplays, beginning with his first,* Short Grass *(Simon & Schuster, 1947). Blackburn's longest affiliation was with the Disney studio where, for a time, he was best known for having written the lyrics for "The Ballad of Davy Crockett," a popular television and then theatrical series based on the exploits of this legendary frontiersman. In his Western novels, Blackburn tended toward stories based on historical episodes such as* Navajo Canyon *(Doubleday, 1952) or* A Good Day to Die *(McKay, 1967). Perhaps his finest achievement as a novelist is the five-part Stanton saga focused on the building of a great ranch in New Mexico from the Spanish period to the end of the nineteenth century. Tom W. Blackburn's Western fiction is concerned with the struggles, torments, joys, and the rare warmth that comes from companionships of the soul, the very stuff which is as imperishable in its human significance as the "sun-dark skins of the clean blood of the land" which he celebrated and transfixed in shimmering images and unforgettable characters.*

*T*he Apache scouts were singing in their compound. Leaving the corrals, where he had been seeing to the care of horses gaunted by three days of hard riding, Alan Brill moved across Fort Huerfano's dark parade ground toward the dozen Indians crouched close to a small fire. He singled out his interpreter, Joe No Bear. Brill knew considerable Apache, but no white man ever really learned the tongue and he couldn't make out the intricate cadences of this song.

"What's up, *hombre?*" he asked Joe.

"It doesn't make sense," the interpreter said. "Working for us makes them traitors to their own kind, and they're scared. They seem to think there are *Tenneh* somewhere near in the brush tonight."

Apaches and their distant cousins, the Navajos, called themselves the *Tenneh*, the chosen people. Legends of Apache daring were legion on the desert. However, Brill grunted skeptically at Joe No Bear's translation of the chant.

"This close to the post? Hardly. There are more soldiers here tonight than there are *Tenneh* in Arizona. Shut them up, Joe. I'll be back later."

Joe No Bear was a singularly fearless man, but Brill realized the uneasiness of the scouts was in him, also. This was Brill's country. He knew the strange currents which often traveled the desert air. He started back across the parade ground as ten o'clock sentry calls sounded. A quarter moon and a blaze of stars were overhead. The fort was more alive than usual, movement focusing about the band blaring for the semi-monthly ladies' night dance being held in the officers' club.

Brill was tired. With the now-chanting Apache trackers he had returned at sunset from a stiff patrol almost to the edge of Baboquivari Basin. He hadn't yet reported. Although he wanted a bath, a shave and bed, he'd have to come back and talk with the scouts when he'd seen the colonel. Band music grew louder as he approached the club. Under Colonel Strang, every aspect of army life was kept polished at Fort Huerfano.

As he stepped up onto the porch of the club, Jane Strang swept by the open door in the arms of a young lieutenant. A tall, slender girl with glossy black hair and the patrician Strang features. Aloof, proud, harsh in her way as the colonel himself. She had been out here nearly two years, Brill remembered, obviously on her father's hope she'd snare a junior officer and marry herself off his hands. She had apparently been hard to please. She wasn't married yet.

Brill scowled at the party going on within the club. These were good soldiers, every man of them. He was sure of that. But not for the desert. He was a civilian scout, not an army man, and he was glad of it. He didn't want a superior officer's daughter tossed at his head, a cold one like Jane Strang, at that. He didn't want to dance little steps to music when the night winds whispered of danger in the brush. There was a senseless-ness and futility to the whole Apache campaign in this area which chafed him. Too much devotion to the traditional, in field campaigning as well as post life. Given a seasoned regiment, authority to break with tradition and freedom to operate with the same iron relentlessness which characterized the *Tenneh* themselves, Brill was certain a competent officer with some knowledge of the country and of Indians could destroy old Rubio and wind up the campaign in a few months. He thought he could do so himself.

The colonel came out on the porch, followed by his adjutant. He saw Brill and crossed to him, an elegant, austere man with the old army apparent in every line of his figure. His eyes touched Brill's brush-stained gear and the stubble on his cheeks.

"Looking for me, Mister Brill?" he asked stiffly. "Rather informal time to present your report."

"This is an informal war . . . off post limits, sir," Brill retorted. "And a nasty one. I brought in three prisoners from Saddler's Well. One of them is Redondo, old Rubio's son."

"So, the beggar's behind bars! We're going to hang that Apache for Captain Sable's murder, Brill."

"I suppose so. No doubt he killed Sable. He's bragged of it often enough among his own people. I'd like to suggest, sir, that sentries be doubled tonight."

"Are you aware my officers have guests on the post tonight, Mister Brill? Hardly a convenient time for extra duty!"

"My scouts are uneasy. So am I. They have a feeling an Apache raiding party is close by."

"Feeling!" the colonel snorted. "Mister Brill, as a civilian possibly you don't understand this. Wars are fought with facts. You were in the brush. Did you see any sign of a party big enough to be of concern to us here?"

"No, sir. But we have Redondo. His father may try to take him back."

"Exactly! That was my real purpose in ordering his arrest. Old Rubio is the head of all resistance. He cuts us to pieces out in the brush. If we can lure him into our laps. . . . Nevertheless, he won't try tonight. It'll take time for him to raise a big enough party to attack Fort Huerfano. I find your suggestion ill-advised, Mister Brill. I propose you freshen up a bit at your quarters and return for a few dances with my daughter and the other guests here. A soldier's duties are not wholly in the field."

The officer reëntered the club. Brill scowled. This post had been planned by a general in Washington with no knowledge of Indian country. Rubio, sub-chief of the Mescaleros, was too wily to operate against the government with an army of his own. He worked always with few tools, very sharp ones. The mile of brush-choked flat north of the post was an inviting highway to those who knew how to use it. Brill thought of the prisoner in the stone guardhouse — a dark-skinned little man with icy eyes and the tensed body of a desert-gaunted animal. Weeks of trail work, hours of thinking like an Apache and luck had resulted in his capture at Saddler's Well. Now he was to be hanged. Death by the noose, however well earned, was a thing no white man relished. To an Apache such a death was an offense against his wild, fierce gods. Rubio would not wait long for the attempt to free his son.

Jane Strang came alone onto the porch as the music inside changed. She saw Brill and spoke coolly. "I saw you come in tonight with your pack of savages at your heels, Mister Brill. You take this game of play-war very seriously . . . a game with ragged, stupid Indians for enemies and the whole army to back you up against them. I'm surprised you don't enjoy the rest of it as much . . . the dancing, and acting the hero before the ladies."

"This isn't a game and the Apaches are a long ways from being stupid. I've no patience with fools who can't see it!"

"You think I'm interested in your patience?" the girl asked, coloring. "The army tailors a lot of uniforms to fit fools, but even they can be gentlemen. Is it necessary to be uncivil, Mister Brill?"

"Honesty is more important than civility in this country. However, I apologize. The music's starting again. I'm hardly dressed for it, but perhaps I may have this dance as proof I'm forgiven?"

He rose, arms extended. The girl frowned but didn't protest. Brill danced well, but never as well as this. The colonel's daughter was the right height and stride and the music seemed to stir the same impulses in her body as it stirred in his. They danced as one, closer than wholly necessary.

"You're an excellent dancer, Mister Brill," Jane Strang murmured. "How many other accomplishments do you hide under that dirty leather shirt? You live in this country. You must like it. At least, you're not after an upgrade in rank, like the rest here. Sometime I'd like to hear what hold the desert has on you. Now I'd like to know why you really asked me for this dance. Not to apologize. You're not an apologizing kind. Mind telling me?"

Brill was aware of the void of superiority the girl kept between them. Her curiosity was a surface thing. She was giving him the same treatment she had given a dozen subalterns. It nettled him. He grinned. "Not at all, Miss Strang. The colonel's orders."

"I'll report you carried them out perfectly!" she snapped. She started down the steps. Brill would have accompanied her, but she waved him peremptorily back.

He found makings for a cigarette and started upon it. He was half finished when a shout, punctuated by a woman's brief, high-pitched cry of fear, sounded across the parade ground. An army issue rifle snapped near the sentry line, followed by another and then the jolt of a heavy old trade musket. Brill discovered he was running toward the sounds in great strides, his belt gun drawn.

Officers piled from the club behind him. Women screamed. Two soldiers were dead in the doorway of Colonel Strang's bungalow. Another figure writhed in the dust like a broken-backed snake. A sergeant ran up with a lantern. By its light Brill saw the headband, booted moccasins, and breech-clout of an Apache twisting and sweating in the silent death-agony of his kind. Seizing the lantern, Brill dodged around the bungalow, knowing the uselessness of looking inside. That trail began at the corner of the house. The toes of Jane Strang's slippers had dragged in the dust as *Tenneh* warriors hauled her into the brush. He heard others shout the discovery of two more dead sentries, silenced with knives. A thorny saguaro stock held a patch of dimity torn from Jane Strang's dress as she was dragged past it. Beyond were the brush and the night. Brill stopped, halting the others also.

"They'll kill her if we press them too close," he warned. Colonel Strang loped up, gray-faced. He seized Brill's arm. "For God's sake, Brill, what can we do?"

"It was Rubio. Knew he couldn't get Redondo out of the guardhouse. Took a hostage, instead. He'll pull off into the hills and wait for somebody to come out and parley. I'll take Joe No Bear and follow him, but you've got to keep every other man on the post inside bounds till I get back. If Rubio thought a trick was afoot, he'd kill your daughter without batting an eye!"

Brill stared at the towering monolith of gray rock in the near distance. Corpus Christi Peak, beyond which was supposed to be the hiding place of the last of the Mescaleros. Rubio had led Joe No Bear and himself a twisting chase. They were two days out of Fort Huerfano and hadn't come up with the old devil. They had no assurance that when they did Rubio would palaver. They might instead run into a pair of rifle slugs from ambush. Killing army men was an Apache pastime and Rubio would know, if his first emissaries failed, Colonel Strang would send out others in an attempt to secure his daughter's return.

Joe No Bear had halted a little distance ahead, listening. He stiffened abruptly and reached for the rifle under his saddle skirt.

Brill barked a hasty order: "No! Leave the gun alone, Joe!"

The interpreter straightened. An instant later the Apaches appeared. Three of them on a ridge, rifles leveled, materializing as though dropped from the sky. Then Rubio himself was in the center of the trail ahead, the erectness of his figure belying his wrinkled face. A trade musket was cradled in one arm. A greasy strip of calico held lank hair from his eyes. His face was expressionless mahogany. Brill dismounted and cut the distance between them in half.

"*Salmann!*" he said, hand out, palm forward, using the Apache word for friend.

Rubio's answer was in harsh border *parlado*. "I know you, *blanco,* and the Indian son of a dog behind you. The *Tenneh* are not your friends. We talk business. I have the white woman. She is too thin and small of bone to be of use in my camp. I trade with her."

"For Redondo," Brill said. "*Bueno.* He'll be set free with a canteen of water and a good horse when the girl is returned unharmed to the post."

"Rubio is big fool enough to trust the *blanco?* I wait here four days. When you return alone with Redondo, I will come for him. When we are gone, the woman will be sent out to you."

"I will bring Redondo, with a cocked gun at his back. When the girl is as close to me as you are and I see she has not been harmed, I will let Redondo go to you."

Rubio was silent. Alan knew he would accept the terms, since the Apache had no more intention of keeping his end of the bargain than Brill had of keeping his. The one hope was that Rubio might believe Brill would return immediately to the post, that his mind would be fixed on killing both Brill and the girl the moment his son was safe.

" 'Sta bueno," the old man agreed. "Ride fast to the fort, now. Try a trick and you die. My people are as thick here as the rocks on the hills."

Brill nodded, grimly amused. There had been the tracks of six in Rubio's party — five of them Indians. It was a safe bet there wasn't another Apache closer than the western slope of Corpus Christi. Rubio moved, vanishing as suddenly and swiftly as he had appeared. The riflemen above vanished also. Brill returned to his horse and re-mounted. With his companion he rode back the way he had come.

From ocotillo shelter Brill studied the canyon floor. Four Indians crouched close to a tiny fire. The girl was sitting apart, her ball dress a stained, tattered ruin. Brill worried about the absence of the fifth Apache. Joe No Bear was worried, too. He had found this camp. They had ridden a dozen miles in the direction of Fort Huerfano, then cut a gradual circle to gain the rim of the canyon in which they had met Rubio in the afternoon. Rubio apparently believed the two of them had gone on to the fort, but Apache caution must have made him station a sentry. There was no other way to account for the missing Indian. With a sentry out, the others could relax and even enjoy a fire. Brush whispered beside Brill. Joe No Bear appeared. "No sign, *jefe,*" he muttered. "This I don't like. We wait for the missing man?"

"No. He may have been sent out to trail us this afternoon. If so, he's apt to show up any time and warn the others we're here."

"I think he's close," the interpreter said stubbornly. "If we ride into this canyon without knowing where he is, it may be to die!"

"If we don't, Miss Strang dies. We'll go together, both heading for the girl. One or the other of us will get through, maybe both. Whoever gets to her first will take her up on his horse and head downcanyon. The other will cover retreat if he can. ¿Sabe, amigo?"

Joe No Bear nodded reluctantly. They remounted. The canyon wall wasn't the kind of descent even a martinet of an officer would assign for training cavalry troops, but a horse could go down it. Rocks clattered ahead of Brill. The Apaches at the fire leaped to their feet. Brill flung one shot among them. Jane Strang sprang up and began to run unsteadily down the canyon. Brill changed his course to intercept her. He bent low and hooked her under her arms. Guns flared. Across the canyon the sentry Joe No Bear had feared opened fire with a rifle.

The girl came up in a flurry of skirts, petticoats, and kicking legs. Bending forward, Brill shielded her body with his own the best he could. The horse under them seemed to understand the urgency of the moment and reached out with tremendous strides in spite of its double load. Half a mile down the canyon, Brill looked back. There was no sign of Joe No Bear. There had been no outcry. The man had likely been shot from his saddle, dying swiftly. Brill hoped so. There were many ways a man could die in an Apache camp. For a brief instant Brill was bitter. The woman in the saddle with him was a poor exchange for the Indian interpreter. Then his mind leaped forward to the ride which lay ahead. It was one thing to be clear of Rubio's camp and another to reach Fort Huerfano before they were overtaken. First they would have to cover as many miles as possible before their horse gave out. Afterward there would be grimmer work.

Jane Strang slept on the sand while Brill unbridled and unsaddled their exhausted horse, turning the animal loose. He knew it would regain its wind and find water and forage in the hills behind them. An Apache would likely catch it up later but he had a saddleman's aversion to trading the life of a horse even for his own. He hunkered down beside the girl, knowing she had slept all the time they could afford, and gripped her shoulder. She sat up. "All right?" he asked. "They didn't hurt you?"

"The Indians? No. But their eyes. . . . For the first time I know what Apaches are really like! You were right, at the post: they're terrible enemies. I know now this isn't a game, Mister Brill. Are they after us?"

"Probably starting now. They don't like night travel. We've built a lead. If we can hold it, we'll make the fort."

"We'll make it!" the girl said.

"In that outfit you're wearing?" Brill asked. "You've got a bolt of dress material stitched onto you. Every ounce of skirt and petticoat will drag on you like it was weighted with lead before we've gone half the way. Shed as much of it as you can, now."

The girl's face lost color. Her neck stiffened angrily. "Aren't you choosing a poor time to take advantage. . . ?"

"Advantage!" Brill interrupted explosively. "In this country a man thinks of something besides women, once in a while. You little fool, I'm trying to save your life!"

Picking up the canteen he had salvaged from the saddle, he started across the sand. Hell lay ahead of them. Jane Strang could dress for it as she damned pleased. He admired modesty and a touch of coquetry in any woman, but like most things it had a place. It didn't belong here. The girl lagged so long she was forced to run to catch up with him. Brill didn't look at her till a half hour had passed and he paused for one of the brief rests he intended to call twice an hour. The sun was high and heating the air and the *malpais* underfoot. He peeled his jacket and tossed it aside. When night came, he'd be cold; but to be rid of the weight during the day was more important. This would be a close thing, at best.

He sat on the sand. The girl sat near him. She had taken his advice. She wore now only her overblouse on the upper portion of her body, retaining its long sleeves for protection against the sun and discarding whatever had been beneath it. She had also removed voluminous petticoats and the generously cut skirt which had swayed so gracefully when he'd danced with her at the post. What remained was a simple pant-legged undergarment reaching a span above her knees and looking curiously like the short hot-weather pants some of the sportier officers wore off-duty.

She kept her face averted but he could see truculence in the set of her features. He was amused. A woman was the vainest creature on the face of the earth, yet each habitually wrapped herself in sufficient swaddling to conceal what she actually was. When circumstance or necessity forced a partial disrobing, she was angry. It made little sense. In this gear, this girl was something. Had this happened months ago Colonel Strang would not have had to order his scout to dance with his daughter. And her superior air was evaporating. It was hard for her to maintain it when she must certainly know her life depended wholly on his skills and his knowledge of the country.

He inventoried his own possessions. He had buried his rifle when he abandoned his horse. He had his belt gun and his knife. And the canteen. Needs were not complex on the desert.

"You'll burn where you're uncovered," he told the girl. "Watch that. And give me those slippers. They're light. I'll fix them so they'll do better on this footing."

She tossed the dancing slippers to him. They were well made, with a thin sole of good leather. He pried the heels from them with his balanced, double-edged *cuchilla*.

"They'll do for moccasins, now. If they get sand in them, empty them. Your feet are soft. You'll have to take care of them. They've got to carry you a long ways."

The girl looked at him as she pulled the slippers on. "You're satisfied with my . . . my dress?"

With this invitation, Brill studied her carefully from head to foot. He made it deliberate and slow. Finally he nodded. "Completely," he agreed with a grin. She flushed, rising as he stood up and shouldered the canteen. They started forward again.

They moved through barren hills while the sun worked higher, a ball of molten brass. Thirst rose in Brill. He assuaged it by giving the girl a little of the water in the canteen; her relief made him feel better. Time was as motionless as the sun. The monotony of the desert closed in on them so that they walked a treadmill without apparent gain. Brill grew astounded at the girl beside him. Her slippers, even without heels, were not good for this kind of going. She had to empty them often. Her strength must be fraying down with each passing mile. But she didn't lag, and she didn't walk with her head down. She looked at the country and the endlessly changing skyline. Once or twice she paused, obviously not to rest but to stare for a moment at one or two of the more impressive vistas. She must understand the desperation with which they traveled, but there was no fear apparent in her.

Brill thought once that she was actually relishing the savagery of their position, the challenge of it. He realized this was more likely a reflection of his own feeling. This was what the desert did to a man. It gave him challenges to absorb every ounce of energy and every skill he possessed. This was its fascination. This and the beauty and the clean emptiness. Because this girl was alone with him here, he was crediting her with the same feeling. He wondered why. A man might do that with a woman he wanted — an attempt to share his own way of living with her. But he knew it would be fruitless to want the colonel's daughter. She was all tradition and legend and pride. Unreal things which meant nothing on the desert. He wanted flesh and blood and simplicity in a woman — a challenge offered which would match the challenge of the country and his own spirit. He decided he was thinking too much of the girl in the heat and he put her from his mind.

At sundown Brill was worried. There was no pursuit. In spite of his best efforts and the girl's doggedness they had not made the kind of time necessary to keep ahead of Rubio and his desert wolves. The unpredictable was an Apache specialty. He held on through the twilight, resting more often but never stopping.

Toward morning they halted to sleep briefly. In spite of the fact that Brill had reserved all of the water in the canteen for her, he saw that the girl's lips and tongue were beginning to swell with dryness and thirst. She didn't, the second morning, study the country as she had the first, but neither did she complain. She grew more unsteady and fell often, but kept moving ahead. There was sand in her. Toward mid-morning Brill pointed out a distant line of hills.

"The ridge beyond the post," he told her. She made no answer. He thought talk would pass time, keep her preoccupied and therefore longer on her feet. He talked freely, talked of things he had never mentioned on the post. Talked of the time when Rubio was gone and the Apaches had no leader able to hold them together, marking the end of the long campaign and the coming of peace.

At noon, mirage-like, the quadrangle of Fort Huerfano hung against the horizon ahead. And with the post in sight Brill had to think of the last problem to be faced on this trek. He remembered Jane Strang's pride, her stiffness, and the gulf of superiority she had tried to maintain between them. He started looking for a place where he could leave her while he sneaked onto the fort to get clothing for her, so that she could make another kind of entry. He knew that if she arrived with him in her present dress and condition, neither the girl nor her father would be able to withstand the impact of the gossip which was a part of normal post life. The army could be merciless on its own kind. However, the girl forced his hand. On a sandy level stretch, she collapsed suddenly between one stride and the next, apparently in a dead faint of exhaustion. He had been careful not to overtax her the last few miles and he was startled by her collapse now. However, she had done better by far than he had expected in the beginning and the important thing now was to get her to the fort dispensary as fast as possible. The hell with reputations and pride and post gossip. Bending, he swung her up in his arms.

Sometime later he looked up from the girl, cradled in his arms and still apparently unconscious, to see a man blocking the trail he was staggering along. A stocky man with a wrinkled mass of emotionless mahogany for a face. In this instant, then, he realized why there had been no pursuit behind them. This was Apache pride, as towering in its way as that of the old army. One man had stolen a prisoner from Rubio's camp. Rubio had come after prisoner and thief alone. And with desert wiliness he had not attempted to trail them but had headed straight for the fort.

Rubio's musket came to his shoulder. The Apache was reputedly a good shot with it. Brill knew Rubio intended to kill both himself and the girl here, to be found by some party from the post. He spilled Jane Strang roughly to the ground, where she would be unlikely to draw the first shot, and took one stride past her before Rubio's musket belched smoke and its heavy ball plowed into Brill's body. It flung him down hard on his side, sick with shock, without wind, and clinging to a shred of conscious-ness. A shoulder wound, high on the left, he thought. He thought also that the girl who had seemed still unconscious had bounded to life like a cat at the sound of

Rubio's gun. He thought she had clawed his own dragoon pistol from his belt and was firing it two-handedly. The gun emptied. Jane Strang continued to pump the already fired chambers of the cylinder past under the clicking hammer. Rubio had not reloaded his trade gun. He carried the bone handle of a knife in his hand. It would do for a woman. Brill stared at the knife. His own right hand moved stealthily to his belt. Ignoring Brill, obviously thinking him done, Rubio reached for the girl. Brill sat up, ignoring the effort and the pain. Both lasted only a moment — only long enough for a swift overhand cast with his right arm. The knife turned over slowly, seeming to travel so lazily any man could have dodged it, but its velocity was so great that it buried itself to the hilt in Rubio's throat. The *jefe* of the Mescaleros fell. A long hard campaign ended as easily as this.

"Alan, Alan . . . are you all right?" Jane Strang demanded, kneeling beside him with her sun-reddened face pressed close to his and her scratched arms about him.

"Hit in the shoulder," he growled. "Surgeon'll have to dig out the ball, but it won't be deep. Apaches always skimp on powder. I'll be steady in a minute. Then I'll go in and send your father out with some clothes for you. You can't go in the way you are."

"I thought you'd feel that way," the girl said, frowning. "The devil with the post! This is the one time in my life I can speak frankly. I want a man. I always have and never could find the right one in uniform. I want to be out in this country . . . but on your ranch. That's why I pretended to faint, so you would have to carry me in. I thought we were closer or I'd have waited a bit. I must be heavy to carry. We'll both go in, now. When my father sees me like this, he'll demand you marry me. And . . . he's still your superior."

With thickened tongue and cracked lips and reddened eyes — with the skin burned from her face and white flesh torn and scabrously scarred, this was still a beautiful woman. The primitiveness and the heat and the limitlessness of the desert were in her and she would demand all of a man, as the desert did.

"Always try to obey orders," Brill said.

TWO QUEENS FOR SKIDWAY EMPIRE

(1950)

☆

by DAN CUSHMAN

Dan Cushman was born in Osceola, Michigan, and grew up on the Cree Indian reservation in Montana. In the early 1940s his novelette-length stories began appearing regularly in such Fiction House magazines as North-West Romances *and* Frontier Stories. *Later in the decade his North-Western and Western stories as well as fiction set in the Far East and Africa appeared in* Action Stories, Adventure, *and* Short Stories. *A collection of some of his best North-Western and Western fiction was recently published in* Voyageurs of the Midnight Sun *(Capra Press, 1995) with a Foreword by John Jakes who cites Cushman as a major influence in his own work. The character Comanche John, a Montana road agent featured in numerous rollicking magazine adventures, also appears in Cushman's first novel,* Montana, Here I Be *(Macmillan, 1950) and in two later novels. Some of these early stories are now collected in* The Adventures of Comanche John *(Circle Ⓥ Westerns, 1996).* Stay Away, Joe *(Viking, 1953) is an amusing novel about the mixture, and occasional collision, of Indian culture and Anglo-American culture among the Métis (French Indians) living on a reservation in Montana. This novel became a bestseller and remains a classic to this day, greatly loved especially by Indian peoples for its truthfulness and humor. Cushman also produced significant historical fiction in* The Silver Mountain *(Appleton Century Crofts, 1957), concerned with the mining and politics of silver in the 1890s. His most recent book is the North-Western,* In Alaska With Shipwreck Kelly *(Five Star Westerns, 1996).*

☆ I ☆

SAMARITAN IN SILK

Buzz Leary stopped for a few seconds, blocking the steps of the beat-up passenger coach, and from that vantage point had a look at Red Bank. It wasn't much like the Red Bank he remembered from five years ago. Then it had been a settlement; now it was a booming railroad construction camp rising false-fronted and tent-roofed from quagmire streets. Only the hills were the same, the limitless hill and forest country of British Columbia, great-chested, rising toward the distant, ice-blocked summits of the High Caribou.

Leary took a deep breath. The air was sharp and forest-scented. It struck his body like alcohol, took the sluggishness from it, placed a tingle in his muscles. Men behind him, trying to get off, were packed tight. They were shouting at him. The huge Swedish construction worker at his back finally lost patience, and bellowing "Har, noo!" charged shoulder first with weight and a momentum that sent Leary staggering. He stayed up for two steps, then sprawled across the rough-plank depot platform.

Leary rolled to his feet, leaving his warbag where he'd dropped it. He was taller than the Swede, a rangy hundred and seventy, but the Swede outweighed him by thirty pounds. Leary was poised with his fists ready, but the Swede tossed up both hands.

"Yumpin yimminy, Ay can't fight wit'out chew snooce."

Buzz Leary laughed and said, "To hell with you. You'll get no snooce from me. It'll ruin your health. But I'll buy you a shot of moose milk."

The Swede linked his arm and they crossed the jam-packed depot station platform with smaller men getting out of their way. A moment later they were over the high heels of their logger boots in muck.

For a while, Leary had forgotten about the Neil boys, but there, with the main street in front of him, he looked for them. It occurred to him that he should have taken his .38 Colt double-action out of the warbag and placed it in some friendlier spot. Inside his mackinaw, for instance. Just in case the Neil boys took a timber-wolf view of his return. Then he said, "To hell with 'em!"

"Yah," the big Swede said, without knowing what he was talking about. "To hell wit' 'em. You show me a Norwegian and Ay skol a cemetery."

They walked into the first saloon they came to. Leary had two drinks while the Swede was having four. The saloon was a little keg-and-tincup affair with frame sides and a canvas roof. A stove flamed hot from a load of pitch-knots, and heat, combined with whiskey on an empty stomach, made him lose the keen edge of his faculties. He'd need them if he ran into the Neils.

He tossed his warbag to his shoulder and left the Swede doing a noisy schottisch on his hobnails, and singing:

> *My name it bane Swanson*
> *Ay come from Wisconsin*
> *To work in the timber land*
> *Bane ride to Shee-boygin*
> *On Yim Hill's red wagon*
> *Wit' axe handle in my hand.*

Outside, following the corduroy sidewalks, Leary could still hear him as he stamped his hobs and bellowed the chorus of the timberjack song:

> *Ay wear a red collar,*
> *Ay drink saxteen dollar,*
> *Wit' axe handle in my hand.*

A big, ramshackle building that had been the general warehouse and office of the Red Bank Lumber Company now bore a sign reading ROCKY MOUNTAIN HOTEL. Leary walked toward it. With the warbag on his shoulders, he looked taller than his six-feet-one. It broadened the apparent width of his shoulders. His was a build one often saw among the timber stiffs of the Pacific slope. His face as well as his body showed strength. He might even have been handsome in an untamed way if it hadn't been for a nose, twice broken and badly knit, and for a right cheek that was puckered from a series of parallel hobnail scars.

The lobby was dim. Leary paused. There was a bleary old man behind the desk; near the window sat a girl almost hidden by an Edmonton newspaper. She wore a tight whipcord dress, and her posture, with one knee over the other, her slim body bent aside to catch the light, made him want to see the rest of her. Just then she dropped the paper and looked at him over it. He could see her eyes. They were dark and lovely. Then the paper hid them, and he walked on to the desk saying, "I need a room."

The clerk waggled his gray head and said, "You timber stiffs better have your own balloon and nosebag when you hit these railroad camps. What rooms we got are for the boiled collar boys. We ain't even got a stray bed. Have to roll your soogins in the bullpen. Two dollars."

Leary tossed his warbag behind the counter, with the .38, too close to the side making a heavy thud. He watched the clerk, but the old man didn't seem to notice.

"How can you get downriver to Skidway?" Leary asked.

"Railroad barge. Tell 'em you're a shovel-punk and you can ride free." He was more friendly after getting Leary's two dollars. "You looking for a job in the woods? Come around next year. Things will be poppin' in this country once the railroad goes through."

"The Neil boys still up there?"

He heard a rattle of newspaper and knew that the girl had again lowered it to look at him. He turned and saw her face. It was everything he'd imagined. Pretty enough to knock a man back on his heels. To hell with the Neil boys, he thought, I wonder who she is. He might have gone over, but she ducked behind the newspaper again.

The clerk was saying, "Sure, Oren and Bill Neil are still up there. Biggest outfit in the country now that the Learys went ka-flop and old man Dardis got killed. Young Mary Dardis, she's still milling, but she's down to one saw. Come to think of it, the Neil boys aren't up there exactly, either. They're right here in Red Bank. Came in yesterday. Staying right here at the hotel."

Leary, signing the register, had already seen their names.

He wrote his own name and, the clerk reading it, said, "Leary! Say, *you* ain't one o' the Skidway Learys are you? No relation to old Logger Leary that used to be the big *tyee* up there?"

"My dad."

The clerk whistled. He drew himself up and said, "In *that* case maybe we do have a room for you, after all. That'll be five dollars more."

"One seat in a crum show's as good as another. For five bucks I'll camp in the bullpen."

He wanted another look at the girl, but he didn't want to seem too anxious. Casually, with a swing of his long body, he turned, but she was gone. He barely glimpsed her leaving the front door. Outside, he had another brief view of her turning down a side street toward the railroad sheds.

He shrugged and dismissed her from his mind. He had a bath and a shave at a barber shop and, with the early darkness of northern November settling, found a stool in a steamy, crowded Chinese cafe. He'd just ordered a caribou steak when he realized that a man had come from somewhere and was standing behind him. He was a big man, very broad, with legs like a stud horse. Hatred went through Leary in a raw shock. The years had made him forget how he felt toward the man — Oren Neil.

Neil had run his father out of business. He'd done it cleverly, by maneuvering Leary and the Dardis Company into a timber war. Buzz knew that now. He knew it, but the Neil boys didn't *know* that he knew it. Buzz had lifted the cup of coffee just placed in front of him. In the steamy, backbar mirror he saw Oren Neil's face. A smile turned the corners of Neil's mouth. He knew Buzz was watching him.

"Hello, Buzz," he said in a silky voice that was unexpected from a man of his rugged appearance. "So you came back to look up your old friends!"

Leary went hot and cold. A clammy perspiration sprang out along his hairline. He was thinking: "Here is the man who killed Steve Dardis, trampled him to death under his hobnailed boots." It had been like this — Dardis had agreed to a night meeting with a Leary representative with a view to stopping the trouble that was bankrupting them. But in the morning, Dardis was found beaten to death, and the Leary representative had fled the country. Everyone blamed the Learys. The Learys even blamed themselves. "I should never have sent Hobs Donahue to talk with him," old Logger had said. But now Buzz knew the truth. Fighting to control his voice, he revolved on the stool and said, "Hello, Oren."

They shook hands. Neil asked pleasantly, "Still in the lumber business?"

He had a good look at Neil, now. Five years hadn't changed him except to enlarge his jowls, but he wasn't fat. He was big and predatory and, if one was to believe a large number of women, he was handsome. His frame was no larger than Leary's. He might have been an inch shorter, but he had a greater depth of muscle. Oren Neil used to brag that he'd never hired a timberjack he couldn't lick, and Leary knew it was true.

"Sure I'm in the lumber business," Leary said. "High rigger. Been working around Bella Colla."

"Heard you were on the Klondike."

"I was on Copper River."

"Back for good?"

"I'll be seeing how things look."

Oren Neil smiled, his narrow eyes showing he knew what was on Leary's mind. "The railroad changes things, doesn't it? It might even make that Caribou white pine of yours worth a piece of change. I dare say you could lumber it at a profit, now." He scratched his jaw as though the idea had just occurred to him. "Yes, but it'd take capital. Twenty or thirty thousand dollars by the time you got your dad's old mill in shape."

There was no friendliness in Leary's voice when he said, "That's the thing of ours you wanted most and the thing you didn't get . . . the white pine."

"What are you talking about? It wasn't *us* that put your dad out of business, it was Dardis. If you came back here with a chip on your shoulder. . . ."

"Don't play me for a fool, Oren. When those cheap lawyers were trying to buy that Caribou stand from me, I knew who was behind them."

Neil decided to laugh. "All right. So it was. How'd you find out?"

The truth was, Leary had thrust a lawyer three-fourths of the way from his sixth-story window in a Vancouver office building, threatening to drop him unless he got the truth. "I used persuasion."

"*I'll* use persuasion. Hold on, don't lose your temper. You're not a kid any longer.

I think we'll get that Caribou pine when you find out you can make more by selling it to us than you can by trying to lumber it yourself?"

"At six hundred a section?"

Neil laughed and said, "Oh, hell! Is that what he offered you? I don't wonder you used persuasion. You should have knocked his teeth down his throat. But this is no place to talk. Come back to the booth."

There were two small, private rooms in the rear. In one of them was Oren's brother, Bill Neil, his elbows on the table, waiting. Bill was shorter than Oren, but heavier. His shoulders were massive, giving him a sloped, gorilla appearance. He was unshaved. Tobacco stained the corners of his mouth and gave his black whiskers a rusty glint. He was dressed like a timberjack in a gray wool shirt, hobbed boots, a pair of tin pants so smeared with pitch and dirt they could have stood in the corner by themselves.

Bill grinned, leaned over to spit, and said, "Well, Buzz, so you're back in the old bush. And just when we was bragging about being shut of the Learys."

The greeting was one he'd have accepted cheerfully from even a casual acquaintance, but from Neil it was different. He felt anger burn through him and had a struggle to control himself. He said, "Us Learys keep coming back for more."

Bill stopped chawing and looked at him with narrowed little eyes. The kerosene lamp on its chain overhead brought out the brutal qualities of his face. Bill liked to effect a clumsy good nature, but the difference between the brothers was only superficial. At the bottom one was just as merciless as the other.

Bill said, "That's the idea! Keep coming back for more. Don't be a quitter. Trouble is, if you look around, you'll notice this country is near run out of Learys."

Oren hooked a chair with his boot toe and said, "That Gateway timber war burned itself out five years ago. Let's leave it that way. Here, kid, rest your hocks."

Leary pulled the chair around so the door was somewhat at his back, and sat down.

Oren said to Bill. "Leary and I have been talking about that Caribou pine. By the way, you know what that cheap lawyer offered him? . . . six hundred a section!" He laughed and struck the table with his hand. "I told him to buy as cheap as he could, *but six hundred!* I don't blame you for getting rough with him. What price do you have on it anyhow?"

"I don't think I want to sell."

Oren had been putting on a good act, but it froze now. Anger started to show in the thickening of his neck muscles, the rise of a vein at his temple. He'd been notorious for his temper, but now he was trying to keep hold of it.

"I'm sorry, Buzz. I thought you'd grown up. Got over being a hot-headed kid. Thought you were here on business. I have a legitimate proposition. A *business* proposition. I'll pay you two thousand a section for that timber, and assume all unpaid liens and taxes. I'll grant that with the railroad going through you'd be able to timber it off yourself. If you were lucky, you'd make that much. But what's the use? I'm offering it to you without risk, all in the clear."

It was a good proposition. Leary knew that. He'd rather it hadn't been so he'd have better reason for throwing it back in Neil's face.

"No, I don't think I'll sell to you." He didn't emphasize the you, but that's the way Neil took it.

"You mean you won't sell to the Neils?"

"That's right. I won't sell to the Neils."

Bill said, "What you got against us? We always tried to keep the peace in that Gateway country. It was your dad and Steve Dardis. They put themselves on the rocks."

"That's what I always thought." Leary felt the tightness that had settled. It was like the steel string of some instrument drawn tighter and tighter until it vibrates at the breaking point. The clatter of dishes seemed very loud out in the restaurant.

Bill said, "Now you're mad because Oren and me saved our money and bought in on Skidway after your dad went ka-flop. You. . . ."

Oren said, "Keep still and let him say what he started to. Go ahead. What makes you think they didn't put themselves on the rocks?"

He hadn't intended to tell about meeting Hobs Donahue, but now all he wanted was to throw the truth in Oren Neil's face. He said, "My dad sent Hobs to make peace with Dardis. He shouldn't have sent him alone. He should have known somebody might be waiting for him on the trail."

Oren Neil was pale around the mouth while his neck was gorged with blood. If Buzz had any doubt that Hobs Donahue had been telling the truth, that doubt was gone now. Usually Oren was the dominant one of the two, but at that moment it was Bill who could laugh and dribble tobacco juice at the floor.

"Now who'd be waiting for Hobs?" Bill asked. "You're letting your suspicions run away with you, putting one and one together and coming up with a double-dozen. Use your head, Buzz. You know as well as anybody that Hobs hated Steve Dardis's guts."

"I should have told you in the first place. I ran Hobs down in the city. The two of you and Claggett killed Dardis."

Oren Neil was half way out of his chair, his legs bent, hands poised. He seemed ready to spring. He spoke through tense lips: "You believe what you want to. I ran your drunken father out of business, I'll own up to that. I hope you turn my offer down. I hope you try to log the Caribou yourself. I hope so, because I'll run you out of the country, too."

Leary stood half turned away. He looked casual and limber-armed compared with Oren Neil. Then he moved and swung a savage right hand to the point of Neil's jaw. It smashed Neil back. He half fell over the chair. His shoulders struck the wall so hard one of the panels ripped loose. He bounced back, grabbed the table with his left hand and upset it, trying to pin Leary against the wall.

Leary had the door back of him. He kicked it open and stopped just outside, knowing that now both men couldn't come for him at once. Bill Neil was struggling over the table. Oren shoved him aside and was through the door. He came with a bull charge, his hands flung far ahead. Leary retreated another step, set his feet, and brought up a one-two left and right. Neil caught part of their power with his arms. They didn't break his momentum. He was heavier than Leary and, in the crowded quarters between the wall and the row of stools in front of the counter, it was his advantage. He carried Leary before him as men bellowed and climbed out of the way.

Leary hit the wall with his right hip. He did it deliberately as sometimes he'd used the boards in a hockey rink. It made him pivot sharply, roll with the charge. It placed him with his back to the wall and Oren Neil close in front of him. He planted his right foot on the wall, feinted high with a left, and brought up a right that snapped Neil's head to one side and dropped him to the floor. He lit in a sitting position, between two of the stools, his shoulders against the counter. For just a second his eyes lacked focus. He lunged to his feet. The force of his doing it rocked the entire length of counter and sent a crash of dishes to the floor. Buzz was on him, slugging with both hands, and Neil, still a little groggy, fought him off, retreating through the door to the corduroy log walk outside.

Neil rolled with a left and came back with a barrage that made Leary give ground. The logs gave an uncertain footing. Something struck him on the back of the leg. He tried to step over it. It tripped him. As he fell, he saw Bill Neil crouched low to the walk with one leg thrust out. Leary tried to twist over and save himself, but Oren Neil saw his chance and was atop him with the speed and ferocity of a great cat. He swung a heavy, hobnailed boot, and it struck like an explosion inside Leary's brain.

He was down. Fragments of consciousness were like voices screaming in his ear, telling him to crawl away, to keep his arms wrapped around his head, but the boots struck again and again as he felt the diminishing shock of them.

He came to by slow degrees. It seemed like hours. There were voices, a man and a woman. Finally he realized that they had him on his feet, and were walking him somewhere. He felt slush underfoot. He was going across a street. He was aware of lights then, and his head commenced paining with repeated stabs, as though a knife was working back and forth, cutting his brain in half. He was thirsty. He tried to say something. His lips seemed thick. All his teeth ached. Neil had really given him the hobs. The crowd looking on had probably saved his life. Otherwise he'd have got it the same way Steve Dardis had.

A girl had hold of one of his arms. He turned and looked at her. Through puffed eyes he could tell she was small, and dark haired, with a lovely, thin face. Even smashed up as he was it seemed strange to him that such a girl would be here, beside him, wading the muck of this tough construction town.

A big Finlander had hold of his other arm. "You got room in ho-tal, kid?"

Leary grinned and managed to say, "Sure, up in the bullpen."

"I have a room," the girl said.

Men sat beneath the hanging lamps in the tiny lobby, staring at them as they walked through, and down a hall to a door with a brass number *8* nailed on it. She opened it with a skeleton key and said to the Finlander, "I'll take care of him now."

He backed away, fumbling with his cap, and she closed the door. It was dark for a moment inside the room, and Leary heard her moving around. Then she struck a match, lit the lamp, adjusted the wick. The underlighting did something to her face. It gave her skin a tawny appearance, brought out the softness of her throat, accentuated her thin nostrils, the delicate, wedge-like shape of her face. Her eyes were dark, but the hair he first took to be black had a rich coppery sheen with the lamplight striking close against it. She turned, and he was aware of the full lines of her body. She smiled at him, and took off her jacket.

"You'd better sit down," she said.

Her voice sounded different, now. Soft and rather husky. He sank down in a straight-backed chair, still looking at the woman. She wore a dress of some soft, woolly material. Wine red. It wasn't tight, it was just cut to fit, and the material hung to the curves of her young body. She was fragile and feminine. It was the way a woman ought to look. A woman who is not ashamed of being a woman. The dress had broad straps over the shoulders, and beneath it she had on a blouse of white silk, open at the throat.

She found a towel, dipped it in the water pitcher, and squeezed it out. "You're cut awfully. Maybe I should get a doctor."

"You'll do." He tried to grin.

She came around behind him and started rubbing the towel gently over his face. Seated, he was almost as tall as she was. He was aware of her closeness, of the subtle perfume she wore. He looked around the room. Her suitcase was open on the floor. She'd hung a couple of dresses on wire hangers behind a rusty-looking curtain that served as a closet. The bed had been slept in. There were no sheets on it. Gray, cotton, blankets, still bearing the impression of her body. She hadn't disturbed much more of the bed than a kitten. It occurred to him that she must have slept through the day and just got up.

"Does it hurt?" she asked.

He moved like a man waking up and said, "Just a little."

"What were you fighting about?"

The battle seemed far away, a nightmare scene, another world.

"We're old . . . friends. Did you see it?"

"Yes!" She whispered the word so intensely that he turned to look at her. Her eyes were bright, and she was biting down hard on her underlip. "Yes, I saw it. It frightened me, but I couldn't stop looking. Even when you were down and he was stamping on you . . . I thought he was killing you, but still I had to watch. Every second of it."

"Ever see men fight before?"

She shook her head.

"You'll see it every night in this town. What are you doing here, anyway?"

"Why should you ask?" There was defiance and bitterness in her voice. "Isn't it enough that I get a man to help me drag you in off the street and. . . ."

"Yes, that's enough. It just didn't seem to me you ought to be here. In a town like Red Bank."

She whispered, "I'm a dance-hall girl. Didn't you notice? I'm wearing a red dress."

"You're not a dance-hall girl!" he said with sudden violence.

She stopped rubbing him with the towel. It was bloody from his face and scalp. She dipped it in the pitcher and squeezed it out, her eyes on the pinkish water that boiled around her white and slender fingers.

"You're just a boy, really."

"I'm not a boy, and you're not a dance-hall girl."

She spoke in a voice that sounded a trifle tired. "I came here to sing in a music hall. I guess there's a difference." She was before him again, bathing his face. Her hands were warm and soft. She said, "You didn't want me to be a dance-hall girl."

"No." He reached for her.

She stopped and let her elbows press down hard across his neck, against his chest. He felt her body against him for a few seconds, and she whispered, "I'm glad."

He got out of the chair. In doing it, his knees turned and almost failed him after serving him through all the battle.

She backed away and shook her head. "Please. I shouldn't have done that. It's just that you're such a nice fellow. Don't get any ideas. Sit down and let me finish cleaning you up."

He took the towel from her and rubbed hard to get the rest of the blood off his face. Then he looked at himself in the rusty mirror. Oren Neil's hobs had cut deep furrows in both cheeks that were still oozing blood. Both his eyes were blackened; his lips were puffed; his face was swollen on one side more than the other. He felt better now, however. Only a slight headache.

He fished tobacco and papers from his shirt pocket and, while rolling one, said, "I'll live. I'll live and give Oren and Bill both another chance at me. I hope the hell it'll be one at a time, though."

She opened a gold mesh bag and took out a packet of cigarettes. "Have one of these." And she added, "I always carry them for my father."

"Where is he?"

She laughed and said, "Last I heard of him, he was dealing faro down in the States." She puffed a cigarette to light over the lamp, put it between his mashed lips, and lighted one for herself. "You don't mind seeing me smoke? After all, this is 1908. The era of women's rights." Her lapel watch was ticking on the dresser. The hands stood at eight o'clock. "I haven't eaten since yesterday."

"Why, girl. . . ."

"Last night at Trout Creek. I came in on the train this afternoon."

He looked at her sharply. He'd been through both passenger cars. They'd been filled with construction workers recruited in towns eastward along the line. Two women, but neither had been she.

Her eyes narrowed, and for an instant she reminded him of a cornered animal, then she smiled, showing the tips of her teeth and said, "You look like you doubted me."

"I came in on it, is all. I didn't notice you."

"But I was there. No, I'm not escaping from the law. But let's not talk about it. You'd hate me if you knew the truth. That's why I wouldn't let you put your arms around me a minute ago. I'm not good enough for a kid like you."

Kid! It sounded funny. She wasn't as old as he was. He started to say so, and she cut him off.

"I'm hungry. Have you forgotten?"

"There's that Chink dump. . . ."

"No. Not there. The variety theater. There's some private booths upstairs. The owner, Klondike Williams, I know him well."

☆ II ☆

HONKYTONK ROAD TO HELL

Klondike Williams was a quick-moving man of fifty with a cockney accent. He spoke to the girl, calling her "Etty," and gave Buzz Leary a sharp, rat-like glance.

"Sing tonight?" Klondike asked.

"No, we're just hungry." She tucked her hand under Leary's arm while Klondike grinned, showing a row of gold-tipped teeth. "How about one of the cubbyholes upstairs?"

"Ow, listen to 'er! Class, w'at?" He shook his head. "Not a chance. We got the gold-plated bunch in 'em tonight, we 'ave for a certainty. Maxwell Phare, travelin' super no less for Dominion Limited. And in the other, Mister Oren Neil *and* a lady friend."

The words, Leary decided, were aimed at him and he made a start as though to grab the man, but Etty got in front of him."

She said to Klondike, "How much you got tied up in those gold choppers?"

"Too much to want 'em knocked out, m' sweet. Now that's a fact. For you and the gentleman . . . a box with a view of the stage. Best in the 'ouse." He gave Leary another sharp look. "It's cash, ain't it?"

"It's cash."

The box was a tiny cubicle with a table and two slim, gilded chairs. A decorated screen covered the front of it, hiding them, but allowing a view of the stage and the floor below. The show hadn't started, but there was music from a violin, clarinet and harp. In a few minutes a Chinese boy entered in soft-slippered silence and placed on the table a bottle of champagne and a large bowl of iced oysters on the half shell.

"I didn't know we'd ordered," Leary said while his puffed, hob-scraped face made him look mean.

Etty gave him a reproachful pout and said, "They expect you to have this when you take a box."

"I don't want to go second class. I just want to order."

"You likee beef steak?" the Chinese boy asked, smiling. "You likee rare?"

"I could use a raw one for my face."

He tore off the sealing wire on the champagne bottle, and sprung the cork so it popped and left a tiny froth mark on the ceiling. He did it with a deftness that showed he'd opened such bottles before and Etty clapped her hands with the delight of a small child. He filled the glasses, drank, and commenced wolfing the oysters. Hungry, the first drink hit him hard. There was more food, a great deal of talk, and the show going on. She kept filling his glass. Without his noticing it, the place had filled up. The floor below was now a solid mass of rough-clad, rough-talking men, a few frilly-dressed women, all swimming beneath a haze of bluish tobacco smoke. The bottle was empty. Afterward he had only a fuzzy recollection of popping a second cork. Wine, tobacco smoke, noise, and music, the closeness of the girl — all of it seemed mixed up together.

It was a warm current carrying him ever deeper and deeper, then suddenly he knew he was getting drunk, and with an effort he brought himself to concentrate on his surroundings. He was like a drowning man who finds it's easier to come up than it is to stay at the surface. His head buzzed; his eyes came to focus on the table. He realized they'd finished one bottle of champagne and were half way through a second; the table bore the remains of steak, and baked potato, and Russian fish eggs. He'd always disliked fish eggs and the people who ate them. He'd been there a long time. It must have been midnight. Down on the stage two men in loud suits, straw hats and bamboo canes were hoofing and singing in brassy unison:

Way down on the o-old plantation
I had eight women makin' love to me;
Now Monday it was Linda's turn,

And Tuesday it was Jane's,
And Wednesday I was merry as could be-e . . . .

He noticed Etty watching him. She had a cigarette in one corner of her mouth. Smoke curled past her face.

He said, "Let's get out of this dive."

"Sure, if you want to." But she didn't move. She seemed to be waiting for him, wanting him to come to her.

He stood and took a single step around the little table. He seized her beneath her arms, lifted her. She remained perfectly passive, her head tilted back, her eyes almost closed. He kissed her, drew her hard against him, and kissed her again. Her lips were soft and slightly wet from champagne.

He came to with the sun shining through the dirty windows of a big room. He'd been sleeping in his soogins on the floor. He sat up. His face was still puffed and stiff-feeling from Oren Neil's hobs. Inside he was worse. He spat and shook his head. Finally he brought his aching eyes to focus on the details of the room. It was square and bare with benches around two sides. Here and there were bedrolls, but no one was in sight. He saw a washstand and a big brass pitcher. The pitcher was empty. He cursed and hurled it at the door. It struck with a clang that was like a pain in his ears. He heard a man running along the hall. The door opened. It was the old white-haired clerk.

"What the hell!" He picked up the pitcher and tried to decide which of its dents was new. "Say, you been out on a dandy!"

"Fill it up."

He did. Buzz Leary stood over the basin, naked to the waist, while he poured it over him. The cold water felt good.

"Face full o' hobs and a gut full o' champagne all in one night. By damn, you Learys can really take it."

"I feel like I took it, all right."

He threw open the window and stood in the cold November draught until he was dry.

"You'll get pneumonia," the clerk said.

"That'd be an improvement."

"You don't hold your likker very good, kid."

He always had in the past. Last night it had hit him between the eyes. That first drink. He'd been sitting there, dipping oysters in tomato sauce, and wham-o! "Proves an Irishman should stick with straight whiskey."

The old man said, "One time I had a pal that got rolled in a plush house over at Kitnik. That's a salmon town out on the coast. Gal knocked some cigarette ash in his drink. You counted your money this morning, kid?"

"If you think that girl lifted my roll. . . ."

"I don't think nothing. I ain't saying nothing against her, either. That big grizzly, Oren Neil, would just as soon knock my head off like he did yours."

"What's he got to do with it?"

"I don't know that either." He looked around quickly. "I wish I hadn't brought it up. Don't ring me in on it, y'hear? But I'll tell you this: some of the boys say he was in a fancy cafe with her down in Vancouver a couple months ago. Then she shows up here."

"Sure she's the same one?"

"How could I be sure? All I know is what some of the boys say. Figure she followed him here. Women have a hankering for him."

Leary looked at the door after the old man was gone. He walked over and found his pants, located his wallet, opened it. He'd hit town with five-fifty in currency and about two hundred dollars in gold. Currency still there — all but sixty of the gold. He hadn't been rolled. In fact, he'd come out of it rather well. Champagne and caviar!

At the railroad office Leary learned that a barge would leave for Skidway next morning at sun-up. He had no difficulty securing passage, put the rubber-stamped *Employee* slip in his shirt pocket, and went back to the hotel. It was mid-afternoon then, and Etty was waiting for him. He'd been suspicious of her, but it all vanished when he saw her — small, smooth and so pretty. He knew he hadn't been drugged, and he decided to ask bluntly about Oren Neil.

"Neil?" she said. "Oh, the man you were fighting with. No, I don't know him. Why?"

"Someone said you were with him in Vancouver a couple of months ago. Said you followed him here."

"That's silly. I haven't been in Vancouver for over a year. I never saw Oren Neil before last night. Not that I know of, anyway." She reached up and brushed her fingers gently on his left cheek. "Does that hurt? The cuts have all turned purple."

"I'm not a very good sight, am I?"

"I think you're a very good sight. How do you feel? I've had a headache all day. I'm not much of a party girl. I haven't had anything to eat. Do you suppose dinner would help me?"

He took her to the Paradise. The place was dim and quiet now. It had been cleaned out, but there was still a stale smell of tobacco. A few men were at the bar and card games. This time they went to one of the private dining rooms she'd asked about last night. The same Chinese boy came in with a tray, put whiskey, glasses and bottled fizz water on the table.

Etty mixed herself a whiskey and fizz, but Leary merely poured himself straight fizz. "Henry Ward Beecher style," he said.

She pouted. "I won't drink mine then." She was like a sulky kitten. "I shouldn't have brought you here. I thought. . . ."

"Oh, hell!" He laughed, filled the glass the rest of the way with whiskey. "There, if it'll make you feel better."

"It will make you feel better. Really, it will."

It did. It took the residue of ache from his head, wiped the resin taste off his tongue. Food was a long time coming. He had a couple more drinks. Suddenly he realized the liquor was hitting him again. He stood and said, "I need some fresh air."

She got up, small and quiet, and walked to the door. Her jacket was tossed over a chair. He thought she was going outside in just her thin, wool dress. She didn't open the door, though. She put her hands behind her, leaned her shoulders against it, and stood looking up at him.

"I love you, you know." Her words were frank and they jolted him to a stop. She was breathing rapidly. She seemed excited. He started to say something but she shook her head. "You're not the first man I've said that to. I swore I'd *never* say it to a man again. But now I have."

"Etty!" he said, and took hold of her arms just below the shoulders. She moved back and forth, trying to pull away, but the door was against her shoulders. "Etty, tell me about yourself. What are you running away from?"

"You want to know? Buzz, let me go. I'll show you. You can *see,* then you'll know what I'm running away from."

He let loose of her. She reached back over her shoulders. She was unbuttoning her dress. She drew it down and held it across her bosom with both hands while revealing the skin of her shoulders. Criss-crossing them were welt marks several months old.

"He whipped me. My husband. Now you know. He was no good, Buzz. He couldn't even hold a job. I sang and he drank up the money. Then he imagined things about me with other men and whipped me. He took his belt off and whipped me."

"You poor kid! That's why you ran away?"

Again, as the night before, she was in his arms. She sobbed and clung tightly to him, her cheek pressed against his flannel shirt. She clung tighter and tighter as though he was the last thing she had and all else was a howling wilderness.

"Yes, I ran away. But he'll follow me. He'll find me. I have to sing in these places to earn a living. Somebody he knows will be sure to see me and let him know where I am."

"Where is this fellow?"

She shook her head. "Don't let him come and take me."

"I'll break his neck if he comes around."

"Take me away from here, Buzz." She let go the front of his shirt and tossed her arms around his neck. "Oh, Buzz, take me away. Take me where I'll never hear of him again. Take me away!"

"You don't have to run away from him. If he comes around. . . ."

"Oh, Buzz, I'm a foolish girl. I've never seen anything. Take me with you. Show me those places you've been. The cities, Montreal. Please, Buzz, take me to Montreal."

"On six hundred and eighty dollars?"

"I have a couple hundred."

"That's not enough. Etty, listen to me. . . ."

"But we can get by. You can play hockey. You must have some way of raising a few thousand. You're a Leary! You're from a great lumbering family."

"Let's talk about it tomorrow."

She flung herself in a chair, bent over, and cried with her head in her hands. "I was a fool. Of course you don't love me."

He tried to comfort her. She asked him to have another drink with her. She poured it. It was a tremendous slug.

"Now, listen, Etty. . . ."

A long time later he'd half promised to sell out and take her away with him. The orchestra was playing, and somehow or other they got back in one of the theater boxes. A voice inside Leary's brain kept saying, "You can't keep this up night after night." It was a box on the lower tier this time, but strangely those same brassy comedians were on stage, hoofing and singing:

Way down on the o-old plantation
I had eight women makin' love to me . . . .

Leary said good night to the girl and went inside the bullpen where ten or twelve men were snoring in their soogins on the floor. It was just commencing to get light outside. Clear and raw, with a gusty wind from the northwest. An engine down on the tracks kept switching around and tooting its whistle. It would be good, he was thinking, to take her to Montreal. The thought of taking her there made him sick and gutless. And the money was easy to get. Just sell that Caribou timber.

He didn't dare see her again. He didn't dare go to bed, miss the barge. He wasn't man enough to say no to her. He'd always had contempt for men who could be wrapped around a woman's finger. He groped across the room, found his soogins, rolled them up with his extra clothes and went outside.

The wind struck him: it felt good to him: good and clean, with a sharpness to it that carried away the fumes of whiskey, tobacco and perfume. He walked to the railroad yards and among the vast, sprawling warehouses to the river docks where a hundred or more men were at work with handcarts and horsecarts hauling construction equipment down and loading it on big square-ended barges. These would run the current down-stream and unload at camps here and there along Gateway Canyon where excavation and grading crews were at work, preparing the roadbed in advance of the rails.

He asked the loading boss about the Skidway barge. It was pointed out to him — a roofed-over boat with its own steam engine. In another hour it was sun-up, and he stood on the barge deck, watching Red Bank as it grew small and was engulfed by forest. For a distance of twelve miles the railroad lay along the north bank, then it ended, and they kept passing construction camps, each with its stretch of partly-finished grade. Late that afternoon, after passing the last of the construction camps, the barge cleared a point and the town of Skidway was in view.

Buzz Leary stood with his elbows on the rail, a cigarette between his still-swollen lips, looking at it. Things had changed. When he was a boy, there'd been seven sawmills operating within a ten-mile radius. Now there were no more than a couple. The barge, swinging close to shore, gave him a brief view of his father's old mill. The big building was vacant and weather-browned brush had sprung up around it.

The docks of the town were a half mile farther. He got off, hoisted his warsack on his shoulder, and walked up the corduroyed walks. Most of the town was old and drab, but here and there a new building was going up in anticipation of the day the division headquarters were moved there from Red Bank. There were lots of men on the streets, a few timberjacks and mill hands, but most of them were with the railroad engineering crew. He walked along the length of Main Street before he saw a man he knew. It was the barber, Jake Culliton.

He shook hands with Jake and asked about his old friends. Most of them were gone, following the timber north and west. Big Torg was still there, however. That was Torg Torgerson, his father's old mill boss. He was operating a little tie mill of his own back in Comas Gulch.

It was deep winter twilight when Leary got there. Torg, a huge, blunt man, plodded down, peering at him. It took him a few seconds to realize who it was, then he almost cried. They had supper together — Leary, Torg, and his three big-framed sons.

"Ay always know those damn Neil boys bane at the bottom of it," Big Torg said when Leary told him about his visit with Hobs.

In the morning Leary and Torg went down to inspect the abandoned sawmill. Most of the equipment was still there, but it would take fifteen thousand to put it in shape. Then, with the shadow of evening settling in the timber, he walked northward from town up a narrow-gauge logging railroad toward the north mill of the Enterprise Company which Mary Dardis had somehow managed to salvage from the wreckage left by the Dardis-Leary timber war.

Big Torg had warned him, "You bane fool to go up there. By golly, that girl she's tougher than man. Shoot gun like man. Long time ago she lose that mill only nobody have guts to go up there and serve bank paper. Her log boss, he's tough, too. Name's Franzen. You look out for him."

The tracks took him up a wide gulch through timber. It had snowed a little since the last train of cars had been down. The tracks, he could see, were in a fair state of repair. After half an hour of steady walking, a sign beside the tracks stopped him. "TRESPASSING FORBIDDEN," and in small letters, "VISITORS PLEASE WAIT FOR WATCHMAN."

He stood for awhile, but it was growing late, and he decided to walk on. The repeated screech of a gangsaw came to his ears; on the air was the sour, pitchy odors of a mill. He kept thinking of Mary Dardis as he walked. She'd been a quiet, scrawny, freckled kid when he last saw her. He couldn't imagine her getting very rough — didn't seem like the same girl Big Torg had described. He was wondering what he'd say to her when a gunshot broke his reverie. A bullet scorched the back of his neck, and the next moment he realized he was on his stomach, scrambling down the railroad ditch.

He felt his neck and looked for blood. There wasn't any. The bullet had missed, but it hadn't been aimed to miss. It had been aimed to kill. He lay in a foot of snow in the railroad ditch, safe only for a moment. He raised himself on hands and knees, took a quick glance around. His only escape was on up the hillside. He sprang, made it in three long strides. The gun cracked again. Its high-velocity slug tore rocks and dirt from under the snow and stung his legs. He lunged through a tangle of fox brush as a third bullet whanged past.

He paused on one knee and looked around. While running, he'd glimpsed the gun flash. It was eighty or ninety yards away, at the shadowy crest of a bank. Whoever it was wouldn't stay there. He'd move and try to cut him off. He'd naturally expect that Leary would turn back toward town. That's where he was wrong. He'd come up there to talk with Mary Dardis.

He grinned as he rubbed his taped-up knee and thought that maybe she was the one shooting at him. Darkness was settling, and that was in his favor. He moved uphill slowly, followed a deer trail across rock and fallen timber. He glimpsed lights through the trees. It was the mill. He sat on his heels, rolled a cigarette, and puffed it cold while looking down on the mill. He'd seen it eight or ten years before when the Enterprise Company was one of the big ones in that part of British Columbia. Now it was only partly kept up, perhaps operating at a scant one-third capacity. Below him were some bunkhouses with tar-papered roofs, a wangan house, some sheds. The saw kept screeching intermittently, and in moments of silence he could hear a man playing an accordion and singing in Swedish. The mill office was farther off, and up a low hillside. That's where he'd be most likely to find her.

He made a circle of the mill, came to the building by a rear path, listened at the door. No lights or sound, but a wisp of woodsmoke was rising from the stovepipe. He rapped and, getting no answer, he went inside, groped through a length of hall and reached the big room which was a combination living room and office. He could see the general outlines of it by the slight glow that came from the open draft of the stove. "Hello!" he said, thinking someone might be asleep in one of the wall bunks, then he went on, found a chair beside the stove, and sat down. The unlighted cigarette had all the while been between his lips. He bit off the sodden end, opened the stove door, lighted up; then he settled back to wait for someone to come in.

He finished the cigarette and another. A loose board thudded out front, warning of someone's approach. He heard voices, the door opened, and a girl came in. She stopped, and was looking around. It was too dark for her to see him, but the air was filled with the smell of a cigarette. Her hand had moved back, the fingers long and slim, pointed downward, just touching the butt of her revolver. Her posture reminded him of a startled animal. She had that kind of grace, the grace of a panther. That was the impression he had, seeing her just inside the door, faintly revealed against the light of a rising moon. He'd been prepared for her — for Mary Dardis. This couldn't be Mary Dardis, he was thinking. She'd been scrawny and bony and skinny-legged. This girl was none of those things.

He said, "Don't draw that gun. I've had enough people shoot at me for one day."

"Who are you?" Her voice was high-pitched. It showed the tremble of nervousness inside her. It was like the vibration of a string drawn too tight.

He said, "Now, just stand there, and I'll show you." He wanted to give her time to steady herself. She was on the point of whipping that gun from its holster and, unless appearances went for nothing, she'd be a wildcat once she cut loose. He leaned over, opened the stove door, threw his cigarette inside. She saw his face then, strongly lighted by the fire, but it was apparent she didn't recognize him.

She said, "Well?"

"I'm Buzz Leary."

The words hit her. She moved instinctively, a light-footed, cat-like pivot, and the gun came from the holster. She checked herself with it rocked back in the heel of her palm, ready to fire.

He cried, "Use your head, girl!" He saw her stop, her legs spread. She wore trousers, regular tin pants, but on her they were different. Even scared for his life, he couldn't help admiring the way her legs molded into them. "You wouldn't want to shoot me. Not on this nice, clean floor."

She let the pistol barrel tilt toward the floor. Her eyes were still intense and a little wild, but he guessed he was safe enough. As safe as a man ever is with a redhead.

She said, "Light the lamp!"

He scratched a match. The lamp was on a chain above. He stood on a chair, lighted it, adjusted the wick. While he was doing it, he had a good look at her. She was medium in height, with hair the color of liquid copper. Her eyes were intensely blue. The tin pants, held up by a belt, were cinched tightly around her waist. She was slim anyway, and the belt made her look slimmer. What she would have been in one of Etty's dresses! She wore small logger boots, a mackinaw, a man's hat. She was Mary

Dardis, though. She still had the freckles across the bridge of her nose, and there was that old mannerism — her way of tilting her head to one side when she looked at him.

He said, "Well, Mary, this is a funny way to meet an old friend."

Her little chin was jutted out, her lips were tight. "Did you think I'd forgotten? Did you think I could ever forget that the Learys killed my father?"

He said earnestly, "We didn't kill him, Mary."

"If that's all you came here to say. . . ."

"It's not. I came here to tell you the whole story."

"Well, I'm not going to listen." Her hand was very tight around the gun. Her finger, clenched on the trigger, had started the hammer back on its double-action mechanism. Her lips were pulled back. He could see her perfect white teeth. She spoke through them, "I know what you Learys are. I know what *you* are. You came back from the city and now you think you can make a simple backwoods girl listen to your lies."

"You're afraid of me, aren't you?"

She reacted as though to a slap in the face. He thought for a second that he'd gone too far, that this time she would fire. Her breast, swelling the mackinaw, rose and fell rapidly. She said, "Afraid of you?" She laughed and jerked her head backwards, swinging the coils of coppery hair that fell from beneath her hat. "You haven't noticed, but *I've got the gun.*"

He got another cigarette going and laughed at her with it scissored in one side of his mouth. "Sure, you're afraid. You're afraid of having to admit the truth. It'd make you feel like a fool, damning the Learys all these years, and trying to kill me on my way up here this evening. Sure you're afraid of me. You're afraid of listening to me."

She hissed, "Get out."

"No, not till I talk. Go ahead and pull the trigger. That's the only way you can stop me. Sure, I was down in the city. I was in Vancouver, blowing in my summer's wages. I never was any good, you know. Well, somebody broke a table over my head and I woke up in the hospital. You know who I found there, in one of the other wards? Hobs Donahue. He was dying. He told me about that night he went to meet your father. My dad sent him to make peace but, when Hobs got to the woods trail where your father was to meet him, the Neil boys and Claggett were ahead of him.

"They offered him five hundred dollars if he'd tell your father to go to the devil. When Hobs wouldn't do it, they slugged him and tied him up. Then your father came, and they jumped him. Maybe they didn't intend to kill him. Not at first. Just beat him up, knowing us Learys would get the blame for it. But your father saw who it was, so all they could do was finish him off. Hobs knew he'd be blamed and end with a rope around his neck, so he got out of the country."

Her lips were closed, slanted down at the corners. She didn't believe him. "More Leary lies!"

"Look around and see who the winners were in that timber fracas if you think it's a lie."

A man had come through the door and was in the shadow, watching them. Leary could tell little about him, except that he was tall, and that he stood with the hunched manner effected by many tall men who wish to minimize their height. The man said in a slightly nasal tone, "You want me to take care of him, Miss Dardis?"

Leary said, "Is that your bushwhack specialist, Mary?"

"What were you talking about . . . somebody trying to kill you on your way here? If you have some sort of lie cooked. . . ."

"It's no lie. Somebody shot at me. I was coming up the railroad."

"Our watchman has orders to keep everybody off. If you walked through our sign, maybe he decided to throw a scare into you."

"Scorch the back of a man's neck at ninety yards . . . some scare!"

The man walked forward then, into the light. He was in his late thirties, very skinny, with a narrow face, a high-ridged nose, and eyes that pressed closely against it. A lever-action Winchester hung in the crook of his arm.

"He's lying," he said for Mary, but Leary could hear him. "I shot, all right. Shot three times to put him on the run, but there wasn't a bullet came within twenty feet of him."

Leary said, "You must be Franzen."

His eyes showed a slight twitch of surprise, "Yah."

Big Torg had mentioned him, said he was tough. Torg had been right about everything. With Franzen backing her, Mary Dardis rammed her revolver back into its holster. Her mackinaw was unbuttoned, but the room was still too hot with the fire going, so she took it off. She looked better the more he saw of her. She threw her hat aside, too, shook out her thick mass of hair, forked it back with her fingers. He knew that she was tired from doing a man's work, but pride wouldn't let her show it.

She said, "What are you doing back here? And let's have the truth this time."

"I haven't had much luck with the truth so far. Always heard you couldn't reason with a redhead." She stood with her hands on her hips, her head up. She was so pretty he forgot for a moment what he was talking about. "You know, I still own that stand of white pine up in the Sag. It'll be worth a quarter-million when the rails go through. No good to me, though, I haven't got a mill. I notice you have one here and nothing much except silvery hemlock to feed it. It's a chance for both of us."

"No. I may go broke, but I'll not go in partnership with a Leary!"

☆ III ☆

THEY'LL TRY WITH FIRE!

*I*n the morning, Leary went downriver to the temporary rail camp at Big Bend. There the railroad survey turned from the river and headed eastward through the Kenaba Sag. The Sag was hilly and dissected by deep gulches, but it afforded no major obstacle to the railroad as did the mountain ranges north and south. A wagon road had been built by the engineering crew and he caught a ride as far as Caribou Creek, camping there, alone, beneath the shadow and silence of the big pine.

It had never been timbered. The Sag had no stream large enough to float such logs. He cruised the timber, blocked it out to decide which section could be timbered with the least cost. Returning, he stopped briefly at Skidway, hired a steam launch to Red Bank, and took the supply train on to Trout Creek. There he saw Dwight Gordon, one of Dominion Limited's vice-presidents, and made a deal to sell one tenth of the entire Caribou stand in the form of sawlogs which the railroad would saw at its own mill at Vermilion Lake. At Gordon's insistence he signed a guarantee to deliver by June first four million board feet to a siding that the railroad would build up Long Tom Gulch. On the strength of that he received an advance payment, half of which he immediately spent on yarding equipment. When he got back to Skidway, a blizzard was on, and the engineering crew had laid off eighteen men whom he immediately hired and put to work, twelve of them at the Caribou constructing winter camp under the direction of Big Torg and two of his boys, the rest at the old Skidway mill.

He lacked capital to reopen the mill, but no one except himself and the railroad front office knew of the deal he had, and he wanted the Neils to assume he planned on sawing the Caribou pine himself. They wouldn't sit back and let him make a profit on the very stand that had been their greatest ambition for twelve years. They'd try to stop him but, not knowing his deal with Gordon, maybe they'd try at the wrong place.

For three weeks things went along without a hitch. He spent most of his time at Caribou where the shacks were up and the crew had progressed to the point of building rollways. It was late December then, with the strong cold setting in. Late one night he came down from Caribou and approached the mill to hear the high, insistent barking of Babine, a malamute belonging to Ole Torgerson.

Ole generally kept the animal inside a large wire pen back of the bunkhouse, but tonight he'd got loose. Leary followed the sound through an area of second-growth spruce. He heard a man then, cursing through his teeth, apparently trying to fight the dog away. A gun exploded, and instantly the dog was silent. The bullet must have struck him in the brain.

Leary ran. He took long strides following the twisted path through the timber, and suddenly the man was right ahead of him. His back was turned. He started to run. They collided. The man fell away, trying to twist as he did so and bring his revolver up, but Leary fell with him, twisting his arm to make the gun fall. He knew who it was. Franzen — that tall log boss of Mary Dardis's. He'd had something in his left hand. A can. The gassy odor of kerosene was on the air. Leary did not pause. He rolled, still gripping Franzen's wrist, came to a crouch, pivoted, and had him in a whip-lock with which he could twist his arm off at the shoulder. Franzen screamed from pain and Leary stopped. He placed a foot beneath Franzen's armpit and jerked the arm little by little, watching his face contort from pain.

"Who sent you to burn me out?"

Franzen panted and whimpered at the end of each breath. "Mary. She said . . . she'd burn you . . . run you out of the country."

It was what Leary both expected and hated to hear. He'd come there to fight the Neils, not Mary Dardis. He let him go. He stood over him for a few seconds. When he got up, Leary hit him with the heel of his palm and knocked him down again.

"Who was it sent you?"

"I hope to die it was Mary. She told me to shoot to kill that night at the north mill, too. What the hell do you want me to do? Lie and say it was Oren Neil?"

The kerosene can he'd been carrying was heavy metal. It had overturned and was leaking slowly. Franzen bent to pick it up. As he stopped he whirled and swung it at Leary's head. Leary knew it would be coming. He weaved away and beneath it. As it whisked over him, he stepped in and smashed a right to Franzen's jaw. Franzen went down on his back. He lit hard and bounced on the pathway. He was out cold with blood running from the corners of his open mouth. Leary picked him up, got him over his shoulder, carried him up to the road. By that time, Ole Torgerson was coming to see what the trouble was. Leary told him to hitch the team. He was going to the north mill.

Franzen came to and sat up in the box of the sled. His jaw had been broken in a couple of places, and he was hunched over, holding it with both hands all the way past town and up the gulch. No one challenged them. Leary pulled in as close as he could get to the mill office and shouted Mary's name until she came to the door with a quilt wrapped around her.

"Here he is, kerosene and all!"

Franzen got to his feet, but he didn't offer to help himself from the sled, so Leary gave him the shoulder, knocking him off the back. He sat in the snow, still holding his jaw. Leary threw the can of kerosene out beside him. Mary shouted something, but he didn't wait. He drove downhill at a stiff trot, his winter collar up, muffling whatever she called after him.

When he got back he learned from Ole that a girl had been there the previous afternoon looking for him. He asked who she was, and had that gutless feeling at the same time knowing it would be Etty. She'd followed him from Red Bank.

"What's she doing in Skidway?" he asked.

"Singin' at the Rialto. Yimminy, what a girl!"

"I know." He went to his room. He had a notion to change clothes and find her that night. Instead he went to bed. He didn't sleep well. He got up before daybreak, had breakfast with the crew, went back to his room, and shaved. His face was in better shape now. A lot better than that first night he saw her. He looked at his watch. Only eight-thirty and Etty wasn't the type who got up before noon.

He stood at the high desk and looked at the surveyor's map that Dwight Gordon had sent him, showing the route of the spur line up Long Tom Gulch. Gordon wanted him to mark his loading point. He took half an hour in figuring it out and was just marking the X when he heard her voice in the next room. He strode over and opened the door.

"Buzz!" she whispered, and the next instant she was clinging to him with her cheek pressed against his flannel shirt. "Buzz, you *are* glad to see me?"

She'd had a drink or two, and the smell of it, together with tobacco and perfume, brought back the memory of those Red Bank nights with jarring realism. Ole had come to the door with her and was staring, a grin on his moon face. Leary tried to let her go, but she cared nothing for what Ole thought.

"Oh, Buzz, why did you leave without saying anything? Why did you do it?"

He waited until Ole had backed out of sight and said, "I couldn't take you to Montreal. You must be able to understand that."

She was pouting again, "You didn't want to. You never really cared for me."

"You wouldn't want me if I was a quitter. What are you doing here in Skidway? Singing at the Rialto?"

"You know why I came. I came because of you." She moved back a trifle, but still clung to him. "Buzz, I was here yesterday to see you. It was important. I wanted to warn you."

"What are you talking about?"

"They are planning to burn you out."

"Who?"

"I don't know. Somebody called Dardis. Some Dardis woman."

"How'd you find that out?"

"You hear things around places like the Rialto. Men get to drinking and they tell you more than they should. There was a man, a sawyer from the Dardis mill. He said his boss was going to burn you out."

"Franzen?"

"No, a woman. Mary Dardis. She was planning to burn you out."

Somebody had come to the door. Leary spun around and saw Mary Dardis. She was looking beyond him, at Etty.

"That's a lie!" Mary Dardis emphasized her words by hurling the door shut. She had a swaggering walk when she was angry, and she was angry now. She was dressed in wool shirt, mackinaw, and stag trousers. The gun was strapped around her waist. She stopped with her hands on her hips, a couple of steps from Etty. "You heard what I said! I said it was a lie."

Etty was frightened. She whimpered something and got behind Leary.

Leary said, "Maybe it was a lie that your foreman was here last night with a can of kerosene?"

She took a deep breath. She stood very straight, with her small shoulders back. Sunlight, coming through a smoky windowpane, brought out the flame color of her hair. By some magic, it looked darker, more like bronze, in daylight.

She said, "I wouldn't know about that. If he tried it, he was doing it on his own hook. *I* didn't send him. Anyhow, when I heard about it, I paid him off and gave him the boot. That's what I came here to tell you."

Etty, cringing behind Leary, whispered, "Don't believe her."

Mary heard her. "Say, who are you? Are you the new girl at the Rialto? I'll not be called a liar by any man in this camp, and it's a cinch I'll not take it from any dance-hall fluff."

Etty whispered, "It's true, Buzz. It is! She's the one who tried to burn you out. Don't let her fool you, Buzz."

He was watching Mary. He wondered what she'd do when she got mad enough. He wondered if she'd go for that gun at her waist. He kept his hands poised to grab her if she did.

She started forward, and he tried to push her back. She was quick as a forest cat. She dodged beneath his arm and seized Etty by the front of her jacket. Etty screamed and tried to claw her way free. She was no match for Mary's strength. Mary kicked her feet from under her in the best timberjack style, and tried to fling her to the floor. But in falling, Etty got hold of her hair with both hands.

They fell and rolled over and over. Fear had given Etty a desperate strength. She tore Mary's hair with one hand and tried to scratch her with the other. Mary got up far enough to swing her fist. She deliberately let the fist miss, doubled her elbow, and drove it to Etty's neck. Etty screamed and fell face down. She wasn't hurt that badly. She was screaming for Leary's sympathy. He stood over them, not knowing what to do.

Etty pushed herself up. She was on hands and knees with her hair spread out around her. Mary was on her feet now. She trampled on Etty's hair with her logger boots, pivoting with each step. Leary couldn't see the purpose in it, but he did when Etty tried to stand. Her hair was snagged in the slivery floor.

The girls had struggled for about half a minute. Finally Buzz Leary decided to take a hand. He grabbed Mary from behind, held her by her upper arms as she twisted back and forth. It was all he could do to hold her. Muscles, beneath the soft flesh of her arms, were like babiche thong. Her head was just under his chin. He could smell her hair. A fresh, forest scent. Her shirt and mackinaw had come open. He could see the white skin of her shoulder. He was strongly aware of her femininity. For a moment he forgot about Etty's harrowing plight on the floor. With a downward, twisting movement Mary got free. She whirled to face him. Her left hand clutched her shirt, holding the front of it closed. Her right, with a practiced swiftness, whipped the revolver from its holster.

"Mary!" he cried. "Be careful." Her finger was too hard on the trigger. Another ounce of pressure would bring the hammer back. "You better get out of here."

"Sure I will. I was a fool to come at all. Once a Leary, always a Leary." She strode over and looked down at Etty. Her feet were wide set, like they'd been when he first saw her at the Dardis mill office; the gun was at her side. "But before I do, I'd like to talk with this *friend* of yours."

Etty tried to turn her head and look up at her. Her eyes were like a frightened weasel's.

Mary said, "Now tell him the truth. Tell him you're a little plush-house liar."

"What?"

"Tell him you're a liar!"

"I'm a liar," she whimpered.

Mary turned away from her and said to Leary, "But you'll believe her, won't you? Sure you will . . . you dumb Irish timber tramp."

She strode out, coming down hard on the heels of her boots. He got down and helped pull Etty's hair loose. When she was free, she clutched his breast and sobbed, "But it was true! She made me say I was a liar. She really did send that man out to burn your mill."

Although he promised Etty he'd see her that night, instead he thought all day about Mary Dardis. He couldn't get over the impression of her closeness when he held her, the feel of her strong body, the fresh forest scent of her skin and hair. So that night, rather than going to the Rialto, he found himself once again walking toward the Dardis mill. No one fired at him this time. A lamp burned inside the house. He climbed the path across packed snow, rapped.

She drew up suddenly at seeing him. Her eyes moved beyond him, and for just a moment she seemed to be afraid.

"Well," she said, "what do you want?"

There was the defensiveness again. Her back was stiff and her little chin jutted out. The gun was strapped around her waist.

"I didn't want anything important. Just thought I'd drop around. Aren't many of us old-timers left. You, me, the Neils. Thought it over a long time and decided I'd find a better welcome here."

She said, "I made a fool of myself, didn't I?"

"Oh, I don't know." He touched his battered nose. "I didn't get that being smart. People that don't make fools of themselves aren't worth knowing."

"You really believe that?"

"Sure."

He followed her inside. She got the table between them and, with a return of tautness in her manner, said, "Is that why you believed that dance-hall girl instead of me?"

"You're not being fair. She thought you were to blame. You ought to admire her for trying to tell me the truth."

Mary made an exasperated gesture and her blue eyes started to dart fire. "She. . . ." Mary checked herself. "I'll not say any more about her. You'll have to find out for yourself."

"That's generally how it is. Pa told me the whiskey would give me a headache, but I never believed him until I tried it."

The easy good humor of his talk had its effect, and she decided to smile. She said, "Well, are you a guest or on business?"

"Think I'd better be a guest."

"In that case, I'll pour a cup of tea."

"Coffee."

"Tea!"

While he drank, he knew she was watching him. After a long period of silence, with no sound except the snapping of knots in the stove, she spoke. "You don't think I tried to burn you out?"

"If I did, I don't suppose I'd be here." He put his cup aside. "I was thinking it'd still be a fine thing if you'd saw that Caribou pine of mine."

"Buzz, you'll never yard it. You'll never get those logs to Skidway, or anywhere."

"Yes, but what if I do?"

"No, I won't saw your timber." For a while she'd been a girl, soft and lovely. Now that was gone. Her little chin was out again. "Maybe *you're* right, Buzz. But the Learys broke my father and caused his death. I know that, Buzz. Everybody knows it. I'm not going into partnership with a Leary!"

He left an hour later and started for the Rialto, but Big Torg was on the street looking for him. He'd just arrived from Caribou with word that the Neils were hiring men away from the camp with higher wages. Leary countered by a raise topping the Neils. When it became apparent that a wage war would be too expensive, the Neils struck in a manner more direct. Their goon squad, led by huge, brutal Jug Claggett, commenced methodically beating every Leary man who showed up in town. They went afield, and waylaid men between Skidway and Caribou. The point was reached when few would take work with Leary at any wage, and he didn't blame them. Then he received word from Torg that the skidways between Caribou and Long Tom Gulch had been blasted. He realized that in some manner Oren Neil had learned the true destination of his timber.

Big Torg said, "We got to get that Claggett. Ay skal call my boys together. You give Swede axe handle, he fight like hell. Maybe we find two-three more. Johnny Bruce, he'll fight, and so will those Irishmen, McGraw and Callahan. Counting everyone, bane have eight. We'll catch Claggett down at the Rialto and. . . ."

"I've thought of that, but he's wary as a two-toed wolf. He keeps showing himself alone, but when he gets jumped those roughs come from everywhere. You get the boys together. I'll go down and see what I can find out."

Claggett was at the Rialto. Leary could see him through the front window — a huge, lumpy-faced man standing with one elbow on the bar and a bottle of beer in front of him. A couple of his men were there too — Myers, and a big Finlander that

Leary didn't know. The others were probably around, within shouting distance. He kept walking, waded snow around to the alley, climbed some outside stairs to the second story. He paused inside a hall and looked at the double row of rooms. Number 11, Etty had told him. He found it. Someone was moving around inside. He rapped, and she said, "Who is it?"

"Buzz."

He could hear her catch her breath. "Wait," she said. He stood a couple of minutes, then she let him in. Her white silk dress clung to the lines of her body. He had an idea she'd kept him waiting while she put it on. She grabbed his right hand in both of hers and drew him inside. "Buzz, why haven't you come before? And after you promised."

"They have me crowded against the wall. I haven't eaten since morning or slept more than four or five hours in the last two days."

He looked it, too. He'd lost weight since coming to Skidway. There was a set leanness in his jaw, a flinty look in his eyes. He got away from her and rested his long body on the edge of her dressing table.

She said, "What's wrong, Buzz? Is it Claggett?"

"Claggett and his toughs. They have the town buffaloed. It's getting so I can't hire a man."

"I heard they were blocking your rollways, too."

"Yes, but one thing at a time. I'm going to run Oren's bully boys out of town first, then I'll see about those fellows out in the hills."

"Oh, Buzz, I'm afraid. . . ."

She was going to cling to him again and he held her off with a long-thrust arm. "Wait. Do you really want to help me?"

"Yes! I'll do what I can . . . *anything* I can."

"All right. I'm getting some of my boys together. I want to catch Claggett when his knuckles crew is somewhere else. He hangs out here most of the time. Here at the Rialto. I want you to. . . ."

"Yes, Buzz. I'll keep watch. Sometimes Neil takes most of them out of town with him. Last Thursday Claggett and Nakola were here, just the two of them, till midnight. Drunk, too. But if you get Claggett, you'll still have to deal with the others when. . . ."

"Those timber toughs are all alike. Once they start getting their skulls kicked in, they hunt softer jobs a long way off. You send me word, Etty. How often does he let his guard down?"

"I don't know. It might be tonight. It might be a week."

He moved toward the door. "Etty, this means a lot to me."

She came to him and whispered, "Even Montreal?"

"Even Montreal. . . ."

Torg had the men together next afternoon. Among others, he'd recruited two Swede timber butchers named Rustad and Christianson from the Dardis mill. The addition of these brought the total to ten. Leary warned them they might be waiting for a good many days, but that evening the half-breed boy came with the message. It was written in a tiny hand on paper strong with Etty's perfume.

Only Claggett and four men here now. Others upriver. Hurry.

He sent the boy away, came back inside. The men stopped their poker game to watch him. He wadded the paper, threw it in the stove.

"That it?" Bruce asked.

"Yes." Leary looked at his watch. Seven o'clock. Claggett would have a bellyful of grub and the variety house crowd wouldn't be around yet. "Right now," he said.

He saw McGraw with a .45 Colt in his mackinaw pocket and told him to leave it behind.

"How about axe handle?" Rustad asked. He was one of those Dardis Swedes. He'd been half drunk when he got there and had been spoiling for a fight all evening. "By yimminy, Ay can't fight wit'out chew snooce and axe handle."

"Go ahead and take it, but don't swing it unless they start swinging 'em first. I don't want anybody killed. I want 'em alive so they can tell how bad this country is for timber toughs."

☆ IV ☆
SATAN'S RENDEZVOUS

*T*he street looked quiet with the thermometer at zero and light from the saloon windows shining bright across the new snow.

Leary stopped and said, "Torg, you take the Swedes down that side. Bruce, you keep your boys across the street. When the ruckus starts, I want about four men outside. They might have a deadfall fixed up for us."

Bruce said, "What about you?"

"I'll go over there."

"Alone?"

"Sure." He made an impatient gesture when Torg started to object. "Keep watch. I might need help in a hurry."

He started toward the Rialto, making a long slant across the street. He was half way when Mary Dardis called him. He spun around and saw her coming down the steps from the Northern Mercantile Company. She came across, taking rapid steps, and stopped to look up at him, her head tilted to one side. Her eyes lacked their fire tonight. They looked scared.

She said, her voice unusually soft and pleading, "Buzz, you're headed for trouble. You're headed for more trouble than you can handle."

He let his shoulders jerk with a laugh. "It might surprise you how much trouble I can handle."

"That girl is going to double-cross you."

"Think she'll have Neil waiting for us?"

"I don't know a thing about that. All I know is you have a couple of my men, drunk and ready to get their heads beaten in, and I don't like it."

"Talk to them, not me. They're over twenty-one."

"How do you reason with a drunken Swede?"

"How do you reason with a sober Irishman? One's as bad as the other." Then he dropped the grin off his face and said, "It would please every drop of ornery Dardis blood you got to see me fold up and get run out of the country, wouldn't it?"

"You'll get run out. Etty and Oren will see to that."

He watched her spin on her toe and walk off. There were Etty and Oren Neil tied together again. He recalled what the old fellow in Red Bank had said. And something else had been in the back of his mind — that survey map had been lying open on his desk the morning Etty visited him, and right afterward Neil moved to block his route to Long Tom Gulch.

He walked on to the Rialto's front sidewalk. The windows were steamed over. He waited for the door to open and got a glimpse of the interior. Not many around yet. Claggett, Myers, and a couple others were sitting around a disused card table. He decided not to go in after all, circled to the rear, climbed the stairs. He listened for a while in the lamplit hall and walked to Etty's room. She was there. He turned the knob, opened the door.

She said, "Oren!" and whirled. She caught herself then, and tried to laugh. She had a silk robe tied around her. It came to the floor and made her look smaller than ever. She took a provocative tuck in it and came to him, saying, "Oh, Buzz, the idea you must have of me! I was thinking about *him*, Oren Neil, and the night he kicked you in the face so awfully. I was worried about tonight, and then the door coming open. . . ."

"Sure." He closed the door with the heel of his hobbed boot. "Sure, I know." He noticed that her lips were smiling, but her eyes were as shifty as a mink's. She tried to snuggle up to him as she had so many times in the past. He looked over her head and saw a cigar burnt out in her dressing table ashtray. "Where is he?"

"Who?"

He pushed her out of his way, took a long step, and jerked the closet curtain aside. Nobody there. He turned then and said, "You know who . . . Oren Neil?"

"Oh, Buzz! Buzz, you don't really think. . . ?"

"I think you tried to make a punk out of me in Red Bank. Tried to get me to sell the Caribou to Oren Neil."

"Buzz. . . ." Her shoulders shook convulsively and she tried to bury her face in the front of his shirt.

"What's he giving you?" He grabbed her, shoved her back. "What's he giving you?"

Suddenly she stopped pretending. Her little mouth was drawn thin and turned down at the corners, twisted, contemptuous. She bared her teeth and almost spat at him. "You fool! You ugly fool! Do you think I'd give you a second look unless I had a reason for it? Do you think any woman would choose you instead of Oren? Of course I made a fool of you. In Red Bank and here in Skidway, too. I got inside your office and you let me see the very thing Oren wanted most to know. And I told him. Oh, how he sat here and laughed, when I told him. And about you, you big stumbling punk . . . you and your poor Etty stuff. I wanted to tell you to go to hell then, but Oren said to hold off a while and get you good. He said he didn't dare get too rough, not with you having the railroad behind you. He said maybe you'd come looking for trouble. And you did. You came pussyfooting to me. Promising maybe you'd take me to Montreal."

He'd never hit a woman. He started and checked himself. Frightened, she screamed, "Oren! He's here, Oren!"

He tried to stop her. She kept screaming. He could hear heavy boots in the hall. The door flew open, and Oren Neil was there.

Neil came to a stop. A huge man, he filled the doorway. Back of him was Bill, and skinny-faced Lyn LaValley, owner of the Rialto. Etty was shrieking, telling him things, but Neil didn't look at her. He back-handed her out of the way and said, "Well. Leary! So this is the place you picked for it." He laughed, his head tossed back, hands on his hips. Then he stopped and the laugh seemed to leave a vile taste in his mouth. "It suits me, Leary. It suits me fine."

Leary said, "Where are your guts?"

"Now what did you mean by that?"

"I mean you haven't the guts to fight me without Bill and that sneaking LaValley at your back."

"Teach you that in the hockey arena? Even up and all sporting, old topper? I fight to win. That's what I'm going to do tonight. I'm going to cave your skull in. And everybody knows you came here with your mob looking for it."

Leary had backed a step away. His left hand was behind him, on the back of a chair. A kerosene lamp was burning on the dressing table at his right. He said, "Sure, Oren," and picked up the lamp.

LaValley shouted, "Look out!" just as Leary threw it.

It struck the wall, shattered. The room was dark, a darkness filled with the fumes of kerosene. He'd expected the kerosene to set the wall afire and drive them all out, but it didn't. A second later, Oren and Bill both charged him. Light from the hall gave him a vague impression of movement. He shifted his position, wielding the heavy chair.

He met Oren Neil with the full force of it and dropped him in one direction. With a return movement he smashed Bill. He ran against Etty. She screamed, "Here he is!" and clung to his arm. He tried to rip free. She hung with the clawing ferocity of a cat. He came around with all his strength and snapped her free. She struck the floor and Oren Neil, rising, trampled her. She wailed his name and he cursed her, booted her out of the way.

Leary turned with the chair to meet him but in the darkness Bill staggered head foremost into it. It dropped him so hard the floor shook. He came up, made a blind grab for Leary's knees, but he took a hobnail boot between the eyes and went down like he'd been blackjacked. Leary lit on him and gave him the hobs. He saw Oren coming with a bull charge. The man's superior weight carried him to the hall. There the hobs on Leary's left heel caught the carpet and he fell backward, caught himself on his hands. Oren went for him with his boots, but this time Leary wasn't the easy prey he'd been on the corduroy walks of Red Bank.

He rolled, felt one of the boots graze his face. Neil tried to turn. Leary rose from beneath him, caught him by his crotch and the front of his shirt, and lifted him high in the air, trying to drive his head against the ceiling. Neil twisted over, fingers hunting for Leary's eyes. His struggling weight carried Leary off balance. He took three lunging, running steps, fell but, in falling, managed to propel the man headforemost down the narrow stairway.

He could hear cursing and the crash of a handrail. Some of those timber toughs had been coming upstairs and Oren Neil's plunging body had taken them down again. A knife pain went through Leary's knee and he steadied himself with his back against the wall. His leg still held him, but he'd have to go easy on it. Then Oren Neil charged back into sight.

He had a segment of banister. A heavy oaken club. He grasped it with both hands and wielded it like a ball bat. Leary moved enough to take it across an upflung arm. A glancing blow. He went to one knee and kept going forward. Oren Neil thought he was going down, backed away half a step, and started a second swing. He saw it would miss and tried to change its direction. Leary let it graze his shoulder, hesitated a fraction of a second with his heels set, and smashed a right to his jaw. It stunned big Oren Neil. His eyes were off-focus like the eyes of a beef under a slaughterhouse hammer. He reeled, hit the wall with his shoulder. His weight crushed lath and plaster. He rebounded as his legs folded under him. He sat down hard, but he wasn't out; he had enough left to get one arm as a shield and grope with his club for the other.

Leary did not hesitate. He'd been raised in the big timber and knew the rules under which the timberjack fights. A man is put down only to make him vulnerable to the real weapons — the boots on one's feet. He sprang when Neil was lunging to his feet. The hobs raked him and carried him down again. Neil rolled over, got up. He didn't realize the stairs were behind him. He fell backwards and rolled to the landing. Leary was atop him in two long steps. Neil stood and was smashed down the next six steps by a right and left to the jaw. He was groggy but not quite out. There was a baffled, beaten look in his eyes. His face was smashed. He coughed and spat out a tooth. His lips moved but the words were drowned out by riot in the saloon beyond.

"You had enough?" Leary asked.

He nodded his head.

Leary seized him by the shirt front and flung him away. His head clumped the wall and he pitched face forward, limp and beaten. Leary stepped over him and reached the lower stair landing that overlooked the saloon and gambling room. It was full of struggling, chair-swinging men. The fight had passed its apex. The place was a shambles, bar overturned, mirrors smashed, faro and roulette spreads heaped against the walls. He could see and hear Big Torg over everyone, a chair in his hands, mowing through the last remnants of Claggett's timber toughs.

Claggett had his men all there, and a few Neil lumberjacks to boot. They should have had Leary's bunch outnumbered. It took him a moment to realize that most of the wrecking crew were from the Dardis camps. They were tough, too. He saw Mary at the door and started toward her. A stray chair struck him on the shoulder and bounded off. He scarcely looked around. Big Torg rammed him out of the way. He was dragging Jug Claggett by the collar. He dumped him at Mary's feet and commenced booting him in the ribs.

"You talk, noo!" he roared. "Talk! Talk!" he repeated, kicking him a little harder each time. "You talk. Tell Mary Dardis who bane kill her father. You talk or Ay skal cave in planty more ribs."

"I'll talk." Jug usually affected a swaggering voice and manner, but tonight he was reduced to a cringing whine. "I'll talk. Leave me alone, I'll talk. It wasn't me. I didn't have anything to do with it. It was a long time ago, and. . . ."

"Talk!"

"He come up and Bill hit him. He'd have let it go at that. He ain't like Oren. He's mean, but he's not crazy. But Oren always hated your dad, and he jumped on him with his boots, and. . . ."

"That's enough," Leary said. "Save it for the police when we get them here from Fort Royal."

Mary said, "I want to hear it."

"That's all I know. He got him with his hobs eight or ten times before Bill could drag him off. He's got an awful temper, Oren has. He goes crazy. I don't know if he intended to kill your dad. He was scared afterward. They had Hobs Donahue tied up and Oren talked about killing him, too, so he couldn't talk. But he thought it over and decided nobody would believe Hobs anyhow. So he turned Hobs loose and told him to hit the skids out o' here. I'd have told. I'd have gone to the law, only them Neil boys would have. . . ."

"All right," Mary said.

Leary took her outside. Men were still running that way to see the excitement. He led her down the snow-covered walks. He was bare-headed, his shirt ripped open. The zero breeze felt good. It washed him of that rotten combination of sweat, whiskey, and perfume that filled the Rialto.

"I've been a fool," he said. "I should have known Franzen was in with the Neils when he tried to burn me. I should have known he was working with them when he tossed that Winchester lead at me that first evening when I went up to the North mill."

She asked about Oren and Bill Neil, and he told her. He noticed that her chin was no longer jutted. Her fear and defensiveness were gone.

One of her hands rested on his arm. He took hold of her arms, just below her shoulders, turned her so she was facing him. He didn't know he was going to kiss her. He didn't know her head would be tilted back, that her lips would be waiting for him.

He said, "I still have a lot of white pine and no mill to put it through."

"We'll make a business appointment sometime." She was smiling up at him. He was surprised to see her eyes swimming through tears. "Who wants to talk about the lumber business now, you big, dumb Irishman, you?"

NO MAN'S RANGE

(1951)

☆

by GIFF CHESHIRE

Giff Cheshire was born on a homestead in Cheshire, Oregon. The county was named for his grandfather who had crossed the plains in 1852 by wagon from Tennessee and the homestead was the same one his grandfather had claimed upon his arrival. Cheshire's early life was colored by the atmosphere of the Old West which in the first decade of the new century had not yet been modified by the automobile. In 1929 he came to the Portland area in Oregon and from 1929 to 1943 worked for the U.S. Corps of Engineers. By 1944, after moving to Beaverton, Oregon, he found he could make a living writing Western and North-Western short fiction for the magazine market and presently stories under the byline Giff Cheshire began appearing in Lariat Story Magazine, Star Western, *and* North-West Romances. *His short story, "Strangers in the Evening," in* Zane Grey's Western Magazine *(10/49) won a Zane Grey Award that year. Although the background of the story that follows is cattle ranching, Cheshire's Western fiction was often characterized by a wide historical panorama of the frontier. Frequently his novels are set in his native Oregon.* Starlight Basin *(Random House, 1954),* Thunder on the Mountain *(Doubleday, 1960) and* Wenatchee Bend *(Doubleday, 1966) are among his best titles. No less notable for their complex characters, expert pacing, and authentic backgrounds are his novels under the Chad Merriman byline, beginning with* Blood on the Sun *(Fawcett Gold Medal, 1952). Several of these titles have recently appeared in hardcover reprint editions in the Gunsmoke series from Chivers Press.*

☆ | ☆

WHAT I NEED I CLAIM

*T*he oncoming riders looked hostile. Bart Tyler sat his saddle and watched them spill out of the gap and spur toward him. Of those four riders, Tyler figured that it was Matt Ginsing he'd have to kill. It had been shaping up that way for a year. Ginsing, Slash 3 ramrod, never rode off home range without a couple of hard-bitten hirelings.

Bart was on a slope, and a big cut of Herefords under his brand was shuffling down onto the bottom below him. It seemed like evening, though it was only a little past noon. The sooty atmosphere lent a glassy sheen to the frozen rock formations all about. The oncoming riders were not swinging over to come around the steers but were holding arrogantly to their course and driving head-on, hell-for-leather.

Bart thundered down in a wide hook to the left. His throat was dry and tight, for this was a thing he should never have run into up here at the edge of the *malpais*. Slash 3 lay well to the south, and Bart had no idea what Ginsing was doing here at the gap.

It was no day for casual riding. A sudden freeze had come two days before. Now it had moderated with the wind in the north and that meant snow.

Bart came onto the flat without speeding up the slow shuffling of the numbed steers and pulled on ahead. Ginsing and his men seemed to sight them and swung off toward him. They slowed, then pulled to a stop, and let Bart come to them.

Ginsing was a tall, stooped man with red hair. The two punchers with him were the ones who usually accompanied him on his riding away from Slash 3. Bart thought he knew the fourth person, a small, slender girl who sat erect in the saddle. She was dark and wore a tailored riding habit. She tallied with the description he had had of Linda Dana, the city girl who had fallen heir to Slash 3. Bart touched his hat out of deference to her, but his face was chilled by more than the frigid wind.

He looked at Ginsing and saw the ghost of a derisive grin on the man's mouth. "What are you doing in these parts, Ginsing?" Bart asked.

Matt Ginsing was pulling off a glove. He fished out the makings and began to shape a cigarette with one hand, in spite of the wind. A flashy handkerchief showed under the collar of his coat and he wore a fine-textured black hat. The girl was watching him shape the cigarette, and Bart wondered if Ginsing had the astuteness to realize her amusement was less at the performance than the show-off instinct behind it. Ginsing sealed the cigarette with a sweep of his tongue and took time to light up before he acknowledged that Bart had spoken. Then instead of answering the question he asked one. "You figure on holding them Herefords up here during the storm?"

"I'm not in the habit of walking them just for exercise."

"There won't be room for you in the brake shelters, Tyler," Ginsing said. "Slash 3 is using them this year. We need the whole Crooked Creek bottom for the cut we brought in there yesterday. Wondered if you figured on it for yourself, so we come out to turn you back."

The icy wind seemed to cut clear through Bart. "Turn me back?" he said. "What are you driving at, Ginsing? What have you got Slash 3 stuff in there for? You know damned well I've been using those brakes every year since I've been here! The whole Crooked Creek bottom!"

"Watch your language!" Ginsing rapped.

Linda Dana smiled slightly. "I don't mind. I've an idea that, in his place, I'd use even stronger language than that."

Bart looked at her desperately. "I take it you're Linda Dana. Do you realize Slash 3's got no rights to the Crooked Bottoms? Ginsing made a play for them last winter, but I talked him out of it. I thought that point was settled."

"Why," Linda said, "I understand that's a primitive area in there, that the government owns it."

"That's true, ma'am. But all these slope ranches have been using the back-country for shelter during bad weather. We've sort of divvied up, each using the country behind it. Slash 3 don't touch the *malpais*. In all the years your uncle run it he never tried to horn in."

"But he had a right to," Linda said promptly. She waved a gloved hand toward the gap toward which Bart's steers still shuffled. "I understand, all right, that you've enjoyed the sole use of that part in there until now. But this winter it's our turn." She had taken the thing away from Ginsing and done it easily, and the ramrod was frowning a little.

Bart's temper let go completely at her easy dismissal of the matter. "By damn, you'll get your stuff out of those bottoms!" he thundered. "And you'll do it fast! I'm going in, and there's no room to spare. Ginsing knew that before he drove up here. You can dock his pay for the time and trouble."

Linda Dana smiled, and Bart saw a deep dimple sink in her cheek. "I was thinking that you should be turning yours back before they get mixed with our cattle in there. Do you want to turn them around and start for home, or do you want my men to do it for you?"

"You're asking for grief, ma'am. Slash 3 never did set too well with us little outfits. Your uncle was a hard-driven man, but he could be reasoned with. He was never as high-handed as Ginsing turned once he took over. Ginsing's got this whole up-country on the prod. He's getting you into hot water."

Ginsing spurred his horse over. His two punchers looked wary. Ginsing nodded to them and growled, "Go head back his steers."

"Lay-off!" Bart thundered. He saw that he had made no impression on Linda Dana with his appeal. She nodded her approval of Ginsing's order. The punchers rode out. Bart was on the point of pulling his gun but held himself motionless. If he gave them the excuse, they would plug him, for Ginsing could shoot the way he rolled a one-handed cigarette and the punchers were gun-slingers.

Thoughtfully, Linda Dana said, "My uncle wasn't a good businessman. Slash 3 took on a lot of new stockers last fall. It hasn't shelter for them. And I don't see how you can argue it hasn't a right to take its turn at using the badlands. I know how you feel. I'm really sorry. But I couldn't help it if I would, could I?" She rode out after Ginsing's punchers.

"In other words," Ginsing said, watching Bart guardedly, "the lady don't care a hoot if you and your critters freeze. She aims to have shelter for hers. I only work for her, Tyler."

"It sure must go against your grain!" Bart rasped.

"I wouldn't say that." Ginsing struck out after the others.

The Slash 3 riders had turned Bart's Herefords away from the gap. Bart stood by his horse, numb with disbelief. There had been mean, over-bearing things from Matt Ginsing all through the year since Will Dana died, the mounting kind of clashes that could lead to killing trouble. The mounting impotence in Bart did nothing to cool his rancor. He sat motionless, letting them turn back his Herefords, only because the ghost of an idea was shaping in his mind. He could drive his herd back down to headquarters, letting it endure the full force of the oncoming storm and beyond doubt losing far more of it than he could afford. He could spend unending hours in the saddle trying to protect and care for it. He could forget Crooked Creek and its long and narrow bottoms, sheltered by the broken rises at the edge of the *malpais,* grassed, watered and so well sheltered that a small herd could make out through weeks of blizzard untended. He could — but he wasn't going to, any more than any other man of pride would. "My uncle wasn't a good businessman," that fragile-looking, stone-hearted female had said, looking at him blandly with her amber-flecked eyes.

When they had turned Bart's steers, the Slash 3 riders headed back through the gap to Crooked Creek. So they meant to stick around and make sure he didn't try to move in there with them. There was the chance that he would enlist the other up-country ranchers to help him, which was why Ginsing had moved in there in force.

And Slash 3 would have to stay with its cattle through the undoubtedly coming blizzard, if that was any comfort.

Bart lacked the time to muster his neighbors, for the black sky showed plainly that snowfall was at hand. He stamped his feet on the hard ground, trying to warm them. Abruptly he swung and mounted his horse. The thing to do was to let them think he was buckling down and driving his bunch back home. But Tyler knew this reach of the badlands better than anyone else in the country. He knew of another way to reach Crooked Creek, farther up its length than Slash 3 was apt to penetrate. He swung in behind his slowly-moving bunch and began to hurry it.

The steers picked up speed because they were moving downwind now. But even on Bart's back the wind had force enough to feel. He knew that Ginsing would be watching from the gap, but there was little chance of the man's guessing what he had in mind. For some reason Bart's anger had moved off Ginsing to center on Linda Dana. He was young, human and fully conscious of her physical attractiveness.

The wind whipped up frequently in bitter gusts. The steers began to trot, to low in uneasiness, with the higher bawling of late calves outstanding and heart-touching. Weather like this always built a heavy dread in Bart Tyler, not only for its rigors and dangers, but because he had had a bad experience with it the winter before. He remembered now how close he had come to dying when he had lost his way in country he knew like the palm of his hand. A blinding snowstorm could do that, confusing a man, and turning him panicky, and destroying him. The first snowflake struck Bart's face. He frowned at the sky and saw the mounting agitation in the upper air. It was scattered with tiny, swirling dots that loomed larger as they fell. Then the flakes began to land on the neck and head of his horse and the ground about, and presently was obscuring the distant point of his little herd.

Bart had moved well away from the disputed gap. Presently, nearly lost in the obscurity, he made out the distant rim break he sought. He knew he would like this better once through it, with the vaulting roughs to break the blast of the wind and help guide him. There should be two or three hours of daylight left, and as long as he could see a little he could find his way where he wanted to go. He would figure out what to do with himself when he had settled the Herefords on the upper Crooked, for he had no camp outfit and might be unable to return home. But this last concerned him little in his hunger to defy Slash 3.

He rounded the herd and headed it through the 'scarp break without trouble. Even in the first long canyon it was detectably warmer. Bart kept the bunch hustling, strung out and weary but as eager as he to move out of the blast. It kept getting darker and the snow was heavier. But Bart was easing, able now to guide himself and knowing landmarks well enough to feel confident of reaching his destination. The canyon narrowed constantly, the going getting rougher. Then suddenly it fanned out. They had come to the end of the big one. Bart halted his horse and sat for several minutes, hunched and with his gloved hands pressed in his armpits. Given a start here, the bunch would drift on into the long, narrow bottomland of the upper Crooked. Ordinarily he would leave them there to fend for themselves, looking in on them only when weather permitted. But with Slash 3 on down the creek and already turned hostile, he didn't dare leave them untended. Poor as the prospect looked, he had to go home and return with a camp outfit and spare horse or two.

He already was cold almost beyond feeling. He swung down and found his legs so stiff they nearly buckled. Holding onto the horse, Bart worked his knees and stamped his feet in the snow, which by now came half way to his ankles. When he had warmed himself a little, he remounted and turned the horse about.

He had got as far as the 'scarp break when the storm struck in full fury. Bart pulled in under an overhang and sat there for a long while, raw fear beginning to rise in him. It was strange how the scare like the one he had had could stick to a man. He was trembling and his shoulder muscles pulled into a hard lump. He knew that he could never make it home in this. He had to wait it out, with nothing much to help him. He wondered what Linda Dana thought of a blizzard now and what business principle she would use to meet it.

Knowing he could find fuel, water and the best available shelter in the upper creek bottoms toward which he had started the herd, Bart turned back. He knew that full night had mixed into the blizzard's blackness long before he reached there. He found another overhang that was sheltered from the wind and big enough to protect him and the horse. He had difficulty in lifting his leg over to slide from the saddle and, when he made it, he fell slackly into the deepening snow. Fear was eating openly at his nerves now, the panicked desire to mount again and ride headlong for home, and this was not mitigated by the unmistakable uneasiness of the animal.

He unsaddled the horse and hobbled it with clumsy, unfeeling hands. He took the saddle blanket, still warm from the horse's body, and wrapped it about himself. He was exhausted, growing languorous, but afraid to let go and rest. A man didn't dare because indifference came, then stupor, and abandonment to the mercy of the storm. He began to walk about.

He didn't know how many hours had passed when he grew aware that the wind's high howl was diminishing. When at last dawn began to lighten the snow-filled canyon about him, he realized that the fall had tapered off and showed signs of quitting completely. A sense of triumph came to Bart then, wiping out some of the bone-weary ache of his punished body. He was still alive; his horse was still on its feet; and this primitive victory gave him a kind of elation. Not till then did Bart come out of his lethargy enough to remember Matt Ginsing and Linda Dana and his defiance of them. He was cheered suddenly. He had kept his hands warm and he took the hobbles off the horse and threw on the saddle. For the first time in hours he rolled a cigarette to take the place of breakfast, then mounted, and rode into the canyon. The snow had completely wiped out the signs of his herd's passing and it was hours later when he broke out onto the creek bottom and saw them there.

They were all right and would be if this was all there was to the storm. The creek was wooded, affording protected grazing and browse, and great patches of the exposed bottom grass had been swept clean. The only danger was from Slash 3. If Ginsing or one of his riders cared to poke far enough up the creek, discovery was certain. And Ginsing wasn't a man to share this restricted, hinterland graze after having laid claim to the shelter for Slash 3. If Ginsing got onto this, he would run the Herefords into the badlands or else out into the open sweeps.

Bart swung his gaze to the south. The creek pinched to a gorge there, narrow but negotiable, and some of his steers might stray that way, instinctively seeking the main bottom, with which they were familiar. Bart doubted that he dared leave them un-herded even long enough to return to the ranch for a camp outfit and the extra horses he needed to spare the one he rode. A spunky, reckless thought came to him. The chances were good that Slash 3 had no idea of what he had done with his bunch. They must have made their own camp in the main bottom. They would have outriding to do there, after last night's fury. Bart had a sudden craving to outfit himself from their supplies or, if that wasn't possible, to destroy theirs and let them sweat it out as he had the night before.

Bart's familiarity with the region served him well as he rode down through the creek gorge and entered the big bottom. He meant at least to take a look at the Slash 3 camp. He swung to the right wall, picking his way carefully along the bottom, now passing large numbers of Slash 3 steers. He was growing tense, but his excitement was high and compelling. Then he pulled his horse down in sudden interest. Far down the bottom three horsemen were riding away from him, heading toward the gap where the quarrel had taken place the day before. Bart couldn't tell who it was at that distance, but three punchers would be plenty to tend the Slash 3 cattle and the lone disputer of its right to this shelter. Bart waited until distance had nearly dissolved the men, then turned his horse out into the bottom.

He came to the creek and moved through the trees, figuring they would have taken the campsite he had used on occasion. Presently he spotted the smoke of a fire ahead of him. He stayed on his horse and soon could see the camp. There was a tent, he saw, heavily weighted with the snow that had fallen in the night. On beyond was a rope corral holding several spare horses. But otherwise the site looked deserted. Bart rode in and swung down at the fire.

There was a coffee pot on a rock beside the still brisk fire, a savory-smelling kettle on a rod above it. Hunger hit Bart then. He found a cup and poured himself coffee. He was drinking it when he saw the tent flaps stir slightly. There was no wind in this sheltered place, and his gunhand brushed the grips of his .45 in a reflex action. He pulled the hand up in embarrassment when the flaps parted and Linda Dana stepped out.

Bart grinned at her, knowing that all the dislike he felt for her showed through the mock amusement. "You nearly made me swallow this coffee cup," he told her. "A man would think you'd have sense enough to hustle back to that nice big house at Slash 3, yesterday. Apparently you've got a taste for roughing it."

"Apparently," said Linda, "you have a taste for other people's food."

"In this country grub belongs to anybody who needs it. I need it. Naturally I expect to pay for it now that I've seen you here." That brought a flush to her cheeks that gave Bart pleasure. "How come you stayed out here?"

"The storm struck sooner than we figured. Ginsing said we didn't dare risk trying to get home till it had blown over."

"Don't blame him," Bart said.

She straightened and her head went back. She had pulled on a wool coat and had a muffler wrapped about her neck, a stocking cap on her head. She had caught his innuendo and was furious but too proud to answer. "I intend to learn the cattle business," Linda said. "That's why I came out with the men. I won't have hired help doing anything I'm too soft to do for myself. However, it was not my intention to play house with three men. And if I were a man, I would rip out your tongue for that remark."

"Where's Ginsing heading?" Bart drawled.

"They'll be back shortly. But if you have any further business with Slash 3, you can take it up with me."

"Fine and dandy, ma'am." Recklessness was stirring in Bart again. He had to act fast and get away before Ginsing and his punchers returned. But his tracks would tell them plainly where he had come from to reach this camp. And an hour's ride would show them the Herefords in the upper bottom. "You and me have got business. I aim to make a camp pack, for which in due time I'll pay you fully. And I don't aim to let Matt Ginsing know who did it."

"He'll know, all right," Linda retorted.

"Who'll tell him? Those horses yonder?"

She stared for an instant. "What do you mean?"

"You and me're going for a ride, ma'am."

"You're . . . abducting me?"

"Don't know about that. But I've got a mighty important reason to keep Ginsing from knowing who raided his camp. Owlhooters ride through here. I figured to make it look like one of them had located the camp and helped himself. I've still got to make it look like that."

"Why. . . ?" Linda's face was white with disbelief.

"Don't worry, ma'am. I'd take you down to Slash 3 if I figured there was no danger of you seeing Ginsing till this storm's blowed over for sure."

"And since you can't . . . what?"

"I reckon we'll figure it out as we go along."

Linda's hand was moving slowly toward the pocket of her coat, a greenhorn movement, for a western girl would have known that he would notice. He stepped forward and caught her wrist. He fished the little gun from her pocket and slid it into his own. He remembered the wild desire that had burned in him the day before, to catch her in a plight as helpless as the one he had been in the day before. Suddenly he felt no pity for her in her obvious fear.

She breathed, "So it's true! Everything I've heard about you!"

He looked at her in surprise. "How come you'd hear anything at all about a measly greasy-sacker like me?"

"I've heard plenty," Linda answered. "About you and all the other little ranchers who've fattened off Slash 3 all these years!"

Bart's eyes had narrowed. "And you heard every word of it from Matt Ginsing. Woman, you're a plain damn' fool. Now, you move out there in the snow where I can look at your pretty figure. If you get wild impulses, I'll do more than wash your face in the snow. I'm going to make up a pack. I'm going to leave a note thanking Ginsing for the grub and blankets and the nice, pretty girl. Then we're going to do some wild riding, meandering so as to keep them busy a while trying to follow. I know this country and they don't. If I can fool them the way I want, I'll figure out a better life for you."

"You. . . !" Linda said savagely, "you're the damned fool if you think you can get away with a thing like this!"

Never taking his eyes off her for long, Bart set about his business. There was a very real need in what he was doing, in addition to his personal feeling in it. He had to fool Ginsing about who had visited the camp, which would be impossible if he left Linda there. But it might be good for her, he reflected. She needed to learn how one of those fat little greasy-sackers had to live sometimes in the interest of his little herd. He took Slash 3's tarp and began to build an outfit, helping himself lavishly. He took their coffee pot, a skillet, and a hand axe. He went into the tent for a second and got the blankets off the cot Linda had used. When he went to the rope corral and snaked out a pack pony and saddle horse, he forced her to accompany him, stumbling through the snow. She was silent, submissive, and genuinely frightened. If there had been any doubt about what she had been told of him, there was none now. Presently he made her step up into the saddle, gave her a blanket to wrap about herself, and they rode out. He had decided against leaving the note he had threatened to leave, figuring he could make the horses' tracks tell the story more convincingly. The single tracks he had made coming down from the upper bottom would be less interesting to Ginsing than double tracks going on in another direction. With Linda missing, Ginsing would be quick enough to assume that it had been an owlhooter coming in from the heart of the *malpais*, finding a chance to reoutfit and acquire a pretty girl as well. Slash 3 would ride the other tracks in the effort to liberate Linda, and Bart intended to make it hard riding. He headed due west, into the roughest kind of country.

☆ **‖** ☆

COLD SOLITUDE

grim satisfaction came to Bart as he considered what he had imposed upon Matt Ginsing to balance the hopelessly unequal situation. There would be the shock and alarm of Linda's disappearance, a sudden dangerous shortage of provisions, and the urgent need of pursuit into wild and forbidding country of which Ginsing and his riders had only the scantest knowledge. Bart knew he could play hare and hounds with Slash 3 for days on end, keeping them always away from his own herd.

They climbed through a rim break, making no effort to hide their trail. Bart wanted to be followed, to force his enemies to exhaust themselves, and taste of the hopelessness they had forced on him. He had no pity for Linda Dana, abject and frightened though she was, because of them all she most needed a dose of that bitter medicine. When he had planted enough trail to keep them busy for a few days, Bart aimed to take her out. If that brought his cattle safely through this stretch of bad weather, he meant thereafter to mobilize his neighbors and force a showdown with Slash 3. If she wanted to sic the law on him for abduction, that was all right with Bart Tyler.

They kept going all through that day and Bart knew he was giving Linda a ride she had never dreamed could be. He pressed even deeper into the roughs, floundering through snowdrifts, wandering with the aimlessness of the lost. Twice he bisected their own trail, once heading south and again going north, to compound the confusion for Matt Ginsing. The day stayed clear and, as the afternoon waned, Bart made a wide loop and began to backtrail. In the thickening twilight he found shelter for a camp and halted. His first stab of sympathy for Linda hit him when he had to help her from the saddle and hold her upright, tramping through the snow until she had worked the numbness out of her body. But he kept his resolve firm. Only the day before she had told him through Ginsing that he and his steers could freeze to death without causing her concern. She was getting a taste of what that meant. Perhaps she realized that she had asked for it and it was that which kept her so tractable and quiet.

Bart unpacked, hobbled the horses, and made camp. They were under another overhang, with a sheer rock wall to the windward. He took the hand axe and found fuel, then set a fire out from the wall to give them the warm space between. It was free of snow, and Linda dropped down in complete exhaustion.

He tossed her the blankets and said, "Wrap yourself up. You'll be warm as a new biscuit pretty soon. I'd give you back your gun except it wouldn't do you any good. If you killed me, you'd only rattle around in these roughs till you died yourself."

Linda seemed to wince, then she threw back her pert head in total hostility. "You should be getting a lot of satisfaction out of this, Bart Tyler!" she blazed.

"I reckon I should," he agreed, "but I don't aim to. Don't forget, ma'am, that you had me completely helpless back there at the gap. You showed no mercy."

"And I don't expect any now!" she retorted.

"You'll get it in the way you keep worrying about," he said, and he grinned at her. "We've laid enough trail to keep that red-headed foreman of yours busy for three or four days. In the morning we're pulling out and I'll take you home."

"Then what? Do you realize I'll have you in jail?"

"Maybe. But not if I can help it. Slash 3 has declared war on the little ranches that lay around it. I aim to have a powwow with them and see what they aim to do about that."

Linda's lips parted in a scornful smile. "So the parasites will now unite to destroy the ranch they've fed on all these years."

Bart had dropped the pack from the pack pony and was making camp. He looked at her sharply. "That's twice you've graveled about us two-bitters. Ginsing sure must have fed you a lot of lies. Just what is it you've got against us, Miss Linda?"

Her answer was prompt, attesting that she had thought a lot about it. "My uncle should have been a rich man with the holdings he had and the hard work he did all his life. And he died from financial worry and close to bankruptcy. Bled white by rustling from you parasites. Harassed and hampered at every turn because you little outfits hate the big ones."

"Slash 3 is near bankruptcy?" Bart asked in disbelief.

"Why would I try to lie about it, if it wasn't?"

Bart was starting to cook their supper, slicing the bacon he had taken from a can, and dropping the slices into a heating frying pan. He filled the coffee pot with snow and set it next to the fire to melt down to water. What Linda had said interested him powerfully and he gave it considerable thought.

"It's sure news to me that your uncle was having money trouble," he said finally. "I reckon somebody's made you believe it, but that talk about rustling and trouble-making from us little outfits is pure hot air."

Her smile was bitter. "What else would you say to me?"

Bart ground coffee beans on a rock, using the butt of his pistol, and started coffee. He had taken a jar of sourdough from the Slash 3 camp, and he poured some into the skillet, and set it to bake in the heat of the fire. He was puzzled, disturbed by what she had said, and she seemed to prefer silence. When he had supper cooked, he filled a tin plate and handed it to her.

"You'll feel better with some hot grub in you."

Temper seemed to prompt her to refuse the food, then she accepted it. Bart nearly grinned at the hungry way she ate. It seemed to revive her and lift her spirits, the way good food could when a person was beaten-out and miserable. But it brought no trace of relenting into her manner. Watching her covertly, Bart was struck with the thought that he might have misjudged her, that she believed what she had been told and had considered her action back there at the gap justified. But that made no difference to his own plans. He had his steers to protect, and he had to keep her away from Ginsing until he could take stronger steps against the man.

It did make a difference in his attitude toward her. In the kindest tone he had used on her, he said, "Since I don't mean to let you see Ginsing for a while, I can tell you why I'm doing this. I ran my herd into the Crooked bottom on up the creek from where you people were. I rode for wages till I was twenty-five, and I've put in five more years trying to get a start of my own. If I lose my herd, it's all wiped out. And I sure stood to lose it the other day, and by your decision. I still stand to lose it if Ginsing finds it in there. So I did what I did to keep him tied up and thinking about something else."

Linda was looking at him and listening and there was the merest chance that she was impressed. But she said nothing whatsoever. Night was about them now, and a cold moon had emerged in a clear sky. Bart took the saddle blankets and let Linda have the better bedding from her own camp. He said, "Now relax and get some sleep. I hope you've got more sense than to try and get away. You wouldn't get far, and if it happened to snow again I nor anybody else could trail you. I need sleep myself and I don't want to worry about you."

"I'm no fool," Linda answered.

"Maybe not," Bart agreed and found that he really meant it.

He bedded down at a respectable distance from the bed he made for the girl. She kept by the fire for a long while but rolled up in her blankets finally and he relaxed. He was certain Ginsing had told her a lot of wild yarns about the neighborhood and its relations with Slash 3. He was equally sure that she had somehow gained the wrong impression about the big outfit's financial standing. A cowman with only one eye could see that Slash 3 made money and always had, that it was managed too closely and well to get itself into trouble, and it had suffered no severe adversities in the years Bart had lived on its border.

He didn't know how her uncle's estate had been handled, by whom administered, or what kind of financial accounting had been made to her when she inherited the ranch. But Bart would have bet his imperiled little herd that she had been fooled, and badly, and for a reason. Somewhere in recent hours his conception of Linda had changed. She was green as a pond frog and suddenly possessed of a vast property. She obviously didn't know just how vast and rich it was. There was only one conclusion and Bart drew it now. Somebody meant to take over what had been kept hidden from her. Matt Ginsing had at least a big part in it. The discovery gave Bart a strange sense of bewilderment. He had bought chips in that game without realizing it and would have to play out the hand.

Bart roused frequently to refreshen the fire and make sure that impulse did not cause Linda to attempt an escape. But each time he rose she lay dead to the world. He was glad of that, for as the night advanced the wind began again and hourly increased its howling intensity. Bart's worry increased with it, his old fear of a blizzard revived in him. He had gambled on fair weather until he had Linda out of here. A sudden change for the worse would catch them in a plight he couldn't bear to contemplate.

Long before dawn he saw the first snowflake drift down through the outer light of the campfire. Alarm ran through him, wild and close to panic. He had made his bet and lost it and they were in for trouble. His glance fell on the sleeping Linda and remorse rose in him. He had gambled a life that didn't belong to him. He had learned too late that he well could have been blinded by outrage and suspicion. But he shook these weakening thoughts out of his mind. He had to meet the situation and second-guessing was of no use.

It meant that they had to strike out at once, heading for the outside. He roused Linda, saying, "It's started snowing. We've got to hit the saddle. With no breakfast."

She made a low, moaning sound and for a moment more lay still. Then she scrambled up, the fear in her jumping to him and intensifying his own. He willed himself to a steady coolness and was glad that somebody outside himself had need of him. He said, "Try to make up the pack while I saddle up. The sky's still pretty clear. It's just that we'd better not risk getting pegged down here."

The need to keep her reassured was good for him, too. Linda made a couple of wild turns around the fire, got hold of herself, and began to gather the pack. Bart unhobbled the horses and saddled them.

They had traveled for an hour when daylight began to lighten the atmosphere. The snowfall was heavier but still little more than a drizzle, a light but steady sifting. Bart was heading directly for the rim gap by which he had sneaked his herd into the upper Crooked bottom. If they made it, he would be in territory more familiar to him and would stand a better chance, even if this thing whipped up to blizzard fury again. He broke trail for Linda, leading the pack horse, and had dropped all worry about her keeping close to him. Her fear of the surrounding wilderness and glowering sky was all too evident. She crowded her horse as close to Bart as she could manage.

To Bart she had become a different personality to the one he had detected at the start. She had firmly believed Slash 3 to be a struggling, hard-pressed spread in the midst of enemies. It didn't seem so callous to Bart now that she had insisted on her ranch taking its turn in the Crooked shelters. And he couldn't censure her for being so badly fooled in a business about which she knew nothing. He had to admit that he was sorry for her and for what he had done to her out of rancor. It was the least he could admit. Bart had his own fears to fight down and he forced himself to pick a careful, strength-saving route. He made no mention of it to Linda, but with each passing hour the visible distance grew less, the snowfall heavier, the sky darker. There was no sign of the sun, but he figured it was late afternoon when they dropped down into the canyon through which he had brought his cattle coming in.

He halted. Linda floundered up beside him. Both saddlers and the pack horse were nearly exhausted from the daylong struggle with the underfooting. Night was just ahead of them. It was a long way to his ranch and a longer way to Slash 3. Only the winter before he had got lost while out in the open and had nearly died.

Before he could speak, Linda said, "We won't make it, will we?"

"Not as far as I hoped," Bart admitted.

"You don't know how I loathe you for forcing me into this." It seemed to be said without passion, and this very coldness struck deeply into Bart.

☆ III ☆
BITTER AMENDS

*H*e turned his horse without answering, knowing that their best chance lay in striking deeper into the *malpais* and coming again to where he had left his steers in the upper Crooked bottom. It was as sheltered as any place in here and in addition afforded firewood and water and even fresh beef if they were storm-bound long enough to need it. Linda followed him numbly and Bart could no longer bear to think of her and what, out of pure resentment, he had done to her.

It was not long after that when Bart grew aware that night and all its greater terrors were coming in upon them again. But by then the snow was a heavy, pelting force, cutting visibility to a point not over a hundred yards ahead of them. He rode on doggedly, only now and then flinging back to see that Linda followed. They came to a canyon that lay with the wind and had the full cold blast to buck. Because she was downwind from him, he didn't hear anything when it happened. He just looked back and saw the empty saddle of her horse.

Bart halted his own jaded mount and flung himself from the saddle. It didn't surprise him when he went on down, landing full length in the heavy snow carpet. He staggered to his feet and wallowed back past the pack pony and Linda's still plodding horse. He couldn't see her because of the snowfall and the night. He followed the dragging trail the animals had made and then found her, still and silent where she had hit the snow when she fell from the saddle.

He bent, self-reproof releasing some spring of energy in him. But she was light when he swung her up into his arms and staggered back along his own path. Her horse had halted behind the pack pony and Bart's own. He had come up to it before he realized that she could not ride and that neither horse was strong enough to carry double in this underfooting. He thought of lashing her across the saddle in dead weight, a punishing and dangerous thing to her in this condition. He tried to think where they were, but landmarks were blotted out. It probably was a considerable distance to the Crooked bottomland. He placed Linda in the snow, then strung her horse and pack pony behind his horse, tied together. He got Linda across his shoulders, his left arm snuggling her knees to him, the hand catching her limp arm. He caught the reins in his free hand and started on, heading full into the wind. Presently he was moving through total darkness. There was no fuel in here but Bart knew then that he had to find the best shelter he could.

He veered to the right, coming to the talus of the wall rise. He followed this, rocky and rough though it was. But the increasing size of the detritus began to tell him where they were and his heart sank. It was a long ways yet to the creek bottom. But it helped decide him. Presently he grew aware that the strong headwind had been cut off. He knew that the canyon narrowed someplace in here between high, nearly vertical walls. Protection from that freezing wind was the best he could hope for. He halted when they came to a rock nest that would be additional protection, and again he put Linda down.

His sense of lightness at the released weight gave him a surprise. He used his numbed feet to clear the snow back from the base of a big boulder. He seemed warmer already from having gotten out of the beat of the wind. He unsaddled the horses but left their blankets on them, his mind dull but remembering to hobble them in case they would be needed again. He used the other blankets to make a bed as far in under the big boulder as he could get it. He laid Linda there.

She was too cold and in this condition her temperature would keep dropping the few degrees it took to be fatal to human life. He had matches and could burn the pack saddle for a fire that would last only a uselessly short while. But he was warm, almost comfortable now from his exertions. He unbuttoned her coat and then his own and slipped into the blankets beside her. He pulled her close to him to give her his body's warmth. The wind howled and shrieked above but could not touch them. The blankets trapped their warmth and presently he knew that her breathing was less shallow.

He came out of a torpor a long time later to realize she was struggling in the tight clutch of his arms. Before he had fully remembered the situation, he felt her teeth sink into his chin. He released her hastily, gasping, "Cut it out, you little fool! You came within an inch of freezing to death."

She struggled away from him, and he climbed to his knees, suddenly furious. If she thought he had taken advantage of her helplessness, he should have let her keep on thinking so. If she preferred to freeze, she could damned well freeze. But the air into which he rose was bitterly cold, its chill going through him in a knifing sweep. The horses needed the flimsy protection of their saddle blankets. Reconsidering, Bart dropped to sit beside her.

He said, "Look, Linda, you blacked out and fell off your horse. I carried you as far as I could but couldn't make it to where I wanted. I had to get you warm and there's no wood around."

"You carried me?" Linda asked.

"It was that or lash you head-down across a saddle. But if you're still of a mind to let me freeze, just consider how you're going to get out of here on your lonesome."

She said nothing and he covered himself again beside her. Presently her relaxing body settled against him and he knew she was asleep. He thought, "If we live, I'm going to have an awful time getting her out of my mind. But I'd have to. She hates me worse than poison. . . ."

The storm was still wild and raging when daylight washed out some of its obscurity. Bart climbed to his feet, knowing they had to press on for the creek bottom where they could have a fire and hot food and feed for the horses. He rose and swore involuntarily.

"What's the matter?" Linda gasped from under the blankets. She rolled out from under the boulder and rose hastily.

Bart pointed to the still and stiffened shape of a horse at a distance from them. "He did what we could have done. Just laid down and gave up and froze to death. The others kept stirring. We'll get on. There's enough light we can get to a better camp."

Linda was staring at the dead horse. Finally she said, "I'm sorry I made a fool of myself. I'm grateful for what you did for me."

He managed to grin at her. "Ma'am, you're learning a little about the cattle business."

Bart repacked the pack pony because it had been less heavily burdened than the saddle horses and was in better shape. But he led his own horse, and they started on afoot. It was brutal punishment when they came again into the full blast of the icy wind, but there was no escaping it. Once more they reached the place where the canyon fanned out, and Bart knew they were close to the bottomland. He turned along the foot of the high bluffs, once more out of the wind. Hope was rising in him. If they could find suitable shelter, they had every chance of coming through.

They kept going. At long last Bart found what he sought, a wind-eroded half cave in the sandstone bluff. The walking since they had got out of the wind had warmed them, and even Linda let out a little cry of relief.

Bart made camp hastily for they had not eaten that day nor the day before. He took the hand axe and went out and presently was back with enough wood to get a fire started. He built the fire and watched her unpack, almost child-like in her eagerness. She had bacon sliced by the time he had a hot frying pan. Without being told, she melted down snow for coffee, and when he started to make their bread she said, "Let me." So he took the axe and went out and brought in a bigger supply of wood.

He had a smoke with his coffee after they had eaten. Something was working on him, and he said, "I gave you a rough time, didn't I?"

She looked at him and now he was quite sure that the bitter hostility had left her eyes. She said, "Maybe."

"That's a queer answer. What do you mean?"

"I gave you a rough one, too, didn't I? Actually, I started all this. And a rough time isn't so bad if you've got the sense to learn something from it."

"What have you learned?" Bart asked with interest.

"That nothing on earth tastes as good as bacon, skillet bread and butter, and sandy black coffee. That it's darned nice to be alive. And that people ought not to get their judgments second-handed."

Bart smiled. "People who make their own can still land a mile wide of the mark."

"If that's an acknowledgment of guilt, I'm glad. I was going to be too noble to say so, but I still don't think I'm the only damned fool in this situation."

They were storm-bound through that day and night, but Bart rose on the following morning to find that the snowfall had stopped. The sky was clear. A long slope ran from the cliffs to the distant creek. Away from the cliffs the wind had kept great patches of grass swept clean. He saw the horses grazing in the near distance, and all along the open reach his strung-out Herefords. A deep satisfaction came to him. His herd was all right, though his concern for it had faded in the anxieties of the last few days. But now Bart would think again of Matt Ginsing and his hard-faced riders.

Bart returned to the campfire to find that Linda had awakened. He hadn't told her how close they were to the Slash 3 camp, and he wondered if he should and let her make her own decision about returning there and exposing him to Ginsing. She had changed greatly, but he didn't know how much nor for how long. Things might look differently to her now that they seemed to be safe.

He decided to feel her out a little before going too far. "Did Ginsing ever say anything to indicate he might like to buy Slash 3?" he asked, "or otherwise take the poor, money-losing proposition off your hands?"

She glanced at him sharply. "Why do you ask?"

"He must have had some reason for lying his head off to you. That outfit's a going concern and always has been. What trouble it ever had with its neighbors, it started. In a country like this, people get to know a lot about each other's business affairs.

Somebody wants to get you plenty sick of your inheritance, Miss Linda, and wants to get the whole of it at a nice cheap price. Who but the man who fed you the lies? Matt Ginsing?"

"All right," she said, "Ginsing wants to buy Slash 3. He thinks that if it was run right, it could pull out of the mess. I know how much cash I came by. It's hardly enough to meet the payroll and other expenses though the winter."

"Because your uncle was a great one to put his money back into the spread," Bart snapped. "That's the way he built it. But what you don't know is how much the place is worth nor how much cattle you could tally if you got honest figures. Somebody gave you a false appraisal."

"You really mean that?" Linda asked. And from her surprise Bart knew she hadn't even suspected such a thing like that

"Who administered your uncle's estate?"

It was a moment before she answered. Then she swallowed and said, "Matt Ginsing. You probably know my uncle was sick a couple of years before he died. He turned everything over to Ginsing and fixed it so the man would run things until I'd learned enough about it to take over."

"And there," Bart said, "is your answer. You don't have to take my word for it. Get the court to order an honest accounting and you'll be surprised at how rich you are and how little need there is for you to fight your way out of the mess your dinky little neighbors got you into. Ginsing wants to start trouble with us to make it all the more discouraging for a greenhorn girl. That's why he rooted me out of my shelter this winter."

Linda's cheeks had blanched and her voice sounded a little shaken. "I just can't believe that!" she gasped.

"Find out for yourself," Bart told her. "Slash 3 camp isn't very far from here. I can take you there and let you spoil my little caper here. Or I can take you on home."

"Take me home," she said, without hesitation.

Bart wanted to take a look at the cattle before tackling that. He took a rope and walked out and caught his horse. It appeared to be in good shape. He brought it in and saddled it, then rode out through snow that was at times knee-deep, at times swept clean, and sometimes piled so high it bogged his horse. He worked his way through the scattered Herefords, finding a few downed cows which he tailed up and a couple of late calves that had died in the storm. That didn't depress him for every storm took its toll and he expected it.

He was down toward the gorge that formed the connection between here and the lower bottom when he pulled down his horse in sudden interest. He wasn't sure what he had seen, but as he studied the dazzling white distance he recognized the small shapes of horsemen. Three of them and coming toward him. Bart's brow knit in a dark frown. It had to be Slash 3, and they probably had sighted the Herefords already.

☆ IV ☆
I'VE TURNED GREASY-SACKER

*H*e knew what had happened. When Ginsing had returned to his camp to find Linda missing, he had seen single horse-tracks coming there from this direction. When the resumed blizzard had cut off the possibility of continuing the search for her, Slash 3 had returned to camp. Now all tracks were wiped out, deeply buried in fresh snow. So Ginsing had remembered and got to wondering what lay in this direction. Bart knew this was the showdown. There was no hiding the Herefords, nor even Linda. Ginsing's wrath would be doubled when he knew for sure who had abducted her. Bart looked at his gun and found it in working order. Waiting, he slipped his hands into his armpits to warm them. The oncomers grew more discernible in the distance.

He saw from their manner presently that they had spotted him. He was sure now that it was Ginsing and both his punchers. Bart knew that gun trouble was bound to come and had the impulse to cut loose at this distance to drive them back out of this bottom and warn them against giving him more trouble. But legally, if not in fact, it was Linda's right to say what was to be done with the Herefords and with Bart Tyler himself. Bart waited.

The others rode up to him, slowly and awkwardly, in the snow. Matt Ginsing's eyes were fairly withering in their hostility.

He growled, "So it was you, Tyler! Damn your mangy hide, you've got a gut-drilling coming!"

"Take it easy, Ginsing," Bart said softly. "I've got nothing coming from you. But if you feel otherwise, you'll get as good as you send."

"Where's Linda Dana?"

"Keeping house for me, Ginsing. And she's got her eyes open to you finally. Your rotten scheme won't work. You'd better let your hackles down and stay away from her unless you're in a hurry to get fired."

"Where's your camp?" Ginsing thundered.

"It could be anywhere," Bart said, grinning. "I came a long piece to take a look at my Herefords. In case you think the three of you can put a slug in me, stop and ask yourselves how you'd ever find her if you did. It's a big *malpais* and a mean one."

"By damn, we'll pry it out of you!" Ginsing blustered. "I see what you're up to. You've thrown sand in that girl's eyes. You figure you can marry her and come by Slash 3. Even if she's willing, you're not going to cut it." Something cold and merciless showed in the man's eyes. Playing for high stakes, as Bart had no doubt he was, the last days must have been an ordeal for him.

Ginsing gave his punchers the merest signal. By habit they kept their horses spread out. Bart saw three hands streaking for gun grips, and he jumped his horse straight at Ginsing, who was closest. He pulled his own gun but doubted that he had time. The two horses crashed together, and Ginsing's went down in the loose footing. Bart hurled himself toward the man, which was the only thing that could keep the punchers from shooting at him point-blank. They rolled free of the tangled horses together, each man trying to use his gun.

Ginsing's exploded and Bart felt its muzzle's heat on his cheek. He used his elbow to hit the man across the chin then, balanced, whipped the barrel of his gun across Ginsing's head. He rolled on into the snow, still clinging to Ginsing. The horses got untangled and scampered away. The two punchers were circling, hunting an angle from which they could shoot at Bart without endangering their leader. One of them tried a shot that went high. Bart shoved his gun into Ginsing's ribs and yelled, "Drop those sixes or I plug him!"

"Plug the son!" the ugly-faced one bawled.

"Shut up, Jack!" the other cut in. "Tyler'd do it. Ginsing lost his head. Tyler, we made a mistake. Me and Jack'll holster our guns and we'll all start over." True to his word, he did it. Though the other puncher still glowered, he followed suit.

Bart rose to a hunker but kept his gun in hand. He rapped, "You two jackdandies light your shucks. I'm keeping Matt Ginsing. He's going to set in on a powwow at my camp pretty soon. Don't try to follow me and don't try to attack my camp or the promises Ginsing must have made you won't be worth two cents."

The Slash 3 punchers stared at each other. The more level-headed one nodded and they rode away, heading back toward the gorge. Ginsing was out cold. His horse and Bart's had not gone far in the heavy snow. Bart walked out and got them. He was less considerate than he had been with Linda. He threw Ginsing roughly across the saddle, tied him there, and started in to camp.

Not until he was on the last slope did Bart realize that Linda could have seen it all and must have heard those gunshots. It didn't surprise him to find her anxious-eyed and waiting when he rode up to the sandstone cave, leading Ginsing's horse and its burden.

"I saw it!" she breathed. "Did you kill him?"

"No, worse luck. But you and me and Ginsing are going to come to an agreement about this bottomland."

"Ginsing has nothing to say about it. Slash 3 is mine."

Bart watched her with a building smile. "Then who's going to use the Crooked bottoms?"

"We are."

The smile left Bart's face. "I thought. . . !"

"Sorry," Linda cut in. "That's the best I can do. Can we go home now?"

Bart nodded and began to break camp. By the time he had the pack made up, Ginsing was beginning to revive. Bart had taken the man's gun and unloaded it and thrown the gun off into the snow. When, groaning, Ginsing shoved to a groggy sitting position, Linda crossed to him.

She said, "Hello. Did you have a nice nap?"

Ginsing's face was heavy with animosity. "So you think it's funny!" he snarled. "Me and the boys go through hell and high water for you, and you think it's a laugh!"

"No," Linda said, "I'm not amused. It's not entertaining to watch three men I've trusted trying to shoot down one greasy-sacker who only wants to protect his cattle. You didn't know I was watching, did you?"

"Tyler started it!" Ginsing growled. "He got tough. We had to pull his fangs to keep him from hurting somebody."

"Tyler didn't get tough," Linda retorted. "He was tough already. Tough enough to take the worst you could dish out and still make a monkey out of you. Ginsing, I'm asking the court to order an investigation of my uncle's estate and the way it was handled while you were administrator. I don't think you and I would be congenial with that going on. Do you want to quit or shall I fire you?"

Shock showed on Ginsing's face. "Who's going to run the outfit for you? Tyler, there?"

"I'll worry about that."

"Everyone of the boys'll quit with me," Ginsing threatened.

"Fine. I'll be a one-woman outfit. A greasy-sacker."

Ginsing got drunkenly to his feet. His horse still stood near and, when Bart made no objection, Ginsing strode to it and swung up. He didn't look at them as he rode out.

Bart looked worried. "Maybe you shouldn't have threatened him with that investigation, Miss Linda. It threw the worst scare into him he's had yet."

"What's wrong with scaring him?"

"He knows he's not going to fool you into selling out to him," Bart answered. "But it's hard telling what he's done and what all he wants kept covered up."

"He's not going to keep anything covered up," Linda retorted. "How could he?"

"He might keep you from ever going to anybody with anything."

Linda's eyes widened, then she swallowed. "He'd have to kill me."

"Yeah," Bart said.

He gave Linda his horse and took the bareback pack pony for himself.

He said, "If you hear a shot, dive into the snow. They'd try to get me first."

"Oh, Bart!" Linda breathed, and it was the first time she had ever used his first name.

They got through the roughs without trouble. Bart hadn't expected it there for Ginsing wasn't familiar with them. But he could guess the point at which Ginsing and his two punchers could be expected to emerge. It was there that Bart feared trouble. But he said nothing of this to Linda. When they reached a rim-break opening onto the outer plateau, he told her to drop behind him a distance, and rode on. He swept out between the jaws of the high rim with his gun in his hand. The wisdom of that was attested when he heard the sharp crack of a carbine. His hat sailed from his head. The man was on his left, still mounted, his horse held close to the rimrock. Ginsing himself. He had a murder to accomplish and apparently didn't want his underlings to have knowledge of it. The carbine was still at Ginsing's shoulder. It fired again, a crowding determined shot, just as Bart chopped down with his gun and pulled the trigger. Ginsing pitched from the saddle. Bart rode over and stood above the dead man for a long moment. His having guessed the situation and swung into it alone and prepared for action had rattled Ginsing or Bart Tyler would by now be dead. He saw that Linda was coming on, regardless, and he didn't want her to see Ginsing. Bart swung up and rode out to meet her. She didn't have to be told what had happened. But Bart said, "He tried a risky thing and decided to do it on his lonesome. His picked gunmen will clear out because they backed him too strongly in too many things. I'll take you to town. You'll have to locate a new foreman and have him pick up a new crew." He caught Ginsing's horse because he wanted a saddle under him, and he stopped to pick up his hat. They rode on.

The sky stayed clear now, and the wind was down. When they were well away from the scene of the violence, Linda said, "Bart, about that bottomland. When I said *we* would use it, you must have thought I meant Slash 3."

"Who did you mean?" he demanded.

"You and me. You've got to help me run Slash 3, or I'll lease it out, or sell it. The only way I can see where you'd have the time would be for us to run everything together and split the profits according to investment. Now, don't look at me that way, Bart Tyler!"

He kept looking at her, a smile breaking on his lips.

THE WOMAN ON THE STAGE

(1952)

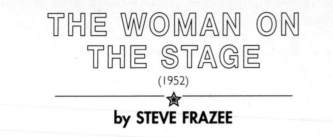

☆

by STEVE FRAZEE

Steve Frazee was born in Salida, Colorado, and from 1926 to 1936 worked in heavy construction and mining in his native state. He also managed to pay his way through Western State College in Gunnison, Colorado, from which in 1937 he was graduated with a Bachelor's degree in journalism. He began in the late 1940s to make major contributions to the Western pulp magazines with stories set in the American West as well as a number of North-Western tales published in Adventure. *Few can match his Western novels, which are notable for their evocative, lyrical descriptions of the open range and the awesome power of natural forces and their effects on human efforts.* Cry Coyote *(Macmillan, 1955) is memorable for its strong female protagonists who actually influence most of the major events and bring about the resolution of the central conflict in this story of wheat growers and expansionist cattlemen.* High Cage *(Macmillan, 1957) concerns five miners and a woman snowbound at an isolated gold mine on top of Bulmer Peak in which the twin themes of the lust for gold and the struggle against the savagery of both the elements and human nature interplay with increasing intensity.* Bragg's Fancy Woman *(Ballantine, 1966) concerns a free-spirited woman who is able to tame a family of thieves.* The Way Through the Mountains *(Popular Library, 1972) is a major historical novel recently reprinted in a mass merchandise edition by Leisure Books. Not surprisingly, many of Frazee's novels have become major motion pictures. A Frazee story is possessed of flawless characterization, the clash of human passions, credible dialogue and often almost painful suspense.*

☆ | ☆

*I*n the Sand City jail a half hour before Shiloh Jennings was due to take the stage up the canyon to Lodgepole, Woody Partner looked down on him with sad patience. When Shiloh drank, he felt good; when he felt good, he felt like fighting. He must have been at the peak of happiness fifteen minutes before. Shiloh was not old or whiskery, neither being a requirement for handling lines on six tough horses. At the moment it was hard to say just what he was. Knuckles had left contusions, abrasions and other things on Shiloh. Blood mixed with dust did not help his appearance either.

"What happened this time?" Partner asked of Marshal Enos Close.

"I didn't think he was so very bad, or else I would've hunted you up," the marshal said. "For a while I thought he was going to make it, even drive the stage. Then this woman passenger for Lodgepole. . . ." The marshal's eyes brightened and he stared at Shiloh's unlovely face as if it were a pleasant view. "Did you see her, Woody?"

"I did not."

Shiloh stirred a little on his cot. He tried to open one eye. "I'll take care of 'em lady," he muttered.

"Blonde." The marshal smiled and cocked his head. "Not the alkali kind but . . . well, you know how the coat of a good buckskin shines when he's oat fed and just rippling along full tilt in the sunshine, with his tail a-flying?"

"She ain't no horse!" Shiloh tried to sit up and swing at the marshal. Woody pushed him back and put one foot on his chest.

"Somebody had better talk some sense around here," Woody said. "Shiloh never could when there was a woman. . . ."

"He called her a horse, Woody. Let me hit him!"

"She's a blonde," the marshal said. "Now as a general rule, you take a blonde. . . ." He saw that Woody was not interested at the moment. "She asked him something about the road. He dusted the walk with his hat when he bowed. Mighty nigh fell on his nose. When she went on, three hands from the Milliron ranch sized her up and made some remarks." The marshal shrugged. "That's when the fight started."

"How did Shiloh do?"

"About usual. We roped one man across his saddle. Another could ride after we lifted him up, and the third one could see well enough to lead the other two back to the ranch."

"A woman," Woody said. "They'll do it every time."

"Yep." The marshal was not unhappy. "One like her, especially."

"You've been married a long time, Enos."

"Sure! But I ain't dead yet. I don't rightly figure just which kind of woman this one is, but, saying I was a younger man. . . ."

"Just say your wife was away visiting her folks. Get me some water and an old shirt or something, Enos." Woody shoved Shiloh's legs over and sat down.

"I can drive all right," Shiloh said. "You won't have to take the stage this time, Woody."

They were partners. Shiloh made a living, and Woody did the work on their placer claims at Lodgepole. Someday, of course, they were going to wade in gold and sprinkle it in the manes of their horses. But not right away. Woody would have to drive the stage today, and the two investors that were due to reach Sand City this afternoon would be grabbed up by mining sharks. They wouldn't be the first good prospects that escaped; and it would not be the first time Woody drove stage to hold Shiloh's job. They were partners and that was it.

Marshal Close returned with a pan of water and a bob-tailed shirt. "There's two kinds of women, I figure. . . ."

"Both poison," Woody said. He was not gentle with Shiloh's face. "Got any arnica, Enos?"

"Yep. You take the first kind of woman. . . ."

"Take both kinds. I want some arnica."

"To hell with you, Partner," the marshal said. "If you were a little more like Shiloh, I'd say there was some hope for you." He got the arnica.

She was tall, if there was anything in that. A good buckskin gleaming in the sunshine. You could say that about the hair under the dab of a bonnet. Horse hair. She knew too much at once with those eyes, brown eyes running to coolness. They could get warm and dark, Woody thought, if the brain behind them wanted something. The bodice of the brown dress was tight, and the front part was cut no higher than the law allowed. About seven petticoats, Woody figured. The hot sun straight into Tumbling Canyon would make an oven of the coach and teach her a thing or two about petticoats.

Buster Arlen, the agent, weighed two-fifty; he came from behind the counter only on special occasions. The fat fool thought this girl would pay attention to him, like the other gape-mouthed idiots standing around in the sun. Marshal Close was there, clearing his throat importantly, as if there were a pile of law to be kept — and he wanted the woman to be sure who was keeping it.

She looked with calm interest at Woody. "You're the other driver Mister Arlen told me about?"

Married or unmarried, they all looked a man over and sized him up for what they might be able to work out of him. Ordinarily, Woody didn't mind. No woman had ever scared him yet. But this one had put Shiloh Jennings flat on his back in jail and had cost both him and Woody a chance to get some moneyed men in on their claims.

"Yeah," Woody said. "I'm the other driver." He went around the coach to have another look at the baggage on the rack, kicking a little more dust than necessary. There was the usual problem here; they fell into two classes, good and bad, with the line between marked like a canyon. He wasn't quite sure about this woman yet, not that it made any difference. But of course a man should know about those things.

There were four other passengers. Buck Harmon and Rastus Wiley were claim-owners, ragged-pants hopefuls like Woody. There was a drummer in a derby hat. He looked as if he had indigestion. He must have, because he didn't seem interested in the blonde at all. The fourth passenger was a slender, middle-aged man. Woody put out his hand.

"Always like to know my passengers, mister. I'm Woody Partner."

The man's smile was a quick wink, as if he did not want the world to observe the expression too long. "Rogers," he said. "John S. Rogers."

The name had the right smell, what with the initial and all; but you couldn't always tell by that. One of the biggest tin horns Woody had ever known was named G. Rodney Dennison. This slender man with the fast smile had not bothered to knock much of the dust from his clothes, but his face was clean, his boots were good, his suitcase on the rack was worn and expensive — and he had a sort of careful look about his eyes that spoke of money looking for a little more money. Rastus and Buck sensed all that too. Rastus held one hand over the buckskin patch on the seat of his pants and smiled his best. A sickening exhibition, Woody thought.

"You interested in mining, Mister Rogers?" Rastus inquired.

"Now, now, let's not say I'm interested in anything, just because I happen to be going to Lodgepole." Rogers raised one hand and his quick smile flashed on and off.

"Well, let me tell you about my claims, anyway. Get in, Mister Rogers." Rastus started to lend a hand. "Now most folks don't care to ride backwards, so. . . ."

"Mister Rogers will ride on the seat with me," Woody said. If there was any talking about claims to be done on this trip, Woody was going to do it.

"I would like that, yes," Rogers said.

"I'll be go to hell!" Rastus said.

Buster Arlen was already helping the blonde up on the driver's seat.

"Hey!" Woody said, "she's going to ride inside."

"Miss Dennison is going to ride out where she can see the view," Buster said. He glanced at Rastus and Buck and the drummer. "She also likes fresh air."

"As the driver, I got the say as to who rides up there," Woody beckoned. "Climb down, lady."

She settled herself, wriggling a little to get her skirts properly arranged. She looked at Woody.

"Come on! Get down from there!"

The woman smiled gently. "No, thank you."

Woody glared at the laughing men. Any one of them would have got hauled off that seat by hand, so they were all showing their ugly back teeth now. "I said for you to get down!"

"You may go to hell," the woman said calmly.

The roar got louder. Woody ground his teeth. At least he knew where the blonde belonged now. "Come on, Mister Rogers," he said. "There's room for three."

Rogers was watching the woman with keen interest. "No, no, Mister Partner, I wouldn't want to crowd things."

"Of course not," Rastus said. "Come on, Mister Rogers, I'll help you inside. Now most folks can't stand to ride backwards, so I'll just move this cigar drummer and you and me can be real comfortable for our little talk."

"Thank you, Mister . . . ah . . . what was your name?"

"Too many misters around here," someone said. "What's the country coming to?"

Woody took the stage away with a lunge that should have tipped the blonde's skirts up and caused her to squeal, but she had braced herself. She smiled. "Have you ever handled horses before, Mister Partner?"

First, she had caused Shiloh to land in jail, all beaten into lumps; then she had made Woody a laughingstock before the men; then she had lost him a chance to interest Rogers in the Rainbow claims; now she was insulting him. Woody sorted over his profanity. The mildest was not good enough and the worst was too much, even for a dance-hall girl. He grunted.

All the way to the mouth of the canyon he did not miss a rock or hole. She rode it out with an amused smile, and that made it all the worse for Woody. Her lips were full and red. From the corner of his eye, he watched the little muscles in her throat and the crinkling of her eyes as she squinted against the dust and glare. It was the little smile that got him. He knew a way to wipe the expression off for her, but the stage line didn't like that sort of business with women passengers. Unconsciously, Woody wiped his mouth on the shoulder of his shirt. He felt his whisker stubble rasp the fabric. He could rub the smile away all right.

The red lips and the tantalizing smirk — that's what it was — were beginning to work on him. They got that way, working around dance halls; they knew how to make a man come to them. The worst of the whole thing was that she seemed to know just what he was thinking.

"Where you going to work?" Woody asked. "Luckey's place?" That was really a fly trap, down by the creek, a hangout for muleskinners and swampers. It gave Woody some satisfaction to toss the insult at her, although he was sure she didn't know what he meant. She would, later.

"Is that a nice place?" she asked.

"Just right for you." She would find out, this Miss. . . . ? What was it Buster had called her?

Rastus Wiley was talking the ear off Rogers, telling him how five dollars invested in the Little Dipper claims would bring back a hundred, maybe a thousand. It was sandy here at the mouth of the canyon, with no place to run horses; and for another mile it was going to be too smooth to bounce the talk out of Rastus.

Woody glared at the woman. Wind from the canyon was running like a little song in her hair, that buckskin stuff. There was perspiration showing on her delicate temple, and a tiny vein was pulsing just below the hairline. She touched her dress front casually with both hands, tugging as if to allow air to wash in. She glanced at Woody full on. Her gaze caught him by surprise. He was disconcerted for an instant because he did not see a dance-hall girl; he saw a woman of another sort, the kind he sometimes allowed himself to think of, somewhere beyond the day when the Rainbow claims had made him rich.

He started to speak civilly to her, to say something about the road ahead. But Rastus Wiley's voice came above the whispering sand against the wheels and the creaking of the coach. "Now, I'll tell you, John S, there's ground all around the Little Dipper, of course, but my claims lie in a sort of natural settling bed where all the gold of the centuries has plumped down, just a-waiting!"

John S. was it? Before they got up the canyon grade, it would likely be Johnny. That miserable Rastus and his lies. Now Woody could have given Rogers an honest statement about the Rainbow placer, if it hadn't been for this woman. Pretty, all right, but. . . . "Look at that road up there, miss. Your side will be hanging smack over the canyon. Don't you want to ride inside?"

"No thank you, driver."

Woody stopped. He climbed down and opened one of the doors. Rastus and Rogers were smoking cigars, and Woody could guess whose cigars they were. Buck was asleep, crowding the drummer, who was also asleep, in one corner.

"Anybody want to ride out in the nice fresh air, Mister Rogers?" Woody asked.

"This is fine," Rogers said. "Mister Wiley has been telling me some very interesting stories."

"Yeah. Rastus, would you like to. . . ?"

"I wouldn't crowd a lady for the world!" Rastus said piously. "Now, like I was saying, John, most of the gold washed down from the Sawatch Range had to settle someplace. . . . Close the door, will you, Woody? It's sort of drafty in here."

"The draft is coming from inside, Rastus." Woody got back in the seat and picked up the lines. He stared at the steep grade up there on the blue granite ledges. For the next two hours it was nothing but a slow haul, with frequent turnouts to let the horses blow. The bumps would merely jar larger lies out of Rastus and less sense into Rogers. Anyway you looked at it, the woman was to blame.

"Is something wrong, Mister Partner?"

That damned little smirky grin. Rules or no rules, job or no job for Shiloh, Woody clamped the lines between his knees and grabbed the woman. She came to him with a gasp, not surprise, undoubtedly, but merely because the breath was jerked from her.

He kissed her savagely, grinding the stubble on his upper lip against her face. He hauled her tightly against him. The pressure of her body against him and a faint scent of perfume were factors that he had not reckoned with. For a moment he half forgot that all he wanted was to smear that smile. One of her hands was free. She worked the other one loose from the pressure of his arm and chest. Both hands crept up along his shirt and clutched there.

The same old story, he thought, *no matter if one did look for an instant way above the general run.* The next moment her thumbs were digging in behind his jaws, against the nerves under his ears. The collar of his shirt was dragged hard against the back of his neck as she used it for grip and leverage. It was an utterly paralyzing trick. Her face was only inches from his. He saw brown eyes dark with anger, and he saw a red flush rising where his beard stubble had raked her face.

"You smelly brute!" she said.

"Let go!" It was a squawk of pain, a cry for help or whatever else was available. "Let go!"

Rastus interrupted himself to yell, "Yeah, let's go. What's delaying things up there, Woody?"

The horrible pressure vanished. Woody's eyes slipped back into their sockets. "Where," he asked, "did you learn a seven-hundred-dollar trick like that?"

"Where did you learn to think you could paw any woman you saw?"

It was her cussing there in Sand City that had got Woody to thinking she wouldn't object. Maybe he was wrong. Smack in the middle of kissing her, something had told him he had made a mistake. Now he was ashamed. "I'm sorry."

She brushed her skirts, as if trying to remove that smell she had accused him of having. She didn't even bother to look at him, and that was aggravating. He tried to change his mind about her again. She had cussed and she knew a fearful trick that numbed a man's whole head. You didn't learn things like that staying home with mother. By gosh he *was* sorry. He had never seen a finer looking woman in all his life. When they got to Lodgepole. . . .

"What's the delay?" Rastus yelled.

"Shut your big blab mouth! I'm driving this stage."

The little smile returned when Woody started up the canyon. *I made a fool of myself*, Woody thought. *I wish I could make that right.*

Before the stage reached the first turnout, Woody decided he had been too long around the wrong kind of women. The first thing he was going to do when they reached town was take a bath and shave. Then he would dig his suit of clothes out of his warbag, if the rats hadn't beaten him to them. Good Lord, maybe she was married! He tried to think of someone in Lodgepole to whom she might be married. There was no one he could think of who deserved a woman like her. He pulled over into the turnout.

Rastus and Rogers got out to stretch their legs. The drummer looked sick. He staggered over to the edge of the road, holding his derby in one hand and bracing himself on a rock with the other to keep from falling into the canyon.

"You got folks in Lodgepole?" Woody asked.

"Perhaps."

Woody grinned. "I said I was sorry. It was just that I'm not used to being around. . . . Well, you see. . . ."

"Yes, I see. You must have cut quite a figure around the dance halls in your time, Mister Partner."

"In my time! You sound like I was a hundred and seven."

"It's hard to say, as filthy as you are."

"I'll be go to hell!" Woody said.

Woody overheard Rastus saying, "I figure, Johnny, that about five thousand will start things off. Later, as things pick up, we can expand a little." Rastus was walking with Rogers along the edge of the road.

"Umm, Mister Wiley," Rogers said. "That's quite a sum."

Rastus tossed an imaginary fifty thousand into the canyon. "Out here it's nothing! Why, one piece of ground no bigger than a preacher's front porch can give you a half million in a month."

"Indeed!"

"That's a start, of course." Rastus waved his hands, and the mountains turned to solid gold.

"Is this your regular line of work, Mister Partner?" the blonde asked.

"I'm a claim owner."

"Oh?" She glanced with disarming interest at Woody and then looked up the road. Part of the buckskin patch of Rastus Wiley's pants had come loose and was flapping. "Of course," she said, "I should have known that at once."

Woody laughed. She looked at him in surprise and then she was laughing. They shared it together, and it came to Woody that here was the kind of woman he had thought to seek out when the Rainbow had made him rich. But why should he wait? He kept wondering about the clothes he hadn't worn for two years. What if she was married? A short time before he had been glaring at her because of the trouble she had caused but now he was worrying about something else. He cleared his throat.

"Do you know anyone in Lodgepole?"

"One person," she said. The cold wind of worry and something else were apparent in her face. All the humor vanished from her eyes.

☆ **II** ☆

ESTABLISHED IN LODGEPOLE

When they crossed the bridge at the lower end of Lodgepole's long street, Woody stretched the horses out for a conventional finish. He scattered dogs and burros and tenderfeet on the run. They flashed past Luckey's place. Two muleskinners were fighting just outside the door, rolling on the ground, gouging and grunting. The bouncer was just going back inside. Woody saw the woman look at the sign, and then she looked sideways at him. He looked straight ahead. Damn the things a man could say when he was sore!

The usual crowd was waiting in front of the St. Clair Hotel: miners with an eye out for men with money, gamblers idly poking their teeth with ivory toothpicks, loafers, and drunks. Lantern-jawed Steadman, the marshal, was watching from the lobby. The blonde was well aware of the eyes on her, Woody knew, but she carried the knowledge easily.

Someone shouted, "Now, there's a looker, boys! That's real color in the pan!"

Even the Panama Kid, a faro bank dealer from G. Rodney Dennison's Placer Palace, lost some of his dead-faced expression as he crowded closer to have a look at the blonde.

"This is Lodgepole?" she asked Woody. She knew it was, of course. He saw her swallow. She was about half scared, he decided.

Woody tossed the lines to a hostler. That pack of staring apes down there, no wonder she was nervous. "Could I \ . . ah . . . um . . . call on you tonight? Supper with me, maybe?"

She looked doubtfully at the hotel.

"Oh, it's a decent place," Woody said. "You'll be staying there, of course?"

"Yes, for a while." She looked doubtfully at Woody then.

He touched both hands against his sweat-stained, dusty shirt. "I won't look like this."

She smiled, but still she was uncertain about something. "All right," she said.

"Stand aside down there!" Woody yelled. He leaped from his side of the seat and ran around to help the woman. She was light on his arm, and the pressure of her hands was warm, and the smell of her perfume made him try to remember how long it had been since he had done any serious courting.

A drunk jostled against Woody, pawing at his shirt. "You missed all the excitement, Woody! You should've been here yesterday. Some tin horn shot G. Rodney deader'n a mackerel over Billie. We had a trial and everything, and the best funeral you ever seen!"

"Too bad," Woody said.

The blonde suddenly was clutching his arm. Her face was deathly pale. "Did he say someone killed G. Rodney Dennison?"

"Yeah. No great loss . . . did they hang the tin horn who shot Dennison, Mell?"

"Naw! It was regular and justifiable. We turned him loose and he skipped. We had the best funeral, with free drinks! You and Shiloh . . . where is Shiloh, anyway?"

"Hey, miss, what. . . ?" She was clinging hard to Woody's arm. She looked sick enough to faint. Something clicked in his brain, and he remembered then that Buster Arlen had mentioned her name, but Woody had been too mad at the time to pay much attention.

"Are you . . . was G. Rodney any relation?"

She took a deep breath, looking at the faces of the men all around her. "He . . . he was my husband." She let go of Woody's arm and walked into the hotel.

"Ain't that a case?" someone said. "That no-good G. Rodney getting himself killed off just when his wife was coming to town. I'd say he didn't have no judgment."

Another miner, watching the blonde, said, "Man, I'd say he had wonderful judgment. I never even knowed he was married or where he was from, but. . . ."

"We know where he went, at least!"

Woody just stood. Rastus was inside with Rogers, carrying the latter's suitcase. Marshal Steadman had turned from the window and was watching the Panama Kid, who was standing with his hat in his hands, obviously offering sympathy to the blonde at the desk. She looked at the Panama Kid and nodded woodenly.

A fine note all around, Woody thought sourly. Here she had agreed to have supper with him, and all the time she was married, or at least thought she was. What kind of a woman would do a thing like that? Just about the time he allowed she was the nicest thing he had ever seen, he had to find out she had been G. Rodney Dennison's wife. No good woman in the world could have been dumb enough or young enough to have married G. Rodney Dennison without knowing what he was. To hell with the blonde for Lodgepole.

Rastus Wiley, the seat of his pants flapping, went up the stairs with Rogers. That Rogers had looked like a tight, sharp man, but something about mountain air made a lie easy to believe. To hell a second time with Mrs. Dennison.

Laurel Dennison slumped down on the old bed in her room. She looked at the dust on her hands and she knew her face and hair must be a mess, but she was too tired and numb to move. There was one silver dollar in her purse. She had just finished telling the biggest lie of her life and now she was frightened to death because of it. G. Rodney Dennison. Of course she had known what he was, from the time he was twelve years old. He had been her third cousin. Uncle Shadrach Dennison had always said Rodney would come to no good end. She could feel no loss in his death, but she could remember that he had written her and offered her a job singing in the Placer Palace. That had not been what he wanted, but that was the bait. Her parents were gone then. The only future had been Rufus Englebright. There was always a little moisture around his mouth, and the back of his stubby hands were covered with coarse black hair. She could not marry Rufus. Someday she would have killed him to get away from him. But she could, perhaps, fend cousin Rod off long enough to get her breath and spy a future.

She had run away from Kentucky in the night. It had taken her a year to get here, slinging hash, working in dance halls. She might have slipped anywhere along the line, but she hadn't. One dance hall was like another; she never thought the Placer Palace would be any better, but it was a goal. Her future, she kept telling herself, would begin when she reached Lodgepole. Now she was here. Rod was dead and she had lied about being his wife. Widow was better than third cousin, a dance-hall girl. There was a respectability in widowhood — and no future.

She thought of the stage driver, Woody Partner. A hundred men like him had made her offers of various kinds, and some of them had kissed her. Not quite like Partner, to be sure. She had not thought any man could jolt her as he had, even though his intention had been based in anger. What was Partner? Undoubtedly a good-looking man, with the dust and beard stubble removed. But he was just another ragged hopeful. They were all going to make it in cattle or land or railroads or mining, the young ones. The men who had already made it had lost too much of themselves along the way to appeal to her.

What did she want, anyway? She had fended off so many men on her way here that they all began to fall into the same category. Women, she had soon found out, were considered either good or bad. How about the men? They could allow themselves all kinds of shenanigans, but when they dragged themselves back into decent society they expected everyone to agree that they smelled like roses. Hang the whole bunch of them, Woody Partner with the rest. She knew he had sized her up as a dance-hall girl right at first; then he had doubted his judgment, but he couldn't change his mind. Still, right in the middle of his rough kiss. . . . No. Woody Partner was just another man. There was no future in him.

Laurel Dennison took her silver dollar from her purse. Standing at the window, she looked down on the street. The noises of the town pounded up at her. This was worse than a cow town for racket. Everybody expected to get rich and liked to say so. If talk were gold, the streets of Lodgepole would be impassable. There were so many jostling men down there seeking wealth. A woman could do the same, using any method that was available, within limits. But she was frightened. She wanted to leave at once. She looked at the dollar and then dropped it into her purse again. If she could go back home, there was no one there but Rufus Englebright or someone like him; and the long trail behind her was to be forgotten. It was Lodgepole or nothing.

She found a chamber maid sweeping in the hall and asked her the way to the bathroom.

"Down to the end of the hall, but it ain't rightly a bathroom. You mean you want to wash all over?" The woman looked at Laurel doubtfully. "I can get a warsh tub. To tell the truth, I just don't remember no one taking. . . ."

"Let's try the tub."

"All right. I'm sorry about G. Rodney, Missus Dennison. The worst husband is still some kind of husband. I've had three and right now I'm fresh out of one. You won't mind a little lye smell in the tub, now, will you?"

For her services Laurel gave the maid, whose name was Candy, the silver dollar. The next bath I take, Laurel thought wryly, might have to be in the creek. The water was harder than the devil's heart, but Laurel finally got lather from the soap. Candy brought more water and a jug of vinegar as a hair rinse.

"Now that's the way I've always wanted my hair, short and handy to take care of," Candy said. "But my third husband . . . you never saw a man like him for thinking long hair was something wonderful." She poured vinegar and went away.

Laurel stood with a towel around her head. Her legs were long and well formed. Her body had never fascinated her, but she was well aware of it. She believed too that a woman was something more than a form, a voice, a look, and motion to be watched. Sometime she would find a man who understood that. The stage driver, Woody Partner — after he began to get straightened out — had looked at her the way she wanted a man to look at her. But there in the front of the hotel, when she said G. Rodney had been her husband, everything had washed out of his face. He would not come to take her to supper now. He had been knocked numb by the idea that a married woman would go to supper with another man, right under her husband's nose. Now he thought she was a widow, and still the wrong kind of woman to suit him.

She put on her one black gown, quite simply cut because there had been only a few yards of the material left in the dressmaker's shop in Dodge City. The faint lye smell still clung to her. She used the last of her perfume.

Candy came to take the tub and water away. "Now that dress is just about right, considering everything," she said. "Never mourn 'em too much, I always say. Get another man while there's still life in you."

"What kind of man is Woody Partner, Candy?"

"Him? A wild one, Missus Dennison. Not as wild as his partner, Shiloh Jennings . . . he's a fright, but . . . well, you know what I mean. You take the average man out here, living alone in a shack. . . ." Candy explained certain failings of men.

"Now they'll be honeying up to you, like that Panama Kid, when it comes to wanting the Placer Palace. Don't you be in no hurry to sell it to the first bidder."

Sell the Placer Palace! The thought that she would now be considered the owner of it had not even occurred to Laurel. As quickly as that came, she knew, also, that no one would believe her if she said the thought of property had not entered her mind when she said she was her cousin's widow. She had done that to protect herself, to give herself some status, a cut above her life of the past year.

After the maid left, Laurel sat down, staring at water splashes on the carpet. She glanced at her purse. She thought of what she had gone through to get here, holding Lodgepole as a goal, as a place to start. If she had the courage to go through with it, what was so awfully wrong? During the last year she had met men who were stealing empires in the West, and bragging of their slyness or their strength. All she wanted was some measure of security, not an empire; and what was so bad about allowing a worthless, dead Dennison to aid a living, hungry Dennison?

Old Wes Dennison, her father, would turn over in his grave if he could know what she was thinking. But he had never been west, or in the fix his daughter now found herself. There was this Billie that the man had mentioned, the woman who had caused Rod's trouble. She might be a big problem. Laurel wondered if she had the nerve to go ahead.

The knock at the door was timorous. Woody Partner? Laurel sprang up and ran to the mirror. A few moments later she opened the door. Not Partner. The man was long-jawed and tough-looking.

"The judge said I ought to call, Missus Dennison. He's busy at his claim. I'm the marshal, Olney Steadman." He began to get red in the face. "I'm sorry about G. Rodney, but. . . ."

"I know. He was lacking in some qualities."

"Well, he was . . . , yeah."

"Sit down, Mister Steadman."

The marshal's eyes jerked guiltily around the room. He let his seat touch the edge of a red plush chair uneasily. Laurel knew by the extreme difficulty he was having ignoring her clothes scattered around the room that he was unmarried. She saw in him some of the qualities of what was called a good, steady man. He had an honest look; he was probably a little dense and completely brave. If he went after a man, he would go all the way. If he married a woman, that would be a great duty also. Her judgment said that Marshal Steadman was a solid man; but not quite what she had in mind. She tried to compare him to Woody Partner. Hang Partner anyway! Who was that whiskered, uncouth lout to be used as a basis for weighing men?

"Now, about the Palace . . . your husband probably wrote you that it's the biggest joint here. It's a money-maker, Missus Dennison. The judge figures there won't be no trouble about you taking over any time." Steadman cleared his throat hastily. "I don't mean to run it , of course. No lady like you would figure on a thing like that. But damn it, ma'am . . . pardon me! . . . how did a fine woman like you ever get tied up with somebody like G. Rodney?"

Laurel looked at the rug. "I was young, Mister Steadman. He seemed so dashing and wealthy, always talking of his father's land back in Kentucky. He turned my head."

"He was a polecat, if ever I seen one!" Steadman clamped his jaw and shook his head. "Begging you pardon, because he was your husband." The marshal seemed to have lost his train of thought. His neck grew redder as he tried not to watch Laurel dragging a dress over underthings strewn on the bed. "Well, now, Missus Dennison, you just rest up a few days and then you send for me. I'll take you over to the judge and we'll have everything straightened out in a jiffy." Steadman clamped his hat on and started out. "The Panama Kid, the one that told you there in the lobby how sorry he was about your husband . . . he's been sort of running the Palace since yesterday. He's not much good. You let me know if he makes any propositions." Steadman blinked. "What I mean is . . . I mean. . . ."

"I understand, Mister Steadman . . . any business offer."

"Yeah!" The marshal ducked out.

There went an honest man, Laurel thought. A trifle thick but plenty strong in other ways. It gave her a twinge to think that she would be betraying his honesty if she went ahead. She had met so many stinkers in the last year, men like the Panama Kid, suave and interesting to a degree. . . . The barren purse lay on the bed. The racket of the town went on. Lodgepole or nothing.

Candy knocked and then walked in. "They're about ready for supper, Missus Dennison. It's best to be early. The stuff gets sort of cold and greasy near the end, not that the general run of hogs mind a bit."

It was the little things that worried Laurel now. She couldn't leave a tip. No doubt Candy had passed along the word that she was generous. Laurel was also hungry. Her appetite had never failed her yet.

The slender man who had been a passenger on the stage with her rose from his chair as Laurel started to pass on her way to another table. "I am deeply sorry, Missus Dennison, to know of your bereavement. Perhaps you remember me? I was on the stage today. My name. . . ."

"Oh, yes, Mister Rogers, I remember. Thank you." He was a kind-looking man. Probably sharp as a hatpin about money, but a gentleman. He was married, she guessed. His deference and his poise before her indicated as much.

"Would you join me, Missus Dennison? I'm not much company, but they tell me you're alone here in Lodgepole."

"Thank you, Mister Rogers."

He handled her chair deftly. She had known gamblers and sports with good manners, but they used them as a tool, as gestures. Rogers was different. She ordered steak. The thought of it gave her a happy feeling. She had eaten no breakfast and no dinner.

"I don't suppose you'll remain here, Missus Dennison, after you dispose of your husband's property?"

"I . . . I don't really know. Perhaps if I could invest in some mining property, or something." How much was the Placer Palace worth?

"I would not advise mining," Rogers said quickly. "Especially for a woman." He smiled. "You must have heard that Rastus fellow today. However, my business is mining, in a way."

"Oh?"

"I don't *buy* property, you understand, I merely get a lease and bond, or an option, on ground that appears to have possibilities. Later, I dispose of my interest to someone who wants to sink his money in the ground."

"But that Rastus fellow said there were millions to be made."

Rogers smiled, and the smile stayed a little longer than usual. "He's right, but it amounts to plunging. It's much safer and surer, my way. I don't want to bore you with business, Missus Dennison. I was always doing that with my late wife."

His wife was dead then. Laurel would bet that John S. Rogers had been a good husband. He was clean, too, the cleanest man she had seen in a long time, except a few gamblers and Chinamen. He had spoken of his wife with a sincere tone. Combine some of the qualities of this man with some of the qualities of Marshal Steadman, but you couldn't do that. You must take a man the way he stood.

The Panama Kid, dark, smooth of face, paused at the table. His tone was deferent and gentle, but his eyes bounced sharply between the man and woman, and then they fixed an instant longer on Laurel's hands. No wedding ring. What of it? she thought. But there was something working behind the Kid's eyes, and it worried her.

"I would suggest you drop in at the Placer Palace about noon sometime, Missus Dennison. I'll see that there is no one to disturb you, and you can look the business over. I imagine, of course, that you'll wish to dispose of it."

"Yes," Rogers said curtly, "she will."

The gambler looked at Rogers briefly. Hostility lay between the two men like a knife on the table.

"Some noon then, Missus Dennison." Panama bowed, walked quickly off.

Rogers watched him walk away. "Pardon me for intruding, Missus Dennison, but don't trust that man a second, in business or. . . ." He cleared his throat. He was the superior male then, believing he knew more of certain subjects than a woman could ever learn.

"You've been very kind, Mister Rogers. I wonder if you would act as my adviser about selling the Placer Palace."

"Gladly."

They rose. It was then Laurel saw Woody Partner standing in the entrance to the dining room. He was dressed in gray. An expression of disgust carried clear across the room to her. She caught up with him in the lobby.

"Mister Partner, I'm sorry. I didn't believe you'd come, after. . . ."

"I see you didn't." Now she was worse than a dance-hall girl; she saw that on his face. "I was coming by to give you my sympathy. Now you got it." He walked away.

"Wait, please!"

He went out the door. The suit was just a trifle small for him, she noticed. His back was stiff and proud. Rogers had seen. He made no comment, and his face showed nothing. He bowed to her at the foot of the stairs. She went up slowly. She had been sure Partner would not come. Now she had hurt him. Of all the people she was hurting and using in her trickery, Partner was the one she least wanted to injure.

I could be in love with him, she told herself. *It doesn't take forever to fall in love.* She remembered how he had held her and looked at her when he helped her from the stage. But the look on his face a few moments ago. . . . She threw her purse across the room. Tomorrow she would be hungry again and every day thereafter. She needed new clothes. There was a hole in the sole of her right slipper, covered with paper. And she had laughed at the patch on Rastus Wiley's pants!

In her time of anger because she had made a mistake about Woody Partner's coming, she could justify everything she was doing. But when she went to bed she kept thinking of the contempt in Woody Partner's eyes. How would he feel if he knew everything else about her?

She stayed close to the hotel for two days. Rogers was looking over mining claims, and she saw him only briefly in the lobby. From Candy she learned that Partner lived in a little cabin at the upper end of the street. And so it was one evening she and Candy walked that way, to see the view. And Candy, humming to herself, went right on by when they happened upon Partner chopping wood before his door.

"I really am sorry about the other night, Mister Partner." She would go that far. The truth, in the middle of everything else she was doing, was a good feeling. But she would not be humble. Partner was clean shaven. His gray eyes looked her up and down, and she saw that he believed that much of what she had said. Now let him say something.

"All right," he said. "You're sorry." He made as if he were going to resume his chopping, but he did not.

Why should she even bother with a man who had no more manners than a lout? Rogers would have reacted much more courteously. But she saw in Partner's eyes once more the look he had given her on the stage; and she saw he was fighting against a barrier in his mind.

"You thought it was odd that I said I would have supper with you, when I was married?"

"Yeah," he said, "it was mighty odd."

It was not all anger. He was puzzled. There was no way to explain. Partner kept watching her, asking for the explanation. "There was nothing wrong in it at all," she said. He half believed her, and he was more puzzled than ever. It was, she thought, as good a time as any to leave. It seemed to her that she was messing up everything she tried to do.

Partner watched her join Candy, and he watched the two of them go down the street. Then he began to chop wood as if he were killing snakes.

☆ III ☆

PANAMA DEPARTS

Laurel had seen many women like the one at the bar with the Panama Kid. She had been one of them. This one was younger, prettier than most, but the mark was there.

"Go on, Billie," Panama said. "Missus Dennison and I have business to discuss."

Billie drank a shot of whiskey slowly, watching Laurel over the glass. "Uh-huh," she said, and Laurel took it to mean almost anything. Billie went up a stairway, along a balcony. A door slammed.

Panama smiled. His glance touched Laurel's ringless hand. "Well, this is the place, Missus Dennison."

Laurel judged the Placer Palace quickly. Roulette, faro bank, poker, a big dance floor at one side, an enormous bar, well stocked, on the other. It was worth something.

"I never would have left a wife like you behind," Panama said. "Where was it you were married?"

"In Kentucky, just a little over sixteen months ago."

"Oh? How much would you say this place is worth?"

"Ten thousand dollars."

Panama blinked. His eyes went sidewise in a flick toward the shadowy balcony. Laurel knew then that Billie had slammed a door but she had not gone into a room.

"Come on down, Billie, if you wish," Laurel said.

"It's interesting enough from here, girlie. Don't forget what I told you, Panama."

Panama spoke lightly. "I suppose you have your wedding certificate with you, Missus Dennison?"

"For the judge . . . when the time comes." Along the way Laurel had learned to play poker. She was glad of it now.

Panama was a gambler too. "Say it was lost or misplaced," he said in a low voice. "We could still get along."

"And Billie?"

"I'm very fond of Billie." Panama's voice carried that time, but his eyes said things to Laurel that Billie could not see. "I would like to lease the place."

Laurel shook her head.

"Suppose a rumor started that you had no legal right to the place . . . Missus Dennison? In view of the respect the miners here had for your late . . . er . . . husband. . . ."

"Respect! Rod was a triple-plated skunk, and everybody knew it! Speak up Panama, or throw in your cards!"

"Ah!" Panama smiled. "You did *know* him then. You didn't learn that talk at the old homestead in the Blue Grass either. I think we can get along."

"No, we can't." Panama was too much for her, and she knew it. If he had not already guessed the truth, he surely would in time. Deception said she should try to make a deal with him, but even in the middle of dishonesty there were principles she could not cast away. At that, she compromised a little. She gave Panama two days to bring her the keys to the Palace, and to get himself and Billie out of there.

"Don't push your luck too far," he said. "I'll drop by the hotel in two days, about suppertime, let's say, but I don't know whether I'll have the keys or not. You think it over . . . Missus Dennison."

He knew. He had found out by some means. He was not bluffing now; he was giving her time to let her own bluff start to crumble.

On the walk outside she paused, half blind with fear and anger. Her hands were shaking. She clasped them around her purse. She bit her lip. She could send the marshal; Steadman was blind enough to do her bidding. But she couldn't bring herself to make the big thickhead do her dirty work. Rogers? His mind was too sharp and orderly; it ran toward law and evidence. He would want her to show her wedding certificate, or other proof, to the judge at once, and have the Panama Kid ousted. Partner? He was the last man she wanted to know about this mess; and the one she wanted most to help her. *I've really trapped myself,* she thought, *and if I can, I'd better get out of it by myself.*

That night at supper Marshal Steadman paused at her table, gulping when he saw everyone in the room watching him. "I see you went to the Palace, ma'am. If that there Panama gives you any trouble at all, you just say the word."

"Thank you, Mister Steadman. Everything is fine." He would never know how many times she had changed her mind while she was speaking. He went on to the long table at the end of the room. Every time her glance touched him casually he lowered his head.

She tried not to watch Partner when he came into the room. He was in the gray suit again, and this time it was not as rumpled as it had been before. He slowed down at her table, nodding civilly; he would have passed but she said, "Why, Mister Partner, will you join me?"

He hesitated, and all the time she knew that this was what he had intended. "Thank you, Missus Dennison."

"Please call me Laurel, Woody."

He was uneasy at first, but there was a drive and force about him that overcame that. "I was like a stablehand last night, Missus . . . Laurel. I'm sorry."

She forgave him with a smile. She sensed the deep strain of seriousness in him; he was no man to flirt with. She found out that he was from Pennsylvania, but this was his country now. He spoke of his dreams. They ran on far beyond the Rainbow claims, which he hoped to sell soon. He had ideas about a smelter, when the lode claims above Lodgepole swung into development.

"I want to settle here," he said. "Build a big house up there on the hill, and. . . ." He stopped abruptly; she knew what he was thinking. "When me and Shiloh sell out. . . ." He stopped again. She was in his future too, but he was thinking she was a widow of only a few days.

If there were only some way she could bring herself to tell the truth. The thought was a dark streak in her happiness. Suppose Panama wrecked everything. Then Woody would find out the worst way possible. *Later I'll find courage to tell him,* she thought. Altogether, in spite of her worries, it was the happiest time she had experienced in Lodgepole. Before he left her in the lobby, he asked her when he could see her again. They looked at each other for an instant that was magic. She said, "Tomorrow," and the magic lasted all the way to her room.

The next day she sent for Panama. He took his time in coming. That, and his easy assurance when he did arrive, told her that he must have something more than a bluff up his sleeve. They met in the lobby. Marshal Steadman walked past the window slowly.

Without an invitation Panama sat down beside Laurel. "Well, have you seen the light, Laurel?" His eyes were bold and raking. She felt color rising in her face. A gambler. You couldn't trust one as far as you could throw a stub-tailed bull with one hand. Yet, she remembered girls in places where she had worked who were crazy about men like Panama. It was only natural to wonder just what the attraction was.

"I could crook my finger at the man who just passed, and he would be happy to run you out of town, Panama."

The gambler smiled. "That would be double O, and the house would win. We don't want that, do we?"

"What about Billie?"

"Don't give me that little girl stuff, Laurel. You've seen the train go by and heard the whistle. You and me and the Palace . . . in a year's time we could light out for San Francisco and live high."

"It's still no, Panama."

Rogers went through the lobby, his clothes muddy. He nodded curtly to Laurel and ignored her companion.

"You say no, but you've still got to find out what my cards are. That's why you sent for me. Suppose we walk out on the hill. A wonderful view, Laurel."

She had no choice. They crossed the street and went over the stream on a foot-bridge. Marshal Steadman watched them bleakly. They stopped among the aspens. Looking far down on the canyon, Laurel was for a moment diverted by the view. She was still alert enough to drive her elbow sharply into Panama's ribs when he came too close.

He laughed. "Don't be so violent near the final resting place of Lodgepole's noble pioneers."

Startled, she looked behind her, noticing then the graves among the trees. One was newer than the rest. "Rod's?" Her lack of honor came hard against her in the silent thicket.

"Uh-huh," Panama said mockingly. "You'll want to erect a shining marble shaft, no doubt."

Whatever Rod had been, he had been a Dennison, her cousin; and Kentucky cousins, even third ones, are not to be spoken of lightly by strangers. "You're a filthy hog, Panama!"

Something crossed Panama's eyes. She caught a flashing insight of some quality long submerged. "I'm sorry," he said. "God rest his soul." Sincerity was there for one moment, and then the careful watching look was on his face.

They moved away from the graves.

"Did you ever see Billie before?" he asked.

The casual tone warned her. Fear tightened up her insides. Panama's face was dead blank. "No," she said.

"She saw *you*."

"Did she?"

"In the Plains in Abilene, six months ago. You were *Miss* Dennison then. She remembered the name because she had just got a letter from G. Rodney to come out here and work for him. Now wasn't it odd that you, married then by eight months, would be working in a dump?"

"It wasn't odd at all. I had no money to get here."

"Oh? G. Rodney sent Billie money to come out. You're way ahead of her, Laurel, in every respect. Why. . . ."

"Shut up! What do you want?"

"You admit it then?"

"No!"

Panama shrugged. "Nobody will believe her if I don't side with her. The two of us, you and me Laurel, can handle the Palace. It's that or else you lose."

"And so will you!"

"Double O. Luck runs that way sometimes."

"I won't deal with you, Panama. I'll have you run out of town." Laurel started away.

"I don't believe you will, Laurel." At the edge of the aspens near the creek Panama took her arm and stopped her. Farther down the stream a burly man who swaggered in his walk came from a stable and led a team to drink. "We'd better settle this thing right now," Panama said.

"There's nothing to settle. She lied!"

"Don't be a child." Panama took her elbows, swinging her in front of him, smiling down at her. He was, she had to admit, a handsome man. "Let's consider ourselves, Laurel," he murmured. His hands slipped from her elbows to her waist. They were warm and strong and the touch of them sent quick excitement through her.

Up to a point she could size up men quite coldly, and then during moments like this her judgment began to blur. He pulled her closer. There was a clean smell of bay rum and laundered freshness about him. The dark eyes smiled at her confidently. His kiss began as a gentle pressure. His left hand went up to the back of her head and his lips crushed into hers. There was a power surging in her then, and a fierceness. After a time Panama drew back. His face was grave, but the mockery was in his eyes, enough for her to know that this had meant nothing to him, that it was only a gesture like his manners. "We can get along," he murmured.

Across his shoulder she saw the man downstream was watching. He turned the horses to go back to the stable, and then she recognized the swagger. It was the stage driver who had been drunk in Sand City, the man who had started the fight with three cowboys when they insulted her: Shiloh Jennings.

She began to beat her fists against Panama's chest. "Leave me alone! Let go of me, you beast! Let go!"

Panama stepped back, surprised.

The man left his horses and came on the run. He splashed across the creek. His face was all cuts and lumps and terrible discolorations, and he had a happy fighting light in his eyes.

"By thunder!" Shiloh said. "The blonde for Lodgepole with a tin horn that can't behave himself!"

"Get out of here, Shiloh," Panama said. "Go. . . ."

Shiloh piled head-on into the gambler. For a while Panama did very well, and then Shiloh butted him in the stomach. Panama went down against a tree. He sat there, breathless, but his eyes were blazing. One hand went under his black coat and came out with a derringer. Shiloh picked up a rock. Laurel screamed. The rock was going to do Shiloh no good. The pistol shot made her scream again. She saw Panama drop his gun and grab his arm.

From across the creek Marshal Steadman, standing with a smoking pistol, said, "Get his hideout gun Shiloh . . . unless he wants to pick it up hisself."

Panama did not want the derringer. He looked at Laurel, half smiling. "You women have got all the aces. But this time I'm going to talk, Miss Dennison. I'm going to tell them all about you."

"You say one word about her and I'll slap all the taste out of your mouth!" Shiloh reached down and tore the front of Panama's shirt loose with a twist and a jerk. "And I'll cram this fancy smelling rag down your throat to boot!"

Steadman came across the stream. Men were running from every direction. "He was going to open his filthy mouth about this lady, was he?" the marshal asked. "I ought to shoot him again right here where he sits . . . begging your pardon, Missus Dennison."

A gambler knows when he has lost. Panama looked at the three of them, his face calm. He held his arm. "The vet can wrap that up while the hostler at Murty's stable is throwing a saddle on that fancy mare of yours," Steadman said. "I reckon that woman, that Billie of yours, that caused the trouble between G. Rodney. . . ." Steadman looked at Laurel and gulped. "Well, she's going with you, Panama."

Shiloh put his arms around Laurel. "You poor little thing."

She shoved him away. He smelled of horses and arnica. She saw Woody Partner standing across the creek, his face grim. How long had he been there? Other miners were splashing over to see what they could see, but Woody was just standing.

"Come on!" Steadman said. He heaved Panama to his feet. The gambler gave Laurel an enigmatic look and then went away with the marshal.

Suddenly Shiloh swooped Laurel up in his arms. "I'll carry you over, ma'am."

She tried to struggle. "There's a bridge. . . ."

"No trouble at all!"

The crowd laughed.

Shiloh put her down in front of Woody. "The poor little thing. She was insulted by that tin horn, Woody. Now. . . ."

"I saw," Partner said. "I saw it all from the stable, Missus Dennison. I was wondering why you didn't use that little gouging trick with your thumbs." He was utterly disgusted; he turned and walked away.

So he had seen how she responded to Panama's kiss. "Woody, wait!" There was no use. She didn't know what she could say if he came back. He did not come back. Damn men anyway! What business had Partner had being over there in the stable, spying! "Woody, wait a minute!"

He went on.

A miner looked at Panama going away with Steadman. "Not that he don't deserve shooting, but who's going to run the Palace for us?"

Partner went back to his cabin and jammed his suit into his warbag. He had borrowed money to get that thing cleaned up and pressed at the Chinaman's. How big a damned fool could a man be? She had said, "Call me Laurel, Woody." He had been right from the start, and then he had let that look in her eye warp his judgment. She was going to have supper with him, and all the time she was married, or would have been except for a tin horn's bullet that she didn't then know about. So right away she got friendly with Rogers.

Even after that he let the memory of the way she had looked at him twist him away from facts. She had been G. Rodney's wife. My God, that should have been enough. He kicked the warbag under his bunk. It disturbed a broken shovel and some tin cans that had held food eaten and unpaid for yet at Craig's store. Dreams, Woody. Marry her and have some kids. Sit in the evenings on the porch of that big house you're going to build and watch the smoke from the smelter you're also going to build.

He stood in the middle of a dirt floor, in a cabin where a man could not straighten to his full height. It was all going to be different someday. The blonde for Lodgepole had given him ideas of making quick changes from things that had seemed pleasant enough before he saw her. She was beautiful; she had seemed sincere enough when they had supper together. And then she had stood there in plain sight and kissed that miserable tin horn. She hadn't even tried to get away from him, or start any trouble, not until she was already free . . . and saw Shiloh watering the team. To hell with a woman like that. If he could get her out of his mind, it wouldn't be so bad. But he couldn't.

Shiloh came in singing. "I'm going to run the Placer Palace until she sells it, Woody! The little thing asked me herself."

"That last drunk cost you the stage-driving job. What'll it be with all that whiskey around you and a fight handy anywhere you want to look?"

"Just for a week or two, Woody. She asked me. . . ."

"She asks plenty and she gets it. She's no good for any man, Shiloh. You saw her hugging the hell out of that gambler, didn't you?"

"Now, Woody, we're partners, but don't talk about her like that. She's a fine little. . . ."

"She's no good."

Shiloh punched Woody in the nose. Woody hit Shiloh twice on his bruised mouth. It was a good fight, and it took most of the steam and anger out of Woody before it was over. They wrecked the inside of the cabin. When they could move, they staggered down to the creek and splashed cold water on themselves.

"She's a fine little thing, I still say." Shiloh was ready to go some more.

"All right," Woody said, feeling a loose tooth, "she's a little angel. Now let's sell our damn claims and get out of here for good!"

Laurel paced her room. This thing had gone too far. Now she had lost Woody Partner. Rogers knocked. He hesitated when she had invited him to come in. "Perhaps in the lobby, Missus Dennison. I have some business to discuss with you." It was not prudishness but instinctive courtesy that made him hesitate.

"Come in. I've already stirred up enough talk so this won't make it any worse."

"I think I have found a buyer for your property . . . two men named Burns. They've gone back to Sand City but they intend to return in a few days."

"That's very kind of you. Won't you sit down, Mister Rogers."

"Do you mind calling me John."

"Not at all. My name is Laurel." She never would get over the little twinge she felt every time she was called by a name not hers. If she could work up courage now, she would tell Rogers the truth.

"I took the liberty of mentioning a figure to the Burns brothers, Laurel. Twenty thousand dollars. You should get at least fifteen before it's agreed on."

Fifteen thousand! Laurel swallowed slowly. What a lot of things you could do with that much money!

"Before the men return there are certain matters we should take care of. The stock and furnishing of the Palace should be inventoried. We should examine your late husband's lease or title, whichever he had to the building. All records should be put in order to determine if he had any large outstanding obligations before his death. A seller owes an obligation to a buyer. I have always conducted my affairs along that premise, and I'm sure that you will wish to do the same."

The shrewd, kindly eyes made her blush with shame inside. Fifteen thousand dollars — where was the courage she had tried to summon?

"If you wish I will take care of the whole matter for you, Laurel."

"Thank you." Was that an admission she was not going to tell the truth?

"Now, the matter of establishing your right to the property. I talked to the judge, such as he is, and I'm sure there will be no difficulty there." Rogers frowned. "You've no idea how brusquely these people take care of legal matters out here that would require a year's time back home."

"Yes, I've noticed that." Marshal Steadman had sent a hulking deputy after Billie. When she tried to protest, to tell what she knew of Laurel, the deputy had clapped a dirty hand over her mouth and almost dragged her away. More than anything about the mess, that part stuck in Laurel's mind. She was no better than Billie, only luckier.

"To give all the protection we can to the buyers, I suggest that a copy of your marriage certificate be presented to the judge and a record of it entered."

"I have no marriage certificate, John." Laurel looked at Rogers steadily. Now that she had said that much the rest of the truth should be easier.

His eyes did not waver. "I would not have believed that," he murmured. He cleared his throat. "However, a common-law wife," he said it hastily, "still has rights under the law." His look was gentle. "In view of the way legal matters are handled here, the matter need not come up again. You did not have to tell me, Laurel, but now I respect you for it even more than I did before." His voice was soft. "You were so very young, of course. You're scarcely more than a child now."

Her courage to tell the truth was gone. She nodded.

"Try to forget it," Rogers said. "Let me help you all I can. In time it will all go away." His face was twisted for an instant. "You have youth and courage and great beauty, Laurel." He rose and went to the door. "You are a very beautiful woman." He bowed and went down the hall.

Utterly sick with self-condemnation, she flung herself upon the bed. Survival and a chance. That was all she had wanted at first. And now she was betraying men like John Rogers and Marshal Steadman. Honor was not the mark of stupidity, as some thought of Steadman. Rogers was honorable too, and she had never known a keener man. Out of it all, on top of everything else, she had lost Woody Partner. She was now on the verge of having more money than she had ever dreamed of, but what was that if she couldn't have the one man she wanted?

She could reduce her problems so far by logic and then emotion disrupted the rest. A weary old dance-hall woman had told her once, "Someday you'll see a man. He may not be anything special that you can tell, and the chances are he won't have a cent. That's the way it happens. But he'll be the one, whether he is fat or thin, tall or short, or even stupid. That's the one, Laurel. I know. I waited for a rich one."

Laurel rebelled against that thought too. Any tired old hag was full of advice. Suppose one of them had met a man like John S. Rogers. You didn't have to love a man wildly to marry him, and maybe you could be very happy just the same. Who was Woody Partner anyway? She knew no more about him than she knew of Rogers; not nearly as much as she had guessed instinctively of the Panama Kid. He lacked Panama's good looks and Rogers's innate courtesy. He did not even have Shiloh's booming friendliness, and for all she knew he might not be half as steadfast as Marshal Steadman. There it was. She could marry Steadman, if she wanted to, and tell them all to go to hell. Steadman would never give her any trouble. But, anyway she worked at the problem, Woody Partner would not get out of her mind.

☆ **IV** ☆

WOODY SELLS OUT

*I*n one month the Lodgepole Mining Brokerage was a solid institution. Rogers and Dennison. Few of the investors flocking up from the railroad at Sand City knew that Dennison was a woman until they walked into the office. Lode mines were beginning to open up slowly. Men took the chocks from the end of the last rails in Sand City and got ready to string iron up Tumbling Canyon. The boom was on. And so far, not even the placer ground had been worked thoroughly.

For the Placer Palace Laurel had received sixteen thousand dollars in cash. Fifteen thousand of it was in the brokerage, but the taint to it had not been changed by transfer from one place to another. Laurel was hurt, and sometimes angered too, because Rogers's careful honesty in dealing with prospective buyers had been recognized instantly. Men accepted her but as a woman. He had taught her how to keep the records and how to deal with prospects who came into the office when he was away scouting claims. She was a partner, but she knew Rogers was always a little amazed by the thought. She doubted that he would have gone into business with any man. Nor did he intend that she be a business partner indefinitely. John Rogers would ask her to marry him as soon as he thought she had been a widow a proper length of time.

Shiloh Jennings had not been hamstrung by any such scruples. During the week he had run the Palace for her, he had asked her to marry him twice a day. And now the marshal was hesitating at the door. His face was already fiery red. He gulped. He glared up and down the street to see if anyone out there could read his mind and dared to say anything. He twisted his gun belt four inches to the left and then four inches to the right again. Laurel knew. He had been working himself up to it for a long time. It would be a frontal approach, as short and direct as he could make it.

Finally he came to the desk. He spread his feet and took a tremendous breath. "I ain't much but I'm steady and can always make a living." He tried to think of something else in his favor. "I'd treat any woman mighty good. Will you marry me, Missus Dennison?"

Revulsion in herself swelled up in Laurel. She came from behind her desk and put her hand on Steadman's shoulder. The muscles jerked. His face grew redder.

"You're one of the finest men I ever knew, Olney." Her sincerity was heightened by the knowledge of her own dishonesty. "A woman would be a fool to refuse you, but. . . ." How could she put it?

"Yeah," Steadman said, "I know. Rogers. He's all right. I know a good man when I see one, Missus Dennison. Well, by God . . . begging your pardon . . . I had to ask." Steadman tramped out again.

He was not greatly hurt, she knew; he might for a while think he was, but it had been a duty with him. He had become attracted to her, considered his reactions for a long time, and then decided it was his obligation to ask her to marry him. Now he had done it and was relieved.

Woody Partner held no such duty. She had seen him around, of course, going his indifferent way. And yet, she thought, he had been over-careful in his ignoring of her.

That in itself indicated something to her. Who was Partner anyway? Just another mud-splashed lout from the creek. If he sold his claims, he wouldn't have as much money as she and Rogers made on one quick transaction. What right had Partner to walk away because he had seen her kissing Panama, even if she hadn't objected to the kiss? Woody probably had been around with every dance-hall girl in town at one time or another. Had he? She wondered.

She piled blame and censure on Partner until she had him buried under the accumulation due all men. But he would not stay buried. He kept popping up. First, he smiled at her; they laughed together on the coach; and then his face was grim with disgust and loathing. She hated him. That was why she kept thinking of him, of course. Over a little thing like kissing Panama. It was really nothing. Nothing at all.

But it was not just that and she knew it. The one act had been proof to him of all the dishonesty in her. You could be hugely dishonest if it suited you. She had not been born that way, and she hadn't been able to develop protective calluses over her conscience. Someday. . . . No, she couldn't tell the truth then or ever. Rogers was dragged in with her now. She sat down at her desk once more, staring at an option on the Freedom Placer. Options, papers, figures — and where was her youth going so quickly? She tore the option into bits. She grabbed up the whole pile of papers, and then she put them down slowly.

After a while she began to write from memory the paper she had torn up. Jim Shelton would be in again tomorrow, asking if, for hell's sake, ma'am, ain't nobody been around to do some buying yet? He could sign the paper again. Everything would be in order. Rogers and Dennison would go right along, making money, being honest. John S. Rogers would ask her to marry him. She would accept. Everything would be fine. It was a much better future than any she had hoped for all those weary months when she was holding Lodgepole as her goal.

Rodney, up there on the hill, soon to get his marble shaft, would have laughed about a deal like this; it was the sort of thing that had always pleased him. Laurel began to check through the papers on her desk. All but one little corner of her mind steadied down. And then Woody Partner was coming through the door. That one little corner of her mind flamed up and destroyed the whole careful structure of her thinking. He had not changed at all. Maybe . . . yes, there was just a hint of shame about him.

Laurel put several more figures on the sheet before her. She said calmly, "Yes, Mister Partner?"

He had expected a little more. Get the hook in deeper, she told herself. Let him wiggle.

"Are placer holdings moving any better?" he asked.

"I'm afraid not, Mister Partner. John says the investment trend is all toward lode mines now. Of course, we're still interested in placers, but they don't last. John says investors. . . ."

"Yeah. I know. I'm thinking of giving you an option on the Rainbow . . . Shiloh and me. We haven't been getting along so well lately. Shiloh wants to pull out."

"I see." She kept her interest very casual. "Well, I suppose we could take an option on the Rainbow, although John says we're in too deep already."

Partner shifted his feet. "What I want is to sell outright, so Shiloh can get away like he wants to."

"We don't make a policy of buying ground ourselves, Mister Partner. John says. . . ."

"I know what he says!" Her frequent reference to Rogers was working on him, sure enough. "We're willing to unload the Rainbow for five thousand. That's a steal."

"Placer ground. . . ." Laurel shook her head doubtfully. She knew how it irritated a man to hear a woman express any opinion about mining. "You're thinking of leaving too, Mister Partner?" She was polite and calm, but her insides were pounding.

"No. I want to try to develop some lode claims I've got near the Liberty Bell."

She nodded. There was something more on his mind. Let him be disturbed. He deserved worse. "I guess we could make an exception," she said. "For four thousand."

"Five," he said.

She frowned. "John will take me to task if I buy ground at any price, but perhaps I can convince him. . . ."

"Yeah. You can, all right."

"I beg your pardon?"

He was a trifle ashamed. "Nothing," he said.

"Four thousand then?"

"All right. We need the money."

She filled out a bill of sale and wrote a check. "Shiloh will have to sign this paper also, Mister Partner."

"He's at the Palace now. I'll get him."

Partner found Shiloh and he signed. Then Shiloh returned to his drinking, telling Woody to hurry and cash the check because the Burns brothers were growling something fierce about the bar bill.

Partner paused at the door of her office. Now something on his mind was troubling him. He put the check in his pocket and entered.

"Laurel, that Panama Kid . . . he didn't mean anything, I know. I got a little sore, I know, but I've been thinking it over and. . . ."

"Oh, yes, Panama. I'd forgotten who you were talking about for a moment. What about him, Mister Partner?"

Woody reached for her hand. She pulled it away. Her heart was singing now. "This is a business office, Mister Partner."

He leaned on the desk. His face was serious. "One reason I wanted some money right away was because of you, Laurel. Ever since the day I saw you there in Sand City, I've been thinking I wasn't going to wait until I made my stake before I asked some woman. . . ."

"Some woman!"

"I mean you. I. . . ."

"*You* weren't going to wait, Mister Partner. You were just going to walk in one day and say to *some* woman, 'I'm ready now.' Ready for what?"

"You know what I mean! Don't be so damned edgy."

"Don't be so damn crude, Woody Partner. I don't know what you mean."

"The hell you don't!"

He would have taken her in his arms then, but the desk was between them and she made no move to rise. She had not planned to be so perverse, but it had served; and she would continue to let it serve for a while. Let him do the stewing and fretting. She had him now. It was all she could do to keep from rising and going around the desk to him. That was what she wanted, but the woman in her — and common sense, she thought — told her to let him dangle.

He grinned at her. "I got some things to do. Then tonight at six o'clock I'm going to get a rig and come by the hotel. We're going to take a ride, Laurel."

"I may be busy."

"I'll come by at six."

"I didn't say I'd go."

"You will."

She stood at the window and watched him go straight to the bank. The bustle in the street gave her pleasure. She had never seen a more beautiful day. She looked up on the hill, up where Woody wanted to build a big house. The only thing was — how much could she tell him about herself and Rod? For once she was able to crowd the thought away. Maybe he should not know, ever.

The two men who came in with Rogers were named Julius Hill and Fletcher Wann. They did not look as if they could make a down payment on a hillside lot, but that was belied by the deference with which Rogers treated them. They accepted his introductions to Laurel and then forgot her. When money was in the air, a lot of men could do that, she had learned.

Hill filled a corncob pipe. "We've got to have everything, Mister Rogers. We've got a lot of work to do before winter."

Rogers nodded. "We have everything but one group of claims." He glanced at Laurel. "Mister Hill is talking about the placers. I managed to get an option out of Rastus Wiley and his partner today. That leaves only the Rainbow."

"Smack in the middle," Hill said. "We've got to have everything, you know."

"I got the Rainbow today," Laurel said.

The three men stared at her. Then Rogers smiled. "You see, gentlemen, you were unduly startled when I told you I had a woman partner. Now what do you have to say?"

"As long as you have the whole works tied up, I'm satisfied." Hill lit his pipe. "How much for the whole batch of options?"

"Forty thousand," Rogers said.

Laurel figured. That was about twenty-five thousand profit.

Hill looked at Wann. They nodded, stony-faced. "Get everything in order and we'll give you a draft this afternoon on the Sand City exchange," Hill said. The two men shook hands with Rogers, nodded to Laurel, and walked out.

"Whew!" Rogers's quick smile winked. "I was getting worried about the money we had tied up in those placers. How'd you ever get an option out of Partner?"

"I didn't. I bought his ground."

"Bought it! How much?"

"Four thousand." She saw Rogers's face turn serious in an instant. "What was wrong in that?"

Rogers gave her a long look. "You didn't know about this combine, did you? I didn't tell you about the rumors."

"No."

"It's like this, Laurel. We only hold options over a set period, two months. We're obliged to forfeit our money if the options aren't taken up during that period. If someone buys our paper, he assumes the obligation to fulfill the agreement or forfeit the option money. . . ."

"I understand all that."

"Hill and Wann and the company they represent, a large and reputable group, will have to deal with each individual claim owner now, on the actual buying price, which means they'll have to deal with us on the Rainbow, since you bought it." Rogers frowned. "You paid about one fourth of what the ground was worth, or will be worth now. It was good business, but. . . ." He had always known, then, about how she felt about Partner.

"But I didn't know this big deal was coming up!"

"I know you didn't," Rogers said gently. "But will Woody Partner believe that? Three weeks ago he wanted seven thousand for the Rainbow. You have beaten him down considerably. What's he going to think?"

"I didn't beat. . . ." She had. A thousand dollars, and at the same time she had thought a thousand dollars was worth the suffering Woody Partner had caused her for a month. She had intended, afterward, to tell him so. Now there was likely not to be any afterward for her and Woody.

"We can quit-claim the ground back to him," she said. "That will prove. . . ."

"No, Laurel." A pained expression crossed Rogers's features. "Do you think he'd take it back . . . from a woman? Shiloh Jennings has told everyone in town by now and by tomorrow, when the news spreads that Hill and Wann are going to buy up the whole creek, there will be two thousand men laughing at Partner because a woman bested him."

"I didn't mean to . . . not that bad, at least." Laurel sprang up. "I'm going to go tell him before he finds out."

"Just a moment." Rogers came across the room. He took her by the hands. "I'm going to ask this *before* you go. Laurel, will you marry me?" His face was almost wistful. He watched her with a patient, sensitive look; and he knew before she spoke what the answer was.

"I'm sorry, John. It's Woody."

"If you can get him," he said gently. "I wanted to ask now, before anger against him might have caused you to make a decision you really didn't want to make, later."

"You don't think he'll believe me? You think. . . ."

"I'm awfully afraid he won't, Laurel."

Not an hour before she had been sure of Partner. She should have let him speak on then, allowed him to be penitent and masterful at the same time. "He has to believe me!" she said.

Rogers released her hands and stepped aside.

Steadman found Woody for her in the Highlands Saloon. When the marshal brought him out, it was evident that the two men had quarreled. Steadman said, "There he is, Missus Dennison," and walked away, hitching at his gun belt.

"Woody, I've got to tell you what happened after I bought the Rainbow. . . ."

"Don't bother, Missus Dennison." His flat-cheeked face showed contempt for her and anger at himself. "The banker told me. He knew about Hill and Wann, even before you did."

"But I didn't know! I'm willing to give the claims back at the same price. . . ."

"Thanks no. I'm a sucker sure enough, but I don't wail when I get caught. Take your money, Missus Dennison. That's what you came here for in the first place. Keep the claims and go back to John-says." He walked back into the saloon.

The marshal hadn't strayed far. He spoke beside her for a few moments after Partner disappeared. "Shall I bring him out here again, ma'am? I can make him stand there and listen to what you want to tell him."

Laurel said, "Go in and tell him . . . to go to hell!"

"Yes, ma'am." The marshal was already moving; then he stopped and stared at her. She was almost running down the street.

She went to her room and threw herself upon the bed.

It was nearly evening, and the racket of the town was mounting when the knock came. Rogers called her name. She did not care about the tear stains on her face or her rumpled appearance. She put her head against his shoulder and cried. He held her gently.

He was a man she could always go to in time of trouble. She began to dab at her face with a wet cloth. Rogers sat down and watched her gravely. If he asked her to marry him now, she just might do it. But he did not ask.

After a while he said, "If you ever get another chance to talk to Woody, how much are you going to tell him?"

"I don't want to see him ever!"

"That's utter nonsense," he said crisply.

"I'm going away from here, John, and I'm never coming back. I want you to do something for me. I want you to take sixteen thousand dollars of my money and do something decent with it."

"That's an odd request, Laurel."

She sat down on the bed. The truth she had wanted to speak for a long time began to come from her slowly. It grew no easier as she went along. She told Rogers everything about misrepresenting herself as Rod's wife.

Rogers looked at her solemnly. "So now you want to do something worthy with the money. Tell me, Laurel, if it were all you had in the world, would you still give it away?"

The thought shocked her. "I don't know. I really don't know."

He smiled. "You're as honest as I always thought you were."

He had held something back, and now she sensed it. "What did you mean when you asked me a minute ago if I would tell Woody everything?"

"I meant about working in dance halls. A half dozen men who came to our office told me later they had seen you in different places, Laurel."

"And all this time you've never mentioned it?"

"Why should I? I know who you are now."

She would never receive a greater compliment, and she knew it.

"I'll see that a school and a church are built with the money," Rogers said. "Give me the check tomorrow." He frowned. "Strictly speaking, that will be compounding breakage of the law, but. . . ." He shrugged. "This country seems to make its own laws as needed. Where do you intend to go, Laurel?"

"I don't know."

Rogers stood up. "You know, of course, that you have been just as big a spoiled brat as Partner. You know that you would have fought and quarreled with him until you both grew up. You know that being young has a lot of disadvantages."

She guessed he was right, but it all didn't matter now.

"He's downstairs," Rogers said. "Waiting."

She could not believe the words.

"He was drunk . . . for a while. He's all right now. I talked to him. There wasn't any emotional barrier between the two of us, so he could believe what I said about that business deal."

Rogers walked out. He was sitting in the lobby when she went down. Woody Partner was waiting in a buggy outside.

They drove above the placers on the creek. Night was settling slowly from the purple sides of the mountains.

"Made a fool of myself again, didn't I?" Woody said.

"Yes."

"Don't be so smirky about it!"

"I smirk as I please."

He stopped the buggy. "I wiped that chessy-cat grin away once, but you used an infernal hold on me. This time. . . ," he grabbed both her hands.

The shadows came down around them. Day or night, it did not matter. They were young. They owned the world and time would run forever.

DECISION IN SUNDOWN
(1953)

★

by BARRY CORD

BARRY CORD, *whose real name was Peter B. Germano, was born the oldest of six children in New Bedford, Massachusetts. During the Great Depression, he had to go to work before completing high school. It left him with a powerful drive to continue his formal education later in life. He eventually earned a Master's degree from Loyola University in Los Angeles in 1970. He sold his first Western story to A. A. Wyn's Ace Publishing magazine group when he was twenty years old. In the January 1939 issue of* Sure-Fire *Western, Germano had two stories, one by Peter Germane and the other by Barry Cord. He came to prefer the Barry Cord name for his Western fiction. When World War II came, he joined the U.S. Marine Corps. Following the war he would be called back to active duty, again as a combat correspondent, during the Korean conflict. In 1948 Germano began publishing a series of Western novels as Barry Cord. They are notable for their complex plots while the scenes themselves are simply set, with a minimum of description and quick character sketches employed to establish a wide assortment of very different personalities. The pacing, which often seems swift due to the adept use of a parallel plot structure (narrating a story from several different viewpoints), is combined in these novels with atmospheric descriptions of weather and terrain. The Sagebrush Kid (Arcadia House, 1954), Dry Range (Arcadia House, 1955), The Iron Trail Killers (Arcadia House, 1960), and Trouble in Peaceful Valley (Arcadia House, 1968) are among his best Westerns. "The great southwest. . . ," Germano wrote in 1982, "this is the country, and these are the people that gripped my imagination . . . and this is what I have been writing about for forty years. And until I die I shall remain the little New England boy who fell in love with the 'West,' and as a man had the opportunity it see it and live in it."*

*C*oming down the old path leading from the Upper Jay, Melina Davis saw the riders on the town road, and her first thought was one of pleasant surprise. *Clay's early!* And because it was unlike the man she was about to marry to be either late or early about appointments, she paused and looked again.

The rider turned toward the ranch, and Melina frowned. She was on a grassy knoll with a stand of jackpine at her back, and she could look down on her father's modest ranch, the neatly-kept buildings, the meadow that separated her from the L-shaped house. This was a scene she had known from early childhood. But the rider coming to the Boxed D was not Clayton Ross.

She had her hands thrust carelessly into the pockets of her blue jeans, her tan cotton blouse was open at her throat, and her brush jacket lay in the crook of her left arm. And through the numbness of her surprise ran the aching thought: *He's come back! Steve Corrin's come back!*

Her face was flushed, for it was a warm day, and her hair, dark brown and alive

417

with highlights, had shaken itself loose from the bun. Some of it straggled across her appearance, and she thought miserably: *I can't let him see me like this!* And then she remembered Peggy Higgens, and the hurt was still there after five years. She pulled her lips in tightly, remembering this man's departure from Sundown. "Yes . . . you've come back!" she muttered. "Four years too late!" And she no longer cared how she looked as she walked down the path to the house.

Steve Corrin was talking to her father as she came into the yard. Tod Baxter, their handyman, was chopping wood in front of the shed. He was working leisurely and, with an old bachelor's curiosity, had his ear cocked to the conversation.

"I'm sorry to hear that, John," Steve was saying. "Somehow, I always linked the Davises and Sundown Valley together."

He was still in saddle, and as he turned to look at Melina she saw the changes in him. Most of the transformation was inside the man. Melina had known Steve well. And now, deliberately studying this tired, dusty rider sitting in the harsh glare of the sun, she saw that something had robbed the man of the gay recklessness that had attracted the girls in Sundown. Steve Corrin was still lean, wiry, dark-headed, and good-looking, but there was a mature hardness to his mouth, and his gray eyes, which had danced to every flicker of emotion, now revealed little.

Though Melina had heard the stories that had come back to Sundown about this man, she was unprepared for the change. For Melina remembered Steve with the eyes of a girl who had been in love. And to her Steve Corrin had remained the wild, reckless youth who, coming to town for the Saturday night dances, would key up the night the same as a strong drink could. That was how he had affected her then. But she had been seventeen — and she hadn't known about Peggy Higgens.

He was looking at her, his eyes somber, and a faint smile touched his lips as he fingered his hat. " 'Afternoon, Melina."

She acknowledged the greeting with a slight nod of her head. "This is a surprise," she said curtly. "You're the last person I'd expect to see ride back to Sundown!"

He drew back slightly, as if he had been flicked with a whip, and his eyes left him naked for a moment, open to her bitter anger. Then he murmured dryly: "Sometimes a man gets a hankering for old scenes, Miss Davis."

She ran her unfriendly gaze down the hard length of him, letting it linger on the dusty holster and the palm-slicked walnut butt above it. "That gun always was your trademark, Steve Corrin," she remarked. "We've heard how you've made yourself quite a reputation with it since you've left Sundown. But really, we have no use for your talents here."

John Davis was frowning. "Now, now, Melina," he interrupted briskly. "Maybe we could use a man who can't be pushed around. A man who's handy with a gun." He turned his attention to Steve, grumbling a half apologetic explanation. " 'Course, it ain't my fight any more, Steve. I'm through in Sundown. But there's others who need. . . ." He glanced sidewise at his daughter and shrugged, his mouth hardening.

Steve murmured, "Sundown won't be the same without the Davises. You've got a nice spread here, John. Seems a pity to let it go."

"Dad's too old to run it the way it should be run," Melina answered coldly. "And I'm leaving the valley in September."

"Leaving?"

John Davis nodded. "Melina's getting married next month. To attorney Clayton

Ross. Would you know him, Steve?" he added heavily. "He came to Sundown two years ago. They plan to move north to Dallas, right after the wedding."

A faint glimmer of the old Steve made its ghostly appearance in the tired man on the weary piebald. "Congratulations, Miss Davis," he said. He settled back in the saddle. "Five years have changed a lot of things in Sundown," he observed wryly.

Davis nodded. "Planning to stay in town?"

"I was," Steve admitted frankly. "But I reckon I'll drift on." His smile was cold, polite. "Like your daughter made plain, John, Sundown ain't partial to my kind."

He nodded shortly, touched his hat brim to Melina, and swung the piebald around. His body was straight as he rode away, and he didn't look back.

John Davis was frowning as he turned to his daughter. "For a gal who used to see a lot of Steve, you were mighty unfriendly. There was a time when. . . ."

Melina's tone was sharp. "He was Peggy's man, Dad . . . not mine!"

John Davis shrugged. "Peggy talked a lot," he muttered, "but somehow I didn't think young Corrin. . . ." He brushed the back of his hand across his mouth and looked after the dwindling rider. "Just the same, Melina, that's the man we need here, now. I don't care what happened five years ago. Sometimes I feel I'm running out on my neighbors just when they need me most. You know how Bollinger's crowding all the little ranchers along the Jay. He's like old Nafzinger was, getting too big for his britches!"

But Melina was thinking of something else, and her bitter thoughts found expression: "He should never have come back!"

John Davis put his arm across her shoulders, understanding pushing aside his worry. "Don't be too hard on him, gal. He was like a boy who'd come a long way to get home, when I first saw him."

Melina shrugged curtly. "Let's check back over your figures, Dad," she said, dismissing Steve. "Clay promised he'd bring a buyer with him when he called. And," she linked her arm through his and smiled anxiously, "I wish you'd quit worrying about Bollinger and the others."

John nodded soberly. "I wish I could," he said simply.

Clayton Ross was a prompt man. He had said he would be at the Boxed D at two, and five minutes before that time Melina saw his dust on the road from town. A heavy man rode with him.

They had been waiting for Clay in the wicker chairs on the verandah. John Davis uncrossed him legs and came to his feet, frowning. "Isn't that Frank Bollinger with him?"

Melina shaded her eyes. She waited, not speaking, until the two riders came into the yard, and even without looking at him she sensed her father's displeasure. The big man with Clay was Bollinger, sitting solid and arrogant in the saddle — a big man in expensive fawn-colored riding britches and shirt, soft suede jacket, and an extra-wide-brimmed cream Stetson.

Ross dismounted at once and came up the stairs. He was barely two inches taller than Melina. A small man, clean-shaven, sharp-featured. A small, energetic, driving man. He put his hands on her shoulders and kissed her with definite possession. "You look lovely," he said. He turned to her father and said briskly: "Good afternoon,

Mister Davis." It was still "Mr." Davis, even though he was marrying his daughter, and John Davis knew there would never be anything closer between them.

"Mister Davis," he began flatly, "I believe you've met Frank Bollinger?"

John Davis nodded. Bollinger swung heavily out of saddle. "Sure," he boomed good-naturedly. "You might say we're neighbors, Clay."

Davis ignored him. He looked at his daughter. "Did you know who Ross was bringing here this afternoon?"

Melina bit her lip. "No," she admitted, "but what difference does it make who the buyer is, Dad? You. . . ."

"I'm particular who I'll sell to," John snapped. He nodded curtly at Ross and turned to the door.

Bollinger stopped short at the foot of the stairs. "Now wait a minute, Mister Davis. I've come prepared to. . . ."

John slammed the screen door, drowning out his words.

The big man's face flushed. He glanced at Ross, and the lawyer shrugged uncomfortably. "I didn't think he'd take it like this, Mister Bollinger." Ross's tone had a shade of servility that annoyed Melina.

"I apologize for my father's rudeness," Melina said. "But it's his ranch, and if he doesn't want to sell it to you. . . ."

Bollinger didn't even wait to hear her out. "He'll sell!" he said, his voice shaking. "And on my own terms now!" He put his angry, uncompromising gaze on Ross. "I'll give you until tomorrow noon to talk to the old fool! Then I'll handle it the other way!"

He went back to his horse and mounted, a big, angry man who didn't intend to be sidetracked.

Melina's eyes snapped. "Clay, who does he think he is!"

"He's a big man in Sundown," Ross said soberly. He had been shaken by the turn of events, and the subdued look in his eyes irritated Melina. He made a quick gesture with his hands. "He was prepared to pay more than the Boxed D was worth, Melina."

"And who was judging the Boxed D's worth?" Melina snapped.

Ross mustered a small smile. "Melina, you're upset." He put his hand on her arm, adding quickly, "We'll be leaving here soon. The troubles of Sundown are not ours. And I was only thinking of helping your father get the best price he could."

Melina had a sudden uncomfortable recollection of Steve Corrin as he had looked that morning, hearing again the quiet disappointment in his voice: *Somehow I always linked the Davises and Sundown together.* Then she blotted out the picture of that man who had come back to Sundown.

"I would sell to Bollinger or anyone else," she said, her voice softening, "but it's a matter of pride with Dad. You must see that, Clay. If Dad sold to Bollinger, he would be selling out Jenkins, Pardee and Meegham. I've heard Dad talk. If Bollinger got the Boxed D, he could cut them off the upper Jay. . . ."

"That's their worry," Clay interrupted coldly. "Not yours . . . not ours. And once I collected my fee. . . ."

She turned on him. "Clay, are you in on this?"

He met her angry gaze directly, and his lips tightened stubbornly. "Well I'm an attorney, Melina. And I've been hired by Bollinger to represent him on this matter."

"Because he thought you could do what he knew he couldn't! Because you're marrying me, Bollinger thought Dad would sell if you asked him!"

"What's wrong with that?" Ross snapped, nettled. Melina saw the sharpness in his eyes, and in that short moment she glimpsed what the future would hold for her with this man. Smoothness, respect, a surface gentility that would turn to heartless cruelty when he was crossed. What this man wanted would come first. It would always come first, even before her.

"We're leaving Sundown!" Ross repeated. "Bollinger's check will set me up in Dallas. You've no stake here, Melina," he added harshly. "Why should it matter that Bollinger hired me to arrange a business deal? Why. . . ?"

Melina cut him short. "Because Dad will still have a stake in Sundown. I'm going with you to Dallas, but Dad will be staying. He'll move to town. Do you think he could face his friends if he sold them out to Bollinger?"

Ross sneered faintly. "Business deals are rarely concerned with friendships. And Bollinger is a hard man, Melina. He wants the Boxed D, and he'll get it. I'm only trying to save your father from getting hurt."

Melina stiffened. "You mean he's threatened Dad?"

Ross frowned. "You know the situation in the valley. If anything happens to your dad, it will either be done so as to appear as an accident, or it won't be done before witnesses. And I don't have to remind you of the law enforcement here. After all, this is still frontier country."

There was a sudden empty feeling in Melina, depriving her even of anger. "Clay," she said thinly, "if I hadn't heard you say it, I would not have believed it."

Ross took her tone for acquiescence. "Now, Melina," he said gently, "you understand I am only trying to help your father. Get him to sell, and we'll leave Sundown with clear hearts. He can come live with us, if he. . . ."

She pulled away from him. "Dad would die first!" she said. She looked into his face, seeing the effect of her words there. "I find this rather easy to say, Clay. I think it's because I've never really been sure. But I know now. And I'm glad I found out before it was too late . . . for both of us! For both you and me."

"Found out what?" he snapped.

"I don't want to marry you. I wouldn't make you a good wife!"

He pulled her roughly toward him. "Melina, what are you saying?"

"I can't marry you, Clay," she said flatly.

"*Why?*" There was a shocked, cruel glint in his sharp gray eyes. "Just because I brought Bollinger up here? If that's the reason, I'll break off. . . ."

"No," she said coldly. "It's not Bollinger. It's because I find that I don't really want to go to Dallas. I didn't realize that until right now. And I don't want Dad to sell the Boxed D!"

His fingers hurt her. "You little fool! If you think you can turn me down and make me the laughingstock in town, you'll regret it, Melina!"

She said flatly: "Take your hands away, Clay!"

His small frame shivered with the sudden ugliness of his temper. But he stepped back. "I'll see you again," he said confidently. "You'll change your mind."

"You know me so little," she said quietly. Then she turned her back on him and went into the house.

Her father was standing by the kitchen table, kneading tobacco in his pipe. They both stood, waiting, until the sound of Ross's departure faded into the drowsy heat. John Davis said quietly: "What changed your mind, Melina?"

She didn't answer. She went to him, burying her face against his rough shirt, and though tears wouldn't come, her shoulders shook with emotion.

Sundown sprawled in a bend of the Jay, a sleepy little town which had existed almost twenty years and had taken its time about growing. Oaks and cedar cast their shade along both sides of the main street, now dignified by the title of Morgan Avenue. But it was still the town Corrin had known — the Sundown he had known as child, boy and young man. The town still retained that quality which as a younger, restless man had fretted him — the peace of Sundown along the Jay. But as he came back now, with the sun slanting its red banners across the road, he had the sour and bitter thought that all things change, even in Sundown. He had seen it in the face of a tired man at the Boxed D and in the unfathomably hostile attitude of a girl he had ridden six hundred miles to see again.

He turned into Morgan Avenue, thinking without importance that this was Friday evening. Several light wagons were clustered around the general store; two saddle horses waited hipshot at the rail of one of the bars. Steve rode past these and turned in at the Four Palms Saloon. He had never been a drinking man, but the ride had been long and dry, and he needed a lift. Besides, a man could pick up almost as much in a bar as in a barber's chair.

Joe Beakes, he found, had changed in five years. Steve remembered him as a jovial two hundred-pounder. He scarcely recognized the sour-faced, thin, unsmiling man who came to wait on him. Beakes barely glanced at him. He said: "What'll you have, stran . . . ?" He was wiping his hands matter-of-factly on his apron when the recognition jerked his eyes to Corrin again. "*Steve!*" He extended a hand. "This is a surprise!"

Steve shook hands. "I've been running into surprises all day," he made talk. "I had to look twice to make sure you were the Joe Beakes I knew."

The barman belched softly. "Sorry," he mumbled. "Bad stomach. More than a year now." The lines down the sides of his mouth were deep. "Hurts all the time, kid." He reached for a bottle of whiskey and a glass, but Steve said: "I'll have a beer, Joe."

The barman drew him a tall one. "On the house," he said. He glanced at Steve's gun. "You've made a name for yourself. El Paso, Cochise, Santa Fe, Taos. All kinds of stories. . . ."

"Stories have a habit of getting better with every open mouth," Steve commented dryly.

Joe shrugged. "You used to be pretty wild. Too much for Sundown, if I remember." He grinned faintly. "But I got an idea some of the folks will be glad to see you back, Steve."

He had looked forward to coming back, he reflected, but a girl had changed that. He had run full tilt into the lash of her hostility, and he didn't know why. All the way into town he had tried to find some reason for Melina's attitude, but had to give up.

"Staying, Steve?"

"Huh? Oh," he shook his head, "just drifting through, I guess, Joe."

"Been a few changes since you pulled your freight, Steve. A big man named Frank Bollinger bought out the Double Rail. Fired the old hands, brought in new faces.

Some of the old settlers along the East Jay moved out of the valley . . . some new ones came in."

"Sam Ulston?"

"Dead. Last year. Drowned trying a crossing of the Jay last spring. Made a good deputy sheriff, but drank too much. Carl Sillman took his place."

Steve drank his beer. Joe moved off to serve a newcomer, and Steve took this opportunity to leave. He found he had no interest in what happened in Sundown.

Out on the walk he had the sudden impulse to get back into the saddle and ride on. But the piebald needed a night's rest. So he rode on down to Wyatt's stables and turned the animal over to a pasty-faced youngster he did not recognize.

"Where's Wyatt?" he asked.

"In the hospital at Benbow," a voice answered behind him. Steve turned to face a tall, bony man with a star on his vest. The man had a nervous way with him. His eyes moved too fast, as if he wanted to see everything, everywhere at once.

"Hello, Carl," Steve greeted. Carl was about his age, twenty-four. He had been one of the bunch Steve had whooped things up with. He had never cared much for the man, considering him somewhat of a weak sister. It was a surprise to see him wearing a lawman's badge.

"Staying in town, Steve?"

"Depends," Steve answered offhandedly.

"We've got an ordnance in Sundown," Carl said anxiously, "about wearing a gun." His tone was almost apologetic.

"Sure, Carl," Steve obliged, "I'll stow it." He unbuckled his cartridge belt, wound it about his holster, and slipped it in his saddle bag. "Kinda get used to packing it and forgot," he said grinning. "Sundown looks peaceful enough."

Carl relaxed. "It is. All except for a few soreheads."

"Soreheads?"

"Yeah. Jenkins, Meegham an' Pardee. You remember them? Got two-by-four spreads along Upper Jay."

Steve remembered. They were neighbors of John Davis. He inquired casually: "What happened to Wyatt?"

"Ate too much," Carl said, grinning. His nervousness was lessened by Steve's relaxed manner. "I always said Wyatt would eat himself into an early grave. He's up at Benbow with stomach trouble."

"Regular epidemic," Steve chuckled. "Say, what happened to Peggy Higgens?"

The grin faded from Carl's face. He said cautiously: "Don't you know?"

Steve frowned. "Know what?"

Carl said hurriedly: "She married that grain salesman from Benbow right after you left. She's living in Benbow now."

Steve grinned faintly. "She was pretty wild herself. Glad to hear she's settled down."

His smile faded as Carl said hurriedly: "Yeah. Well, I'll see you, Steve." The deputy turned and moved off down the walk.

"Well, what in the hell bit him?" Steve growled.

He was alone in the dining room of the Drover's Hotel where he had signed for a room when Jenkins came up to him. A bitter-cheeked, small, narrow-shouldered man of fifty-odd years now, a man who had married late in life and now had five children, all of them too small to help out much. Jenkins, Steve remembered wryly, had been outspoken in his opinion of Steve Corrin.

"Steve!" Jenkins said. "Heard you were back." He grabbed a chair and sat down without waiting for Steve's invitation. He was dark from the sun, and weather and worry had not been kind to him. He looked old and withered, but there was a fight in his blue eyes. "I ain't gonna beat around the haystack," he said bluntly. "You were a wild kid, an' pretty cocky, too, an' I was glad when you shucked out of here."

A faint anger stirred in Steve. "Thanks," he said dryly, "you want me to ride on?"

"No, I want you to stay." Jenkins grinned sourly. "Let me have my say, Steve. Then, if you kick me out through the door, maybe you'll be right. But let me have my say."

Steve leaned back and spread his hands.

"I was glad to see you gone," Jenkins repeated, "but I am glad to see you've come back. If the stories we've heard about you are fifty percent true, you're the man we need here now. We're being shoved around by a range hog named Bollinger. There ain't a one of us who can stand up to him, or the hardcases he's brought in. He's bought Carl Sillman, body an' soul. . . ."

"And you want me, the wild, bad boy who was no good for Sundown, you want *me* to fight your fight?"

Jenkins nodded. "Reckon that's what it amounts to," he said. "The fight's mine an' the rest of the folks along the Upper Jay."

Steve's grin was bleak. "Go to hell!" he said softly.

Jenkins jerked. His lips came down tightly over his stubby teeth. "I don't blame you much," he said slowly. "But this was your town once, Steve. You grew up here. I thought. . . ."

"I'm leaving in the morning," Steve said coldly.

Jenkins hesitated. Then he got to his feet and walked out without another word. Steve let his anger simmer down and then found he had lost his appetite. He got up and drifted out to the street.

The shadows merged almost quickly into the darkness of night. Steve rolled a cigarette and felt lost and lonely, as if he had never grown up here, and knew no one. Outwardly the town looked the same. But it had changed. Or he had changed. He wasn't sure. But he suspected the change was more in himself. It had come to him suddenly, as he walked up to his dingy room in a distant hotel, what he wanted. Tired as he was, he had come down, saddled, and headed for Sundown. Inside him a cynical voice chided him. What reason had he had to expect Melina Davis to wait five years for him to find out what he should have known before he left? He had seen a lot of her. But then, he had seen other girls, too. Why should she have waited? He had promised her nothing.

Two riders came by, moving at a jog, and he glanced up to see that they wore guns openly. They rode past and headed for the Ace of Clubs Saloon. Steve saw Carl standing on the corner, but the deputy made no move to intercept these riders who were openly breaking the town ordnance.

Hell with it! Steve thought wryly, and turned back to the hotel.

Sundown seemed to expand on Saturday. Wagons, buggies, and riders started coming in, making Sundown a busy little place. Steve ate a leisurely breakfast. He had no destination in mind, but he had definitely decided to leave.

He came out to the walk and started for the stables. A big, important-looking man in fawn-colored riding britches rode in, flanked by two hard-bitten riders that brought a frown to Steve's face. The big man parted from his companions further up the street and came riding past Steve and turned in to the rack just ahead. He dismounted and came up to the walk and brushed past Steve, a heavy, florid man too important to be polite to strangers. He went into an office that had CLAYTON ROSS, ATTORNEY AT LAW across the window.

Steve walked past. Three doors down a tall, dour-faced man with big hands and feet stood in the doorway of his dry goods store. Steve nodded. "Howdy, Higgens," and Higgens bobbed his head in acknowledgment, a red flush darkening his face. He was Peggy Higgens's father, and Steve paused. "Heard Peggy's married."

Higgens mumbled: "Yes, she's living in Benbow, now," and turned abruptly, disappearing inside his store. Steve stiffened. He knew Higgens as an inarticulate man but, damn it, what was biting him? He remembered Carl's reaction when he had mentioned Peggy. What was there about Peggy that even her father should react so strangely?

He looked out across the sun-beaten street, and disgust rose to taunt him. *All right,* it said — *you've come back! Satisfied?* He stretched his legs to get to Wyatt's stables.

The pasty-faced hostler watched him saddle the piebald. "You're Steve Corrin?" he said, and Steve grinned sourly at the note of awe in the boy's voice. "What's it like in El Paso?" the boy asked. There was a light in the boy's eyes that Steve remembered. It had been in his eyes five years ago. "Someday I'm gonna shake this town," the boy said solemnly. "There's nothin' doin' here."

Steve grinned. " 'Luck on the trail," he said, and swung the piebald away.

Melina Davis was worried. She sat beside her father on the spring wagon seat, and she could tell by the thin line of his lips that her father was headed for trouble. They arrived in Sundown just before noon and a faint warning roused her as she noticed Bollinger talking to Clayton Ross in the doorway of Ross's law office. Her father didn't even glance at them. But Clay looked up as they drove past, and she felt the sharpness of his glance. Bollinger gave them a slow, insolent look. Melina's face felt hot.

John Davis swung his team in toward the walk and tied up at an open space along the crowded racks. "I'll see you at the hotel at two, Melina," he said. She watched him head for the Four Palms and she felt helpless and a little frightened.

Two men in dusty range clothes came out of the Ace of Clubs directly across the street from the Four Palms. They were Double Rail men and they openly wore their guns in holsters thronged down on their hips. They watched John Davis push through the Four Palms doors with close-lidded interest. Melina shivered. Sundown had an element of tension this day, of violence that hung suspended by an uneasy thread of a man's greed. She turned away. Coming to town today had not been her idea, but John Davis had hitched up the team, and Melina at the last moment decided to accompany him.

A rider came out of the stable yard by Johnson's Warehouse and turned up the street toward her. Melina stopped. She felt cold and yet flushed, confused and frustrated and hating, and she despised herself that this man could still do that to her.

Steve saw her. He reined in sharply and dismounted, stepping quickly up to the walk in front of her. Close up now she could see the strain about his mouth, a grim seriousness in his eyes. "I was about to ride out to the Boxed D to say good-bye," he said.

"I'm glad I saved you the trouble," Melina replied coldly. "Good day, Mister Corrin."

A stubbornness crept into the angle of his lean jaw. "I have no intention of forcing my presence on you, Miss Davis. But I am curious. We were good friends before I left Sundown. What have I done since then?"

"I assure you, Mister Corrin, that what you did away from Sundown doesn't interest me in the least. I'm sorry if I appear abrupt." She started to step past him, but he put out a blocking arm.

"Sundown's changed," he said harshly. "That didn't surprise me. But you've changed, too, and somehow that hurts. Lying doesn't become you, Melina. When I knew you, you spoke your mind. I guess that's what I remembered most about you. Even when I no longer had a clear picture of how you looked, I remembered that you were different from other girls in our group. I remembered your steadiness. . . ."

"How touching," Melina said, and she felt the sneer on her lips. "In all those five years you thought only of me. Never of Peggy Higgens?"

He frowned. "Sure, I thought of Peggy Higgens sometimes. But not in the same way."

Melina laughed bitterly. She felt taut and flushed, and she knew, though he kept discreetly out of sight, that Peggy's father was listening from the doorway of his store. "I think it would have been better if you had thought of Peggy a little more often. It's several years too late now, isn't it?"

Steve stiffened. "Too late for what?" he snapped. He put his hand on her shoulder. "What about Peggy Higgens?"

There were footsteps behind her. Clayton Ross's sharp features loomed up. "Melina," he intruded, "I want to talk to you."

Steve shouldered him aside. His lean face was drawn tightly against his high cheeks. "What about Peggy Higgens?" he repeated harshly.

Melina stepped past him and put her arm out to Ross, who was standing with an uncertain frown. "Good day, Mister Corrin," she flung back curtly.

Steve let his hands drop to his sides, balled his fists helplessly, then turned sharply off the walk. He got into saddle and jerked the piebald's head around in a savage, unthinking gesture.

Down the street Abe Jenkins and John Davis pushed through the doors of the Four Palms. Jenkins was drunk. His voice carried up the street, thin and strident. "I'm gonna start packin' a gun again, John. Ain't had use for it for fifteen years. But no range-hungry hog is gonna crowd me out of Sundown. You can sell out if you want, but me, I'm stayin'!"

Melina had turned at the first sound of his voice. She had a sudden numbing sense of impending violence, sharpened by the sight of the two Double Rail gunmen lounging on the Ace of Clubs steps. They had come alert as her father and Jenkins appeared. Desperately Melina looked for Carl Sillman, but the deputy was nowhere in sight.

Beside her Ross said with relish: "The drunken fool's asking to get hurt." He took her arm possessively. "Come into my office, Melina. I want you to reconsider. . . ."

She pulled away from him, too concerned with her father's danger even to reply. Davis was trying to shut Jenkins up, but the bitter old man was beyond caution.

"Look at 'em!" he shouted, wagging a finger at the Double Rail men. "Just waitin' to run us out! All of us! They're newcomers to Sundown, but already they walk around like they own the valley. Damn their swaggerin' bullyin' way . . . I'd like to. . . ."

Davis's sharp voice called up the street. "Damn it, Abe, shut up!"

There was a difference of twenty years in the two Double Rail gunmen coming slowly down the saloon steps. The older man said sharply: "You accusin' us of somethin', Jenkins?"

Melina was rigid. She heard Ross suck in his breath sharply, heard his barely audible whisper: "So that's what Bollinger had in mind."

The scene down the street seemed suddenly unreal to Melina. The Double Rail men came on at a menacing shuffle; but they stopped as a slim figure astride a piebald reined in by them. The older Double Rail gunnie's shoulders gave a queer jerk.

The hot, sun-bright stillness seemed to act as a perfect conductor of voices. Clearly Melina heard Steve's quiet voice. "I see you've changed stamping grounds, Harvey."

The gaunt, round-shouldered man looked up. He held Steve's glance, dropped his eyes to Steve's gunless hip. He seemed to consider this a long moment. Then he shifted his glance to Frank Bollinger, still standing in front of Clayton Ross's office.

Steve's voice carried an iron suggestion. "I don't think you'll like it here, Harvey. Sundown ain't the kind of place you'd like. Nor your friend either, from the looks of him."

The younger man scowled and his hand drew his gun half out of the holster. "Just who in hell are you?" he demanded insolently.

Harvey laid a hand on his companion's arm. "This your stamping ground, Steve?" he asked nervously. Steve nodded slightly. Harvey drew a deep breath. He glanced again at Bollinger who was frowning. "I was gettin' itchy-footed," he said quietly. "I think we'll ride. In the morning?" It was a question.

Steve nodded. "Fair enough. In the morning, then." He remained in saddle, waiting while Harvey pulled the younger, puzzled man back into the saloon. Then he dismounted. Jenkins had sobered somewhat. "I wouldn't start packing a gun, Abe," Steve advised flatly. "Let the law handle your trouble." He turned to Davis. "See you sometime, John." He got back in saddle and rode out of town, without looking back once.

The tension ebbed out of Melina, leaving her momentarily weak-kneed. Ross was still staring after Steve. From the dry goods doorway Lemuel Higgens called to her. "Melina, come here, girl." She turned, puzzled. He was standing in the doorway, a bony, uncomfortable, inarticulate man. "There's something I must tell you," he said. His voice was tense, strained.

She followed him inside. She smelled bolts of cloth in the semi-darkness of this narrow, cramped store, and she found herself wondering why so big and clumsy a man should have chosen such an inappropriate business. What had been weighing on this man's mind came blurting out, with no preamble. "I should have told you before, Melina. But I didn't think he'd ever come back to Sundown. And it was better, easier to let you and all the valley folk think Steve was the cause of Peggy's shame!"

Melina felt the hot blood in her cheeks. "Lem, whatever are you saying! What do you mean?"

Higgens's voice labored. "I wanted to kill her when I found out! But she was . . . my daughter. And she told me the truth. She told me who was the father of her child!" Melina waited, shocked into silence. Pityingly she waited, while this stern, terribly ashamed man stumbled to find the right words. "But it's been five years, Melina. And Peggy married the man who was the father of her child. That's what I wanted to tell you. Things turned out all right. She's living in Benbow with the man she married . . . the man I. . . ." He faltered.

Melina's voice was small. "But why? Why did Peggy tell me what she did? Why did . . . ?"

"I know because I made her tell me," Higgens said harshly. "She always wanted Steve. She wanted to hurt him, to hurt you, too. She said you . . . you thought a lot of him."

Melina turned away. She stopped in the doorway to look back at the big, broken, sad man who had shown greater courage than she would have ever believed him capable. She said softly, humbly: "Thank you, Lemuel."

Then she was out on the walk and hurrying toward the wagon. Her father saw her as she climbed up into the seat and took the reins. "Wait a minute, Melina. . . ." She ignored him. She swung the team sharply around and drove past him, barely aware of his stunned surprise, barely aware of anything.

She overtook Steve on the bluff above the river, two miles out of Sundown. He had pulled off the trail and was looking down the length of the valley, and she saw the controlled surprise in his eyes as she drove up. All the way from town she had tried to decide the words she would use, how she would explain it. But now she sat numbly on the seat, looking into his face, knowing how she had hurt him, and understanding the guarded appraisal.

"Steve," she said. "Come back, Steve. Sundown needs you . . . and I need you. I need you, Steve!"

For a moment he held back, his eyes searching her face. Then the hard barrier this man had built up crumbled, and he rode to her. She stood up in the wagon and came into his arms, standing there, feeling the yearning in this man. There would be time, later, to tell him about Peggy — to explain why she had hurt him. Now it was enough Steve Corrin had come home!

TOO TOUGH FOR TEXANS!

(1954)

★

by WILL C. BROWN

Will C. Brown is the pen name under which Clarence Scott Boyles, Jr., wrote most of his Western fiction. Born in Baird, Texas, and descended from Texas cattle-raising families on both sides, Boyles's early career was in newspaper journalism. Although he did publish a couple of Western stories in pulp magazines in the 1930s, it was first following his discharge from the U.S. Marine Corps after World War II that he began his writing career in earnest. Texas is the principal setting in nearly all of Boyles's Western stories, including his first novel, The Border Jumpers (Dutton, 1955), which also served as the basis for the memorable motion picture, Man of the West *(1958) starring Gary Cooper. Dell Publishing, which reprinted this novel, selected it for the Dell Book Award as the best Western novel of 1955.* The Nameless Breed *(Macmillan, 1960) won the Golden Spur Award from the Western Writers of America in the category of best Western novel and is still considered Will C. Brown's* magnum opus. *In these novels, as well as in* Laredo Road *(Dell First Edition, 1959),* Caprock Rebel *(Macmillan, 1962), and* The Kelly Man *(Dell, 1964), a high level of suspense is established early and maintained throughout, often by characters being pitted against adverse elements and terrain. Boyles is particularly adept at making his readers feel the heat, dust, wind, desolation, deprivation, and dangers of the land in his stories. When violence does occur, it is logical and handled with restraint and brevity. The story that follows appeared in the final issue of* Star Western.

The new teacher whipped the overgrown Tucker boy on the third day after the opening of the Windmill school, and two dozen awe-eyed nester kids hurried home with the news of it as though reporting sight of hostile Indians. That night at the supper tables of sheep spreads and cow outfits up and down Catclaw Valley, people said that the young teacher, Bowie Jones, should have been told about the Tuckers.

Holly Ellis, who rented a room to the pale young teacher from Tennessee, was already itching with curiosity when Jones rode back to Holly's 'dobe ranch house in late afternoon.

"Heard you licked Orvie Tucker," Holly said without preamble.

"Caught him cheating," Bowie Jones said.

"Is that bad?" Holly shifted his rheumatic frame in the porch rocker.

"Same as stealing."

Bowie Jones balanced on the porch rail and took a deep breath, looking across the mesquite shadows that dappled an eternity of prairie distance. "By gad!" he exclaimed to Holly, grinning, "a man can just *breathe* better out here. I haven't had a touch of asthma since I left Tennessee. No foliage . . . you have no trees in this part of Texas except those mesquites. It's air a man can breathe!"

"Then get a belly full now," Holly retorted. "You're just one-third through whipping Tuckers."

The grin partially disappeared. Bowie Jones gave Holly a quick look.

"How do you mean, Mister Ellis?"

"Call me Holly, son," the grizzled nester complained. "I've told you that ten times. What I'm talking about is Bog Tucker and his oldest boy, Dutch. They're not gonna like it, you whippin' Orvie. Bog and Dutch're the reasons Orvie is dad-blamed near grown and still in the sixth grade. They've run off school teachers faster'n the settlement could hire 'em."

Jones looked out into the prairie again and ran a hand over his head to throw a dangling crop of light-colored hair out of his blue eyes. He was thinking of Orvie Tucker, a sullen hulk of a boy, nearly as old as Jones and fifty pounds heavier. The Windmill school wouldn't be a bad place if Orvie hadn't started to be a school room problem almost from the first hour. But when he had felt compelled today to lay that strap across Orvie's burly back, he had not thought of the kind of repercussions Holly seemed to be worried about. He unconsciously worked his hand muscles and asked Holly what about Bog and Dutch? Were they as no-good as Orvie?

"Bog will go for his likker jug and Dutch will start sharpenin' a nine-inch pocket knife he puts a lot of pride by," Holly said. "That give you an idea?"

"Bad ones."

"Scum of the country. I don't want to alarm you, but you better be told. Bog and Dutch will sure as hell jump you for whippin' Orvie. They'll think it's some kind of personal insult. That's the kind of low-down ignorant galoots they are, figurin' that the teacher whipped Orvie so now they got to whip the teacher. Supposed to prove the Tuckers don't take no messin' with or something. You follow me?"

Holly's wife called from inside and Jones said quickly, "Sit still, Holly. I'll get it!" He vaulted agilely over the banister, dog-trotted to the woodpile, and loaded his arm with split stove wood. When he came back from the kitchen, dusting his sleeve with his right hand, his left was clutching a fat slice of apple pie. He winked at Holly. "There was method in my madness."

Holly's eyes twinkled. "Anybody else, I'd say you was spoilin' your supper, but not you. You eat like a horse. Bet you've put on five pounds in a week, and you're beginnin' to get a little sun brown over that pekid white you come here with."

"Came here," Jones corrected. "Past tense, Holly."

"Anyway, you know what I mean," Holly retorted. "The pekid look you showed up with."

"I'd been indoors quite a while," Jones said, sampling the pie. "Finishing my education. All I could think about was trying to get a teaching job out in Texas, and here I am. How's that for luck?"

The worried frown came back on Holly. He said soberly, "You may not think you're so damned lucky, now you've riled those Tuckers."

Bowie Jones chewed thoughtfully, his mind seeming to consider some distant thing. He said slowly, "I've know some bad people, back where I was. The way I see it, I'm paid to teach something to about twenty kids of all sizes and I can't teach them if I can't have discipline, and I can't have that if Orvie Tucker is running the school instead of me. The first day I put him on a front seat because he was a big boy and he looked like a trouble-maker. He just got up, moved to the back, jerked some scrawny little kid out of a seat, and took it over himself. I let that pass."

Holly cocked his head and eyed Jones with keen interest. "You didn't contest him then, huh?"

"I was just trying to get the school started. But it was plain that Orvie was out to run the room and me with it. The next day he poured a bottle of ink down Nelly Stephens's back. He grabbed one little boy by the arm and twisted it till the kid screamed bloody murder. I told him to stay in, that I wanted to talk to him. He just walked out with me calling to him. But today he was sitting there copying all the arithmetic answers off a paper he had grabbed from a desk across the aisle."

"So that's when you whipped him?" Holly asked.

"Cheating is the same as stealing," Bowie Jones said doggedly. "That's one thing I can't take . . . cheating. I figured this one had better be my round before he had me on the ropes. So I went back with the strap. You could have heard a pin drop. Orvie tried to get up, but I held his wrist, and that took care of that. I was still wielding the strap when he twisted away and ran out the door. It will suit me just fine if he doesn't come back."

"I'm afraid he'll be back," Holly grunted, "Bog and Dutch flankin' him."

They jumped Bowie Jones on Saturday afternoon in front of the Catclaw Mercantile down at the cross-roads. The first he knew, he faced a black-whiskered man of larded girth who smelled of whiskey and sheep.

"You the feller that whupped Orvie?"

There was no time for an answer. Bog didn't wait. The anvil-heavy fist that had jerked Jones about had a doubled-up mate that was already coming at him with all of Bog's two hundred and thirty pounds behind it. Red and white streaks exploded in Jones's head, both then and when he hit the plank wall. He lay there stunned. When he tried to sit up, shaking his head to clear the blindness out of him, he saw from one eye the towering wrath of Bog and a younger copy of the big man. Dutch had the same kind of hate on his map as his pa, with his right hand shoved down in the knife pocket of his overalls.

"I'll teach you to hit my boy!" Bog muttered. He turned to the store's buggywhip rack beside the door and jerked out a buggywhip.

Jones struggled dazedly to his feet, feeling his right eye already swollen half closed. Bog's mammoth arm descended and the buggywhip lashed across the professor's shirt. Bog raised the whip again and Dutch's hand came out with the pig-sticker.

Jones ran. In that befuddled moment, it was in his mind only to get away. The onlookers on the porch and clustered at the store door watched silently as Bog followed a few steps down the walk, then stood with the whip still cocked as Jones got to his horse, mounted, and rode for home.

That night, in the kitchen, Holly Ellis shifted to peer down critically at Jones's eye in the lamp light.

"Past tense or present tense," Holly reported, "it's swoll to beat hell."

"Your cussing is worse than your grammar!" Mrs. Ellis scolded.

"The meat's helpin' it some," Holly said, turning over a cut of raw beef in his hand. "I'll put the other side to it now. It's gonna be black a while, but the meat's takin' down the lump, a little."

"We never had beefsteak back in the . . . back at the academy where I was," Bowie Jones said. "I always used half of a fresh-killed chicken for a black eye, if I could get the chicken. They had a doctor there but there were so many black eyes around he wouldn't pay any attention unless your eyeball was half out."

Mrs. Ellis, fussing around Bowie like a riled-up bantam hen, kept saying contemptuously, "Those low-down Tuckers! Somebody ought to *do* something!"

"Guess nobody's itchin' for the job," Holly said matter-of-factly. "Bowie, I wouldn't go to school for a day or two, till this blows over a little. Let the kids have a holiday."

"I must have looked great," Bowie commented, gingerly feeling the reddish-dark mass of his swollen eye. "Running like a fool with that big ox after me with a buggywhip."

"What about staying home tomorrow, like Holly says?" Mrs. Ellis insisted.

One side of Bowie Jones's thin mouth formed a tight grin as he sought and found Mrs. Ellis with his good eye. "Tomorrow is the *one* day I've got to be there," the teacher murmured. "It's likely to be the most important day in the history of the Windmill school."

He flexed his muscles while Holly made the beefsteak secure to his eye with a wrap of dishtowel. Holly's glance followed Jones's hand movements. They were big-knuckled hands with traces of old scars. "That academy you went to back in Tennessee," Holly said carelessly, "it probably didn't have no books to teach you how to run a school that had a Orvie Tucker in it."

"Not exactly," Jones agreed. "They did know how to teach you quite a lot of things not in any books, though."

Jones faced the school room from his desk at the blackboard, looking over his charges with his good eye. This had involved, all day, extra twisting of his neck and turning of his head to bring his vision to a focus. The room of assorted-size nester kids had been painfully quiet and well behaved. The furtive looks they stole at the unlovely countenance of the damaged professor were a mixture of amusement at his black eye and awesome tension over the magnitude of the violence that had come into their midst. Jones could see that the Tucker affair had unquestionably made Windmill school life an exciting thing, like death or a barn fire in the community.

From where he overflowed a back seat, Orvie Tucker had spent the day belligerently looking about for somebody to notice him, and became sullenly resentful when the younger kids gave him wide berth.

"I'd like to speak to Orvie Tucker a moment after school," Professor Jones announced. "Orvie, you stay. The rest of you are dismissed."

But the others tarried, after their first hurrying exit to the school yard. They delayed their usual rush for the road and prairie paths, looking back fearfully and curiously to the sun-bleached frame structure where some mysterious catastrophe might be in the making, with Orvie and Professor Jones in there.

"I want to tell you that I am sorry about our little trouble," Professor Bowie Jones said. Orvie leered, seeing that the teacher was trying to make peace with the Tuckers. Professor Jones walked on to the back of the room where Orvie stood with feet planted apart, his fleshy face screwed into a pattern of surly triumph. "But, Orvie," Jones said, "you are within four years as old as I am, and you're a head taller and a good many pounds heavier. You're not really a boy, Orvie . . . eighteen is old enough to be a man. So I have got to teach you like a man."

He knocked Orvie down. Orvie never saw the fast footwork, the right uppercut. Jones's tight knuckles rode into Orvie's right eye and Orvie fell so solidly that the kids in the road thought the cast iron stove had tumbled down.

Jones went to the corner and got a bucket of water and sloshed it into Orvie's face. When Orvie stirred and sat up, Jones went out and mounted his horse and rode home to the Ellis place.

Both Holly and his wife were on the porch, seemingly busy patching some harness, but anxiety and curiosity were written plainly on them.

"How'd you make out today?" Holly asked casually, giving close attention to sewing a strap on a backband.

"No trouble," Jones said. "No trouble at all."

Those who had seen it from the road told the unlucky ones who had missed it — with embellishments — and everyone re-told it with additional embellishments at the Catclaw supper tables. Not a pupil, from first-graders to "seniors" in the sixth grade, was tardy next morning. None, that is, but Orvie.

A hush fell over the room when Orvie shuffled in. Twenty-odd necks craned, first to Orvie's coming in with a black eye and to Professor Jones and *his* black eye.

"Up here, Orvie," Jones said quietly. "This front seat. I've moved Tim Bridges back to your old seat."

There was a prolonged silence, then Orvie plodded down the aisle and clumsily slid his bulk into the front desk. The two black eyes faced each other across the six feet of intervening space. Orvie wiped his nose with the back of his hand and buried his head in the first book he touched.

Bog Tucker and Dutch rode up just before the noon recess. They dismounted in the road and methodically tied their horses to the fence posts. They came on at a purposeful plod across the dusty school yard, with Dutch just a step behind and to the side of his pa.

Bowie Jones sighted them through the open doorway and abruptly ended the fourth-graders' spelling lesson. He looked at Orvie, catching the big Tucker boy tenderly feeling his swollen eye, and Jones's hand came up in unconscious duplication of the movement as he felt his own puffy eye flesh. Then he massaged his fingers and moved unhurriedly down the aisle. As if they had smelled the Tuckers coming, all heads turned to follow Bowie. The pupils, a row at a time as he passed, gasped audibly when they caught sight of what was looming up in the thin September sunlight of the school yard. Bowie met them just outside the door.

Dutch moved around to flank Bog. The big man started the proceedings by first holding his black whiskers down and spitting carelessly to one side, keeping his red-rimmed eyes slits holding to Jones. Dutch sunk his fist down in his knife pocket. Jones moved two paces aside so his feet would be clear of the rock step. He was thinking that they were awfully big men, over two hundred pounds apiece, and were going to be hard to put down, and that he had better be at it.

Bog was just opening his mouth and his two beefy hands were forming mighty fists when Jones stepped out with left foot, weight rocking forward, then back to the ball of his right, chin down to left collar bone. He feinted with his advanced left hand, although he did not need to, with Bog so solidly planted flat-footed and wide open. When Jones's right swing then flashed out of nowhere to connect with Bog's upholstered chin, the impact was like a sledge breaking rock. Bog melted down as if his sinews had unraveled, and it took all the speed Jones could turn on to catch him one-two with right and left jabs to right and left eyes, before Bog was just a pile of overalls, meat, and whiskers in the red dust.

Dutch's knife was coming out as Jones pivoted in rhythmic shoulder swing to smack first Dutch's right eye with a left jab and then, in the return shoulder swing, planted a right fist in Dutch's left eye. Dutch had time to mouth a curse and start one blind haymaker which Jones ducked. Then the teacher waded in with rights and lefts to Dutch's stomach, nose and chin.

Jones sat on the rock step, looking at his bloody knuckles. When Bog at last lumbered to his feet, followed by the almost sightless Dutch, Jones stood up too, and again moved away a step. Bog and Dutch made circling motions with their heads, trying to see each other. Bog glared hard at Jones for a long moment with his good eye. He raised a hand and felt carefully of his whiskered jaw, holding the hair down to spit aside, then he said, "C'mon, Dutch."

Dutch was already turning, stumbling off ahead of his pa, looking back a little, and Bog crowded after him. They went to the gate and untied bridle reins from the posts. It was then that the commotion broke out behind Jones — sounds that ripped the heavy prairie silence apart and made him whirl in real fright. The pupils were jammed in doorway and windows, yelling at the Tuckers in high and nervous shrieks of taunts and laughter. The little ones squealed and made faces, and the bigger boys yelled suddenly brave and daring insults. The jeers mounted in volume — in roars and squeaks of jubilant hysteria. The Tuckers mounted and rode away.

Jones reëntered the school house. The pupils hurried to their desks. In complete silence he walked down the aisle. Orvie Tucker's head was buried in an arithmetic book.

Jones paused alongside his desk. "Tell 'em to use raw beefsteak on those eyes, Orvie. That's what I used."

"Yes sir," Orvie said, and bent closer to the book with one dirty fingernail underlining the words he intently read.

Holly Ellis was so busy cleaning a currycomb on the front porch that he hardly had time to notice Jones when the professor came home in the late slants of the September sun. Mrs. Ellis likewise seemed intent on running a black thread through the eye of a needle over a lap laden with garments to be patched. Jones waited, facing the prairie pasture and taking great gulps of the dry Texas air.

"Moon Sellers come by a while ago," Holly mumbled.

"*Came* by," Mrs. Ellis corrected.

"Dammit, he was *here!*" Holly exploded. "Said his kid flew in from school with quite a story to tell. Where you been?"

"Down at the store," Jones said, "just sitting on the store porch, visiting with loungers. Funny thing, they're all right interested in the Windmill school."

"Let's see those hands!" Mrs. Ellis ordered.

Quickly he put his skinned knuckles behind his back.

Holly said, "This is the gol-dangdest black-eyed community in Texas." Then, dropping the currycomb and fixing Jones with a direct stab of his little eyes, he demanded, "That there academy back in Tennessee teach you to fight?"

"Yes," Jones said mildly, "I guess you might say that was their main course." His voice went to a far-away tone. "I guess I should tell you, Holly, and you, ma'am," nodding to the upraised eyes of Mrs. Ellis, "about that school where I was educated. The Buckle Mountain Academy is not a regular college. It's . . . well, it's the state reformatory. You might even say, a prison . . . for that's what it amounted to. For boys . . . kids that got into trouble. Like me."

Holly said, "The trustees thought it was a college."

"They helped us get jobs," Jones said. "I got my education there during my sentence. Came out with a teaching certificate and asthma. And one other thing." His mouth twitched. "I was lightweight boxing champion . . . and there were some right rough fighters in Buckle Mountain."

"So you wanted to come to Texas to teach and get over asthma," Mrs. Ellis said sympathetically.

"Yes, ma'am . . . and away from fighting."

"Moon Sellers says the Tuckers will never want another fight as long as they live," Holly said. "The community will be ready to help them keep that idear, I expect. Folks're gonna be right itchy to side with the professor, after today. Only wish I could have seen it."

But Mrs. Ellis was still staring up at Bowie Jones as if she might be searching out the heart of her own son. She said softly, "What did they . . . why had you been sent to a place like that, Bowie?"

"For stealing, I'm ashamed to say," Bowie replied. "It started by cheating in school, then stealing stuff from stores. I've got to teach Orvie Tucker that cheating's bad . . . if I can get that over to him, something might be made out of that boy in spite of Bog and Dutch."

Holly coughed. "You made a fair start, teaching Orvie. I wouldn't be surprised if he shuns cheatin' from now on like Bog shuns soap and water."

"There's some apple pie in the cupboard," Mrs. Ellis said, poking futilely at the needle eye.

"If you hadn't offered it," Bowie Jones said as he headed for the kitchen, "I'd have stolen a slice . . . your pie's one thing that justifies theft." He took a big breath of the good night air deep down into his lungs and gingerly touched his swollen eye with his swollen right fingers and went inside, already smelling the apple pie.

Jon Tuska is author or editor of numerous works about the American West, including *Billy the Kid: His Life and Legend* (Greenwood, 1994) and with Vicki Piekarski co-editor-in-chief of the *Encyclopedia of Frontier and Western Fiction* (McGraw-Hill, 1983) now being prepared in an expanded second edition. He and Vicki Piekarski were the co-founders of Golden West Literary Agency and the first westerners in the history of the Western story to coedit and co-publish thirty-six new hardcover Western fiction books a year in two series, the Five Star Westerns and the Circle Ⓥ Westerns.

COPYRIGHTS